Earthwork

by

Mark Crutchfield

Copyright

First published as an ebook in 2015
First published in paperback in January 2017

Earthwork Copyright © 2007 Mark Crutchfield
Cover photograph Copyright © 2014 Mark Crutchfield

Mark Crutchfield has asserted the moral right
to be identified as the author of this work, which
cannot be copied, reproduced or sold, in whole or part,
without the author's permission.

All characters in this publication are fictitious.
Any resemblance to real persons, living or dead,
is coincidental.

ISBN 978-1-520-15127-4

Who watches the watchmen?

Juvenal

Part One

February

*'And I have felt
A presence that disturbs me with the joy
Of elevated thoughts; a sense sublime
Of something far more deeply interfused,
Whose dwelling is the light of setting suns…'*

William Wordsworth
*Lines composed a few miles above Tintern Abbey,
On revisiting the Banks of the Wye during a tour.
July 13, 1798*

Prologue

Brother Carreg escaped the cloistered ennui of Glastingberie Abbey on a bright morning in 1191, never to return. He ran south-east without incident for most of the day, his stamina fuelled by nervous energy, occasionally by panic, but always by the strongest sense of purpose.
Carreg was relieved to be free of his meagre life as a monk, but he held no hopes for his future. He had stolen a relic intended for the new Angevin King of England, thereby exchanging his own presence at the blessed End of Days, which many years of Christian eschatology had taught him to expect and crave, for a much earlier, lonelier, and far more certain doom.
As late afternoon deepened the revealing light, the outlaw began to feel a little less fearful of finding somewhere to rest. Yet the site of his first pause among the treacherous waterways of the mere was to be the scene of his first brush with capture.

Carreg sank into the tall grass of a wild meadow beside a deep, reed-lined channel. He groaned relief. He knew that a rest in open ground was risky, but it offered him a good view of the route already travelled. It was from the north-west, Carreg decided, that men would follow him.
The monk wiped sweat from the crown of his tonsure. He rubbed his aching knees and blistered feet. Minutes passed in silence. Carreg began to feel reassured by the isolation of the fen. He set aside the cloth-wrapped prize he had carried from Glastingberie and lay back in the grass.
Despite the danger of falling asleep, Carreg was about to let his eyes close when an intimate breathlessness – at first gentle, but now faster, harder and louder – seemed to rise from the grass around him.
He sat up cautiously and scanned the view, trying to pinpoint the source of the needful gasping. But, just as his gaze settled on a leafy bower in the furthest corner of the meadow, horsemen appeared at the edge of sight.
A troop of three lightly armoured riders, consisting of two sibling knights under the orders of Abbot Henry, and a rather more richly dressed courier for the crusading King Richard, cantered into view from the north-west. The pace at which they travelled made them appear confident, yet they had no cause to be sure that Carreg had passed this way, nor that they were less than a hundred yards from their quarry.
Wanton tones continued to emanate from the hazel border until the vocal throes of an orgasm startled a magpie from its nearby roost.
'Sshh!'
A frustrated gasp and then, 'Don't stop!'
Airborne, the magpie soared across the meadow in a wide bobbing arc, clacking as it came, and drew the suspicious attention of Sir Baldwin of

Glastingberie. He reigned his horse to a walk and signalled for his companions to do the same, all the while eyeing the meadow's western border. Baldwin raised a finger to his lips in anticipation of questions. He pointed across the field at the magpie's rejected roost.

Within the hazel thicket at the corner of the meadow, a young couple lay satiated. Where gaps in the lush growth of leaves offered windows on the sunset beyond, slanting rays of the sun's fading light infused the bower with a florid glow, creating the illusion that these young people were themselves exuding the crimson radiance as an expression of their release. Here and there, the light ignited beads of ticklish sweat that moved across their skin in time with the pulse of racing hearts.

'I know you're there. Stand up.'

The young couple flinched and clung to each other in panic as someone swiped at the branches above them.

'We've found him,' the dismounted Baldwin announced. 'I can hear breathing.'

Sitting patiently astride their horses, William of Glastingberie and Sir Walter Giffard glanced at each other, and then turned back to watch the bringer of law to these fenland hides talk impatiently to the hazel trees.

'Don't waste any more of our time. Out you come.'

But those hidden by the hazel did not speak the language of the ruling Norman, and when his order went ignored for a second time, the knight drew his sword and chose a likely-looking gap in the trees through which to plunge the blade. A strained grunt and the appearance of a shivering hand satisfied the swordsman's lust for proof of his find. Baldwin withdrew the sword and wiped it clean with a handful of grass. He slid it back into its scabbard and dragged the partially dressed young man into the light.

A grief-throttled shriek alerted Baldwin to a second presence among the welling shadows. A girl leapt free of the thicket to swipe and stab hysterically at the killer with a small knife of her own. Easily avoiding the attack, Baldwin knocked the dead man's lover to the ground with a sideways blow of his gauntlet, breaking one of her cheekbones. Stunned by the pain, the girl seemed to forget the men's presence and threw herself over the body of the young man to cry against his punctured chest.

'He wasn't a monk,' said Walter Giffard, needlessly. 'At least, not a very good one.'

'But they were hiding from us,' reasoned the killer, 'and we're looking for someone who's hiding from us.'

'We can see why,' William replied. 'And besides,' he added, 'everyone hides from us.'

'Don't laugh at me. A treasonous monk has taken something wanted by the King and is carrying it effortlessly across our father's land. It will be my more *strenuous efforts that Sir Giffard will remember when the Abbot asks for a report of our search for the thieving Welshman.'*

Receding from the meadow's scene of murder, Brother Carreg took advantage of his pursuers' distraction. He broke cover and ran, further distancing himself from the mammary outline of Glastingberie Tor on the fiery western horizon.

Sweating in the weighty restriction of his habit, Brother Carreg thought he might reach his rendezvous by nightfall if he could maintain such a pace. Only a few more miles, he had been promised, and he would find someone who knew what to do with the leaden weight he clasped to his chest. He could bury the object himself, or cast it into the next body of water he encountered, but is that what his waiting ally had planned? And could these acts performed in panic reassure others that the relic would never be found? If recovered and carried as a standard at the head of English armies, such a prize might prove capable of breaking Britain's surviving Celtic heart.

Carreg followed a route south-east from Glastingberie along an alignment of ancient monuments, whose age and purpose were already forgotten by the year of Carreg's final journey. It was towards the shire's grandest megalithic site that his flight was aimed.

The outlaw sought a wooded hill at the edge of the mere. He had heard it described as crowned by a ring of eleven standing stones, forming an ancient temple of the Earth and of the sky, named The Meeting by the Anglo-Saxons and watched over, it was said, by a fearsome Twelfth Stone, which roamed at will to protect its rooted siblings.

Carreg saw heavy slate-grey clouds massing in the southern sky, and he crossed himself against the malignancy of their omen. Then he lifted the hem of his habit and lengthened his hasty strides.

*

But for the annual attentions of the seasons, Meeting Hill survived without alteration the eight centuries since Carreg sought its wooded sanctuary, as did the Neolithic circle of stones at its summit.

One freezing February evening in 1999, a lingering patina of snow breathed the late afternoon light as an amber radiance, and frost crystallising the trees on Meeting Hill reflected the setting sun as myriad pinpoints of diamond brilliance. A man entered the clearing at the summit of the hill and waited in the company of the standing stones. Ian Longe was there to test his friends' devotion to a popular local cause, and the timer on his watch counted every second that he remained alone.

While he waited, he paced the two-hundred-and-fifty-foot circumference of the ring of stones, increasingly aware of how quiet the summit's wildlife had fallen. No birds sang, and nothing moved in the trees or bushes around him.

(Two minutes, thirty seconds.)
Legend says that the stones of Meeting Hill cannot be counted. Legend says a lot of things about The Meeting. The megaliths cast lengthening shadows over the snow as Ian walked the circle against the tree-framed twilight, and he decided that he disagreed with Legend about many claims concerning The Meeting's behaviour. Yet he counted the stones again, just to be sure, and to distract himself from the oppressive silence that seemed to be thickening the air around him.
(Two minutes.)
...Nine, ten – still eleven.
Still, as reassuring as a confirmation of their number may have been, Ian remained unnerved. Glancing frequently at his watch, he raised one suspicious eyebrow and stared at his granite companions, as though expecting one of them to slink off into the trees at any moment.
In fact, misbehaving children in Little Arlingham are warned that this is exactly what the menhirs of The Meeting do every evening. As a child, Ian himself had been told that the stones creep around the village in the form of vicious demons, which demonstrate an appropriate talent for sniffing out misbehaviour. Able to smell the stench of youthful misdeed from their vantage on the hill, the Meeting Monsters feast on the flesh of naughty kids all night, and then they return to the hilltop, where they are turned back into stone by the first rays of the rising sun.
But what if it's cloudy, Mummy?
Then you'd better behave yourself.
(One minute, forty seconds.)
Though the twilight panorama of the frosty monument could not have reflected more innocently, with nothing in sight to justify Ian's sense of unease, the evening calm of the deserted clearing had assumed a sinister potential, perhaps a little more in keeping with the mood that many would expect from an ancient site of such brooding presence.
Ian had been born in Carreg's End, the southern tip of the village at the foot of Meeting Hill, and like every local child had become immersed in the monument's rich mythology long before he read of its more probable origins. Even at the age of twenty-nine, Ian was still capable of feeling spooked on Meeting Hill, especially when he caught sight of The Meeting's wandering Twelfth Stone, who sometimes watched silently from the shadows of the undergrowth, his weathered features crudely camouflaged by mud beneath a crown of twigs and leaves. But such sightings were rare, especially in recent months, and Mad Dog's presence did not usually scare the wildlife.
Ian wondered who else might be hiding in the trees, and why.
(One minute, twenty seconds.)

The setting sun scraped the distant horizon and turned Glastonbury Tor into a conical silhouette with a corona of fire. This is a view achieved so precisely only twice a year from Meeting Hill, which would be a meaningless observation if both occasions did not also fall on the dates of pre-Christian festivals. Scholars cite this alignment as proof that the choice of location upon which to erect The Meeting was not arbitrary, and that the monument was built as a calendar to mark the stations of the seasons.
(One minute.)
It was this spectacular alignment that a woman hidden by trees on the dusk-burnished side of the hill was present to witness. She had come to Carreg's End to celebrate a Gaelic festival she knew as *Imbolc:* the first springtime observance of an ancient faith.
Sitting contentedly on a bed of damp leaf-mould, and somehow seeming to belong in these surroundings, the lightly dressed woman was oblivious to having caused the pensive silence that her veiled presence had imposed over the hilltop. Conjured by the combination of just a few personal items and this unique solar vantage, the intense experience in which she felt immersed had soothed her usually restless thoughts. For only a few blissful moments she was calmed by a sense that she had fully communicated the depth of her reverence, and that the world she worshipped had recognised her presence in return. The glowing peace she experienced within and without was, she believed, her priceless reward, and deep gratitude brought tears to her eyes.
(Thirty seconds.)
The meditating woman considered this ecstatic experience to be an achievement of mystical grace. Compared to the irrationally low mood by which she was periodically visited, her peace during these moments was transcendent, though cruelly short-lived.
Wrenched back into a colder state of mind by the crispy tread of footsteps on nearby leaves, the young woman glanced over her shoulder and assessed the threat to her sanctuary. She saw a man of approximately her own age standing just inside the clearing, and he seemed to be sharing her difficulty in finding time alone outdoors. With no intention of giving up her own search that evening, she quickly gathered up the personal tokens laid on the ground before her and dropped them into a leather pouch. She speared the remaining length of a smoking joss-stick into the damp earth and began to creep further downhill into the trees.

(Fifteen seconds.)
Ian caught the smell of incense. He ran his nervous gaze along the silhouettes of the trees and jumped when the last fraction of the sun winked as a shadow flickered across it.
His suspicion confirmed, Ian considered his response, wary of provoking

defensive measures from someone – some people? – caught hiding in the trees.
(Ten.)
But a response was exactly what the villagers who funded his efforts demanded. People without respect for the site are not allowed to lurk on Meeting Hill.
(Five.)
Summoning confidence to confront the creeping unknown, Ian laid one hand on the radio holstered on his belt and took two hesitant steps toward the trees.
(One.)
With a heralding roar of its V6 engine, an off-road vehicle leapt into the clearing through a gap in the eastern trees. It landed hard on its front wheels and swerved to avoid the passage of a Land Rover that flew in behind it.
Ian's expression betrayed relief. He paused and checked his stopwatch. Not a second over the target time, he noted, but did not respond when the engines were silenced behind him. With his confidence reinforced by the arrival of friendly numbers, Ian's cautious investigation of the tree-line became a bold advance.
The driver's door of the Mitsubishi swung open and Ian turned to signal frantically for silence.
The broad smile of Alan Forrest broadened further at this indication of what he would call 'a situation'. Ian's earnest wide eyes infected Alan with a sense of unease, which he eagerly passed on to the driver of the second vehicle through its muddied windscreen.
Clearly annoyed at having to turn out in such a low temperature, Craig Pearce pulled up the collar of his fleece uniform and wound down the window.
'S'up?'
Alan put a finger to his lips and pointed after Ian's advance on the shadows. Craig rolled his eyes, pulling on a pair of thick gloves as he clambered out of the car.
The three men fanned out across the clearing through the stones, leaving trails of visibly bated breath in the freezing air. When they reached the border of winter branches, they paused to exchange silent glances of companionable reassurance.
Craig whistled for attention from the nearest of his friends. 'Is someone hiding in there?'
 Alan nodded happily.
Craig frowned and hissed, 'Why would anyone want to freeze their arse off hiding up here?' He reached discreetly into his jacket for something he kept to hand for whenever he felt vulnerable.
Alan returned the smug expression to which Craig had become accustomed. 'We're Earthwork,' he replied, as though Craig needed reminding. 'On Meeting Hill, everyone hides from us.'

The shrill expletive of a robin reduced the men's confident stance to a farcical drop for cover.

They wrestled self-control from the shaky grip of nervous energy and exchanged embarrassed glances as they rose. Recomposed and mindful of their duty, each member of Earthwork chose a gap in the western treeline and stepped warily into the woods.

Estate

It rained the next day when Ben Marchen returned to the village.
His cigarette had gone out two minutes ago, but he noticed only when he dropped his battered backpack at the edge of Arlingham Road, pushed his dripping fringe back over his head and tried to draw on the soggy filter. He spat it onto the tarmac when nothing happened. Ben pulled his collar up around his neck and felt cold water stream down his spine, soaking into his shirt.
'We'll arrive in sunny Arlingham in just a few minutes now, ladies and gentlemen,' he grinned at the muddy road behind him, in humourless imitation of coach drivers who bring tourists during the summer months. 'But we'll have to park outside the village when we stop for fags because this bus is fucking huge, and the road into Market Square is tighter than a badger's arse. But it's only a short walk to Arlingham's exciting retail complex: Frank Morley's Tobacco and Provisions, established in the year of our Lord, Eighteen-Sixty-Five. Now don't forget to view the Thirteenth-Century church, the maypole on the green, and of course the Rural Heritage Museum – which is exactly what this whole village is, come to think of it. Honestly, man, the fun never starts.'
Ten years before, Ben had been proud of his reasons to leave the village of his birth: he was terrified of a predictable future and the trappings of domestic routine; he fostered an acute hatred of authority and unthinking conformity, and he espoused an arrogant certainty of the imminence, benefits and permanence of a socialist revolution. Now, standing less than a mile from the 'Please Drive Safely Through Our Village' sign, Ben knew – but would never admit – that a need to rediscover those feelings was the reason for his return. He had always considered nostalgia the nemesis of rebellion: a process better at fossilising worthy tracts of his past than preserving them. And yet, as his thirtieth birthday approached, he was shocked to realise that nostalgia was the only thing keeping those rebellious feelings alive.
Even at the height of his discontent, Ben would not have altered Little Arlingham, or its local hilltop monument, in any way; but, as a younger man, he had reasoned that the village was there to be lived in, and that any urban environment will prove asphyxiating to modern life and attitudes if its residents pretend that Britain has not yet left the 1950s.
Hypocritically, Ben himself had changed little in the last decade. His characteristic urge to protest against anything planned by anyone he perceived to be rich or (but more probably *and)* powerful provoked from him the same old invective, updated only by its practised delivery after years of repetition. He also remained instantly recognisable to anyone who had known him as a teenager. His tall, slightly awkward frame had gained little of the tan and tone

he had hoped might be the reward for years of adventurous travel, while his dark hair maintained a bushy resistance to taming; and, though his dress-sense had always possessed a grim, hard-wearing practicality, the grey waterproof overcoat, thick jean shirt and black combat trousers in which he returned to the village may well have been the same ones he left in.

He flexed his fingers, cold and creaking after carrying bags from Castle Cary. Then, his spirits lifted a little by his own derisive humour, he re-shouldered the backpack, fixed his gaze on the ground before him and trudged on, northbound, towards the village. The rain had been persistent since he stepped off the train. It had finally melted the last of the weekend's snow, but the drizzle felt just as cold.

A further five minutes' walk brought him to the ornate western gateway of the expansive Wyre estate. Standing well over thirty feet high at its vertex, the Eighteenth Century archway is still impressive, despite the ravages of age and weathering. The roof of the edifice is crowned by three upwardly tapering tiers, upon which two granite eagles have no choice but to remain vigilant, their wings stretched forth as though concealing fresh kills from other predators. From up here, the patient birds have a clear view over and around Little Arlingham. Fields and patchy woodland stretch away to the south-east, until the A303 interrupts the greenery like the slash of a scalpel across a map. Beyond this sits the platform outline of Cadbury Castle, rendered ghostly that morning by low cloud.

In the opposite direction, the foreground is dominated by the dome of Meeting Hill, whose wooded slopes give way to the valley in which Little Arlingham nestles. The Somerset Levels stretch away from the village to the north-west, and this flat expanse of fields and criss-crossing rhynes and ditches is a reminder that this part of the country was once flooded, accessible even from the sea. And, just at the edge of sight, seemingly stranded upon the well-drained Levels like a ship at low tide, Glastonbury Tor sits distinctly against the sky and offers a distant focus for dreamers.

As Ben happily reacquainted himself with this view from the shelter of the archway, the metallic expletive of a car's botched gear-change reached him on the breeze. Seconds later, a white four-wheel-drive vehicle approached from the north. The car slowed as it neared Ben. He assumed that it did so for him. He waved an apology and stepped aside, but the vehicle indicated left and swerved into the Wyre estate, its driver playing music so loudly on the stereo that it was audible through the bodywork.

Ben peered through the window of the muddy Mitsubishi and immediately recognised its driver, despite the years that Alan Forrest's face had collected since Ben last saw him.

Alan returned the glance, but he had no clear view of the watchful man in the rain.

Ben considered the encounter as he watched the car accelerating along the avenue of trees beyond the archway. Seeing Alan had not surprised Ben: he had always thought of his childhood bully-turned-friend as an extrovert who seemed surprisingly happy within the confines of the sleepy village, and he had fully expected to find him here on his return. In fact, it was the unexpected nature of the sighting that interested Ben. An off-road vehicle entering the property of Little Arlingham's wealthiest locals would not have distracted Ben for more than a moment, even decorated as the car was with eye-catching Celtic crosses, had Alan Forrest not been driving it.

The car disappeared from view, leaving Ben alone with the archway's raptors poised above him like a twin visitation of recall and regret, and he remembered scenes both temporal and geographical within the estate, granted him so long before by his childhood friendship and teenage romance with a member of the youngest generation of Wyres. He recalled the mile-long avenue of poplars leading into the heart of Wyre land, interrupted less than a third of the way along by a property on its southern side in which Eleanor Wyre had lived, and which Ben remembered as a modest dwelling for people of such famous wealth: a red-brick, three-bedroomed house issuing vines of honeysuckle and climbing rose in the warmer months, and sweet wood smoke from a tall chimney in the winter. He remembered an orchard only a little south of Meeting Hill in which he and Eleanor Wyre had met to lie in silent union at night, or else discuss the social difficulties of their coupling. He remembered escaping his eighth birthday garden party with four friends, each of them eager to run and laugh through the Wyres' fields and woods in any direction as long as it was Away, to become lost and yet so happy until herded by the estate's gamekeepers.

Replayed increasingly frequently during the nine years of his travels, these memories had finally lured Ben home, though they had assumed the jaded, time-capsule distaste of pictures in a dog-eared holiday brochure. Now, though, resuscitated here in the scene of their birth, they were less like recollections than vivid revisitations, and Ben experienced a giddy, infinite-mirror vertigo as he felt pulled into the memory of a memory-in-making. He found it intoxicating, and these few minutes alone seemed to justify his decision to abandon the nomadic nature of his adult life, as well as rewarding the time, money and effort he'd committed to this return.

Still, though: standing here and remembering also felt like stalling. Ben had an apology to make, and the things he planned to say to his parents would be difficult after nine years away. But then, Ben reasoned with the indomitable confidence of Famous Last Words, he had come home to see his family. How painful could it possibly be?

*

Gazing up at his father in disbelief, Ben dabbed at his mouth in search of blood and tried to stand.
The 'WELCOME' mat on the doorstep of Hill View had been lying.
'Ow.'
Geoff Marchen's face was thunderous and throbbing with red pressure. His shoulders were back and his fists were raised. The senior Marchen wondered at Ben's failure to retaliate, but he could not summon enough sympathy for his fallen child to back down. 'I thought I'd come to terms with the way you left,' he seemed to chew and choke on the words, clenching and relaxing his fists, 'and I've even tried to understand why you didn't contact us for nine years – but now you turn up here like nothing happened, still spouting the same old shit?'
Insensible, Ben could barely focus on his father's face. The ability to form a reasonable defence, if such existed, was beyond him.
'Do you have any idea how worried your mother's been? Even after all these years, she wonders where you might be and how you are, and what she might have done to deserve the way you treated us.'
'Mmh?' Ben managed, raising himself on both elbows at this hint of a more forgiving parental presence. 'Look,' he began, wobbling to his feet, 'let me see Mum, just for a minute. I'll say hi and be out of your way. I came home to apologise.'
'No,' said Geoff, folding his arms tightly against the request. Marchen still exuded formidable strength but, Ben was surprised to see, Dad was getting old. 'How do we know you won't do the same again? Another disappearing act would destroy your mum.'
'You won't let me see her?'
'I'll tell her I've seen you.' Geoff took a step back across the threshold of his house. 'And I'll tell her you're safe.'
Ben dabbed at his swollen lip and spat blood at the dishonest doormat, frowning at the garden path as his plans crumbled even faster than his father's reserve. 'Safer away from you, man,' he mumbled.
Of all the likely responses to his return, Ben had never considered that being punched to the ground might be one of them. Neither had he entertained thoughts of finding himself without a place to stay.
With nothing more to say, Geoff Marchen closed the front door of Hill View. Meanwhile, Ben contemplated a long walk. He had nowhere to shelter except the pub, but he did not want to stumble into a bar, and possibly into old friends, with a nosebleed.

To Guide

Over an Eighteenth Century folly at the foot of a Snowdonian mountain, a dark and heavy cloudscape dominated the sky in vaporous imitation of the mountains below. But the rainclouds were now breaking up, and became gilded by the light of the emerging sun.
Brightening though the day was, a woman wearing a loose white gown began lowering shutters across the windows of *Pen Annwn's* attic room. She owned this ancient property in Wales, though she was not Welsh. The woman was named Jill Baynes at birth, but at the age of forty-three she was addressed by many hundreds of people as Roedan, their Priestess and Leader.
At the summit of the tower, Roedan attempted to bring about a change in her life with supernatural aid. Many people might have called such an act a prayer. Others might consider it magic. Roedan thought of it simply as negotiation. She recognised, named and praised the many forms and forces within Nature. In return, she occasionally asked these elements for a little help with her own ambition.
It was a semi-reliable trade, she would have admitted, but she held a strong conviction that her pleas were always heard.
With the shutters of the octagonal tower in place, Roedan lit several candles in the branches of a black iron stand, which was wrought in the form of a simple tree. The candelabrum had only a table, a chair and a plain wooden chest as allies in minimalist occupation of the room.
As an occult traditionalist, Roedan believed in the flickering glow of candlelight as the correct medium with which to illuminate theosophical intention. However, the ritual she performed when the mood was set was always of her own devising. Roedan believed that the motives and methods of adepts should vary. She knew that the sacrifice of living things could be an effective bribe to hungry deities, but Roedan was taught – and now taught others – that creative effort invested in new and interesting rites was of equal value to the forces addressed. 'Go ahead and slit the throats of lambs,' Roedan once said to her followers, 'light candles and dance around pentagrams, or kneel and chant the same old litany, as long as your intention is to bore your gods into ignoring you.'
However, Roedan remained obsessive about the candles, and her innovation was not so exclusive that aspects of well-known ancient mythologies were unwelcome in her practice. Roedan was born in Hampshire, but she was drawn to the Celtic fringe and traditions as both her home and her ethos. She had also gleaned the art and legend of ancient Greece for the symbol she now traced in chalk across the polished floorboards of the room. It was a single-path labyrinth: a spiralling route first traced in the classical world as a symbol of the winding path of life, as a trail of Experience, and even as a map of the

afterlife that the dead may tread, and then retrace, towards rebirth.
Roedan used it to represent the course of an ongoing search.
The Llugwy valley north-east of Moel Siabod was flooded with light as the sun emerged, and through a narrow gap in one of the window's shutters a single streak of the sunburst entered Roedan's ritual space, for a moment rendering the room's airborne dust-motes incandescent. From a ceiling hook near the window, a single teardrop crystal span slowly on a length of cotton, refracting the beam to send tiny rainbows drifting around the room.
Roedan hopped lightly across her chalked artwork and opened the chest beneath the western window. She removed from it a collection of objects recommended by another occult tradition. Spiritual alchemy, Roedan had discovered, used this romantic apparatus to represent the four classical elements, and she placed these items around the labyrinth at the primary compass points.
Starting and rotating clockwise from the north, Roedan placed a pentacle inscribed in clay for Earth, a feather to symbolise Air, the dull blade of an extremely old sword for Fire, and a wooden goblet to represent Water.
Roedan also lit a tall white candle, which she placed in the centre of the spiral to symbolise the goal of her search. Then she unfastened and stepped out of her loose white gown.
Roedan harboured few inhibitions. She was alone at that moment, but it would not have mattered if trusted others were present. If asked why, Roedan would have explained that she preferred to be naked during ritual acts because she despised any barriers, literal or figurative, between herself and the forces she sought to reach.
If questioned further, Roedan might also have admitted to pride in her body. She had maintained a consistent weight throughout her life, her belly had never been stretched by pregnancy, and she exercised to maintain a shape and tone that held power over men. Her body was the tool with which she had secured achievements of her will over several intractable opponents.
Ready to begin, Roedan lowered herself onto the floor at the mouth of the labyrinth. She never had found the clichéd lotus position particularly comfortable, so instead opted for a less disciplined slouch in which she could relax.
Sitting this way, facing into the path of the maze, Roedan closed her eyes and focused on her breathing. She intended to set her thoughts travelling upon a visionary path, represented by the chalk maze before her, towards the light of discovery at its centre. She could achieve this much herself, of course, but any genuine insight as to the whereabouts of her prize would, she hoped, be supernaturally inspired.
Roedan could not simply reason her way to the discovery of a long-lost artefact: she had already tried it. She had failed, and had been ridiculed by the

academic community in consequence.

The will of Nature did not always grant her requests, but at least it did not humiliate her for trying. She had nothing to lose, so with the focus of her desire held firmly in mind, Roedan stepped imaginatively onto the path of the maze.

*

Dusk on Meeting Hill.

Casual visitors to the wild hilltop usually leave before sunset. At this time of the evening, when the half-light seems to suffuse the clearing with a pale ether in which the stones counsel, people are unlikely to be found on the hill. Ben Marchen knew this, and he was very happy about it.

He let his backpack fall to the ground beside one of the stones, choosing to ignore the sound of something fragile shattering within. Bitter rumination over the encounter with his father had hardened Ben's bruised features during his walk from the village, but his expression softened in ecstatic relief as he nestled into the secure familiarity of his surroundings. Entranced, he crossed the clearing for the first time in nine years, and then eased his weary frame into a crouch against the base of a standing stone.

During his decade away, persistent memories of a childhood spent in pursuit of boundless imagination amongst these patient stones had finally brought Ben face to face with an invulnerable opponent: a sense of regret. It had been on Meeting Hill that Ben first met an inspiring, intelligent, sulkily persuasive man, whom Ben had thought of as homeless until sharply corrected to think of him only as 'free'. The man's name was Kennett. He had embodied and expressed the nineteen-year-old Ben's distrust of village life, didactic parents, possessive girlfriends, wealthy landowners, the Capitalist West and its imperialistic military-industrial complex, and Ben had followed him, out of Little Arlingham and on to casual work in Kent, raising funds for travel and migrant labour around Spain, Gibraltar, Greece, Goa, Mauritius, Israel, and then Egypt, in the company of four other people similarly in the thrall of Kennett. But it was not until the day the travellers stepped off an over-crowded train in Cairo behind their increasingly self-righteous leader that Ben had finally succumbed to his homesickness.

During an evening visit to Giza, Ben had turned to stare at Kennett, who was lecturing his followers about the way in which the touts offering camel-rides around the Pyramids will trick tourists into paying twice, and about how he would *never* fall for something like that. At that moment, Ben began to feel ashamed of having lived for so long under the spell of this self-appointed guide. He also realised three other very important things: firstly, that Kennett had no right to insist upon 'looking after' the passports of his fellow travellers; secondly, that he desperately missed Somerset; then, finally, that dreadlocks can only ever look like an affectation on a white man – particularly so on Kennett. Ben had sensed the elder traveller's pathological insecurity for years, but it was only during those final weeks in Egypt that Kennett's anger at the world, and his jealousy of its more contented citizens, became disturbingly zealous, even for people – like Ben – whom he had recruited as a travelling audience.

In fact, Kennett's regular (and, by then, annoyingly familiar) diatribes against hereditary monarchy, globalisation, monogamous relationships and marriage, American cultural hegemony, nationalism, property ownership, celebrity-worship and genetically modified crops allowed the other members of his company to view their own lives from a fresh, and freshening, perspective. Despite the rebellious feelings that had put them on the road to start with, they realised that none of them was as angry about everything as Kennett was, and – despite Kennett's assertion that Permanent Revolution was a state of affairs to be applied equally to the self – that being a little more relaxed about the world and its ways was no bad thing at all. When Ben forcefully reclaimed his passport and abandoned Kennett that day in Cairo, his travelling companions did the same.

But even these recent memories could not compete with the vivid images of his childhood, which filled Ben's mind as night descended upon The Meeting. It was as though the stones had absorbed the very essence of his younger years, and were now allowing him access to the wonder and enchantment of that distant innocence.

For Ben, The Meeting had shrunk. The circle of stones is around eighty feet in diameter, and the clearing in which it stands is one-hundred-and-twenty feet across; but twenty years before it had seemed capable of housing a garrison of several thousand soldiers under the command of King Ben and his best mates, the fearless Sir Ian and the haughty Lady Wyre. But life had not been easy for this army. Meeting Castle was regularly invaded by a tribe of local savages, who held a distinct advantage over the defenders: Alan Forrest and his barbarians were several years older than Ian, Ben and Ellie, and there were more of them.

'Get off, Alan! It's our turn to play here! You promised! I'm tellin—'

Ben blinked the memory away. Towering castle walls, thundering hooves and the clash of weapons faded into the misty night sky.

During his confrontation on the doorstep of Hill View that day, Ben had felt the first pang of concern about the wisdom of his homecoming. He had wandered the village in search of accommodation, but had found Arlingham's guest-houses closed at this time of year, despite the prominent B&B signs displayed in their front gardens.

Then he had walked to Morley's for cigarettes and discovered the most conspicuous recent change in Little Arlingham. Despite frustration at his home town's white-knuckled grip on a staid past, Ben was disappointed to find that Morley's Post Office & Tobacconist had been taken over and expanded by a national chain of convenience store. It's bright fascia, window adverts for cheap lager and multi-buy deals on chocolate bars seemed entirely out of place. Teenagers wearing baseball caps and hooded tops leaned against the window outside, spitting, swearing and smoking self-consciously. Ben immediately decided that he hated the place, but stepped into the store to buy cigarettes anyway.

The transformation had brought Ben a little lower. It was not until he reached the summit of Meeting Hill that he experienced any feeling of welcome at all, and so he resigned himself to sharing a damp night with the stones on the hill. Ben raised the collar of his jacket around his neck and lower face. He rummaged in a pocket for his cigarettes and pulled one into his mouth, finding it easier to play the rough-sleeping outcast with a Marlboro between his lips.

'They don't suit you.'

Ben spat the cigarette nearly halfway across the clearing as a firm hand gripped his shoulder. He leapt up and around to face the owner of the hand, but lowered his guard when he saw an old man in a dark cloak and hood standing behind him. After a moment's examination of the figure, Ben began to laugh.

'Hey, man, who are you supposed to be? Merlin? Herne the Hunter? Gandalf? Obi-wan Kenobi?'

The figure shook its head inside the hood.

'I don't suppose the name matters,' Ben grinned. 'I recognise the archetype.'

'Very predictable, Ben.'

Ben feigned surprise. 'And you know my name! Impressive entrance,' he conceded, but then voiced a more natural response. 'Seriously, you fucking weirdo – who are you?'

'You're clearly a man of wide experience and many horizons, Ben Marchen, but while a sense of irony may provide an individual with valuable insights into the future, the cynicism and pop-culture references really are beneath you.'

Ben gaped at the old man and thought it over. 'You're fucking full of it! But let's see: an old man in what looks like a monk's habit hanging around The Meeting at night, appearing without introduction or manners and spouting cryptic judgement – you're Mad Dog.'

The new arrival's silence revealed nothing, which Ben decided wasn't a denial.

'Wow, man – you're a living myth! I suppose I should be honoured that the Twelfth Stone of Meeting Hill has finally decided to talk to me, rather than watching me from the trees like you did when I was nine. By the way, about that: you know you can't hide in the woods watching children play without people getting suspicious, don't you? When I find out what's stopped the villagers from coming up here and lynching you, I'll let you know.'

Y Deuddegfed Maen, correctly identified, was silent for a moment. Ben sniffed and turned away, searching the grass for his cigarette.
'You're right.' The Twelfth Stone raised a hand and pulled the hood from his head. An extremely old man, whose sparse hair, slim face, sunken features and weather-lined skin could only have been sketched accurately by Brian Froud, looked apologetically at Ben. 'I suppose the silent arrival and unsolicited wisdom was unnecessary. Be warned: this is what happens when you spend too much time by yourself, wrapped up in your own narrow purpose.' He reached within the folds of his cloak without breaking eye contact with Ben. 'So, what are your plans?'
'My plans?'
'I just wondered where you'll be staying until you patch things up with your father.'
'You know about that?'
'And more besides, but it's not my place to say. Not yet. No matter how insightful you are, you won't listen to me at this stage. You're too arrogant, and you have no reason to trust me.'
The cloaked man held Ben's gaze as he pulled a pistol with an unusually wide barrel from his robe. Ben shook his head, squinting through the gloom at whatever the man was holding. 'I thought I might head off, you know, somewhere else. Things haven't really turned out as I'd hoped... Christ, man – is that a gun? Are you going to shoot at me?'
The old man glanced down at the pistol as though he had not realised he was holding it. 'A gun? Oh! I see what you mean. It does look that way, doesn't it? But no – and I find it sad that you need to feel threatened before you show a little humility.'
He raised the pistol and pointed it into the night sky. Ben tried not to show his relief. 'What is it?'
The old man smiled. 'I'm afraid I can't really explain without using words like Fate, or Destiny.'
'Ah,' Ben nodded. 'You're right: I won't listen.'
'Sorry,' the cloaked man shrugged, 'but I need you to stay awhile in Little Arlingham. It'll take you some time to realise what you're meant for, and I'm afraid that process might be painful. But I promise you'll know it was worth it when you discover the love, the time, and the meaning of your life. The Meeting has been waiting for you, Marchen.'
Ben turned away and stared silently at the surrounding stones. The Meeting returned his gaze intently. Behind him there was a click, a sharp explosion, and then the effervescent whoosh of a rising firework. Nightfall in the clearing was reduced to a skeletal shifting of shadows as the violet glow of Mad Dog's flare forced the dusk into retreat. Darkness on Meeting Hill was temporarily banished by the piercing light, forced to cringe and shudder behind the

standing stones.

Ben was not surprised when he turned and found that the old man was gone, and he did not bother to search the clearing for him. He decided that a spooky old man in a hooded cloak could probably disappear without trace whenever he ran short of cryptic things to say.

The flare drifted away on the cold February breeze until its flame died somewhere over Orchard Ridge beyond the Wyre estate, leaving Ben crouched expectantly against a standing stone in the dark. With Mad Dog's words fresh in his mind, a strong sense of anticipation held back his need for sleep with a polite but firm hand, like a bouncer outside a club.

But anticipation lacks the dutiful commitment of door security. Ben's sense of expectation became complacent and sloppy, and sleep stole in the moment it was distracted. Disappointed that Destiny had not immediately pointed its finger his way as Meeting Hill once more surrendered to the night, Ben allowed his increasingly heavy eyelids to fall as his body demanded its due for the long day's hike. With one arm looped through his backpack's straps like a cautious traveller, Ben dozed against The Meeting's largest stone.

*

In the centre of her labyrinth, the north-facing edge of Roedan's candle melted and collapsed. Clear molten wax spilled down its length and began to cool against the floorboards. Unrestricted, the flame dwindling upon its wick rose to dance jubilantly, and its amber strobe pulsed against Roedan's eyelids.

Alive with candlelight and the visions procured in dream, Roedan's eyes flickered open. She sat up and noted her position around the path of the maze, but frustration competed with satisfaction at the progress she had made.

After an hour of meditation on her search, concentration had carried her thoughts into the realm of semi-consciousness, where random images and disembodied voices stalk the borders of sleep. This visionary chaos became fused with her sense of purpose, creating a twilight world of restless reflections for Roedan to explore, until sleep had finally consumed her focus, and had she allowed her body to lie across the floor.

Shadowy figures moved against the periphery of dream. Roedan had walked a rural route by the light of a candle she could not see, searching every dark and hidden place for a treasure as valuable as it is ancient, and as real as it is lost.

A messenger had appeared in the form of an indistinct man. She could not identify him, but the figure had carried an object that Roedan believed to be the artefact she craved. A hand reached out towards her, barely penetrating the sphere of golden light by which she searched, and Roedan had thought that this denizen of dream was offering her the cruciform plate it carried. But the hand had refused to relinquish the item. Instead, the outstretched limb served to prevent any further movement along her chosen path. She could only gaze at the brandished cross in frustrated desire.

Roedan blinked away memory of the dream that woke her. She rose from the floor and reached for a glass of water on the table. Roedan knew that many of the world's mythologies are populated by figures who flit between Heaven and Earth carrying the prayers of mortals and the messages of gods. Early cultures often considered inspiration to be of divine origin. Roedan had read of Eshu, a West African god and trickster, who was appointed mediator between humans and heaven by the High God as punishment for the anarchy he caused on Earth. She also knew of Thoth, the Egyptian Moon god, who imparted the skills of prophecy and magic to his worshippers. The angel Gabriel imparted the will of Jehovah. Hermes, in winged hat and sandals, bore the messages of the Olympians to the ancient Greeks. In Scandinavian lore, Odin was the god of magical change and inspiration; and a little further south, the Germanic peoples praised Wodan for their moments of spontaneous insight.

Roedan thought she had felt the presence of this archetype during many pivotal moments of her life: it had brought the opportunity that led to her meeting with Mad Dog, many years before; it had inspired and often aided her present search, and its favour had attracted her many hundreds of followers. Everyone, she surmised, must have a name for the notable coincidences in their life. Serendipity, she liked to call hers in helpful circumstance – but in the dark obstructive form it had taken in her dream, no name was offered with its appearance. Even the cross it bore seemed to be brandished as a warning, or as a bar against her progress.

She had heard friends with similar interests talking of mischievous sprites that interfered with their journeys upon the Etheric Plane. Tom Sutherland, her closest friend and confidante, had described such distractions as a pain in the astral arse, and Roedan laughed a little at this memory of his brash American wit. The humour helped restore her motivation.

She drained the glass of water, rubbed at her goose-pimpled arms, and then returned to her position within the maze.

*

'He can't be. It's only eight o'clock.'
'Wake him up.'
'Don't. He must be knackered to be sleeping up here. How would you like it?'
'I don't, and I don't like having to turn out when it's this cold. I'm not leaving till we find out what he's doing here.'
There was a pause. Then, 'Oi!'
Ben ignored the voice.
'Told you. He must be knackered.'
'Or drunk. What do we do? Walk away and let him set fire to the place with a few more flares?'

'He's asleep! What harm can he do? Snore too loud?'
'I'm not standing here freezing to death while you two bitch about it.'
'What are you doing?'
'Waking him up.'
'Hang on, Craig—'
'It'll be Christmas before you think of something!'
'But what if it wasn't him?'
'Then I'll read him a bedtime story and kiss him goodnight. Can you see anyone else up here?'
Ben stifled a snigger. A moment later he was hauled roughly to his feet and pinned against the megalith by a strong pair of hands and a hot huff of alcohol.
'What's so fucking funny, Guy Fawkes?'
With his jacket pushed up around the lower half of his face, Ben was incapable of a clear answer. He opened his eyes, but could only squint in the beam of four powerful headlights. Cast as silhouettes against the cars, two figures were standing side by side while the third – the impatient younger one with the bad breath – held Ben up against the stone with an unrelenting grip.
Ben wriggled his mouth free of his collar. 'Calm down, kid. You've got nothing to prove to me.'
'You don't tell us what to do up here! Do you know who we are?'
'Earthwork?'
The three men looked at each other.
Ben nodded. 'Thought so. I saw a picture of you on the agenda board outside the village hall. You've been busy while I was away.'
Craig stepped back. Two more torches dazzled Ben as he straightened his jacket and wiped the sleep from his eyes.
'Ben?'
Ben nodded. 'Could you drop your torches?'
'I thought we'd never see you again.'
With the torches lowered, Ben identified the taller figure as Alan Forrest. The shorter one had Ian Longe's profile. Ben shrugged and ran a hand through his matted hair. 'Kennett let my respect for him go to his head,' he replied, reciting the brief explanation he had composed on the train that morning. 'On good days after I left home we were like Sal Paradise and Dean Moriarty on the road, but on the bad days we barely acknowledged each other. Shame really, after the years and countries we worked through together.'
'*Together*?' Craig repeated.
'Grow up,' said Ben.
'So you came home.' Alan raised an eyebrow. 'Has the rebel been tamed?'
'No chance,' Ben posed. 'But he does have a few apologies to make, as soon as his Dad calms down.'
The group became quiet, even uneasy, until Craig cleared his throat. Alan took

the hint. 'Sorry. Ben, this is Craig Pearce. Craig moved here from Devon last year. Craig, meet Ben Marchen, who you've heard us talking about.'
Craig nodded and burped quietly into his hand. 'Yeah, great. Can we get back now?'
Craig walked away, leaving the three old friends alone. 'He's young and it's past his bedtime,' said Ian. 'He can be moody.'
'Who isn't when they've drunk that much? Don't let me keep you. Your friend's right, it's cold,' he said, returning to his seat against the stone.
Ian and Alan offered him a bed at either of their homes. Ben gratefully informed them that he would bear the offer in mind, but he refused shelter that night. He felt that Little Arlingham had already sentenced him to a night on its wild periphery, and that accepting domestic comfort now would somehow rob him of his achievement over the day's trials.

With this masochistic reasoning as justification, Ben spent the night on Meeting Hill. It helped him retain a sense of the non-conformity he had chosen as a lifestyle, if only for a little while longer; though he had been tempted to return to the village with Alan and Ian, where he would have laughed about old times, and probably cheapened the experiences of his travels by talking about them like a gap-year holiday.

Nestling up against the megalith, Ben knew that a compromise would have to be reached: a way of returning to the village without betraying the statement he had originally intended by leaving it. It would be some time before Ben could comfortably think of the village as Home.

Meanwhile, Meeting Hill was his home for the night. As the Earthwork cars disappeared from view over the brow of the hill, the distant ringing of church bells in the village provided Ben with an outdoor lullaby. The sound seemed to fill the cold air around him, occasionally amplified or silenced by the varying strength of the breeze. The leaves of Meeting Hill's trees moved with a steady flow of air, giving Nature a voice with which to whisper the replies to pagan prayer, or whistle songs of lament for the shrinking Wild Wood. Few listen, and even fewer understand, though the rising urgency of the creaking branches and rustling leaves might have identified this as a wind of change; a natural herald for the unleashing of creative potential, epic discovery and unthinkable transformation.

Impasse

The first rays of the rising sun found slim gaps in the frames of *Pen Annwn's* window shutters through which to stream, replacing the extinguished glow of the room's votive candles. A puddle of melted wax from the centre of Roedan's ritual maze had reached almost to the skin of her thigh, but had hardened before it could disturb the woman sleeping nude on the chalk.

A polite knocking from beneath the floorboards initially went unanswered. It was repeated, this time more urgently, and accompanied by a cry of 'Coffee!' in an American accent. Roedan was forced to recover a little faster than she might have liked. It would take some time to warm and stretch the cramps from her chilled body after hours spent lying on the cold hard floor.

Rising awkwardly with chalk-dust smeared across her left cheek and temple, she leaned aside and unbolted the trapdoor, allowing entry to her ritual space. A similarly aged man climbed the last few rungs of the ladder through the floor while Roedan paced slowly around the room. She worked the stiffness from her joints, stopping at each of the eight windows to open the shutters.

Her coffee-bearing companion said nothing as he set a steaming mug on the table. Then he leaned against a window to appreciate the view of Moel Siabod beyond. The middle-aged American, dressed flamboyantly in patchwork jeans and a multi-coloured woollen, did not spare Roedan's nudity a second glance, and Roedan would not have cared if he had. Tom Sutherland and Roedan had united as casual lovers three times when the need had overtaken them, but, beyond these rare one-night couplings, theirs was a professional relationship.

Roedan surveyed the room and considered clearing everything away. A fresh start to ritual meditation always felt good, as if every avenue of opportunity was still open, and anything was possible. However, packing up at this point would have been like clearing away a half-finished jigsaw. She decided to leave the room as it was.

Roedan stepped back into her white gown and reached for the coffee, rubbing at her stiff neck as she eased herself down into the room's only chair.

Tom spoke quietly, moving behind Roedan to massage the knotted muscles of her neck and shoulders. 'How did it go?'

'All right at first,' she replied, relaxing into his touch. 'Oh, that's good.'

'At first?' The American pushed aside Roedan's tan-brown hair to knead the flesh beneath her ears.

'I got stuck,' she said. 'Something got in the way, but I don't know if it was meaningful, or just dream bullshit. At first I thought I'd reached the end of the search. I thought I'd actually found it, Tom. I saw a cross, but it wasn't my cross – and it was stopping me, not showing me anything.'

Tom breathed deeply in concentration as he worked to relieve Roedan's tense upper back. 'It'll come,' he reassured her in his warm way, the manner that had earned him Roedan's trust since their introduction years before. Tom Sutherland offered effortless empathy and genuine, always credulous, attention. 'But we really should get you warm now,' he added. 'Come on back to the house.'

Tom helped his friend and employer up from her chair, across to the trapdoor and down the ladder from the room.

A light breeze entered the attic space as the door lowered and latched behind them, breathing chalk dust across the floor to collect in shallow drifts against the objects surrounding the maze.

A simple diagram of this ritual path – of the clay pentacle, the feather, the ancient short-sword and the wooden cup, all positioned around a circular labyrinth – was one of the pennant motifs beneath which Roedan's followers regularly gathered.

This is the route by which Roedan led her followers to worship, dance, and pray.

This is Geophagia.

Committee

This is Earthwork.

Packed into Little Arlingham's Edwardian village hall, the governing members of the Meeting Hill Preservation Society spent ten minutes on a needless introduction, reaffirming everything that the group was already known to stand for. The villagers present were also subjected to the acceptance speeches of several local figures who, as a sycophantic opening to the February meeting, were invested as honorary members in thanks for their donations to the project.

And they deserved it, some had argued – but what about the Field Operations Team? others wondered. Alan Forrest was employed full-time by the committee, and therefore received a salary; but two other men devoted not only money to the cause, but a majority of their free time. These men had never received such a public show of appreciation, and while the volunteers clearly found the job-satisfaction reward enough, the people of Little Arlingham saw them as far more deserving of gratitude than certain others, who threw money at the cause only for recognition.

Commander Balton, Little Arlingham's Public Representative and Committee Chairman, returned to his seat beside the five Earthwork governors on stage, the Wyre siblings, Georgina and Brampton, who owned Meeting Hill, prominent among them. Balton had delivered an uninspiring speech to the stony faced villagers in the hall, and, as their polite applause faded in anticipation of something a little more interesting, the Commander (who would not to respond to anyone unless addressed as such) consulted the meeting agenda. He traced down the page with an expensive pen and then gazed down into the front row of the public seating.

'Field Operations Team Leader, Alan Forrest, to report.'

The audience sat up with renewed interest. Never mind the speeches of the dusty governors, the fund-raising plans from the treasurer, or Georgina Wyre's seasonal threat assessment, the people of the village wanted to hear from the real Earthwork: the men who kept watch over the stones in all weathers, and who selflessly accepted the responsibility of driving around the countryside in powerful off-road vehicles wearing specially commissioned uniforms.

Alan took the stand to a round of enthusiastic support from the public, as well excited whistles from two young women in the second row. Alan waited out the applause, seemingly humbled by the crowd's attention. Yet, in the front row of the gallery, Ian Longe and Craig Pearce knew just how much Alan enjoyed his role as front man for the team.

Alan had always looked a little awkward in the Earthwork uniform of khaki polo shirt, grey trousers and fleece jacket, informal though it was. His straw-blond spiky hair and thick goatee beard made him look more at home in his

off-duty wardrobe of loose surf-wear. He was nearly thirty-three-years-old, and Ian regularly accused him of demonstrating a premature mid-life crisis.
Alan acknowledged the governors and then addressed his eager audience. 'Mr Chairman, ladies and gentlemen—'
A wolf-whistle from the second row – disapproving glances from the governors' bench.
'Only two minor incidents to report since last meeting,' he read from a typed sheet. 'Field Operations were called to a disturbance on Meeting Hill on the twenty-eighth of last month. A party had begun when we arrived. A small fire had been started and—'
A familiar face at a window beyond the public gallery caught Alan's eye. It briefly met his gaze but then disappeared from view.
'...And...and while the situation was resolved with no trouble or damage to the site, the group of around twenty teenagers we found on the hill, all of school age, had been daring each other to graffiti the stones.'
A murmur of dismay crossed the gallery.
'Local youngsters?' Commander Balton voiced the crowd's surprise.
'Yes, Commander.'
'From the village?'
'Mostly, I think.'
'Are you sure?'
Alan nodded. 'I recognised a few who live in Carreg's End.'
Commander Balton leaned back into his chair, shaking his head. 'Has the committee made no impression on the local youth? Doesn't Earthwork mean anything to them?'
Alan nodded. 'Definitely, sir. The children in the village think we're heroes.'
Alan's immodesty sent a ripple of laughter across the audience.
Sitting beside the Chairman, Governor Georgina Wyre emerged from a daydream with a suggestion. 'Perhaps a visit to the village schools might be in order—'
'Certainly,' the Commander agreed. 'A word with the head-teachers might produce the names of those responsible.'
'No, no,' Georgina cut in, 'perhaps the field team could visit the schools, particularly the Carreg's End Secondary, to run through an Earthwork presentation. If we can give the youngsters some idea of what the committee aims to achieve, they might take us a little more seriously. Perhaps one of the cars could be taken in for the pupils to look at, keep things interesting.'
With neither agreement nor protest from the distracted Alan, Balton accepted the proposal as a plan for later discussion. He turned to the frantic secretary, who was transcribing the meeting at the end of the table. 'Make a note, Miss Lewis?'
'Noted, Commander.'

'Please continue, Mr Forrest.'
Alan stared blankly across the heads of the seated supporters.
'Mr Forrest?'
'Mh?'
'Did you not agree with the school visit idea?'
'Oh. No, it's not that.'
Ben entered the village hall as quietly as its heavy door and his hiking boots would allow, his eyes bloodshot and his hair wild. Everyone in the hall turned to follow Alan's gaze. Ben stopped and cringed. Several people recognised the dishevelled new arrival with conspiring murmurs. Ben edged past several people to a mid-row space.
''Scuse me, 'scuse me, 'scuse me.'
Sparing Ian and Craig an expressionless glance, Alan returned to his report.
'Second,' he resumed, 'during our monthly time-trial exercise at the weekend, Ian became aware of someone hiding in the trees while he was alone on the hill. I wouldn't have bothered mentioning this if it weren't for a number of other villagers who think they've seen or heard people hiding in the trees.'
'Madog?' Georgina Wyre suggested.
Alan shook his head. 'I don't think so. He doesn't hide that well.'
'Deer?'
'Possibly. When you're alone on the hill, it's easy to assume that every noise you hear is someone hiding – but we're country folk,' he exaggerated his Somerset accent for the audience, raising a dutiful chuckle, 'and I think we know better than that. But there are people who've seen at least one person wandering through the trees on the western slopes, usually in the evening.'
'Children?'
'Again, maybe, but how many youngsters are that quiet? Without scaring ourselves and starting a witch hunt, I think it might be worth bearing in mind that The Meeting attracts all kinds of people, and we can't predict everyone's motives in such a remote spot.'
'Good point,' the Chairman addressed the village. 'Can we suggest that people visiting The Meeting be aware of this while alone? Surveillance?'
Carl Harper, Little Arlingham's retired police constable, rose unsteadily to his feet in the public gallery with only a little support from Ian. 'Commander?'
'Increased watch hours if you would, sir, every evening after sixteen-hundred hours until this blows over. That all right?'
'No troub – trouble at all, Comman –' Harper slumped back into his seat.
'We're busy enough maintaining preservation of the monument,' Commander Balton muttered bitterly, catching Ben's eye as the younger man yawned widely in the third row, 'without having to worry about the intentions of every vagrant who passes through the village.'
Balton held Ben's eye for just a heartbeat too long. Ben took the comment

personally and returned the insult silently by scratching his nose with a middle finger. Balton missed the gesture as he glanced away.

Across the hall, Alan Forrest cast Ben an apologetic glance. Ben nodded once and then rose to his feet. He pushed his way back along the row against the knees of his irritated neighbours. He strode along the aisle and out of the hall, letting the heavy door swing shut behind him.

'Mr Forrest?'

'Sorry?' Alan turned back to the governors.

'I said, what are your plans?' Brampton Wyre repeated.

'Today?'

Wyre nodded.

'Full Moon's due in a few days, so we'll expect The Meeting to be busier after dark. Field Operations have the usual checks to make. We'll also be having a look at the footpath fencing around Meeting Hill as soon as we've finished here. All damage to fences on estate property will be reported to Governors Brampton and George Wyre – and if the horses are available, we'll cover the ground much faster if we can ride.'

Georgina Wyre, who detested her first name and insisted upon being addressed by this abbreviation, nodded a polite consent.

Sitting beside his sister, Brampton Wyre looked bored.

'Settled,' Commander Balton asserted. 'Any questions from the gallery before we adjourn for the month?'

One cautious hand was offered in timid response, as if its owner was afraid that someone might notice. 'Mrs Willis?' Balton asked.

'Was someone letting off flares on the hill last night?'

The Chairman looked at Alan. Alan looked at Ian. Ian raised his eyebrows.

'Ye-es...' Alan admitted.

'Did you find out who?'

'No,' he replied truthfully, but unconvincingly. 'Can I report on this next month when we have all the facts?'

Commander Balton raised his hands. 'Until next month then. Thanks to everyone for coming.'

Meeting Brook

Ben had entered Little Arlingham twice since his return and found himself unwelcome on both occasions. In an echo of his feelings from ten years before, Ben felt driven to the social and spatial fringes of the village. Aimless and alone, Meeting Hill quickly reasserted its place in his affections as a site of elevated sanctuary. Up here, enjoying his first sunlit view of The Meeting for a decade, Ben nestled into its comforting preservation like a memory. Unlike urban space, Meeting Hill was not required to bow to the forces of modernity to justify its continued existence in this, or any other, century.

Ben scaled and sat upon The Meeting's tallest standing stone. Stability in any form had been absent from Ben's adult life – he'd made sure of it – though he was now prepared to admit that a degree of it seemed inviting as he neared his thirtieth birthday. Quite how stability was attained and maintained remained a mystery to Ben, but this particular megalith was setting a good example. Like all the menhirs on Meeting Hill, more than a third of its total length had been driven into the ground by its prehistoric builders, giving the site a durability that even a surge of Seventeenth Century Puritanism had struggled to compromise. Sitting cross-legged on top of the stone with a can of cider in one hand and a cigarette in the other, Ben offered a portrait of effortless enlightenment. He drained the cider but frowned at his cigarette. After a few seconds of critical examination, he pushed the Marlboro into the can and dropped it nine feet onto the grass below.

On the opposite edge of the clearing, where the trees surrounding the monument offer a single opening onto the summit, three men on horseback ambled easily into the space occupied by the stones.

'Fawn has wind,' said Craig Pearce with concern for his horse, somewhat spoiling the grandeur of their mounted arrival. 'And she's jumpy.'

'Farty and jumpy?' Alan scratched at his goatee. 'Sounds like the equestrian fever George mentioned. It can make horses unmanageable. They start biting and throwing their riders, but I think the violent stage comes a while after the flatulent phase. It's contagious but not fatal in humans, causing only impotence in men.'

Ian Longe, characteristically dour, kept pace with Alan as Craig clutched protectively at his groin and leapt from the saddle. Ian asked, 'Where do we start?'

Craig eyed his colleagues and the mare with equal suspicion.

'It's the hill's border fencing needs checking,' Alan replied, capable of a professional manner when his colleagues looked to him for leadership. 'We saw the western road on the way here,' he went on, reaching into his fleece pocket for a plan of the site, 'which leaves us a stroll along the eastern wire to the estate, starting over...' Alan scanned the tree-line for a give-away

fencepost: '...there. You and Craig do that while I check on the brook and go over the stones. Should only take twenty minutes. Everyone carrying a radio?'
'Fuck knows what I'm carrying now,' Craig muttered, tethering the horse to a low oak bough. 'Alan, this fever, it's—'
'Horse shit,' Ian informed him. 'You're too gullible.'
Armed with their maps and a sense of purpose, Earthwork set off in pursuit of their separate missions. Ian and Craig checked their belts for radios and then turned towards the trees. Alan patted his horse and made off alone across the clearing.
'Not very good, are you?'
Craig span on his heel. 'What?'
'What did I do?' Alan replied.
Ian, the most intelligent man on Meeting Hill at that moment, realised that not only did the critical voice belong to a fourth, previously unseen party, but that it had emanated from somewhere overhead. He looked up into the triumphant grin of an old friend. 'All right, Ben?'
'I mean,' Ben went on, 'I don't know much about your club, but the little I've learned is that you're a rural vigilante group set up to look after these stones – or is there more to it?'
'Vigilante? No, but we look after the site,' Alan agreed.
'Then you're not very good at it,' Ben repeated, jumping down onto the grass to stand amongst his old friends. 'You didn't consider the possibility that someone might want to hide up here in plain sight?'
'But we weren't looking for anyone,' Craig protested.
'Sorry, man,' Ben shook his head, opening a second can of cider and offering it to Craig. 'Not impressed.'
'I don't care what you think—'
'What are you doing?' Alan asked.
'How do you mean?'
'Have you travelled the world just come back and sit around up here taking the piss?'
'I'm hiding,' Ben admitted. 'The village hasn't been too welcoming.'
Craig sneered. 'Why do you think that is?'
'Because somehow I've always felt excluded from society and everything that it expects from its citizens,' Ben said, disarming Craig with an honest answer. 'I've always been happier away from concrete and people, but I'm not popular because everyone hates a drop-out, don't they? I'm just sceptical and dispossessed, though, not a thug like you. Actually, Alan, I don't know what I'll do.'
'So you'll leave again?'
'No,' Ben said, turning to the older man when he was sure of Craig's self-restraint. 'Not if I can sleep on your sofa. It seems like I might have a family

problem to sort out.'

The three villagers exchanged uncomfortable, and not particularly discreet, glances. 'Well,' Alan tried to change the subject, 'if you're free, you might want to help us out with—'

'Wait,' Ben pointed at them all in turn. 'You all know something. What is it?'

'About?'

'About my parents.'

Ian watched Alan's response with quiet interest. Craig stared at his own feet. Alan shrugged and gave in. 'You know what the village is like, Ben: if someone sees or hears something, everyone knows about it sooner rather than later.'

Ben nodded. 'And who was it? Who noticed? I passed Hill View on my way up here and saw the district nurse leaving. The way she kissed my Dad on her way out didn't look very clinical.'

Craig owned up, seeming to take an almost gloating satisfaction in his confession. 'I couldn't help notice,' he said firmly. 'The district nurse visits your house almost every day for an hour or two, so unless your Dad is *really* ill…'

Ben fought to restrain himself when Craig left the statement open like a sick joke. 'And my Mum? Does she know?'

Ian stepped a little closer to Ben, breaking the impression that the three uniformed men were interrogating a prisoner. 'Do you want to hear all this from us? It's not really our place.'

'I'd like the truth,' Ben replied, unable to make eye contact.

'OK. Then no one has seen her for years. We talk to Geoff – your Dad, I mean – in the pub sometimes, but we haven't let on that we know about... about his new friendship. We ask after your mum, but he always just says she's fine. That's all.'

The news was almost a relief. Ben leaned back against the megalith on which he had been sitting and felt a little of his anger drain away. Tortuous images of his mother living at home, oblivious to her husband's infidelity, were allowed to slip away. Perhaps his Mum knew of the affair and had left. Perhaps she had met someone herself and was happy.

Ben realised that he had only himself to blame for being the last to know.

Alan, Ian and Craig watched Ben close his eyes for a moment as he breathed the cold midday air like an opiate.

'Look,' Alan felt compelled fill the silence, 'forget about it for a while.' He looked at Ian and pointed discreetly at Ben with an open expression.

Ian shrugged.

'We could use a hand this morning,' Alan went on, his offer a tactful distraction. 'We promised to check the hill's fencing. I'd appreciate some company.'

Craig tensed at the suggestion. Ian gave him no chance to protest. 'Most people in the village would pay, kill, or donate a testicle to work with us,' he boasted. 'In fact, those are the only three ways you get to join Earthwork. I paid. Alan sacrificed a bollock.'

Alan shrugged. 'I wasn't using it.'

'And I killed,' said Craig.

Ian grinned. 'We're local heroes.'

Ben opened his eyes, a little humour returning to brighten them. 'You? And since when did The Meeting need watching?'

Craig groaned and turned away. 'I'll be looking at the fence. Catch me up if you find time for some work.'

The three friends watched Craig disappear into the trees.

'Wow, man. Insecure, isn't he?' said Ben.

'Craig hasn't lived in Arlingham long,' Alan whispered, 'but he started acting like a jealous local as soon as he moved in. His parents took over the Mitchell farm.'

'The Mitchells have gone? Shit.'

'I'll be with Craig,' Ian said. 'He might miss something while he's in that mood. Ben, I'll see you back here if you can hang around that long.'

The author of his own reputation, Ben had no reply.

Concealed in shade beyond the evergreen fronds of a yew at the clearing's eastern edge, the cloaked figure of The Twelfth Stone watched and listened. He realised that the youngest Marchen had been made to feel unwelcome in the village of his birth, and he feared that Ben was already preparing to leave, despite the meeting with his old friends, which the old man had contrived the night before. But Mad Dog did not yet realise how much Ben appreciated cold shoulders as evidence of his proud non-comformity. Instead, he was reassured when he saw Ben leave his backpack at the foot of one of the stones and follow Alan around the circle. Mad Dog relaxed against a bough and settled into his familiar habit. For decades, *Y Deuddegfed Maen* had watched countless visitors pace similar weaving routes between the stones. Most of them were fair-weather, camera-wielding tourists, who enjoy the hill's peace and scenery but who do not really care what places like The Meeting were built for. Many others were defiant, solitary mystics convinced that they alone know what places like The Meeting were built for. Few visitors to The Meeting were sufficiently clever or modest to admit that, actually, we may never know what places like The Meeting were built for.

'You're up here one night with some friends,' said Alan.

'Am I?' asked Ben.

'Hypothetically.'

'Ah.'

'You've decided to find out how long it will take you and your mates to topple

one of the stones – manly stuff, prove what a bad boy you are.'
'Doesn't sound like me.'
Exactly as Ben remembered him doing as a teenager, Alan pointed a finger to silence him. 'You're digging at the earth around the base of the stone. You're having a great time: wait till those crusty fuckers in the village see what we've done! *Golly gosh! Some blighter has debauched our monument!* There's no one around, it's going to be easy.'
Alan suddenly stopped, stood up straight and theatrically cupped an ear. 'Then, in the distance, only quietly at first, you think you can hear the sound of engines. But what's that got to do with us? You get back to digging.'
Ben began to enjoy the performance.
'Hang on, though – those engines are definitely getting louder,' Alan frowned, assuming the cautious expression of his imaginary vandals. 'You try not to show how nervous you're getting. You've got a lot to prove to your gangster mates. But then, out of the night, this massive car roars into the clearing! And a Land Rover! And then another one! Are you going to hang around to see what they want?'
'Me?' Ben asked. 'I might.'
'*No,*' Alan corrected him, 'of course you're not. So the whole thing's been worthwhile. But Earthwork members never know what they're going to find till they reach the hill. There could be any number of idiots who'll turn violent if we get preachy, and the best way to scare twats,' Alan concluded, 'is a big entrance.'
'So you drive huge noisy cars,' Ben said.
'Paid for by contributions from Brampton and Georgina Wyre,' Alan explained, 'who bought The Meeting for the estate a few months after you left. It was Brampton's idea to set up the committee.'
'Why did he do that?' Their meandering route around the stones brought the men to the northern edge of the clearing. 'Why does Meeting Hill need protecting?'
Surveying the monument in the sunshine, Alan seemed lost for words. Ben hadn't posed the question as a challenge, so the silence it provoked was awkward, though Alan justified the pause by considering his answer to be conclusive. 'Because it's beautiful.'
To Ben, sentimentality seemed like the strongest, and yet somehow least reasonable, foundation for an environmental project. He did not disagree, but Alan had not answered his question. 'Fine. But why *now?*'
Alan patted the nearest standing stone. 'Brampton Wyre made us realise how vulnerable this site is. Let me show you.'
He led Ben beyond the ring of stones to its border of winter trees. The woods presented a deep tangle of knitted branches and thorny undergrowth, but Alan raised his collar and then his arms over his head and pressed forward. There

was no path offered to the brow of the hill, nor down the steep northern slope, only a slow, stinging route forced through the mesh of trees and brushwood. Ben followed closely enough to listen to Alan, though far enough away from the branches whipped back in his wake.

'Brampton wanted to level this ground and build on it a few years ago. He saw just a pile of rocks on a hill, standing in the way of estate expansion. There were plans to develop the eastern edge of the estate, with Meeting Hill as the only obstacle. But if the land was to be turned into a retail park or a trading estate, like the rumours said, then not only was The Meeting at risk, but also Little Arlingham as the village we knew. The area would have been carved up and polluted with new access roads, heavy goods vehicles and trade traffic. Earthwork is Brampton's apology to the village for his mistake.'

Alan stopped talking and walking, suddenly aware that Ben had fallen behind. 'Where've you gone?'

Ben reappeared a few yards uphill, pushing through a stand of dormant hazel as he brushed clean a book he had rescued from the damp ground. He examined the leather-bound volume and the tiny padlock securing its cover.

'Everything you've said sounds strange,' Ben decided.

Alan turned back downhill. 'Why?'

'The Wyres' plan. It seems out of character. When we were kids, Ellie Wyre talked about her Granddad. She made him sound all right, and she made her Great Aunt Georgina sound even nicer – definitely not like someone who'd want to wipe out the local scenery.'

Alan slid on a small avalanche of leaf mould but side-stepped to surer footing. 'George didn't. She saved the hill. The day after notices for planning permission were posted, Brampton woke up to a massive protest by the villagers. It attracted local media attention, but not even that bothered Brampton. As joint owner of the land, George was the only person who could block the plan, and she did. They still share Arlingham House, though they don't really get on any more. Brampton's wife died a few years ago and Georgina never married, so there's no social buffer to stop it getting awkward when they're together. But Brampton kept the peace with his sister and the village by founding the Earthwork project. The estate provides us with a base on Wyre land, three vehicles, and regular permission to borrow from the stables. We even have a part-time watchman to keep an eye on the hill from a distance.'

'Who?'

'You remember PC Harper? He's retired now.'

'Carl Harper is your watchman?'

Alan nodded.

'But he's a pisshead. Always was.'

'He's never let us down. It was Carl who called us out last night when you were up here messing about with flares.'

'That wasn't me. It was Mad Dog. He wasn't happy that I didn't seem impressed by his materialising-out-of-the-night routine. Where are we?'

The men had battled nearly a third of the way down the northern slope of Meeting Hill, which was 'Almost there, I think,' Alan announced, peering through the trees ahead.

'Where are we going?'

Alan forced a final reverse-facing charge through the brittle lattice of winter branches until he was able to stand upright. The trees parted where the ebbing tide of the previous year's bracken ended on the lip of a concave hillside glade. The men stepped down into a bowl of exposed and ancient roots, encircled and canopied by oak, beech and sycamore. From a vulviform fissure between boulders at the highest edge of the hollow sprang a busy flow of clear water. It pooled in an elliptical basin eroded into the granite, swirled and eddied beneath a loose flotilla of twigs, and then overflowed onto a shallow channel of pebbles to cascade downhill beyond the glade.

Ben stood in awe of the sanctuary. 'I never knew this was here.'

Alan sat down beside the rippling pool and enjoyed his friend's surprise.

Ben was truly surprised, and happy that his difficult return home was now offering a genuine sense of discovery. 'I thought we'd been all over Meeting Hill as kids. Strange we missed this place.'

'I'm glad we did, we'd have spoiled it.' Alan pointed to the ledge of soil and exposed roots above the spring. 'A few heavy footsteps across that might bring it down, and I don't think it would take much to block the water. This hollow takes some finding so it's usually safe from tourists, but we keep an eye on it. So does Harper.'

The diamond-hard sunlight of February bejewelled the bubbles and ripples of the pool. Ben drew closer and stared into the sparkling water, his face the landing for a pale blizzard of reflections. 'What kind of people does Carl look out for?'

'It depends on the time of day, month and year. Different people are attracted to the hill for different reasons. Tourists usually arrive on weekends during the middle six months, but particularly July to September. They want to spend an hour walking the site and then head downhill to the village for postcards, cream-teas and the pub. The only threat they pose is numbers. The place hardly gets a break in summer. Any full moon, solstice or equinox will bring some interesting characters. They're mostly harmless, except that some of the people who argue loudly for their right to worship on the hill, which we have no problem with, believe that their rights include being able to build bonfires, paint symbols and melt candles onto the stones. But anyone visiting for any reason at any time might turn out to be an impulsive vandal – not committed to destroying the place, just careless: thinking it's all right to chip lumps off the

stones as souvenirs, that kind of thing. We can use reasonable force to evict anyone who might cause damage to the hill or monument, and we've had to a few times. Not the Battle of the Beanfield, or anything, but still messy.'
'Really?'
Alan returned a strychnine grin. 'Don't worry, it's not our favourite way of dealing with things.'
Ben's mesmerism by the flickering spring gave Alan a chance to study his profile. The younger man had no more than two days of stubble growth, and yet his face appeared to have lacked a wash for much longer. A decade of travel had sharpened Ben's features, particularly his nose and the muscles behind his eyebrows, perhaps by weight-loss, or perhaps by frowning, and his lips were dry and split. The vacant expression he wore at that moment was the one Ben had always worn in Alan's memory, but it sharpened further when Ben saw something unexpected in the pool.
'Hey, man, there's money in here.'
Ben plunged a hand into the spring water without trying to keep the sleeves of his sweatshirt or coat dry. He showed Alan a pound coin. 'Look.'
Alan knew why. 'Craig threw that in the last time we were here.'
'I wouldn't have thought him the type.' Ben pocketed the coin. 'Mine now.'
The radio at Alan's hip made a startling noise. He fumbled at something to reduce its volume and listened to the confused broadcast. '…steal Bucephalus! …coming your…'
 Irrationally, Alan shook the radio before sending a reply. 'Calm down and repeat, Craig.'
'Steal Bucephalus?' Ben asked. 'Is that an Earthwork code? Does it mean you're due a coffee break but Craig wants to make it sound cryptic?'
'Bucephalus is one of the horses.' Alan winced as his radio produced an extended stream of senseless speech and static. 'But this might be an Earthwork situation.' He gradually became aware that Ben was also distracted, but the confusing broadcasts of his radio represented Earthwork business, which he felt obliged to give his full attention while on duty. '...essed in black...heading nor—' He wrestled with the radio until a sudden movement and the disappearance of Ben made Alan leap to his feet. The sounds of Ben's headlong flight through winter branches directly downhill began to fade, but similar races down the wooded hillside at either side of the spring could be heard nearing and then passing, and Alan leaped into a panicky descent of his own.
He had not travelled far before he lost his footing and sprawled forward. The landing hurt his chest and hands. He rose but immediately repeated the fall and decided that slower progress was better than injury and no progress at all, so his slower and quieter downhill trek allowed him to hear the unfolding of events in the field directly below: shouting; shouting by other voices, the

raising of at least one voice in pain, and then the sharp crack of a firearm.
The rhyne carrying water from the spring of Meeting Hill left the trees where the land levelled off and became the farmland of the Wyre Estate. Alan emerged beside it and made his way towards the gathering of five men in the middle of a ploughed field. He saw Ian and Craig, both of whom gestured at him to hurry, and then he recognised Gary Basildon, the estate's head gamekeeper, near a tangle of struggling limbs. Its focus was a man Alan did not recognise.
As Earthwork's salaried director, Alan became Basildon's target for a conversation about such an occurrence on Wyre land. The keeper had been staring with bored disdain as the three younger men tried to pin down a dark-clothed stranger, but he crooked a finger at Alan and led him a short distance away to talk. 'What is this bullshit, Alan? And why is it happening on the estate?'
'I don't know what's going on yet. Who's that guy?'
Alan immediately regretted these words.
'You don't know what your team is doing?' Basildon leaned a little closer to him in theatrical disbelief. He was older than Alan by only a few years, but with his contractual authority and proudly sported firearm he flaunted a stern arrogance and paternal intensity of judgement. 'You don't know who they're fighting, or why?'
'Who did you shoot, Baz?'
'I'm a professional. No one is shot.' Basildon nodded at the sprawl of struggling men beside the brook. 'Your friends from the happy stone circle club are only volunteers, but they're also supposed to be professionals. This means I shouldn't have to fire my gun into the air to get their attention when they're chasing bickering children across private land. Do you think I'm not already busy enough?'
It was only confusion that suppressed Alan's anger at being spoken to in this way. Beyond the inescapable fact of the Wyre family's inheritance of a large tract of Somerset, neither Brampton nor Georgina had ever considered their wealth justification for assuming aristocratic superiority over their neighbours, so Alan had always been surprised that Gary Basildon, one of their many employees, sought to do so in their stead. Gary's familial roots were no more privileged than anyone else's in the village, and less wealthy than most, yet he affected a precise accent of received pronunciation over the orchard-ripened tones of his peers, and insisted on being addressed by his surname. Everyone he knew, except his wife and his employers, foiled him in this request by calling him Baz, which he hated. Alan had on occasion felt sorry for Gary, suspecting that the keeper must be an unhappy man at heart, but he struggled to find any sympathy for him at that moment. 'I'm sorry, I know you're busy,' Alan brightened forcefully. 'Is it killing pheasants or hatching them that you do

at this time of year? You get back to that, I'll sort this out.'
'You have one small hill with eleven rocks to keep trespassers off, but I have over fifty square miles to watch, and when—'
Alan could not have dreamed up a conclusion to their exchange more satisfying than Ben's failure to restrain the man he'd taken such a surprising lead in pursuing. The stranger escaped Ben's exhausted grip and aimed a sprint further into the estate. Baz noticed and abandoned his conversation with Alan to run for the Land Rover he'd left idling at the field's edge. Craig followed with a speed and ferocity that threatened a very different outcome to the proportionate response Basildon would achieve, but Alan called him back with a sharp order. Craig was keen to justify his anger. 'That prick was going to take your horse.'
'Why?'
'I don't know. We saw him on the hill and he ran. We chased him but Ben got down here first. I think they know each other. I wanted to help, but Ben kept saying it was nothing to do with me. I know he's yours and Ian's mate, but he's been back here a day and—.'
Alan pointed at Craig's right hand, closed in a grip at his side, and lowered his voice. 'I don't want to be your boss, Craig. I didn't take on this job for a power trip. I hope you didn't either, but I have to wonder when I see you still carrying that knife around.'
Craig admitted no wrong-doing, nor shame at the suggestion, but Alan's reasonable tone did silence him.
'As Team Leader there's a list of daily responsibilities I have to check off. Making sure that people I work with aren't carrying weapons shouldn't be one of them, but I will if I have to. I need to cover myself in case a knife you sneak into a scene like this doesn't end up reappearing and getting used later. Carrying a blade on duty would be worse for you, me and the whole project than any trouble that Ben Marchen, or even a horse thief, could cause us. I shouldn't have to explain that. Should I?'
Craig's embarrassment became apparent when he smiled awkwardly.
Alan stepped away. 'We're going to chat to Ben and see if we can make sense of this, and you're going to bite your tongue. Get rid of the knife. Well,' he addressed Ian and Ben as he approached. 'I suppose that was one way of demonstrating what Earthwork is for.'
Ben offered a humble smile to the three men, and then turned to watch Baz's terrain-bounced Land Rover and the trespasser until the pursuit ran out of sight. 'I'm sorry. I think that episode was my fault.'
Craig asked why.
'That guy's name is Kennett,' Ben replied. 'Alan and Ian saw him once, briefly, just over nine years ago, when he travelled through Little Arlingham.'
'You left with him to go travelling.' Ian remembered. 'But you're not friends

anymore?'

'No way, man. It took me several years to realise that all he wanted was his own following. I finally walked away from him in Egypt, but Kennett tracked me down to a hostel in Jerusalem last year and lobbed bricks through the window.'

'You think he came to Arlingham for this?'

'I don't know, but I know he blames me for losing the gaggle of travellers he enjoyed preaching to. Given the chance, he'll have a go at me for coming back here. He'll say I've crawled back to a cosy middle-class property in the countryside, stolen from The People by the landed elite, so that I can wear a Barbour jacket and kiss my parents' arse and worship money. Or something like that.'

Alan made a connection with recent Earthwork call-outs. 'People have been seeing someone hanging around in the trees on the hill for the last couple of months, mostly in the evening. Could it have been him?'

Ben produced the leather-bound book he had discovered above the spring on Meeting Hill. A copper labyrinth had been worked into the front cover and it was lightly secured by a small padlock. He had never known Kennett carry a book like it, but Alan's suspicion seemed reasonable. He hooked a finger between the book's binding clasp and the pages it sought to protect and pulled until the padlock snapped. The book fell open, presenting Ben with pages filled by neat handwriting. He turned to the last entry, written only two days before.

> FEBRUARY 5th Imbolc
>
> The energy forced to my hands by this rage is destructive, and almost uncontrollable. It makes me want to lash out and scream. Resisting the urge makes me grip until I can feel fingernails piercing my palms, like the energy needs an escape. But I know that such power must be meant for something more creative, if only I could channel it.
>
> The fury demands further expression. I find I need to clutch at the things that are faithful to me, dedicated to me, and which are nothing without me. Frustration makes my attention introvert. Inside, I approach some precipice that I'm sure I've glimpsed before at times like this. I'm on the edge of something devastating. Getting too close could release me or destroy me, but I need it, and it needs me.
>
> It's terrifying, but so exciting, and it's mine.

Ian took an interest. 'Kennett's?'

Ben shook his head, and for a reason he could not articulate at that moment

felt protective of the compromised diary's author. He pocketed the book.
'Then whose?'
The adrenalin of his chase and struggle with Kennett began to ebb and was replaced with pain in his face, and Ben realised that he was bleeding. 'Can I use someone's bathroom? I need to clean up.'

Favours

By 1999, Arlingham House had been the ancestral home of the Wyres for over two hundred and forty years. It was a stately retreat unseen by the majority of even the area's most deeply rooted natives, hidden by its distance from the estate's borders, by the gentle contours of the land, and by the tall English elms surrounding the house.

The poplar-lined avenue from the western gate ended at the front of Arlingham House in a circular drive, which skirted the pillars of a dramatic porch around the front door. To the rear of the house, a cobbled courtyard accommodated buildings at each edge: a garage for Brampton's and Georgina's cars to the south, stables and a workshop to the north, and facing the manor itself, a dark-timbered barn, whose doors opened out onto the courtyard.

It was into this cobbled space that Ben was led by Earthwork and their horses. Despite Ben's historic attachment to the youngest of the Arlingham Wyres, he had never travelled so far into the estate. 'Hmm,' he scratched thoughtfully at his chin, gazing up at the grand façade of the house. 'I'm guessing Professor Plum, in the library wi-ith... the candlestick?'

Ian, Craig and Alan left Ben alone while they stabled the horses. Glancing around the courtyard, Ben's gaze was drawn to a symbol painted in white across the double doors of the barn. It was the same Celtic cross he had seen displayed on the Mitsubishi driven by Alan the day before, though a little less professionally rendered. Ben crossed the courtyard to the barn, split the cross exactly in half as he pulled open one of the doors, and peered inside.

It took some time for his eyes to adjust to the interior gloom as he entered. A single bulb swinging gently from the centre of the roof created more restless shadow than useful light. Filling the barn to Ben's left were three vehicles: two Land Rovers and the larger four-wheel-drive he had seen the day before.

There was nobody inside the barn, but Ben could tell that this was no mere storage space. It had been made as comfortable as an unheated timber building could be, and one of the far corners was clearly being used as an office. On a large oak table in the corner was a computer. The screen faced away from him, but a faint blue glow against the wall revealed that the machine was in use. Ben crossed the floor and paced around the table, flicking through sheets of paper spread across its surface, until he reached the keyboard. A reasonably detailed map of Somerset was displayed on the screen. Ben touched the mouse beside the keyboard and watched the map scroll smoothly to the north. He read the function key definitions at the bottom of the page and pressed F1 for the option it promised. The display was updated in less than a second: tiny coloured symbols appeared across the map. A white star and the number one now covered Glastonbury in the top left corner of the screen. Further consecutive numbers were positioned on a straight dotted line arrowing south-east across the map. The numbers stopped at Southwood, but the line continued, crossing East Lydford, South Barrow, and terminating at Little Arlingham.

Ben lost interest and wandered away to the wall opposite the cars. More maps of varying scales were pinned up here, each of them displaying numerous, but unidentifiable, symbols, with the position of the Wyre estate marked clearly on them all by the Celtic-cross design used frequently around the barn. A collection of photographs filled the spaces between the maps, most of them views of the stones on Meeting Hill, often pictured at sunset or cloaked in mist, while others pictured The Meeting from above, or with smiling strangers posing proudly around The Meeting as though they had just built it.

Ben paid closest attention to the largest photograph on that wall: a group portrait picturing at least twenty five people on Meeting Hill, all of them clustered around three large vehicles that were parked in a row between standing stones.

'I'm stood somewhere at the front, beside Alan, I think.'

The female voice was unfamiliar. Caught uninvited in someone else's building, Ben reacted reflexively. 'OK, I'll leave,' he said, raising his hands submissively as he turned towards the door.

The friendly face Ben found behind him looked hurt as it squinted into the photo. 'Well, it's not the best picture of me, but it doesn't usually scare people away.' Then the woman smiled. 'Hello Ben.'

Ben returned the greeting with an uncertain wave.

'Wyre,' the woman revealed, offering Ben her hand. 'Georgina Wyre – but, for god's sake, don't ever call me that. George is all right. I was always a tomboy.'

'Hello.' Ben shook Wyre's hand suspiciously. 'You know me?'

'I do,' George nodded. 'The boys mentioned you last night. They said you were home and sleeping on the hill. My great-niece only ever had one boyfriend in Arlingham before the family emigrated: a wilful young heart-breaker named Ben Marchen I never had the chance to meet before he ran off in search of himself with some passing vagrant.'

Ben lowered his hands. 'That was me.' He managed a tone that conveyed a certain embarrassment, but no regret.

George turned off her computer, glanced around the barn and turned back to Ben as if awaiting an opinion. 'So?' She nodded encouragingly. 'What do you think? The village has been busy while you were away.'

'I don't know what to think,' Ben replied, quickly feeling so comfortable in George's company that his answers could only have been candid. 'I just got back. I've had twenty four hours of drama and my head's still spinning.'

Alan, Ian and Craig stepped into the barn. Alan greeted George and stated how thirsty he was.

'Coffee everyone?' George offered. Everyone nodded. 'Lovely, me too,' she

replied. 'Ian, get some from the kitchen, would you?'
Ian retreated from Alan's laughter and disappeared across the courtyard.
'You've met Ben?' Craig asked, sitting on the bonnet of a muddy Land Rover as Alan and Wyre chose chairs around the table.
'Just,' George replied with a grin that eased twenty years from her face. 'And I can see what Eleanor saw in him.'
'Don't get too fond,' Craig said. 'He'll run off again if life seems difficult. That's what you're good at, isn't it, Ben?'
Sensing confrontation, Ben's frame seemed to expand within his jacket, as if enjoying a spontaneous testosterone surge. He stepped forward, touched the weeping cut above his eye with only a brief wince to spoil the gritty display, and held his reddened fingertips before Craig's eyes. 'I didn't get this by running away, man – and where were you while Kennett was stealing your horse? You were close enough to see it happen, but all you did was radio Alan for help. You're full of shit, and you haven't been around long enough to criticise me. Shut up or grow up.'
'Boys, boys,' came a new voice. 'Such hate!'
Ben turned to give its source a face and attempted to make light of the exchange. 'And we'd only just started...'
Craig nodded stiffly. 'Mr Wyre.'
'Craig,' Brampton Wyre returned the gesture, but eyed Ben with all the geniality of a gargoyle. 'And...?'
'Ben Marchen.'
'Ah, Georgina mentioned your return. The name Marchen is not unknown in the Wyre household. I saw you arrive with the other lads, just thought I'd say hello on my way out.'
At first Ben was not sure what to say. 'You're George's brother?'
Brampton nodded. 'And you, Mr Marchen, are a mess.'
'Oh.' Ben unconsciously wiped his stained fingers against his jacket. 'It's nothing.'
'Just an Earthwork thing,' Craig expanded considerably. 'Ben wanted to do his bit.'
Brampton watched Craig's mouth as he spoke, as though he could actually see the words emerging. Judging by his expression, Mr Wyre didn't like the look of them.
Brampton Wyre was formally dressed in a suit and tie and highly polished shoes, and his face seemed equally neat, as though it had just been ironed. His grey hair was short and tidy, with a parting that looked as if it had been carved out of his skull. Like his younger sister, he possessed a vitality that lessened the impact of his age. Brampton Wyre projected confidence, authority, and a certain indiscriminate contempt.
Ben was grateful for Wyre's arrival. He did not think he could best Craig in a

fight. The younger man was broader and better built. 'Good to meet you, Mr Wyre. If you don't mind,' he backed away, 'I'll clean up. Where's your bathroom?'

Ben was directed to a small brick building beside the barn. It was a lavatory out-house referred to as The Last Resort by Earthwork: infrequently used and even less frequently cleaned. But there was running water, and a cracked mirror above the sink provided Ben with a chance to examine his wounds. The basin was soon rimmed by diluted redness as he splashed his face with freezing water.

Behind him the door opened and Ian appeared. 'I found these in our first-aid box.' He laid a strip of fabric plasters on the sink.

'You make your first-aid box sound like the last place you'd find plasters.'

'What was Brampton talking about?' Ian asked.

'He was telling me what a mess I am,' Ben replied, pulling various expressions at the mirror in search of a gritty one that suited his now grazed appearance. 'Perhaps he's right. Do you think I should have my hair cut? It's been almost three months.'

'You think that's what he meant?'

'He's right. I am a mess. What do you think, man? Should I admit that whatever I went around the world looking for is probably the result of some chemical imbalance up here?' He tapped at his temple. 'Or should I keep believing that I'm chasing my destiny, and head off again like everyone expects me to?'

'You haven't changed.' Ian replied. 'It seems to me like you could do one just as easily as the other.'

Ben nodded. 'That's exactly how I feel.' He looked into the mirror to apply a plaster, but paused as he met his own gaze. 'I just wish I understood why.'

Ian watched him become lost in his own reflection.

'I sometimes feel like I don't fit my skin, and I have to get away, somewhere wild and quiet, like I'm being pulled away from people – or pushed out by them, I can't decide which. Either way, I end up hating them for it. I've travelled through so many different countries and stayed months in each one, finding shit work, or staying with people Kennett knew, and then moving on because whatever I'm looking for wasn't there – and now that I'm home, I feel closer to whatever I need than I've ever been anywhere else.'

Ian watched a deep darkness fill Ben's eyes. There was bitterness in his stare, but also hope, and a vulnerability that pierced Ian's watchful composure. He clapped Ben on his shoulder, bursting his friend's recollection of so many different cultures and ever-changing landscapes. 'It hasn't been the same here without you. Carreg's End has no one else so committed to offending everyone. There's a new generation hanging around the shops annoying the pensioners, but you were a crusader. Your insults were creative, and your rebellion was a statement against the complacency of the village. Perhaps you should head down to the Co-op and show the wannabe gangsters loitering outside how it's really done.'

Ben shook his head with a self-conscious snigger. 'I was never on that kind of mission,' he said, applying the plaster to his grazed temple. 'I was just selfish. I didn't want to be around people. I suppose that is offensive, but not on purpose. I can't say I feel much different to when I left, but travelling gave me a new perspective. I found the need to come home. I suppose the real trick now will be learning to stay.'

Ben rinsed the blood from around the sink. Then he lit a cigarette and stepped out into the sunshine.

'I know part of your trouble, Ben,' Ian declared modestly, but confidently. 'It occurred to me in the pub last night when I was talking to Alan and Craig about the all the ways we've earned a living. I think you've always made the mistake of believing that staying in one place, taking a house and getting a job, is the same as giving up. You think that being settled means burying your ambitions, waiting around to grow old and then die. To be honest, I'm a bit offended by that. Do you think the rest of us have just given up by staying in Carreg's End?'

'I'm not getting into this while you're defensive, man. What happened to Mr Island of Calm who used to drag me out of fights with Alan?'

'But is that what you think we've done?'

Ben stopped and became sincere. 'I don't know,' he replied sadly. 'I wouldn't know the difference.'

Ian looked away to dull the edge of his observation. 'Since you left, Alan has had about twelve different jobs around this area. Now he works for a charity created to protect a Stone Age temple from vandals. He's a serial monogamist, but failing to act his age and worshipping Seventies rock music means that he can't keep a girlfriend for more than about three months.'

Ben nodded and smoked thoughtfully. An occasional horsey *hmmph* echoed from the stables.

'In the last ten years I've been to university in Bristol and worked for two different firms, and now I work from home running a sign design and manufacturing company. But I haven't settled down with anyone yet, because after work I spend half my time volunteering to help Alan chase idiots off Meeting Hill.'

Ben was starting to realise how thirsty he was.

'And as for Craig,' Ian went on, 'he proves my point better than anyone. He loves the village, volunteers more time for Earthwork duty than he does his own job, and meets a different woman in a different pub every weekend.'

'So what is your point, Ian?' Ben grinned. 'I'm sure there's coffee in that barn getting cold.'

Ian shoved his hands into his pockets and turned to amble across the courtyard. 'We haven't been away from the village for more than a week at a time in years, but all of us have lived as hard and as fast as you, wherever you were.'
Ben doubted that, but he nodded anyway before they reached the barn, offering Ian some return on his show of concern. 'I've always thought of Little Arlingham as home,' he admitted, crushing his fag-butt underfoot, 'and I suppose I was always heading back towards it. I just decided to take the journey the long way round. I wanted to feel like I deserved the rest when I got here.'
Inside the barn there was coffee and sandwiches. George, Alan and Craig were discussing committee affairs, but they greeted Ben in a way that strengthened his resolve for a reform of his reputation.
'Ah, you're still here,' George observed. Ben searched her glance for any trace of mockery, but instead found a genuine curiosity. 'As your first day back in Arlingham has been so challenging, will you be staying with us for more?'
'With you?' Ben blinked. 'Are you trying to recruit me for your club? Will there be badges and secret passwords and ginger beer for meetings?'
'No,' Craig rumbled. 'I don't think George meant that.'
George fell silent. She was a charismatic and creative marshal of the field team members. She liked to refer to herself as one of the lads, and the three men respectfully accepted her as such. George was also exceptionally active, and her daily dress-sense reflected her willingness for involvement with the group outdoors. Earthwork had never seen George in a skirt, although she often threatened to accompany the men on one of their many sorties wearing a twin-set and pearls, simply for their horrified reaction.
Ben was offered a glimpse of this playful vitality now. She seemed to be enjoying the tension between himself and Craig.
'Please, don't let me disturb your business,' Ben said. 'I was going to suggest that we head for the pub – I owe you all a pint – but I'll just grab a snack here and hide in the corner until you're finished.'
Ben helped himself to a sandwich and a mug of coffee and retreated to a chair beside the computer on the other side of the table.
Over the course of the next twenty minutes, Earthwork discussed topics that ranged from the mundane maintenance of boundaries and grass length on Meeting Hill, to the apparently unpopular issue of the team expanding its protective role to answer tourists' questions. 'I'm not a museum curator,' Craig growled.
Ben was happy to remain on the periphery of the scene, and the others seemed confident enough of Ben's contentment to become fully absorbed in their debate. Ben turned on the computer and was presented with the map he had seen earlier. He stabbed experimentally at the computer keyboard and found that pressing certain keys initiated an animation sequence on the screen. Over

the shaded urban space that represented Glastonbury, a cartoon image of the Tor appeared, complete with miniature tower at its summit. Likewise, pictograms of other familiar landmarks appeared at appropriate points across the map. Flashing lightning bolts connected the spaces between each site. Ben was so impressed that he wanted to know what it all meant, but did not want to interrupt Earthwork's conversation, until a particular item of discussion roused his curiosity beyond restraint. 'What job?' he asked, breaking the group's flow. 'What's too risky for you?'

Something seemed to occur to George, who looked at Alan for sanction. 'Why don't we tell Ben about our puzzle, Team Leader? A new face might prove useful.'

Ben followed the various expressions of the group. He was surprised to see Craig nodding approvingly. 'You want my help? With what?'

'Just a routine committee issue,' he replied.

Ben emerged from the darker corner to wander around the barn, here and there stopping to peer at the maps or photographs on the walls. He was flattered at being thought useful, but did not want to appear too eager. 'Oh? Then why doesn't the committee deal with it?' he suggested airily.

Craig swallowed the last of his coffee and stretched back in his chair. 'Because we don't want to get into any more troub—'

'*Because* we've tried before,' Alan moderated, 'and this job requires a little more stealth than our heavy-handed experience caters for.'

Ian tried to look hurt.

Ben nodded, exchanging his idle wander for a smug stance against one of the cars. 'Doesn't sound so routine.'

Alan was unrepentant. 'We could use your help,' he admitted.

Ben's expression contained a relaxed air of good-humoured, though conditional, submission. 'Is it something illegal?'

A brief consideration by the team. 'No-oo...'

'Unethical?'

'Not if you consider the bigger picture.'

'This'll be my second heroic favour of the day.'

'We'll owe you,' Ian nodded, ignoring the uncertain glance from Craig.

'Ah,' Ben grinned, rubbing his hands together as he rejoined Earthwork at the table. 'I was hoping you'd say that. Well, there are one or two things I might ask for help with in return.'

'What do you want?' Craig sneered. 'A lift to the nearest airport?'

Ben ignored the comment and addressed his old friends. 'I want to find my Mum.'

No one knew what to say.

'The only way I can think of finding her, without risking more trouble with Dad, is to see my Gran, if she's still alive. She was living in Shepton Mallet

ten years ago, so I could do with a phone book and a lift to town to find her.'
'Of course,' Alan agreed. And then, cautiously, 'Anything else?'
Ben nodded apologetically. 'I need a job,' he sighed. 'I suppose I was counting on Dad to shoulder me back into the family business, but I think I've killed that career. Do you know of anything in the village I could apply for?'

Ben set out cheerfully on Earthwork's errand, travelling west across the estate to Meeting Hill's southern border with Carreg's End while the cold February day suffered the ageing of its light. From a modest winter zenith, the sun appeared to mature in keeping with the advancing hours. After the steady glare of sober afternoon, the aesthetic warmth of the reddening sky deepened into wizened evening. Ben followed George Wyre's instructions precisely, though they involved a minor trespass and an indeterminate wait in the freezing air. He climbed a fence, found a hiding place and made himself as comfortable as he could.
With the sun then low enough to rest peacefully in crimson finality behind the silhouettes of distant trees, Ben felt safe enough among the lengthening shadows to emerge a little from cover. He wanted a clearer view of his target through the zoom lens of Ian's camera.
Squatting just inside the garden of an isolated cottage near Meeting Hill's wooded slope, Ben could not resist an opportunity to capture the twilight scene on film while awaiting the chance to complete his task.
'We've tried, you see, but Mr Crane knows us too well. He knows we're watching him – but not you, Ben. He doesn't know you.'
Focusing on the ivy-lined porch of the bungalow as if to project his will upon the man within, the cold nipped spitefully at Ben's bare and stiffening fingers.
'He sells logs.'
'Logs.'
'Firewood.'
'So?'
'So we'd like to know where he's harvesting his supply.'
A smile. *'I think you already know, Alan.'*
A nod. *'But the trick, Ben, will be to catch him at it.'*
Widening the camera's aperture in the failing light, Ben scanned the cultivated plots of the garden surrounding the house, framing magnified views of bean frames, tilled soil and dirty stacks of plant pots, and then a robin that alighted upon them to watch and sing. He also noted the lack of trees in the garden to support such a steady trade in winter fuel.
'Pay him a visit. You can take my car.'
'A perk of the job, is it, your Fiesta?'
Indifference. *'Buy all his firewood and then hang around. See where he goes to restock. Take Ian's camera.'*

'Is this some kind of initiation?'

'I'm sorry?'

'This job: going undercover to take photographs of your neighbours – is it something all new Earthwork members go through to join?'

'You want to join us, Ben?'

'Well, man, it seems like you want me to.'

The camera's viewfinder was suddenly invaded by moving feet, which Ben framed and followed along the garden path. Then, at the fence that marked the boundary between Graham Crane's garden and the Wyre estate, Ben filled his sights with the watchful caution of his quarry. Mr Crane peered cautiously in both directions along the fence. The camera's rapid auto-drive kicked in to capture Crane's actions in stop-frame animation: a photographic storyboard documenting the trespass, from his initial footing upon the lowest rung of the fence, to his heavy landing on Wyre soil. One more wary look around him, and then Crane was away, pacing the short distance across the adjoining field to the forested slope of Meeting Hill.

'Gotcha,' Ben smiled, his breath rising as a cloud of satisfaction in the twilight calm as he focused on the double-headed blade that Crane began to swing.

With the axe and its oblivious owner captured in their incriminating partnership, and with the freezing air of dusk filled with the steady rhythm of distant chopping, Ben rose from his cover and congratulated himself on the smooth execution of his mission.

But visions of a heroic return to his friends were interrupted by a hostile, deep-throated, and almost certainly canine, growl from nearby. Ben flinched with a nervous giggle, searched for and spied a dog only a few feet away, and then flung himself over the garden fence with a German Shepherd lunging at his heels.

Part Two

June

'Now I: let God and man decree
Laws for themselves and not for me;
And if my ways are not as theirs
Let them mind their own affairs.
Their deeds I judge and much condemn,
Yet when did I make laws for them?'

A.E. Houseman
Last poems

Closer

The sun had set.
Almost exhausted, Brother Carreg emerged from tall rushes at the edge of a pool near the southern limit of the fen and was greeted with the sight of an isolated homestead. Smoke rose from the timber roof of a low stone building in one corner of an enclosure.
Ill-prepared for such exercise by monastic life, Brother Carreg wore the strain of his exertion as a deep flush to his weary features. Breathing heavily, his legs and lungs screaming their protest against such long-distance punishment, Carreg decided to seek a few moments shelter at the edge of the enclosure.
Heavy rain clouds approached from the east, accelerating the descent of dusk. Carreg eyed them dismally as he hurried across a short stretch of open ground for a broad oak on the inland side of the dwelling, stooping as he ran. Rounding the border of the homestead in this way, Carreg narrowly avoided running into three tall stakes arranged in a row at the entrance to the enclosure, each bearing a severed head. Carreg met the empty stare of a male face in the centre of the row and was unable to tear his eyes from its frozen expression of terror.
The decapitations were recent work. The heads still dripped blood and tears into the mud. Carreg retched and turned away. He still saw the contorted horror of the impaled head when he closed his eyes.
He saw someone else when he reopened them. A soot-smudged girl, probably no older than fifteen or sixteen years, had appeared before him. Her features were dirty, slim and sharp, as if moulded by pinches. She wore damp woollens and wielded a thick branch as a club.
Carreg jumped in fright – his linen-wrapped burden slipped from his arms. He glanced past the girl and saw another four nervous faces peering out of the rushes at the edge of the mere.
'They died because of you,' the girl said, grasping her club with both hands and levelling it at the quailing monk.
Carreg swallowed heavily. 'I—'
'Three men came, looking for a monk. We hid, but they tried to run,' she added, nodding at the row of heads.
Carreg opened and closed his mouth several times as he focused fearfully on the end of the young woman's club. 'Men on horses?'
'From the church in Glastingberie.'
'Which way did they go?'
The girl shook her head and stared into a nearby wood. 'They're still here.'
Carreg's breath became caught in his throat as he glanced in every direction.
'They think we're hiding you,' she went on. 'They're searching the copse.'
The monk gibbered.

'What's this?' The girl stooped to pick up Carreg's parcel. 'Is this why those men want you?'
'It's not mine,' he muttered, thankful that the girl could not unwrap his prize without releasing the club. 'It's for the keeper of Meeting Hill.'
This statement forced a change in the young woman's threatening stance. 'Y Deuddegfed Maen?' she whispered nervously, looking around fearfully as she crossed herself twice. 'Is it here?'
Carreg sensed an advantage. 'I don't know,' he replied airily. 'I'm looking for it.'
The girl crossed herself yet again. She lowered her club and retreated a step. 'It's a demon,' she spat. 'It wanders. We live on what we can catch, but it steals from us – food, clothes.'
'If I can find it,' Carreg ventured, testing the depth of the girl's superstition, 'what you're holding might drive it away.'
The woman stared reverently at the muddy bundle in her left hand, but the whinny of a horse made her stoop for cover. Carreg dropped to his knees in panic and supplication. 'Help me!'
'Hide,' the girl whispered. 'There – the tree.'
Carreg did not hesitate. He dodged the row of heads and stumbled for the nearby oak. When he looked back from the shade of its low-hanging boughs, he saw the woman knelt in the attitude of prayer before the dripping remains of her companions. The scene was perversely tranquil against the twilit western sky. Such grisly silhouettes against a crimson dusk stood at so great a remove from Carreg's sheltered experience as to seem much further than a short walk away. Even when three riders and their mounts cantered into view from trees to the south, Carreg felt irrationally distant from the approaching threat, as though idly viewing the kind of verdant scene he had enjoyed from his cell in the abbey.
The horsemen stopped beside the kneeling girl. Carreg saw one of them draw a sword from its scabbard. He could not hear what was said as the blade was placed against her neck, but a threat must have been issued because Carreg saw the kneeling girl raise an arm to point.
The monk closed his eyes and held his breath. He crossed himself. Despite his instinctive urge to run, he knew that there was nothing else he could do. Tears forced their way past his eyelids; and yet, when Carreg opened them to face his pursuers, what he saw made the water in his eyes fall as tears of relief. The horsemen were riding briskly away to the west, as indicated by the girl's outstretched arm. Carreg rose and stepped out from the shade of the tree, only then realising the price he might have paid for his survival. He had left the cross that marked the grave of Arthur, Dux Bellorum, in the conspicuous grip of the interrogated girl.

The monk exhaled shakily and gazed up through a gap in the clouds at the *evening's first star. The twilight was reflected in Carreg's weary eyes as he shook his head in defeat and gazed mournfully at the kneeling girl. Her pointing arm folded at the elbow to become a gentle wave, and when she lifted her other hand from between her thighs it revealed a muddy roll of cloth.*

Carreg's further relief was clear, but jaded by its cost. The girl offered him the return of his parcel, but she did so from behind a row of severed heads, and the monk was bound to wonder whether his objective was worth their sacrifice. He had not realised that his actions would have such a devastating effect on people unconnected with his cause.

*

'George?'

'Alan.'

'You wanted to see me?'

'I was hoping to see you all. Close the door,' replied the interior shade. 'I have something to show you.'

Alan's eyes adjusted gradually to the barn's low light. The interior was dark and stuffy, but despite the heat of June, George preferred the doors shut when working alone. She turned on the computer, cleared a little space amongst her papers on the table and pulled up a chair for the new arrival. She leaned back contentedly in her own, and the blue glow of the computer screen picked her smile out of the shadows. 'When can we expect to see your troops?'

Alan moved warily through the darkness of the barn, but he still walked into a chair. 'They're busy,' he replied, fumbling to upright the fallen furniture. 'Can't you get a brighter bulb in here?'

'They're busy?'

Alan reached the seat beside Wyre at last. 'I couldn't contact Ben,' he explained, 'and Ian has a date.'

George raised her eyebrows. 'Tonight?'

Alan nodded.

'With whom?'

'You wouldn't know her,' Alan evaded.

'Who with?' George persisted.

'It's Sarah,' Alan admitted. 'The girl from Glastonbury. She opened Tantric Trading, that new shop in the village.'

Wyre rose from her chair and strode purposefully across the room to sort testily through an untidy stack of books. Alan shuffled his feet. He felt guilty for disclosing Ian's plans and for failing to reach Ben. When Wyre returned to the desk with several volumes relevant to her news, she could no longer refrain from comment.

'And he's seeing her tonight,' she muttered, stabbing spitefully at a few keys on the computer, 'when he knew I wanted to see you all.'

'He'd already made plans,' Alan replied, mindful of his tone.

'But this is important.'

'I know what's bugging you, George, and I understand,' Alan said, 'but I don't think we have any right to judge the company Ian keeps.'

'But she runs a New Age gift shop,' protested George; 'just the sort of place we all agreed gives Meeting Hill a cheap, theme-park feel, and we're desperate to avoid that. People buy candles and charcoal in shops like hers and leave them all over the sto—'

'Apart from us, George, Earthwork is made up of volunteers,' Alan interrupted to remind her. George's mouth remained frozen in the shape of her last syllable. 'When the governors decide that the committee can afford to pay every team member for their time, then I'll order them to cancel their social lives.'

George conceded the point. 'Perhaps we have no right to judge. If Ian wants to court a young woman who feels the need to wear a *shawl* in this weather...'

'If you want volunteers to give up their Sunday evenings, just give them a little more warning.'

With Alan's grievance accepted, George asserted herself once more. 'Threats to The Meeting rarely give us warning.'

'Threats?'

'Yes, like this one,' George nodded, slipping easily back into her role. She leaned forward to patter at the keyboard. 'Have a look.'

*

In the lounge of the house in which he rented room, Ben Marchen set aside his dinner plate and opened someone else's diary for company. He felt lonely, and had often felt this way since he resettled in Little Arlingham.

Protracted periods of time alone had never bothered Ben during his nine years of travel, but here at home the rift in his family and the absence of his mother remained a concern. Ben's visit to his grandmother in Shepton Mallet in February had offered him no fond reunion, nor any information on the whereabouts of his mother. Granny's palliative care had been placed in the latex-gloved hands of care assistants some time before, and Ben found her lost in senility. She remembered little and understood even less.

Ben's working life was also a cause of alienation. He had earned a living since February by pursuing casual labour on the Wyre Estate, and on other farms around the village, but this was an occupation that often left Ben little time for his increasing involvement with the Earthwork team. Labouring was so poorly paid that he was obliged to accept every available hour of work.

However, Ben was eventually able to reduce this unpredictable employment to a supplemental form of income when Ian Longe offered him the chance to train with his small business. Ian made the offer in mid-April, claiming that he had planned to recruit an apprentice to his small village practice around that time anyway. Ben boasted no previous experience or aptitude in graphic design, but he responded well to Ian's tutoring, and Ian was pleased to have his friend aboard when it became clear that Ben possessed imagination. What he lacked in technical experience he made up for in creativity, and two recent commissions completed by Ian's company, creating logos and sign work for two Somerset businesses, were founded on Ben's original ideas. Happily, Ben was often able to work at home. He rented the small extension of a detached house at the northern tip of the village, opposite the church of St. Michael.

But despite this reasonably secure foundation for a future in Little Arlingham, Ben's reputation amongst the villagers was not fully restored. Not that Ben minded notoriety: he routinely played up to his rebellious image, reinforcing his contradictory social standing as The Outcast by reacting rudely or comically to the judgemental glares of Arlingham's elder generation. Here, the sinister raising of an eyebrow against suspicious scrutiny; there, a suitably devious smile to a window in response to its twitching curtain. In fact, Ben came to believe that many of the villagers would have been thoroughly disappointed had he not played up to their negative expectations of him.

On the afternoon of Georgina's meeting with Alan on the Wyre Estate, however, Ben was unaware of even the most scornful stares from the villagers he passed. Unable to spend such a beautiful evening indoors, he picked up the diary he had saved from the frost on Meeting Hill in February and set out for a walk. Ben had learned Lea Granger's name from the diary, but not her address, so had been unable to return her book of lonely, seemingly tormented days.

He became engrossed in the words of the diary's owner as soon as he opened the book. Ben thought her the most interesting women he had never met, and even their lack of acquaintance presented no obstacle to a growing affection for her.

Without looking up from the journal, Ben left the garden and wandered the quiet outskirts of the village with regard for neither direction nor destination, ignorant of all but the monosyllabic conversation of nearby sheep, and the closest potential obstacles to his aimless route.

> January 21st
>
> It's hard to feel much safer than this. I reach the countryside south of Bristol and nothing else matters. None of those fuckers can intimidate me in such a familiar and peaceful environment. But security is a temporary state of mind, and these wavering moods lead me to one sad and fundamental question: What am I? Sad, because I've come this far without knowing – but fragments, I suppose, of a struggling whole that finds it so hard to reconcile all the conflicting pieces (at least, those I've

identified so far). In one dim corner of my head is a face wearing the uninhibited lust of a dark sexuality; in another (a lighter, greener corner that defies its boundaries of Mind by falling away into an unspoilt panorama), a wide-eyed young girl sits beneath a blossoming tree and threads a crown of buttercups. In yet another, I recognise the non-entity that is my employed persona, and it grinds its teeth as it says, 'How can I help you…?'

Watching over them all, of course, is misanthropic Lea Granger, who sits on Meeting Hill and raises two fingers to human company. I need no one, and fuck them all if they can't deal with that.

Anyway, fragments or whole, I am no less than I was. Accepting limitations seems so challenging when I suffer this doubt; but perhaps, just occasionally, I need this pain. I don't think I'd be Me without it.

Ben snapped shut the journal and looked up. He discovered that he had almost completed a circular route around the village, and was standing among the graves of St. Michael's.

Many of the ancient tombstones looked more like gothic growths of stalagmite formation than anything man-made, and the weathered uprights were well established as support for rampant ivy, furry rashes of variously coloured fungi, and for a while also Ben, who needed a seat after his long walk. He leaned gratefully against an antique headstone to gaze up at the Fifteenth Century chapel, resisting the urge to smoke.

Ben kept an unopened pack of cigarettes in his pocket and called it the Comfort Twenty. He had decided that, since it is usually the things in life we consciously deny ourselves that we crave the most, his need for nicotine might be satisfied by knowing that he always had cigarettes to hand. It had worked so far. Ben had not smoked for over a month. He was keen to lose at least a couple of the personality traits that had earned his unsavoury reputation. Ben was cautiously (and pessimistically) attempting a gradual change of image, starting with his formerly dark and strictly practical wardrobe. In a grudging effort to conform, and even to appear approachable, Ben wore light-coloured shirts instead of hard-wearing black tops; he exchanged his worn black boots for a pair of blue and white pumps, his loose combat trousers for jeans, and his leather wristbands for a watch. Even his unruly hair was subdued with some effort by a barber at least once a month.

Ben transformed himself from a traveller into the boy next door, but it made him very self-conscious.

Cooing contentedly amongst the timbers overhead, two doves were using the vented space of the belfry as shade from the sun. The male of the pair strutted back and forth along the ledge, his breast plumage inflated proudly, until both birds were terrified into flight by the toll of the chapel's bell, calling Arlingham's God-fearing to prayer.

The village's northern edge was situated on slightly higher ground than the southern end, and the plateau on which St. Michael's was built almost matched Meeting Hill's height above sea-level. From here, the Sunday toll of the chapel's ancient bell carried easily across the view and reached most of the surrounding farms and hamlets.

This prominence at the edge of the Levels had also made it a favourite site for the building of a one-hundred-and-twenty-foot-high tower to broadcast television, radio and mobile-phone signals. Villagers concerned about the health risks associated with microwave emissions had protested against its construction, but the tower was erected anyway, and was set in an acre of land behind the church of St. Michael. The grounds were kept off-limits to local youths by a security patrol that arrived around early evening.

Noticing it as if for the first time, Ben examined the lofty pylon from the churchyard while pretending to ignore the judgemental glares of the arriving Christian faithful. Indiscreet whispers were exchanged by several of those who passed, and they awoke in Ben the kind of defiance which, once aroused, would not be satisfied until it had challenged those who provoked it.

*

Georgina's computer screen displayed a map of Somerset littered with symbols that flashed rhythmically, and Alan had started to blink in time with them. Staring at the monitor in the dark hurt his eyes.

'You see?' George concluded, removing a pair of spectacles to gauge Alan's reaction, as if the glasses were not to be trusted. 'Another festival, another step closer. I couldn't say anything until I was sure, but I've kept an eye on this since December and I think it's time we took it seriously.'

Alan rubbed at eyes weary of the monitor. 'What kind of festival?'

'Members only,' George replied. 'They're music events for subscribers to this magazine, but given the nature of the organisation, there must be more going on than dancing.'

Alan accepted a copy of the publication that George had been chewing distractedly, avoiding contact with the damp dog-eared corners, which now bore an impression of Wyre's dentures. Repressing a sigh that might have betrayed boredom, Alan studied the artistic lettering forming the title, *Geophagia*.

'The organisers have been applying to various landowners across the county for permission to hold huge gatherings since December last year. Geophagia writes up the meetings as celebrations of the Celtic Eight-Fold Year. They form a Neo-pagan group. They seem interested in most New Age clichés, but they show particular interest in Arthurian legend and so-called Earth mysteries, which is no great surprise given the mythology of this area.'

Alan shook his head as he frowned into the computer display.

'What's puzzling you?' George asked him, misinterpreting the frown.

'Nothing, I can just feel my eyes turning square,' he replied. 'And I have to check something.'

Alan grabbed a partially folded map of Somerset, wary of the accuracy of George's small-scale digital version.

'I can't make it much clearer for you,' George said. 'They're coming our way.'

With space on the table-top already consumed by Wyre's computer, books, maps, and a large collection of used coffee mugs that harboured a variety of colourful cultures, Alan rose from his seat and sprawled the crumpled cartography over the bonnet of a car. Visibility was significantly reduced away from the glow of the screen, but horizontal slices of sunlight pierced the gloom between gaps in the barn's timbers to illuminate the map in streaks.

George picked up a wooden rule and waved it casually in Alan's direction. 'Need this?'

Alan glanced up and was not surprised by Georgina's offer. 'You read my mind, Boss, but I don't need it.' He shook his head and turned back to the map. With a pencil he circled four sites north-west of Little Arlingham. After a few moments contemplation he gave a gentle snort, confounded. 'Do you think anyone has ever noticed this before?'

'Apart from me?'

'Apart from *us,*' Alan nodded, tracing his finger diagonally across the map.

'And Geophagia?' George added.

'Geophagia?'

George held up the magazine.

Alan nodded. 'And them.'

George laughed. 'Of course!'

'So what do you know about it?' Alan asked, smiling at the wonder of his discovery. 'Is the straight line a coincidence?'

'You mean you've not heard of anything like this before?'

'Why is that a surprise?' Alan returned, a little defensively. 'Is this sort of alignment common?'

George leaned back into her chair and smiled the tight-lipped humour of the superiorly informed. 'Ever heard of Alfred Watkins?'

'Nope.'

'Well,' George decided, stabbing at her keyboard until the map was cleared from the screen and replaced by a three-dimensional animation of the Earthwork symbol as a screen-saver, 'I think you should read up on this yourself and gain some background knowledge of Geophagia and their interests. Time is still on our side. True to their religious nature, the people who lead Geophagia are creatures of habit, and hopefully predictable in the long-term.'

'So this is a Glastonbury thing,' Alan realised, folding the map in all the wrong creases.

'Well,' George shrugged, 'we do live near Glastonbury.'

'But living near Glastonbury doesn't automatically make us all keepers of arcane wisdom and mystical secrets,' Alan replied. 'You're the researcher. Being an expert on the spiritual bollocks is your business.'

George placed a hand on a pile of colourful pamphlets and magazines. 'It wouldn't hurt you to look at some of the alternative local papers. There are quite a few religious groups in Somerset with an active interest in sites like The Meeting. Their beliefs are harmless enough, but an obsessed minority can prove damaging. It's always worth keeping an eye on what might come out of Glastonbury and head our way.'

Alan pushed his hands into his pockets and kicked his way idly around the barn's interior. 'This is worrying,' he decided.

'Certainly,' Wyre agreed, examining several coffee mugs in search of the vessel most recently used. 'Geophagia's first festival was huge. A gathering of that size near Meeting Hill could be—'

'No,' Alan cut in, pausing to stand before an updated photograph of the Earthwork team. 'Forget the hippies and their parties. I'm more worried about the rabble you've given me charge of. They're all friends, George, but as a team, we don't always... I don't know.'

George drained a coffee mug and winced. 'Ur! Wrong one.'

'We all argue a lot, don't we?' Alan continued, staring into the faces of the group photo. 'Earthwork should be more than just the sum of its parts, but there's always conflict. Our only strength is that each of us is devoted to the cause, even if we can't always agree on the best way to deal with things.'

'You don't think the team is doing its job?'

'No, I'm sure it is,' he reassured her. 'But our personalities are so different, and the voluntary nature of the work doesn't always keep the same discipline as paid employment. Look at Ian: he surprised us all in the beginning with the way he got things off the ground, running about making the contacts we needed, but he's slipping back into his shell. You must have noticed?'

Wyre shrugged. 'He always was quiet.'

'And Craig,' Alan considered, shaking his head in frustration. 'Craig!'

'What about him?'

'He's a bit unlikely, isn't he?'

'How?'

'As a respectable member of the committee. How did we end up recruiting a farm-hand with an unhealthy affection for knives and SAS survival books?'

Georgina's eyes narrowed as Alan's summary sharpened her attention.

'Really?' she replied slowly.

'Well,' Alan attempted to soften his judgement before George became concerned: 'just a boys-and-their-toys thing, I suppose. And then there's Ben,' he concluded, turning back to the Earthwork portrait to study the vacant expression of the committee's newest member. 'Whose idea was it to get him involved?'

George pointed an accusing finger in the younger man's direction with an unreadable expression.

'Maybe,' he admitted, and shook his head at his own reflection in the glass of the picture frame. 'How did sleepy Little Arlingham create someone like Ben Marchen?'

*

Ben completed his slow ascent of the narrow ladder with a nervous and humourless laugh, perhaps as a distraction from the mild vertigo that was beginning to weaken his knees, or perhaps in denial of the shock that hit him when he realised that such reckless impulses were still able to influence his actions.

The ladder ended on an exposed platform at the top of the broadcasting tower. Ben stepped out onto it feeling breathless but triumphant. The tower moved just enough beneath him in the light evening breeze to be sensed, but to Ben, dizzy with the effects of emotional release, it seemed that the entire construction was gaining steady impetus at the first stages of collapse. The sunset view and shadowed landscape became an uncontrollable blur of emetic motion and he span unsteadily, blindly groping for any support to steady his legs and level his reeling mind.

Ben stumbled to his knees and tightly gripped the safety rail. He had to breathe deeply for two minutes before he was able to open his eyes without nausea. He had never experienced a fear of heights before, but began to rationalise the stupor in terms of his precarious exposure. He was kneeling on a thin mesh atop what was, essentially, little more than permanent scaffolding.

Ben's weakness receded as he learned confidence in the tower's stability. Two minutes more and he recalled his motivation for the climb. He cheerfully believed that he had achieved in minutes something that most others would never even contemplate, and this was important to Ben. He did not think that average people (as he imagined average people to be) would appreciate the satisfaction to be gained from enacting even this modest, though highly visible, trespass.

Beyond the barbed wire boundaries of the grounds below, a growing number of villagers leaving the evening service gathered in the churchyard to gaze up at Ben. Someone pointed, uselessly.

Emerging at a humble shuffle from the musty sanctuary of his chapel, the

Reverend Matthew Norton was eager to project the friendliest of parting expressions to each of his parishioners in turn, and did so by greatly exaggerating the piety of his farewell gestures. Every nod became a theatrical bow, followed by a steady rise towards the perpendicular, which he never quite achieved before the next of his flock departed, sending him into another forward assault of unsurpassed humility.

But Norton eventually noticed the chatter of the sizeable crowd among the graves. He followed the raised voices of mutual condemnation to where he could share the villagers' view.

Thriving on the attention, and savouring the opinion that he knew the spectators would be forming of his behaviour, Ben was inspired to further feats of abandon. He climbed over the safety rail at the summit of the tower. He leaned out into the air with what appeared to be the lightest grip on the rail, and – the villagers suspected at hearing his laughter – an equally tenuous grip on his sanity.

Norton hurried around his parishioners to stand at the border between the churchyard and the tower's grounds. 'Hold on, young man!'

The words drifted up from below to reach Ben's ears as a parody of reassurance. This, Ben could tell, was a voice unused to being raised much beyond a volume required to wake a snoozing parishioner in the chapel's rear pew.

'Don't give up!' came a sequel offering. 'Nothing is ever as bad as it seems!'

Ah, Ben realised, flashing a wide grin of satisfaction: sentiments of hope for the potential suicide. Which one next? he wondered, swinging out into the aerial domain where Gravity promises a swift return to Earth for her flightless deserters, and only the tips of five sweaty fingers prevented free-fall into the company of a newly arrived security guard and his dog.

Any minute now, Ben decided, the vicar would try to tell him that he had everything to live for.

From below, contradictory verbal offerings competed for some sign of their intended effect above the sound of Ben's laughter. 'There is always hope!' Norton called from the churchyard.

'Get down 'ere now!' the guard hollered from the foot of the tower.

'Help will often manifest itself in the unlikeliest of forms,' Norton suggested.

'You know you're in big trouble, don't you, lad?' the guard informed Ben. 'I'll have the police here!'

'Climb down slowly and join us,' Norton suggested politely, hiding his annoyance with the patrol's compromising sentiments. 'It's all right – you have everything to live for!'

'Yeah, man!' Ben exulted, arching his spine and throwing his head back to view the remains of the sunset upside down. 'I know!'

This response rather stunted Reverend Norton's consolatory momentum. He fell silent, accepting the absurdity of trying to talk such a clearly happy man out of suicide.

'Do you think I'd climb up here only to throw myself off?' Ben asked the crowd, straightening up for a surer grip on the railings.

Unsure of an appropriate answer, Norton resorted to a simpler line of enquiry. 'Are you all right?'

'Yes!' Ben crowed. 'I'm all right! Don't you ever want to do something like this? Just for the hell of it? *Any* of you?'

Norton exchanged a look with the villager beside him and shook his head. 'As you might imagine, Mr Marchen, hell is not my business, but your reckless disruption to this community is very much my concern. I've been more than fair, I think, and now I'd appreciate an end to this nonsense. Come down.'

Three adolescents standing to the rear of the crowd wore wide-eyed expressions of awe as they watched Ben's provocative display in respectful silence. Little Arlingham's rare public-order offences were usually perpetrated by idle teenagers, but here they saw a grown man daring to challenge the elder residents' hatred of independent expression. The three friends, consisting of two male school-leavers and a girl just a little older (though not yet old enough to defy her parents' order to accompany them to church), were silently rooting for a more satisfying end to the drama. They exchanged conspiratorial glances beneath the critical scrutiny of their parents.

The youngsters carried themselves uncomfortably, suggesting self-consciousness. Each week, as if having to sit through church was not trial enough, the three were forced out of their hooded tops and baggy jeans into clothes deemed suitable for church.

It was from these heavy chains of parental constraint that they sought to free themselves as they slipped away from the crowd, though not unnoticed. Their parents issued stern orders for the trio to return. When their shouts were ignored, the orders became face-saving compromises in the form of reminders for the teenagers to look after their best clothes.

When Ben reached the foot of the ladder ten minutes later, he winked arrogantly at the security guard who, like the dog straining at the end of its leash, was restrained by Reverend Norton's polite request for forgiveness. But any words of tactful reason that Norton might have been about to impart were drowned by the sounds of an accelerating car engine, and a bass-heavy stereo. The polemical lyrics of a rapper filled the northern end of Arlingham High Street, and then began to approach the church.

The village was stirred by the rapidly spreading news of Ben's defiant act, and youths who considered Little Arlingham devoid of the medium – and the tolerance – for the forms of expression they enjoyed felt suddenly liberated by Ben's example.

Sounds of the approaching car made the small crowd in the churchyard turn in collective condemnation towards the noise. Taking advantage of this distraction, Ben threaded his way through the unevenly spaced gravestones at a jog and leapt unseen over the cemetery wall.

Insults

Sarah Conrad span on her toes in a field of barley, laughing with innocent pleasure as the cereal brushed at her down-turned palms. The air breathed like a sigh of ecstasy through the crop and blew strands of Sarah's dark hair across her smile.

Ian Longe experienced a moment of hypnotic pathos as he watched her. Perhaps every man craves credit for the happiness of the woman in his company, but after witnessing Sarah's simple enchantment with her surroundings, Ian knew that he could not compete with the author of such elemental joy.

Sarah looked up then, and for a moment was surprised by Ian's presence. She dropped her gaze too soon, betraying a shyness Ian was surprised by after watching Sarah surrender so fully to her senses. She denied her embarrassment with a smile and made her way back through the swaying crop to the blanket at the field's edge. Blinking away the glaze of his thoughts, Ian held aloft a bottle of red wine by way of explanation for his brief return to the car on the lane.

Sarah dismissed his offer by dropping lightly to her knees and cupping Ian's face in her palms. She kissed him, something Ian had not expected, nor even dared hope for from Little Arlingham's newest and, in his opinion, most attractive resident.

Sensing hesitation in his response, Sarah pulled away to search for an answer in his eyes, only to see Ian blink and turn away. 'Something wrong?' she asked.

'No,' he replied, recovering sufficiently to meet Sarah's gaze once more. 'Only—'

Sarah waited patiently, but she had to prod Ian into finishing his reply. Ian shrugged and surprised Sarah with his openness. 'It's been a long time.'

'It didn't show,' Sarah smiled.

'Perhaps sincerity can make up for a lack of practise.'

Sarah laughed in a way that Ian felt cheapened his statement. 'Don't get too sincere, I only just met you!'

'Are you saying we've known each other long enough for you to put your tongue in my mouth, but not long enough for me to say that I really like you?'

Before them, Somerset stretched away in feminine contours of graceful perspective, its horizon ill-defined by a bank of cloud to the distant west. Sarah turned to gaze into the view, which became the couple's chaperone during a briefly awkward moment.

'Can I ask a blunt question?' Sarah asked.

Ian did not seem surprised by the question. 'Please.'

Sarah excavated a pebble from the soil and tossed it into the barley. 'Do you

enjoy saying things that shock people?'
'Like what?' he requested.
'Like the other day when you said you think I'm bi-sexual.'
'Why were you shocked when you said I might be right?'
'And like last week when we met for the first time in the village: you and your friend stopped by my shop, and even then I could see that you enjoy stirring things.'
'Stirring things?'
'You don't remember?'
Ian's mouth curled at one corner. 'Remind me.'
'You don't need reminding. You just want to hear me say it.'
'Remind me!' Ian grinned.
'I asked Alan if he's married. He told me there's a girl he's seeing, and then you said "But they're just fucking".'
Ian smiled and nodded. 'It broke the ice.'
Sarah shook her head.
'I find it easy to say what everyone else only thinks. Is that always a bad thing?'
'Perhaps it's just none of our business?'
'Then why did you ask him?'
'I didn't, really. It was just small talk. I wanted to know why you both started conversation with me. Would Alan have stopped to chat if he was married or living with someone? Would you?'
Ian was shaking his head. 'I don't care enough about what people think of me to examine things like this.'
'You don't care what I think of you?'
Ian cradled the wine in his arms paternally. 'I might, but now you've made me afraid that we haven't known each other long enough to say so.'
'You might want to get to know me first.'
Ian raised the wine bottle to his eyes and viewed the remaining daylight through a filter of distorting rouge. 'Perhaps I don't need to.'
Sarah suppressed laughter. 'What are you talking about? Love at first sight?'
Ian leaned back on one elbow and sought eye contact. 'I couldn't admit it now if I were! For someone who runs a shop selling dream-catchers, you're quite a cynic. I bet you thought I was going to say I love you to get you into bed.'
Sarah, as embarrassed by hearing the observation spoken as by the truth of it, giggled nervously.
'You're probably right about how blunt I am,' Ian conceded. 'I don't like offending anyone, I just like saying things that get a reaction. I suppose that's something I have in common with my friend Ben. Have you met him yet?'
Parallels between Ian's and Ben's behaviour had been drawn by Alan Forrest and Eleanor Wyre many years before, but there was a distinct difference in

their characters. Ben had always seemed keen to challenge the boundaries of what anyone will allow others to do or say, while Ian displayed a more intimate delight in provoking frowns from those closest to him, as though testing fidelity.

The chirp of a mobile phone demanded attention from somewhere beneath Ian's shirt. Sarah pulled an expression of surprise and peered into Ian's lap in search of it. Ian looked a little uncomfortable beneath such scrutiny and put a hand to his belt, gripping a rectangular outline through the material of his shirt as if to deny the unwelcome interruption.

'You brought a phone with you?'

'No. Yes – I'm sorry. Force of habit. I didn't think anyone would try to reach me, but it's not long till the Solstice, and we all promised George Wyre that we'd be ready if anything comes up.'

'Doesn't matter. Aren't you going to answer it? Might be important.'

Ian chewed thoughtfully at his bottom lip. The decision of whether to answer or ignore the call troubled him for a moment, but Ian felt that he had made no secret of his priorities. 'Ian Longe,' he spoke into the phone by way of an answer.

A brief pause hinted at the caller's disbelief. 'Aren't you with Sarah?' Alan asked.

'Yes.'

'And you took your phone with you?'

'For Christ's sake, Alan—'

'How long will it take you to get back?'

'We're only out at Restharrow.'

'Do you mind cutting your evening short?'

'Trouble?'

Ian heard Alan's chair creak as he leaned back into it. 'We could use you here.' Sarah might have been justified in feeling offended by Ian's excuse to leave, but she demonstrated only an idle indifference to the interruption. She rose from the blanket beside Ian and wandered slowly back and forth along the hedge while he spoke with Alan. Eventually, Ian stood to join her, folding the mobile and tossing it carelessly into the basket of barely touched food, his manner begging the chance to return to the easy humour the couple had enjoyed before their first kiss. 'I'm sorry,' he shrugged.

'Are we leaving?' Sarah asked.

Ian nodded uncomfortably. 'I'm sorry,' he repeated.

Sarah believed him, though she struggled to suppress her disappointment. She smiled. 'We could try again tomorrow,' she suggested, 'on one condition.'

Ian nodded happily.

'That you won't bring your phone?'

Ian was relieved to be offered a second chance, but he was impatient to join

his colleagues on the estate. He reached into his pocket, retrieved his polished Earthwork badge and pinned it to his shirt.
Sarah stepped forward to read the lettering engraved across the horizontal bars of the Celtic cross. 'I bet you had to pay for that if you're a volunteer.'
Ian shook his head. 'The budget stretched far enough for a sheriff's badge each,' he said dismissively, though the light in his eyes betrayed his pride in the badge. 'No expense spared. Come with me now, I'll show you what we do.'

*

A red 1990 Vauxhall Nova was pulled up to the low stone wall surrounding the chapel of St. Michael. Its wheel arches had been widened, the windows tinted, the exhaust enlarged, the car's aerial lengthened, the paintwork embellished with oriental letters, and a spoiler had been added to the rear hatch. Its stereo speakers had been upgraded and, at that moment, were broadcasting Dr Dre at a volume that made the windows of nearby houses shudder. Many young people who identified with its aggressive lyrics thought of such music as the voice an oppressed minority. However, the unoppressed majority of Little Arlingham simply dismissed it as a loud thumping noise.
From the door of his rented room opposite the church, Ben had watched the eruption of this unprecedented disorder and was shocked into an uncharacteristic humility. The national news had recently become filled with stories about the many urban areas across Britain ravaged by the behaviour of anti-social youth, but Little Arlingham had never seen anything like it.
Only twenty minutes before, Ben had protested strongly against Reverend Norton's accusation that he had incited these teenagers, but his argument was fuelled only by instinctive defiance. He knew that he would have to accept a degree of blame, and he had effectively admitted it by phoning the committee for help – though he immediately regretted the call, and had thrown his mobile phone across the lawn. Ben was angry with himself for wanting help, adamant that he should not have given his neighbours any chance to accuse him of leaving a mess for others to clean up. Whether or not he received help, Ben decided that it was his own responsibility to intervene.
Animated by this resolve, Ben left the garden of the house and stepped out into the road to make his advance on the church. The shouts and whistles of young people followed him. For any Arlingham teenager bored and embittered by their rural seclusion, Ben's trespass atop the nearby mast had been a rallying cry. For his teenage audience in the churchyard, the urge to rebel had been unleashed, though in a way very different from Ben's form of self-expression. Once free of parental scrutiny, these teenagers sought out a number of like-minded peers with whom to demand respect by demonstrating a blunt and reckless hatred. In all, fourteen destructive youngsters, who had previously

limited expression of their non-conformity to being a mild nuisance outside the Co-op, or commandeering a bench on Arlingham Green to drink cheap cider, became involved in a brief wave of vandalism.
Ben ignored the masquerading and jeering of the youths. Determined to add their own name to that day's list of Arlingham's fashionably notorious, five teenagers were climbing the war memorial in a steady swarm of struggling bodies, and the roofs of nearby cars were being used by hooded boys as platforms upon which to mime the lyrics and aggressive gesticulation of rappers.
And then Ben began to realise that what he had thought were leers and insults were actually calls of respectful greeting.
'Forget it, I'm not here to join you maggots,' he muttered, heading directly for the open doors of the church, from which came the sounds of greatest disturbance. He heard echoing shouts interspersed with thuds and crashes, betraying an intensity of destruction that made even a few of the teenagers within earshot exchange uncertain glances.
Ben paused for a few deep breaths before plunging into the church. He glanced along the road in both directions and saw parents and other adults striding the lane to reprimand (and, in two extreme cases, restrain) the adolescents for whom they were responsible, or those teenagers fearful enough of a raised voice and an accusing finger to curb their behaviour.

*

That evening, only Craig Pearce was fulfilling the Earthwork duties for which he had volunteered. Though Alan and George were immersed in research and threat assessment, Craig believed that the best way to ensure protection of The Meeting was to actually climb the hill and keep an eye on it.
There were cars that Craig did not recognise parked at the foot of Meeting Hill. He recorded their registration numbers, just in case, and then walked the winding footpath through the woods to the summit. Here, scattered across the clearing with regard to respectful spacing, visitors pursued idle distractions that seemed somehow disrespectful to a site of such archaeological interest and brooding majesty.
As tourists may read in the village guide book, the antiquarian William Stukeley visited Meeting Hill in 1723 and, mistakenly, attributed its erection to the Druids. Edmund Bolton expressed his own opinion later the same century, asserting that "The Meeting was a worke of the Britanns, the rudenesse it selfe perswades". In more recent years, The Meeting has been surveyed by any number of students of orthodox and alternative sciences to explore every avenue of interest, from geological study of the hill, to a controversial testing of the stones' reputed healing powers. But this evening's visitors to the monument had arrived with no academic ambition. The Bradleys, a family of

four (plus dog) from Yeovil, had driven to Little Arlingham to eat a picnic and play football on the hill. Around them, three couples of varying ages were stretched out on the grass enjoying the balmy dusk after a day of sunbathing and alfresco intimacy.

Craig regarded these ten people jealously. He paced the perimeter of the clearing beneath a cloud of sullen resentment while the tourists remained oblivious to his scowls and scornful glances. Craig eyed every movement of the scattered parties suspiciously, though would have been baffled by the suggestion that he was officious. Nevertheless, Craig was extremely eager to spot any action that fell within the disturbingly broad parameters of "Behaviour detrimental to a site of fragile natural beauty and scientific interest" (as defined by the committee), from the dropping of litter, to the damage debatably caused by ball games. As representative of a council that reserved the right to remove undesirables from Meeting Hill, Craig felt that this sweeping clause effectively offered him authority to act against anyone who did not seem sufficiently impressed by his presence.

Throughout the lifeless winter months, the ring of stones stood as a skeletal frame of congruous grey against the wild tangle of barren border trees. In summer, however, the weathered megaliths contrasted strongly against the surrounding growth of deep green oak, lush beech and the warm blue sky, and Craig decided that only people who have visited The Meeting regularly throughout year, during each season and in all weathers, may be justified in feeling that they have glimpsed every face and mood of the monument. The stones of Meeting Hill stand immutable, accentuating the diversity and cyclic mortality of the life around them.

'Excuse me.'

Craig became aware of two new distractions at once. Firstly, the male half of the nearest couple had stepped forward to look a little closer at Craig's uniform. Simultaneously, the merest shifting of shadow among the trees within his peripheral vision hinted at a previously unseen presence.

'Are you a guide?' the tourist asked.

Using a sleeve to buff the pewter Earthwork cross pinned to his shirt, Craig glanced briefly into the trees. He seemed unconvinced by the stillness of the shadows, but he temporarily dismissed the hidden figure to answer the tourist. Mindful of the potential for added weight to Earthwork's donation box at the foot of the hill, Craig summoned his limited reserves of geniality. 'Yes,' he managed.

The tourist, expecting a little more from a self-confessed retailer of local knowledge, nodded expectantly. Uncomfortable in the ensuing silence, Craig tried to smile and nodded in return.

'And are you free?' the man prompted with a forced smile – an expression that elevated the thirty-something-year-old flesh of his face and emphasised a dimple in his chin.

'No charge,' Craig replied, 'but the Meeting Hill Preservation Committee will always welcome a donation.'

Momentarily confused by Craig's interpretation of 'free', the man recovered himself by patting at his pockets, listening intently for the give-away chink of spare change. Gutted by a promising jingle, the man offered Craig several coins, who raised a polite refusal. 'There's a box at the bottom of the hill,' he explained, unable to resist another fruitless glance into the trees. 'It'll be safer in there.'

'So,' the tourist nodded again, unconsciously following Craig's distracted gaze, 'what can you tell me about the site?'

'Well,' Craig replied, shifting his weight from one leg to the other as he contemplated the question, 'I suppose that depends on what you want to hear.'

The man shook his head. 'Meaning?'

'Meaning,' Craig allowed himself the beginnings of a smug smile, 'that I could describe this area's geology, and how the land north of here was flooded until less than a thousand years ago, which made high-ground like this valuable, and even sacred to prehistoric and Dark Age peoples. I can describe various theories of how Neolithic man moved the stones so far cross-country and erected them here, and I can list significant historical events covering eleven-hundred years.'

The tourist's expression suggested that the offer was about as welcome as a collapsed lung.

'Or,' Craig offered seductively, narrowing his eyes and dropping his tone to a conspiratorial murmur, 'I could conjure visions of a site alive with folklore and legend. I can tell you stories of the ancient heroes rumoured to be sleeping in the hill beneath our feet. I can describe the moonlit rites of druids, standing stones that turn into child-eating demons, and how villagers have been known to go missing at night after investigating strange lights over the circle. I can recite a mythology so rich that you'll swear you can hear nature spirits calling from the depths of the Wild Wood around us...'

The tourist's face assumed an expression of rapture. 'Really?' he breathed. 'Has anything strange ever happened up here?'

Craig folded his arms, turned away and sniffed. 'Thought so.'

The visitor did not know how to interpret Craig's change in mood. 'Have villagers ever gone missing?'

'You mean you believe all that shit?' Craig replied, imitating the man's disappointed tone. 'Why did you come here?'

The visitor's expression had taken on a shade of angry colouring. 'What's the matter with you?' he reasoned. 'Aren't people allowed a little imagination?'

Craig shook his head. 'Not if you can't appreciate the site without it. I think it's sad that so many visitors might never have taken an interest in Meeting

Hill if they didn't think they'd find a landing pad for UFOs when they got here. Without the ghosts and elves, The Meeting's just a pile of old rocks to you, isn't it?'

The tourist backed away, shaking his head. 'You're going to destroy the tourist trade here,' he said by way of a parting shot.

'That'll make my job easier,' Craig agreed, watching the man signal to his partner that it was time to *Pack up, we're leaving*. 'Does this mean you won't be making a donation now?' he called after them, unwounded by the couple's response of a one-fingered reply.

Craig's sullen stance was finally noticed by most of the other visitors, and the ring-tone of his mobile phone announced his presence to the rest. Unhooking the mobile from his belt, he moved to stand out of view behind the nearest standing stone and answer the call. He was keen to show any onlookers that his business had absolutely nothing to do with them.

'Craig,' he answered, and listened intently for a few moments. 'Where?' he exclaimed. 'Why don't they call the police? Or if it's just kids, let their parents sort it out.'

*

The leering mediaeval sculpture over the door was not the warmest of welcomes to Arlingham's Fifteenth Century chapel. Ben peered up at the gargoyle and nodded politely as a gesture of superstitious respect before stepping into the church.

It took some time for Ben's eyes to adjust to the dimly lit interior after the tangerine phosphorescence of twilight. Once they had, the scene was revealed as one of chaos. The vandals did not notice his entrance, giving Ben time to look around. The first thing he saw was a young couple engaged in a tight clinch against the nearest pillar. Their dramatic hunger for each other was contrived in the manner of the sexually inexperienced, as though acting out an esoteric adult ritual with no idea of what it was supposed to achieve. But Reverend Norton strongly disapproved of their coupling, thereby reassuring them that such behaviour was suitably shocking in church.

A dart of folded paper drifted sedately along the aisle from the altar. The projectile, formerly Psalms Seventy Two to Seventy Four from the chapel's antique leather-bound bible, startled the couple from their breathless embrace as it landed against their cheeks. The author of the missile, an adolescent already known in the village for his worrying lack of conscience, cheered and strode a swagger of victory around the alter, and then returned to the scriptures for more ammunition.

'Oh Gary, that is silly – and Jonathan, this is so unlike you. Please Melissa, do put that down.'

The Reverend Matthew Norton, pacing the aisle in restrained despair, addressed each of the seven teenagers in turn as they dismantled the chapel's décor. But, barely audible against the teenagers' anarchic laughter and the music from the car outside, his voice held a tone of defeat. The cleric realised that his objections were useless against the gang; his protest was now as much a stand against his own surrender as the youths' desecration.

Up to this point, liberal-minded observers might have been able to present a reasonable case for sympathetic judgement of these teenagers, perhaps citing the High Spirits so often conjured in defence of Youth's excesses – but Ben realised that the boundaries of such leniency were about to be breached.

He did not see who threw it, but Ben did see a blunt metal candleholder strike the Reverend Norton across the side of his head. Ben looked in the direction from which it had flown and saw several young people standing beyond the pews. When he turned back to Norton, the vicar had fallen heavily onto the flagstones of the aisle.

Too numb to respond in any way, the adolescents stood their ground, experiencing the mingled feelings of regret and disbelief that seek to deny the terrible Now. Even they realised that the limited immunity of their age might not protect them from the consequences of a serious injury or a fatality.

Ben dashed forward towards the fallen man. He shared the teenagers' growing sense of detachment from the crisis, though felt sufficiently less responsible for it to be able to react. He crouched and stared at Norton's shocked expression, but without even rudimentary first-aid skills he was powerless to do anything more than ask, 'Reverend?'

The bass rhythm and expletives broadcast by the car outside the church ceased abruptly. The depth of silence that followed created a vacuum that sucked the chapel's interior free of levity and momentum and replaced it with gravity and frozen consequence. With a wounded man as its focus, this horrifying void induced in everyone present a leaden powerless that remained even after the silence ended a few moments later, and the air was then filled by music from the same car stereo. This time its speakers were challenged by a new genre as *Still D.R.E* (featuring Snoop Dog) was replaced by the Electric Light Orchestra's *Believe Me Now*.

Alan Forrest appeared in the chapel's doorway and surveyed the damage. 'Fucking hell!'

The new arrival provoked an instinctive response from the teenagers. They ran in every direction at the mercy of their panic, finally identifying the only other means of escape from the chapel. They competed against each other to be the first through the vestry door, which Craig Pearce opened from the other side and blocked with an expression of threatening immobility. 'Stop!' he barked.

The mob complied momentarily, but then turned to charge back along the aisle, shoving past Ben, who fell backwards over a row of toppled pews. By now, Ian had joined Alan at the front entrance, the pair making up in number

what they lacked of Craig's grit. Alan caught and restrained the first seventeen-year-old. Ian, characteristically restrained, merely blocked the door and shrugged in mock sympathy to the teenagers' confinement. 'Sorry,' he lied.
Expecting only more of Alan's physical example, the group could arouse no motivation to rush Ian's cool. Losing their steam, the youngsters slowed to a defeated shuffle and stood motionless at the end of the aisle. One or two covertly scanned the walls for the faintest hope of alternative escape.
Craig, who had chased the teenagers, was a little more enthusiastic in his restraint of them than his Earthwork companions. He grabbed the collar of the nearest male and pushed him roughly against a pillar. The assault unleashed a defensive reaction from the boy's friends, who had nothing to lose. A confused scuffle ensued, into which all four of the older men were enticed as months of committee companionship contributed to a defence of one another as unrestrained as that of the teenagers. Hasty, badly aimed blows were thrown and occasionally received by each of those involved, with heavy grunts of effort and pain, and stunned gasps of unexpected contact echoing around the chapel, until: 'Enough!'
The tangle of bruised and winded bodies stalled in almost perfect freeze-frame, with the effect spoilt only by a youth who struggled for breath at the wrong end of Craig's temper.
'Yes,' the Reverend Norton croaked, rising painfully to his feet with one hand pressed protectively against his head, 'this certainly seems true to the character of the Earthwork I've heard so much about. Your methods of preservation are notorious across south-east Somerset, you realise?'
A combination of surprise and relief was expressed by the blank stares of the combatants as they examined the elderly priest.
'The Earthwork committee has no business here,' Norton continued. 'It's insulting that the Wyres consider the parish unable to handle a little disagreement like this—'
'Disagreement?'
'Sending hired thugs into the village to interfere in our affairs without consultation!'
'Consultation,' Alan intoned.
'You heard me,' Norton replied.
'You needed help here,' Alan said. He glanced at his companions for endorsement of his conviction and received it. 'You think there might have been time for a village meeting while these yobs destroyed your church?'
Someone nearby made a weak struggle for breath. The Reverend Norton identified the source of the squeaking and cuffed Craig around the back of the head. 'Let go of the boy! And you,' he stabbed a trembling finger at Ian, 'go outside and turn off that noise!'

Alan frowned. 'You don't like E.L.O?'

Norton suppressed an irreverent explosion, instead channelling the anger into an impatient round-up of the teenagers. 'All of you,' he muttered, 'home!'

'Or the police station?' Craig suggested.

Norton's expression broke into a victorious grin. 'Then perhaps you'd like to accompany them?' he offered, snatching at the blade sheathed into Craig's belt. 'And while you're there, you can explain this,' he seethed, dangling the knife before Craig's reddening features.

Alan slumped visibly and closed his eyes.

At such an admission of guilt, Norton rediscovered his venom, tossing the blade out through the open door of the chapel past Ian's surprised (though impressively unflinching) gaze, before turning to address the other men. 'You dare to bring your weapons and your arrogance here? At whose command? I assume your committee did authorise this action?'

Their silence only confirmed the Reverend's suspicion. He eyed each of the Earthwork members in turn, finally turning to Ben, who nodded a confession. 'It was me,' he said.

Outside, the music ceased abruptly.

'You?' Norton shook his head. 'You sanctioned this?'

'No, man,' Ben replied. 'I couldn't do that. But I did make the call. I asked the others for their help.'

The vicar nodded. 'Help in clearing up your mess.'

'Me?'

'Yes, Mr Marchen – you think people haven't noticed the effect you've had on the village since your return, culminating in this evening's farce after your charade on the tower? These impressionable youngsters have been turned into disciples of your reckless example, and you're not even man enough to assume responsibility. Your reputation is well known locally. We've all heard tales of your teenage promiscuity, about the way you abandoned your family and girlfriend to disappear with some passing vagrant, as well as various activities since your return: playing with fireworks on Meeting Hill, fighting your father, trespassing on Wyre property, drunkenness… Do you deny it?'

'I'm struggling to fit in,' Ben admitted.

'You struggle to conform to a way of life that is not meant for you,' Norton declared, and stepped close enough to Ben to whisper a threat meant only for him. 'You are irretrievably wild, Marchen, and I will hound you until you are back on the path that takes you out of Arlingham and into the wilderness. But you,' he turned on Ben's silent companions with a shout, 'you should have known better than to become involved. I thought that Earthwork was only devoted to the civil defence of Arlingham's borders?'

Ian sniggered. 'Not exactly,' he said.

'No!' Norton remembered enthusiastically. 'It's just stones, isn't it? Little

Arlingham has committed time and money to the preservation of a Pagan monument – but now you've brought your mockery of local Christian faith to my door!'

'That might be going a little far,' Ian protested.

'Get out of my church!' Norton bellowed.

'We can help,' Ben suggested. 'Take you to hospital, maybe get checked over—'

'Get out!' the Reverend repeated.

'We can tidy up.'

'Out!'

'But—'

From above the altar came a metallic twang – the snapping of brackets weakened by the teenagers' barrage of missiles – and then the scrape of wood against stone. Earthwork and Norton turned to see a six-foot crucifix fall from two decades' suspension and smash itself on the flagstones.

'Can't you see?' Norton hissed, his voice strained with an edge of hysteria that startled even Craig. 'God does not want you here!'

Earthwork complied, and Norton slammed the chapel's wooden door heavily behind them. An echo of the impact made the church sound many times larger from outside, and the porch briefly shuddered.

'Well done,' Craig growled at Ben. 'That fuck-up will give the committee great publicity.'

'Hey, man, it makes me look worse,' Ben replied, contemplating his feet.

'I don't think anyone cares about that,' Craig said. 'It was your mess – but I don't think anybody here is surprised that you needed help with those children.'

Ben jumped at this opening. 'The children you couldn't face without being armed to the teeth? Were you afraid those sixteen-year-old girls would be too much for you?'

'So,' a sceptical voice observed from the churchyard gate, 'this is what you do, is it?'

There was a woman reclining in the front seat of Earthwork's Shogun. She recovered something from the dashboard and tossed it to Alan. 'The boy-racer didn't seem to like your introduction to Seventies' rock, but I managed to get your tape back before he drove home to his mummy.'

Ian turned to his bickering colleagues. 'Ben, Craig: this is Sarah. She doesn't like E.L.O either.'

Ben nodded a stiff hello, but he had nothing to say.

'Can we go?' Alan requested.

'All of us?' Ben asked hopefully.

Alan nodded. 'We need to talk. The Solstice is only a week away, and Georgina has asked me to give you some news.'

Earthwork climbed into the car, but Craig loitered in the churchyard to search the path with an expression of disappointment.
'Craig?' Ian called from the front seat. 'You with us?'

Destiny

Alan drove his four passengers around the northern edge of the Wyre estate to the high ground of Orchard Ridge. It was the magic hour before darkness. Across the Somerset lowlands, a sedate flood of vapour rose to turn lone hills into islands and the Mendips into a peninsula. In the north-west, the distant Glastonbury Tor rode the tide of mist like an anchored schooner.

Alan brought the Earthwork volunteers to this twilight vantage because he wished to present George's concerns in a style that resembled an outdoor multi-media presentation, with himself as the lecturer, the view as his blackboard, and *Argus* by Wishbone Ash playing quietly on the car's stereo as a soundtrack. Unfamiliar with Alan's mildly theatrical ego, Sarah assumed that Ian, Craig and Ben felt as patronised as she did when the team leader parked the car facing west, asked his passengers to sit on the bonnet of the Shogun or in front of it, and to remain quiet. He then strode a little way ahead and began pointing out landmarks in a commanding tone. In fact, the other men did not feel patronised. Sarah watched them quietly humouring Alan, and they were able to do this cheerfully because they had learned that a demonstration or enjoyment of power was not Alan's motive for his low-key exhibitionism. The Earthwork team's leader wished to be the focus of attention on occasions such as these only to be sure that necessary information was offered quickly, clearly and – if possible – humorously.

'Anyone know what a ley line is?' Alan asked his audience.

Made to feel as though she had returned to school, Sarah raised a hand. Alan acknowledged her response but seemed disappointed about it. 'OK.'

'It's an alignment of prehistoric places like burial mounds and stone circles and henges.'

'Correct,' Alan said, which made Ian laugh. 'And according to George, we're standing on one.' Alan turned sideways against the lilac view and pointed out Glastonbury Tor. 'The so-called Avalon Ley starts here and travels south-east, terminating behind you at Meeting Hill. A lot of people believe that these kinds of alignments are common, deliberate, and mark channels of 'Earth energy', like a kind of life force, or something. Sounds like the National Grid for trees.'

No one else thought so.

'Now, anyone ever heard of Geophagia?'

Sarah glanced at the blank expressions of the men around her and again raised her hand.

'Thanks, Sarah,' Alan chirped.

'Geophagia is a Neo-pagan group. A woman called Roedan created it a few years ago. They used to hold monthly meetings at the Assembly Rooms in Glastonbury, but Geophagia became too big for the venue. So Roedan led the group outdoors and they started holding dance nights in a field between the Tor and Chalice Hill. I have a friend who joined them last year. They seem all right. They produce a monthly magazine called *Maze*. I stock it in my shop.'

Alan's response seemed less an expansion or summary of Sarah's answer than a correction. 'I can't say I know much about them myself, but George became aware of them months ago. They're a Pagan relic cult. They follow a philosophy that their leader – Rowden? Redden, is it? – has used to attract a massive following. They regularly hold large festivals, with two thousand or more people turning up each time. They worship nature, prehistoric monuments, Arthurian characters, the weather, rainbows, sheep and all that.'

Craig fidgeted. 'What do we care? They've never been to Meeting Hill.'

'George thinks they might do.' Again, Alan turned side-on to the view of the fading landscape like a TV weather presenter. 'Look again at Geophagia's last four festival venues.' Adjusting for his friends' perspective, he pointed at Glastonbury Tor, and then dropped his hand a few inches with each new place name: 'Kennard Moor, Baltonsborough, Southwood. There are plenty more sites between Southwood and Meeting Hill that might qualify as a ley marker, like barrows, roadside crosses, a couple of ancient enclosures, an old well, a standing stone, stuff like that. What we don't know is which of these places Geophagia might choose to meet at next. They don't advertise the festivals publicly, it's members only. What we do know is that every time they get together, they get a little closer to Meeting Hill – and we can predict *when* they'll meet. Who's ever heard of the Celtic eight-fold year?'

Everyone looked at Sarah. Sarah laughed and counted down on her fingers from left to right: 'Midwinter Solstice, Imbolc, Vernal Equinox, Beltane, Summer Solstice, Lughnasa, Autumn Equinox, Samhain.'

Alan viewed his team with disappointment. 'Thank you, but everyone here knows that – or should do. We're all used to visitors lighting fires on Meeting Hill, or covering the stones in candle wax, every December 21st, February 1st, March 21st, etcetera. And knowing more about the beliefs of people who might want to hold massive dance festivals on our hill is exactly what George expects of us now.'

'Fuck,' said Craig. 'Why?'

'Because we're facing the risk of having a large number of Pagans arrive all at once later this year, and George has spent the afternoon talking dramatically to me about *knowing our enemy*. We've always respected peaceful religious access to The Meeting, and only ever come into contact with destructive worshippers long enough to sling them downhill. Perhaps if we understood their motives better we could find ways of deterring vandals from coming here at all, rather than having to fight them. Can you imagine what an invasion of a couple of thousand people might do to our monument?'

Craig had no wish to argue this point. He would have felt very happy if Little

Arlingham outsiders were banned from Meeting Hill entirely. 'But if we're seen taking too much of an interest in hugging trees and burning wicker men, people might started thinking we've gone crusty ourselves.'
'I think a few people already see us that way,' said Ian. 'You heard the vicar earlier. Think of our title. To anyone who doesn't know us, Earthwork could be an order of druids.'
Knowing Ian a little better than she knew the others, Sarah felt able to challenge him. 'Why would you see that as a bad thing? Earthwork isn't a religious group, but that doesn't mean your motives can't be personal. Most of you grew up here, which makes your interest in preservation of The Meeting quite an intimate – even spiritual – one.'
The men avoided looking at each other.
Ian raised an eyebrow. 'Careful. You might provoke somebody into a pseudo-psychological interpretation of Earthwork's aims. We don't want to hear any fatuous comments about how protecting Meeting Hill is really just a way of clinging desperately to our childhoods.'
Ben looked guilty.
Perhaps feeling a little silly about something he'd said to Ben in February, Alan picked up and ran with Ian's point. 'We can all feel how we like about Meeting hill in our free time. Anyone here can head up to the clearing, strip naked and dance like Kate Bush around the stones like to Stravinsky or Kula Shaker, but while we're on duty our reasons for doing what we do have to be objective and professional.'
'Then why would you want objective, professional Earthwork members reading mumbo jumbo and memorising hocus pocus?'
Ian and Ben groaned at the exaggeration.
'I didn't say that,' Alan protested.
'How do we keep our distance from the hogs if we're just going to wallow in the same shit?'
'Hogs?' Sarah frowned. 'Shit?'
Ian laughed in a way that he usually only managed when he was drunk. 'That's a crude and offensive analogy, Craig, but still the cleverest thing you've ever said.'
Craig chose to accept this statement as a compliment, but Sarah took the conversation personally. 'I have a shop full of the kind of *shit* you're talking about. I make a living out of selling it to people who like that kind of thing, but I don't think that makes me one of them.'
'No?' Craig pointed at her clothes. 'So wearing a kaftan and driving a 2CV with a bumper sticker that says "My other car is a broom" is all just part of the sales pitch, is it?'
Sarah had no answer to this.
'Maybe Sarah's an arch-capitalist *deep* under cover trying to bring down the

counter-culture with materialist hypocrisy from the inside,' suggested Ian.
Craig did not understand this statement. 'Whatever, the disguise fooled me.'
'Do you think it would fool Geophagia?' asked Alan.
'You want to sneak into their next festival to find a list of future venues,' Ian said.
'You thought of it as well?' Alan smiled to hide a hint of envy.
'Long before you, boss,' Ian returned the grin.
'You're joking,' said Craig.
'I think George was joking when she said it this afternoon,' Alan nodded, stroking his chin philosophically, 'but if we're serious about heading off the threat of a big party on Meeting Hill, and if Sarah could kit us out to look like we live in treehouses, I don't think it's a ridiculous idea.'
Craig folded his arms. 'I do.'
'Craig,' Alan despaired, 'where's your vision?'
'Wait,' Craig replied in an awe-struck whisper, squinting at the fading horizon, 'a vision is forming now: I see a journey in a horseless carriage; a man with a stupid goatee beard holding paper money, and a row of brimming glasses... Take us to the pub, Alan. You're buying.'

*

Ben returned to the village with his friends, but he chose not to drink with them in The Bolthole. He made an excuse about having work to do at home, but he really just wished to be made conspicuous by his absence since he'd made no real contribution to the evening's discussion.
In addition to this, Ben had felt compromised by talk of his friends' motives for involvement with the Earthwork project. After only a little consideration, Ben realised that his motivation for helping with the preservation of Meeting Hill was entirely personal. This did not mean that it was selfish or different from any of the other members – if asked why he chose to volunteer, his answer would have matched the Carreg's End Monument Preservation Committee's mission statement almost word for word – it was just that Ben believed in Earthwork's cause so passionately that he could no longer describe his interest as objective or professional.
Ben had also been made to feel a little uncomfortable by the team's condemnation of certain beliefs carried by a minority of The Meeting's visitors. He harboured no belief in the supernatural nor faith in any religion he'd ever heard of, and yet the ancient circle of stones that crowned the hill in whose shadow he had been raised did inspire in him a form of thinking that could only be described as fatalistic. Ben felt that a childhood spent within sight of Meeting Hill was a life unavoidably nurtured by a sense of hopeful providence. Fateful promise radiated from the stones like heat from a bonfire, though whatever it offered would undoubtedly stand in opposition to the

conformity he had been striving to achieve since his return to Little Arlingham earlier that year, which meant that the hand of Fate had seemed absent from his life since February. In fact, working on the assumption that Destiny's tools for guiding its Chosen are instinct and proclivity, Ben had been actively betraying his own nature, thereby forcing him out of favour with the Fates, perhaps sending them off in search of a more committed prodigal. This thought made him feel lost, and memories of the day's regrettable events even made him question the value of his attempts at change.

'Fucking bollocks,' Ben whispered. For a moment he hung his head, but decided that if he was going to surrender to these feelings of aimlessness and dejection, then the summit of Meeting Hill would be a more satisfyingly dramatic place in which to do it.

It took Ben twenty-five minutes to reach the monument.

Once there, stood alone beneath the clear night sky among moonlit stones, the scene seemed perfectly set for the arrival of something providential.

'Hello, Ben,' Destiny greeted him.

Ben turned to face the old man. 'Where have you been, man? It's been months since you materialised for me.'

'Materialised?' the cloaked figure repeated like he was attempting the word for the first time.

'You have that feel about you.'

The Twelfth Stone nodded as though used to such an observation. He allowed the hood to fall away from his head with the gesture, and his face seemed suddenly familiar. 'You know, you look like someone else,' Ben said, 'but I can't think who.'

The cloaked man stepped forward from beneath the trees and offered his impassive profile to the moonlight.

'What exactly are you, Mad Dog?' Ben asked. 'The village humours you, and after haunting so many Arlingham residents since they were old enough to climb this hill, don't you think we deserve an explanation?'

Madog shook his head. 'I'm a tired old man hiding behind an archetype,' he replied dismissively, 'and I want to retire soon. Our paths will cross under less dramatic circumstances soon, but you have a little further to go before we can compare notes. Meanwhile, The Meeting will demand a lot more of your attention over the coming months.'

Ben shrugged and eyed the stones gloomily.

'What?' the old man said. 'Don't you care?'

'I don't know,' Ben mumbled, experiencing an uncharacteristic urge to justify himself, 'but I can't help feeling as though I'm a bit out of touch.'

'Maybe, but you've only been back a few months after an absence of years.'

'I think there's more to it than that. When I left home with Kennett, I knew I'd

miss The Meeting, but I thought that travelling would expand the way that Meeting Hill makes me feel. It's like the stones offer a glimpse of something untamed and adventurous. I wanted to travel and experience the rest of it.'
Madog nodded encouragingly.
'In my head,' Ben recalled, focusing upon his memories, 'there was always a perfect sunset, and a quiet hill I could climb to watch it when I was in trouble, or when I felt left out.' Ben fixed the Twelfth Stone of Meeting Hill with a candid gaze. He looked vulnerable. 'I travelled the world in search of that sunset,' he said. 'I saw hundreds a bit like it, and I enjoyed the search, but I never found what I'd grown up dreaming about.'
'So you came home.'
'But I hadn't given up. I rediscovered parts of life here that I'd missed, especially The Meeting.'
He wandered a little way across the grass, mounted a slight raise in the earth and stared up into the sky.
'So why the navel-gazing now?' the old man asked. 'What's up with you?'
Ben shrugged. 'The trouble is,' he continued, a little sulkily, 'it's been so long since I felt like I did as a kid, I've forgotten what I was looking for. My imaginative sun finally set, if you know what I mean, and I think I've been a bit broken-hearted ever since.'
'Ah,' Destiny nodded at last, assuming an expression of relief. 'Is that all this is?'
'What, man?'
'Sounds to me like a bad case of growing up.'
'Oh. And is there a cure?'
Madog shook his head sadly. 'I'm afraid not. Sooner or later it's going to kill you – but,' the old man raised a conspiratorial eyebrow, 'I've heard of a way of reducing the symptoms...'
'Yes?' Ben feigned hope, rejoining the Twelfth Stone near the edge of the circle.
'You see,' the Madog explained, 'innocence is a state of mind. You've grown out of the sense of novelty that Meeting Hill offers, but the lasting impression this site had on you at an early age has lasted into adulthood, and now it's been expanded by your mature reasoning. You can't relive your childhood, but why on earth would you want to? Doesn't life as a grown-up hold fascinations of its own? Ben Marchen Junior laid a creative foundation to your psyche, but now he can be laid to rest in the baby photos your Mum used to show your girlfriends to embarrass you.'
Ben closed his eyes and shook his head at this uncomfortable reminder. 'You said exactly the wrong thing when you were starting to make me feel better.'
But Madog was unapologetic, even ruthless. 'Don't forget what the vicar in the village was trying to tell you today. You do know what he was saying,

don't you?'

'How do you know about that?'

The Twelfth Stone had disappeared. Ben found this trait annoying. 'And what else do you know about my Mum?' he asked the silent darkness.

Alban Heifia

Night had passed, though darkness remained to preserve a quality of stillness impossible beyond the hour before dawn. The sun was not yet risen, but an assurance of its approach was offered by the brightening eastern horizon, and the pre-dawn glow grew strong enough to coax the Somerset populous from its period of deepest sleep, like a mother wooing her child from bed with promises for the bright new day.

In part, it was the maternal qualities with which we might imbue the body and role of the Earth that inspired Roedan's spirituality and environmental campaign. As the conceiver and nurturer of life, the Earth was viewed by Geophagia as a mother, as the womb from which Life emerged, and the breast from which it continues to suckle: simple metaphors that require no faith for their relevance.

This, Roedan believed, was why prehistoric cultures interred many of their dead in neat domes of earth. The British and European landscape is embellished with barrows that mark the burial of ancestors who hoped that their enduring memory, and perhaps even rebirth, would be conceived and gestated by monuments of womb-like aspect. Roedan respected this way of thinking, and many people respected Roedan's way of thinking, and so it was that on June 21st she led her followers onto the Somerset Levels to dance. Transported cross-country in a convoy of vehicles to a large field near three Bronze Age barrows, Geophagia arrived with the dawn.

Their unpublicised intentions were announced to the agricultural hamlet of South Pennard by the rumble of heavy goods vehicles, diesel-fuelled generators and a wash of electric floodlighting. The early arrival of site-planners and construction crew was followed closely by the first of four juggernaut loads, and then a team of well-dressed security personnel.

Though clearly chosen for their formidable stature, the security staff seemed incapable of moving much faster than the sleepy cows viewing their appearance. Stepping confidently and watchfully from the cavalcade of cars in which they arrived, with each of the security personnel wearing sunglasses to reflect the amethyst suggestion of sunrise, here was a face of Geophagia that Earthwork had not yet seen, nor even had cause to consider. The committee had no reason to suspect that the founders of a Neo-pagan group would need to employ such threatening (though immaculately dressed) manpower. To date, Geophagia's promotional literature had concerned itself principally with environmental awareness, questions regarding the whereabouts of certain Arthurian relics and discovering gateways to the Celtic Otherworld, so quite how intimidating security aided these interests was unclear. However, if a way into the realm of Annwn was ever discovered by the Geophagia Foundation, these men seemed likely to be the bouncers employed to stand at the portal.

A hive of construction activity erupted across the rural acres hired for the event, and ten minutes before sunrise a silver Audi drove smoothly into the crowded meadow. The security personnel at the gate nodded respectfully as the car passed them. Its driver threaded a route between the unloading lorries and stopped inconveniently amid the construction work. The engine was silenced, and then the lightly robed Roedan slid with feline grace from her car to breathe the gentle easterly breeze.
Oblivious to the many busy people around her, Roedan closed her eyes, sighed slowly in appreciation of whatever she was able to sense, and began to pace smoothly across the meadow. Trance-like in expression and movement, Roedan followed some irresistible airborne lure, and continued even when someone reversed a transit van into the open door of her Audi. There was a crack of shattered brake lights and crumpled bodywork, and horrified shouts from the employees nearby.
Oblivious to the incident, Roedan continued to walk. She headed east, but could only travel so far in this direction. A border of hawthorn proved to be a challenge, even for a woman who claimed such intimacy with the natural world. Roedan reached out to stroke several leaves of the hedge with patronising sympathy, as if the hawthorn might actually be to blame for standing in her path, but was to be forgiven this time.
'Miss Roedan?'
The founder and leader of the Geophagia Foundation closed her eyes tightly to control her displeasure at this address, and then turned to face a nervous young man.
'I'm sorry,' the van driver began, 'but you parked your car behind me as I was reversing, and your door—'
Roedan shook her head, but the driver did not know how to interpret the gesture. 'It can wait,' she smiled patiently, almost genuinely, and then returned to her counsel with the hawthorn.
The driver backed gratefully away, but remained fascinated by Roedan's intentions. She had closed her eyes with an expression of relief, as if sight had been obscuring her vision, and was reaching into the hedge before her. Then she took a step forward.

Alan Forrest checked the road in both directions before raising a pair of binoculars. He stepped up onto the footplate of the Earthwork Shogun and gazed south. Geophagia's preparations lay half a mile and two meadows away. A gentle downward sloping of the land to the west worked in Alan's favour, and the festival field was laid out for telescopic study.
Alan was unsure of what might constitute the 'suspicious intentions' George had sent him to watch for, so he chose to survey the activity and compile a list of the structures being built. Alan considered such idle observation a waste of

time when the rest of the Earthwork team was busying itself with a watch over The Meeting, so he felt obliged to return with something written down.

Work in the meadow proceeded quickly, and Alan thought that he could already identify the forms of fairground rides emerging from the piles of unloaded equipment. Now able to appreciate the scale of Geophagia's operation, Alan was able to share Georgina Wyre's concern over the prospect of having such an expansive festival set up near, or even on, Meeting Hill. However, though Geophagia's impact upon the land and local serenity would undoubtedly prove considerable, Alan did not witness any behaviour more disrespectful than three or four of the contractors urinating into the field's hedges. George had already anticipated everything Alan saw: fairground rides, a sound-stage, lighting rigs, marquees and decorative banners; but she also suspected Roedan's organisation of planning something else, though Wyre refused to reveal what she thought Geophagia may be up to at this stage. She had seen Alan off that morning with a simple instruction to 'Just watch them'.

Which he did, though he quickly tired of the task – until he spotted a woman swathed in loose white robes struggling to push herself through a tangle of thorns along the eastern edge of the festival field.

Bronze Age round barrows, unobtrusive monuments to the ancient dead, offer pregnant focus to Britain's rural panoramas. Though often only glimpsed from nearby roads as curious green islands amid ploughed or cultivated fields, these burial mounds exude age and enigmatic purpose in a way not easily described, unless equal attention is paid to the environment in which they are set. Sterile speculation as to the inspiration of their prehistoric builders will fail if an observer has not experienced these lonely landmarks during wilder moments, at the edge of night or the break of morning.

Study the barrows impersonally, and you may prepare a thesis on the methods and manpower employed to construct them, on their contents, and the social importance of those interred within, compared to similar examples around the country.

But sit alone with the barrows at dawn as the sun sweeps the land with rays of golden light, igniting feathery fronds of swaying grass like an ethereal bush-fire across the ancient domes, and you may experience the awe and wonder with which a previous culture was inspired to compliment the fertile miracle of the world.

Roedan emerged on the other side of the hedge with her clothes pulled and torn into a state of immodesty. Her skin was grazed and bleeding in several places, but she cared only for the imminent sunrise. Roedan gazed along the line of barrows towards the horizon with a rapturous grin as the sky brightened visibly by the second. She kicked off her sandals and strode barefoot through the long grass to climb the slope of the nearest barrow. There, Roedan greeted the first sliver of the rising sun with a jolt of ecstasy, and then a moan of satisfied need that even the most masterful lover would have struggled to coax from her.

In the festival field behind her, one of the generators exploded in a bright plume of ignited diesel fumes, spinning machine parts and then startled cries from the nearby workers. Men ran forward through the smoke to kick hot metal away from the marquees.

Roedan's senses were overwhelmed by the experience, though she managed a breathless smile as the world seemed to spin around her. She taught her following that this intoxicating passion is not just a heightened emotional response to natural beauty, but a tangible force in its own right: an energy flow whose intensity varies with the seasons, just like seas slave to lunar will.

Supernatural phenomena, Roedan maintained, are not to be dismissed by the narrow-minded or feared by those who have encountered their flickering epiphanies. That some manifestations of what is possible choose to remain elusive does not render them alien, hostile, or incompatible with our everyday reality. By definition, she convinced her enraptured audiences, nothing can exist outside of Nature, so why should a lover of Nature fear or doubt its rarer aspects?

Synchronicity is no coincidence. Earthshine is no trick of the light. A prod from the finger of Fate is as tangible as a kick in the groin, and, as an abstraction comparable to any of these illusive phenomena, the exposed sanity of the lonely ascetic on a spiritual path is laid bare to the misdeed of daemons.

But the construction crews in the adjacent meadow did not share Roedan's euphoria that morning. They would have argued that only people who believe that transcendent energies are unleashed by the Solstice sunrise can be affected by them. The workers felt nothing, of course, and Roedan would not have argued with them – she would have just pitied them for their ignorance.

'Jill? Sorry – Roedan,' the new arrival mumbled, 'the DJ wants to run a sound check.'

Running a hand through her hair as she sat down in the grass, Roedan nodded her assent. The employee's face sank out of view behind the hedge as its owner hopped down from the bonnet of his van.

With a skylark trilling jubilantly overhead, and a light breeze breathing waves of swaying pattern through the grass, Roedan allowed herself to melt into the dawn. She heard large speakers on the nearby platform brought to life, and then the DJ introduced the Weekend Players' *Pursuit of Happiness* to the Solstice dawn. The music rose into the clear summer sky, and Roedan allowed her imaginative perspective to fly with it in a steady arc of lucid vision, as though her consciousness had been transferred to the slipstream of the eastbound breeze like a mythological sylph, moving on, up and away across the fields in a cinematic marriage of musical tempo and imaginative motion.

From the relative cover of its parking space below, a white Mitsubishi Shogun rolls back onto the road and drives east, remaining in view for only a few seconds before this soaring narrative view overtakes even Alan's acceleration and flies straight for the unblinking eye of the rising sun.

A wide vista of meadows, snaking streams and blossoming orchards pass by smoothly below until all sense of locality is lost, and our sylph's-eye-view is filled with equal proportions of earth and sky. The sun brightens steadily as its globe clears the horizon, and then the tree-lined hemisphere of Meeting Hill becomes visible against it.

Drawing closer, we find the eleven standing stones devoid of human company on the summit, and the hilltop sanctuary is a lure for our roaming perspective, which skirts the treetops around the clearing in a smooth circular descent. The narrative enjoys unhindered passage down through the branches and leaves, finally emerging at ground level, where a lone roe deer is alerted but untroubled by the arrival of our oneiric presence, and a light mist lingers on the summit, blurring the megaliths' emergence from the soil and lending diaphanous substance to golden beams of the sun's waxing light.

Into this view canters a horse and rider. The mount's hooves glisten with dew. The pewter Earthwork cross pinned to Ian's jacket catches the sunrise as a flash of diamond brilliance and casts a wavering reflection onto the Monk's Pillow, the largest of The Meeting's stones.

The watchful rider slows the horse and rubs his eyes. Ian is unused to rising so early, but he gazes over the site with a smile of quiet satisfaction. His Earthwork duty brings him regularly to the stones, but Ian does not take the privilege of frequent access to The Meeting for granted, especially at times of the day and year reputed to hold such significance for megalithic monuments. However, Meeting Hill will be forsaken by the Pagan community until much later this Solstice morning. Ian has found the summit deserted, so he concludes his dawn patrol with one slow circuit of the clearing and then descends the southern footpath at a steady trot.

*

May 1st Beltane

Time marches on and away, regardless of my contentment with the way things are, or were. But Glastonbury Tor is a rock – literally, and as an anchor for my soul when everything seems to be slipping away. Today I find the hollow tower standing alone. The view is perfect, the breeze is a friend, and the whole world is somehow purified by my distance above it. From the summit of the Tor, Glastonbury and the countryside around it lose the detail that defines recognition and identity, and instead become generic, like archetypes. This could be any rural market town, anywhere in England, and I – a kindred principle amongst manifest dreams – can be involved in all, and yet none.

But peace is short-lived. All too soon I am reaching for my diary and pen, compelled to examine my thoughts and feelings in case any of them occurred while I wasn't looking. I surrender to the urge to document every moment of experience, desperate to save even the most trivial observation in case I break the thread of my recorded existence and lose control over it.

The day is coming to an end, but I have to laugh, even in front of the people who are arriving on the hill around me. Everyone here wants to see the sun set, but I find it ironic. Sunsets are a natural symbol of finality: the blaze of glory before darkness and cold, and yet I see such inspiration and optimism in its blood-red glow.

Like tourists, the other people here disappear as soon as it starts to get dark, and I'm happy with that. I relax in the fading light and plant my heart in the memory of stolen innocence, hoping beyond all sanity that the soul of the past may nurture seeds to its own rebirth.

Ben looked up from the diary to reach for his tea, but immediately tossed the book aside and jumped out of bed when he saw sunlight against the bedroom window. 'Shit, man!'

Unable to sleep in the clinging heat of the shortest night, Ben had made himself a drink and picked up the previous year's memoirs of the girl named Lea. He continued to find her words compelling, and so addictive that he had let his tea go cold as he lost track of time.

Ben got up and dressed in less than a minute. He was expected on the Wyre Estate for committee duty, but that morning he rejected his uniform for the cool freedom of shorts, trainers and a T-shirt bearing a humorous slogan concerning the superhuman alcohol consumption of its wearer. He retrieved his Earthwork badge from a shelf, pinned it to his chest and then descended the stairs three at a time.

In the driveway of the house was Ben's vehicle, an ageing Toyota pick-up he had chosen for its rural character and bargain price.

'Your car needs a silencer, Mr Marchen. Engines this loud are illegal.'

The unexpected advice was offered by Reverend Norton, who was passing on his way to the church. Stood at the end of the drive with a dog that looked at least as old as the vicar himself, Norton confronted Ben as he closed and locked the front door behind him and made for the offending vehicle. Ben nodded reasonably, determined to be polite

against all expectation. 'The exhaust is loose, or holed, or something,' he

admitted, 'but I have a friend who can sort it.'
'That noise has disturbed us all week,' Norton laboured the point.
'Hey, man, I bought it only two days ago,' Ben told him, unlocking the door.
Norton evaded the contradiction. 'It needs silencing,' he repeated, relishing the last word, but apparently reluctant to move on having brandished it.
Ben started the car and revved it gently. Norton did not move. He stood his ground at the end of the drive and lectured Ben inaudibly through the pick-up's windscreen. Ben glanced at his watch, found no time for the confrontation that Norton seemed keen to provoke, so tried to look as though he might be having trouble with his gears. He made a show of struggling the car noisily into first and then lifted his foot sharply from the clutch, stalling the engine with a thud. The car lurched forward a foot as it died, forcing Norton and the aged dog into a reflexive backward jump.
Ben wound down the window and leaned out. 'Sorry!' he grinned dopily. 'I'm still getting used to it.'
Norton nodded slowly, as though the encounter had thoroughly vindicated his opinion. He whistled a low summons to his decrepit pet and marched resolutely towards the church.
Ben had accepted a degree of responsibility for inspiring the disorder of the week before, but the villagers' treatment of him ever since was so irrationally determined that Ben was not only bored of it, he had started to consider himself the aggrieved party, which eased his conscience.
As soon as his exit from the driveway was clear, Ben released the hand-brake, rolled out onto the road and accelerated south through Carreg's End.

*

From the open doors of the barn in the courtyard of Arlingham House, Craig Pearce watched a silent confrontation between the Wyre siblings.
Georgina Wyre had been heading across the courtyard in the direction of the Earthwork barn, reading a book as she walked, when she noticed a silent presence at the back door of the house. Opposite the barn, Brampton Wyre stared at his sister with glowering disapproval. They made eye-contact, and George paused for a moment to challenge his piercing gaze.
The spell was broken a few seconds later by the emergence of the estate's mechanic, Abel Mild, who was well past retirement age but refused to admit it, from the nearby workshop. Brampton looked away and stepped back into the house. Similarly, George dismissed the encounter with a blink and returned to the contents of her book. She wandered sedately past an entertained Craig to her table in the barn.
Before Craig could turn to join her, he was approached by the jittery form of Abel, who begged attention wearing his familiar expression of nervous insistence. Craig glanced down at the man and considered ignoring him.

'You're down motor 's mornin'.'
'Pardon?' Craig frowned. The depth of Abel's West Country accent made him the butt of jokes about rural isolation.
'Knackered.'
'Slow down, then, you're always sprinting about the place.'
'Not me,' Abel winced.
'Eh?'
'Y' jeep.'
'What about it?' Craig frowned.
'Buggered.'
'What's wrong with it?'
Abel blinked. ''S technical,' he muttered, acutely possessive of his role and expertise. 'You didn't put an' oil 'n it.'
'You mean *you* didn't put any oil in it? You're the mechanic. Have you told George?'
'I'm tellin' you.'
Ian appeared on horseback on the other side of the courtyard. Abel danced a panicky shuffle in response to the arrival, so possessive was he of the estate, and so terrified of strangers, though he brought his nerves under control when he recognised the rider.
'Least 'e rides nicer 'an 'e drives, else 'e'd stuff t' an'mals too,' Mild muttered, retrieving a cigarette from behind his ear as he walked away.
Despite the hour, Ian had begun to feel good after his ride across the fields, and especially deserving of whatever breakfast might be on offer.
'All quiet?' Craig asked as Ian slid off the saddle.
'As we like it,' Ian nodded, rubbing Bucephalus' damp neck and guiding him to the paddock behind the stable.
'No dawn sacrifice to the stones?' Craig replied. 'No naked Pagans dancing to worship the rising of the Great Yellow Hot One? Why did we bother getting up at three this morning?'
Ian hurried back across the courtyard and peered into the barn. 'Has George sorted out the toast yet?'
Craig shook his head. 'Brampton's up and about so I think she's avoiding the house. He's keen to know how we work, isn't he? He had his spies out since before dawn.'
From the cramped workshop adjoining the stables, Abel Mild scanned the courtyard on cue, but Ian was too hungry to care. 'No breakfast? George promised.'
Alan returned only a short time later, manoeuvring the car back into the barn as Brampton had instructed the Earthwork team to do at the beginning of May, despite George's protests. Allowing for the availability of drivers, George knew that the committee's response time could only be improved if the

vehicles were positioned ready in the courtyard, facing an open gate. But Brampton Wyre had insisted that the cars be kept inside Earthwork's headquarters, at the same time reminding the team of his generosity in having devoted the barn, vehicles, and occasional use of the horses to Earthwork service at all. The courtyard itself was primarily the focus of a busy agricultural enterprise, he said, and should not be made impassable to the estate staff.

As joint owners of the family estate, the Wyres might have foreseen this overlapping of interests and its potential problems, and no one was quite sure why they had pressed ahead regardless (although, based on his own experience, Ian had suggested that wealth and/or maturity were no obstacles to the natural state of mutual provocation between siblings). As a result, their competing priorities widened an already daunting rift between them. Brampton, who had yet to renounce his ambition to adapt and expand the estate's business interests, despite his public support for the committee, sought substantial acreage for commercial development, and Georgina doggedly opposed him.

But it was clear, as Craig had seen, that open enmity between brother and sister was avoidable, and this failure to confront each other directly over contentious issues left Brampton feeling free to shape his plans, and George at liberty to join her Earthwork colleagues and devise their own.

Lea Granger

The sun was well established upon the route of its Solstice display by the time Ben reached the ornamental gateway to the Wyre estate. He pulled off the road through the eagle-crowned arch, drove too fast for a further minute beneath the leafy canopy of the estate's poplar drive, and finally emerged with a dusty skid from the trees in the deserted courtyard. He rehearsed his excuse for being late as he parked the pick-up and climbed out of the car.

As always, it was dark inside the barn, but Ben could make out four familiar figures around the table as he entered, each nursing mugs of coffee and apparently waiting for him. Unless the pendulous bulb hung from the rafters had blown, Ben could only assume that the darkness held some purpose for his colleagues. 'Are we holding a seance?'

Craig mumbled something sardonic about it being easier to raise the dead than some members of the living. 'I'm sorry I'm late,' Ben replied, 'but I was involved in a little research.'

Again, Craig had something to say about the kind of thing Ben would probably study while alone in bed, but Ben just gazed with unconcealed interest at the other men's drinks until George pointed to a large flask and a spare mug. 'Really?'

'Mmh,' Ben nodded, enjoying brief command of the group's attention as he poured himself a cup, 'I've been reading up on the records of a Geophagia insider.'

'The diary?' Ian remembered. 'The book from Meeting Hill.'

'The same,' Ben replied, taking his seat beside Alan, 'and I'm starting to feel a bit guilty about the conclusions we've jumped to, man. It might be our job to suspect the intentions of these kinds of groups, but I think we might be wasting our time with Geophagia. This woman, Lea, has filled her diary with fierce environmental argument and concern for megalithic monuments, which only leaves us her obsessiveness to worry about. But I don't think *we* can criticise the girl on that score.'

George nodded but remained quiet.

'Are you really expecting trouble?' Alan asked her. 'We've read up on everything you've collected about Geophagia and I've seen the group at work this morning, but we've seen nothing to justify suspicion.'

Wyre laid her hands flat on the table and leaned back into her chair. She had earned the respect of the men with her easy leadership and democratic approach to decision-making. Even Craig said she was 'cool'. However, upon hearing the younger men's reservations she became defensive. 'You want to see the Geophagia Foundation hold a rave on Meeting Hill?'

'No,' Ian replied. 'But not for any good reason. I think we might just be wanting to find one so that we don't seem prejudiced. Geophagia have earned a decent reputation so far by cleaning up after themselves at previous festivals, and we have no proof that they're anything less than respectful to the sites they visit. I think we're being a little possessive of The Meeting and jealous of people who come here – unless there's more, George? Perhaps there's something you haven't mentioned yet?'

'Perceptive as ever,' she commended him.

'Well?'

George shrugged. 'Perhaps,' she admitted, 'but it's too soon to say with any conviction. You might all accuse me of paranoia, or of looking for ways to justify the possessiveness that Ian's talking about. I think that what we already know about Geophagia is reason enough to worry. Alan? What did you see this morning?'

'Nothing remarkable: plenty of vehicles and a lot of people setting up tents, a fairground, stage and electrics. Lots of security on the gate, and some woman who seemed to get emotional on one of the South Pennard barrows at sunrise. Nothing dodgy, though you gave me nothing specific to look out for. But this is a huge event. They might tidy up after themselves, but the fields they've occupied will be churned up. I think that's as much as we can know without getting in there and asking questions.'

'Well now, there's a plan,' George observed, reaching beneath the table to retrieve a metal briefcase, the likes of which a cinematic assassin might employ to carry a high-tech weapon. George flipped open the clasps and raised the lid to reveal a set of four tiny, flesh-toned units encased in protective foam, and a larger gadget whose function Georgina would undoubtedly enjoy explaining.

Apparently quicker on the uptake than the others, Ian raised his eyebrows and gazed at the committee leader in surprise. 'Just what does our budget stretch to, George?'

Wyre seemed offended. 'These not good enough for you?'

'That's not what I meant. I didn't think we'd finished paying for the cars yet, and you're splashing out on expensive radio gear.'

'What are they?' Craig asked, straining across the table for a better view.

'A way of co-ordinating your visit to Geophagia's Solstice festival tonight,' George replied, lowering her voice to a conspiratorial volume. 'With only one minor let-down, this equipment will keep us in touch over a wide area, allowing me to direct you when we split up to explore. You each wear one of these in your ear, eliminating the need for bulky radios that security would spot a mile off.'

The men could barely contain themselves. Each of them made a grab for their share of the new toy and set about squeezing it into their ears.

'Fantastic, George!' Alan enthused, though he winced a little at the size of the ear-piece. 'You've really planned ahead. What's the minor let-down? And how do we talk to you while we're wearing them?'

George chuckled as Alan answered his first question with the second. His face dropped. 'These are only receivers? So how do we update you without a two-way system? Your information will be out of date the moment we leave you.'

Georgina accepted this criticism of her plan, but she knew that the alternative would be unpopular. 'Would you rather risk the radios?'

The men looked at each other and accepted that anonymity would be pivotal to the success of their task. 'We can't advertise ourselves as gatecrashers and expect people to answer our questions,' Ben observed. 'It's a shame more people don't carry mobile phones, we could have taken ours without standing out.'

Wyre shrugged, lacking other options. 'Then these are the next best thing. At least I can watch the gate and keep an eye on Geophagia's security staff – you'll want to know where they are, whether they've noticed us and what kind of mood they're in. And we only need one-way communication for me to guide you around the field.'

'You have a map?'

'I have guides from the previous festivals. Geophagia publish nothing like that before the event – I only knew where today's festival would be held because I have a friend with his ear to the ground in South Pennard. But Geophagia prints site plans in its *Maze* magazine to illustrate their biased reviews later, and they're all similar. There are certain things that I want you to look at, but you'll know what I'm interested in by now if you've read up on the texts I suggested.'

Three of George's colleagues nodded solemnly, so Craig's lack of response was conspicuous. 'Mr Pearce?' Georgina frowned. 'Did you spend some time with the magazines and books I recommended?'

'Oh yeah,' Craig sniffed dismissively, avoiding eye-contact with anyone. 'Fairies and spirits, rainbows and crystals, Avalon mists and the Lady of the Lake. Oh yeah.'

Wyre shook her head. 'You haven't read a page,' she accused him, her stern tone surprising Earthwork for the second time that morning. 'What's the matter? Too macho for a little research, Craig?'

'Something like that,' Craig replied eventually with a confrontational stare. 'Actually, I'm just too embarrassed to admit that I took your idea seriously and read everything I could find. *Know your enemy,* you said, so I read all the books and magazines, and now I've got ley lines, path-working techniques, Arthurian romance, Celtic wisdom, triple-goddesses, Feng Shui and alchemical jargon coming out of my ears. I'm thinking about setting up my own little cult now. I could sound so wise, or just so cryptic, that people would have to assume that I'm a messenger from the Pelaides, or a reincarnated shaman.'

Ian thought it a good point. 'We could read about this stuff for months, but we can never know enough to keep up. Geophagia have one or two running themes that come up in all their magazines, but none of them relate to a consistent aim or purpose, and they don't like to identify themselves with any established religions. In fact, there's not much they won't print in Maze magazine. Anything associated with the occult is thrown in to create a collection of unrelated New Age clichés and empty feel-good messages.'

A tractor rumbled past the open doors of the barn with a trailer carrying fresh bedding and feed for the stable. The throaty chug of its engine silenced the team's debate for a minute, giving them time to sip at their coffee. When the tractor moved on and peace was restored, George and the men spent a further few moments in silence, collecting their thoughts. In the roof space above the table, a trapped bee droned ceaselessly in search of the open sky but discovered only a forest of rafters and a mouldy skylight, against which it flew repeatedly with fuzzy bumps of frustration.

Ben drained the last of his coffee and leaned back to watch the unlearning persistence of the bee. For a moment, Earthwork allowed the weak interior light and the timber-scented heat to lull their minds into idle thought, until Alan remembered some sense of the morning's responsibility. 'I think someone should look at The Meeting again. All these plans will mean nothing if people are vandalising the stones while we're sitting here gassing.'

George reassured Alan as she replaced the tiny radio receivers in their case. 'Mr Harper is on duty.'

Ben exchanged a look with Ian. 'On duty? But we can't rely on the man to stay awake.'

'Fine,' Wyre replied, and with Ben's late arrival in mind accepted his concern by sending him out on a patrol of Meeting Hill. The other men volunteered to stay behind, finalise the evening's plans and drink more coffee. Georgina even hinted at the possibility of hot croissants, making Ben's duty even more unwelcome when he considered his empty stomach. Ian raised his mug in cheerful farewell and winked as Ben made for the door with the keys to the Land Rover. 'We're here if you need us,' he reassured him, patting his radio. 'Just shout.'

Exactly one year before, Ben had been staying at a friend's flat in Southwark, and he had not realised that it was a solstice day until the evening when he sat down in front of the TV with an Indian takeaway to watch the news. There was a report about a dawn gathering at Stonehenge, and the arrest of a number of people who expressed their self-proclaimed reverence for the site by fighting each other, and climbing the trilithons to urinate into the crowd.

The report had aroused in Ben a surge of something wild and untamed: a restlessness he had sought to crush by abandoning his life of travel with Kennett. Ben had put aside his dinner and crossed the tiny lounge to the window. Lifting the nicotine-stained net curtain, he gazed out across a fume-choked city at the last of the sunset and yearned for a view in which the landscape reflected the rosy passion of the sky. He was suddenly sick of the claustrophobic urban sprawl, with its hard concrete edges and artificial horizons. Ben had tried to convince himself that the glowing dusk was a natural presence that sanctified the city, but he could not. Twilight and endless rooftops were incongruous as halves of the same view. The city was an unnatural grey pile that reached up to despoil the sky.

One year on, and Ben reflected happily on having returned to the environment he had craved. He wound down the window of the Land Rover as he negotiated the narrow winding route to Meeting Hill. He turned on the radio and found one of Alan's tapes in the player. It came to life halfway through the Ozric Tentacles' *Jurassic Shift*.

Over the roadside hedges, the forested vault of Meeting Hill steadily filled the rectangular view through the windscreen. Framed in this way by the metal border of the window, Ben was able to imagine the hill as being immutably preserved in a secure portrait world, safe not only from those who might threaten The Meeting's physical integrity, but also from the sight of pylons, houses and roads that would defile its natural aesthetic.

Meeting Hill's vulnerability outside this slim perspective was a fact particularly unwelcome in comparison. Ben preferred to think of the site as a free and unspoilt domain, whose dense flora and teeming fauna were inviolate to the disrespectful, but whose branches reached out as agents of the Wild to beckon to those who feel the pulse of the *anima mundi* as keenly as trees.

And Ben experienced their lure as he gazed up into woods at the foot of the hill. He made a sharp right turn off the road to negotiate Meeting Hill's only path, but stopped for a moment to contemplate one of the site's many ancient oaks. Here was a tree so old, gnarled and twisted in its antiquity, Ben thought it must be a remnant of the primeval forest that once covered Britain. The wizened growth embodied a stately mystique, but even while he was absorbed by the personality of this familiar form, Ben experienced a nagging frustration at his inability to define it. The sum of its qualities defied description, unless its own noun was offered an adjectival role. Ben could cite characteristics such as its age, strength, vitality, enigmatic presence, and many more, but nothing on his list came close to describing the tree's essential *oakishness*.

On the summit, Ben found The Meeting in its familiar mood of patient anticipation, and he considered time alone with a site of such renown as comparable to an exclusive audience with an admired celebrity. The Meeting was a popular attraction for many people, but, at that moment, the stones belonged to Ben.

He had not expected to find the clearing empty, though. A motorbike parked at the edge of the road below had hinted at a visitor to the site. Idly suspicious,

Ben reversed the car carefully into the cover of the southern trees, turned off the engine and waited for the unseen guest.

Ten minutes peace lured a roe deer from the trees, and it grazed amongst the stones. Ben watched the animal contentedly, until something beyond the range of Ben's senses startled the deer into rigid vigilance. It stared into the trees opposite Ben's position. It saw nothing to cause further alarm, but was terrified from the open hilltop by Ben's emergence. He locked the car, jogged across the clearing and then paused at the edge of the northern tree-line, listening intently for whatever had disturbed the deer. He heard nothing, which was reassuring, but not a reason to avoid further investigation.

Beneath the canopy of beech and oak, clouds of midges swarmed in vertical shafts of leaf-filtered sunlight, and Ben felt a little guilty for breaking their contented flight with his passing. He crept through the trees to the edge of the northern slope, and then quietly on and down, stepping carefully over exposed roots where the slope's gradient could no longer cover their creeping expansion.

Ben soon found himself directly above the glade that sheltered Meeting Hill's hidden spring, whose chattering flow he could hear through the trees. He stopped and stooped among the ferns to peer into the gradient dell. There, sitting beside the water, Ben saw a woman of around his own age, or perhaps a little older, whose silent crouch beside the fragile waterfall gave him no cause for concern. But Ben stayed to watch her anyway; he was curious, and despite the woman's rather hard exterior of motorcycle leathers and heavy boots, Ben thought her beautiful.

Highlighted by roving beams of sunlight that stroked and explored her skin as the treetops through which they shone swayed to the whim of a humid breath, the young woman's actions of simple grace turned Ben's interest into captivation. He saw her reach into a bag and retrieve a crystal pendant, which she suspended from a low oak bough above the spring. Then she lit an incense cone and placed it on a flat pebble in the shallow water. All this seemed meaningless to Ben, but these reverent arrangements revealed such clear devotional intent that the actions themselves seemed imbued with meaning, as if the innocence of the moment served its own fulfilment. A ritual for its own sake, it appeared to Ben in his ignorance of the girl's motive; perhaps an enjoyment of the act of humility and reverence which, ultimately, turned a selfless observance into a quietly selfish one.

The breeze became a little more forceful, for a few moments penetrating the grove. Every leaf of the surrounding trees flickered to life and whispered the joy of its wind-driven animation. The blond-haired stranger looked up and responded with a smile to the elemental presence, which passed across her impassioned features like the caress of an unexpectedly intimate stranger.

Ben enjoyed the scene with hidden impunity, but he was no keener to become a voyeur than he was to find himself being watched in a similar manner, so he retreated as quietly as he had advanced, though not quite clear of the trees. Far enough from the spring for his footfalls to sound distant, Ben turned and headed carelessly back downhill, intending to stumble into the glade and discover the girl with all the surprise he could muster. He made his progress especially noisy, treading intentionally upon dry twigs, and allowing the branches he pushed aside to catapult behind him. In this manner, he received a cut to his right hand from one sharp branch, as if by way of revenge for his treatment of the trees.

As Ben had expected, there was no sign of the crystal pendant or the incense when he ducked beneath a bough and stepped down into the glade. There was only the young woman, who had composed herself at the sound of his approach. She sat beside the spring as before, though now only preoccupied with a cigarette, and acknowledged Ben's arrival with an expressionless glance.

Having been regarded so disdainfully by the kind of person who might otherwise have found herself confronted by the Earthwork team and a lot of questions concerning her business here, Ben was tempted to exercise his invested authority. His attraction to the woman prevented him, but Ben offered the stranger no particular acknowledgement in return. He paced silently to the edge of the stream a little further downhill and gazed patiently into the water at his feet.

'Not too close,' the girl warned him. 'The sides of the stream cave in easily.'

Ben resisted an urge to laugh at the irony. 'I know, man,' he replied instead. 'Everyone has to be careful up here. The locals are quite possessive,' he added, able to meet the young woman's gaze only briefly, though long enough to make his comment seem like a mild threat. 'They keep an eye on the place.'

The girl was expecting more, but none came. She nodded slowly. 'And you're local?'

'Yep.'

The girl drew on her roll-up. Her eyes narrowed as the smoke reached her face. 'Do you keep an eye on the place?'

Ben's response was blunt. 'Do you come here often?' he asked, and regretted the cliché even before he had finished the line. He sucked on his oak-sliced finger as though the distraction might delete his mistake.

'What?'

'I mean, the villagers have been talking about someone hiding in the trees up here, at least as far back as February. I just wondered…'

The girl thought about it. 'I like it here,' she said eventually. 'Its—' she shrugged. 'It's peaceful,' she decided, as if the statement was such a poor expression of her true conviction that it left a nasty taste in her mouth. 'I didn't ride all this way to damage the place.'

A seed of suspicion germinated in Ben's mind and was nurtured steadily by the girl's manner. Thanks to his recent reading material, Ben felt as though he was already acquainted with her, and he struggled to avoid addressing the girl in the familiar. 'No, of course not,' he nodded positively, stepping uphill to offer the girl his hand. 'I'm sorry. Ben Marchen.'

The young woman thought about it. She swapped her cigarette from one hand to another, wiped her palm against her jeans and grasped Ben's hand. 'Lea Granger,' she introduced herself, and something of the initial distrust was dispelled – though Lea still considered Ben's arrival an invasion of her privacy in such a concealed place.

'Hello,' Ben nodded, stepping back some polite distance to contemplate something – anything – else. He found her gaze penetrating.

Lea examined the smudge of redness he had trailed across her wrist with his finger. Then she looked up to consider how awkward Ben appeared as he crouched beside the stream. 'You shouldn't be so eager to give away your blood, Ben Marchen,' she advised him, immersing her arm into the pool at her side. 'There are people you can't trust with it.'

Ben glanced at his bleeding finger, and then in surprise at Lea. 'You know any?'

Lea did not miss the trace of mockery in his tone. 'They're out there.'

'And what could they do with it? No one who knew me would want to clone me.'

Lea was pleased with this opportunity to touch on the territory of her own interests. 'A drop of blood is a link to its host,' she replied dramatically, 'and bridging the gap from sample to source is just a simple matter of will.'

Ben nodded as he recognised the reference. 'As above, so below,' he quoted, robbing Lea of her advantage.

Lea stared back at Ben through sleepy eyelids and drew heavily on her cigarette. 'You walk Roedan's maze?' she asked with some surprise, exhaling smoke.

Ben shrugged. 'I don't know what that means, man,' he lied, 'but I read a bit about hermetic text once: *The Emerald Table* or something, I think.'

Lea blinked and looked away uncertainly.

'*Walk Roedan's maze?*' Ben repeated.

'Oh, nothing,' Lea said quickly, rising from her place beside the spring.

Ben realised that the encounter was in danger of ending far sooner than he would have liked, and on a note in stark contrast to the result he had hoped for. He sought frantically to contrive some delay. 'You're leaving?' he managed weakly as Lea stepped across the stream and faced the route uphill.

She hesitated, unwilling to confirm the obvious, but not quite capable of ignoring the harmlessly attentive stranger. 'Is that all right?'

Ben shrugged again and gestured at the glade around them. 'It's just that—you seem compatible here. You don't look out of place.'

'Compatible?'

'With the trees, in a way...' Ben struggled, trailing off, self-conscious to the point of pain. But Lea banished his diffidence with a smile. His awkward observation had somehow landed as a compliment, and Lea seemed disarmed as she glanced appreciatively around the glade. Satisfied, she rewarded Ben with sparkling eye-contact. 'Nice to meet you, Ben Marchen,' she said, and then ducked beneath the low bough of a sycamore to climb the slope.

Ben cringed and cursed in whispers as he repeatedly relived the encounter, enjoying the memory of the better lines of the exchange, but substituting his feebler quotes for what he knew he *should* have said. But his mood following the encounter was one of regret, despite Lea's smile. Ben stepped up to the rippling basin beneath the spring, splashed water across his reddened features and drank deeply from his own cupped hands as though he might drown the recollection of his performance.

Post Meridiem

Beneath the broiling eye of the Midsummer sun, Somerset shimmered in the afternoon light. Roads softened, and motorists sentenced to pursue the sticky tarmac distance as slaves to the convenience of mobile metal withered behind the wheel. All around them, even along the verges beaten by the hurricane slipstream of HGVs and impatient drivers, the flora of the West Country's rural vista screamed its vitality in colour and strained for the deep blue sky.

Earthwork reconvened after lunch. Craig was the last to arrive, and upon his return to the barn he found Ben standing on the table. Around him, George, Ian, Sarah Conrad and Alan were contemplating the theatrical poses he assumed to disguise his embarrassment. His colleagues spluttered mocking laughter.

As the first to have shown an interest in the large parcel Sarah had delivered at George's request, Ben had been volunteered to help unpack the clothes within. Then, as punishment for a sexist remark he had made about accepting the garments un-ironed from a woman, he had been chosen as the guinea pig to model them.

'Mmh-hmm,' Sarah nodded. 'Just the job.'

Ben gazed down at his baggy new attire and yelped, 'What? You mean I really look like a guinea pig?'

'You look like a hippie,' Craig said.

'I'm supposed to look *ethnic,* I think,' Ben explained. 'But ethnic to where, or when, is anyone's guess. I'm betting Woodstock, 1969.'

'Then I'm doing OK,' Sarah replied. She rummaged through a set of pin badges and pendants for accessories to garnish Ben's outfit of patterned trousers, tie-dyed T-shirt, and a pair of purple boots with multicoloured laces. She handed Ben a shark's tooth on a length of leather to hang around his neck. 'George asked me to make you all blend in with the crowd tonight.'

Craig, who was thoroughly enjoying Ben's ridicule, found the situation less amusing when it became clear that Ben was modelling clothes he was also expected to wear. 'You won't catch me dead in those rags,' he growled.

'Then I'm glad you're still alive to dress yourself, Mr Pearce,' George snapped, belittling Craig's reluctance as similar clothes were handed around to each of the men in turn.

'Forget it,' Craig said, folding his arms against Sarah's offer. 'This has been a bad idea from the start. You want us to stroll around an event held by people that you don't want us to trust, but you won't say why. We know very little about Geophagia; they haven't invited us to this festival, and we're expected to dress up like twats to fit in? No. We should be here watching the hill.'

'Who'd have thought it, man?' Ben jeered as he jumped down from the table. 'Craig *I-pity-the-fool-who-steps-on-Meeting-Hill* Pearce as the voice of reason!'

'Come on, Craig,' said Alan, 'we've been through all this.'

'And I was never convinced,' he replied, glaring icily at Ben.

'We'll need you there.'

'The Meeting needs us here.'

'But if there's any chance that Geophagia poses a threat, shouldn't we see what they're about?'

'Of course, just as soon as that threat has been explained to us,' Craig reasoned, turning meaningfully to George. 'We're being sent to spy on people that our researcher only *suspects* of some sinister plot. We could land ourselves in trouble, so forgive me for thinking that we're just being paranoid until someone justifies the risk.'

George nodded reasonably. Either side of her, Ian and Alan exchanged their everyday clothes for Sarah's New Age disguise, relying only on the length of their shirts to defend their modesty against Sarah, who gawped happily.

'I've already told you,' George replied, 'I'll explain everything, but I'm afraid it'll all seem weak and tenuous until you've been out there and seen Geophagia for yourselves. You'll come back with questions that will make my research more relevant – and besides,' she added, 'the treasury has been generous with the budget for this project. These clothes were expensive, especially the boots.'

Craig and Georgina faced each other silently as the others arranged themselves. Sarah handed out the wristbands and accessories which, she had decided, would identify the Earthwork members as Pagans. Ian frowned at the brooch he was given. The pattern of three interconnecting circles held no real meaning for him beyond an adherence to the required image, and he felt a little uncomfortable about wearing an occult sigil as idle decoration. 'I hate to be awkward,' he said, 'but I try not to wear magical symbols unless I have some idea of what they might turn me into.'

'Superstitious?' Sarah asked, and not without some surprise.

'No,' Ian denied it. 'I don't think I'm superstitious. What if I asked you to wear a crucifix? Or a swastika?'

'It's a disguise, Ian, not a personal statement, but if you're that worried about it just wear your committee badge,' Alan suggested, pinning his own Earthwork cross to the paisley waist-coat he had been given. 'It looks the part.'

Craig had followed the conversation intently and gleaned much by implication. 'That's where all this is leading, isn't it?'

The others looked at him.

'Being afraid of Geophagia.'

His colleagues returned to the fitting of their clothes. 'Oh,' Alan said, 'you're still on that?'

Alan's rebuke only strengthened Craig's resolve. 'I bet that the superstition

Ian's talking about is exactly the kind of shit worrying George. We're expected to risk trouble tonight for the sake of a crusade inspired by someone's *vision*, or the message a crusty saw in his cannabis smoke.'

George had retreated to contemplate copies of *Maze* magazine at the other end of the table. She made no response. Similarly feeling that the conversation was exhausted, and that their own commitment was confirmed, neither did the others rise to the argument.

'Well, George?' prompted an unexpected new voice, whose owner had interpreted the group's silence as awkward complicity with Craig's complaint. 'I think we all want to know what you're keeping from us. With respect, Craig, it's nice to see you so restrained and reasonable.'

Briefly pleased to find an ally in even this surprising form, Craig turned to see Brampton Wyre at the door of the barn. He was wearing formal shirt and trousers, but in deference to the heat, Wyre had rolled up his sleeves and rejected a tie.

'Perhaps Craig's right,' Sarah added timidly. 'I know I'm not really involved here, but I don't want to see you all in trouble for this. Ian, don't you want to know that the risk is worth taking?'

It seemed that only a disclosure from George could bridge the impasse. Alan, Ian and Ben remained motivated by a concern for The Meeting that required no further justification from George. That Geophagia might converge upon Meeting Hill at all, whatever their intentions, was enough to commit them to the night's undertaking, however risky. But Craig, true to his simple philosophy regarding the monument's preservation, saw less value in such distant espionage than in a direct confrontation on home turf.

Alan noted Georgina's disappointment at this apparent mutiny. Having been accused of paranoia, George did not believe that revealing more unconfirmed suspicions would act in the best interests of the committee's morale. Nevertheless, she nodded in resignation to the pressure and turned the monitor of her computer to face the silent audience. She tapped at the keyboard until a digitised map of Somerset appeared on-screen.

'I'm sure we all recognise home,' she began, stabbing at a series of the function keys to make various markers and animated diagrams appear across the map. 'Starting here,' she pointed, 'at Glastonbury, and working south-east across the map, all prehistoric sites known to date from the Iron Age at the latest are marked by a white star.'

The silent audience nodded dutifully. Brampton Wyre stood amongst them and exchanged smirks with Craig.

'Now compare the positions of these sites with this blue line of consecutive numbers, which mark all Geophagia's previous festivals. The higher yellow numbers indicate locations discussed in *Maze* magazine as sites of Pagan interest.'

Alan noticed that 'They overlap.'

'It's a ley, or ley line,' George continued. 'Some people believe that these early monuments were purposely built in alignment. Others believe that a ley indicates, or perhaps even guides, a vein of some kind of energy, or life force, and that the current can be tapped through ritual at these sacred centres.'

Craig slumped into a chair. 'See?' he moaned. 'You see what you'll be chasing tonight? I can't believe we've fallen for this.'

'On the strength of this belief, amongst other things, the Geophagia Foundation has chosen to dance on each ancient site in turn, trying to *raise the energy,* as they put it.'

Despite provoking George's lecture, Craig shook his head, rose from the chair and left the barn wearing an expression of contempt for all that the dispute had revealed. George peered after him and turned to the others with a shrug. 'This is why I didn't want to go into more detail until you'd seen these things for yourselves.'

'And this,' Brampton pointed to the screen with its flashing cursors and animated scenery, 'is your reason for risking trouble? To spy on people who might – just *might* – want to come and dance near Meeting Hill? Have you considered your chances of being arrested for trespass tonight? Wearing hand-made clothes doesn't make you one of them. At best you'll look like posing *dilettantes,* and at worst like idiots – except Ben, perhaps. He'll fit in. Are these suspicions really worth it?'

'But I haven't finished explaining them,' Georgina protested.

'Do we really need to hear more?' Brampton seemed almost to choke on the idea. 'Don't waste our time.'

He made an exit after Craig's example. The barn remained silent until Ben could no longer resist an ice-breaking apology as a way of distancing the majority faithful from the doubters. 'Sorry, man. What the hell can you say to Craig in that mood?'

Wyre's expression was unreadable as she passed over the chance to gloat. 'It's no one's fault,' she decided, 'but I knew that none of this would make any sense before you'd seen Geophagia up close. It's like reading the instruction manual to a gadget you don't own.'

'But there's more?' Ian asked cautiously.

'Yes, there's more,' George admitted, taking off her reading glasses and polishing them with a loose corner of her shirt. 'There's the stuff that Craig really wanted to hear, but I can't prove any of it, and I've resisted discussing it in case you think I'm obsessively paranoid.'

'Then perhaps now's the time,' Craig suggested, reasserting his presence as he leaned casually against the frame of the barn door. 'What do you have to lose?'

*

Almost five in the afternoon, and the sun blazed on in earnest.

An elevated stage at the eastern end of Geophagia's festival field had been erected that morning, and Roedan spent the afternoon rehearsing a speech as the site neared completion. Thanks to her habitual attire of loose, often immodest gowns or robes, the toned surfaces of her body were used to year-round exposure, but Roedan's skin had tanned an even deeper shade of olive beneath the Solstice sun.

She paced the platform, contemplating the insides of her sunglasses for inspiration whenever the torrent of her indulgent wisdom lost its cadence, sense or momentum. Before her, completion of the festival's constructions sent an increasing number of contractors to seek approval from their preoccupied director.

Even as the founder of the Geophagia Foundation, Roedan chose not to delegate responsibility, such as supervision of fairground layout, or the placement of security staff, which others might consider a waste of time for one so enlightened. She told her associates that all these things, from the promotional merchandise on sale in the marquees to the arrangement of attractions around the field, were facets of one vision: her vision, and while others might follow it religiously, only Roedan could shape it.

A growing crowd of staff gathered around the stage awaiting attention, eager to declare completion of their work, but all too aware of her temper when disturbed at such moments. The employees waited quietly, until a chorus of impatiently cleared throats from several members of the expanding group pulled Roedan from her trance. She blinked twice, removed her sunglasses and eyed the staff resentfully. Many members of the group were private contractors with work orders and receipts to be checked and signed, but Roedan merely cast her eye over the site. Her view from the podium covered a wide arc of vision, from the tumuli beyond the hedge to her left, over the festival arena before her, and to the narrow South Pennard road on her right. Roedan saw the lane filled with cars, forming a queue that receded out of sight.

'Ms Bain—' began a man nearest the stage, but stopped in time to correct himself. 'Roedan,' he resumed, 'we're ready.'

The director nodded silently.

'Roedan?' the man persisted, apparently familiar with his employer's moods, and aware of the limits to which he might press her in this one. 'People are arriving. We're blocking the road out there.'

This news seemed to have a little more effect on Roedan. She closed her eyes and tilted her head to receive the warmth of the sun evenly across her face. Her staff resisted expression of their impatience, and some of them even took an interest in her graceful actions as it seemed that she might be about to say something inspirational.

Most of the delivery and construction crew were older, more cynical individuals than Roedan's followers, and these employees were less likely to display the same awe with which members of the Geophagia Foundation viewed their leader. A few of the contractors had been discussing the legitimacy of Roedan's claim to mystical insight, though many more had bluntly asked how anyone could live so far up their own pretentious arse.

But most of the gathering agreed that Roedan was an impressive individual, who exuded the worldly sagacity of middle-aged confidence as qualification for authority. A few individuals even suspected that the content and direction of her speeches mattered little to anyone who sought the passion, and the sense of inclusion, that following such a woman might promise.

Still Roedan was silent. She opened her eyes again and scanned the view to her right, where hundreds of her followers were queuing in car and on foot along the narrow lane.

'Roedan?'

Eventually she nodded, thereby ending the mild torture of her staff. Roedan indicated the field space before her that would, within minutes, be filled with the expectant hordes of her devotees. She confirmed the gesture with a simple order.

'Let them in.'

*

Beneath the trees around The Meeting, Ian and Ben lay silently against the earth with only a short screen of bracken to conceal their scrutiny of a lone female on the summit.

Regular checks on the site throughout the day had been planned by Earthwork, and this routine helped distract the group from their nerves as the evening's task drew nearer. But this was not a routine check: the men had been called to Meeting Hill by the watch in the village, and Ben admitted to preferring this kind of spontaneous duty over the more mundane patrol. Better to be called to trouble, he had said, than to be accused of going out looking for it.

Upon arrival, Ben had seen a familiar motorbike parked at the foot of the hill. He and Ian had then climbed the southern slope under cover of the trees. On the summit the men had found a woman walking alone around the clearing, apparently following a path dictated by the swing of a pendulum she held at waist height.

'We've been called here for this?' Ian breathed.

Ben's gaze remained fixed on the drifting grace of the visitor. 'I've seen this girl before, man,' he murmured.

Ian attempted to make himself comfortable against the slope, wary of spoiling the new clothes given him by Sarah, and wiping profuse sweat from across his brow. Tiny flies and itchy living things danced in the forest's narrow sunbeams, occasionally straying too near the men's damp skin and finding the

stickiness impossible to escape. 'Is she trouble?'
'I don't know,' Ben replied, chewing his bottom lip thoughtfully. The creases of skin at the corner of Ben's eye tightened slightly with a glimmering of amusement. Ian perceived more than just recognition of the girl in that gaze, but he questioned Ben no more on his interest.
A little to the west, the sun had reached a point halfway between the uppermost leaves of the tallest oak and its roots within Meeting Hill. Ben and Ian fidgeted impatiently amongst the ferns for nearly fifteen minutes until the sound of a match being struck some distance away offered them a sense of safety in which to creep closer to the summit. They watched Lea Granger drawing on a hand-rolled cigarette at the northern edge of the clearing. She glanced at her watch, and the time it told seemed to induce some forgotten sense of urgency. Lea pulled a stub of pencil from a pocket and used the nearest megalith as a surface against which to scribble something on a king-size Rizla. She folded the paper, pushed it into a crevice within the standing stone and slipped on her beaten leather jacket as she strode across the clearing for the footpath.
Ian stood and brushed himself down as soon as the girl was out of sight. Ben rose and followed Ian until they emerged from the trees. The day's relentless heat added a watchful pressure to the monument's solitude. Standing in air possessed of such palpable substance created a sense of having indirect contact with the surroundings, like sensing the lightest touch through clothing. Ian stopped to appreciate possession of the Meeting's attention. 'It's just like years ago, Ben,' he breathed, 'when we first came here as kids.'
Ben nodded absently, but left Ian to his reflective moment. He crossed the clearing to where Lea Granger had stood only minutes before and retrieved her scribbled note from the niche in the standing stone. Earthwork had discovered many pieces of paper secreted in the stones' most accessible crevices, mostly devotional in nature, and addressed to an entire pantheon of supernatural beings, including Gaia, Dionysus, Isis, Pan, Herne, the Tuatha De Danann, and Cernunnos.
Ian strolled contentedly through the stones, his hands shoved deep into his pockets, and peered at the tightly folded note. 'What's it say?'
Ben unfolded the cigarette paper and made no outward expression of his surprise at the message.

Ever let the fancy roam,
Pleasure never is at home.

Ben passed the paper to his friend, though reluctantly. He did not like sharing it – the scribbled words seemed imbued with the same intimacy as the lines of Lea's diary.
'Keats makes a change from the usual selfish wishes,' Ian decided, and Ben

was cross was himself for not recognising the reference. '*Dear Satan, please kill my ex-boyfriend* was getting boring, wasn't it?'

'That girl,' Ben replied, surprised to see Ian replacing the note within the stone's crevice: 'were you watching her? She was so lost in this place, you could see that nothing else mattered while she had time on her own up here.'

Ian gave the slightest shrug, but Ben was not put off.

'Nothing would have distracted her,' he said, as though afraid of overstating the observation. 'She's just like I might have been if I hadn't—' Ben paused and cast Ian a guilty glance. 'If I hadn't settled back here.'

'Which part do you aspire to? The thing with the pendulum or the letter to the fairies?'

Ben looked up at the sun through the trees, as though the softening light of late afternoon might clarify his meaning. 'Neither, man. I just think that girl looked composed, as if she thought of The Meeting as polite company. But at the same time she seemed euphoric, like she'd found exactly what she came here for. When I'm up here, I feel like whatever I'm looking for is always just out of reach. I wonder what she has that I'm missing?'

Ian watched Ben struggle to articulate his thoughts. 'It helps if you know what you're looking for,' he said, shaking his head wearily as he tired of Ben's self-indulgence. 'You travelled the world looking for the answer, but that's no use if you didn't even know the question. You have no idea what that girl was feeling – and who cares?'

'Let's follow her.'

'Who?'

'Motorbike girl.'

'Why?'

Ben brushed past Ian and headed for the footpath. 'Where do you think we might end up if we follow someone like Lea today? We might prove George right about Geophagia's interest in The Meeting.'

'Ah,' Ian nodded, understanding more than was intended, though he did not question Ben's use of a name. 'But we don't have time. We have to get back to get ready with the others.'

'Why, man?' Ben laughed. 'We're already *deep* under cover in this brilliant disguise.'

'But we can't be sure about her, Ben. After everything Craig said, we can't justify paranoia.'

Ben began to seem swayed by Ian's caution as the men made their way downhill, but Ben was driving, and once back on the road he simply ignored his friend's protests and aimed the Toyota west out of Carreg's End. He sped along narrow, pot-holed roads which, in places, were little more than dusty tracks connecting local farms. The windows of Ben's car were wound down, the radio was loud, and the tempo that influenced the pace of his driving startled the cows they passed.

'You're sure she came this way?' Ian asked.

Ben nodded, absorbed in driving. His negotiation of every bend in the road seemed to demand a dramatic skid and a cloud of dust, which required concentration.

'We're supposed to be back on the estate,' Ian protested in vain, glancing at his watch. 'George has the evening all planned out.'

'But you don't care,' Ben told him, throwing the car into a blind turn. 'You're enjoying this as much as I am.'

'Might be,' Ian admitted with a crooked smile, 'but I've been a member of Earthwork much longer than you, and I feel like I should be setting an example.'

'Hypocrite! Who borrowed an Earthwork Shogun to carry their windsurfing gear down to Newquay last month?'

'Left here,' Ian cut in, pointing ahead to the next turning.

'Eh?'

'If you want South Pennard, turn left here.' Ian settled back into his seat as Ben took the left turn and accelerated. 'It's bad enough that we've spoilt George's plan,' Ian justified himself, 'without ending up lost as well.'

The view from this road was unobstructed by hedges, allowing Ben to spot a motorcycle some distance ahead of them. 'There!' he stabbed at the windscreen. 'There she is.'

Ian nodded. 'So you were right. Now what?'

'If this girl turns out to be a member of Geophagia, then we have proof that their interest may reach as far as Meeting Hill. Perhaps,' Ben added airily, 'she knows something George hasn't uncovered yet. She should be watched if she visits The Meeting again.'

'And you want to watch her?'

Ben said nothing, pretending to have missed the tone of Ian's reply. He reached for the volume dial of the stereo and turned it up until conversation was impossible.

*

A bank of violet cloud low in the western sky somehow seemed much further distant than the sun glowering above it. Smothering the horizon where the Earth met the sky, the cloud threatened to swallow the sinking sun before it reached the distant hills.

The cobbled courtyard between Arlingham House and its surrounding buildings was now steeped in the lengthening shadows of the avenue's trees. Alan had thrown open both the barn doors to treat the gloomy interior to the early evening light. Then, perched on the edge of the table while George, Sarah and Craig distracted themselves around him, he glanced outside at the poplar-lined drive, and then at his watch as Earthwork's two absent members failed to appear.

Sarah also glanced at Alan's watch. 'They're late,' she said. 'Do you think they had real trouble on the hill?'

Her voice disclosed a note of concern. Alan turned to Wyre for reassurance. 'Did Mr Harper say what was going on?'

Sitting beside Craig at the computer, George also checked her watch. 'It was actually Mrs Harper who called,' she replied. 'She probably took over the afternoon watch because the old piss-head was comatose – but you know what she's like: she'll flap about anyone who sets foot on the hill. I don't think that one female tourist hugging the stones would make Ian and Ben this late. Did I give them a time to meet us here?'

From inside one of the Shoguns came the chirp of a mobile phone. 'Mine!' Alan claimed the call, and hopped down from the table to reach in through the window. 'Alan Forrest.'

'Guess where we are.'

'You should be here, Ben.'

'Just to get directions to South Pennard? We don't need them,' Ben replied. 'We had our own guide.'

'Why didn't you wait for us?'

'Because Ian says we're young, reckless and vastly intelligent, and we can do whatever we like.'

Alan listened to a struggle for control of the phone at the other end. Eventually, a sober-toned Ian resumed: 'Tell George she's right. We followed someone here from Meeting Hill. Geophagia is definitely interested.'

'The tourist on the hill?' Alan asked.

Behind him, George made some sense of the conversation and gestured frantically for the phone. At the table, Craig snorted a wet bubble of mocking laughter as he stabbed idly at the keyboard. Alan surrendered the phone, hopped up onto the bonnet of a car and traced a finger around the outline of the Earthwork cross.

'I didn't want anyone near the festival until it was dark,' George told Ian. 'I had everything planned. Tell me what you're doing – are you waiting to get in?'

Ian tried not to sound scolded. 'No queue now,' he replied. 'They've opened a field for parking and we've tucked ourselves into a dark corner.'

'Good,' George nodded to herself. 'Don't move until we meet you there.'

'Done,' Ian agreed. 'Craig coming?'

'Doesn't seem likely,' she murmured, watching Craig feign concentration in the computer monitor. 'But if we can't convince him, I don't think Sarah has much planned this evening.'

Craig and Sarah looked up at George wearing contrasting expressions. 'See you within the hour,' Wyre concluded the call and handed the phone back to Alan. 'We'll take Alan's car,' she decided. 'We can't turn up in an Earthwork vehicle, the markings will attract attention. Craig? Are you up for this?'

Craig leaned back in his seat and made a show of thinking about it. 'Well,' he began, 'I'm still not sure that you've explai—'

'Fine,' George cut in, dismissing Craig's opinion with time running short. 'Sarah? We could use your eyes and ears for a few hours.'

'They're yours,' she agreed.

'Right,' George smiled, her more characteristic affability returning. She reached beneath the table and retrieved the case full of radio equipment, as well as a small pile of various leaflets and copies of *Maze* magazine. 'We no longer have the time I'd planned, so I'll make this brief. It's Midsummer's night, and the Geophagia Foundation is halfway here. Observation is your only objective this evening. The information we pool tonight will tell us what we need to know about their intentions, about possible weaknesses, and perhaps even ways of changing their minds if they intend to congregate on our hill. Do you understand? And do you agree?'

'Sound,' Alan nodded.

'Each of Geophagia's meetings are about music, dancing, and selling crystals and dowsing pendulums to the gullible, but at the solar festivals – equinoxes and solstices – Geophagia's founder gives a talk on her magical theory. Tonight,' she continued, 'I think you can look forward to a lecture on The Simple Power and Creative Scope of Metaphor and Imagination, according to this issue of *Maze*.'

'Wonderful,' Craig intoned from behind the computer. 'How do we join?'

George turned back to Sarah. 'You still want to be involved?'

'Do I get to wear an Earthwork cross?' she bargained.

Sensing an imminent question concerning the availability of Earthwork badges, Craig immediately placed a protective hand over his own. He turned the computer monitor around to face the other three. To reaffirm his commitment to the cause, despite his disagreement with this particular project, he had typed, 'ON DUTY'.

Sunset VI

Viewed from above, the press of bodies filling the South Pennard festival arena seemed to shift and ripple in waves, like oil moving over an uneven surface. To the south, a field reserved for parking trickled a slow ooze of new arrivals out into the lane, a short distance north along the road and into the gateway of the Solstice celebration.
The sun was setting, though not quite gone, but floodlighting blazed from the borders of the festival ground, and torches of fire atop pillars either side of the entrance gate made an imposing ceremonial portal, through which the Foundation's members passed to witness Roedan's recreation of British tribal ethnicity. Designed to resemble the meeting ground of a Dark Age war council, or perhaps the ritual site of an even earlier people, more torches of naked flame lined the hawthorn borders of the field. Filling the spaces between them, banners of pale fabric bearing Geophagia's identifying symbols were draped from T-shaped frames, hanging without a ripple in the still evening air.
Over half the field space in front of the stage was left clear to accommodate an audience of at least two thousand. A large proportion of that number would occupy this space to dance as soon as the music began, and the rest would follow when Roedan claimed the stage to speak. The rest of the rented field was given over to marquees and adrenaline rides. Filling the gaps between rides like the gravity wheel, cyclone, waltzer, frisbee and reverse-bungee, a rash of tents and stalls provided drink, food and distractions until the main events.
At one such stall – a tent devoted, like so many others, to the sale of Pagan and environmental literature, incense, pendants in the shape of famous crop circles, and candles of various shapes and sizes – a young man edged himself sideways through the browsers to peer critically at the goods on offer. A book about the marriage of ecology and socialist politics caught his eye. He was about to pick it up, wanting to appear involved, when he noticed something about the people standing around him, particularly their clothes. Ben began to feel self-conscious.
A major part of Earthwork's plan to pass unnoticed through this exclusive event was an imitation of what they imagined to be the habitual attire of the Pagan community. Generalising wildly, the committee had accepted George Wyre's vision of an unshaven mob sporting combat or patterned trousers, brightly coloured boots, T-shirts contrived of hand-spun, tie-dyed fibres, comically oversized hats and/or dreadlocks. But this, Ben suddenly realised, was a crowd unfamiliar with the psychedelic cliché. He felt indescribably stupid and hopelessly exposed.
Earthwork's negotiation of gate security had itself been a scene of impressive, though attention-drawing, theatricals, involving a sorry tale (as told by Sarah,

with much flirting) of four young travellers who, in the excitement of their cross-country pilgrimage, had lost their tickets and membership cards. Dressed like this, Ben decided, the four would be remembered.

Alan, Sarah and Ian were feeling equally awkward as they plunged into the crowd in pursuit of their own goals. They were directed by George from the car via radio, but with only a vague instruction to 'mingle' as motivation for their advance.

The DJ hired to accompany Geophagia's 1999 tour – the increasingly famous Van Planer – provided an opening soundtrack of down-tempo cultural and ambient dance, indulging his characteristic taste for relatively little-known artists.

The bass-heavy rhythms made it hard for Ben to concentrate on George's transmission. He tried discreetly to push the ear-piece nearer his protesting tympanic membrane, and silently cursed the group's lack of two-way communication. From the back of Alan's car, hidden in a corner of the next field, George broadcast a steady succession of instructions for each member of the team. However, Ben's own directions had been drowned out when he passed the generator driving the Big Wheel, so his only hope of finding George's target – an information and subscription-renewal tent – was to wander between the stalls in idle search.

Also alone, Sarah had been directed towards the front of the arena towards the stage, while Alan and Ian had stayed together to stand watch over the hedge bordering the tumuli in the next field.

'If anyone goes near the barrows,' George spoke directly to their ear-drums, 'try to remember everything that happens, and whether the organisers are involved.'

This request made little sense to the men as they wandered between tents at the field's edge, but they did not question George's motives. They obeyed, attempting to disguise the intensity of their scrutiny as they wandered, perhaps a little too aimlessly to be truly aimless, and returning the polite greetings of passing Geophagians.

Ben hardly bothered to acknowledge the sociable nods of anyone he passed, if he noticed them at all. Paying little heed to George's advice concerning the dangers of ignorance at an event laid on for people with a common passion, Ben had become occupied with a personal search. At one of the merchandise tents he noticed the sale of leather-bound, maze-embossed journals, identical to the one he had coveted since its discovery on Meeting Hill in February. To whom the original diary belonged, where she had acquired such a novelty, and whether or not she was allied with Geophagia were no longer causes for speculation. Ben knew that he had exchanged introductions with the author herself that morning, and glimpsed her again that afternoon.

Ben had not disclosed his interest in Lea, and Ian had not pressed him on the subject – a behaviour typical of Ian, whose discretion may have been born of a quiet confidence in his own interests and a respect for privacy, or else an arrogant self-assurance that no one else's business was worth prying into.

Ian and Alan were distracted from George's instructions by separate diversions at the field's edge. Ian was gazing up at the banners that displayed symbols of Geophagia's interests, trying to make sense of the various designs. He recognised Geophagia's labyrinth logo: the single-path maze that appeared on all of its literature; and also the straight line connecting simple representations of local landmarks, which he decided must demonstrate the group's interest in ley lines. However, a design that resembled the molecule models he had seen at school meant little, and neither did the tall symmetrical outline of a cross filled with the rigid letters of an archaic text.

Standing beside Ian, but facing in the opposite direction, Alan considered a puzzle of his own. 'Where did all these incredible women come from?' he wondered, nodding and smiling at any female who happened to catch his eye. 'Is this why I can never meet women in the clubs at weekends? Because they're all out here praying to trees?'

Ian tried to ignore him. Alan's discussion of women was often too sexist to be taken seriously, and since Alan had recently responded to a call for greater female involvement in the committee by suggesting recruitment of 'young blonde talent to keep the lads motivated', Ian thought it best not to encourage him.

A few yards from where the men stood, the flap of a tent was pushed aside by a woman who moved with feline grace and a confident, self-satisfied air. She emerged sedately to gaze at the stream of passing people. Eventually, she made eye-contact with Alan. The woman, who Alan estimated to be aged a little over forty, wore a white gown fastened at her left shoulder by a bronze brooch of Celtic knot work, and she seemed immaculately composed in such simple attire. Her daring classical dress, combined with the novelty of her maturity among so many younger people, offered her an aura of authority that Alan could not resist.

'Ian!' he nudged his companion to point out the expressionless, sleepy-eyed woman. 'How young would a man have to be to be too young for a woman like her?'

Indiscreetly, Ian turned to follow Alan's gaze, but quickly glanced away, feeling somehow intimidated by such a level return of attention. 'Alan,' he murmured, resuming his contemplation of the flags, 'don't get noticed.'

'But I'm following orders,' Alan attempted to justify himself. 'George told us to *mingle*.'

Mutual interest between Alan and the woman continued a little longer, until the spell was broken by a communication from George. Alan instinctively pressed a finger to his ear and glanced away. When he turned back a few moments later, the woman was gone.

Now a little more confident that she would not be disturbed, Georgina pulled a packet of biscuits from a bag, made herself comfortable in the back seat of Alan's car and scanned a page of notes through her reading glasses. Contemplating a list of interests and priorities for her scouts to pursue, George considered the past few minutes' radio-silence time enough for the team to have completed their previous observations, and so raised her radio to broadcast the next. Around the festival site, four fingers were pressed suddenly against four straining ears.

'Dates, please,' George requested of her radio, glancing at the surrounding cars in search of unwanted observers. 'We need to confirm dates and venues for Geophagia's future meetings. Look out for leaflets or new *Maze* magazines – but Geophagia is an exclusive club, so this sort of information might not be left lying around.'

Aware of how long they had stood conspicuously in one place, Ian tugged at Alan's sleeve, signalling the need to move on. Alan followed him, gazing thoughtfully up at the big wheel in the fairground ahead of them. The illumination of the rides was now able to compete with the warm glow of the setting sun.

Above the hedge along the field's western border, Ian saw the tip of South Pennard's largest barrow. Across the summit of the dome, tall grass swayed against the fiery horizon and blurred the definition of the sun's vivid outline, creating from Ian's perspective the illusion of a distant inferno.

In search of the information Georgina required, Alan and Ian drifted among the ranks of Roedan's faithful, tempted by the growing conviction that such a benevolent gathering could pose no real threat to sites chosen as dance venues. All around them, people were possessed by the lure of the ale, merchandise and literature stands, while others formed cliques of social groups and laughed openly in their companionship, or just danced where they stood to form isolated pockets of movement. The music from the stage was increased in volume every ten minutes or so.

'I like it here,' Alan decided, and then looked at Ian for any reaction to this heresy.

But Ian nodded in agreement. 'I feel guilty for spying on these people. They're doing nothing wrong, but we should keep looking for whatever George needs.'

'Skipping from tent to tent reading everything we find is so dull and conspicuous!' Alan quietly protested. 'We look like we're searching for something.'

'What else can we do? Come on, let's get it over with.'

'Can't we just ask someone?' Alan suggested. 'We can be subtle – it'll just seem like we're mingling.'

Ian stared at his friend. 'And blow our cover?'
Alan laughed without restraint. 'We blew our cover when we turned up dressed like Jimi Hendrix!'
Ian found it difficult to deal with Alan's unexpected impatience. He remained silent to avoid further debate, but Alan had seen someone in the crowd that only heightened his enthusiasm for an easier option.
'Look,' Alan nudged him, pointing through the stream of moving bodies to single out the woman he had spotted a few minutes earlier. 'There she is again, and she's looking at us. I think she's interested.'
Ian refused to stare. He turned to the nearest souvenir stall and faked fascination with a pack of tarot cards. 'Alan, *interest* is the last thing we want to attract. Just leave it.'
But Alan turned back to gaze at the robed woman, whose exotic dress-sense only helped cement his commitment to a more direct form of investigation. 'Come with me,' Alan said, 'we'll talk to her, and you can ask for the dates George needs. Your line of questioning will probably be more subtle than mine.'
Frustrated by his inability to protest with so many people around them, Ian could only offer his indomitable partner a level gaze and make a final candid appeal. 'Alan,' he replied firmly, 'I don't agree with this. We didn't come here for you to try and chat up the first woman who looks at you twice, or to run around advertising our ignorance as a way of getting out of the job we volunteered for! We can't risk giving anything away.'
In stubborn response to Ian's chastising tone, Alan's idea to escape the monotony of their search became a resolution. 'Look,' he countered, stiffening his frame to assert an inch of superior height, 'I don't want to spend a minute longer than I have to snooping around here like a rat. I'll finish what we've started, but I'll do it without having to spend the rest of the evening going through volumes of *Donga Magazine* and *Space Cadet Weekly* to find what George needs.'
Alan strode away into the crowd. Feeling helpless, Ian watched him go.
Now choosing to ignore the man with whom she had started talking, the watchful woman turned and viewed Alan's approach with some interest. Her friend continued his side of the conversation regardless, even as she turned away from him.
Ian considered the presence of the woman's similarly aged companion another cause for alarm. The man, perhaps a little older than the woman Alan wished to talk to, was the only other person Ian had seen dressed in a way that resembled Earthwork's disguise. Pony-tailed and bearded, he also wore a T-shirt bearing an image of a Sioux Indian, a leather waist-coat, black jeans and Converse trainers, and was carrying a mobile phone at his side as though expecting a call at any moment. The man's age and prominent possession of a

phone gave him an air of authority, and possibly even managerial involvement with Geophagia, making Ian ever more nervous. The lights of the fairground rides projected an ever-shifting mosaic of restless colour across Ian's anxious expression. 'You prat,' he murmured as he watched Alan's arrival interrupt the man's one-sided conversation.

The unidentified pair offered Alan and his questions their full attention.

Ian did not linger to observe Alan's introductions. He melted into the endless stream of people and moved with them around diesel-blooded generators and the rides they fuelled. He paid for a seat on the Big Wheel to avoid aimless wandering. He was secured into his seat next to a much younger girl, who cooed and waved at friends in the chair behind them as the ride circled on, up and around. Ignoring the excitement of his young companion, Ian was eventually able to gaze down over the festival in relief. With this view he was able to plan a route back into the heart of the crowd where, he knew, Ben and Sarah would be pursuing goals of their own.

As Ian reached the highest point of the Big Wheel's cycle, the last sliver of the Solstice sun set into the Polden Hills, leaving only a tangerine glimmer of its daytime power to settle across the horizon.

Genius Loci

In the claret twilight of Midsummer's Day, Craig made one final, narrow-eyed survey of the clearing on Meeting Hill and pulled shut the door of the Land Rover. With his view framed by an arboreal tangle of oak and beech beyond the stones, Craig had watched the sun set on the first half of the year. Then he had tensed himself for a dusk invasion of the site by an army of satanic revellers who, almost certainly drugged to the unfocused eyeballs, would have been intent on celebrating the shortest night with an orgy of vandalism.
Craig waited for nearly an hour in watchful anticipation of these bacchanals, even willing their arrival to satisfy expectation, until finally resigning himself to an evening of lonely suspense in the barn.
With the car already facing downhill, Craig turned the key into ignition instead of starting the engine, turned on the headlights and released the handbrake. He coasted gently down the footpath, thoroughly enjoying the satisfying crunch of the tyres' crispy tread over dust and gravel.
Craig left the Land Rover parked outside the barn, determined to be prepared for emergency call-out, even if leaving a vehicle in the courtyard defied the orders of Brampton Wyre himself, who Craig glimpsed in silhouette at an upstairs window of Arlingham House.But Craig ignored the watchful figure. There was no tense moment of competitive scrutiny across the courtyard – at least, not from Craig. He looked away, refusing to be intimidated, and retreated into the barn.
Craig set his radio down on the table and wandered into the untidy corner where George spent time with her books; piles of them, which Craig assembled in stacks across the cluttered surface to browse while he waited. He lit the remains of a candle, which spluttered and popped as the flame consumed the candle's coating of dust in a shower of sparks, and then he picked up the nearest of many ageing volumes.
Without the hand-written notes and comments scribbled in their margins, Craig never would have pieced together the truth of Georgina Wyre's fears. Craig found that each text contained lines underlined, highlighted or commented upon, thereby presenting the patient reader with an evolution of Wyre's concerns. This pool of information not only linked the themes George had already mentioned, but introduced elements of mythology not yet discussed.
Craig was captivated. George's notes identified a motive for mercenary archaeological zeal that disturbed him. Then, having gleaned a notion of what George thought Geophagia might intend, Craig was introduced to uncomfortable emotions concerning his earlier objections. He felt guilty about his protest, and for having dropped out of the group's efforts. He decided that he had made a fool of himself.

Craig closed the last of the books and rubbed his eyes, pleased with his hour of self-motivated study, and then wondered how he might best make amends. Before him was laid a heavy text documenting the travels and battles of a Dark Age legend; he thoughtfully traced his fingers around the bold italics across the front cover, *Rex Quondam, Rex Futurus,* and quietly considered his options.

*

George instructed Earthwork to regroup.
Ben located Sarah at the edge of the crowd, not far from the stage. Sarah smiled in relieved recognition as he approached, but they did not discuss their business in this crowded space.
While surveying the crowd for Ian and Alan, Ben spotted Lea Granger for the third time that day. She had emerged with several companions from a marquee behind the stage and, to Ben's surprise, was climbing the steps to the platform. He wanted to push forward and capture her attention in the hope of a more successful exchange than their first that morning, but this was clearly not the moment.
So, quietly proud of his devotion to duty, Ben turned away and searched the expanding crowd for his friends, though his gaze returned frequently to the stage. To the delight of the crowd, Lea and her companions positioned themselves around the platform with musical instruments: Lea assumed the lead at the front of the stage with an acoustic guitar, and the others with drums, keyboards, electric and bass guitars, and microphones for them all to support Lea's vocals.
Sarah nudged Ben with an anxious expression. 'Can you see them?'
'Yeah,' Ben nodded absently, eyeing each member of the band in turn as the DJ began to reduce the volume of his own music. 'I wonder what sort of stuff they play.'
Sarah stared at her distracted companion. She prodded his shoulder, but Ben could hardly tear his eyes from the stage. 'Not them,' she snapped. 'Ours!'
'Oh,' Ben gave the crowds a cursory glance and turned back to the stage. 'Not yet.'
Sarah raised herself on her toes to peer above the sea of faces around them, feeling as alone with Ben as without him.

Roedan blinked in response to what was, from someone who claimed to be a member of her own loyal ranks, a ridiculous question. She considered the younger man's uncertain, though hopeful, expression, and stared in disbelief at the clothes he was wearing. Then she glanced over his shoulder in search of the similarly dressed man who had shown nervous interest in his friend's actions before he had disappeared.

But despite his relentless questions, Roedan felt no obligation to answer the determined man, who seemed capable of smiling encouragingly for an impressive length of time without looking pained, and who absolutely refused to show any discomfort under her closest inspection. Roedan turned to her own male companion and raised her eyebrows. Tom Sutherland glanced at his watch, nodded a silent understanding and paced confidently away into the crowd.

'Hello?' Alan prompted the woman. 'I was just asking,' he repeated, 'if you knew where we can expect to see the next festivals held? Do you know?'

Roedan began to stare at Alan's chest, or so he initially thought. After a few moments, he tried to follow her gaze and discovered that his committee badge was the source of interest. Alan made as if to scratch his chest, attempting to cover the Earthwork cross. 'Isn't this music loud!' he observed, charitably offering the robed woman an excuse for her lack of response. 'Listen,' he floundered cheerfully, 'have you heard where they're holding the next few meetings?'

Roedan waited patiently until the frustrated man had satisfied the itch across his upper-torso and then renewed her scrutiny of his badge.

'I'm sorry,' Alan continued without any hint of apology, 'you are in Geophagia, aren't you?'

Roedan frowned in contempt. '*In* Geophagia?'

'You're a member?' Alan repeated.

The woman considered her position with a wry smile. 'You could say that.'

'Great,' Alan nodded his relief, but the effort of the conversation was starting to tell in his voice. 'Then perhaps you can remind me of a few dates?'

Roedan thoughtfully studied the Earthwork badge and seemed not to hear the question. Alan rubbed at the back of his head impatiently as the last of his composure drained away.

'Jesus, lady,' he muttered, 'what are you on?'

The woman's eyes flickered up to meet Alan's critical regard with an unexpected intensity, as if she was peering into his head. 'Tell me, friend,' she began, placing one hand in the small of his back and the other lightly against his ribs, encouraging him to walk with her, 'you did receive this year's *Rites Of Passage* festival visa?' Then she stopped and smiled forgivingly. 'Mmh,' she purred. 'Of course you did.'

Alan cleared his throat nervously. 'Uuh,' he winced. 'Of *course* I did...'

Roedan nodded with satisfaction.

'But I lost it,' he added in a heart-rending tone of childish regret.

Roedan was optimistic. 'Oh, not to worry, your copy can't have gone far,' she reassured him. 'I mean, how could you have known about this evening and been allowed in without it?'

Alan's mouth went dry. He tried to swallow but couldn't. The pair looked silently at each other for some time: Roedan at Alan with an unblinking gaze of confident intent, and Alan at Roedan in a series of jittery glances. He began to pat the sides of his trousers uncertainly, and then contrived an expression of relief when he found something in the left pocket to rustle. 'Oh!' he rolled his eyes with comical realisation. 'Look at that – I had it with me all the time.'

Roedan nodded in relief for him, but said nothing. Alan took one step back and glanced at his watch. A single bead of sweat had crept from his blond hairline and became poised at the left temple. 'Well, thanks for your help—'

'Are you sure?'

Alan stopped and breathed slowly through dry lips. Across the arena to the south, the dance music began to fade, and the lights around the stage dimmed to an ambient glow. 'I'm sorry?'

Roedan shrugged and pointed at his pocket. 'Are you sure you have everything you need?'

Alan patted at his trouser pocket. It contained the pencil and scrap of paper he had used to note anything remotely likely to interest Georgina. Roedan nodded encouragingly and gazed with unwavering interest.

Alan felt compelled to produce the paper for inspection, and was just planning his dismayed reaction at discovering that, *Oh, no, that's not it! That's my shopping list! Now what have I done with that damned* Rites of Passage *thingy?* when: 'Alan! Are you Alan?'

Alan nodded blankly at the excited girl who emerged from the crowd to hang provocatively on his arm.

'Your friend's been looking for you *everywhere!*' she sang, pointing through the press of shifting bodies to where Ian waved a weary greeting like a phlegmatic, but perfectly timed, epiphany. 'Come on! Ian says you've got his money and he said he'd buy me chips!'

'Oh? *Oh!* And how long have you known Ian?' he asked, now a little uncomfortable as their names were voiced within hearing of the suspicious older woman.

'Since the big wheel,' the girl replied. 'I spilt my drink over him and he took it so well!'

The girl fell silent when she became aware of Roedan's watchful presence. She released Alan's arm and smiled politely, but was too awe-struck to voice a greeting. Roedan nodded an imperceptible return of the recognition, an action that seemed to double as a curt, but not impolite, dismissal.

The girl turned back to Alan and tugged at his arm. 'Hey! Come on!'

Alan tried to appear reluctant, as though he really would have preferred to stay and arouse further suspicion with Roedan. But, 'Oh, all right,' he intoned submissively, and followed the bouncing girl into the crowd with a parting nod of triumph at the woman they left behind.

A bearded man appeared beside Lea at the microphone as the lights dimmed around the stage. Ben turned to Sarah to point out this development, but found his companion still engrossed in a search for their colleagues.

With some relief, Ben noticed that the man on stage wore an outfit not dissimilar to the clothes worn by Earthwork that night. Tom Sutherland tapped at the microphone as though unsure of what to do with it, but compensated for this modest display with a confident address to the crowd. He slid his clipboard beneath one arm, leaned forward as if to embrace the microphone and breathed, 'Geophagia has the answers, people.'

The crowd roared an enthusiastic response. Ben was so impressed by this opening promise that he wished he had come prepared with the questions.

'Thank you,' Tom calmed the crowd, glancing at his clipboard for spontaneous effect while he waited for the cheers to fade. 'Thank you. Roedan will deliver her second speech in the Vitalism series in less than an hour's time – but first...' he murmured, stirring cheers of anticipation from his audience, 'we're going to hear from the band providing a stunning live soundtrack to the Geophagia Tour. Described by *New Vox* magazine as Somerset's drum'n'bass answer to The Cocteau Twins, they're here now to raise the Solstice energy, so put your hands in the air and make some noise for Kundalini!'

Light flooded the stage as Tom retreated and Lea opened the band's first track with a succession of rapidly strummed chords. The bass guitar began a throbbing accompaniment, and then the drummer introduced a high-tempo wave of percussion that set the crowd moving in the only way that such a tightly packed mass was able to. More than a thousand people began jumping, and Ben jumped euphorically with them.

Sarah was not so happy with the sudden activity. She could no longer search the crowd. In frustration she turned and tapped Ben moodily on one bouncing shoulder. 'What are you doing?' she demanded above the music.

'Mingling!'

The rest of the band brought their instruments into play, filling the night with a soaring, anthemic melody, and uniting every member of the crowd in worship of amplified sonics.

Just as Brampton Wyre had predicted, Ben fitted in.

Sarah received Ben's reply as an inference that she did not, and she was about to start hopping in reluctant conformity when, some distance away, a single face became conspicuous as the only stationary feature in the forest of bobbing heads. A man was smiling at her. Sarah struggled to identify him, but then groaned inwardly when she recalled a name she would have once murmured in the tone reserved for lovers.

Sarah tapped Ben's shoulder a second time – and again, harder, when she could not get a response.

'What?' Ben asked irritably.

'We have to go,' Sarah told him, tugging at his T-shirt.
'Go? Why?'
'I've been recognised.'
'Who by?' Ben demanded, turning to gaze at each of the dancers around them like a deer caught in headlights. 'And where will we go?'
'Doesn't matter!' Sarah hissed, turning away and pulling most of Ben's shirt with her. 'Just walk.'
The pair struggled back through the restless crowd for a full five minutes, covering a distance of only around fifty feet, before Sarah finally broke out of the moving mass and into a quieter area of the field. Ben did not share Sarah's urgency to distance themselves from the stage and its performers. He continuously glanced back over his shoulder at the vocalist, who happened to catch Ben's eye only once, but whose momentary expression of recognition was dismissed by her band's change of chord into a lively chorus. It was an easy, infectious theme, and Ben hummed along as he squeezed himself free of the jumping crowd.
He found Sarah standing beside Alan at the edge of the audience arena. Alan stood beside Ian, and Ian glanced nervously between Sarah and the girl clinging to his arm. 'Hi,' Ian waved with his free hand. 'We found you.'
Sarah nodded. 'You did,' she replied, unable to prevent a trace of mockery from entering her tone. 'And who's *we?*'
'Oh, this is Amy,' Ian introduced the excitable nineteen-year-old, and Ben did not miss the note of pride in his voice. 'She likes to spill drinks over people.'
'Yeah!' Amy snorted. 'And after a ride on the big wheel, Ian bought me chips!'
Alan resisted the urge to cover his face with his hands. Instead, he crossed his eyes at Ben, though Ben was already losing interest. The band was finishing its first song and he wished he could be closer to the stage to cheer.
'Well,' Sarah nodded, her arms folded defensively and one eyebrow raised in rehearsed cynicism, 'isn't Ian just the soul of benevolence?'
'Cool,' chirped Amy, who did not know what benevolence meant, though guessed it might be something good if you got food out of it.
'Amy helped Ian rescue me from some difficult company,' Alan explained, and then a little more quietly to Sarah: 'You won't believe who I started talking to!'
Kundalini's next song started with a heavy roll of drums and a sequence of electronic chords, and the crowd's energy was renewed. The quieter area in which Earthwork had regrouped shrank rapidly as more of Geophagia's membership arrived.
Ben was still absorbed in Kundalini's performance, and far too distracted to pay much attention, when George Wyre broke radio-silence from the car park.
'I'll assume you've all found each other by now, somewhere near the stage I

hope, and it's best that you stay there. When the band finishes, you can look forward to a speech from one of the organisers on sentient metaphors, or something.'

'Ooh!' Alan cooed at his silent colleagues, attracting confused attention from Ian's new friend.

'Sarah? *Sarah!* I thought it was you!'

Sarah flinched at the sound of her own name. The man she had struggled through the crowd to avoid had caught up. The others saw her close her eyes, inhale deeply, and then spin on her heel to face the new arrival. 'Hello, Michael.'

Michael was older than Sarah and her Earthwork colleagues – even older than Alan, who considered his few years' seniority over the others an advantage as Field Operations Leader. Michael leaned forward to kiss Sarah warmly on both cheeks, and then took a step back to look her up and down with an expression of approval. 'Sarah! You look so well! How have you been? *Where* have you been – and what are you doing here? I didn't know you walked Roedan's maze! Did you read up on everything Roedan recommended at Alban Eilir? What did you think?'

Sarah struggled to keep up with such questions. Powerless, Earthwork watched her floundering. One fumbled reply, they knew, would rob them of their cover. But when she heard Amy ask Ian for his phone number, Sarah decided that she longer wished to face this challenge alone. 'Me? With Geophagia? Didn't you *know?'* she replied, and then turned confidently to face the others. 'Alan? Ian? Just how long have we walked Roedan's maze?'

Blissfully absorbed in Kundalini's performance, Ben remained ignorant of the events behind him.

Ian and Alan looked to each other for support in carrying the weighty buck Sarah had so deftly passed them. 'Well,' Ian frowned as he decided how best to evade the question, 'I can't think. Alan? Just how long has it been?'

'Oh,' Alan shook his head, shuffling uncomfortably on the spot as though he might physically dodge the question, 'I'd have to say, at least—'

'Ages?'

'Oh yeah,' Alan agreed with feeling. 'At least *ages.*'

Sarah looked pleased with their discomfort. She flashed them each a satisfied smile and then turned back to Michael. 'Does it matter?' she asked dismissively, 'when you and I have so much to catch up on?'

'I can't believe I've not seen you around town before now!' he replied. 'Where have you been hiding? Did you move, or something?'

'Yes, actually,' Sarah nodded, taking one of Michael's arms in the same way that Amy clung to Ian's. She led the older man away towards the lights of a nearby food stall. 'Buy me some *chips*,' she suggested with a vengeful glance at Ian, 'and I'll tell you all about it.'

Ian returned a respectful nod in appreciation of her move, but regretted having initiated such spiteful sport. He knew from experience that this kind of game has no rules and no winners, and the only consolation is the potential for passionate reconciliation between losers.

He and Alan remained silent until the pair disappeared into the crowd. Amy swung impatiently on Ian's arm and sucked habitually on a strand of her own hair, gazing up at Ian with an expression of innocent pleading that a man of lesser principle might have found painful to resist.

But Ian was clearly distracted. He ignored Amy's gaze and leaned a little closer to Alan. 'I hate these fucking mind games,' he murmured quietly. 'Still,' he added, struggling to find something positive to say about seeing his girlfriend walking arm-in-arm with an ex-boyfriend, 'I think Sarah's done us a favour. A few more cryptic questions like those and our friend *Michael* would have seen straight through— *ow!* What are you doing?'

'I love your badge,' Amy said, pulling at Ian's T-shirt to study his Earthwork cross. 'Did you buy it here? What does it say? Ear—? Eart—'

'Earthwork,' Alan finished proudly, raising a hand to point at his own committee badge. 'It's a kind of local club.'

'Cool!' Amy chirped. 'Like Geophagia?'

'Ye–es,' Alan nodded uncertainly, glancing down to examine his shirt when his hand failed to locate the badge. 'Shit.'

'S'up?'

'It's gone,' Alan said, stepping back to study the grass around his feet. 'I've lost it.'

'Oh, Alan,' Ian scolded him wearily, 'you know we can't let you into the club house for secret meetings without it.'

'Not funny,' Alan replied, stroking at his shirt as if the action might force a reappearance of the badge. 'I'm serious.'

'When was the last time you had it?' Ian asked, taking Amy's hand in his own to stop her pawing at his shirt.

'Not long ago,' Alan struggled to recall, but became too distracted by vigorous movement beside him to concentrate. He turned and stared incredulously at Ben, who was dancing alone, oblivious to the concerns of his friends.

'What the hell is he doing?' Alan asked Ian with a nudge.

Ian shook his head, like dancing was the last thing he would expect to see someone doing at a music festival. 'Don't know,' he replied. 'Fitting in?'

Ben danced euphorically, captivated by the music and Lea Granger's voice, until he caught a glimpse of his grinning audience. He gradually forced his uninhibited moves to disintegrate into a more modest jig; then an embarrassed shuffle, and eventually to the restrained tapping of one foot.

Finally he turned to Alan, Ian and Amy as though he had only just remembered they were there and asked, 'What?'

Ethos

Craig paced the barn for some time, considering ways to ease his conscience. He could not imagine being of much use to his colleagues at this late hour, but then reasoned that joining Earthwork in South Pennard a little late was certainly better than not all, if only for appearances. He decided to go, and he picked up a set of car keys in the same moment that he became aware of someone watching him.

Craig heard the scuff of a boot against cobblestones outside the barn door, and he was not surprised by the presence of a spy. Brampton Wyre had sent employees to observe Earthwork's conversations and activities before.

But Craig did not act on his awareness of this presence immediately. Intending to use the Land Rover outside, he put the car keys in his jeans' pocket and then, with unexpected energy, took a running jump onto the table. He sprinted the length of it, leapt for a hold on a rafter near the doors and swung himself feet-first towards them.

Abel Mild's surprise at Craig's disappearance from his view through the gap in the doors left him no time to move away. The doors burst open, knocking Abel backwards across the cobbles. Craig landed neatly in a watchful crouch and looked at the mechanic in disgust.

'You rightfully have the reputation of being the strongest and most athletic member of Alan's team,' called Brampton Wyre, who was standing at the back door of Arlingham House, 'and I appreciate that you are young and full of energy, but none of these are excuses to assault my staff.'

Craig rose with slow, deliberate confidence. 'I didn't know he was there,' he replied. 'Sorry about that, Abel.'

'I thought you and I were of the same opinion earlier today,' Wyre went on, approaching Craig and the recumbent mechanic, who clutched at his nose, whimpering. 'But might I guess that you've changed your mind about Earthwork's plan?'

'You might,' Craig muttered, turning away from Wyre and the mechanic to unlock the Land Rover.

Brampton watched the vehicle roar away across the courtyard and along the tree-lined avenue. The crimson rear lights of the car faded between the parallel rows of poplars as it accelerated west.

Brampton offered Abel a hand and helped the old man to his feet.

"M I bleedin'?' the mechanic asked, raising his nostrils to Wyre's view.

Brampton squinted at Abel's top lip and shook his head. 'Did the kid call anyone?'

'No,' Mild replied, testing the bridge of his nose for fracture. "E's readin', then jus' got up, walked 'bout and jumped on me.'

Brampton peered into the dimly lit barn. He seemed about to step inside, but a stern voice and heavy footsteps caught his attention, so he waited patiently for the new arrivals to appear.

Alerted to the possibility of strangers in the courtyard, Abel Mild paced nervously.

Into the courtyard from the fields strode the intimidating bulk of the estate's gamekeeper, and a much younger figure dressed entirely in black, who reluctantly kept pace at the whim of Gary Basildon's grip. The keeper carried a shotgun in the crook of his left arm, open and unloaded, while the other hand clenched a fistful of the younger man's shirt.

Brampton nodded curtly at Baz.

'Mr Wyre,' Gary returned, and then shook his prisoner. 'Trespasser.'

'Oh?' Brampton addressed the silent man. 'Just taking a short-cut, was he?'

The keeper shook his head. 'No, he's set up camp in the middle of Parker's Copse. Been there a while as well: camp fire dug, well-built shelter, rubbish everywhere.'

'Really?' Brampton nodded, apparently amused by the discovery. 'How industrious. Torch?'

Baz produced a heavy rubber flashlight and handed it to Wyre. Brampton clicked it on and shone its beam into the eyes of the trespasser, who blinked against the light, but did not attempt to hide his face. Brampton stared thoughtfully at the man for a few moments and then switched off the torch. 'You've lived on my property for some time, though I doubt you'll tell me how long. You've paid no rent, so you owe me.'

Brampton and Baz exchanged a glance. It was this silent exchange that broke their prisoner's reserve. 'You're calling the police?'

Wyre shook his head. 'No, not if we can decide on another arrangement.'

The trespasser took no comfort in an exclusion of the law. He tried to back away, but was grabbed smartly by the keeper. 'Just call the police. I'm not repaying debts with favours for you and your gimp.'

'I can't begin to understand what you mean,' Wyre dismissed the man's fear. 'Tell me your name.'

'Fuck off.'

'Baz?' Wyre prompted his employee.

The gamekeeper lifted his captive by the shirt collar until the man's toes barely scraped the ground.

'Your name?' Brampton repeated.

'Kennett,' the man replied quickly.

'Kennett what?'

'Just Kennett.'

'Oh? Bizarre. Well listen, Just Kennett, I'd like you to work for me. If you work well, I'll forget about your stay on my property, and even come to an arrangement about what I might owe you.'

Kennett pretended to consider the offer, like he had a choice. 'What do I have to do?'
Wyre turned to glance briefly at the barn. The Earthwork cross painted across the doors reflected light from the windows of Arlingham House. Brampton seemed to dismiss whatever he had initially thought, and then gazed northwest at the silhouetted dome of Meeting Hill. 'Well first,' he began, passing the torch back to Baz, 'I'd like you to forget that we ever met.'

*

Kundalini concluded their set on stage. The audience surged forward on a wave of euphoria raised by the climax to the final song, and Ben followed them.
Alan and Ian stood their ground against the people that pushed around and between them, but Amy was happy to release her grip on Ian and vanish with the flow.
Eventually, Alan and Ian found themselves alone in a sizeable area of empty field. 'Do you think Ben wanted the lead singer's autograph?' Alan asked.
'I think he wanted the lead singer.'
Any plan that Kundalini might have had to reprise the most popular of their tunes as an encore was swept away as the crowd pushed up and over the platform. The music stopped abruptly after a few bad guitar chords, an amplified rattle of fallen drumsticks, and then the feedback whine of toppled microphones. But the music was soon replaced by an ambient number from DJ Van Planer.
Most of those who reached the platform stayed only long enough to seek out their favourite band member for an autograph, or await their chance to throw themselves bodily back into the crowd and be surfed away upon a forest of supporting arms. A number of others remained to dance, and Ben was among them. Lights pulsed around the stage in time to the music, and those left on the platform by the forward surge simply danced wherever the rush had left them.
A strobe light replaced the sequence of coloured lights, and it was in this play of flickering animation that Ben came face to face with Lea. She had just retrieved her guitar from beneath several pairs of dancing feet and was examining its broken neck with an unreadable expression. At his own feet, Ben noticed a small leather pouch he had seen before. He picked it up and waved it in front of Lea's face to catch her attention. She snatched possessively at the pouch before paying its rescuer any attention. 'Thank you,' she nodded after checking quickly through its contents, and then looked up at Ben. 'Oh. Hi.'
'Hi. That's sad, about your guitar.'
Lea lifted the broken instrument and gathered up its loose strings. There was nothing else she could do. 'I've had it so long, I can't remember being without it.' She shrugged and lowered it. 'I didn't realise you were one of us when I

saw you in Arlingham this morning.'
Ben shrugged. 'Why would you?'
'Because you blanked me when I asked you.'
'You asked me if I was a member?'
Lea looked confused. 'In our way.'
Ben could think of nothing else to say. 'Sorry.'
'Why? Being in the same club doesn't mean we have to talk about our business.'
'You're not interested in getting to know other members? I'm actually quite new to Geophagia.'
Lea seemed a little more interested. 'And your friend?'
'Who's that?'
'In the trees with you this evening.'
'Ah,' Ben looked away, but was not put off. 'Just boys' games.' He scratched at the back of his head and exaggerated his embarrassment. 'Men can't visit a place like Meeting Hill without wanting to run through the woods and pretend they're Robin Hood.'
Lea smiled a rare flash of appreciation and humour where, usually in the company of men, expressions of suspicion and cynicism reigned. 'I can relate to that. I think it's healthy to react imaginatively to your environment.'
'To hunt orcs in the forest,' Ben grinned.
'To pretend that the wilderness goes on forever, and that you're alone in it,' Lea nodded.
'And look up at the stars from a high place and feel like you're standing on the edge looking down.'
'Or spend nights on Meeting Hill and really believe that the stones are watching over you.'
'And leave messages in the cracks of the stones for the gods to find?' Ben attempted.
Lea stopped and smiled in silent understanding. 'If I didn't want my messages to be found, I wouldn't bother leaving them.'
Three members of the dark-suited security team appeared on the opposite side of the platform and began to herd the revellers from the stage. Unaware of much beyond their own exchange, Ben and Lea were surprised to find themselves being pushed off-balance by the unexpected pressure against them. Lea reached for Ben's shoulder for stability but succeeded only in initiating a domino effect: Lea into Ben, Ben into those behind him, and so on, until a dozen people were forced over the edge of the stage.
Ben and Lea landed among them in an untidy heap of limbs. They floundered for nearly a minute in a show of helpless clumsiness that kept them tangled long after those around them had stood and brushed themselves down.
'I'm sorry,' Ben lied breathlessly through his laughter, pulling an arm out from

beneath Lea's legs and checking that it was his. 'This is like Twister without the mat.'

Lea shook her head. 'My fault,' she declared, touching experimentally at Ben's chin. 'Does that hurt?'

'A little.'

'That's my fault too. It was me who elbowed you.'

'It's OK,' Ben replied, supporting himself on one elbow, 'but I do have one small problem.'

'What?'

'Trying to decide if kissing you on the day we met would be pushing my luck.'

Lea blinked. 'That's a problem?'

'Well, in a position like this,' Ben began to explain, 'it's practically expected, which might be a good reason not to – much too predictable. But then,' he went on, 'if I don't, I'll only regret missing the chance.'

Lea said nothing, but her silence was eloquent. She gazed at Ben with shining hazel eyes.

Nearby, speakers taller than the people around them vibrated to a relentless tempo, thudding in contrast to the unhurried pace at which Ben raised a hand and ran his thumb lightly across Lea's lips.

Keen to blend in, Alan and Ian attempted to dance like other people, but without looking as though they were dancing together. With each other, not *with* each other.

Ian, a little more relaxed about such appearances, enjoyed the expressions of discomfort he could provoke from Alan by pointing at him and singing along as they danced.

Alan was pushing Ian away for the third time when Sarah reappeared, alone and watchful. 'You've lost your girlfriend?' she observed.

'You've lost your boyfriend?' Ian countered.

'Just the last guy I went out with,' Sarah replied.

'And Amy just helped us out of a difficult corner,' Ian sniffed defensively, 'but then I couldn't get rid of her. Don't worry, Sarah, she was too young for me. Nineteen-year-olds are no challenge at all.'

'And the challenge is important?'

Ian thought about it. 'No one wants a potential partner to fall into their arms ten minutes after meeting,' he grinned. 'Someone like that would seem much too needy, bound to have issues.'

'Is that what Amy did?' Sarah asked.

Ian's smile widened. 'You'll never know.'

'You wanker,' Alan responded on Sarah's behalf.

Ian said nothing more, though looked like he wanted to, but Alan and Sarah were relieved by the distraction of fresh animation around the stage. Two spotlights were trained upon the empty platform, and Van Planer faded out his music for the second time that evening.

'Listen,' Alan broke the silence, reasserting his leadership of the group, 'there's been nothing over the radio for twenty minutes, so we'll have to assume that George has lost the plot or fallen asleep; but we can't stand here dancing around our handbags until she wakes up. Ben's run off looking for autographs, and we've found nothing that George seems to want.'

'George hasn't really told us what she wants,' Sarah reminded him. 'Does anyone know why she's so set against these people?'

'She must have proof of something naughty. I don't care what Craig says, George isn't paranoid.'

'Maybe we should stay a little longer, listen to whatever the guru has to say. But if it doesn't sound like anything that might concern us, we'll head back to the cars.'

'And Ben?' Sarah asked.

'He can take his chances,' Alan replied. 'He's chosen to follow his own agenda.'

The space around Earthwork was steadily reoccupied by Roedan's followers as the moment scheduled for her speech approached. Ian turned and gazed expectantly at the stage. 'How do you think the wonderful mystical marvel will arrive? Astral projection? Teleportation? Or just on foot so as not to intimidate us mortals?'

Distracted by the floodlit podium, Alan, Ian and Sarah were facing in the wrong direction to see the crowd part itself behind them, allowing light from the fairground to penetrate the centre of the gathering.

In preparation for the imminent arrival of its host, powerful spotlights had been placed at the forward corners of the stage and angled up to send vertical beams into the night. From elevated pyres alongside them, glowing embers released incense smoke into the light to form pillars of seemingly tangible florescence. Simultaneously, a frame to the rear of the platform unfurled a row of decorated banners, and Earthwork was impressed by the simple display.

'Could have been worse,' Alan decided. 'Anyone able to pull this kind of crowd might have been tempted to go for the full showbiz glitz: fireworks, sequinned girls, lasers, maybe a couple of pumas lying around the stage.'

'We're not here to write a review,' Ian murmured, and then blinked in surprise when the dark press of bodies before him brightened around the outline of his own deepening shadow.

Alan paused to consider a caustic reply, but he too became aware of how unusually light it was growing in the midst of the crowd. Before he could turn around, a growing suspicion of activity behind him was confirmed by the people in front, who suddenly rotated where they stood and gazed into the lights. What the crowd saw made it part itself smoothly through the centre like

Old Testament waters before a prophetic divider.

For an uncomfortable length of time, Alan, Ian and Sarah found themselves standing alone and exposed against the perimeter lights between parting walls of the awe-struck audience. They glanced in panic at one another, and then turned to follow the reverent stare of the crowd.

Bearing down on them from the west, Roedan strode toward the stage through the widening avenue of her followers, flanked by bulky minders and preceded by three bobbing shadows. The floodlights behind Roedan filled her thin white robe, creating a pale aura that flickered as she walked.

Earthwork quickly side-stepped into the crowd and watched Roedan's majestic passing with a curiosity that blended seamlessly with the expressions of wonder around them. Then the patient crowd fell in behind their leader as she neared the stage, and by the time Roedan reached the stairs, the audience had healed the rent through its centre and jostled those at the front to the edge of the platform.

Roedan gazed across the crowded arena from the elevated podium. Geophagia ecstatically cheered her arrival.

Earthwork resisted the forward surge in an effort to stay some distance from the stage, but they, like those stood beside and behind them, felt the weight of her stare as keenly as those who were able to touch her feet.

'It's good to see that our numbers swell with each new meeting,' Roedan began, her sonorous voice suffusing the night air like drifting steam from the speakers. 'All of you will be recognised and rewarded by whatever divinity you seek, and by even greater powers besides, but I will not speak of those now. I prefer not to invoke the will of the Invisible before I am sure that those who flock to my banner fully appreciate the miracle of the material world, and the power of their own imagination.

'First, my friends,' she smiled warmly as lights all around the arena began to fade, 'please kneel. Kneel before the view and receive the blessing of the breeze.'

There were no signs of surprise or protest from the attentive crowd. Without hesitation, people lowered themselves to kneel silently before the platform as the field darkened. Only a faint red glow from the incense pyres either side of the stage remained to burn through the gloom.

It took one silent minute for the eyes of the crowd to become accustomed to the darkness. The clear night sky, myriad stars and the shimmering brush stroke of the Milky Way were revealed as an infinite vista of breathtaking perspective, and a dim twilight effulgence lingering in the west offered distinction between Earth and Sky over the undulating Mendip horizon.

The Earthwork members were sufficiently impressed by the scene to feel justified in having dropped to their knees with the rest of the crowd, even though Roedan's request seemed to infer that she was somehow due credit for

the glittering cosmos.
But then the breeze came: a warm breath that lightly touched the upturned faces of the crowd like the blessing they were promised.
'Jammy,' Alan whispered, but quietly remained impressed.
A spotlight somewhere behind the crowd cast diffuse light over the stage, picking Roedan out of the darkness between the glowing incense pyres. The strength of the lamp increased slowly, allowing Roedan to resurface from the gloom like a haunting.
'A landscape lying in shadow beneath the clear Solstice night,' she observed. 'Just one of a million simple experiences whose grandeur is failed by words. These experiences are a magic we enjoy through our usual senses – pure magic,' she breathed, 'and yet people search for more – for the *invisible*, no less, when it is the visible that defines our perception of this world and the next.
'What is magic, after all, if not the animation, or the will, that moves and shapes our universe? Here we may truly use the word *spirit* in the way that it was originally meant, as the animating principle, my friends: the form of the landscape, the sigh within the breeze, the power behind the waves and the hunger of the fire. It has become cliché to consider only the novel and rarer aspects of Nature as somehow sacred: the lightning strike, the shooting star, vivid sunsets, eclipses of the sun, or the sighting of some rare animal – but what of our everyday surroundings? Think of the mesmerising repetition of pattern amongst leaves upon trees, the phases of the moon, or the evolution of every species of life on Earth. All is animation, friends – all is *will*.'
Seeing this brief pause as a chance to stand without seeming inattentive, the crowd rose steadily to its feet. Earthwork stood with them. Sarah gazed forward with interest, but Ian and Alan exchanged tedious looks. 'What a swizz,' Alan murmured. 'People come expecting visions and energies, and Roedan feeds them the lunar cycle. Do they pay to hear this stuff?'
'It's a big crowd. She must be saying something they like.'

Following their fall from the stage and recognition of mutual attraction, Ben and Lea retreated to the darkened interior of Kundalini's back-stage marquee, barely able to resist each other before reaching the privacy of the tent. There, after five minutes alone with the woman who had occupied his thoughts for several months even before meeting her, Ben spent a moment reflecting on this unexpected turn of events.
'Are you all right?' Lea asked him.
'Are you joking?'
'You seem distant.'
Ben and Lea knelt face to face inside the opening of the tent, both having lost their T-shirts to each other's breathless groping within moments of stepping

inside. But their coupling was no farce of urgent fumbling. Ben's near disbelief at the evening's fortune had checked his excitement, offering his advances a tender control, while Lea's confidence in returning his attention gave the exchange a steady momentum, the pace and course of which she determined according to her own growing need.

Ben exhaled a slow shaky breath, betraying either a barely restrained lust or perhaps a hint of nerves. Lea considered that both deserved a response of quiet sympathy.

'It's OK,' she reassured him, laying one hand against his chest and the other at his waist as she pressed her lips into his neck. 'You're not afraid of me, are you?'

The curiosity underlying her tone hinted that she wanted him to be, though Ben would not have admitted to thinking so. Instead, he might have begun to speak of the added meaning this encounter held for him beyond the thrill of spontaneous passion, if only such an admission didn't involve revealing his possession of Lea's diary.

'No,' Ben shook his head slowly against her kisses, 'I just feel like I've known you much longer than— well, you know what it's like when you see someone famous in the street? You can't quite believe they're there, or that you're there, or something...'

'Yeah?' Lea whispered, running her tongue from the centre of his chest to the pulse of his jugular.

Ben's eyes rolled back into his head. 'Doesn't matter,' he muttered, and then eased Lea down onto the grass beneath the canvas.

'In any discussion of disembodied will, words like *spirit, essence* and *animation* are unavoidable, as is our conclusion that the subject is rooted in our natural surroundings. Therefore, it is upon the Earth herself that the attention and respect of Geophagia is focused.'

Roedan's statement provoked an enthusiastic response from the audience, but Alan yawned and glanced at his watch.

'It is the lure of the freedom and power of wilderness that sets us on the road away from a layman's idle appreciation of Nature, leading to the initiate's interaction with the mysteries. And we celebrate in the home of this tradition.'

Roedan paced the platform to address each half of the crowd, and her movements grew increasingly dramatic, as if to throw physical weight into the conviction of her words. 'The Earth should be appreciated in its wondrous entirety, of course, but our purposes require focus – in this case upon one small, green island in the northern hemisphere of our planet.

'Now,' she gazed at the people nearest the platform as though to gauge their ability to absorb the next of her profundities, 'we gain insight into personality through physical characteristics, which everything manifests to express itself.

For example, my interests and experiences express themselves through my choice of clothing and mannerisms, allowing people to label me as a pacifist, a liberal, a vegan, a Billy Bragg fan, and a Greenham Common veteran.'

A dutiful chuckle from the audience at this rare flash of self-effacing humour.

'And we may apply this simple principle on a far greater scale,' she continued. 'I assert that the essence of a country can be defined in this way. We can come to know the identity of a land through its landscape, climate and wildlife. Viewed in these terms, the British Isles are unique.

'The Earth is awesome, breathtakingly beautiful to every sense, but the British wilderness offers an unparalleled depth of fascination, and this is our focus. Thanks to our country's climate of opposite extremes, the flora and fauna of Britain manifest themselves in rugged forms: from the gothic growths of ancient yew and gnarled oak, whose spreading branches creep moodily against dramatic skies, to the familiar species of British wildlife, whose faces, furs, horns and antlers have become the classical symbols of Pagan divinity.

'The natural forms, patterns and colours of our land have become entrenched within our psyche, inspiring the folklore of countless generations. In turn, this rich mythology has augmented its geographical personality, whose essence I have come to know as Avalon – the spirit of wild and ancient Britain.'

With a pause in her speech came an encouraging cheer from the crowd, and Sarah Conrad also appreciated Roedan's sentiment. Sarah quickly drew parallels between Roedan's statement and Earthwork's cause. After all, what was the committee's purpose if not the preservation of its own corner of ancient Britain?

Alan and Ian had also noticed this common interest, but while Sarah was able to nod silently in reasonable agreement, the men decided that an appearance of weary boredom was the appropriate response for a dutiful Earthwork member.

A gasp. 'Do that again.'
Ben paused. 'Where?'
'Just where you were— Oh. That's it...'
'You're amazing.'
'Hardly started. Gets better.'
'No, I mean anyway. You're just amazing.'
'Don't go soft on me.'
Ben became defensive. 'Never been a problem before.'
Lea sniggered. 'No, I mean sentimental.'
'If the position we're in isn't a good time to get slushy, I don't know what is.'
'Waste of breath. Kiss me here.'
'All right,' Ben agreed, and his tone of surrender sent Lea into a fit of laughter.
'No question,' she said, 'you're funny.'
'I'm not really known for my wit.'

'No, *funny,*' Lea repeated. 'Odd.'
'Cheers.'
Lea was not deterred by his wounded tone. She was encouraged by it. 'In fact,' she decided, 'I think a you're a bit of a lost soul.'
Her statement sounded a little too much like sympathy, and it made Ben retreat. 'I don't need mothering.'
So Lea reached forward with her other hand and waited for a give-away breath. 'What about that?' she asked. 'Is this what you need?'

Van Planer accompanied Roedan's speech with ambient chords of electronic strings as the orator paced the platform. Along the borders of the arena, soft showers of glittering ashes drifted from the overhead beacons and danced upon the breeze.
'Avalon,' Roedan repeated the name affectionately, 'is not just the nostalgic dream of a wilderness that once was, but the reality of a land and a way of life that may still be. Avalon is easily achieved as a state of mind, but the reality for which we campaign offers more to its faithful restorers than a merely psychological haven: Avalon is the eternal essence of British wilderness, my friends,' she continued, now softening her tone. 'The diverse and dramatic properties of these isles inspired the pre-Roman population to tales of the deeds of gods and heroes, and the soft rolling landscape inspired reverence for the feminine properties of the Earth itself – a female presence so tangible that we might truly consider our Britain the land of the Goddess. Every distinct natural feature is a symbol of her majesty, like a jewel in the crown of a monarch.'
Following prods from Sarah, the Earthwork members forced themselves to appear a little more receptive to Roedan's words.
'But Avalon may prove to be an exclusive club,' Roedan warned her followers, changing mood with a conspiratorial glance at the crowd. 'The rune-carved gateway to the Wild Wood of primeval Britain will be barred to those with selfish motives. The true seekers of Avalon wish to work at recreating a traditional way of life, and achieving close, self-sufficient communities. But people whose interest in Avalon is preoccupied only with rumours of magic and hedonism should – and will – be identified for all to recognise. These people don't want to live – they want to exist in the reflected glory of those who they think will do their living for them. These are the people who seek Avalon solely for its gods and their favours, not for its offer of the freedom to run, to learn and to excel as humans. It will be the spirited amongst you that the gods notice: those of you who are prepared to live and to risk, even if such passion involves living at the expense of those who can't be bothered.'
This provoked the greatest response yet from the hungry crowd, but Roedan had no time for a validation of her opinions. She positioned herself in the

beam of a spotlight to fully reflect its brilliance and then reached into her robe. Roedan waited until the applause was reduced to a background murmur before subjecting the crowd to a penetrating glare of intimidating scrutiny. Back and forth across the throngs of Geophagians her gaze swept like the beam of a lighthouse, and those nearest the platform had to blink and look away.

'Just how do we recognise the selfish, the lifeless and the undeserving amongst us?' Roedan asked as she studied her silent faithful. 'What would the uninvited look like if we could pull them from our midst?'

These questions inspired the crowd to a search of its own. Heads turned, and neighbours studied each other suspiciously, as if Roedan's uninvited might display some distinguishing mark.

'They'd look like a parody of us,' Roedan hissed into her microphone, relieving the crowd of its responsibility to answer. 'I suspect that anyone with a desire to fit in will try to look like us. But people imitating a group to which they do not belong would try too hard, and their ignorance would be the key to their exposure. Every crowd contains an element of the uninvited, my friends. Do we know ourselves well enough to spot them?'

Despite Ben's submission to his lust, Roedan's words had continued to register at some auxiliary level of his pleasure-flooded mind, until the possible direction of her speech finally struck home like a cold suppository.

'What's the matter?' Lea whispered.

Ben strained to listen to Roedan's words as he rose from a prone position.

'What?' Lea persisted. 'Where are you going?'

Ben groped about on the grass in search of clothes he had shed, but remained painfully conscious of how he was making Lea feel. 'Look,' he improvised, 'shouldn't we be outside where we can hear the speech? Isn't Roedan the reason we're here?'

'We're in a *tent,* Ben. We can hear the speech. '

'You can?' Ben replied. 'And what do you think so far?'

'I think I'm happy in here with you. I'm not missing anything so far. Roedan always kicks off like this – though I can't remember a talk about uninvited guests before.'

'Really?' Ben swallowed, pulling on a boot and fumbling at the laces.

'Really,' Lea nodded into the gloom, but then paused to think about it. 'Why? Does that worry you?'

Ben stopped. 'Why should it worry me?'

Lea shrugged. 'You're new to the scene,' she suggested. 'You might find it a bit intimidating.'

'Well, maybe.'

Lea reached out in the darkness until she found his arm, and then shuffled forward to press her cheek against his. 'Are you so fragile, Ben Marchen? It's

all right. We're all friends here.'
Ben wrestled with conflicting desires as Lea stroked one of his ears – but he flinched in panic when he felt something become loose and then slip at the passing of her fingers. The sudden movement helped dislodge his ear-piece, and Lea was left holding a slightly greasy radio receiver in her upturned palm.
'Oh!' she jumped, sounding startled and embarrassed, and all Ben could do was sink back and kneel before her in weary defeat.

Earthwork attracted not only wary glances, but also the kind of glares that suggested a hardening of suspicion into unblinking conviction.
On the stage, Roedan pulled a metallic token from within the folds of her robe and held it up to the light. Ian watched her move until the object projected the intensity of the nearest spotlight towards them from the platform, and Earthwork's position in the crowd was indicated by a thin beam of light through the incense smoke. The dazzling reflection danced as a pinpoint in Alan's eyes, puncturing his swaggering confidence in Earthwork's charade.
Roedan pointed with her other hand, and a spotlight at the southern edge of the arena beamed into the crowd at the intruders' position. People turned and strained for a view of those exposed.
A few seconds later Ian, Alan and Sarah found themselves standing alone inside an expanding circle of unsmiling faces.
'You see, my friends?' Roedan said with patronising sympathy. 'The uninvited stand among you. So,' she glanced at the reflective face of Alan's committee badge, '*Earthwork* – is that really how you thought Geophagians like to dress?'
Alan, Ian and Sarah feigned ignorance, glancing down at themselves and each other with no indication of noticing anything unusual.
'Like what?' Ian called defiantly in the accusing silence.
'Like twats,' Roedan replied, and her argument was superior with a microphone as its ally. 'Who are you, Earthwork? What are you doing here?'

Lea was silent for some time, contemplating the echo of Roedan's words and the ear-piece in her up-turned palm. 'Ben,' she asked eventually, 'what are you wearing?'
'Not much now,' he laughed with a note of hysteria, 'you took my—'
'I think you know what I'm asking,' she interrupted. 'Is Ben your real name?'
'What kind of question is that?'
'I might have reason not to trust you, can you see that?'
'Yes,' he conceded.
'Thank you. Now tell me I'm wrong.'
Distanced by a few feet of space and a widening gulf of suspicion, Ben and Lea knelt and gazed at each other's silhouette. 'I could tell you that you're

holding the hearing-aid I wear for deafness in my left ear. I could say that I always dress in this kind of gear, and I could claim not to know which people Roedan is talking about out there.'

Lea sniffed but made no reply.

'I can't, though. Not honestly. Despite all that, I told you my real name because I wanted you to know it, and I'm in here with you because I've known you a lot longer than you think.'

Ben saw Lea shake her head. 'Have you been spying on me?'

In the grip of his conscience, Ben placed his freedom in Lea's hands. 'I'm not going to run,' he said calmly. 'If you want to call someone or—'

Lea slapped him hard: a lucky shot in the darkness, but a stinging blow that caught him flat across his cheek with an audible clap. 'I wasn't insulted until you said that. I was really impressed when you didn't try to lie, but you can't claim to know me if you think I'm going to forget everything we've just shared and scream like a little girl.' Lea softened her tone as Ben wiped a watering eye. 'I don't know why you and those other people have come here dressed like clowns and kitted out like spies, but it can't have been just to get close to me. Are you police?'

The tense silence over the festival arena was broken by the roar of an approaching car and angry use of its horn.

'I'm sorry,' Ben replied. He rose and stepped away.

'You can go, but I want some answers. Remember, I know where you live, Ben Marchen.'

Ben sought the door of the marquee. 'Good.'

The Uninvited

George turned in her saddle and wondered why Ben had fallen quiet. 'Don't stop there,' she ordered him. 'What happened next?'
Ben slowed Bucephalus and listened to the sounds of distant gun fire. 'That's when Craig turned up. He drove straight past gate security into the arena and pulled the others out of the crowd. It was so cool. This isn't the season for shooting things, is it? What would Baz want to kill today?'
The Solstice had been a very hot day, but the next was even warmer. The relentless sun silenced birdsong, robbed crops of their lustre and beat the air into breathless submission. George led the Earthwork team on a mounted tour around Meeting Hill's estate borders and eyed the stunted barley through which they rode. 'There's always pests to control. Why didn't you come and find me last night? I waited in the parking field until nearly midnight.'
'Because you weren't in trouble like the rest of us. Geophagia didn't know you were there, and the way they chased us didn't give us a chance to stop in the car park and wave at you.'
George adopted a playfully scolding tone. 'That's a very dramatic description, Ben. You were spotted gate-crashing a New Age festival, not threatened for infiltrating a controversial cult.'
Ben dragged his gaze from eastern stretch of the estate to pay George more attention. 'Geophagia was annoyed with us for sneaking into their party, but Craig drove an Earthwork car through a crowd of thousands to pick up Alan and the others, so I don't think I'm being *dramatic* by saying that they turned nasty. Geophagia threw anything they could lift. The Land Rover needs new rear lights and two new windows, and if the police don't turn up later to tell us that Craig crushed eighty people last night, he deserves a highly paid job as a stunt driver.'
'What about you? I suppose Craig drove round until he bumped into you?'
'In a way. I'd had the same idea as Craig of trying to reach the others. I managed to get back to my car, but he barrelled into me on his way out.'
Ben had thought the others out of earshot some way behind him, but he heard Craig holler a defensive account of the night's events from his own point of view. 'You T-boned *me*, dickhead! Tell George that! You're paying for the bodywork. Who needs bull bars on a fucking *pick-up?'*
Alan, Ian and Craig caught them up at a trot. George noticed their wary glances at Ben and regretted asking only one member of the team for an account of their night's work.
'The others should tell you the rest,' Ben said. 'They saw more than me.'
Alan allowed himself only one resentful comment about the way in which the evening had turned out. 'We did.' He pointed an accusing finger. 'You're lucky you missed it. What did you do after you left?'

'Headed home,' Ben said, trailing after the others as George took the lead to resume the tour. 'I was tired.'

And ecstatic and frustrated and impatient for a chance to see Lea again.
And angry because one of his car's front tyres was rubbing its wheel-arch on tight corners, and because when he got home at midnight he discovered that someone had planted a nine-foot crucifix outside his lounge window.
Ben got out of the car but kept its headlights on to gaze at the cross, mystified. He recalled having seen a cross like this one displayed in the neighbouring churchyard at Easter, yet here it was in June, erected in the small lawn of his rented extension.
He scanned the borders of the garden as he approached the timber frame, aware that those daring enough to have planted a large crucifix outside his home might think nothing of hanging around to witness his reaction to it. A bat blinked past overhead as Ben ripped a handwritten message from a pin in the centre of the cross.

> *It is written, 'You shall worship the Lord your God,*
> *and him only shall you serve.' Matthew 4:10*

'Fucking mental,' he laughed at the note, crushing the paper into a ball and tossing it at the frame.
A gentle voice behind Ben said, 'That's very offensive to my faith.'
Ben flinched and turned. 'I can say what I like in my garden in the middle of the night.' He peered closely at the new arrival, which he was surprised to notice was not wearing a hooded cloak. 'Are you bored of haunting The Meeting? Or am I overdue a talk about my relationship with destiny?'
'You're confusing me with someone else.'
'Hey, man, is that the *very* Reverend Norton? Sorry, I'm used to a different guy appearing to me at times like this. There's too many religious old fanatics in this village. By the way, have you misplaced a huge crucifix? There's one in my garden. I bet that's the last place you thought of looking.'
Matthew Norton chuckled warmly as he stepped forward into the beam of the headlights. 'I like you, Ben. You struggle against your anarchic tendencies, but you're vulnerable. You didn't find whatever you were looking for while you were travelling, and you came back just as lost.' Norton stepped sideways and affectionately patted the cross. 'But we can help.'
'Leave me alone, and take the stage prop with you.'
Norton changed tact as Ben returned to his car and turned off its lights. 'Then I'll avoid the religion and try this as a friendly neighbour.'
'Don't pretend to be my friend. You only talk to me to lecture me.' Ben slammed his car door. 'It's harassment.'
'So why don't you bow to pressure and leave Little Arlingham? Everyone

would be happier if you lived elsewhere, even if it was only a mile out of town. The village doesn't want you here if you can't change. Putting this cross here did seem a bit militant at first, but I must be seen doing my utmost for your soul. You're a confused young man and I don't want to see a member of my parish, no matter how unpopular, go off the rails during a vulnerable time in his life.'
'I'm nearly thirty.'
'It's difficult to lose your mother at any age.'
Ben walked toward his front door. 'My Mum isn't *lost.*'
'You've not seen her for months.'
'Is there anybody in Somerset who *doesn't* know my business?'
'And your father won't tell you.'
'We don't get on.'
'On top of that, your involvement with Earthwork is in danger of exposing you to ideas which are, I think, destabilising for a young man with no fixed ideas of his spirituality – or at least, of how he might approach the subject, as we all eventually do.'
'And *you* hold the key to my peace of mind?' Ben asked from his doorstep.
'Your transformation is something that many individuals would like to see, even those who have signed up to a different covenant than my own. But I am here to assist in that aim. Know thyself, Ben,' Norton intoned like a sermon. '*Knowledge preserves the life of him who possesses it.*'
'Ooh,' Ben breathed, 'Bible quotes. They always win an argument. I'd better go indoors and rethink my life. Now piss off.'

Ben didn't notice that he'd been left alone with Ian until his friend asked him what he was smiling at. Ben looked up and saw a trail of dust at the other end of the desiccated field kicked up by the other three horses. 'I told the local vicar what to do with himself last night. Where are we going?'
'George thinks travellers might have moved into Parker's Copse, wants us to have a look. She's taking the others up the hill. Someone painted something on a few of the stones last night.'
Side by side, Ian and Ben rode south along the wire boundary around Meeting Hill. From the east came further reports of a shotgun: two shots in quick succession and a distant yelping.
'Did you speak to her last night?'
'Who?'
'*Who?*'
'Was it that obvious?'
From the wilting crop suddenly ran a ragged and blood-stained animal. Ben's horse reared in surprise and had to be calmed. A fox, struggling to breathe through foam and a drool of gore, cowered wide-eyed between the two horses,

flinching with fear and bleeding from its trembling haunches.

'Has it been shot?' Ian asked, but expected no answer from Ben, who slid out of his saddle to crouch near the wheezing animal. The fox cowered lower against the dust and snapped at him.

Ian backed Sable away. 'It's dying, not worth losing a finger for.'

Ben did not listen. He shuffled forward, hoping to cradle the failing creature in his arms.

'It's too scared to be helped. It'll have your throat out.'

Ben was not hurt when he picked it up. The fox died at that moment. Ian thought that the shock and pain of being held probably finished it off, but did not say so.

Ben shook his head sadly over the animal before returning it to the ground. He noticed but did not mind the mess it had left on his T-shirt. He looked up to scratch behind the ears of Bucephalus, who retreated from the smell Ben now possessed. Ben turned away and stared past Ian with an expression of sadness that bordered on grief, and then shock. Ian shared a degree of emotion for the fox, but considered Ben's horrified reaction disproportionate.

'Come on, mate. It's not like we didn't grow up around this kind of thing.'

But Ben waved Ian's words away and pointed past him into the sky. 'Is Meeting Hill on fire?'

Ian turned in his saddle and was stunned by the illusion that the forested dome of Meeting Hill had grown by several times its original height. An immense tower of black smoke as wide as the hill itself rose from the summit and cast a shadow like a stain across the fields.

Breath

The men galloped headlong. Ben feared that his horse would stumble or put a hoof down a rabbit hole, but he knew that Ian feared worse. Sarah had planned to spend her day reading on Meeting Hill.
Ian began the journey well ahead of Ben, but Bucephalus was a far stronger runner than Sable and soon caught up, drew alongside and overtook.
Ben jumped a narrow ditch between fields in the southern shadow of Meeting Hill and joined the road just north of Burrow Corner. The ascending lane from the road to The Meeting lie only a few hundred metres ahead. Ben saw George, Alan and Craig at the junction, though Craig did not remain with them for long. He jumped from his horse to run uphill, and it wasn't until Ben reached the leaders of the Earthwork team that he realised he rode alone.
George asked, 'Where's Ian?'
'He was behind me.' He cast around in his saddle. 'Shit. Must've headed uphill from the field. What's Craig doing?'
Alan wore an expression of helplessness and looked at George. Wyre's presence during this crisis relieved him of the weight of leadership. George shared a helpless expression, though hers was animated by anger. 'He's doing what I told him not to. *No* one else is to go up there. I know Sarah might be on the hill, and who knows who else. But a roasted hero is no hero.'
Alan looked up into the shadow of the smoke, and then back at the others. 'So—'
'We wait here,' George ordered. 'We've called 999. Whoever turns up will want to know where they're going. Isn't Ian asthmatic?'
The horses skittered on the tarmac at the sounds of heat-splintered and falling wood from overhead. The three friends stared into the trees and saw a slow avalanche of smoke rolling downhill. George said, 'Idiots.'

A storm of soot and racing sparks rose from marauding flames in the northern and western trees. In the summit clearing, the smoke slowed and gathered as a suffocating fog.
Ian found Sarah unconscious in the thick of it, lying near a standing stone with a grazed forehead. Having almost collided with the same megalith as he blundered through the smoke, Ian guessed how Sarah had received the wound.
Ian could not see the surrounding trees, but he could feel the intense heat of the flames that devoured them. He had entered the clearing from the top of the south-eastern slope and felt the blaze nearing as he ducked beneath the perimeter branches. Ian discovered fire attempting to advance on the clearing and its ring of stones by crossing the circumference of tall dry grass.
He laboured to breathe. His eyes stung and watered.
Ian shook Sarah's shoulders and called her name, but he choked on the effort.

His lungs felt seared. There appeared to be no chance that he might revive his girlfriend and walk her out of danger. With panic rising to frustrate his efforts, Ian gripped Sarah's arms and hauled them over his shoulder. But the effort used his last comfortable chestful of air, and so he slumped, with strength remaining only to stop himself from smothering Sarah.

Craig arrived on the summit moments later, faring little better in the smoke. He called the names of his friends but found the sound of his voice muffled by the cloud of ash. Craig hurried past the unconscious pair and became disoriented.

It was the fingers of a much older man that came to feel for a pulse at Sarah's neck, and then at Ian's. 'Idiot,' the owner of the hand muttered, and cringed when he saw that Ian held Sarah's hand. Madog hacked noisily at the contents of his throat, lowered the damp rag tied around the lower half of his face and spat into the grass. An indistinct phantom passed through the smoke nearby, weakly calling its friends like the shade of a lost soul.

'Here!' Madog croaked when the figure seemed about to fade back into the grey.

'Ian?'

'Follow my voice,' the old man ordered. '*This* way!'

Craig appeared beside the standing stone, smudged and coughing. Madog cleared his throat and spat again. 'Is this the best Earthwork can do?' he growled, watching Craig kneel at Ian's side.

'What?' Craig asked, and pulled Ian into a sitting position.

'You take him,' the cloaked man wheezed. 'I've got her.'

'Save your breath,' Craig rasped, slipping one arm around Ian's back and another beneath his knees.

Alan directed the first of three fire engines uphill. The driver of the third stopped to speak to him, and Ben heard them discuss the site's limited access and the likelihood of casualties. Behind him, George waved at an approaching police car. The fire engines ascended the steep zigzag path. With George now usefully distracted, Ben and Alan jogged uphill behind them.

By the time the men reached the summit, each vehicle had spilled fire fighters, hoses and equipment in every direction. Facing west, the scene was lit only by a muddy half-light from the sun's smoke-dimmed disc, and much of the clearing was hidden behind a sliding wall of smog. Methodical, well-rehearsed industry filled the space between the eastern trees and the dense screen of airborne ash, but Ben's gaze was drawn by a particular concentration of uniforms beside The Meeting's largest megalith. The legs of two prostrate individuals emerged from either side of the huddle. Alan hurried their way as soon as he noticed.

Hoping to be of some use but finding none, Ben stared around the scene until he spotted Craig sitting a short distance from the friends he had helped rescue, requiring minimal support from of a lone fireman and a dose of oxygen. Glancing beyond Craig to the north, Ben watched with visible grief as a blackened oak bough wilted and fell with a brittle crack. Then he saw the flames that had razed it, just before a jet of water was directed their way.

A glance at the southern edge of the circle revealed an equally watchful figure. *Y Deuddegfed Maen* stood hooded and motionless among the untouched trees. For some time, Ben and Madog stared at one another other silently, communicating fluently. The old man broadcast blame, and Ben could only absorb it.

A short burst of siren forced Ben to side-step from the path of an arriving ambulance. A fourth fire engine followed it. The fire fighters treating Ian and Sarah waved at the ambulance, which turned, parked beside them and ejected paramedics.

*

One mile away to the south, Brampton Wyre watched a man dressed in black approach him through a field of barley in the shade of the towering smoke. Kennett glared expectantly at the impassive Wyre as he closed the remaining distance between them. Brampton watched the man climb the gate at the field's edge and join him on the road beside his Range Rover. Kennett lit a cigarette as Brampton reached into a pocket of his linen trousers and pulled out an envelope, which he handed it to the younger man. Wyre gazed up at the column of black smoke and chewed at his bottom lip while Kennett counted a sheaf of bank notes. But he must have betrayed some sign of discontent because Wyre raised an instructive finger and pointed east along the lane, out of the estate via another distant gate. 'That's what you were promised. Now you can go.'

Kennett smiled without humour and waved the money in the air between them. 'When the revolution comes, it'll be me who takes the heads of entitled pricks like you and uses them as—'

Brampton interrupted Kennett's statement by stepping into his car and slamming the door. Kennett concluded by shaking a fist and mouthing *Wanker* at the Range Rover as it drove away. Then he pocketed the money and began a careless retreat. He strolled east, as ordered, but only until Wyre's car disappeared from view. As soon as he saw the lane clear in both directions, he vaulted back into the barley field, set his sights upon distant Parker's Copse and walked contentedly in a light shower of ash.

Roots

The bare feet of this former resident had not trodden the descending contours beneath Meeting Hill for many years, but Chiron Dell had not changed. The only gate, weighted into its closing swing by a rock and a length of twine, still creaked an unoiled announcement of visitors. And here, just inside the meadow, the old man still relied on a crude wooden frame, strewn with pendulous carrion and crowned with the sun-bleached skull of a ram, to unnerve the uninvited.

Madog lived in a barely weatherproof hut in one corner of the field beneath an ancient oak, and it was towards this meagre dwelling that Roedan strode through knee-high grass and rampant yarrow in the vain hope of surprising The Twelfth Stone.

A diffuse pall of smoke lingered over Meeting Hill in the limpid air, prematurely dulling the late afternoon light. Roedan was just wondering at its cause when she heard the unmusical clacking of a lone magpie. The bird landed on the roof of Madog's hut, but it immediately dived to safety from the flight of an arrow, which embedded itself in the timber of Madog's hut and quivered with the impact.

Roedan turned in search of the bird's attacker and saw a familiar old man emerging from the northern hedgerow. The cloaked man lowered his bow and viewed his visitor with contempt. Roedan pointed after the terrified magpie and raised a mocking eyebrow. 'You still blame your bad luck on the wildlife?'

Madog strode past Roedan without looking at her. 'What are you talking about, girl?'

'*One for sorrow...*'

'I taught you that,' he replied, spitting another mouthful of smoke-flavoured phlegm into the grass.

Roedan laughed.'And I used to believe it. I used to believe everything you told me.'

'What are you doing here? You lost your right to be in my home when you broke your promise and left. You should be married with kids and growing fat in front of a television by now, not still trying to convince yourself that you're any kind of player in my way of life.'

Roedan began to shake her head even before Madog had finished. 'I'm not here to go over these old arguments with you,' she replied, following Madog towards his hut.

'So?' Madog growled, shrugging off his cloak. From a woodpile against the shed he tossed a few timbers into a rock-lined fire pit and brimmed a metal pot with water from a rain-filled barrel.

'A Geophagia meeting was infiltrated last night. I want to know what you can tell me about it.'

'*Infiltrated?* Jill, your group is a money-spinning New Age sham for weekend hippies, not MI5.'

'There were people,' Roedan continued: 'two men and a woman. They called themselves Earthwork, according to a badge one of them wore. The whole thing has your reek about it. Is this something you set up?'

Madog sat down on a six-foot log in front his fireplace. He set aside the bow, tugged off his dusty leather boots with grunts of effort and eventually looked Roedan in the eye. 'No.'

Roedan nodded, watching Madog produce an oversized hanky to wipe at the soot deepening the creases in his face and hands. 'Let me rephrase that: might your influence be at work here? Have you *inspired* anyone to organise something they think they dreamt up themselves?'

Madog inspected his hands and tossed the filthy rag aside. 'I'll admit this much, girl: if these people have pissed you off, they have my blessing, whoever they are. What did they actually do?'

'They weren't members of Geophagia,' Roedan said quietly. 'They shouldn't have been there.'

'Doing…?'

'Asking questions.'

'Bastards,' Madog gasped.

'But they weren't invited, and their infiltration of my festival was an organised operation,' she explained while Madog laughed. 'They even had a marked vehicle waiting to break through my security and drive into a crowd of my friends to pick them up. I want to know what part you played in all this.'

'Oh?' Madog tried to sound insulted. 'And I thought you'd come to ask for my help.'

'Your help.'

'Aye.'

'With what?'

'You know what. Still looking?'

Roedan glanced away. Then, 'Yes,' she admitted, 'but I don't need help from you. That's why I left.'

'It's beyond you, and well beyond your *foundation* of gullible saps,' Madog declared. 'Carreg's bane should be buried and lost. The monk died to achieve that.'

'But I'm close.'

'Don't kid yourself.'

'I've researched this for years—'

'And been ridiculed by every academic in the field. You're chasing myths and fairytales.'

'My leads run deeper than that.'

'*Ha!* You mean you've chosen an intuitive path? You're going to meditate until you *guess* where it is?'
'Don't mock it,' Roedan warned him. 'You taught me to do it.'
'But you couldn't! Stick with a metal detector.'
'Like I said, I didn't come here to be lectured. That's a pleasure you can save for your next student.'
Roedan stopped and considered her last statement for a few moments. Then she turned back to where Madog was arranging kindling in the pit at his feet.
'Is that who Earthwork are? Some collection of misfits you've been appearing to in the middle of the night, like you did to me, in the hope that one of them will be your next apprentice?'
Madog did not react as angrily to Roedan's insight as she thought he might. He considered her question and nodded truthfully. 'You meet some promising people on the summit at night.'
Roedan clapped triumphantly. 'I knew it! So it'll all begin again. You're going to indoctrinate some restless, daydreaming soul into your shamanistic fantasy.'
'You disagree with the tradition of *Y Deuddegfed Maen?*' Madog asked, and made it sound like a dare.
'Oh no,' Roedan humoured him, 'I'm actually very grateful for my roots here. I outgrew your tired superstitions and restrictive ethics, of course, but the grounding you gave me was a good place to start until I was ready to strike out by myself.'
'In search of something that we're not even sure exists anymore, and with no idea of where to start looking.'
'I have more than an idea. I have my research, and my pathworking.'
The Twelfth Stone shook his head and surprised Roedan by producing a copy of *Maze* magazine from a pile of papers behind the log. 'You're a joke as an archaeologist, and you're certainly no oracle – but you're becoming quite the demagogue, I see? Ranting about imposing on the country *an environmentally sustainable society based on the tribal culture of the Iron Age?*' he quoted happily from page four. Then, just as happily, he tore the magazine to shreds as kindling for his fire. 'Politics seems to be more your line. You get to impose your will on everyone else, spew your interminable sound-bites for a few gullible voters and line your pockets in the process.'
Roedan turned away and resisted her fury. She spent a few seconds considering some worthy reply, but instead chose to make a dignified exit.
Madog searched the pockets of his faded, frequently patched jeans for matches; found some, lit one, and held it to the paper beneath his firewood. 'Don't ever come here again,' he called after Roedan, but did not look up until he heard the creak and closing impact of the gate.
The Twelfth Stone blew into the shallow hole at his feet and watched flames begin to lap at the firewood. Then he retrieved an unlabelled bottle of spirit

from amongst things scattered behind the log. He unscrewed the lid and raised his drink to the play of golden sunlight through oak branches extended like a protective hand over his hut and fireside seat. Then he saluted the warm evening breeze, which moved the tall grass and wild flowers like an aria.

And finally, expressing a difficult combination of childish apprehension, paternal love and acute sympathy, he looked up at Meeting Hill, where a shroud of darker air still clung to the wounded summit.

Ben and Lea

June 13th

> Every breath of wind a sylph, every wave an undine, and every contour in the landscape a striving of industrious sprites… After learning to perceive the force within the Elements as wilful, how can I consider the day's first sunbeam as anything less than an epiphany, and as a friend?

He had met its author at last, and Ben reread Lea Granger's journal with fresh insight. From its first entry on April 6th the previous year, to the last one written nearly five months before, every sentence was revitalised.
Sitting on Meeting Hill among the scorched northern trees the day after the fire, Ben studied a passage that reflected his own feelings about the damage to the woods around him.

> I remember the past with disproportionate nostalgia. I'm sure it used to be sunnier. I remember lovers with depths of affection I'm sure I didn't feel at the time, and I seem to remember the landscape as an endless horizon of unspoilt wilderness, as if I could know what that would have been like.
> But summers now seem cloudier and wetter. Boyfriends seem ever more selfish, and the horizon is just a limit to my view of the scars people have left across the Earth.
> 'The spirit of Wild Avalon lives on in our hearts and minds,' Roedan teaches us.
> 'Kill it and it's gone,' say I.
> I can't resuscitate the wide-eyed girl I left behind, but I see no reason to let the natural landscape in which she first found inspiration be eaten away by concrete 'progress', or allow my soul to be further eroded by cynicism and hate.
> Kill it and it's gone.

'I wrote those words on an evening like this last year, sitting almost exactly where you are now.'
Ben resisted the urge to jump up and face the stealthy new arrival, instead trying to hide the book beneath his crossed legs.
'I wondered where I'd dropped my diary,' Lea said in a self-deprecating tone.
'I was so sure I'd lost it here but never could find it.'
Ben pointed at a scrub of withered fern nearby. 'I found it over there,' he replied airily, '...just now.'
'Just now?' Lea remarked, crouching beside Ben to reclaim her book and examine the cover. 'Wow. Hasn't suffered has it? No weather damage or

anything. It's funny,' she went on, 'I always wondered if maybe someone had found it, taken it home and read it. I had this embarrassing idea of someone getting to know me so well through my writing that, if ever I met them, I wouldn't really be a stranger to them, and they might drop hints about secretly knowing me.'

Ben held Lea's gaze with an expression of sincerity for some time and made a show of contemplating the fantasy. 'That's a romantic idea, man,' he nodded. 'Make a good short story, one of those you could end with an unexpected twist.'

'Like?'

'Something surprising,' he suggested. 'You expect the couple to meet and get together, but then the character who found the diary chooses not to get involved.'

'Oh?' Lea narrowed her eyes.

Ben picked distractedly at the blackened bark of a tree beside him. 'Or perhaps the character doesn't want to give the owner of the diary a face,' he shrugged. 'He might worry that the flesh can't live up to the soul of the writing.'

Lea frowned. 'Is that what you—?'

'Course,' Ben continued before Lea could voice the doubt worked into her expression, 'it's not a situation I'd know about, so I'm probably not the best person to write a story like that. Yeah, man, you're right,' he added. 'This book's in amazing condition, considering. When did you leave it here?'

'February.'

Ben nodded at the book. 'Amazing.'

Lea studied Ben's profile as she stuffed the diary into her motorcycle helmet and pulled a decorated tobacco tin from a pocket. She spread her cycling leather on the charcoal-littered ground and sat beside Ben. She began rolling a joint. 'Want to do this with me? I wondered if I'd see you here today. I had to come. I saw the smoke yesterday, but I didn't realise it was Meeting Hill until I heard it on the news last night. What happened? Sun too hot for dry woods?'

'No.' Ben flicked the bark he had picked from the tree downhill through the withered undergrowth. 'Probably arson. The firemen found a half-melted petrol can on the slope where the fire was worst.'

Lea's face changed dramatically. 'I thought this was one of those summer fires that no one can be blamed for. I don't feel too bad when I hear about those. I think of them as Nature's way of having a clear out.' She spoke slowly to hide the tremor in her voice and fumbled an attempt to light the joint. 'But if someone did this on purpose—'

'I'm sure we'll find lots of people to blame,' Ben declared as he studied the horizon through the trees. 'We're a suspicious bunch.'

Lea looked up. 'We?'

'We,' Ben nodded as he turned to face her, but was suddenly wearied by the thought of labouring through a conversation in which he had to maintain the lies spun at their last meeting. 'The Carreg's End Monument Preservation Society,' he said, 'but the locals call us Earthwork. We're a village committee set up to look after Meeting Hill. As you can see, we're doing a great job.'

Ben rose in a fit of anger blended uncomfortably with embarrassment. He left the denuded trees and paced into the circle of soot-coated stones.

Lea watched him from the edge of the clearing. 'You're angry with yourself?'

'Yeah, man, you could say I'm angry with myself, about a lot of things.'

Lea wanted to hear about them, and she hoped they included regret about the actions of Ben and his friends in South Pennard, but the appearance of two vehicles in the clearing silenced Lea's questions. She and Ben turned together. Lea noticed the emblems displayed on the doors of the Land Rover and the Shogun as they passed between The Meeting's gateway stones, and then she pointed at the identical symbol pinned to Ben's shirt. 'Stonewatch, or whatever you call yourselves?'

Ben nodded and spied the Wyres in the back seat of the larger car. 'It looks like our sponsors have come to survey the damage.'

Lea said, 'I don't want to be here with them,' and she backed downhill into the trees.

'Hey,' Ben frowned, 'it's all right.'

'No,' she said firmly, 'it's not. I know nothing about you or these other people, or what you were all doing at Geophagia's meeting the other night.'

'Then let's talk.'

Lea nodded. 'OK. Where do you live?'

'What?'

'Where?'

'The extension on the house opposite the church, other end of the village.'

'One hour,' Lea gave him. She picked up her cycling leather and helmet and disappeared from view over the crest of the western slope.

Engines were silenced and car doors opened in the clearing. Ben saw Craig and Alan step onto the summit and lean casually against the bodywork of the Shogun. Brampton and Georgina Wyre also emerged to nod grimly at the blackened half of the hilltop. Ben left the trees and joined them, but his unexpected appearance from the shade provoked no particular surprise.

'How's Ian?' he called.

'Enjoying Sarah's attention,' George replied. 'Taking him to hospital was a mistake. The nurses are treating him like a wounded hero. He loves it. Good job he's only in for a couple of nights.'

'Terrible, terrible,' Brampton Wyre shook his immaculate head at the grass. 'This suggestion of arson seems mild. Perhaps it should be an investigation into attempted murder. The police will want statements from everyone near the hill yesterday, which includes all of you, and it would be helpful if you can remember everyone you saw nearby in the hours before the fire.'

George and the three younger men exchanged glances amongst themselves. Brampton stared meaningfully at Ben. 'You, Mr Marchen? Who have you seen up here recently?'

'No one memorable, before or since,' he replied too quickly.

'Oh? Then can you think of anyone who might hold a grudge?'

The reply seemed so obvious that Craig could only laugh. 'Yeah, Geophagia.'

Brampton nodded, and it seemed smug. 'Your trespass must have really pissed them off.'

'There's no *way* it was them,' Alan said. 'Geophagia worships places like this. Literally.'

Brampton seemed to have had been hoping for a statement like this. 'First you terrorise the Geophagia Foundation, and now you defend them?'

Alan glanced guiltily at George, and then back at her brother. 'I'm not a bigot, Mr Wyre. I'm allowed to change my mind when I have good reason to.'

Brampton looked at each of those present in turn as though seeking support. 'Then we'll end up dismissing this fire as the work of kids clumsy with matches, but it seems like a lazy conclusion. You need to sharpen up your act, lads. Perhaps the committee should spend a little less time swinging from rafters in the barn,' he suggested with a glance at Craig, which provoked mystified expressions from the others, 'and avoid gate-crashing local parties so you can be here watching the site. You might also use the time you spend posing around the estate on horseback keeping an eye out for people carrying petrol cans onto our hill. Mr Forrest, I'm ready to leave when you are.'

Alan waited until Brampton had stepped back into the Shogun and closed the door before pulling a sloppy salute. 'I won't admit it in front Brampton, but I think he's right.'

Ben asked, 'What now, George?'

George appeared hurt by her colleagues' doubts and surprised by Ben's question. 'We're all feeling a bit bruised by the last couple of days, but Earthwork's purpose hasn't changed. Meeting Hill will recover, the stones can be cleaned, and we need to remain focused on threats to the site. I believe that the Geophagia Foundation intends to hold a dance festival here on October 31st. I believe that the lectures, music and dancing you saw the other night are a cover for something. I've written up my reasons for thinking these things, and I'll have a copy to you all by tomorrow. If you're not convinced after that, then maybe Earthwork and The Meeting will get on better without you.'

Couples

Madog's words at their parting the day before spoilt Roedan's mood for her five-hour journey home. She drove north aggressively through Somerset, Bristol and South Wales, her anger exacerbated by heavy evening traffic.

At dusk Roedan had parked the Audi outside the front door of *Tan Y Bryn,* her home amongst the foothills of Moel Siabod, but she found no relief from her temper that evening. Several messages on her answering machine incensed her further: two of a hurtful nature from a close friend; one from her personal assistant in Somerset, who was struggling to secure a venue for Geophagia's August festival, and another from Tom Sutherland, who had yet to identify the activists known as Earthwork.

The next day made Roedan no happier. She drove into Betws-Y-Coed early that morning for groceries, and when she returned just before midday she discovered that nationalistic Welsh slogans had been sprayed across the walls and windows of two Pont Cyfyng properties, both of which were used as part-time residences for English owners. One of them was *Tan Y Bryn.*

After a visit from the police at two in the afternoon, Roedan sought to resolve the problems brought to her attention the previous evening, but her lack of success provoked in Roedan the kind of irrational, but commonly reached, conviction that she must lie at the centre of an intricate conspiracy. Like most people caught in even a short run of bad luck, Roedan could not remember the last time anything had turned out well for her.

The final mishap in this series occurred late that afternoon, around the same time that Lea Granger discovered Ben Marchen in possession of her diary on Meeting Hill. *Tan Y Bryn's* twice-weekly cleaner from Capel Curig arrived and set about her duties. But Mrs Edwards, a woman already acquainted with Roedan's fragile temperament, made the surprising and ill-timed mistake of taking on the added task of cleaning the two rooms of *Pen Annwn,* the folly built within the grounds of *Tan Y Bryn* that Roedan used exclusively as a ritual sanctuary.

Mrs Edwards returned to the house after twenty minutes work to inform her employer of these additional efforts before leaving, but was given no chance to depart with her usual cheery call of '*Nos da,* Miss Baynes!' before Roedan's mood erupted in a volcanic tantrum.

*

The humid evening air above Carreg's End held a faint memory of the previous day's fire, as though the dome of Meeting Hill itself continued to smoulder. A charcoal mist like dark gauze tainted the sky.

From the vantage of higher ground along Little Arlingham's northern border, the Reverend Matthew Norton studied the scene with satisfaction, though he

did not quite betray the good humour with which he had received news of the blaze. Viewed from the grounds of his chapel, the smoke-smudged hill was a wounded and humbled opponent upon which to gaze and gloat.
During his more passionate sermons, Norton liked to claim that the villagers who showed the greatest affection for The Meeting —especially those actively engaged in its preservation — were responsible for the town's slipping Christian standards. He believed that the visitation by fire upon Meeting Hill offered his opinion Divine sanction.
The minister leaned contentedly against the lichen-coated wall, faced the deepening sunlight and breathed the warm scent of the nearby yew.
The drone of a motorcycle approached from the south and shattered the moment. Reverend Norton turned to watch its passing with all the interest of someone with nothing else to do. A female rider appeared over the brow of the hill, leather-clad and with blonde hair streaming from beneath her blue helmet. She slowed as the road levelled between the church and houses, and Norton watched her eyeing each address in turn. Then the cyclist pulled into the parking space before the churchyard. Lea Granger removed her helmet, ran a hand through her hair and silenced the bike's engine.
'Lovely evening,' Norton nodded.
'Oh, well,' Lea considered the observation, taking in the cleric's view of the scarred Meeting Hill. 'Nearly.'
The elderly owner of a house neighbouring St. Michael's chapel played a classical recording loud enough to be heard by friends in his garden.
'Looking for something?' Norton asked helpfully.
'I am,' Lea replied distractedly, picking up the rhythm of the Strauss waltz and tapping in time to its pulse, 'but I think I've found it, thank you.'
Norton nodded and observed the girl's recognition of the tune. 'You're a dancer?' he asked after several fascinated seconds.
She turned back to him. 'Once, ages ago,' she admitted. 'My parents put me and my sister through a few lessons.'
'Ballroom?'
Lea nodded. Norton pushed himself away from the wall and smiled, impressed. 'Wonderful! I'll bet you made your parents proud.'
Lea's expression tightened. 'I'll never know.'
Norton steered a deft avoidance of this clearly sensitive issue. 'Ballroom is a rare talent for one so young these days.'
Lea shrugged and touched gingerly at her sun-reddened neck. 'Sometimes don't feel so young.'
Norton frowned. 'I hear that from too many twenty-somethings, but believe me, you've hardly lived.' Then he paused to consider a light-hearted impulse.
Lea saw the cleric's eyes brightened by a playful gleam. Norton paced a few steps to the Blue Danube Waltz from the nearby house and then offered the

young woman his hand. 'Would you do me the honour?'

Lea's own expression relaxed gradually from indifference to uncertain surprise, and then into the diffident smile of someone humbled by flattery. She swung herself off her bike, accepted Norton's hand and joined him at the gate.

The pair danced outside the churchyard for more than a minute as the sun sank behind the steeple of St Michael's. Norton and Lea danced long enough for a member of the neighbouring garden party to pick up a camera and capture the impromptu waltz before the music faded. A copy of this portrait would eventually become part of Norton's 'Community News' display on the notice board beside the churchyard gate.

Norton retained Lea's hand as he clicked his heels smartly and bowed a gallant finish, and then turned the contact into a firm handshake. 'Reverend Matthew Norton,' he introduced himself, 'pleased to meet such a natural dancer.'

'Lea Granger,' the natural dancer replied. 'Nice to meet you.'

'So what address are you looking for?'

'Ben Marchen's house,' she said, and did not miss the sudden change in Norton's expression. 'He told me it was the house opposite the church.'

The minister released her hand and took a step back. 'You're a friend of Ben Marchen?'

'It's looking that way. Are you not?'

'Ben is an impulsive fool, committed to nothing and no one for long,' Norton said, retreating for the gate of the churchyard. 'He's in denial of his inability to conform to the lifestyle he has chosen, and he simply refuses to accept his natural place in the world, away from Christian society where he cannot offend us.'

'What's he done?'

'Probably nothing you would find offensive,' he decided, and strode for the doors of his chapel.

Ben's Toyota appeared over the brow of the hill only a few minutes later, cutting short her considerations of Ben's possible offences against the cleric. She watched the pick-up slow as it drew level with the house, and then saw Ben flap a wave of self-conscious greeting as he pulled into the drive.

Feeling a contrasting blend of concern and indignation in the wake Norton's warning, Lea glanced back at the chapel and saw the vicar nodding sagely at her from beyond the closing door of his chapel. She returned an apologetic shrug and strode across the road where she returned Ben's enthusiastic embrace.

*

Tom Sutherland stopped abruptly in the driveway of *Tan Y Bryn* when the door flew open and a woman he recognised as Roedan's cleaner rushed out in tears. 'Mrs Edwards?'

But she did not reply, or even acknowledge his presence. Tom watched her hurry away downhill towards the houses of Pont Cyfyng before he ventured inside through the open front door. There he stood motionless, listening intently in the hallway.

The house was silent, but the American knew that Roedan was home. He was her closest associate and most frequent visitor, and he had encountered circumstances like this in the past. Tom explored the deserted ground floor, gently calling Roedan's name as he paced from room to room. Then he proceeded upstairs.

Tom discovered Roedan lying in a state of immodesty on the first landing. Shards of pottery were scattered across the floor beneath an impact mark on the wall above the staircase, and Roedan had cut herself on their edges as she lay motionless across the fragments, her eyes open.

'Roedan?'

The shoulder fastening of her familiar pale gown had been loosened by the violence of her fury and fallen into blood-spotted disarray. Tom waved a hand across Roedan's unblinking stare to no effect. He breathed deeply in weary recognition of her condition and sat cross-legged on the floor beside her. He lifted her head gently into his lap, smoothed patiently at Roedan's hair and sighed disapprovingly at the devastated ornamentation around him.

*

Ben's eyes ached for sleep, but Lea's naked form lay outlined against the window's view of fading twilight, and he refused to let mere eyelids interrupt his appreciation of her profile. Lea's silhouette began to blend with the darkness as night made itself at home in the room. Then, just as the dusk became incapable of casting even the longest shadow, the radiance of the red light atop the nearby communications tower replaced it. The white walls of Ben's bedroom lost their corners and vertices to the encompassing warmth of the beacon, becoming an effulgent womb for the recovering couple. The room's furnishings surrendered their colours to the dominant crimson hue, and Lea's body became a world of delicate curves that reflected the vermilion glow.

Lea whispered something insensible in her sleep. Ben responded by licking the perspiration from across her top lip. She opened her eyes. Ben saw her frown momentarily, disoriented – and then a smile in the darkness as recent memory was restored. She rolled over and toyed distractedly with Ben's exposure. She kissed his eyes and bit playfully at his nose.

'It seems you have an enemy in Arlingham,' she said suddenly.

'Only one?' Ben replied, relaxing into his pillow. 'I'm getting popular.'

'It's not just the vicar who doesn't like you?'

Ben's teeth were pink in the light of the beacon as he smiled. 'Little Arlingham is a haven for prudish people and judgemental Christians. They don't want to know you if you're not at church three times a day. The vicar's taken a particular dislike to me, except he claims to be trying to help me.'

'How?'

'Don't know, but nothing he says seems very helpful. Whenever I see him he raises the issue of my parents. I don't get on with my Dad, and I don't know where my Mum is. I haven't seen her since she left Dad – or since he kicked her out, or whatever happened.'

'Your Mum hasn't tried to contact you?'

'She probably doesn't know I'm back.'

'From…?'

'Everywhere,' he went on. 'I was restless for a long time. Norton says I still am, or that I should be, or something.'

'And why would he want that?'

'To see me give up my self-imposed rehabilitation and leave the village,' Ben muttered. 'It's not just him: he seems to be speaking on behalf of lots of people who feel strongly about it, though he won't name names. Anyway…' He dropped the subject and leaned forward to kiss Lea.

'No,' she stopped him, 'enough distraction.'

'Distraction?'

'You're avoiding the things I came here to talk about. I found myself in bed with you barely ten minutes after arriving, and now you're changing the subject. What were you and your friends doing at South Pennard the other night?'

Ben brushed aside the sheet and reached to the floor for his jeans. 'You *found* yourself in bed?' he repeated, pulling on the trousers. 'Cheers.'

Lea blinked in silent apology and lay forward with her chin on her hands. 'Interrogating you was my excuse to end up in bed. But we've not had the interrogation yet.'

Ben nodded. He realised he hadn't eaten since breakfast; he'd spent hours on or around Meeting Hill; the day had drawn to a close with emotional and physical demands his body was not fuelled for, and fatigue was now having the same effect on his weary consciousness as alcohol. 'Do you ever have those moments when you want to tell someone everything – I mean *everything:* all the things that matter, all the things that don't; and no matter what you end up saying, nothing seems like enough to satisfy the need to open up?'

Lea nodded. 'Yes. And I'm not so honourable that I won't take advantage of yours.'

'OK then. Earthwork suspects Geophagia of something that even our boss hasn't told us, but we were at South Pennard hoping to get some idea of when —and especially *where* – your group will be holding other festivals. We want to know what the chances are that two thousand people will turn up to make a mess of Meeting Hill.'

Lea nodded thoughtfully. 'I can appreciate that. But Geophagia has never left a mess at any of its venues – not a single fag butt – and if you'd done your homework, you wouldn't have needed to ruin our festival to find that out.'

'I think we did know, really,' Ben admitted. 'But like I said, Georgina Wyre doesn't think it's that simple. I just can't tell you why.'

Lea rose to face Ben in the same cross-legged pose. Ben immediately became distracted. 'You've been truthful, so I'll do the same.'

Ben looked up quickly.

'Geophagia will be holding other meetings, just like the one at South Pennard, on each of the solar and cross-quarter festivals, using prehistoric sites on a straight line—'

'A ley line.'

She nodded, 'Along a ley south-east from Glastonbury as venues. The line terminates on Meeting Hill, just like this year's Geophagia tour. Roedan will apply to hold a dance festival just outside Little Arlingham at Samhain.'

'Sow— when?'

'October 31st. Celtic New Year.'

'Ah.'

'Will you be telling Earthwork about this?'

'Oh yes. It'll save us the trouble of hatching another farcical plot to spy on the Geophagia Foundation.'

Lea smiled in appreciation of their honesty and wondered how far she could push it. 'This truth thing seems to work for us. Now, what will the committee want to do about it?'

'Stop you,' Ben replied. 'We're dead possessive. Can't you see why we'd be worried about an invasion of your people?'

'No,' Lea was blunt. 'I know my people, and I shall be sticking by our right to free religious expression.'

'I think I'm in love with you, Lea Granger.'

'That's a little more than I want to hear from you, Ben Marchen, but I'm certainly enjoying your bedside manner. Come here.'

*

'Ah, Tom. Good. You always understood me.'

The American looked down and saw life returning to the woman's features. 'Understand you?' he laughed. 'I've seen these episodes before.'

'And what are you doing here?'

'I was invited – something you wanted to show me? I think it's a good thing I came. Your temper scared the housekeeper again.'

Roedan patted one of his hands as she sat up.

Tom rose to lean against the banister. 'Still mad about those people spoiling

Midsummer?'

'No,' Roedan shook her head, rearranging her robe in no particular hurry. 'Whoever they are, we can track them down and find out what they were up to. No,' she went on, rising carefully to her feet with only a little help, 'it's something else. Someone I know, someone I trusted, has refused my request for help. I've been ruminating on it since yesterday, and combined with a few other recent mishaps I allowed his arrogance to push me into a tantrum.'

Tom nodded silently. Roedan gazed at him expectantly. 'You're not going to ask me who I've seen?' she asked.

'You'll tell me if you want to.'

'I need a drink. Do you want one?'

'Sure.'

'That's no answer. Typical American. Come on.'

Roedan descended the stairs thoughtfully, as though trying out her feet for the first time. She retrieved a set of keys on the way through the kitchen, led Tom out through the back door and onto the sloping lawn.

On top of the rise at the end of the garden, Roedan's octagonal tower, *Pen Annwn*, originally built by an English gentlemen with consumption in the Eighteenth Century as a lofty refuge in which to take the restorative mountain air, cast a priapic shadow across the garden. Roedan unlocked its door in the eastern wall, flicked on a series of lamps lining the spiral staircase and led Tom upstairs. They passed the only first-story space, climbed through a trapdoor and into the windowed attic room.

Mrs Edwards had mopped the floorboards clean of Roedan's ritual maze and placed everything she found on the floor back in the ornate wooden chest. Tom watched while Roedan redrew the outline of a labyrinth on the floor with a piece of chalk. Then she hopped lightly over the spiral path, reached into the wooden chest and produced a bottle of vodka. There was one glass placed over the neck of the bottle, and as a second drinking vessel Roedan used her ceremonial wooden chalice.

'I invited you here to show you this,' she said, pouring two generous measures of spirit and handing her friend the chalice. 'I've been experiencing some trouble.'

'What are you working on?'

'A meditation.'

This much Tom had realised. 'I know you're usually working on something visionary. What is it this week?'

Roedan was startled by the question. 'This *week?*' she grinned. 'Tom, you were consoling me over my trouble with this spell back in February!'

Tom gaped at her. 'What are you working on? Your pathworkings usually last days, not months.'

'This one requires a little more commitment,' she replied, stepping carefully around the path of chalk. 'It's a search for something valuable lost a very long time ago, but I don't think it wants to be found. I made steady progress at first, but then all I got was interference that only started to make sense the other night. I made the mistake of trying the easy option: I visited my old mentor to see what he might be able to give away, but he just laughed in my face.' Roedan drained her glass with one swallow. 'The old fucker knows something,' she murmured, rubbing her chin slowly with the rim of the glass, 'but he's making me work for it.'

Tom sipped cautiously at his own drink. 'What meditation are you using? Something hypnotic, or just a pathworking?'

'*Just* a pathworking?' Roedan reacted as she returned to the bottle on the table. 'The system of pathworking I've devised allows every member of Geophagia to experience a little magic for themselves. It remains the most effective, and by far the easiest form of divination available to the Neo-pagan. There's nothing *just* about it'

'And what about this interference?'

Roedan seemed humbled by the reminder. 'The image of a shape – a cross – keeps blocking my path, and until the Midsummer festival there was no way I could have known what it represented.'

'What did you find?'

'Blood and sand, Tom! You were *there!* At least one member of that group, Earthwork, wore a Celtic cross. A symbol just like theirs appears during my meditations and it's wearing me down.'

Tom finished his vodka and agreed to more. 'Is the search so important you can't take time out to clear your head?'

'Yes,' Roedan replied directly.

Tom shrugged. 'A break is the only thing I can think of that might help. I'm not sure what else to advise.'

Roedan carried a large candle and a box of matches out of the chest. She placed the candle at the centre of the chalk labyrinth and struck a match. 'What if you were to take up where I left off? I need a fresh perspective. You might not encounter the same obstructions, and you may notice something I've missed. I've been chasing this relic for so long now, I'm impatient, trying too hard, wanting it too much.' Roedan gazed steadily at Tom as she spoke. His face expressed uncertainty. 'Think how satisfying it would be if we made it a team effort.'

Tom nodded, but only because he was sure he could not refuse. He set his drink down on the floor. 'What are we looking for?'

'A link,' Roedan introduced it passionately. 'A tangible conduit to the time and place I've described to you all as a memory, or an ideal.'

'Avalon?' Tom frowned.

'Britain before the historical invasions,' Roedan hissed a little in her excitement. 'I believe in an artefact possessed by the principles and ideals of Avalon. It was in contact with the figurehead of late Celtic mythology.'

Tom frowned even harder. 'The Pendragon?'

'Arthur!' Roedan clenched a fist as though to lend the name physical force. 'A relic of Arthur!'

'The burial cross...'

'The cruciform plate over his grave. It was always an important symbol for Geophagia. We've had it emblazoned across our festival flags since the start – but I believe it possesses something greater than symbolic value.'

'And it still exists?' Tom asked carefully.

Roedan also set her empty glass on the floor. 'I have no proof, but I have intense faith, based on the limited history of the cross. I don't believe anyone could just misplace such an artefact. It exists,' she nodded confidently. 'I have several places noted as best contenders for its location, and we can gain access to them with the festivals. We just need the patience to discover a clue that indicates one of them, and then we can take the search a stage further.'

'Permission for excavation could prove difficult,' Tom pointed out. 'These are fragile places.'

Tom looked at her intently, and then a little fearfully, as Roedan made no reply.

EW.Doc#54

Lea woke and rose long before Ben began to stir. She left him to his jumbled dreams in the disarray of the bedclothes and used a search for the bathroom as an excuse to explore his home. She found the bathroom behind the very first door she tried, but quietly closed it again and moved on to make the most of her freedom. She found an airing cupboard and a tiny kitchen, and then she stumbled into a room that might otherwise have been used as a lounge.

But this room – or studio, for want of a more accurate description of the cluttered space – contained the tools, materials and sketches of a man who seemed not only fascinated by symbols and their design, but who must be making a living out of them. On a frame near the window, an angled easel bore an unfinished commission for Blackmoor House Activity Centre: a logo comprising the outlines of rock-climbers, abseilers and canoeists, circling a compass face. Other completed designs decorated the walls of the room in matching frames.

Lea nodded with unqualified approval as she left the room and paced lightly to the front door in response to the postman's visit. Two letters lay on the mat, and Lea thought nothing of examining both envelopes. She entered the kitchenette, sat down at the table and helped herself to an apple from a bag on the fridge.

The first of the letters was clearly a bill of some sort, and Lea tossed it away. The second was a brown A4 envelope bearing the familiar Earthwork cross above the initials C.E.M.P.S. The envelope was addressed to Ben, of course, but Lea had neither the willpower nor the inclination to leave this correspondence unopened. Neither did she care to conceal her invasion of Ben's privacy – she simply tore the envelope open and pulled its contents out onto the table.

EW.Doc#54 23/06
Author: **G.Wyre**
To: **Field Operations**
Re: **Confidential**

In his book *Liber de Principis Instructione* (1193), Gerald of Wales stated that an excavation of a cemetery within the grounds of Glastonbury Abbey was carried out by Abbot Henry of Sully and his monks in 1191, investigating rumour of the legendary King Arthur's tomb. The rumour is said to have been passed to the Abbey's monks by King Henry II before his death in 1189, who 'himself heard from an ancient Welsh bard, a singer of the past, that they would find [Arthur's] body at least sixteen feet beneath the earth'. Gerald reports that the rumour was confirmed by the monks. A grave was discovered, and the 'giant' bones of Arthur's body were identified by a foot-long lead cross laid above them bearing the inscription:

HIC IACET SEPVLTVS IHCLITVS REX ARTVRIVS IH IHSVLA AVALOHIA.
Here lies buried the renowned King Arthur in the Isle of Avalon.

We'll never know if the cross truly marked the grave of 'the renowned King Arthur', but the discovery is generally thought to have been a hoax. Glastonbury Abbey suffered a huge fire in 1184 and needed revenue from pilgrims. A political motive for such a hoax is also noted below.
The only thing we can be certain of is that a cross like the one Gerald described did exist. A replica of it survived long enough to be drawn for William Camden's book, *Britannia,* in 1586, but the cross was lost a couple of centuries later. The body of 'Arthur' was interred in the abbey until 1539 but did not survive the Dissolution.
Much of this information is common knowledge. Local history books are full of it, and the abbey in Glastonbury displays information concerning the legend. But the details of the story that interest us are more obscure. Only Somerset locals and people familiar with the county's oral folklore tradition might have heard our fireside stories and playground skipping rhymes, which answer a few more questions.
Henry of Sully commissioned a replica of the lead cross immediately upon its discovery: he wanted a souvenir for display in the Abbey after the agents of King Richard I came to claim the original. The King was more interested in crusading, of course, but he planned to have the Arthurian relic displayed publicly while he was away, intending it to be a weapon of demoralisation against the restless Welsh. The Celts still sang of their hero, Arthur, who they believed would return in their hour of need. The English knew that proof of Arthur's death would be a crushing blow to spirited Welsh armies.
A replica of the cross was made, but a young monk named Carreg, apparently a Welsh nationalist on the quiet, is said to have stolen the original before it could be delivered to the King. The monk fled directly south-east from Glastonbury (along what Geophagia calls a *ley*). No one is quite sure where Carreg thought he was going, but the story says that riders were sent after him, and after terrorising homesteads in their search along

the way they found Carreg asleep on Meeting Hill.

The pursuers did not find the stolen cross. The riders presumed that Carreg had buried the relic somewhere between Glastonbury Abbey and Meeting Hill, perhaps at one of the prehistoric sites that mark the ley, or perhaps even on Meeting Hill itself.

Most committee members have grown up in the outlying part of Little Arlingham known as Carreg's End, but how many of us have wondered at the origin of its name? Most people assume that Carreg was someone who owned the land beneath Meeting Hill, on which the village is built. Now, though, the title 'Carreg's End' takes on new macabre meaning.

My fear for The Meeting in this matter began when I first saw an issue of Geophagia's *Maze* magazine. The group holds a deep interest in Arthurian legend, and an image of the cross found with Arthur's grave is printed on the cover of *Maze*. We also saw it on the banners hung around Geophagia's Southwood festival arena.

I'm sure you can see where my reasoning leads, and I'm sure you'll agree that, if there is any chance that Roedan is staging festivals on the landmarks of Carreg's route to search for this Arthurian artefact, we have clear cause to worry about our monument.

But such concern does not mean that our preparation and response need be anything other than considered and proportionate. Given the outcome of our first encounter with Roedan's group, I believe we owe Geophagia every chance to prove themselves above our suspicion.

Lea returned the Earthwork document to its envelope in no particular hurry when sounds from next door announced Ben's rising. She tossed both items of the morning's post back onto the mat at the front door and returned to the bedroom with a bowl of breakfast cereal.

'Breakfast in bed?' Ben smiled wearily as he emerged from the bathroom, scratching feverishly at the back of his head. 'Thank you.'

'Good idea,' Lea managed between mouthfuls. 'This is mine. Plans today?'

Ben sat on the edge of the bed. 'Work, I suppose. I'm falling behind on a commission for Ian. And you?'

'Likewise.'

'You?' Ben pointed in surprise. 'The lead singer of Geophagia's very own Kundalini has a day job!'

'You think I don't work?'

'Well, yes. I mean no— I mean, I'm not sure what—.'

'Perhaps you think I live in an overcrowded caravan on a travellers' site?'

'I didn't think that, but it's not as if you don't look—'
'Like my life is one long mud-bath of a rock festival? I work, Ben. I work—'
'Behind a bar?'
Lea looked away. 'Yeah.'
'Had to be. It's the only other thing you look like you fit. Are you ashamed of it?'
'No,' Lea stared into the milk remaining at the bottom of the breakfast bowl. 'I'm not ashamed of it, I enjoy bar work. I just hate it that you pigeon-holed me.'
Ben was unrepentant. 'I wasn't judging you by your appearance, I just can't see you committing to anything except Geophagia and your music. You'd be insulted if I called you a career woman.'
Lea had no chance to reply. An assertive rapping at the front door interrupted their exchange.
It was Craig. Sweating and panting (though determined to control his breathing in accordance with the belief that an individual under stress should betray neither fear nor pain), Craig turned to look at the motorbike parked opposite the house as Ben picked up his mail and opened the door.
'Hi.'
'You have a visitor?' Craig asked, nodding at the bike as evidence.
'I have,' Ben nodded, studying his colleague's face for signs of judgement. 'What do you want?'
'Sorry,' Craig made a show of remembering himself, 'I was jogging past and I thought it'd be rude if I didn't stop to ask if you want to run with me?'
'Sometime. Not today.'
'Who's your visitor?'
'Is that why you called? Because you saw the bike?'
'Someone stayed the night,' Craig pressed him. 'That girl! It's the singer from the festival.'
'There, you got what you came for. Happy?'
Craig offered Ben a familiar scowl. 'Everyone knew you were keen. We could all see it – but just remember who she is. Remember who she works for and watch what you say.'
Ben did not answer. He stood at his front door in a pair of boxer-shorts and a faded Oasis T-shirt looking guilty and vulnerable as his swaggering colleague backed away and left the garden at a jog.
Lea had dressed by the time Ben returned. 'What was with the homo-erotic tension there? That guy was checking out your legs.'
'No he wasn't. That's a cheap shot.'
'I suppose he's a member of— what do you call yourselves? *Birthmark?*'
'Earthwork.'
'I heard everything,' Lea admitted. 'I don't think he likes you much.'

'This is not news to me.'

'I can see why you'd be concerned, but I still say you and your friends are wrong about Geophagia.'

'So change my mind.'

Lea rose and crossed the room to Ben. 'The Geophagia Foundation,' she began carefully, 'is an organisation in which members – *students,* really – are free to specialise and study their own interests, whether it's the teachings of the Eastern philosophies, the effects of subtle energies on consciousness, the history of tree worship, or the many religions whose faith centres on the Earth herself. And all the time, Roedan is there to unite us all in—'

'In an incense-burning, crystal-sucking, tree-hugging free-for-all?'

'—*In a fellowship* of alternative studies that I would love to introduce you to.'

'Mmh,' Ben melted as Lea slipped her arms around his waist. 'All right,' he made a show of submission. 'But only because it's you.'

'Deal,' she said, 'and I'll hold you to it – even if you've agreed only to annoy that man at the door.'

'I'm not so shallow,' he laughed. 'I'm just being attentive and broad-minded, not irrational and moody.'

'We'll see.'

'You don't trust me?'

'I expect a cynical response to every idea I challenge you with.'

'I'll be good.'

'My ideas will offend every incredulous and hard-boiled bone in your body.'

'I'm in love with every bone in yours.'

'That's a little more than I want to hear from you, Ben Marchen.'

'So we're both going to say challenging things to each other. Who do you think will crack first?'

'I'm not easily scared. Kiss me here?'

The Art of Ceres

Craig Pearce was recognised as the physically fittest member of the Earthwork team. After leaving Ben's flat he ran the outskirts of Little Arlingham and Carreg's End, covering the mileage at a comfortable pace in the easy rhythm of someone used to far greater distances. His progress was occasionally accelerated by bursts of flat-out sprint and frequently interrupted by the performance of press-ups on the tarmac or chin-ups from the branch of a tree.
He jogged along a lane peripheral to the village through orchards and meadows full of sheep that bleated wearily against the heat, and past estate fields whose flagging crops craved rain. He ran until the lane rejoined Arlingham Road just south of Meeting Hill, and there he turned north for the village.
Half a mile from the eagle-crowned gateway to Arlingham House, Craig became aware of an engine behind him. The bonnet of a car appeared to his right and kept pace with Craig's easy rhythm. One of its passengers lowered a window and pointed enthusiastically.
'Wow! You must be the hero everyone's talking about,' Ian Longe cried with exaggerated reverence. 'You're the one who carries asthmatics and concussed sunbathers out of raging infernos without a singe! Look, Sarah, it's the man they say can dance in flames and swim through smoke!'
Sarah waved from behind the wheel of her Nova. Craig nodded without changing pace. 'If this is your way of thanking me for fearlessly saving your life, you sarcastic prick, then don't mention it. Did the nice doctors and nurses get sick of you?'
'They did seem keen to send me home.'.
'Are you stopping at the barn?'
'Is there much going on?' Sarah called.
'George sent us the news she promised,' Craig replied, 'and the Wyres have brought someone in to set up surveillance cameras while they're away.'
Ian raised one curious eyebrow. 'Worth a look,' he decided, and then extended an arm through the window to point theatrically along the lane. 'To the ranch!'

Few committee governors realised how much time and effort the Field Operations volunteers sacrificed to Earthwork duty. It was clear to only three or four observant individuals that if Alan Forrest, Craig Pearce, Ian Longe and Ben Marchen had not shown such commitment to the cause, the Midsummer fire might not have been the first catastrophe to have befallen The Meeting. The Monument Preservation Society had been extremely effective in its role; the fire was obviously an embarrassment for Earthwork, but its governors never considered apportioning blame amongst Field Operations, as Brampton Wyre seemed determined to do. The men could not be expected to spend their time endlessly combing the forested Meeting Hill for would-be arsonists or vandals, so a surveillance system that saw Meeting Hill monitored by at least one person during the hours of daylight was mooted.

Except for Alan, who was paid a salary for his role as Team Leader, no periods of uniformed patrol were set for Earthwork members. The governors had always been satisfied with the team's agreement to consider itself 'on call' during free time, rather like a Lifeboat crew. But, in reality, Earthwork's commitment extended far beyond this simple contract. The team members had discovered that their time would be claimed by some form of committee duty if given more than an hour to themselves. Even their paid employment was occasionally disrupted by panicky calls from Carl Harper, the village watchman.

In consequence, at least one item of uniform was usually included in the daily attire of each volunteer. The Earthwork members had lived in their winter issue of grey fleece pullovers and sleeveless jackets through the colder months, and in summer they wore their grey polo shirts which, like every item of Earthwork uniform, had the committee's stylised Celtic cross symbol embroidered in red at the left breast.

So when Craig encountered an angry crowd at the gateway to the Wyre estate that morning, he considered himself appropriately dressed to react in an official capacity. Each member of the gathering was around the same age as Craig and just as energetic, and their mood was such that, had the crowd been twice its size, Craig might have considered the situation to be a predicament. But with the demonstration (as it would soon prove to be) numbering only seven men and four women, Craig arrogantly decided that he could probably handle them all if things turned ugly. He felt for the folding knife in his back pocket for reassurance.

Craig slowed from a run to a strut, and then a swagger, to approach the group with the composure, dignity and hint of threat that only a measured step may convey. He recognised most members of the group as either villagers, or else people who lived so close to Little Arlingham that they considered them as such. In return, Craig was instantly recognised by most people in the crowd as a member of a certain village society. 'Craig?' called the most confident of the group, a woman two years older than Craig himself. 'Craig Pearce?'

'Sorry, no autographs,' he forced a friendly Ambassador of Earthwork face for the group, pre-emptively seeking to justify the claim that *They Started It* in case a dispute broke out. 'Can I help?'

'You're a member of Earthwork?' the girl asked.

'I am,' Craig smiled, all gritted teeth. 'And you are...?'

'Pissed off,' she glared at him. Her friends shuffled closer.

Craig noticed that three members of the gathering wore T-shirts sporting the labyrinth symbol of the Geophagia Foundation. 'Oh.' He took a deep breath, as though inflated lungs might elevate him clear of this uncertain ground. 'I don't suppose you're all here to volunteer your services or make a donation?'

'We're here to see someone in authority. We want whoever's in charge to apologise for threatening Geophagia members with dangerous driving at our recent festival.'

'Certainly,' Craig maintained his buoyancy. 'The Earthwork governors are holding a public meeting this evening in the village hall, though the Wyres can't attend. I think they're in London on business. You're all local so you can raise the issue there.'

'*Now,*' the woman demanded. 'I can't make tonight.'

'Then if you'll excuse me,' Craig asked, motioning to pass between them, 'I'll call someone who gets paid to deal with complaints.'

To Craig's surprise the group parted, allowing him to pass through the archway beneath the eternal gaze of its heraldic eagles and along the avenue.

The courtyard behind Arlingham House was free of its usual agricultural traffic, but three vehicles were parked there. Recently vacated, Sarah's car had been parked before the open doors of the barn, and beside it was a white van that advertised itself as the property of 'Wincanton Sentinel Security'. The third vehicle, the ageing committee Land Rover, was parked near the adjacent workshop with its bonnet raised. It seemed that the Land Rover was growing a pair of short legs with booted feet from beneath the front axle. As well as issuing tapping and wrenching sounds from the bowels of its engine, it also cursed quietly to itself. 'G'in dere y'*bastard!* Wha—? You bitch!'

From within the shadows of the barn came a burst of stifled sniggering, and then a sound new to the courtyard. Abel Mild wriggled out from beneath the engine of the Earthwork car and squinted suspiciously at the whirring of a tiny motor. After spending several seconds trying to pinpoint the source of the noise, Abel's gaze came to rest on an unfamiliar fixture above the barn door. A tall radio antenna had been attached to the roof of the barn a few days before, which Abel had grown used to, but he considered this addition of a camera an affront to the architectural character of the house and its surrounding buildings.

He rose and stepped forward for a closer look. The camera's nose dipped and span to follow and focus on him. The mechanic stopped in surprise. He edged left like someone experiencing their first encounter with a mirror, and the camera swivelled on its bracket with a low hum. Abel shuffled right, a little faster, and cursed when the camera responded likewise.

More sniggering from inside the barn. The old man flung a spanner at the camera with clumsy aim and scuttled angrily away into his workshop.

Perhaps a rural community so concerned with preserving its implausibly quaint pastoral aesthetic and time-warp charm should have respected Abel Mild as a local treasure, rather than treating him as a figure of fun. But any ridicule of him as a toothless bumpkin was born not of the broadness of his accent, his mistrust of technology newer than the internal combustion engine, nor of his unfashionable devotion to his work. Abel was disliked because he offered Brampton Wyre the kind of obeisance serfs would have been required to show their feudal lord. So, as soon as Mild had been dubbed 'Gollum to Brampton's Sauron' (probably by Ian), Abel's insecurity and poor social skills became fair game for his detractors, and especially for younger people unimpressed by provincial manners and faithful deliverers of a hard day's work.

The youngest Earthwork members were among Abel's critics. Vying with each other for the best view of George's computer monitor behind the system's installer, Alan, Sarah and Ian watched Abel trying to escape the attention of the electronic eye.

'He'll get over it,' Alan said.

Ian straightened up. 'He might not. Abel's worked here nearly all his life. He must feel overwhelmed by these changes.'

Sarah and Alan looked at Ian in surprise. 'You feel sorry for one of Brampton's spies?'

Ian folded his arms. 'He's an old man, and he keeps our cars up to scratch.' He turned back to the computer monitor. 'How do we control these cameras?'

The man from Wincanton Security indicated several buttons across the keyboard and the mouse. He demonstrated how to flick between views from each of the five cameras, how to display all five at once in smaller windows, and then the method of remotely moving each camera.

'Where are they all positioned?'

The technician responded by indicating the view on the monitor and cycling through the available images. As the group had seen, camera one was positioned over the courtyard; camera two was aimed north across the paddock, while number three gazed down from a tree just inside the estate's western entrance, watching over the archway and gate-house. The fourth camera commanded an elevated view across the western fields towards Meeting Hill, and camera five was stationed as close as possible to the road and hill itself – though not so close as to invite complaints concerning the electronic surveillance of land beyond estate boundaries.

Sarah asked, 'Do you think Mr Harper knows he's been replaced?'

Ian shrugged. 'Do you think he'll been sober long enough to understand?'

Across the courtyard, Craig emerged at a run from the avenue's green canopy of poplar trees. He weaved his way between the parked vehicles, entered the shade of the barn and allowed his eyes very little time to adjust to the gloom before reporting his news. 'We might have trouble outside.'

Alan scratched anxiously at his goatee wearing an expression of panic. 'Christ, who have you stabbed?'

Craig ignored him. 'We should have realised that a few Geophagia members would turn out to be local. We were recognised at the festival the other night and now there's an angry mob waiting at the gate.'

Sarah typed at the keyboard and opened the view from camera three. Ian and Alan stared at the screen with a frown. 'There's no one there.'

Craig cuffed sweat from his temples. 'Good. Not so desperate to complain, were they?' He backed out through the barn doors to turn on an outside tap and throw water over his head and neck. 'Less hassle for us.'

In their recharging rack on the wall, the team's radios burst to life with the unusually sober tones of Carl Harper. No one present failed to guess that his communication would have something to do with the people Craig had mentioned. Alan looked for his mobile phone. 'How many out there, Craig?'

'Eleven, max.'

'I'll call Ben.'

'That's a comfort.'

Ian pulled a radio from the rack with characteristic stoicism. 'Earthwork receiving.'

Sarah picked up Ian's committee badge from the table and pinned it to her T-shirt. 'Need a hand?'

In the oily darkness of his workshop, Abel Mild pressed one wide eye to the gap between the door and its hinges. He muttered inaudibly when he saw the security contractor leave the barn, but hissed in excited response to the hasty departure of Earthwork.

Choosing to make their journey together in one vehicle, the Shogun left the barn at reckless speed. As the roar of the Shogun's engine faded along the avenue, Abel emerged from his workshop and considered the inviting vacancy of the barn.

Despite his notoriety as a man in thrall to Brampton Wyre, Abel had only ever entered the barn in the company of a committee member. But his ridicule beneath the glare of the new camera had granted his curiosity dominance over respect for Earthwork's privacy. Abel scuttled like a nervous but determined scavenger across the cobblestones until he reached the barn. Inside, the mechanic viewed the gloomy interior with hungry interest. As a man of little education beyond his engineering expertise, Abel saw the many piles of books and research materials as so much esoteric bafflement, so he satisfied his curiosity elsewhere.

The computer was an oracle of equal mystery, but as the brightest source of light in the barn it was an attractive target for attention. The monitor still displayed the view from camera three. Abel sank slowly into the chair before the screen, his face wearing an endearing expression of awe that was picked out the barn's darkness like an anthropomorphic moon.

Several random stabs at the keyboard – too hard, in the way of people unused to computers – eventually triggered a change of display, and Abel bounced happily in the chair as he discovered an all but miraculous ability to summon views from around the estate at will: from the eagle arch to the courtyard, and from Meeting Hill to the western levels where, the mechanic noticed, there seemed to be something in the fields. Abel leaned closer to the screen and studied the view of several large impressions in the barley: a series of marks connected by lines to form a clear pattern that no wind could ever contrive, but which remained indistinct from the camera's low perspective.

Abel began an excited monologue of garbled panic, and its momentum stirred him into hasty retreat. The old man hurried out of the barn towards Arlingham House.

Earthwork arrived on the summit of Meeting Hill a few minutes later, the last time that this line-up of the Field Operations team would ever do so together.

Ben had responded immediately to Alan's summons, agreeing to be picked up from the village for a well-rehearsed call-out to the ring of coveted stones. There, as Harper had observed, eleven young people were 'arousing suspicion'.

'Why?' Ben asked.

'They want us to apologise for invading their disco the other night,' Craig replied, 'but we didn't respond quickly enough. This must be their way of grabbing our attention.'

Ben laughed. 'Predictable, aren't we?'

'Harper noticed them. He must have heard about the new cameras and needs to prove himself,' Ian suggested. The Shogun emerged from the trees and onto the summit at an intimidating speed.

Alan glanced into his rear-view mirror from the driver's seat and noted the countenance of his passengers. Sarah studied the people amongst the stones before them. She did not appear worried about the imminent confrontation, but neither did she seem as relaxed as the others.

Craig, sitting beside Alan, glared at the crowd from beneath a heavy frown, unconsciously chewing the inside of his left cheek.

Ben seemed happy and unable to hide it; sitting in the back between Sarah and Ian, he appeared content as he was rocked in his seat at the whim of the bumpy terrain.

Ian, meanwhile, appeared even more relaxed. Unconcerned almost to the point of boredom, he glanced at his watch and chewed a fingernail.

Alan sniggered quietly, but loud enough for his passengers to notice. The others turned toward him, but Ian prevented them from voicing their curiosity. 'Nobody ask what he's laughing at. That's what he wants. He made the kind of not-too-quiet laugh that says, *Hey everyone! I really want to make a witty observation, but you have to ask me because it won't be cool if I just say it.*'

'Come on,' Alan begged. 'Someone please humour me.'
Craig took an interest, but he was not humouring Alan. He just wanted to know what the team leader was laughing about. 'What?'
Ian shook his head in defeat.
'Have you noticed,' Alan began, 'that we don't care about confrontation anymore? The scraps we got into when we were younger were all adrenaline, shaky legs, hyperventilation and crap insults – but look at us now. We're seconds away from facing a mob and you're all yawning.'
'My first fights weren't terrifying,' Ian said, 'they were with you. And I still owe you a slap for the years you spent kicking Ben and me around. I might just take the side of these people.'
Alan slowed the car as it neared the group. 'Perhaps some tactful diplomacy will be enough. Craig, Ian, Ben: stay visible, but hang back while Sarah and I handle the public relations.'
Acting independently of Geophagia itself, these members of Roedan's foundation had gathered peacefully to protest against the Earthwork Committee's intrusion at their recent festival. As members of a Pagan organisation, they explained to Alan and Sarah, they intended no harm to site, but they had realised that appearing rowdy on Meeting Hill was the best way of initiating contact with the committee. As promised, their demonstration and opening dialogue with Earthwork was peaceful, but it was not to remain so under provocation from the youngest member of the Earthwork team.
Before that, however, a more personal drama began to unfold on the hilltop.
Ben noticed a cloaked and pensive figure lurking among the charred trees at the eastern edge of the clearing. A hooded old man requested Ben's attention with a beckoning finger and then disappeared into the blackened woods.
Standing passively beside the Earthwork car as instructed, Ben considered himself sufficiently free of responsibility at that moment to pursue the invitation. He left his friends without explanation and followed Mad Dog into the trees.
But the old man had materialised only long enough to bring two estranged members of the same family face to face. Searching the forested slope in the green-filtered sunlight, Ben did not find the Twelfth Stone of Meeting Hill. He discovered his father.
The Marchens stared uneasily at one another. With the memory of their last meeting still vivid and raw, both men were wary, Ben of another assault and Geoff of reprisal.
From the clearing above came the raised voice of a demonstrator, soon joined by the angry solidarity of her friends.
'Hot day,' Ben observed blandly, 'but nice in the trees.'
'Especially when you're avoiding *them,*' Geoff Marchen nodded uphill, chewing gum noisily. 'There's going to be trouble.'

Ben did not reply for some time, and when he did he measured his words and tone carefully. In a tense stand-off of mutual suspicion, Ben could not help considering his father's last statement a threat. He nodded slowly, suddenly very aware of his own perspiration and the insects that seemed to be attracted to it. A fly landed on his cheek, but Ben did not want to make any sudden movements. The men exchanged intense eye contact. 'Possibly,' Ben agreed, 'but it could be avoided. The team know they'll have to watch what they say. These people have already proved to be very opinionated, intolerant, and volatile.'

Ben almost gagged on these words when he saw their effect on his father. It became clear that any reference to the confrontation in the clearing was likely to be interpreted as an insulting parallel to their own meeting. Ben began to consider a less complicated form of expression. Direct, even impertinent questions, he reasoned, could at least be delivered without fear of menacing misinterpretation.

Happy with this logic, Ben asked, 'Where's Mum?'

Geoff Marchen blinked, caught off guard.

'What happened between you?' Ben went on. 'Did you force her to leave? And where did she go? Has she been in touch? I looked for her, but she wasn't where you said. Granny hasn't seen her.'

'You won't hear from your mother again,' Geoff said quietly, closing his eyes and rubbing the bridge of his nose between a forefinger and thumb. Suddenly looking older than Ben could ever have imagined his father becoming, Geoff felt for the earth of the slope and sat down slowly. 'Neither will I – and it's your fault,' Geoff added with a flash of anger which, to Ben's relief, faded just as quickly. 'She took your leaving so hard. She took it as an insult, like I did, and people who feel insulted want someone to blame. Your mother and I blamed each other. We felt like we'd failed as parents, and that seemed to kill everything that our marriage meant. For me, your mother just became a living reminder of my faults. I don't know. It already seems so long ago.' Geoff blinked heavily several times as he gazed down through the trees. 'I never wanted to see her again.'

'But she wasn't with Granny Sherman when I looked for her,' Ben said. 'The last time Gran saw Mum she was with you. Where else would Mum go?'

'I told you all I know!' Geoff barked, starting to his feet. Ben backed away.

The short-tempered father noticed the wariness of his son. He regretted his aggressive impulse, and was even considering some peace-making small talk when Ben asked, 'Are you still seeing the district nurse?'

Geoff Marchen's face tensed and reddened, giving Ben a sense of victory over his senior. He felt triumphant at having discovered a raw nerve in the man he had always perceived to be so strong. He felt perversely encouraged by the risk of violence that his father's anger began to threaten. 'Was an affair with her what drove Mum away?'

The negotiation on the summit deteriorated into violent disorder when Craig produced his knife. Earthwork knew nothing of Craig's offence and would forever be mystified by the Geophagians' violent eruption (though Sarah harboured an instinctive suspicion).
Sensing no immediate reward to Alan's and Sarah's attempts at explanation and apology, Craig had unfolded his pocket blade, buffed it affectionately against his T-shirt and then used its surface to reflect the midday sun into the eyes of a male protester. The man became distracted, and when he glimpsed the knife, Craig offered him a toothy grin of wide-eyed mania across the clearing before quickly concealing the weapon.
The damage to diplomacy was done. The protesters were incensed.
However, even after such criminal provocation, open battle might have been avoided by Sarah's calm mediation if, at that moment, Ben had not crashed free of the trees and sprinted towards them, closely followed by Geoff Marchen, who rushed headlong in furious pursuit. To the increasingly edgy members of the Geophagia delegation, this eruption of men from the fire-razed forest was interpreted as a timely onslaught of committee reinforcements.
Alan sighed deeply and exchanged a look of resignation with Ian, as though he should have known better than to expect any other conclusion to Earthwork's efforts.

The time Ben Marchen spent settling into his Earthwork role, which was a period of five months since his surprise return to the village of Little Arlingham, had been a period of dynamic consolidation of the committee's role and practises. After months spent trying to justify their cause to doubters within the village, parameters of responsibility had been drawn, sources of genuine allegiance and support identified, and then an alarming new level of threat to Meeting Hill's wild sanctuary filtered from paranoia and false alarms. The committee would prepare with jealous connivance for Geophagia's approach over the coming months.
In the meantime, the team had still to wrestle with the everyday challenges that were a greater reality of Earthwork's existence. The committee enjoyed the esteem in which the majority of villagers held their efforts, and they considered themselves fortunate to be actively involved. Yet shielding The Meeting from the effects of inconsiderate tourism, the modern tide of concrete that flows across wilderness, agriculture and heritage alike, and from the ritual smoke, candle wax and symbolic carvings of zealots, did often mean having to confront large numbers of angry people.

So it was that day. The aggrieved delegates of Geophagia hurled insults, and then a readily available arsenal of pebbles and charred branches at the bewildered committee members.

Earthwork contritely refrained from returning fire, but stopped short of offering itself as a passive target for the demonstrators' missiles. The team swallowed its collective pride and hid behind the Shogun.

'We should drive away and forget the whole thing,' Sarah said as charcoal and rocks rained down around them. 'None of this is their fault.'

'No?' Alan asked. 'Then whose?'

'We've been a bit provocative recently,' she reasoned, slicing a suspicious glance at Craig, 'and I think these people are only reacting as anyone would.'

Sarah spoke as someone who considered herself removed from the subject of discussion. She flinched and pressed herself against the car as one of its window shattered, raining nuggets of glass into her hair. She shook her head carefully, and then pointed east across the clearing at a man making a stealthy clockwise tour of the stones. 'Ben? If your Dad's over there, who's that?'

All except one member of the cowering team turned to follow Sarah's quizzical stare, just in time to glimpse a watchful figure wearing an unseasonably heavy robe amongst the trees. 'Isn't that Mad Dog?' Ian said. 'Didn't you say you'd seen him, Ben?'

Ben was inattentive to the situation, sitting a little way from the car with blithe regard for the shower of objects around him. 'Dad blames me for breaking up our family. Maybe he's right.'

His friends did not know how to react, other than to suggest that this was not the moment for pessimistic revelation, though they didn't say so. Sarah squeezed his shoulder, but Ben's grip on the moment remained tenuous for a few minutes more.

Ian risked a glance at the protesters through the shattered car windows when the shower of missiles began to ebb. He assessed the view for several seconds and then leaned closer to Alan. 'We might find ourselves in debt to Geoff Marchen,' he reported quietly, though not softly enough to avoid being overheard by Ben, who looked first at Ian, and then up over the bonnet of the car. He saw his father in discussion with the Geophagia party.

Marchen had approached the group, caught the attention of its established leader and was pointing mysteriously downhill through the north-western trees.

With this unexpected intervention, the protest was suddenly over. The anger of the group was replaced by obvious excitement, and they disappeared into the trees to descend the wooded slope.

'They're off the footpath!' Craig yelped, jumping up and pointing after them like a jealous sibling. 'Trespass! We can evict them for that!'

'Shut up, Craig.'

Alan stepped out from behind the car. Sarah and Ian followed him, and Craig sauntered dejectedly behind them, leaving Ben to observe their investigation through the car's jagged window frames.

'Hello, Alan,' the senior Marchen responded to his approach.

Alan nodded politely, stepping up alongside to share Geoff's perspective. With the trees stripped of their foliage by the recent fire, the view downhill was clear, and Alan was saved the need to question Marchen about what had distracted the protesters. He gazed in comical disbelief.

'I pointed out something I thought might interest them,' Marchen said. 'It worked, but I suppose this'll be something else for your committee to deal with.'

At the edge of the barley field, the Geophagia members emerged from the trees and began wading through the barley.

'Predictable, weren't they?' Geoff said.

But Earthwork was left contemplating an unwanted new attraction to the site. Pressed into the crop of the nearest field was a pattern of perfect circles and connecting lines which, eventually, someone would notice resembled the constellation of Orion.

Ben appeared beside Ian and picked a small shard of glass from his hair. Not wanting to litter the site further, he put it in his pocket. Then he followed his colleagues' gaze downhill and saw the Geophagians leaping and dancing in the expansive riddle of crop circles.

Part Three

August

'...Whoever fair and chaste
Rejects Mankind, is by some sylph embrac'd'

Alexander Pope
The Rape of the Lock

The Rainmakers

With the dusk came rain, but Carreg's hope that darkness might protect him proved overly optimistic. On a muddy track rising gently from the fen to drier ground, Carreg held his breath and listened intently, convinced that beyond the drumming of the rain he sensed the rhythm of hooves.
But the monk was now suspicious of his senses. Fear, paranoia, exhaustion and hunger had begun to conjure danger from the very air around him. Carreg wanted to be sure: he had already been hurt throwing himself from the path of phantom threats.
There it was again, close behind him: a rattle of hooves, harness and reins delivered by the shifting breeze, with a vibration underfoot to confirm the suspicions of his ears – and suddenly his view of the path already travelled became filled with the dark maelstrom of a galloping horse and its resolute rider.
Adrenalin flooded his veins and Carreg ran, though he knew he must have been seen. The heavy object he cradled in his arms like a helpless infant set his sprint off balance, so Carreg was able to run for only seconds before the snorting of the horse's flared nostrils filled the world from only a few yards behind.
Tears came. The monk cried childish sobs of misery at the injustice of this fate: to feel it all end with the sweep of a sword so close to his goal. Helplessly, he realised that the silhouette of Meeting Hill and its crowning tonsure were to be the last things he would ever see. He blinked rapidly to clear the tears from his eyes, but each blink became a flinch as he anticipated death or lightning dismemberment with every heartbeat. His sprint deteriorated into a flailing momentum of instinctive cowering, and the monk pressed the hatefully inscribed cross against his chest with his last ragged breath. The horse and rider closed the remaining distance between them, but then galloped by in a storm of mud, pounding hooves, billowing cloak, bewilderment and then reeling, dizzying relief.
Carreg sank breathlessly to his knees in a puddle, barely able to raise his head and watch the horse disappear around a bend in the lane. Then he closed his eyes, crossed himself several times with the ease of habit, and laughed with an unexpected realisation that only two very different kinds of soul – the very arrogant and the very fearful – must feel that they attract the interest of every passing stranger.
The monk remained kneeling a while longer and prayed fervently as the last embers of dusk faded, and light was drained from the land.
It was therefore in darkness that Carreg reached the wooded slopes of Meeting Hill. He picked his way uphill through the trees, but weariness and the night made progress slow. When he reached a glade that sheltered a spring just

below the summit, the monk almost succumbed to an urge to nestle into the roots of a tree and close his eyes. Sleep would have come quickly.

But duty remained the stronger urge that night, combined with the desire to rid himself and the world of the stolen cross. Carreg blinked sleep away. At the top of the hill would be a friend, he had been promised, someone to whom he could pass his burden.

So dark was the night without moonlight that it took Carreg moments to realise he had escaped the trees and reached the summit. Stars became visible through a narrow break in the rain clouds. For a few moments Carreg could see the belt of Orion above the treetops. The momentary streak of a falling star made Carreg gasp and shudder in the silence, and then his eyes widened when a tall, bulky figure loomed ahead of him. The monk realised that the ground had levelled underfoot, and he had entered a clearing.

'A grim night,' Carreg nodded anxiously at the silhouette. With no response from the figure, the monk took one deep, shaky breath, stepped forward, reached out and touched cold, wet stone.

Carreg found himself alone in a temple erected to gods that were not his own. He reached inside his mud-spattered robe to caress the well worn, reassuring familiarity of a wooden crucifix hanging from his neck on a rosary, and his lips moved fervently with the pressure of whispered prayers.

*

The man questioning Craig had long chestnut hair, and it was tied back in a ponytail that he flicked across his shoulders with a twitch whenever he turned his head. He wore meticulously tended stubble and mirrored sunglasses.

'Do you believe in crop circles, Craig?'

If pressed, Craig would have admitted to liking the man, who had introduced himself as Bere. He was, Craig considered, a townie who had nothing in common with any of the diverse personalities of the Earthwork team, but who seemed to aspire to the rural hardiness with which Craig now patronised him.

Craig looked puzzled by Bere's question, but pointed over the shoulder of the self-titled Bio-energy Research Engineer into the field. 'Yes, there's loads of them over there,' he said, as though the pattern pressed into the barley was not the reason for Bere's presence. 'They all join up to make a big pattern of a constellation.'

Bere glared at him with the kind of judgemental expression that Craig was used to giving, not receiving. That Bere's physique easily matched Craig's own was the only reason that Craig did not take issue with it.

'I know that,' the Londoner replied sharply, slapping at his clipboard with a pen as he grew frustrated with Craig's flippancy. 'I mean, do you accept that these patterns are created by a non-human agency?'

'Like what?'

'Which ones do you accept as plausible?'
'Give me some to dismiss.'
Bere sighed and read down the list on his survey. 'Attempted communication by extra-terrestrials?' he began.
'No.'
'Attempted communication by the Earth itself?'
'Nope.'
'Intelligent micro-tornadoes?'
'Ha ha ha!'
'Fairies?'
'Nah.'
'Will-o'-the-wisp?'
'Doubt it.'
'A convergence of telluric energies at the junctions of ley lines near prehistoric monuments?'
Craig thought about it long enough for Bere to recover his optimistic expression. Then, 'No,' Craig replied. 'Are you making these up?'
'What about mischievous elemental forces?' Bere resumed.
A snigger. 'No!'
'Manifestations of gravity-free, bio-form light-masses composed of sym-bio energy?'
'Ah *ha!* That wouldn't be *your* field of interest, would it?' Craig asked, glancing at Ian and Sarah, who sat on the bonnet of one of the Shoguns nearby, and then at Alan, who was inspecting one of the Sym-bio Research Forum's three unfathomable machines. Craig's expression begged rescue, but his friends were absorbed in their own distractions.
'Well, yes,' Bere admitted. 'I specialise in—'
'Is this going to take much longer? I'm here to chaperone your visit to the Wyre estate, not become a research subject.'
'Wait,' Bere held up a hand, 'please. I appreciate your time. One last question.' He pointed into the field at the crop circles and gave Craig a stare that he must have thought was mysterious, but which actually looked like the onset of migraine. 'Have you seen anything?'
Craig rested his chin on a fist and furrowed his brow, staring thoughtfully at Bere until the visitor began to look hopeful. 'Well, actually,' Craig began, 'I've seen a lot of people trespassing on Wyre property, trampling fragile crops to stand in the field and get excited about this hoax. It's criminal damage, you know.'
Georgina Wyre was standing in the centre of one of the crop circles with two other visitors, a woman named Carla and a man named Paul. George seemed very interested in everything they had to say – a fact that gave the younger committee members some cause for concern. Earthwork quickly decided that

the Sym-bio Research Forum members were poseurs attempting to disguise simplistic animism and New Age leanings behind a thin façade of pseudo-scientific jargon, cosmopolitan fashion, and impressively scaled (if unidentifiable) equipment.

Yet George seemed convinced by them, and the Earthwork members were not happy about seeing their leader and chief sceptic absorbing the group's ideas so credulously.

Carla, the researcher talking to George, was an animated young woman wearing a sleeveless black T-shirt. The man beside her was a reserved character of similar age who seemed faintly embarrassed by the enthusiasm of his companions; but he need not have been, because George was listening intently, nodding when she thought it appropriate, and interrupting with questions even when it was not.

'Not only is the scale and accuracy of this manifestation of particular interest, the setting is also remarkable,' Carla was saying, pushing her unnecessary sunglasses back over her head to act as a hair-band. 'Somerset is an infrequent host to this phenomenon. I wish we'd heard of this pattern's appearance earlier – the state of the crop tells me that this field has been a tourist attraction for some weeks.'

'My only concern is the weather,' replied Paul, glancing warily at the overcast sky. 'We're going to make it rain.'

The first day of August had dawned with a promise of sunshine, but soon clouded over. Rain was forecast – a prediction that offered relief for anyone who grew crops that summer. By midday it still hadn't rained, though the air clung to skin like damp tissue paper. Weeks of uninterrupted heat had resulted in a dense humidity that filled the sky with an oppressive ceiling of grey cloud and sweaty haze. Yet apples ripened bountifully in orchards across the Levels, even as soil lie as dust underfoot. Vehicles travelling off-road across the estate left a sandy cloud in their wake.

'I don't understand that, I'm afraid,' George cut in: 'The bit about you making it rain.'

'It's a meteorological side effect of a focused sym-bio presence,' Carla said dismissively, assessing the sky for herself. 'Sym-bio is not only the manifest life force within all living things, but also the force that acts to promote and preserve the best possible conditions for life. The biosphere of the Earth is simultaneously it own cause and effect. It's symbiotic.'

Craig listened to this speech from the edge of the field with his hands stuffed into the pockets of his shorts, and he turned to find out how much of it Ian and Sarah overhead. 'There's always someone talking like that within sight of Meeting Hill, isn't there?'

Perched on its bonnet, Sarah bounced her heels against the bumper of the Shogun. 'Is any of this true?' she asked. 'I can't imagine real scientists talking about *life force*. Sounds more like a Geophagia thing.'

'And what about the machines?' Alan pointed past Bere, who was pretending to ignore them. 'What do they do? They look like anti-aircraft guns.'

'…And with moisture so essential to the nurturing of life, any intense introduction of symbiotic biological energy – which we are about to attempt – will promote precipitation. I predict rain later today.'

Georgina expressed her first attack of scepticism since the Sym-bio Research Forum had arrived on the estate. 'This is not a revelation to us, young lady,' she smiled pleasantly at Carla. 'The weather forecast has predicted rain since last week. It's already looking likely,' Wyre observed, indicating the low, dark cloud, 'and you've not even started yet.'

'Rain is forecast here?' Carla replied, and even Craig would have grudgingly admitted that she seemed surprised. 'Then we'll probably make it worse. Will Little Arlingham mind a storm?'

'Does thunder and lightning offer the best conditions for life, then?'

'Sym-bio is an electro-magnetic energy. Driving it up into an already unsettled atmosphere might provoke a few flashes – although that's not our aim,' Carla added quickly. 'We actually hope to achieve a focused concentration of life force which, in turn, should create a bio-form light mass: a sentient entity that we believe is responsible for the crop circle phenomenon. Rapidly moving lights, sometimes only the size of a golf ball and sometimes as big as a car, have often been seen above fields where crop patterns were later found.' Carla indicated the earth and air around them. 'You've had one here. We would like to encourage the local environment to produce another, and then monitor the effects on our consciousness.'

The Earthwork team understood little of what the research team was trying to explain, and believed even less of it, but their priority consideration was that it all sounded harmless. Bere requested that the three machines they had towed onto the estate, which he called 'sym-bio accelerators', be placed in positions forming a triangle around the field of crop circles: one furthest west on Meeting Hill, another to the south-east in the paddock near Arlingham House, and the third in a field to the north, where Ian and Ben had roamed the outskirts of Carreg's End as children. Bere patiently explained to the frowning Earthwork that from these positions, each accelerator would simultaneously aim a 'beam' of sym-bio energy at the sky over the pattern in the barley.

Craig spluttered hysterically, almost choking on laughter. Georgina cast him a disapproving glare. Earthwork did not have to share the Rainmakers' beliefs, of course, but as Wyre had granted their request to perform an experiment of some kind on her land, she did expect the team to show her guests common courtesy.

'This sym-bio life force,' Craig managed eventually, 'is a *theoretical* energy, you said?'

'Yes,' Bere nodded, making the most of a chance to flap his ponytail about. 'But a case for the existence of such an element has been demonstrated by greater men than us, the first being Wilhelm Reich, of course. Look him up.'

'Oh, I won't,' Craig assured him. 'So how do your machines produce an energy that you can't prove exists?'

'My young friend here is clearly excited by your research, Bere,' George cut in. 'Why don't you give us a demonstration?'

Chance

A flame reached the end of its wick and went out. Smoke began to drift around the ritual space of the folly's summit room, smudging the air above Tom, who was sleeping, and above Roedan, who watched him. Both were undressed, their clothes piled untidily at the edge of the chalk maze. The shutters were open, but there was no sunshine to brighten Roedan's mood.

Tom opened his eyes, his head against the floorboards. One half of his face had become matted with a mixture of chalk dust and perspiration, but he did not move. He felt unwilling to turn and face Roedan, who he was sure would be staring at him.

He already regretted their intimacy, which had been very different from their previous couplings. Tom felt manipulated, but it had been impossible to say no to Roedan. She had made her advances seem full of an affection that belied her selfish motive. Tom had convinced himself that Roedan truly wanted him, and so he tried to enjoy the feeling while it lasted, which was only until the weak climax of their mechanically performed intercourse.

Weeks had passed since Tom Sutherland agreed to help Roedan with her search, and during that time he had hoped Roedan would not need him after all. Despite his unwavering respect for Roedan and her philosophy, he had never been fully convinced that making choices through meditation was any more effective than flipping a coin. But Tom had deferred confessing those doubts until Roedan reminded him of his promise, and summoned him to *Tan-Y-Bryn*. Just two hours before, Tom had finally expressed his scepticism, though not articulately at first.

'You've lost faith in my methods? In the search?' Roedan accused him. 'You no longer believe in me?'

'It's not that. I just don't think I'm the best person for the job. You have a following of several thousand people – any of them would be better at this than I am. I'm not so intuitive.'

Roedan cast Tom a wary glance. 'But you're the only person I trust with knowledge of this search, and you appreciate why. Besides, you've done well so far – and you've been my most loyal follower, confidant and friend,' she breathed earnestly, taking a step forward to hold his wrist. 'I don't want you involved only for your help, Tom.'

She had then reached for his other wrist and ran her hands up his arms. 'I want you to be involved so you have an equal claim to the achievement, and share my euphoria at the end.'

Roedan had noted Tom's awkward, silent expression and laughed at the doubts she imagined him to be entertaining. 'This search doesn't make us unusual, Tom! Who else, given the knowledge and opportunity, could resist going out of their way to find such a treasure? Look, I already have the search narrowed down to only three accessible sites – you'd be an idiot to walk away when we're so close. Imagine how it will feel, Tom: you and me,' she added quietly.

Tom had been able to resist her coaxing until that moment, until she began stroking his neck with her fingertips. Her tone had seemed caring, though Tom knew her advances to be a form of persuasion – and worse, that a return of her affections would seal his promise to meditate on her behalf. But she was caressing his neck and crooning into one tingling ear with that voice – *that voice!* – so how hard might it be to seem a bit more enthusiastic, and even credulous, to fulfil his promise? The favour involved little more than sitting around describing the random images that flit effortlessly through a relaxed mind.

And so Tom had been led across the lawn to *Pen Annwn*, his doubts drowned by arousal. Tom knew he would probably regret having been seduced, but such foresight does not extinguish the tingling of caressed skin, or the glowing anticipation that follows. And as Roedan had let her gown fall in the centre of the chalk labyrinth, Tom was able to reason that any shame would lie only in his lack of willpower, not in the act itself. Roedan and Tom were too companionable to let casual sex spoil a mature relationship.

The couple's brief hunger traced a route of smudged chalk across the floorboard maze and on around the room. Tom had fallen asleep on the floor soon afterwards. Roedan had not.

Now, awake and wondering what would happen next, Tom heard Roedan moving behind him. She shuffled forward and kissed him in the small of his back. 'I've always wanted to know: what's it like to fuck your boss?'

Tom thought the question as much a statement of triumph over him as a lover's playfulness. Either way, Roedan did not seem to be expecting an answer. 'I'll be back in a minute,' she said, rising to her feet and pacing towards the trapdoor. 'Then we really need to press on with our search.'

Tom questioned her urgency and reached for his trousers.

'It has to be today,' she replied, her expression suggesting that Tom should have known better. 'Finding our goal on the harvest festival of Lughnasa seems so powerfully symbolic, it can only be an aid to the search. To miss a chance like this would unbearable for me.'

Tom did not respond. He knew he did not need to. Roedan was too confident to look for validation of her statements from anyone. Tom watched her descend the ladder and listened to her pacing the spiral staircase. Then he hurried around the room after the rest of his clothes. He dressed quickly, feeling able to work through the expected regret more rapidly than he had hoped, and then contemplated the room and the rest of the day that he would spend in it. Tom struggled to remember each step of Roedan's meditative technique: the inspired best guess, her Visionary Conjecture, which she had devised and taught her following. He recalled vague instructions and

recommendations, and he remembered that they thoroughly bored him.
As the front man for Geophagia, Tom Sutherland was used to promoting Roedan and her teachings, but he had little interest in practising them. Tom was certainly a Pagan, but he was also a traditionalist. He knew no foundation for the practice Roedan had created. Moreover, the search he found himself committed to was not, in his opinion, an occult quest: it was a puzzle for scholars.
As Tom understood Roedan's claim, the location of Arthur's burial cross had been narrowed down to three geographical contenders. During meditation, these sites were represented on the chalk maze by three wine glasses, each bearing a paper label. Tom had no opinion or instinct as to which of these three places might actually conceal the relic – assuming that the legendary object existed at all. And without ardent faith in Roedan's assertion that he would be *inspired* to the correct answer through mediation, Tom now wondered how he was going to fulfil his promise.
It became clear to Tom that he would have to enter Roedan's visionary quest with a destination already in mind. For his progress to seem inspired, it would have to seem purposeful.
Tom glanced south through the shutters and saw Roedan, still naked, stepping into the house through the kitchen door. Feeling confident in his solitude, Tom opened the wooden chest that stored Roedan's ritual tools and found the three labelled wine glasses. He noted the names displayed on each and immediately dismissed the glass marked 'South Pennard Barrows' as a contender. Geophagia had already visited this site, and Tom did not know why Roedan still considered it.
While contemplating which of the remaining pair to reject, he picked up Roedan's short-bladed sword – clearly an antique – and fenced an imaginary foe with it. As he sliced and stabbed the dagger through the air before him, he realised that he had about as much chance of making an informed decision as he did of miraculously being inspired to the correct one. An entirely random choice, he began to reason, would be as valid as one selected by his own careless whim.
'Now *that*,' he decided happily, 'is inspired.'
He reached into a pocket of his jeans and produced fifty pence. He decided which of the two finalists in Roedan's search would be named Heads and which Tails, and sent the coin spinning into the air with a flick of his thumb.
He caught it and opened his fist on the back of his right hand. At that moment he heard Roedan ascending the spiral staircase to the attic room.
The American lifted his hand and looked at the coin.

*

Chance was not allowed to play such a prominent part in the events that were to unfold on Meeting Hill that evening. The old but animated figure who walked purposefully among the stones did not believe in chance. He believed in Destiny.

It was an attempt to assist Destiny that Madog intended here, and this he undertook by placing objects around the site in a way that would have seemed meaningless, if not quite random, to anyone else.

From the hillside spring on the northern slope, Madog had peered down through the trees to watch Earthwork and their guests examining the crop circles. He saw enough to feel convinced that the committee members, who were the most frequent visitors to the summit, would not be likely to travel uphill in the very near future. Madog realised that Ben Marchen was not with the Earthwork team that day, but his distraction had already been arranged, and the old man did not expect to be disturbed by anyone of consequence for some time.

Satisfied, Madog pulled a dead magpie from within the folds of his robe, dangled the bird by string tied around its neck, and crept up to the clearing. Sweating profusely as the day's humidity made the climb an even greater effort, Madog glanced into the sky and noted with relief that the heavy cloud finally threatened rain.

Back on the open hilltop, he checked for any presence more aware of his purpose than the stones themselves, and headed for the southern edge of the summit. Here, the branches of an oak untouched by the Midsummer fire reached out over the grass of the clearing. Madog's gaze searched busily through the leaves and then settled on a stout bough, up to which he was able to climb, even in his cloak, with only a further minute of sweaty effort. Madog tied the string to the branch and let the magpie swing. Then he scrambled, groped, cursed and jumped his way back down to the grass.

Madog pulled his hood up over his head and paced into the space enclosed by the eleven weathered sentinels, reaching into his robe a second time. He walked until he reached the centre of the clearing where the ground seemed a little uneven, and where the grass did not grow as tall. Here Madog appeared more thoughtful, more deliberate, even reverent, and he spent some time staring down at the earth.

A buzzard soared on thermal tides high above him, circling watchfully while Madog stood motionless in the ring of his silent brethren, his head bowed within the shadow of its hood. He remained in this silent stance long enough for the bird overhead to spiral sedately out of view. Then the Twelfth Stone produced a glass jar and a single shard of broken mirror from within the folds of his robe. The contents of the jar seethed ceaselessly as Madog slid the triangular piece of mirror edgewise into the earth.

Satisfied that the shard was hidden, Madog picked up the jar, peered at the rustling activity within and unscrewed the lid. He took a step back, and with

one wide swing of his arm flung hundreds of red wood ants across the space before him in a whispering cloud. The ground at his feet for a moment gained the animated appearance of rippled water; then the insects found their feet and moved together, melting smoothly into the grass.
Madog sniffed and shook off the concentration required by this unusual behaviour. His lips twitched a brief, stubble-rimmed smile, and then he pulled the hood back from his face. He glanced around the clearing, nodding occasionally as though ticking items on a mental list, and slipped one hand into a pocket of his robe. His fist re-emerged clutching the last oblation necessary to his purpose: a handful of daisies, which he cast across the earth before him in a delicate shower of drifting white petals.
His task complete, the Twelfth Stone of Meeting Hill quickly vanished into the trees.

The Meeting has received countless offerings from visitors since the 1960s, some placed in honour of festivals; some as gifts to the site, to the Earth, or one of many deities; and others left to mark rituals performed in the hope of magical change.
Offerings have included handmade pottery, crystals, straw dolls, ornamental blades, flower garlands, incense and candles. And the kinds of people who left them were as varied as the gifts themselves: avid Tolkien fans, self-proclaimed Druids, purported alien-abductees, and even a 1980s' pop star-turned-antiquarian, who had visited the week before.
Watching silently from the shade of the surrounding trees, Madog had seen many of these gifts offered and was always fascinated by the demeanour of the visiting supplicants, which usually differed from the stoical manner in which Madog himself performed his rites. The Twelfth Stone often struggled to stifle laughter when visitors knelt before the stones wearing expressions of imploring piety to make melodramatic speeches and gestures, and fumbling to cast imaginative, though otherwise useless, spells found in books from the Mind, Body & Spirit section of a high street chain.
As a man who snugly fits the parameters of a certain stereotype, Madog was well used to performing acts of occult significance, just like the one executed on Meeting Hill that Lughnasa afternoon. But he had never displayed the needless theatricals and droning liturgy adopted by weekend dabblers in the art. Madog's relationship with the world and its will was a businesslike and, he believed, mutually beneficial exchange.
This afternoon's request would, if granted, cause the suffering of at least two local people. Ordinarily, Madog would have regretted such an outcome, but this pain was not just an unfortunate side effect: it had been his intention all along. The Meeting demanded it, he believed, and – if his timing was right – then the stones would help bring about the circumstance to achieve it.

Orion

By mid-afternoon the Sym-bio Research Forum, escorted by Earthwork and inundated with their questions, had positioned itself around the Wyre estate. They performed calculations and set the aim of their machines – the mysterious devices Bere had proudly referred to as 'sym-bio accelerators' – which had been arranged in an almost perfect equilateral triangle around the crop circles.

The Research Forum, a team of nine people including the three to whom Georgina Wyre had been introduced, worked within sight of a fleet of combine harvesters, which throughout the morning had rumbled into place at the edges of the fields and then loomed over the dehydrated barley in hungry anticipation of its thunderous reaping. The work of the researchers was an eleventh-hour reprieve for the condemned acres of crop; but the rumbling red masters of harvest did not resent a moment as they lowered their threshing blades in smug readiness, inevitability fully on their side.

The sym-bio accelerators were car-sized devices, a little over eight feet in height when mounted on their two-wheeled trailers. Each accelerator comprised a turret that rotated on a plate central in the trailer, an operator's seat, and handlebars that controlled the rotation and aim of what Bere called a 'beam array'. The array was two parallel banks of twenty-five alternately iron and wooden prongs, each five feet long, which extended outwards from the rotating turret. Clad with metal plates and painted battleship grey, the sym-bio accelerators resembled military hardware.

One of these devices was parked in the southern-most field of the estate near Arlingham House. Another was wheeled into position a little less than a mile to the north on the outskirts of Carreg's End, and attracted a crowd of youths. The last appeared on Meeting Hill and aimed its array into the grey eastern sky.

At Georgina's request earlier that afternoon, Craig Pearce had left the estate in the Land Rover to drive surreptitiously past the preparations for Geophagia's Lughnasa festival near Wheat Hill, but found the venue (disclosed to Ben Marchen by a climatically persuaded Lea Granger three weeks before) devoid of any activity. Lea had divulged the correct location of Geophagia's harvest celebration but, playfully, not its precise date. Roedan was not due to return to Somerset until the evening of August 3rd.

In fact, Georgina Wyre had not explicitly instructed Craig to make the trip to Wheat Hill. She had simply asked him to show the Sym-bio Research Forum, her guests on the estate, much more respect. Then, realising that the young man was probably incapable of that, she politely asked him to leave the estate in search of some other way of being useful.

Since Lughnasa fell on a weekday in 1999, tourist visits to Meeting Hill did not increase much beyond their normal number. However, each of the committee members except Ben had made themselves available for duty that day, including Sarah Conrad, who was officially invested in the role of Earthwork Field Team member in recognition of her contribution to the group's efforts, and because several prominent villagers had complained about the male domination of Earthwork's ranks.

Other than escorting the sym-bio researchers around the estate, Earthwork had little else to do that day. The team's greatest concern remained a deep suspicion of the Geophagia Foundation and its incremental approach to Meeting Hill. Georgina Wyre maintained her reasons for regarding the group a threat to The Meeting's sanctity, despite accusations of paranoia and struggling to justify the committee's funding. But since Earthwork's humiliation at Geophagia's Midsummer festival, for which the Field Operations Team had been publicly berated at the committee meeting in June, George rarely mentioned her concerns, deciding that little else could be done until her suspicions were confirmed.

Ian, Sarah and George joined Bere and Carla on the summit of Meeting Hill. The sym-bio researchers spent some time preparing the accelerator, and then Bere started the generator at its base and climbed into the seat behind the array. This was clearly Bere's favourite stage of the experiment. 'The trick now,' he called down to his audience over the din of the generator, 'will be to aim at the same point in the sky over the crop circles as the other two accelerators.'

Wyre nodded encouragingly.

Ian observed no particularly fine calibration of the device by Bere or Carla, so he simply assumed that these wondrous machines were either self-guiding, or that they might emit dazzling beams of the spectacular energy Carla had described earlier, thereby allowing Bere to visually direct the stream into radiant union with the output of the other accelerators.

George and Sarah entertained similar assumptions, but all three Earthwork members were to be disappointed. In response to Bere's aggressive twisting of a throttle on the handlebars, nothing seemed to happen, except a change of pitch in the generator's rumble as it channelled power to unseen effect.

However, Bere displayed the tense posture and concentration of someone riding a motorcycle at dangerous speeds, and when he began to whoop and yell with excitement, Ian, Sarah and George frantically searched the machine and the sky above in confusion, sure that they must be missing something obvious.

The expectant gaze of the people among the stones was eventually aligned with the aim of the machine. There was nothing to see, but their imaginations were stimulated by what Carla had suggested would be happening high above the cereal rendering of Orion at that moment. The audiences around all three rumbling accelerators stared up into the same area of oppressive grey sky, each searching for any hint of the phenomenon described earlier by Carla.

Though nothing visible occurred above the estate that day, the novelty of the event and the expectation it provoked did expand the imaginative horizons of the spectators. As word of the experiment spread, a cloudy pinpoint in space above the Somerset landscape became the focus of attention for more than three hundred people. All over Little Arlingham and Carreg's End, people went in search of places with a view over the estate. With eyes and minds open wide, they all gazed up into the sky.

If it had been possible to look down from the perspective of the theoretical bio-form's conception, an observer would have been better able to appreciate the complexity of the pattern of crop circles below. It was instantly recognisable as the constellation of Orion, but the scale of its layout was too great to be contained by a single field. One knee of the hunter lay in an adjacent meadow, and it was only from above that a crop circle representing Aldebaran, the eye of Taurus, would have been noticed two fields away to the north-west, pressed into the barley with stalks bent neatly in a smooth anti-clockwise swirl, before this cereal mirror of the heavens was lost forever to the threshing blades of the estate's harvest machinery.

Had the day's pervading tone of ritual, which had inspired Madog's actions, possessed Roedan's efforts and infused the sym-bio researchers' experimentation, played a part in an environmental response to these proceedings, then perhaps the sun would have chosen that moment to break through the cloud where the gaze of the spectators met. Or perhaps the wind might have risen to whip the dusty earth into swirling eddies, animate the hilltop trees and introduce an impressively timed squall of rain, thereby giving the stones of The Meeting their first soaking since the fire service hoses at Midsummer.

But there was no sun or dramatic wind. And although there would be rain as forecast later, it would not arrive until darkness fell and events unfolded that made Earthwork's daytime distractions seem frivolous.

A Wet August

Ben Marchen's shape-shifting angst assumed a form that he recognised that day, and its name was nostalgia.
Lughnasa's spirit of observance possessed not only those whose attentions were captured by the occult, or by the pseudo-scientific. For Ben, ritual was manifest in its domestic form as the structure of his working day. He began the morning, as he did most weekdays, by making the most of the autonomy Ian allowed him in his contribution to their commissions. This week he worked at home to complete a logo for an organic farming business near Castle Cary.
And yet, despite his best efforts to conform under pressure, Ben's veneer of working discipline disintegrated around mid-morning that day. He started to see the walls of his makeshift studio as a cage, and the work on his easel as the guard who kept him there. The longer Ben walked the circular route of conformity, the more it looked like a rut, and then a trench, and he glanced up ever more frequently from the gloom of this furrow at the open fields of his earlier freedom. It had seemed sunnier back then.
But the view into distant recollection seemed sunnier still. Ben had been experiencing the spontaneous surfacing of childhood memories for a while now: a reflective process he believed was triggered by confrontation with his father in June, and which had grown in intensity each week since. Everything reminded Ben of something. Everything he did, saw, smelt or heard seemed redolent of some aspect of his youth. His sleep was interrupted and his concentration compromised until his thoughts reached an almost feverish state of fixation, and he began to feel that the barrage of memories must be building to a cathartic finale.
On August 1st, Ben finally surrendered to the whispering sprite of truancy and turned away from his work. He decided to trust his growing conviction that, by exploring the memories flooding his mind, he might be led to the beginnings of an answer – and perhaps even to the name and the cause of an angst that had disrupted the adult years of his life.
Ben left his rooms and walked into Little Arlingham. He was not particularly hopeful of finding everything he wanted to buy in the village, but he was reluctant to drive further afield, so settled on a trip to the newsagent in Carreg's End, which was the only shop in the village with a few shelves of books for sale. He resisted the temptation of a liquid lunch in The Bolthole as he passed.
Pre-dating his fascination with authors such as Kesey, Kerouac and Bukowski during his years of travel, Ben's youthful immersion in worlds preserved by books meant that vast tracts of his memory were filled with the dramatic landscapes, diverse peoples, fantastic creatures and incredible events described in literature; and now he sensed that, beneath the untidy pile of recent years,

the seeds of his desultory lifestyle might lie unexamined within the major preoccupations of his formative years.

Ben picked up as many familiar titles as the shop had to offer, and by the time he had finished browsing his arms were full of books, whose authors ranged from Adams to Grahame, from Kipling to Marryat, and from Milne to Tolkien. Then, even as he was paying for them, Ben began to recall favourite scenes from each of these novels, and such glowing memories had an immediately assuasive effect on his restless thoughts. Ben scolded himself for having allowed the source of this comfort to lie forgotten for so long.

He hurried back along Arlingham Road with two bulging carrier bags assaulting his legs at every stride. As he crossed Market Square he was passed by three vehicles towing contraptions of military appearance, aiming south on their way into the Wyre estate – but Ben was too excited by his purchases to notice. And with his rebellious streak appeased by exploration of its roots, neither did Ben feel any need to wink with goading presumption at his elderly neighbours. He headed straight home and filed through his modest music collection, searching specifically for memorable songs from his first twelve years of life. Then he sat cross-legged on the carpet of his lounge and surrounded himself with the literature of timeless fantasy.

Ben swam for hours through music, pages, words and imaginative vision like a pearl diver through clear warm water, exploring nostalgia and emotion whose depths left him breathless. Picking albums, books and pages at random, Ben rediscovered Grahame's *Piper at the Gates of Dawn* while Jon and Vangelis insisted *I Hear You Now* from the stereo. The Children of the New Forest came to the care of Jacob Armitage during Barbara Dickinson's *January February*. Roxy Music lamented *My Only Love* as the rabbits of Sandleford Warren listened to Bluebell's retelling of the trial of El-ahrairah on their journey to Watership Down. Renaissance sought *Northern Lights* while The Hobbit spoke with Smaug. Kate Bush considered a moody old man and a night on the water in *Delius (Song Of Summer)* just as A Bear With Very Little Brain in search of honey climbed and climbed, and as he climbed he sang a little song that eventually became Carly Simon's *Why,* and Puck of Pook's Hill appeared to Dan and Una while Gerry Rafferty recounted life as a *Night Owl.*

Ben resurfaced from an ocean of memories with tears in his eyes as Andrew Gould's *Lonely Boy* faded with the daylight, which was sucked from the room by the looming dusk. Lost in regression, Ben had missed the passing of the grey afternoon; but, as he closed the cover of Sendak's *Where the Wild Things Are,* a light the colour of straw found a chink in the cloud through which to render the surrounding sky oppressive in comparison.

Ben stared out through his lounge window into the distant golden light, and it seemed to him that every possible exciting thing in the world must be happening all the way over there. He dismally remembered feeling this way all too often, and it made him repent of the way in which he had spent his years since youth.

Regret, Ben observed, offers the most luxurious moments of self-indulgent poignancy.

But it seemed that these hours of nostalgia had served a positive purpose. Ben was surprised to find himself in a state of dreamy relaxation: a peaceful frame of mind he glimpsed so rarely that it made any notion of leaving the flat unthinkable for the rest of the day.

Ben felt at home in his thoughts and in his skin. He reclined in the darkening silence of his lounge for a few minutes more, and then switched on a lamp, tidied the books and albums scattered across the floor and made a coffee.

Of course, Ben was not convinced that a single afternoon of communing with his inner child (as he would later describe it) would be enough to understand the sense of displacement that usually denied him such contentment, or allow him to comprehend the melancholy yearning that inspired his aimless travels. Yet, clearly, the experience had calmed his agitation that day. Ben thought that he might even manage few more hours of work.

This unprecedented peace was disturbed by a knock at the front door. Ben considered ignoring it, but he realised that the caller would have noticed the lamplight from the lounge.

The Reverend Matthew Norton was the last person he expected to find when he opened the door. Ben's contented mood was immediately compromised.

'Oh – hello.'

'Good evening,' Norton nodded. He was dressed as casually as Ben had ever seen him and somehow seemed more affable for it, though Ben decided against inviting his most ardent critic into the house on the strength of his sweatshirt. 'How are you? Were you about to go out?'

Ben shrugged. 'Fine, fine. No, I'm in for the night.' Then, after a pregnant pause, 'Why?'

'Don't be so surprised to see me, my office is only across the road,' Norton smirked, nodding at the silhouette of the church.

'Of course I'm surprised,' Ben replied, considering his own aggrieved perspective to be self-evident. 'I know what you think of me.'

The older man nodded. 'Well, I'll admit that my opinion hasn't changed – but then, neither have you,' he winked.

Ben flinched. Norton seemed to be baiting him on his own doorstep, and until he found out why, Ben could not bare to lose face by bowing to such arrogance. He accepted the duel, and it was in this way that the balance of mind and mood he had achieved minutes before was toppled forever.

Ben stepped outside and politely gestured for Norton to take a seat on the garden bench. He felt that being able to remain civilised while engaged in vitriolic exchange would add a theatrical menace to his response. Ben sat next to him and asked, 'Why did you want to see me?'

'Call it professional courtesy,' Norton smiled with the contrived warmth of someone paid to care. Ben decided that sincerity must be one of the first things ministers are taught at God School. Norton's was almost convincing, and Ben had not expected it. He was disarmed. 'You are one of my parishioners,' Norton went on, 'whether you like it or not.'

'I have no problem with that. My residence in your parish has always been harder for you to deal with than it has for me – your *cross to bear,* if you like,' Ben returned, enjoying it.

'Only since that day in June when you proved to everyone that your restlessness is a bad influence on the vulnerable minds of the village.'

'Restless?' Ben folded his arms, but then immediately unfolded them to avoid a defensive posture that Norton might see as a sign of weakness. 'I feel very settled, especially this evening. I'm a new man. I've never felt less likely to incite adolescents to riot.'

Reverend Norton raised an eyebrow, as though he had been awaiting such an opening. 'Good. Time away from your rock'n'roll girlfriend must be therapeutic for you,' he suggested, his smile wolfish and his tone sly. 'Sporadic relationship, is it? Been a while since you've seen her?'

Norton had aimed well and hit a sensitive target, but Ben avoided asking how he knew of Lea's recent lack of contact, considering that such a question would be a further betrayal of weakness. 'It's not like that at all.' Show no fear, he thought, and show no pain. 'I wouldn't even call our time together a relationship for fear of scaring her off. We have an understanding. We trust each other, but she's a free spirit, and sometimes I don't see her for a few weeks at a time.'

'Well, that's one less trouble-maker in Little Arlingham, isn't it?' Norton replied with satisfaction. 'Don't get me wrong,' he added in response to Ben's angry glance. 'I like her – good dancer,' he chuckled, 'but someone unstable like her can't be good for someone like you, not when you're trying to fight your personal demons.'

Ben shook his head and stared wistfully into the amber dusk. 'No, she's good for me,' he said quietly, unable to deny his feelings, even to score points against Norton.

'So her prolonged absences *are* of concern to you?' Norton dived at the contradiction. 'You didn't seem bothered just now. What about your parents? Seen your Mum recently?'

Ben had dropped his guard and Norton had been ready. 'I don't want to talk about that.'

'Why? Because of your guilt?'

'Guilt?'

'Yes, at breaking up your family when you left home,' the minister reminded him. 'The conscience of even someone like you must be heavy after what you did to the happy Marchen home, what with your mother's disappearance, and your father starting an affair even before the marital bed was cold.'

Ben's composure collapsed and the game was over. Ben stood up. 'You cunt.'

Norton smiled and seemed about to make himself even more comfortable on the bench. 'So much for the new you. What happened to that inner calm?'

Ben began exhibiting the physical signs of a man preparing for violence. His face became flushed, his breathing rapid and shallow, his fists clenched, and his feet set themselves apart for the balance that breaking Norton's nose would require. 'Did you come here to provoke me?'

'Yes,' the older man said, nodding in a way that celebrated his achievement. However, Norton did rise from the bench and edge cautiously away. 'Tell me, are you still planning a quiet evening in?'

Ben's voice betrayed a tone of pleading as he asked, 'How did I make you hate me?'

'I don't, really,' Norton said. 'I just speak for my parishioners, even those who might worship at a different altar. When prayers for change go unanswered, my intervention becomes necessary. I'll see you later.'

Ben looked away in disgust and happened to glance at his car. The vehicle invited him to express his anger in the form of aggressive acceleration, and Ben accepted gratefully.

Norton hesitated as he reached the gate. The minister hung his head for a moment and then turned to meet Ben's glowering stare. The older man's expression had softened considerably, and Ben began to think that an apology might be imminent.

'I'm used to steering *teenagers* away from becoming the Catcher in the Rye, but how old are you? Thirty? Look, if I didn't think that encouraging you to move on was necessary, for your own benefit, as well as for the sake of my parishioners, I would never—' Then the cleric seemed to wrestle with himself and his words. He laughed suddenly and then opened the gate, pointing at the Toyota with a final glance at Ben. 'Don't miss your cue.'

'You're starting to sound like Mad Dog. Now fuck off.'

Ben disappeared indoors and re-emerged seconds later carrying his car keys. He slammed the front door, unlocked the Toyota, slumped into the driver's seat and started the engine. The car's tyres smoked and squealed as the vehicle passed Norton, who stood at the gate of the churchyard wearing an expression of infuriating satisfaction.

Storm

Dark towers of smoke stretched up into the evening sky like a gothic forest as the stubble of harvested fields was burned all across the Levels. Each shifting pillar met the low ceiling of grey cloud at a breeze-blown slant, and fields glittered as flying sparks danced like manic sprites in the heat above the burning straw. Rather than marking the end and renewal of the cereal year, this ancient practice looked like the aftermath of a pastoral apocalypse.
Combine harvesters, tractors and grain-laden trucks rumbled across farms all over Somerset, leaving rural roads littered with drifts of dust and straw, and fields occupied by giant golden bales.
Ben Marchen drove with wild ferocity for over an hour, the acceleration of the Toyota barely able to match the headlong momentum of its driver's rage. These feelings of anger and confusion, ignited by his conversation with Matthew Norton, kindled in Ben an urge to provoke confrontations with complete strangers, upon whom he might unleash disproportionate blame to achieve a cheap sense of control. He wanted to feel like a martyr. He drove too fast around the blind bends of narrow lanes; drove unreasonably slowly with impatient traffic behind him; over-reacted to other drivers' lack of indication at turnings, and used the Toyota's horn mercilessly against every other road-user.
Ben drove until, during a ninety five-mile-per-hour run along the A303 near South Cadbury, he was overtaken by the boredom of sitting behind the wheel. His anger cooled to sullen resentment as the prolonged dusk was pierced for only a few moments in the west by the dying embers of the sun. Its crimson rays breached the grey haze above the horizon, striking the Mendips in slanting shafts between the dark spires of smoke.
Ben left the A303 at Sparkford and adopted a less hazardous manner of driving, but he was still not prepared to return to the village. Instead, he took the A359 north, planning to stop short of Little Arlingham and drop into the Wyre estate. He had not made contact with Earthwork for three days.
Upon arrival, Ben found the courtyard deserted. The three Earthwork vehicles were parked inside the barn, and Georgina Wyre, who seemed to spend so much of her time there engrossed in hefty tomes of local history, archaeology or mythology, was nowhere to be seen.
Ben had no reason to linger – until he glimpsed one of the estate's harvesters presiding patiently over the barley beyond the grounds of Arlingham House. If the field had not already been cleared, this would be his last chance to walk among the crop circles below Meeting Hill.
He had been as excited by the pattern in the crop as everyone else when it first appeared. It was the first time Little Arlingham had seen crop circles. Ben had entered the field at the end of June with an excited throng of other visitors, and so many trails were trodden through the crop by the pilgrimage of sightseers,

tourists, self-titled cerealologists and UFO-spotters that, when viewed from above, the pattern of circles gained the impression of being tied to the field's borders, like coins arranged across a spider's web.

But Ben had not yet walked among the circles alone. Surrendering to the familiar lure of a lonely place at a lonely time of day, he left his car in the courtyard and crossed the adjacent paddock, passed the silent red harvester and found the barley still standing. An easterly breeze caressed the ripe ears of golden crop.

Ben did not know why the harvest machinery had progressed no further than the edge of this field, but it was clearly too late for the workers to start now, and he was able to view the constellation these acres boasted without fear of disturbance. The last trace of murky twilight faded as he strode contentedly into the thigh-deep barley.

Ben found Lea Granger sitting in the second crop circle he happened upon, and he saw that she was bleeding. Lea had extended her left arm out over the flattened cereal and was watching blood drip from a cut near her elbow. Leaning back on her other arm, she vacantly watched herself bleeding. Her face seemed a little paler, and certainly more drawn, since the last time Ben had seen her.

As yet unnoticed, Ben dropped his gaze and shook his head sadly. Not only had he seen Lea perform such an act before, he now knew her well enough to have discovered more intimate scars.

By way of explanation, Lea had talked to him about 'meaningful sacrifice,' though even after lengthy consideration of this response, Ben still struggled to discern the difference between ritual blood-letting and compulsive self-harm. He noticed that some of Lea's scars, one of which jaggedly traced the curve of her left breast, and others that crossed the dangerously vascular surface of femoral intimacy, were clearly very old wounds – older, he suspected, than the acts of Pagan piety cited as justification for her more recent cuts. But Ben would never discover the cause of them. Lea did not like to recall the difficulty of being fifteen-years-old; of changing, of being misunderstood and unpopular and unheard, or of failing to discover more satisfactory outlets for nihilistic thoughts.

Ben crouched in the barley to remain unseen while he watched Lea's silent distraction. The strengthening breeze swept the crop with heavy strokes.

'Hello,' he chirped eventually, rising to his feet and stepping into the flattened circle with an easy smile. 'Oh Lea – are you leaking again?'

Lea showed no sign of embarrassment or regret. She did not even lower her dripping arm. 'The body of the Earth is spent at Harvest Tide.'

'Draining your limbs isn't going to feed next year's crop, priestess.' He knelt down beside her. 'Let's tie that up.'

'I wasn't trying to fertilise the field,' Lea snorted. 'It's symbolic – I'm showing

sympathy for the land. The Earth gives and gives and gives of itself, and we just take and take and—'
Ben silenced her with a kiss. 'I love it that you're not afraid to talk this way.'
Lea pushed him away. 'Don't try to shut me up by patronising me.'
Ben was unrepentant. 'Ooh! A temper tantrum from the original hippie chick,' he laughed, more pleased to see Lea than he could express. 'That'll dent your karma for at least three lifetimes. You're going to be reborn as algae until you learn some manners, but it'll be worth it: you'll be the most well-mannered and respectful moss that ever covered a rock—'
Ben rolled backwards beneath Lea's attacking weight, and the wrestling, laughing couple rolled clockwise around the flattened barley.
'What do you think of the crop circles?' he asked, catching his breath and removing his T-shirt to wrap around Lea's sliced arm. 'Local hoaxers or alien joy-riders?'
Lea became serious as Ben tended her forearm. 'Either. I don't know. Take your pick,' she replied quietly. 'But they feel *inspired*, don't they? Even if they're man-made, they feel like they're supposed to have happened. There's something here, just like on Meeting Hill – a very subtle energy, maybe, or something in the air that has an effect on consciousness.'
'That's just the weed you've been smoking.'
Lea grinned. 'Want some?'
'Of course not! In fact, I'm going to phone the proper authorities right now and report your possession of grubby illicit substances.'
'Well then,' Lea replied defensively, 'I won't give you all the inside information on Geophagia, which is a shame because I know just how much your jealous little gang would love to get its greasy paws on news like this.'
Ben renounced his humour. 'You have news?'
'Might have,' Lea teased him, producing a tobacco tin from within her motorcycle helmet.
'Are you turning double-agent? Or just telling me what you want my side to hear?'
'It's your risk,' Lea replied, her fingers working deftly at tobacco and papers, 'but if you think I'd lie to you, Ben Marchen, then the time we've spent together can't have meant much.'
'I never said I didn't believe you,' Ben replied carefully. Lea seemed to walk an emotional tightrope when discussing issues of trust, and her balance above a dark, bottomless drop seemed wobbly. 'You know my principle: there's the rest of the world, our friends, jobs, Earthwork and Geophagia – and then there's us.'
Lea was silent for a moment. 'Yuk. Sentimental shit. Do you want the rumour or not?'
Ben nodded humbly, lay back on the flattened crop and accepted the first pull

EARTHWORK

on the joint. Lea glanced down at him with mischievous delight. 'Roedan wants to meet Earthwork. She knows who and what you are, and she's coming to Little Arlingham.'

Ben choked on the smoke. 'How did you hear that?'

Lea looked insulted. 'I'm the lead singer of the band fronting Geophagia's dance festival tour – I have my finger on the pulse, country boy.'

'So what does Roedan want to talk about, gypsy?'

'About why Earthwork wrecked our Solstice meeting, perhaps...?' Lea replied airily, taking her turn with the joint. 'She rescheduled and down-sized the Lughnasa festival because of the panic you caused last time.'

Ben shook his head, thinking about the news. 'It's useful to know,' he decided uncertainly, 'but if Roedan is serious about meeting with the committee, we would have found out soon enough. Are you spitting at me?'

'No, why?' Lea laughed. 'Is that something you're into?'

A drop of tepid water the size of a hazelnut landed heavily on Ben's chest. From the surrounding field came the sound of raindrops falling into dry earth. The frequency of these impacts increased quickly to a muffled applause, and soon to a drenching downpour. Ben sat up and gazed into the sky, attempting an estimation of how long the rain might last, but the cloud was of uniform darkness. 'I don't think this is a shower,' Ben said, surprised at how much he had to raise his voice to be heard over the rain, 'but my car is just—'

Lea silenced Ben by pulling off her T-shirt and then tugging excitedly at his shorts.

*

Geoff Marchen left his home in Carreg's End and strode purposefully through the village. He passed Alan Forrest, Sarah Conrad, Ian Longe and several friends on their way to the pub. They were in high spirits. Geoff overheard Alan say how 'strung out' he thought 'Ben's old man' was looking. He lowered his gaze and kept walking.

When he reached the summit of Meeting Hill it began to rain heavily, but Geoff welcomed the downpour. He had heard the weather forecast and he was wearing a jacket. He hoped that the wet weather might allow him time alone on the hill in the darkness.

Geoff strode to the centre of the clearing and gazed down at the ground. There were daisies in the grass, and their scattered white petals were brilliant in the darkness, like a constellation at his feet. Geoff kicked idly at the earth, shook his head and looked up. The tallest of The Meeting's megaliths, known by the villagers as the Monk's Pillow, caught his eye. It was a sinister presence in the night, but Marchen felt no threat. He let his gaze travel clockwise to the next megalith, and then the others, idly counting each of the sentinels in turn. Twelve?

Geoff felt uncomfortable. He pulled his hands from his pockets and focused suspiciously on the twelfth stone. It was much smaller, and a shade darker than the others.

Then it moved. Geoff raised his hands and peered closer at the outline before him. The figure of a man wearing a cloak and hood became clearer as it approached. 'Feeling restless tonight, Geoff?' the old man intoned, taking another step forward. 'You do, don't you? Like something crawled over your grave.'

Geoff lowered his hands, but his expression remained wary.

'You have an itchy conscience tonight, and it's making you scratch so fiercely at the past that your fingernails have broken the surface. But what did you hope to find up here? Unearthing the past won't change it.' Madog pulled the hood from his head and fixed his gaze on Marchen's face as he stepped closer still.

'I bet you've been practising that speech,' Geoff replied quietly. 'But it was a waste of time. You don't need to appear like this to remind me of my position. If you want to ruin me, just make the phone call.'

Madog stepped much closer to Geoff Marchen than any other villager would ever dare. 'You know I won't, but you don't know why,' he declared. The older man stooped to his knees and ran one hand through the grass, searching carefully. With a grunt he exhumed the shard of mirror from the soil at Geoff's feet. 'You came here tonight because you felt your secret disturbed, and there's nothing like paranoia to give someone ants in their pants. So you've come all the way up here to check – but confronting your secret means confronting your guilty self,' the old man observed, holding the mirror up before Marchen's stony features, 'and that never gets easier, does it?'

Madog took a step back, pocketing the mirror. 'Until tonight you've been free to live with your secret without my interference, for two reasons. Firstly, I choose to live outside society and its rules. I live by a stricter, and perhaps less just, law than you, and for that reason I am generally hated, or at least feared. But I'm no hypocrite. I will not report a man to the authority of a system to which I do not belong.'

Geoff Marchen accepted the precariousness of his position, but he could not silence his pride. 'You're so full of sh—'

'*Secondly,*' Madog barked, and smiled slowly and broadly until the rain was able to collect in the well above his cheekbones, 'the Law to which I'm subject does not secure my obedience by threatening punishment. Instead, it repays my humility with opportunities to use situations, like this one, to my advantage – *not,* like Her Majesty's laws, to pursue public interest.'

'So you're the vengeful type?' Geoff accused him, though struggled to meet Madog's intense stare. 'I didn't think that was your way.'

'Then ignorance of my ways is your weakness. You're going to repay me for keeping your secret, and for preserving your liberty for more years than you deserved. I am very much the vengeful type – as is Nature, whom I serve, whose justice I respect, and by whom I profit.'

Marchen tried to seem bored. 'Which means...?'

'Which means that it no longer serves my purpose to let you live here in peace. I want you removed from Carreg's End, and gone from my sphere of influence and interests. They don't concern you, and you don't understand them – you just blundered into this chain of events when your wife came to take my place. You will leave,' Madog concluded, 'so that you never have to face your son when he discovers what you are.'

Geoff groped with one hand in the darkness, as though seeking support. The old man's words were a half-expected, but no less shocking, revelation. 'You're going to tell Ben?'

Madog shrugged. 'I might not have to. He'll find out what became of his mother soon enough, and the timing suits me.'

Geoff Marchen sagged visibly in stature and in will, his head hanging and his legs weakening. Beneath Madog's triumphant glare, Ben's father sank to his knees in the wet grass. 'But where should I go?'

The robed old man shook his head thoughtfully. For a moment his eyes entertained a flicker of sympathy for the figure kneeling before him. 'That freedom is yours,' Madog replied quietly, 'as it has always been. It'll depend on how keen you are to avoid prosecution by your law, and judgement by your son.'

Marchen leaned back on his heels, raised his face to the rain and breathed deeply. He felt sick.

Madog turned away. Finding satisfaction in the fulfilment of his aims did not extend to taking sadistic pleasure in the suffering of another. He raised his hood against the rain and took several steps backwards into the darkness.

Geoff reached out and grasped with sudden panic at the space the old man had vacated. Marchen did not like Madog, but as soon as he felt the consequences of his past begin to stifle his freedom as surely and as finally as a noose, and when the air itself suddenly seemed too dark, wet and full of his own cloying guilt to breathe, Geoff realised with horror that Mad Dog was the last and only man able to help him.

But: 'Goodbye, Geoff Marchen,' *Y Deuddegfed Maen* said, and then he disappeared into the saturated night.

*

Ben and Lea made love in the crop circle and the rain, and they cared nothing for the irritations that might have seen less creative lovers off in search of shelter. The saturation of body and clothes, the tearing of underwear, the discomfort of flesh against barley stalks, and the exposure of intimate anatomy

to grainy mud was an enhancement of the experience for characters of their nature.
'Come away with me, Ben,' Lea surprised Ben by asking at the peak of their excitement. 'Let's get away and see Britain together.'
Dressed again, but still high on the expression of their passion, the couple clutched at each other in surprise when they heard riotous laughter emanating from somewhere nearby.
Ben and Lea decided to follow the sound over the first deep tremor of that evening's thunder. They crept north through the rain-lashed crop until they found another circle pressed into the barley. There, after a cautious and slightly bewildered approach, they spied Craig Pearce lying on his back in the darkness. He was laughing up at the rain with a half-empty bottle of vodka in his left hand.
'Craig?' Ben asked from the edge of the circle. 'You all right?'
The younger man fell silent at this unexpected announcement of company. He sat up slowly, searching the gloom for the source of the voice and burst into renewed laughter when he recognised the unexpected faces. Craig spent further moments in the throes of hysterical laughter, interrupted only by fumbled efforts to sip from the vodka bottle, until he regained enough control to support himself on one arm and attempt an explanation. 'I'm sick, Ben – sick of being left out when— when we deal with the stones.'
'What do you mean?' Ben asked, sitting on the flattened crop beside him. Lightning flickered to the north, and then there was a distant rumble. 'You've been involved with Earthwork longer than me.'
'No, not with the *actual* stones,' Craig slurred. 'I mean, when we deal with the mystical bollocks that comes with 'em. From my firs' day with Earthwork, everyone just seemed to get it – you know what I mean? No one *talks* about it, but you all— all seem to appreciate, and *feel* the place in a way I don't get.' Craig enunciated the words *appreciate* and *feel* with exaggerated precision, and with exaggerated distaste. 'What is it with you all? Everyone who comes to The Meeting – even the people we send away – see or feel something that mos' of them can't even name! Or if they try to describe it, you hear words like *energy,* or *Celtic,* or *spiritual.* But what the fuck do they actually *mean?*'
'But why—?'
'And then there's Ian,' Craig went on, waving the vodka bottle through the rain, 'who used to be a proper God-botherer until he started spending half his life on the hill, and going out with a girl who wears Pag'nism like a fashion 'sessory – and he has that knowing, *arrogant* little smirk! And him and Alan understand the stuff George goes on about when she's explaining whatever Geophag'a's up to, or those people with their non-bio machines— and as for you two: you're neck-deep in this whole fairy-shaggin', otherworldly bullshit, and p'rhaps—' Craig paused to compose himself as far as the drink would

allow, lowering his voice and pointing with considerable disorientation: 'perhaps I want to understand it too. I want to find meaning in things that I didn't put there. You all belong together because you just *get it,* even if you don't discuss it. 'S like a fuckin' conspiracy. I want to belong too, and I have to thank Dr Vladivar here for giving me the guts to admit it.'
Craig raised the bottle and drank deeply, giving Ben time to swallow his pride in preparation for his reply. Lea watched the exchange with amused concentration.
'I'm not drunk, Craig,' Ben said, watching Craig's eyes roll with the impact of the alcohol, 'so I haven't got the same excuse for being so honest, but I think everyone recognises the effort you make for the committee. We haven't always got on so well – me and you are very different. But here we both are, sitting in a crop circle in the dark. You don't know what you're looking for, and to be honest I can't say I know what I'm here looking for either.'
Craig listened with an expression of soft, glazed gratitude which, again, he might have been incapable of revealing without the vodka. But Ben had said something that Craig needed to hear, and it made Ben a little uncomfortable. This was as close as the two men had ever come to friendship after months of rivalry and sarcasm.
'So,' Ben tried to restore a less sentimental tone to his voice, 'has it worked?'
Craig frowned. 'What?'
'Getting pissed in the rain in a field at night. Has it opened the door for you? Do you feel enlightened now?'
Craig grinned widely and maniacally, holding the vodka bottle against his cheek and leering, 'Oh *yeah!'*
The attentions of all three people were captured by a sudden light in the sky to the west. An amber flame, trailing sparks, shot up out of the trees crowning Meeting Hill and climbed swiftly into the night sky. Ben, Craig and Lea watched its steep trajectory, their faces raised to the rain. The light reached the zenith of its flight, hovered, and then fell back towards the Earth, drifting slightly on the breeze, until it struck the ground near the edge of the field.
'Well, I don't see that very often,' Craig muttered, glancing at his vodka bottle, and rising shakily to his feet. 'Wassit? A flare?'
'Don't think so,' Lea replied, turning to gaze at Ben, who of all those present was the only person not to show any surprise. 'Flares last longer. What do you think, Ben?'
Ben also stood to consider the silhouette view of Meeting Hill against the street-light glow of the village. He shivered slightly. 'I think it means I have to go up to the stones,' he said. He glanced at Craig and Lea in turn, and then strode into the barley.
'There!' Craig pointed after him, swaying dangerously. 'You see? *Summoned* to the hill by a light in the sky! This is what I'm talking about, and Ben acts

like it happens all the time.'
Lea looked at Ben, then Craig. 'You need to go back,' she told him. 'You're pissed and wet and cold. I'll see what this is about and tell you later. Go on.'
'Wahey!' Craig cheered as Lea hurried away. 'Never thought the bossy type would turn you on, Benny!'
'Ben,' Lea called, wading through the crop in his wake. 'What's happening?'
Ben stopped and turned, his expression revealing nothing in the darkness. Craig's laughter reached him through the rain. 'I'm sorry, Lea. I'm having a very strange day. Are you coming with me? I think you're the only person in the world who'll appreciate this.'
Lea was excited by the turn of events, and by this mysterious new facet of Ben's life. 'All what? What's up there?'
Ben thought about it for a moment. 'An old man, probably. This happens sometimes, but things have become stranger lately. He might try to give me some cryptic advice or— look, it'll be easier if you just see for yourself.'
Lea required no encouragement. She followed Ben and cast frequent glances at his resigned expression as they strode briskly towards the hill.
At the edge of the field they discovered a smouldering arrow embedded point first in the soil. Lea reached for it, but Ben pulled her on into the deeper darkness of Meeting Hill's wooded slopes.

Craig watched the couple disappear into the night, their progress revealed sporadically by jagged tridents of lightning, and he felt as excluded from his friends' mysterious instincts as ever.
The fire in the sky had not been meant for him, and Craig was very disappointed about it. He knew that there would be a rational and all too human cause to the fiery summons, but even so: witnessing such an event in this wild circumstance was enchantment itself.
At least once in their life, Craig concluded, everyone should see a light in the sky meant only for them.
A male figure appeared at the edge of the crop circle.
Craig stepped back in fright. 'Ben?'
A pause. 'Why? You wish it was?' The voice was unfamiliar and sounded uncertain for a moment. Even in the darkness, Craig could see that the man was dressed entirely in black. 'You like hanging around with that boring twat?'
Craig did not need to identify the stranger to become defensive.
'You can't trust him, you know,' the man went on, 'or rely on him for anything. And people like him hang around their own kind, so I wouldn't trust his friends either.'
'You shouldn't,' Craig said, wishing he hadn't drunk so much. A dim spark of suspicion had been struck by the stranger's tone and was swiftly igniting

Craig's spirit-soaked thoughts. He reached into the pocket of his jeans for a knife, and he did not try to hide it. 'I remember you now, and what you do to horses.'

Craig was surprised by how quickly their strained conversation was cut short by violence. Fights, in Craig's experience, are usually preceded by a much longer exchange of insults before blows are swung. Both sides of a confrontation use angry verbals to judge their opponent's strength, and to talk up the adrenaline required to throw punches. In this instance, though, Craig was given no time to adopt a firmer stance. The dark stranger launched himself into the circle of flattened barley and forced Craig to the ground.

The two men fought for some time, both of them fit, both strong, one numbed by alcohol, and the other steeled against pain by the power of his jealous and obsessive anger.

They fought for pride in what both men believed to be self-defence, and for possession of the blade that would decide the outcome of this encounter, their grunts of effort and strain drowned by the quakes of the storm overhead.

Kennett and Craig rained gratuitous threats and insults upon each other as they struggled, their lunges and counter-attacks causing the men to travel a little distance across the field. Twice they were forced to release their hold upon each other as the minutes of hostility slipped by, both men wearied by the unparalleled exertion that physical confrontation demands of the body.

'You thought I was Ben, didn't you?' Craig breathed heavily as he wiped the rain from his eyes, and he laughed at his attacker's mistake.

'Doesn't matter now,' Kennett said, clenching and flexing his fingers.

After the brief and breathless pause, Craig and Kennett threw themselves back into the fight with an greater ferocity, both heartened by signs of the other's growing exhaustion. Punching distance was maintained for a further minute, but when Kennett managed to force one of Craig's arms into a painful lock, the pair collapsed into a struggling heap once more.

Insults were hissed through clenched teeth as the men grappled in the barley, and the first sign that a victor was beginning to emerge came when the exchange became a one-sided stream of obscenities. One of the men began to sense his strength failing, and the pitch of his voice rose with the pressure of escalating panic. While his opponent fell silent in renewed determination, the weakened man gasped and cursed his adversary and the outcome of the fight with a flood of ragged and incoherent abuse. These insults were then replaced by a single expletive repeated in flinching panic, and finally by breathless pleas for release when it became clear that the other had achieved a clear advantage, sitting astride the defeated man and pinning him to the ground.

Two rapid stabs of lightning illuminated the last few seconds of the fight. The first revealed the raised hand of a man, gripping something sharp and reflective.

The second flash revealed the silhouette of a trembling figure bent over the thrashing torso of his bellowing prey.

Silence fell as the darkness returned, but the fury of the Lughnasa storm continued to thunder the glory of the stronger man's victory, and lent voice to the agony of his victim's grievous wound.

Y Tŵr

Roedan considered the arrival of a heavy electrical storm to be a portentous and satisfying climax to the final hour of her meditation.

Tom Sutherland decided that the occurrence of thunder and lightning over *Pen Annwn* during their enactment of hopeful, if slightly desperate, magical ritual was simply a sign that the universe appreciated melodramatic cliché.

Their meditation proceeded without incident or obstacle, but Roedan sensed a silent scepticism in her friend's businesslike participation in the rites. It also troubled her that she had required the use of intimate persuasion to gain his co-operation. Still, though, he was co-operating, and contributing the kind of effort that showed an attentive, if spiritless, engagement.

She watched him carefully as she considered her suspicion. Tom sat cross-legged on the floor of the tower's attic space. The maze outlined on the floorboards had received a fresh definition of white chalk, and Tom was positioned near the centre of its winding route with his eyes closed.

But Roedan blinked her frown away and refocused on Tom's words when his quiet speech resumed. He methodically described everything he encountered in the depths of his trance: the choices he was presented with, the decisions he made, and the path revealed.

Tom Sutherland conducted the visionary search Roedan had begun, but Roedan remained his guide as to how this aim was achieved. She had struggled in vain to travel the imaginative geography Tom described, but she believed that he was granted access to the plane of ethereal landscape and waiting answers with her careful instruction, and in her name.

The candlelight filling the room's humid interior was a poor defence against shadow as the daylight began to fade, and it offered the ritual space of the folly a deep throbbing glow. Preoccupied, Roedan had neglected to close the windows' shutters. Dancing candle flames were reflected, refracted and distorted endlessly in the panes of antique glass, and occasionally dimmed by the storm's flickering white light, which etched the peak of Moel Siabod in epic profile.

Roedan seemed energised by the storm, and by Tom's steady progress around the last few feet of the labyrinth's path. Tom was also animated, though his excitement was wholly unwelcome. He was trying not to laugh. The timing of the thunder and lightning was stagy, and Roedan's pleading encouragement of what she thought was his inspired soliloquy threatened to spoil the earnest conviction required to conclude this charade.

The spine of the American's dialogue over the past few hours had been a slavish, though faithful, description from memory of the countryside south-east of Glastonbury, but he occasionally embellished his imaginative journey with fantastic features, whose descriptions were faithful to Roedan's own portrayals of the Astral Realm. During this narrative, Tom became sensitive to the enjoyable irony of his chosen conclusion to the search. The disruption to Geophagia's Midsummer celebration had caused Roedan to send her foundation's employees out in search of a certain Celtic cross design, and a name. Both, of course, were discovered in Little Arlingham – it seemed that Earthwork was closely affiliated with The Meeting, the monument at Carreg's End. Contemplating this fact in the light of his earlier decision gave Tom a glow of ironic pleasure.

A series of lightning flashes strobe-lit the room like silent machine-gun fire. Rain rattled at the surrounding glass and a rising wind began to whistle through the window frames, making the candles flicker as Tom edged into the centre of the chalk maze.

Thunder rolled. Tom nearly choked on a snigger.

Interpreting his shudders as a response to some visionary shock, Roedan leaned toward him in a gesture of concern, but restrained herself from making contact for fear of breaking his trance. 'What? What do you see?'

Tom knelt back on his heels and inhaled deeply, raising his head and allowing his expression of concentration to relax into a broad smile, as though in relief. With his eyes still closed he extended a hand to reach for the labyrinth's centre candle, homing in on its heat. 'Things have become easier. I think I'm close now.'

'Good,' Roedan encouraged him. 'Good. The path is coming to an end and revealing its destination. Don't strive any further, just look ahead of you and describe what you see.'

Tom's brow creased in contrived concentration, his eyes shut tight and his hand wavering slowly before the tall flame of the candle. 'I see… a hill, among fields.'

'Good,' Roedan replied. 'Now, let the presence and personality of this hill possess you; let it absorb you, express itself through you, and offer its name to you.'

'It… it's a green, peaceful place,' Tom said, his voice for the first time betraying a note of surprise. 'There are fields, not yet harvested. There are thick woods on the slopes of the hill, but a path winds up through them to the top, an d there are stones, huge stones, all stood in a circle, quite a few – but one of them moves, and there are—'

—Wings, suddenly, suffocatingly everywhere, beating inside and around his head; an angry clacking and a flash of black and white plumage—

'A magpie! And trees! And—' Tom's voice cracked in fear as he flailed uselessly at his own head. He had opened his eyes, but the dark place he described was not removed from sight. 'Oh fuck I don't want to see this! Blood! There's blood here— and that smell! Take it away!'

Roedan shuffled forward to support her friend, but did not yet want him to withdraw from such insight. 'Where, Tom?' Roedan touched lightly at his neck. 'Where are you?'

'Just help me away from it!' Tom's voice began to lose strength, shrinking from an angry holler into a frightened whine. 'It's dark! It's fucked up and there's nothing to stop me falling!' He flinched at Roedan's touch, knocking her and the labyrinth's centre candle away with a sweep of his arms.

Roedan landed hard on her back. The candle landed on the lower folds of her linen robe. Its flame leapt from the wick to the fabric with unhesitating passion and Roedan screamed in panic – a cry so fraught with terror that it gave Tom's senses the shock required to dispel their nightmare.

Roedan flapped at the fire but the action fanned the flames. Tom rose and held her still with one hand while he ripped the burning linen away with the other. Then he stamped on the rags until only smoke remained. He quickly turned back to Roedan, expecting her to need reassurance, or even first aid, but she was already distracted. She had picked up the fallen candle and was holding it reverently before her.

'I don't know where you were,' Roedan said, as calm as Tom had ever seen her as she replaced the now misshapen candle in the centre of the labyrinthine path, 'but tell me where you think it was.'

Tom felt a tremor in his chest as he breathed. Against his will, the American had unexpectedly found himself in a shadowy, hostile place, and although he had considered himself in control of his imagination throughout, he blamed Roedan, her practice and the powers she championed for leading him there. 'It was Meeting Hill,' Tom replied bitterly, 'but like we've never seen it, and I don't ever want to think of it again.'

'But you were meditating on the resting place of Arthur's funerary cross, and the path led you there!' Roedan replied, surprised by Tom's despondent tone. 'Your single vision is more convincing than facts gathered from a thousand scholarly texts—'

Tom cut her short by turning away. 'I don't doubt it,' he said, glancing through the window at the heaviness of the rain. 'You're right: there's definitely something buried on Meeting Hill. Whatever it is, it responded to our probing by treating me to a fucking hideous nightmare. Perhaps it doesn't want to be found.'

'A trick,' Roedan said dismissively, conscious of her nudity now that Tom seemed less of a friend. 'The stones of The Meeting are watched over by the old man I told you about, and he can conjure—'

'I don't care!' Tom barked, stepping towards the trapdoor. 'This is beyond even obsession now, and it's all become too real.'

Tom pulled open the exit. The smoky air was disturbed by a draft from below, and the room's other candles shivered at the touch of the cooler air. Tom paused briefly to glance at Roedan before stepping down through the hatch.

She looked hurt, vulnerable, and twenty years younger in the candlelight.
'Don't go back in there,' he advised her, nodding at the chalk maze as he descended the ladder. 'I'm not going to be here to pull you out.'

Summons

Pacing uphill against the net of branches in the darkness, Ben was assaulted not only by the trees and the undergrowth in his path, but also by the temptation to resist his own curiosity. The flight of the flaming arrow had been a summons, he was sure: a call so clear that Ben could not doubt its meaning. His instinct was to feel flattered at being the target of such an august signal – but after only a little more consideration, Ben began to think of it as a display of infuriating presumption. *Y Deuddegfed Maen* had aimed one arrow into the field east of Meeting Hill: not only had Madog known when and where Ben would be, he had been confident of a response.

Ben felt that he was being toyed with, and that his behaviour was being predicted and exploited by someone manipulative: a man who moved only in shadow or in smoke by day and thrived in the depths of night, as though to shroud himself with a perception of supernatural capability and influence. Worse, Ben could only conclude that rebellion against such a force was an aspect of behaviour accounted for by Meeting Hill's elusive Twelfth Stone, and perhaps even encouraged by him.

Lea remained silent throughout the difficult climb, even when Ben emerged from the blind darkness of the ascending woods. He stopped without a word beside the first of the megaliths he encountered and pressed one hand against the wet stone. The rain had stopped by then, but from all around them came the sound of water dripping from the highest branches into the grass. Lea stepped up beside Ben and ran a hand down his arm.

But the couple was given no chance to linger until impatience or questions materialised. A match was struck on the opposite edge of the circle and applied to a primitive torch – a thick branch covered at one end by a spirit-soaked rag – carried by a robed man. The flame jumped and grew until a quarter of the clearing flickered with amber light. Lea's grip on Ben's arm grew a little tighter, but Ben shook his head and led her on through the tall wet grass of the clearing. At their approach, the old man planted the brand upright in the ground and began to remove his saturated robe.

'Bringing a battery torch not easy or mysterious enough for you, Mad Dog?' Ben asked with the insolence he had perfected during these nocturnal encounters.

'Fire is cheaper.' The older man stepped out of the robe. Ben was surprised to find him wearing dirty jeans and a creased dark shirt beneath. 'But I can't indulge your cynical banter tonight, it would be disrespectful. I have difficult news.'

'What? No riddles?'

Madog retrieved the torch at his feet and studied Ben sternly for a moment, the play of the flame twinkling brightly in his deep dark eyes. He pulled a folded

sheet of paper from a pocket of his jeans and offered it to Ben. 'Your father has left Little Arlingham and I don't know what will become of him.'
Ben looked at the proffered note.
'You can't pretend that this news doesn't bother you,' Madog said quietly, raising the paper a little. 'You've not been friends with your father for some time, but that doesn't mean you haven't spent months missing him.'
Ben blinked a concession to this insight and accepted the letter. He unfolded it and angled its hand-written lines towards the light of Madog's torch. Then he glimpsed the curious expression of Lea, silent and watchful beside him, so he read his father's message aloud. 'Ben. There are things you will soon learn about me,' he quoted, 'and I don't want to be around when you do.
'I have not been a good man. Even my strongest apology will mean nothing when everything is known. I cannot even explain the things I have done. Pride and anger seem to justify themselves so well at the time, but they don't mean anything when they're not yours.
'I miss the way things were before you went away. I would have done anything to go back and change the way I dealt with it, but it's too late now.
'Hill View is yours, it's in my will that way. I hope you will be well and happy.'
Lea watched Ben refold the note and fix Madog with a searching glare. The letter had meant nothing to Lea, and little more to Ben himself, but the emotion that rose to his throat, swelled, and for a moment prevented him from voicing a response, had been stirred by the final two words of the message, which he chose not to read aloud.
Love, Dad.
'Where's he gone?'
'I don't know.'
Lea slipped her hand into Ben's and gazed overhead into the heavy oak boughs. The flickering light of the flame was reflected as a thousand golden stars by the dripping leaves. Ben followed her gaze and spied a magpie, hanged by its neck from a bough halfway up the trunk. A little further along the same branch was the weathered remains of an old rope which, Ben remembered fondly, had been tied there by his father when he was nine. Ben and Ian used it as a swing for several weeks, until a spiteful Alan had hidden in the tree and cut the rope near the top while Ian was riding it.
Ben was immediately struck by the coincidence of this reminder with the subject of the old man's news, but he quickly scolded himself for such naivety. Meeting Hill's Twelfth Stone was the author of coincidence, not a witness to it. 'How are you involved with this?' he asked, waving the folded paper in the torchlight.
'You need to be listening now, Ben, not asking questions,' Madog replied. 'Things have been building towards this for months, and now you need some

straight answers.'

'Isn't that what I ask for every time we meet? Why do people in this village enjoy sounding like crossword clues? Even the vicar sounds like the Delphi Oracle when he gets going.'

Madog smiled in satisfaction. 'Well, my brother has done only as I've asked him, and it led you here.'

It took a few moments for the statement to make sense. Then, 'Your brother,' he said, nodding as though the news had completed a puzzle he had only just become aware of. 'Of course.'

'But I need to reassure you, before your questing mind finds a way of blaming itself for your father's departure, that you have played no part in his decision to leave,' Madog said in such a sympathetic tone that a damp, fragile bubble rose from within Ben's chest and seemed ready to burst behind his eyes. 'Your Dad was a deeply unhappy man, and the reason for his removal from your life is the only secret that I will not tell tonight. You'll find out for yourself, which is as it should be.'

Lea achieved a clearer understanding of Ben's loss when Madog spoke of Geoff Marchen's absence with such finality. She gripped Ben's hand a little tighter.

'But why did *you* need to be the messenger?' Ben asked. 'I'd have found this out for myself eventually.'

'Not soon enough for me,' Madog admitted. 'I needed to see you receive this news, and for you to know the place it holds in my plan for you. I also needed your friend to be here. She needs to see how far out of her depth she is here before you follow her out of my reach.'

Lea stepped nearer the old man's pointing finger. 'Me? What about me?'

Madog answered her question, but as though Lea had not asked it. 'I don't blame you, Ben. Quite naturally you've fallen for a woman who displays characteristics you recognise in yourself: a degree of self-obsession, jaded naivety, a nomadic state of mind, and the grandiose delusion that you exist on the periphery of society to receive glittering destinies at the will of wild gods.'

Ben was almost flattered by the portrait, though when he glanced at Lea to share the appreciation he found her wearing an expression of rigid anger.

'But what concerns me is how close you are to adopting the childish, feel-good philosophy Lea has been taught by Geophagia. She's your girlfriend, so you can't be blamed for taking an interest – but you are meant for more. You are untamed and restless, the original fish out of water, and tonight we've reached the point where I can offer you everything you've proved yourself worthy of. I can justify your refusal to conform. I can restore and preserve the halcyon sunset you though you'd lost, and I can give your passion the purpose it has searched for. You belong here amongst the stones. Your friends protect the monument, but you can become a part of it.'

'So much for the straight answers,' Ben said peevishly to Lea. 'Listen Mad Dog, or Dungeon Master, or whatever your name is, who exactly are you? And what do you want?'
Madog locked his jaw with a visible clench, as though afraid of responding with knee-jerk insults to Ben's irreverence. It made his features gaunt and fierce in the torchlight. Faced with this expression, Ben expected a rebuke instead of an answer, but after a few moments' consideration, Madog met Ben's gaze and declared, 'I am *Y Deuddegfed Maen,* the Twelfth Stone of Meeting Hill, which is a title held by The Meeting's custodian for centuries. The Twelfth Stone is Meeting Hill's awareness of itself, and the site's means of expression and change. *Y Deuddegfed Maen* protects the monument, ensuring its preservation in a way that Earthwork cannot, and it is an honour to do so. The Twelfth Stone also manages the site's relationship with its neighbours, exerting a level of interaction that ranges from the kind of mutual suspicion I share with most villagers, to the more influential and protective presence I have shown you and your friends since before you were old enough to notice it.
'The choice of successor to this role is always made by the previous guardian of the site, and whoever accepts the title then holds it for life. Candidates are studied over a considerable period of time for signs of interest, aptitude, passion and commitment to the role, before finally being offered it. This is exactly what I have done as I've grown older and less capable. My conclusion is that you, Ben Marchen, are well suited to this duty. My brother and I have worked on a subtle – and often not so subtle – campaign of influence to bring you to the same conclusion, although I understand that my offer will be hard to believe at first.'
This statement had an effect on Ben that Madog was neither expecting nor hoping for.
Ben's afternoon of cathartic, insightful, though wearying, nostalgia had made the timely attack of the Reverend Norton particularly bruising. Then, as evidence of the severance of his last family tie, his father's letter had induced in Ben competing feelings of isolation, regret and confusion. Now, as the final but most punishing of the trials he stood that day, Madog's surreal confession was an additional assault on his weakened defences.
The collaborating priests of Little Arlingham had laid siege to Ben's commitment to live quietly in the village. His resistance was not yet breached, but he was tired, and his tolerance was sorely tested. Ben was vulnerable, and he sensed that he was beginning to buckle under the onslaught.
Madog and Lea saw Ben's attention waver and glaze. He turned away and seemed to focus on something among the flame-lit stones. He released his grip on Lea's hand and drifted away.
Lea watched him wander into the flickering shadows at the opposite edge of

the clearing. When she was sure that Ben sought only a little distance from their gaze, Lea rounded on Madog with an icy stare. 'Who the fuck do you think you are?'
The Twelfth Stone blinked and raised the torch safely above their heads as Lea closed the distance between them. Beneath the firelight, her rain-soaked hair reflected a smooth golden sheen. 'I thought I'd just explained,' he said carefully, but then remembered his words against her. 'Ah – now you shouldn't be offended by what I said, young lady. I have no criticism of you, only the cheap philosophy that Roedan has filled your head with.'
'Don't *young lady* me, granddad,' she protested, 'and don't mock my beliefs. Are you using Ben as a way of competing with Roedan? Is it some kind of guru rivalry?'
Madog seemed impressed by the idea. 'Guru rivalry? I like that. But you must already know that Roedan was once my student.'
Lea tried not to show surprise.
'A long time ago, even before I started thinking about retirement, a young lady named Jill Baynes was keen to take my place here, before more selfish interests led her astray. She wasn't here long. She decided that getting paid and becoming famous by spinning philosophical candy floss for the weak-minded was more important.'
'None of this excuses what you've done to Ben,' she replied, side-stepping Madog's defeat of her accusation. 'He's mentioned you a couple of times. At first I thought the idea of a mysterious old hermit watching over the stones was harmless folklore, but this—' she indicated the magpie above them, 'and all the interference with Ben's family is just sadistic.'
'You don't know enough about me, Ben or his family to make that kind of judgement,' Madog declared severely, and for the first time Lea glimpsed the old man's latent strength. 'You think I make decisions lightly? A Twelfth Stone has watched over The Meeting at great risk for generations. Two of our number have died in the bonfires of witch-hunters to uphold the dignity of our rank, and many more have been injured in the act of defending the site they loved, so if you think I don't know my business after so many great predecessors suffered to define success in this role, then—'
Madog paused to calm himself and swallow the threat that seemed ready to follow. 'Then you and I can never be friends,' he finished gently, glancing past Lea as Ben re-entered their sphere of flickering torchlight. The younger man's eyes were damp and bloodshot, and he seemed aged by a haggard expression.
Lea cast Madog a piercing glance and then turned to take Ben's hand. She studied his weary features, ran a hand through his slick wet hair and hugged him protectively.
Madog also stepped forward and attempted an apologetic smile. But, as though able to sense the end of their encounter, the flame of the torch began to splutter

and fade. 'My offer to you will remain open for as long as you need to consider it,' he said softly. The woodwind hoot of an owl came from somewhere above them. 'I won't push you for an answer tonight, but I want you to remember something: the meaning of your life was defined here on your eleventh birthday. You came and greeted these stones with a respect unusual for someone so young. You ignored the horror stories told by Christians to demonise the site, and you accepted The Meeting like a friend. Meeting Hill embraced you in return, and these stones poured their personality, majesty and allure into your innocent little soul. I saw you – you were captivated. Ian was there as well, but he's the most intelligent lad of your generation, and his rational thoughts drowned out whatever the stones had to say in the light of that sunset.

'Your life has been spent pursuing the memory of that communion ever since. It's no surprise you've been restless, and you won't be happy until you've devoted yourself to the place where your spirit was awakened and your life's priorities defined.'

A clear recollection of this childhood memory was conjured for Ben as Madog spoke, and tears came to his eyes at last. Lea felt moisture against her cheek, but as she pulled backed from their embrace to look at Ben's face, the flame of Madog's torch died, plunging the couple into darkness. No noise betrayed the old man's retreat, but Ben did not doubt that *Y Deuddegfed Maen* had withdrawn the moment his light had expired.

'Ben,' Lea said against his cheek, enveloping him so fully that his tears were prompted to rain freely into her hair. 'I'm so sorry about your Dad. What can I do?'

Ben shuddered once in a silent sob and sniffed stickily. 'I've not known my Dad for years. Since I've been home I've had reasons to avoid him. But now I know he's gone, it hurts to think I won't be able to patch things up. Both my parents are gone and I don't know why.'

Retreating into the south, the evening's storm rumbled and flickered through distant thunderheads with diminishing anger.

'What can I do?'

Ben breathed deeply against her. 'Didn't you say we should get away for a while? I think I'd like that. It's all getting to me, and I'm finding it hard to think straight. I think I'm even starting to see things.'

'Like what?'

'I can't— I don't think I can—'

Lea felt him tense as he struggled to answer. 'It's all right,' she silenced him. 'It doesn't matter. You don't have to explain. Everything will be all right.'

'Come on, let's just go.'

Hiatus

The events of Lughnasa marked a nadir in the committee's fortunes and were followed by a lull in Earthwork activity. Alan, Ian and Sarah considered it a period of respite in which to reflect, though Georgina Wyre felt no relief, only pressure to take stock of the committee's conduct, its failing support from the village, and other pressing issues in light of damaging public attention.

Late in the morning of August 4th, George spent time in the courtyard barn studying the headlines of two local newspapers, and an entry on page two of a national tabloid. Each of these articles concerned the arrest of Craig Pearce for the attempted murder of a man of No Fixed Abode known only as Kennett. The media was presenting the case as a landmark incident in the history of rural class-war. Kennett had suffered a stab wound just below his left collar bone and was described as being in a 'stable' condition.

George was not surprised by its interpretation as a violent foray across the social divide, but she knew that this was not the reason for the confrontation. Kennett had not suffered his injury at the hands of possessive gentry after ignoring an order to Get Off My Land. And, to Wyre's knowledge, Kennett had intended no direct action in the name of anarchy by his presence on the estate.

The Somerset Tribune also mentioned the coincidental disappearance of an entire family from Little Arlingham. Geoff Marchen and his son, Ben, had left the village without a word on the same day as the stabbing. According to the Tribune's local source, Geoff's wife, Sian, had also been 'missing' for several years.

George was not surprised by Ben's disappearance. He was notoriously wilful – yet he was selflessly passionate in his duty to help preserve Meeting Hill, and it was for this reason that George felt concern for him. Wyre liked Ben and hoped he would return. But George's concern was also for the committee: Lughnasa had cut two hard-working volunteers from the Earthwork team at a stroke.

As though these things were not enough for her to worry about, three further issues affecting the committee came to light, and George was accused of tactlessness by her peers when she called a meeting to discuss the first of them the day after the stabbing.

A faxed letter from Roedan, Founder of the Geophagia Foundation, was received in the estate office on the morning of August 2nd. The self-styled mystic requested a meeting with the Earthwork Committee to discuss the team's presence at Geophagia's Midsummer meeting. However, where the letter had said 'discuss', George had read 'complain about'. But Roedan gave the Wyres no chance to refuse. As a thinly veiled threat, Roedan expressed 'warm anticipation of informal conversation to avert recourse to legal channels of communication'.

Alan Forrest then announced that he was departing on a month's holiday. It was inconvenient, of course, but George could not deny that Alan had requested and been granted the time off back in May.

And, that morning, the Wyres received a letter from an archaeologist requesting permission to study the 'superlative' prehistoric monument on their land. A 'preliminary, non-invasive geophysical survey' would be made of the site. Then, depending on the results of this examination, permission would be sought to dig several sections across the hilltop to confirm The Meeting's age and search for clues as to the purposes, beliefs and methods of the circle's architects.

With her only full-time Earthwork companion flying to Peru to trek in the Andes; with Ben missing, Craig pleading for bail, and Ian and Sarah spending their free time offering the Pearce family emotional support, George felt lonely and a little overwhelmed by the decisions she faced. She did not know which to deal with first. As these concerns threatened to induce a headache, she swept the newspapers off the table with the wave of an arm and huffed sulkily back into her chair.

She stared past the cobweb-guazed eaves of the barn, through the algae-stained skylight and into the grey beyond. Rain pattered lightly across the timbers, and Wyre noticed with an expression of irony and resignation that, in several places, the roof was starting to leak.

*

The weather brightened on the eighth day of August, though remained changeable during the rest of the month. Any day during the following weeks might have dawned with sunshine, entertained showers and lightning by lunchtime and then cleared again in time for an idyllic summer evening. Yet the spell of oppressive humidity, which had drained Somerset of motivation and perspiration in equal measure for several weeks before, had been broken by the epic Lughnasa storm.

The absence of three Earthwork members was felt keenly from the moment they took their leave.

Alan Forrest's return was not in question, of course, and the date of his homecoming approached swiftly. But since he was George Wyre's only full-time committee partner, she missed his help with her concerns. There was nothing he could do that George was not already doing, but the reliable levity of his mood made difficult days easier. With Alan around to regard any looming crisis with his grinning irreverence, no situation ever seemed so serious. Anyone else involved knew that they would soon find themselves in The Bolthole with Alan cogitating upon nothing more serious than which Led Zeppelin song to request next from the jukebox.

Craig Pearce's return was not guaranteed, nor even expected. Though arrested for the attempted murder of Kennett, the prosecution did not believe that Craig's possession of a weapon was sufficient proof of his intent to kill, so he was eventually tried on an undeniable charge of Grievous Bodily Harm. Of course, George publicly condemned Craig's actions when required, and she wished that her previous exhortations for the young man to discard his knife had been stronger and more frequent. Yet she missed his dogged devotion to Earthwork duties. The youngest member of the committee had spent far more time on the hill simply watching over The Meeting than anyone else in the group.

Ben Marchen's absence was perhaps the least problematic, for both George and the wider team, but it was by far the most fascinating. As days and then weeks crept by since his disappearance, Ben's few friends in Little Arlingham became increasingly concerned. They even missed his entertainingly moody attitude towards work, committee duty and just about everything else that he was faced with on a daily basis. Ben Marchen could always be relied upon to tune into the emotional undercurrent of any situation, whether light or dark, high or low, and allow it to rule his mood for the rest of day.

But other residents of the village, who had staunchly maintained a muttering dislike of Ben since his return in February, now seized his renewed absence as a chance to state Told You So with triumphant vindication for a few of weeks. And then they happily forgot about him.

Sylph Embrac'd

Ian watched Sarah enjoy a peaceful moment that reminded him of their first date in the barley field in June. He considered both occasions to have been rare unveilings of the profoundest depths of a woman. Sarah Conrad's composure and reserve, worn daily to face even trusted society, was set aside for a few moments to reveal a bearing inexpressibly finer.
Sarah wandered barefoot through tall grass in vibrant sunshine, sedately weaving a path between the stones of The Meeting in a spell of silent grace that she wore like a companion sylph. Ian watched her from the shade of the bordering trees and felt no guilt for hiding. He felt only gratitude for this second sighting of something he knew he could not describe, and which would make him feel stupid if he tried to.
Ian did not consider that Sarah would have been inestimably flattered by such an attempt.
He felt, thought and recognised beautiful things about her, but he did not say them.
Neither did he realise that Sarah was growing bored with waiting for an expression of his feelings for her beyond commonplace endearments. The sentiment he voiced could have been said by anyone to anyone else, when what she wished to hear was something that could only have been said by Ian Longe to Sarah Conrad.
By the time Ian came to realise just how much Sarah might have needed to be shown this kind of recognition, Sarah had begun to interpret Ian's piercing foresight and bone-dry wit about other people as a tiresome, and extremely unattractive, cynicism.

An hour and a half before, Ian and Sarah had arrived at the entrance to Little Arlingham's village hall. They were immediately amazed by the media attention that the committee meeting had attracted. Ian quietly noted two television crews, several reporters and numerous photographers. 'Alan will be gutted he missed a chance to get his grinning mug on TV,' he whispered to Sarah, his face expressing indifference as a camera flashed in his direction.
Sarah nodded with an absent smile. 'Not exactly a film première, is it?'
Owing to the advertised attendance of a woman with the unusual name of Roedan, who was famously pissed off with Earthwork for some reason and rumoured to be present to give the committee a public drubbing that day, the number of villagers queuing for the public gallery was vastly increased compared to previous Earthwork meetings.
Ian saw people in the queue who had always shown faithful interest in the Earthwork project. But also waiting (and by far the noisiest element of the crowd) was a large number of teenagers attracted by the media presence,

mixed with Arlingham's members of the Geophagia Foundation, who were displaying placards and banners condemning Earthwork's invasion of their festival, and accusing George's team of heavy-handed control of access to a Pagan temple.

All this was further fodder for the journalists. Among them was a crew from the BBC, who saw the demonstration as an amusing instance of local squabbling, and who filmed it as a quaint backdrop to the story of rural violence by which they had been attracted.

Brampton and Georgina Wyre arrived together, Brampton dressed characteristically in a dark suit and tie, and George dressed in the way that Earthwork was used to seeing her. She had seen no reason to let the formality of the event interfere with her practical outdoor dress-sense and looked as though she might be about to go on safari.

Brampton had no greeting for Ian and Sarah, choosing to sweep straight past them into the hall to join Commander Balton and the other committee governors. George, however, stopped beside the Earthwork volunteers and surveyed the crowd and cameras. She looked tired.

Ian tapped the thick file she carried beneath one arm. 'Have you been up all night writing this?'

'Just a few bullet points for my speech – but whatever I say in there,' she murmured dejectedly, 'I think Brampton has much more, and much worse. This is exactly the kind of slip-up he's been waiting for to crucify us.'

Sarah watched George's expression sink from weariness into sadness.

'We've all worked hard and we've believed in what we've done, but Earthwork's reputation has been dented badly by one error of judgement and an incident beyond our control, so I don't think talking about *best intentions* will do us any good now. I think that public support – assuming we still have any – is the only thing that will allow us to continue watching over The Meeting.'

At that moment Roedan made a conspicuous arrival. She drew up to the kerb outside the village hall in her silver Audi and gave the motor a final rev before silencing it. Faithful Geophagia members in the queue greeted Roedan's graceful exit from her car with ecstatic cheering, while teenage boys whistled and made lewd observations about her preference for a large engine.

'I wish I hadn't agreed to this,' George muttered wearily, prompting from Ian and Sarah heartfelt though useless sympathy. 'But we have to be accountable to our sponsors,' she declared, and paced with heavy resignation into the hall.

Roedan stepped lightly into the space George had vacated and nodded a formal, and certainly not unfriendly, greeting at Ian and Sarah. Wearing a neatly ironed Earthwork uniform, Ian's committee affiliation was clear, but Roedan paid Sarah the most attention. Even though the weather was clear and warm, Sarah seemed dressed against a cooler clime in an ankle-length skirt of

patterned blue and brown, Doctor Marten boots, an orange T-shirt and a violet tasselled poncho. She wore the outfit to advertise a new range of clothing (hand-woven by the indigenous tribes of somewhere Sarah had never heard of) on sale in Tantric Trading, just across the green from the village hall. Her shop was popular with Little Arlingham's younger, identity-seeking generation, with tourists lured by The Meeting, and with the village's elder eccentrics. Roedan would not have looked out of place shopping there.
The Geophagia leader smiled at Sarah like they were sharing a private joke and then gestured for the couple to enter the hall before her. Ian turned to step inside, but stopped when Sarah gripped his arm.
'I can't go in,' Sarah said with a start. 'I feel smothered. I'll see you later.'
Ian responded with a shrug – a careless gesture he would soon regret – and then stepped into the hall, followed gracefully and watchfully by Roedan.
Sarah walked briskly across the green. Behind her, the media and public were allowed to file eagerly into the village hall, and the Earthwork Committee's August meeting was declared open.

Considering the public's heightened expectation of spectacle, the presence of local celebrity and the unusual issues due for discussion, no one expected the gathering to maintain its usual order for long. It lasted only until the Chairman, Commander Balton, announced the morning's agenda.
Alan Forrest's uniformed presence usually provoked approving whistles from one or two female members of the public at these meetings, but such excitement now seemed like dusty sobriety compared to the furore that erupted when Roedan, as a guest of the humbled committee, was introduced to the gathering. Cheers of support from local Geophagia members, who managed to occupy the two front rows of seating, brought disapproving glares from the governors facing the crowd on the stage. There were also unexpected jeers from senior local residents, who blamed this arrogant-looking outsider for the invasion of media and noisy teenagers, and knew that Roedan had arrived to criticise the committee they helped fund.
Roedan's presence on stage above the judgemental assembly bore no resemblance to the stance she assumed before her followers at Geophagia's festivals. From the way in which she had dressed in dark trousers and a businesslike blouse to the way she greeted the governors and attending villagers, Roedan's address was polite and formal, and even carried a convincing embarrassment at bringing her grievance to this audience. Roedan was not, her supporters in the front rows noticed with disappointment, playing the crowd – or, at least, not in the hypnotic style to which they were accustomed. Her speech was brief, concise, and – given the justification for her complaint – carried an unnecessary weight of humility.
Ian Longe, sitting pensively alongside the governors as the lone representative

of the Field Operations Team, could only concede Roedan's grievance, though he continued to feel that his team's actions were justified in the light of George's suspicions.

'So I regret to say,' Roedan concluded after only a two-minute speech, 'that I cannot accept the actions of The Meeting Hill Preservation Committee as merely the high-spirits of young people in search of a cheap night out. Too many Geophagia members claim to have been questioned by certain men – the same men we all saw jump into a vehicle marked with the Earthwork symbol a little later. This large vehicle was then driven recklessly through a crowd of hundreds of my followers. These trespassers were clearly part of an organised, and very dangerous, incursion into a private gathering. Governors, ladies and gentlemen, thank you for your time.'

The audience erupted as Roedan returned to her seat beside Brampton Wyre. Ian watched her fold her hands in her lap and gaze indifferently into the mingled support and hatred of the crowd.

Then she glanced at him, expressionless. Ian saw her blink, but was not sure if both her eyes flickered, or just one. He looked away.

The crowd's anger was not only directed at the stage. Various factions within the public gallery harangued each other furiously, but an observer would not have been sure what opinions were being expressed, or by whom. Ian saw satisfaction framed by the faces of Roedan's followers; he saw disbelief in the scowls of older villagers, and expressions of delight from the youngest of those present. A few wags at the back of the hall were chanting the anthem from *The Italian Job*, 'The Self Preservation Society'.

A sharp rapping from the stage demanded order, and Georgina Wyre took the stand with a prepared speech. Ian had no idea of its contents, but when George glanced his way while awaiting silence, Ian nodded support for whatever needed to be said. He kept his seat until George was able to speak, but then he stepped silently down from the stage.

Ian's retreat did not reflect his interest in the proceedings, and he felt confident that George knew him well enough to realise that.

Ian was suddenly worried about Sarah. He had not given his girlfriend's early departure from the meeting much thought at first. Her excuse for leaving had seemed reasonable at the time. But a recent conversation between the couple, which had taken place just as Roedan's attendance at the meeting was confirmed, had made Ian aware of something he had not previously suspected: Sarah felt extremely guilty about the committee's action at South Pennard, and especially about her part in it. Sarah did not share whatever justification the other Earthwork members had discovered to relieve their collective conscience.

But this was not Ian's greatest cause for concern. The nature of his anxiety was

far more personal. When Sarah disclosed her guilty feelings, Ian had responded with the kind of dismissive, and even derisory, comments more suited to the laddish banter he enjoyed with Ben, Alan and Craig. Such blunt humour had been a poisonous reply to the honesty of a trusting woman, and it had taken Ian some time to appreciate the depth to which Sarah might have been hurt.
Until that moment, Ian had thought his relationship with Sarah capable of facing and mastering any difficult situation. While sharing periods of watch over Meeting Hill, even encounters with confrontational people had seemed effortless as a couple. But now, Sarah's departure – not only from this landmark committee event, but from Ian's company and her own previous humour – inspired in Ian a need to find his partner, to talk to her, and apologise for not playing the part that relationships demand at precarious moments.

In the village hall, the attentive silence that greeted George's speech seemed palpably deeper than that in which Roedan's grievance had been received. George sensed it, and as a person unused to such a public role within the committee, was visibly unnerved by it. Her speech faltered beneath the weight of its own honesty. George's words were cautious, and her gaze flickered defensively. She spoke for a full two minutes before the assembly began to appreciate her comprehensive acceptance of Roedan's accusations. Earthwork, they began to realise, was simply confessing its guilt without any attempt at an excuse.
'With the benefit of hindsight, I can only concede that our trespass was unforgivable, irresponsible, and at one point even dangerous. I can also state that the action was not suggested or sanctioned by the committee's governors. In fact my brother, Brampton Wyre, quickly expressed his disapproval of my plan to infiltrate Geophagia's event when he learned of it. Furthermore, the five members of the Field Operations Team who assisted me in this plan were acting under my instruction, so it follows that all responsibility for this regrettable act must be assumed by—'
'I,' a firm voice declared from somewhere within the audience, 'have something to say about that.'
Georgina Wyre, her mouth still framed around the last syllable of her interrupted sentence, stared down into the public gallery from the stage with a startled expression.
An elderly man in the sixth row rose from his seat. Dressed in a white shirt, blue tie and brown trousers, and sporting a fresh trim of his remaining hair, Madog appeared ancient, yet vital. 'Miss Wyre, Mr Chairman, Governors: I would like to testify, with your permission. Miss Wyre is apologising for charges that she has no business answering.'
Commander Balton, straining for a view of the unexpected speaker, but as yet

unaware of his identity, was clearly annoyed by the interruption, though reluctant to deny such a civilised request. 'Your name, sir?'

'I am Madog, *Y Deuddegfed Maen,* The Twelfth Stone of Meeting Hill,' he replied formally as he edged his way to the end of row six. 'But most people here know me as Mad Dog, the lunatic from Chiron Dell.'

Cautious laughter accompanied Madog to the stage. People were not only surprised to hear the bluntest truth voiced, they even seemed impressed by it.

Cameras flashed around the hall. The media, particularly the local reporters, could hardly believe their luck. Anyone who had heard of this eccentric recluse, and who recognised him as the furtive presence that haunted the borders of Carreg's End, would have realised that Mad Dog's unbelievably well-groomed public appearance was nothing short of a revelation.

George Wyre, still overawed by this beautifully timed reprieve, almost forgot to step aside as Madog approached the stand. The old man, as weathered as an old oak and apparently as hardy, nodded politely and smiled at her. 'You and I should have spoken long before now,' he said quietly. 'We have a lot in common.'

George finally closed her mouth and returned the smile, silently agreeing with this unexpected, but most welcome, new-comer. She offered Madog the stand and retreated to her chair.

Madog wasted no time with pauses for effect. He glanced once at the seated Roedan, whose composure at Madog's appearance did not seem compromised, and then turned back to the expectant crowd. 'I do not venture into polite society very often, but I'm here today – with respect to Miss Georgina Wyre – to say the things that she cannot.'

George, who had reclaimed her seat beside Brampton, appeared self-conscious and uncomfortable, but even then could not suppress a flinch at the unabbreviated use of her first name.

'Earthwork is not directly responsible for its infiltration of Roedan's audience on the night of June 21st this year. In fact, Earthwork cannot accept much credit or blame for many of its recent acts. Any group of people which has pledged to act in good conscience, as this preservation committee most certainly has done, could not have acted in any other manner when in possession of certain facts.

'Until today, Georgina Wyre has been unable to prove her suspicions concerning Roedan's intentions, but I am only too happy to confirm those suspicions for her. Georgina and her team of custodians were *inspired,* shall we say, to find a way into Geophagia's Solstice meeting for very good reasons, although I will not attempt to explain those reasons now. Very few people here would understand them without background knowledge, and I suspect that fewer still would accept such a testimony from someone as strange as me.'

Madog eyed the crowd with a raised eyebrow, as though enjoying his notoriety. Ben Marchen would have understood that stare.

'But I can confidently state,' he continued, pointing accusingly at Roedan, 'that this woman represents a dual threat to our monument.'

A low murmur of varying emotions rippled through the gathering.

'Firstly, in the guise of Roedan, creator and leader of the Geophagia Foundation, she will return to Carreg's End with thousands of followers sometime before the end of the year, and anyone who has ever loved Meeting Hill will come to wish that they had voiced their protest here and now.'

The crowd's discontent increased in pitch and volume.

'Secondly,' Madog continued, having to raise his voice somewhat, 'introducing herself as a woman named Jill Moira Baynes at birth – an archaeologist of poor academic standing with a history of undisciplined and unpublished theories – she will request permission to visit Meeting Hill even sooner, if she hasn't already, only this time she'll come with shovels. She'll come in the name of scholarly interest, but let me assure you that her intentions are very selfish. She's just a scavenger.'

With what sounded like the support of the assembly, Brampton Wyre rose to Roedan's defence. He crossed the stage to stand and loom over the animated Madog. 'This meeting will hear no more of your unsubstantiated accusations,' he declared with a baritone that carried to every corner of the hall. 'As someone who lurks on the hill dressed as a plant to spy on people, your self-righteous attitude is outrageous!'

Madog showed no sign of submission to Brampton's icy glare, nor to the laughter of the audience. 'I'll stand down because I've said what I came to say, not because you're taller than I am. You're a hypocrite, Wyre – this committee was created because of the threat that your development plans posed to the stones. Your position as a governor is a joke.'

Madog turned away from Brampton Wyre with an expression of disgust and addressed the gathering once more before leaving the hall. 'In the future, when distinguished-looking people like those behind me talk to you of the need to *explore the secrets of Meeting Hill*, try to remember how vulnerable the site is. Remember the scars it already bears, and realise that the last thing Meeting Hill wants or needs is any more attention.'

Madog's final words to the assembly were received with a respectful, and perhaps even tentatively apologetic silence, followed by a thoughtful murmur as *Y Deuddegfed Maen* left the stage.

But only George betrayed any satisfaction with the old man's statement. She settled back into her seat and smiled with a contentment that eased the creases of tension from her face.

Ian looked for Sarah at Tantric Trading, and in her flat above the shop. Both premises were locked, and her car was parked outside, so he took Sarah's bicycle from the rear of the shop and pedalled around the deserted town. He passed the village hall but ignored the din echoing within. He pedalled into Carreg's End to look for her at his house, but did not find her there either.

Now sweating with the effort of riding an ill-fitting bike in the heat of his rising anxiety, Ian drifted back into the centre of the village and let his gaze drift slowly across the buildings surrounding the green.

The committee meeting reached an untidy conclusion. People began spilling out into the sunshine, and Ian studied the milling crowd for a few minutes in case Sarah had attended the meeting after all. But with no sign her, Ian surveyed the local horizon until his eyes focused on Meeting Hill's crowning trees.

It was an eight-minute cycle ride to the foot of the hill. He pedalled as far up the steeply ascending track as his fitness and the terrain would allow, and then pushed the bike into the trees on one side and continued on foot.

On the brow of the hill before the summit, the oak-framed view into the clearing from the footpath gave Ian a glimpse of the scene that would form a distracting memory for weeks to come. He saw Sarah drifting peacefully alone around the stones; but his relief was overshadowed by a sudden certainty that he was too late, and that whatever had come between them was already impassable.

Ian could not summon the nerve to attempt an approach, and yet neither could he bear to retreat and lose her from his sight, so he edged sideways into the green border of the clearing, moving silently through the trees until he found a position hidden from both the path and the stones. Through a low screen of fern and brambles, Ian witnessed a moment of Sarah's deepest serenity, and of her greatest vulnerability.

He realised with tearful awe that she was radiant.

After being alone on Meeting Hill for just over an hour, at first unsettled by troubling thoughts, doubts and questions, the affable midday Sun and the chatter of birds began to induce in Sarah a state of quiet reflection: a comforting sense of removal from the village and her own anxieties, and an intense, uninhibited appreciation of the moment.

Sarah would never know that Ian was sitting only a short distance away.

Half an hour past midday, soon after taking a seat against the largest of The Meeting's stones, Sarah became aware of a new presence on the hilltop. She heard the brush of leisurely steps through tall grass, whispering closer. When she leaned forward for a clearer view, she saw a familiar figure pacing steadily around the clearing.

After the dog days of June and July, in whose heat life in all its forms had withered and panted, and then the humidity and storms of early August, in which life and land had perspired the prayed-for rain as quickly as it fell, the comfortable warmth offered by the sun that day made the Earth respond with renewed vigour. Plants exploded in a climax of swollen blooms: celandines, ox-eye daisies, musk mallow, buttercups and Queen Anne's lace blossomed in a festival of colour to compete with the soft, seed-tipped grasses for sunlight. Roedan paced lightly through this knee-high abundance, stroking each megalith that she passed in turn, and her expression entertained a reassuring smile as she approached. She held the younger woman's gaze intently, and Sarah became sure that Roedan intended to speak.

Sarah rose from her crouch against the stone and smiled in return. Her conscience concerning Earthwork's previous conduct would not let her treat Roedan as the villain George Wyre considered her to be.

Roedan stopped to stand much closer to Sarah than the younger woman would expect a stranger to do, but Sarah was afraid that a backward step might appear rude.

'Hello,' Roedan greeted her with a slightly breathless smile. 'Sarah, isn't it? You know, the walk up here never fails to take the puff out of me, but it's always worth it. What a lovely day.'

Sarah responded easily to Roedan's warm and open greeting, just as most people did. 'I love it up here.'

'I know you do,' Roedan replied presumptuously, though agreeably. She held Sarah's eye and said nothing for an uncomfortable length of time. Then she seemed to remember herself and turned to wander slowly into the centre of the clearing. 'That's why you joined the village committee.'

'Partly. Well, yes, of course,' Sarah nodded, wondering at how she was able to speak so openly with a woman she had spent months suspecting of threatening this very site. 'But I first became involved with Earthwork because of Ian.'

Roedan turned back to her and smiled with what Sarah would have sworn was sympathy. The older woman ran a hand backwards through her hair. The sun glinted across the golden spiral pendant around her neck, and Sarah saw that Roedan was beautiful. 'Being in love opens so many unexpected doors, doesn't it?'

Sarah nodded. Roedan noted her silence with a rapid flicker of her eyebrows. 'Why didn't you stay to see the meeting? You missed a circus.'

Sarah laughed and looked guiltily at her feet for a moment. 'Because I knew it would be a circus,' she admitted, 'and I didn't want to hear the details of the stabbing again.'

Again, Roedan was direct. 'I wasn't sorry to hear of Craig Pearce's arrest,' she said. 'I know that he drove the Earthwork car through the crowd at my festival. He's clearly a reckless young man.'

Sarah became lightly defensive. 'I'm sure you don't know the history of the man Craig hurt. It was complicated... but you're right, Craig does have a temper. He's insecure, and he doesn't hide it too well.'

'And why are you prepared to discuss these things with me when your

Earthwork friends look at me like I just kicked a puppy?'
'Because I feel guilty about what we did back in June, and if— if the committee hasn't apologised for our behaviour that night, Roedan, then I would like to now. I've never done anything like that before, but even knowing all the things that George is worried about, I don't think we should have be trespassed on a private event. I even dressed the group up in what I thought would be a *disguise!* I'm so embarrassed. I just got caught up in it all. It seemed exciting, and I thought it was harmless—'

Sarah's voice broke under the weight of confession, and as tears escaped each eye to run either side of her lightly freckled nose, Roedan touched Sarah's shoulder. 'You can let go of that guilt now,' she said. 'I didn't want my grievance with your committee to provoke tears from someone so repentant. Now *I* feel guilty!'

Sarah sniffed, wiping at her eyes and nose. 'I suppose I'm upset about other things as well.'

'About your feelings for Ian,' Roedan said confidently.

Sarah blinked. 'How could it be so obvious?'

'Outside the hall earlier? It was obvious.'

'I don't want to hurt him. But I suppose that Earthwork is such a commitment for us both, and I associate Ian so closely with the committee that I can't have negative feelings for one without tainting the other.'

Roedan glanced up and down at Sarah's clothes. 'If I didn't already know better, I never would have thought of you as a vigilante like them. You seem more like a member of Geophagia than someone who would want to spy on us.'

Sarah could not voice her agreement with these words for fear of the changes that such an admission would bring about. So Roedan said it for her with what resembled concern. 'You'll be resigning your place in the committee, I suppose?'

Sarah felt choked by the emotion that rose to her throat again. Fresh tears spilled down her cheeks. 'Yes,' she managed as a hoarse squeak.

'But really you're crying because you think you want to leave Ian,' Roedan continued softly, and she stepped a little closer.

Sarah cried quietly behind her fingers, but Roedan placed her hands over Sarah's and lowered them from her face. 'Never hide your tears,' Roedan whispered, and Sarah realised how this woman was able to enchant a crowd of thousands. 'A woman is never more true to herself than when she cries without shame, and I doubt that many women are as gorgeous as you are when your cheeks and your eyes are glistening with tears.'

With a skipped heartbeat, stalled breath and unexpected elation, Sarah stopped crying and gaped at Roedan when she became aware of what was beginning to happen. Roedan brushed a finger across the corner of Sarah's mouth and stroked a damp strand of auburn hair aside. Roedan said quietly, 'Women always leave their men.'

Sarah frowned and shook her head, her breathing and pulse quickening as Roedan's fingertips touched the wrist of her left arm.

'They do,' Roedan responded to the denial, 'even if their relationship lasts a lifetime. Men can be unfaithful and restless in the short-term, but then, as the years wear on, they become docile, dutiful, and very, *very* dull. But there is longing in the souls of women that deepens with time. Men can't reach it, or barely even conceive of it, and after many years together, a woman can find herself as far from the man she shares a bed with as from a stranger. It's only when she looks deep inside to the source of tears, to find true shelter from the eyes of the world, that a woman may discover the demons she wishes to fight, the ecstasy in which she would wrap herself, and the fantasies that life buries inside her like guilty secrets. What part can a *man* hope to play in any of that?'

Sarah sighed heavily and nodded. She had only vaguely understood whatever Roedan was describing, but in Sarah's state of mind, the words sounded reassuring, positive, and right.

Roedan perfectly understood the effect of her speech. Sarah looked up and laughed, a little nervously. 'You know, I can't believe it's just us up here on a day like this, especially—'

Sarah's sentence trailed off as she felt Roedan's breath against her cheek.

'These stones are extremely old and very wise,' Roedan murmured. 'They realise that people wanting to know each other need time alone.' The tip of her nose traced the curve of Sarah's cheekbone. 'The Meeting knows that we are strangers.'

Ian closed his eyes and looked away. He clutched at his chest as though in pain, squeezed his eyes shut against simultaneous spasms of regret, anger, frustration and disbelief. The sight of the kiss left him so hurt that he barely reacted when a hand came to rest on his shoulder.

Ian opened his eyes and found Madog standing beside him, staring into the clearing.

'It would be best to try and accept this as soon as you can, young man,' Madog whispered. 'If you didn't already know it, all women leave eventually – if not always in body, then certainly in spirit. She might even be doing you a favour. If you were still together ten years from now, she'd probably be acting all distant, dreaming about the feelings and fulfilment that men are just too thick-skinned to realise women need, or whatever it is they believe.'

'Wow. Thanks, Mad Dog.' Ian raised the grin of an electrocuted man. 'You're a tower of strength and a champion of the underdog. Is there anything you don't know about, or does being The Omnipotent Old Fucker of the Hill make you an authority on everything?'

'No,' Madog said sharply, but softened his tone in light of the circumstances. 'No, but I always have something helpful to say to anyone who shows commitment to The Meeting.'
'It's not helping.' Ian glanced back into the clearing and saw the women strolling towards the footpath, talking quietly, Roedan with one arm around Sarah's waist.
Madog cleared his throat and studied Ian's forlorn gaze. 'If it's any consolation —'
'I doubt it.'
Madog flinched. 'Neither of them is acting as they truly want to,' he went on, his eyes following the progress of the women across the view.
'Yeah, they looked like they really hated sucking each others' faces just now.' Ian ventured out from beneath the trees as Roedan and Sarah disappeared from view. 'So what was it then? Ah, don't tell me – the mystical enchantment of the stones, maybe, oozing some sexual spell to make them sail happily to the island of Lesbos. Or maybe this is something you've inspired them to do to fulfil your great plan for us all?'
Madog's face became carved with grave sincerity. 'I'll forgive your tone, given the situation, but not for much longer. No, I think that Roedan is being savagely opportunistic, and Sarah is being spitefully vengeful. They both have a sense of being let down by Earthwork, and it's just pure luck that they've found each other as a way of getting back at you. That's all they have in common, and Sarah will come to realise that – even if it's too late to turn back when she does.'
'No,' Ian decided after a few moments' consideration. 'None of that is much consolation.'
Madog glanced away, for the first time seeming to wonder why he was making the effort. 'Then the only comfort left to you will be that there remains an Earthwork for those women to want to hurt, even after this morning's gladiatorial display of a committee meeting.'
Ian glanced at Madog beneath the green shade of the beech tree and finally noticed the revolution in the old man's dress sense. 'You were there? At the meeting?'
Madog nodded. 'Roedan's speech required a certain tempering with the truth that only I could provide. Whether or not they'll heed the warning, well…' he shrugged.
'The committee should feel privileged that you even appeared, and grateful that you spoke up for them.'
'Of course they should,' Madog smiled a flash of rare, but sparkling, humour. 'People should be grateful that they even caught a glimpse of me in daylight.'
In fact, Ian did, despite the circumstances. 'So if that wasn't the last monthly meeting of the Earthwork committee, what was it that saved us?'

When Ian's question received no reply, he did not even bother turning around to confirm Mad Dog's characteristically sudden departure from the scene. He set his question aside to be discussed with George later on, and then allowed himself the chance to appreciate what was, on such a fine day at the height of the tourist season, an unusually quiet moment on Meeting Hill. He wandered into the centre of the clearing in the glare of the afternoon sun, allowing the scene of his partner's infidelity to begin the first of a thousand replays in his mind. It was a necessary process, he realised gloomily: the sooner this memory became familiar to him, the sooner its recollection would begin to lose its painful impact on his heart and senses. When that happened, Ian knew, he would be able to talk seriously to his friends about getting over Sarah. Wasn't that how it happened in the past?

Eventually. But Ian also knew that countless nights of sleeplessness and a spectrum of emotions followed significant break-ups, long before the magic words 'over her' could be spoken with any conviction, and without feeling that those words were a betrayal of the woman they concerned.

Part Four

Autumn

'Come away, O human child!
To the waters and the wild
With a faery, hand in hand,
For the world's more full of weeping
than you can understand.'

W.B. Yeats
The Stolen Child

Alban Elfed

One of the hottest summers since the 1970s began to ebb. A freshness to the air hinted at the cold to come, and the breeze carried the faintest musk of turning leaves. The days would remain mild for one more month, but an urgency in the industry of local fauna confirmed that a rumour was being whispered in wild places: something vital was waning, and darkness was coming.
The vibrant pinpoints of blue, indigo and red offered by wild flowers on Meeting Hill bowed to the rusting, but no less dazzling, colours of the trees covering the slopes. The hill's cloak of sycamore, beech, oak, horse chestnut and birch gradually yielded bountiful shades of cherry, lemon and tangerine.
Such a premature ageing of the leaves came as a surprise to many locals after consecutive years in which the lush greens of trees lasted into November, and newspapers had been able to dust off their annual headlines concerning Indian Summers. But the people who bemoaned this year's comparatively early autumn were the same individuals who had, during the years when the sun's strength had outlasted people's appetite for it, talked nostalgically about chillier Septembers and frost at Hallowe'en.

Ben returned in mid-September after six weeks on the road with Lea. Their money ran out at the end of August and Ben had sold his pick-up to fund another few weeks of rail fare, camping and an occasional stay in a guest house. Yet despite expressing their wish that such travel could last forever, neither Ben nor Lea had intended the getaway to become a nomadic way of life, and both became conscious of the disparate demands that the approaching Autumn Equinox would make on their own interests.
The couple returned to Somerset and separated at Castle Cary Station. Lea stepped on to a bus heading for Bristol, and Ben walked home to Little Arlingham. Entering his rented rooms and closing the door behind him had felt like an immediate and traumatic divorce from the world, and he discovered that the only way of softening the impact of this sudden isolation was to relive and record his travels with Lea, recalling highlights of their journey around the West Country in a long letter that he wrote to her. Yet it was only as he completed the letter that he realised: Lea had never told him her address. This worried him since he did not know when he would see her again.
Villagers who proved keen to cite Ben's brief disappearance as evidence of a return to his wilder ways were grudgingly silenced when he pointed out that he had been away only a little longer than Alan Forrest, whose own guided trek in Peru had been far more adventurous and perhaps less likely to see its participant safely home.
It was around this time that Georgina Wyre discovered a renewal of motivation for her role with the committee as its members were reunited,

though conspicuously lacking Sarah Conrad and Craig Pearce. As the Autumn Equinox approached, George addressed the Earthwork team at a meeting one Saturday morning in the estate barn. 'If we can't beat them, we're going to join them,' she declared.

'Wicked,' Alan nodded, tanned and toned by his weeks in the Andes. His wide grin of infectious humour made up in levity what the team now lacked in numbers. 'What are you talking about?'

'I'll get to it. Firstly, I've commissioned signs to be posted on the footpath at the bottom of Meeting Hill. They politely request that no charcoal burners or candles are to be lit by visitors to the monument, on pain of being tarred and feathered by you boys. The stones are in danger of disappearing under a thick multi-coloured layer of wax.'

'They'd be nicely preserved under that,' said Ben.

'It's only a minor problem, but most of these and more serious acts of damage to the site, from people bringing tools to chip souvenir chunks off the stones to having pentagrams painted all over the hill, occur around the time of Celtic or solar festivals, summer orgies, Pancake Day, the Pope's birthday, Arthritis Awareness Day or what have you. Which is why I think we should join them.'

'Cool, man,' said Ben. 'I'll get a hammer.'

'*Join them,*' George continued, 'in the sense of being on the hill at the same time as the visitors. I propose than whenever a greater number of people wish to visit The Meeting, we should already be up there holding a village gathering of our own. We can get everyone involved, from the schools to the Cross-stitch Club, starting with the Autumn Equinox. It's Harvest Festival, and what do the children usually do? Take tins of out-of-date pilchards into school as a donation to the old folks' home? I think a traditional village dance on the hill would be a great improvement on that, and it would cover the hill with people we trust. Only the most committed, psychopathic vandal would attempt to graffiti or harm the site with forty school kids sitting around them making corn-dollies.'

'Genius,' Ian nodded. 'We deploy the villagers as a human shield.'

'Our own festival sounds like a good idea,' Ben agreed, 'and it'd be great PR for Earthwork to be seen involving the community that funds it.'

Ian made a face. 'What, we're a community charity now? What's next? If it's good PR you're after, what about the Earthwork Soup Kitchen?'

'You've turned into a bitter man, Ian Longe,' said Alan. 'Please don't ever fall in love again. You turn into Kevin the Teenager when you get dumped.'

Ian ignored him. 'Who can we call to get a harvest shindig off the ground?'

Georgina Wyre met with the head-teachers of the Carreg's End Primary School and the Little Arlingham Comprehensive, as well as the Women's Institute, Guide and Scout groups, Arlingham's folk bands and the Somerset

Small Traders Union. After only two days of negotiation, George was able to confirm and advertise the staging of a Harvest Festival and Ceilidh Dance to be held among the stones of The Meeting on September 22nd.

'It's like the Mayday festival we hold on the village green,' Commander Balton observed in conversation with George on the afternoon of the Autumn Equinox. 'We should hold more gatherings like this, Miss Wyre. Look at the local history books,' he went on, as though George didn't spend most of her time doing just that: 'Arlingham villagers used to find any excuse to dance up here when Meeting Hill was still common land, '
George smiled. 'I already have ideas along those lines.'
All around them on the summit, at least two hundred villagers browsed stalls of handmade crafts and foods, with all the tents and trailers positioned in the ring of space between the stones and the trees. Two marquees selling the ciders and ales of local microbreweries enjoyed brisk trade at the eastern edge of the clearing, and it was here that Alan, Ian and Ben stationed themselves with plastic pints of Levels Best (the South Cadbury Brewery's most popular ale) in hand as a procession of Little Arlingham's youth completed their ascent of the footpath. A long train of children and young teenagers filed onto the summit wearing circlet-crowns of woven wheat and barley, and linen gowns overlaid with sports tabards displaying each child's harvest-themed artwork. Two by two they moved into the centre of the clearing to dance to reels played by Weirdy Beardy, the local ceilidh band, around bale-mounted effigies of the sun King and the Corn Queen.
'Tokienesque, isn't it?' Ben said too loudly, pausing to burp under his breath. 'I feel like I've walked into *The Long-Expected Party*, or *The Revel* in that Hardy book – *Tess,* was it?'
'*Madding Crowd,*' Ian replied, taking too frequent sips of his beer. 'We did it at school.'
Alan sniggered when two dancing children bumped into the effigy display, making it wobble precariously. 'It's a good job we're here to get drunk and take the piss or else this whole countryside celebration of scarecrows and manure and haystacks would be in danger of disappearing up its own pastoral arse.'
The children's display lasted ten minutes, and then an invitation was made for everyone to join the dance. A member of the ceilidh band, a middle-aged man of old-school showmanship, rose to lead and instruct the willing dancers, most of whom had discovered their willing at the bottom of their third pint of Country Belcher.
Lanterns suspended between standing stones were lit as dusk began to fall and the dance went on, with silhouetted figures moving happily against the reddening sky and glow-worms flickering in the trees about them. The coming

night would have as many hours of darkness as the day had enjoyed light, heralding the beginning of the year's final quarter.

The fair was a success. The dance went on far longer than expected, as did the drinking.

Each of the afternoon's revellers fell into one of three camps: those who did not discover the strength of the local ales until it was too late and went home with headaches; the majority, who stayed on the hill and inured themselves against the cool evening air with even more Levels Best and dancing; and the rest, including Alan and Ben, who headed for the pub because they thought it too chilly to stay on the hill but too early to head home.

Ian Longe, his mood lifted and rendered slightly careless by the beer and the chance to dance with equally drunken women, remained on the hill until the end. The last frantic reel wound down, despite many villagers' cries of *More,* and the exhausted band gratefully began to pack away their instruments. The dancers bowed to (and into) each other, and then stumbled towards the footpath downhill.

Arm in arm for mutual support with a girl he knew from school, Ian saw enviously sober villagers begin to dismantle the stalls and lights around the darkening clearing. 'So, Karen, why is it that when you're drunk, dancing is the easiest thing in the world, but walking home seems impossible?'

The pair managed as far as the edge of the clearing before Ian had to stop and crouch in an effort to steady his spinning head. 'Fuck, what do they put in that stuff?'

'It's not what they put in it,' Karen said, 'it's how much you put in you.' She looked around unsteadily for support and happened upon one of her friends.

'I'm sorry, Karen, I don't have the stamina to be a real man and escort you home,' Ian mumbled, his eyes closing as he leaned back against the trunk of a tree. 'Do you have someone else to walk with?'

But Karen was already gone, leaving Ian free to concentrate on resisting his nausea. He raised his face to the breeze and gulped at the cool evening air.

'Make yourself sick now, or drink lots of water,' said an unexpected voice from the darkness behind the tree.

'Probably a good idea,' Ian nodded slowly, carefully, not thinking about the source of the voice, trusting only to the camaraderie of a fellow drunk. 'But I don't like puking.'

'Do it now to clear your head and then go to the pub. Ben and Alan are there, but don't get comfortable, you'll all be up here again in a while when the hilltop is empty.'

The last few words faded as the voice receded into the night, and then there was no one to answer him when Ian asked, 'Mad Dog? Why don't you give yourself a night off?'

Incite

Comfortable at their corner table in the Bolthole, Ben and Alan drank pints of a less potent brew. From the jukebox, Neil Young's *Old Man* competed with the jumble of voices and laughter that filled the bar. The pub was crowded: far busier than usual and – since most of the drinkers had already spent the afternoon together breaking ice – much more sociable.

'...And then he practically *admitted* that he and his brother have been playing mind games with me since February, man!' Ben explained, pausing occasionally to draw deeply on a cigarette. 'Me being so predictable and moody, they knew exactly how to play me, and what direction to push me in so that I'd end up in a state where I'd agree to— well, whatever Madog thinks I'm so suitable for.'

'It's like a conspiracy theory,' Alan drawled into his rapidly emptying pint glass. 'I don't know that much about the old man – you and Ian always took more interest than me – but he always seemed harmless, at least.'

Ben waved a hand. His own intoxicated gaze seemed surprised by the movement. 'You're right, man, I don't think Madog means any harm. I think he's just selfish, a bit mad, but perhaps ruthless when he thinks it's necessary.'

Alan frowned. 'So it's *necessary* for you to become the sorcerer's apprentice because he says so? Are you defending him? You can't just give up your life for— what? You don't even know what he's asking of you.'

'What life?' Ben stubbed out the butt of the Marlboro and lit another. 'I threw away any career prospects I might have had a long ago. I get only temporary work and I have no family contact. The only interest I might call a life is involvement with Earthwork. And from the way Madog was talking that night, I think that's all he's asking me for. It sounded like he wants me to commit to Earthwork duty twenty-four-seven.'

'Sounds like you're halfway there,' Alan replied after draining his glass. 'Madog's pushed you to a point where you're thinking of accepting – so call his bluff, dude! Don't let him play you.'

Ben exhaled a cloud of smoke slowly and contentedly. 'But he hasn't, has he? He's clever, but no one can *make* me do anything. He hasn't hypnotised me. Everything I've done has been my choice, and I haven't done anything out of character. All the old man did is make me see what I am, what I'm really about, and why. He's made me admit it and face up to it, and realise that I have nothing to lose.'

Alan shook his head. 'S'your funeral, buddy. Have you seen Madog since you got back? Has he hassled you?'

'No, man. Been avoiding him. If I've had to be on the hill, I've always been with you or Ian. Being away for a month helped put my head back on a bit straighter, but I'm not ready for him yet, and I've avoided the vicar completely.'

Alan blinked several times. 'The vicar? Why?'

Ben rolled his eyes. 'Have you been listening? Madog said Norton is his *brother.*'

For the first time in half an hour Alan sat up straight in his chair. 'You kept talking about Madog's brother, but you never said— shit, Ben! Does everyone know that, d'you think? I can't wait to see how the Bible-bashers react when they find out that their *man of God* is related to the local shaman!'

Ben laughed happily, pleased with the effect of his news. 'We're involved in surreal stuff nearly all the time, man – how can any of this still surprise you?'

'Come to think of it, the two old guys do look similar. You wouldn't think of it, though, would you? They're worlds apart – and why would a professional Christian want to push you into being the next bone-shaking witch doctor of Meeting Hill?'

'I'll tell you when I find out,' Ben said, waving over Alan's head as Ian stumbled into the pub.

Ian bought a round of drinks on his way past the bar. He threaded his way around the narrowly spaced tables and trailed a steady stream of beer down the backs of seated drinkers before he reached his friends. 'Hey, losers!'

'Word up!' Alan greeted him at this appearance of an unexpected refill. 'Did you get dizzy doing the *do-si-do*, you country dancing lightweight?'

Ian pulled a stool from beneath the table and changed the subject abruptly. 'I've been thinking,' he began, wiping at the beer spilt across the table with a jacket sleeve: 'you know that old saying, about how tomorrow is the first day of the rest of your life? I think we should find the prick who made that up and shoot him.'

'Ha!' Ben cried. 'This sounds like Mr Island of Calm's long-awaited rant about losing Sarah. Nice of you to open up to your mates at last, even if it has taken alcohol to bring it about.'

'First,' Ian continued regardless, 'the arrogant arse must have decided that what the world needed such a naïve, simplistic philosophy – and if he thought that, he must have thought that most people have fucked up so badly, they're capable of seeing the dawn of just *one* more day as some kind of rebirth. Well it's horse shit. There's no starting over. Tomorrow is just the *next* day of the rest of your life, after whatever you did wrong today.'

Ben encouraged him. 'This isn't bad for a drunken rant. Deep. So…?'

'So,' Ian went on, 'like everyone else who's ever been dumped, I've been waiting for the day when I can wake up and find myself in the position of being over Sarah, as though she was never there. But that's bollocks. I can't make my feelings for Sarah not have happened. I can't make her *not* have left me. The very act of waking up and checking to see if I feel over her is proof than I'm not. When that morning comes, I shouldn't even realise it because I won't be checking because I won't care anymore.'

Ben nodded, but he had finished humouring Ian. He simply agreed with him.

'But it's not just me I'm thinking about,' Ian said. 'What about Craig? Telling him that tomorrow is the first day *blah blah blah* is not going to cheer him up, or make things seem better. He'll still be in prison tomorrow, and the days and months after, and still have a criminal record with GBH stamped all over it.'

This statement silenced the friends for a few moments. Alan shook his head sagely. 'How many times did we warn him not to carry a knife?'

'Craig said Kennett attacked him in that field. I believe him,' Ben declared. His conscience had troubled him since he learned of Craig's fate. He had left Craig in a drunken state on the night of August 1st, and he felt as though he had inflicted Kennett on the village. 'Kennett was asking for it.'

'I'm sure Kennett had it coming,' Alan said mildly. 'But if Craig hadn't been carrying a knife that night, he'd be here now boasting about how he kicked Kennett's arse, and we'd be cheering him. But Craig made his choice. If anyone here deserves this year's Hard Cheese award, it's you.'

'Arse kisser,' Ben sniffed.

Ian nodded. 'Might be true.'

Alan frowned at the younger men. 'We might not be teenagers anymore, but I can still knock your heads together.'

'Not the arse kissing. I'm agreeing with *you*, Alan.' Ian turned to Ben. 'You've had a rough time. I lost a girlfriend and it was my fault, but you've lost your family and you don't even know why.'

Ben started on his new pint and smiled. 'On the bright side, I've inherited a house. And Kennett said private ownership of property was a *bad* thing!'

'What about your Mum?'

If the question bothered Ben, it didn't show. 'I've reported her missing to the Police, but I'm not expecting blue lights. I'm sure Madog knows something about it, but he's cagey.'

Ian was reminded of Madog, but as he was about to speak there came a request from the bar. 'Are the Earthwork lads here?' Carl Harper called. Ian, Alan and Ben turned in their seats to see Little Arlingham's retired constable wave at them. Ian was the first to appreciate the irony of being caught drunk by a notorious alcoholic. He stood warily, checked his balance and then crossed the room to the door. 'Everything all right?'

'Light on the hill,' Carl said urgently, clearly proud to have brought the news. 'Candles, maybe, but definitely flames – lots of them.'

'Aren't they still clearing up the harvest dance?'

'It went dark nearly an hour ago, but now there's firelight on the north slope.'

Ian nodded. 'Did you drive here? Can you give us a lift?'

Carl addressed only Ian during the drive through Carreg's End because Ian sat up front beside him in the old BMW. The Earthwork sentry celebrated the failure of the estate's new CCTV to spot firelight on the hill. 'Yes, I know I like my drink, and there's no point in a serious set-up like Earthwork relying on me as a watchman when I'm crammed into an armchair pickling myself.' Sitting behind him, Alan and Ben struggled to suppress laughter. 'But even though you've got cameras everywhere watching everything, who's watching what's on the cameras?'

'Good point.' Ian managed a quick punch at Ben's leg as Harper glanced into his wing mirror.

'How's married life?' Harper blustered happily. Ian jumped as Carl slapped him heartily on the shoulder. 'I hear you're moving in with Ben. What a pair!'

'Ben was very kind to offer me a cheap room when he realised that— that Hill View was free,' he replied carefully.

'But *Christ* – you two must be miserable under the same roof after all the knocks you've had. You must be walking round with faces longer than bog brush handles, eh?'

Ben could no longer control his laughter.

'You're not dropping us here, are you?' Ian asked.

Harper aimed the car's headlights up Meeting Hill's footpath and tugged on the handbrake. 'Does the committee allow vehicles up there?'

'We're pissed and we don't have torches,' Ian said. 'I don't fancy knackering myself on the walk up there before we've even seen what the trouble is.'

Alan leaned forward until his head appeared between the front seats. 'As Earthwork Field Operations Team Leader, I can authorise the entry of this vehicle for the purposes of the Committee's response to—'

Alan fell back into his seat as the car accelerated uphill.

'So *that's* how we silence your egotistical bullshit!'

Harper slowed his car for both tight turns of the ascending zigzag and entered the clearing at a crawl. The beams of the headlights reflected softly against a fine mist that drifted through the stones like a memory of the evening's gathering. All four men leaned forward in their seats to gaze out into the mist. The nearest megaliths were rendered stark and bleached by the headlights.

Ben said, 'There's no one here.'

'The lights were on the hillside,' Harper replied in a needless whisper, turning off the engine.

It took a minute for the men's eyes to grow accustomed to the darkness. When they had, each of them discerned an amber glow reflected by the branches above the northern slopes. 'I'll go with you,' Harper offered, opening his door.

'Could you wait here for us?' Alan asked. 'We might need you to drive for help if we're out-numbered by muscle-bound warlocks looking for Equinox sacrifices. Here's my mobile in case you hear screaming.'

Earthwork stepped out of the car and mustered around the bonnet. 'Stay

together,' Alan ordered. 'Act sober and let's not get into any scrapes. We're not fit for it. First sign of trouble, we run.'
'Didn't Churchill make a war speech like that?' Ian asked, but the others had started across the clearing. They passed the stones, crept into the trees, and as quietly as they could worked their way downhill until, lit from within, the glade sheltering the source of Meeting Brook rose into view.
Beside the clear and constant flow of the spring, bathed in the light of countless tea-light candles, a shaven-headed woman piled incense onto glowing charcoal in a clay censer. Its sweet smoke rose around her like a djinn released, smudging the candlelit space between trees and sliding through the overhead leaves like water around pebbles. Lea Granger chanted softly, her words offered up to the night with the incense like a prayer.
The men immediately felt that their presence jaded the innocent scene, and they did not wish to interrupt her recital.
'For when the fair in all their pride expire,
To their first elements their souls retire:
The sprites of fiery termagants in flame
Mount up, and take a salamander's name.
Soft yielding minds to water glide away,
And sip, with nymphs, their elemental tea.
The graver prude sinks downward to a gnome,
In search of mischief still on earth to roam.
The light coquettes in sylphs aloft repair,
And sport and flutter in the fields of air.
Know further yet; whoever—'
None of the men thought they had made a noise, but something disturbed Lea's verse. She picked up and threw a fist-sized rock at Alan through the trees in a blur of movement that gave him no time to react. He yelped and stumbled backwards, clutching at his chin. Lea aimed another stone.
'Don't!' Ben called, jumping down into the tiny clearing. 'It's just us.'
Lea glared angrily at the three men and reluctantly lowered her arm.
'Wankers,' she snarled, tossing the rock aside. 'Is he all right?'
Alan cast her a like-you-care glance.
'What are you trying to do?' Ben indicated the nearest of many candles. 'Give Meeting Hill its second roasting of the year?'
Lea sneered. 'Please, you think I'd risk that? When I'm cleared up you won't even know I was here – just like your room in the village, Ben. I went there. Thought you could lose me by moving, did you?'
'I had to move,' he explained, and a hint of pleading entered his voice. 'I had a chance to live rent-free. I would have told you, but you haven't been around for weeks, and you've never given me an address or a phone number—'
'Hey,' Alan cut in, stepping down to stand beside the spring, 'don't distract my

colleague with personal matters. We're on duty. Why are you being so aggressive? Does being a skinhead make you need to lob stones and mouth off?'

Lea seemed almost chastised. Ben winced, expecting the explosive fury of a cornered animal. But: 'I'm sorry about the rock. You could have been anyone.'

'If you're nervous, here's some advice: don't sit by yourself in the trees at night advertising your presence to the world with four million candles.'

'I wouldn't be here in the middle of the night if you boy scouts weren't restricting religious freedom.'

'How's that?'

'The village dance and piss-up on the hill today – that was organised by your group, wasn't it? Thought you'd keep alternative visitors to the site away by crowding The Meeting with friendlies, did you? Well it worked. And just when I thought I had some time alone up here I find you lot perving at me.'

Alan relented a little. 'We're doing our job. *You* could have been anyone.'

Lea stepped up to Alan with a threatening finger raised almost to his nose. 'I know what you *think* you're doing, racing around in your jeeps and uniforms kicking us *undesirable* types off the hill; but if you felt even half the devotion that people like me feel for this place, you'd be up here on your knees every spare minute thanking The Meeting for such sacred ground on your doorstep. You call yourselves *custodians* of the site, but you've made conservation a mercenary and soulless hobby. It's just macho posturing.'

'We have nothing to prove to you,' Alan declared. 'I refuse to talk about conservation with someone who probably has ethical issues about mowing the lawn. Ian, Ben: I don't care if she stays up here, but I want these candles out.'

Alan turned away and paced uphill into the darkness without another word. Lea seemed pleased by the result. 'I think I hit a raw nerve.' She smiled at the remaining men. 'He's such a poser.'

'You know what we're trying to do here,' said Ian. 'And walking around all starry eyed and worshipful won't preserve the site. We get idiots with tins of paint up here sometimes.'

Lea's expression softened. 'You're different to Alan,' she said, picking up a candle and blowing it out. 'Your relationship with The Meeting seems more personal, like you mean it, and I think you'd be far more emotionally involved if Ben hadn't beaten you to it.'

Ian seemed not to understand. Instead he turned to Ben and made a decent impersonation of Alan. 'Ben, I don't care if she stays up here, but I want those candles out.' Then he too disappeared uphill.

Now alone with Lea in the candlelight, it was Ben's turn to take issue. 'I think you set this up on purpose,' he said, gesturing around him. 'You wanted us to come up here so you could get all self-righteous and shout at us. The speech about religious freedom was well rehearsed, but you know you're preaching to the converted. You wanted us to see you with your head shaved and these candles near dry trees, just so you could pull yourself out of whatever pigeon hole you're afraid I might have stuffed you into.

'I know you hate hearing it, but I've been in love with you for months, even though being in love with someone so moody is hard work. Decide what you want from me – and blow these fucking candles out.'

Lea did not watch Ben walk away, but she did listen to his brisk uphill step through the branches and undergrowth until silence returned to the glade. She gazed resentfully at the candles, heard the retreat of a distant engine, and then stooped to spend the next minute or so blowing the tea-lights out – save one. She sat cross-legged beside the stream with the single light between her knees, lit a cigarette from its flickering flame and blew smoke thoughtfully up into the autumn leaves.

Forgeries

Ben awoke the next morning on a settee in the lounge of Hill View, which had been home to generations of the Marchen family. He heard someone hammering on the front door. Ben raised his head, winced when pain erupted inside it, and glanced at his watch. He was late for a committee debrief, but was unable to hurry with a hangover. He groped about on the floor beside the settee until he found his cigarettes, lit one with a groan of relief and rose slowly to his feet.
Lea was sitting on the porch step by the time Ben reached the front door. 'Thought you were out already,' she said. 'I was just waiting for those people to pass by before I broke in for a bath.'
Ben noticed that Lea was red-eyed and dew-damp, and despite the pain in his head he felt the beginnings of arousal. 'You slept on the hill?'
Lea nodded. She stood to inspect Ben's round-shouldered stance and photophobic expression. She cringed. 'I've never seen anyone more in need of analgesics.'
Ian, also awakened by Lea's arrival, hung over and aware of being very late for the Earthwork meeting, stumbled out of the front bedroom. 'Hi, Lea,' he managed with a rigid wave. 'Thanks for calling, but you've given us our fair share of challenging observations this week. Now don't slam the door on the way out. Bye.'
Lea stepped into the hall and closed the door behind her. 'I'm not going to apologise for last night,' she said. 'Deal with it.'
'There, there,' Ian mumbled, trailing sarcasm into the kitchen. 'Don't be so hard on yourself.'
'Stay here, get clean and warm if you like,' Ben croaked. 'I'll see you later. We're late to meet George and Alan.'
'I'll come too,' Lea said. She encircled Ben's neck with her arms and kissed his nose. 'There's something I'd like to discuss with Earthwork, but I'd love a bath first.'
Ben and Ian had no stomach for breakfast. After getting dressed they sat facing each other across the kitchen table like grim survivors of something horrific. Ian was a little more composed than Ben, at whom he stared blatantly.
'What?' Ben asked, growing bored of pretending not to notice.
'I'm worried about you.'
Ben laughed.
'I'm serious,' Ian said, watching Ben smoke his third cigarette of the morning down to the filter. 'Put the fag out. Drink some water. Eat something green. What's wrong with you? It's like you're on a warm-up for some self-destructive rock'n'roll climax.'
Ben met Ian's critical gaze. 'That sounds really good.'

When Lea emerged from the bathroom she was wearing thick black eyeliner, brown lipstick and a black T-shirt that revealed a new tattoo of Celtic knotwork on her left arm. Ian scratched thoughtfully at his chin and raised an eyebrow. 'Hmm, something's different...'
'Me and the band are trying a new sound: something darker. I'm getting in character.'
Ben leaned back in his chair wearing a smile as proudly corrupted as Lea's new image. He stared hungrily into her flattered gaze until Ian rose from the table and scraped the legs of the chair across the tiles to break the spell.
'Who's driving?'

When Lea Granger arrived on the Wyre estate and claimed to have thought of a way of helping the committee, George Wyre became suspicious. But as soon as Ben had introduced Lea unceremoniously to those already assembled in the courtyard barn, George attempted to disguise the effects of the newcomer's mild affront to her capabilities with grandiose humour. 'Well?' she asked when the group was seated around the table: 'What have I failed to think of?'
Sitting among them with a mug of coffee, Lea glanced confidently at the people around her. Ben, Ian and Alan were slumped either forward over the table or backward at an angle that threatened a downward slide. But Lea did not recognise the other two men present. A short, shrivelled, fidgety old man wearing oil-stained overalls and a dirty neck scarf eyed her with malevolent suspicion. Sitting beside him was a tall, well-built man of around Alan's age who was wore a wax jacket and looked as though he was chewing shotgun cartridges.
'This is going to sound strange coming from me,' she began, choosing to look Ben in the eye rather than face the unblinking stares and intimidating jawing of the strangers, 'because you know me as a prominent member of the Geophagia Foundation. But with Samhain only a little more than five weeks away, I want to know what action you're taking to protect Meeting Hill.'
George exchanged looks with each of the men in turn. 'This is depressing. Up until now I've taken some comfort in Ben's assurance that you, as our only influential Geophagia contact, had completely dismissed any suggestion that Roedan poses a threat to our monument.'
Lea nodded. 'Don't panic. I still have no reason to think that Geophagia means to tear The Meeting down in search of Arthurian relics. Ben told me that Roedan applied to you for permission to dig on the hill under another name, but I don't think that makes her a potential vandal. Still, being close to Ben, I've tried to see things from your point of view, and having reached this frame of mind, I'm wondering why you're not doing more to dissuade Geophagia from landing here. If I was as convinced of this sinister plot as you are, I'd be more proactive. It occurred to me last night that if a group was heading this

way for the reasons you suspect, they might not be so committed to digging here if they could be convinced that whatever they're looking for is elsewhere, or that it doesn't exist.'

'Maybe,' Ben said, puzzled by the knowing glances exchanged by George, Baz and Abel. 'But even if we could do that, Roedan wouldn't want to make herself look guilty by suddenly cancelling her festival plans here.'

Lea reached into her shoulder bag for a tobacco tin and papers. A roll-up began to take shape in her fingers as she spoke. 'No, she'll want Geophagia to play here anyway. She lives to stand in front of an adoring crowd, and what better venue than The Meeting for a talk on occult power on the Celtic night of the dead? So yeah, Geophagia might still turn up – but at least they'll have no reason to bring JCBs.'

'How do we know you're not here taking notes for Roedan?' Ian asked, his voice desiccated by his hangover.

'I've come here to help and all you can do is assume the worst of me? Why not go all the way and say that Roedan seduced your girlfriend to leave a gap in the Earthwork team and sent me to fill it as a double agent.'

For one brief, memorable moment, Ian's face displayed an expression of shock.

'*Touché,*' Alan whispered at Ben.

'But you don't need to think that,' Lea continued. 'I don't want to join a club for people who hide their paganism behind uniforms and Land Rovers. I'm just concerned for The Meeting, and I admit that I'd rather not see Roedan bring thousands of people here to dance on the hill. It's not just another muddy field. So because of this – and perhaps also because of what she did to Ian and Sarah – I've decided to withdraw my band from future Geophagia festivals, and cancel my membership.'

This statement very quickly and clearly affected its audience in the way Lea had hoped. She smiled as she was showered with a chorus of *Really?* and *You?* and *No!*

'Excuse us,' Ben's voice rose above the murmurs. He left his seat, motioned for Lea to follow and led her outside. Beyond the barn's double doors, Ben glanced around for eavesdroppers, particularly in the direction of Arlingham House, and searched Lea's expression for any sign of insincerity. 'What have you done?'

'Ben not pleased?'

'Does that matter? Up until now your commitment to your music and your beliefs has defined you. What about your band? Won't they be angry?'

Lea looked uncomfortable. 'They might be. If they can find a replacement singer I'll be happy for them to play for Geophagia, but I can't be involved anymore. Anyway, Roedan doesn't own my spirituality or my music.' She shrugged, lighting her roll-up and picking a strand of tobacco from her tongue.

She examined Ben's earnest expression for a few moments and seemed to arrive at a decision. 'All right, listen – I lied in there. I said I have no reason to suspect Roedan of anything sinister, and that's true. But after everything we've heard about – like the committee meeting she attended while we were away, the dig application by Jill Baynes, and that business with Sarah – how can I help thinking that she might be capable of *anything?* If George Wyre is still suspicious after all these months, maybe I think I should be too – but I don't want anything more to do with Earthwork. The cause is cool, but you're all a bit too fucking Enid Blyton for me.'

Lea turned away.

'Where are you going?'

'I said what I came to say,' she replied. 'Your friends don't trust me and I don't need to be here.'

'No, don't go,' Ben said quickly. 'Why shouldn't they trust you after what you just said? And I'm afraid to let you walk away until you've given me an address. I wrote you a long letter I can't even post, and every time you leave I'm terrified I'll never see you again.'

Lea rewarded Ben's sentiment with nothing more than a shrug, but she finished her smoke in silence and returned with him to the barn. Inside, everyone had begun examining something laid on the central table. Ben and Lea waited patiently behind the huddled Earthwork until George turned to greet their return with a proud smile. 'This is why I wanted to speak to the team this morning,' she said, gesturing at the tabletop display. 'Your visit was well timed, Lea. I think this answers your questions about our continuing efforts.'

There, laid in a row across the table, were three foot-long cruciform plates. Of all those present, Lea Granger was most familiar with the design reproduced in triplicate before her; and, thanks to George's research, everyone else recognised the crosses instantly. Lea stepped forward wearing a delighted grin and touched all three lead plates in turn, gently running her fingertips over the words engraved in each.

The outline of the cross crudely resembled the way in which children often draw women. The edges of its horizontal arms and vertical 'head' tapered gently outwards towards rounded ends. The outline of its lower, much longer limb was also wider at its outer end than at the central junction, but this length ignored the convex curves of its neighbours to end with an angular spur, giving the cross a narrow central 'foot'.

'*Hic iacet sepultus inclitus Rex Arturius in insula Avalonia,*' Lea murmured as her eyes followed the words engraved across each plate. 'The cross that marked King Arthur's grave in Glastonbury. And the letters look just the same as Camden drew them.'

George shook her head modestly. 'There's nothing particularly scholarly here,' she said, touching one of the crosses as Abel Mild watched and listened intently. 'We just copied the drawing by Camden that you're talking about – but they are convincing, aren't they? Mr Mild produced the lead plates, and Mr Basildon, our Head Keeper here, turned out to be an accomplished engraver.'

'When he's not shooting things,' Ben added quietly, and then grinned brightly and widely when the keeper cast a frown like a thunderclap in his direction.

Baz had previously seemed more attentive to Brampton Wyre's commanding presence, and had regarded Earthwork with disdain. Similarly, Abel Mild was known for his persistent scrutiny of the team's activities, and for the whispered counsel he kept with the elder Wyre. These patterns of hostile behaviour had, understandably, led George to believe that both employees served her brother's wish to see Meeting Hill flattened into profitable land. As an employer, Brampton had always been the more assertive and vocal of the Wyre siblings, so it had seemed safe for George to assume that someone like Baz would be more likely to respect the determined leadership of Brampton. As for the engineer, Mild was an insecure man, nervous of anyone who did not live or work in the safe and ordered world of the estate, which had been his home for forty six years.

George was therefore as surprised as her colleagues when Baz and Abel allied themselves with the cause of The Meeting's preservation. George had been right: Baz respected Brampton Wyre, but clearly not as much as he respected the rural borders and heritage of the estate itself. Abel was always wary of relative newcomers like Alan, Ian and Ben; but when compared with Geophagia – a horde of several thousand strangers who intended to descend on the estate for a party – the Earthwork lads started to seem like close family, and previous rivalries were more easily laid aside.

The favourable reception of his work made Abel visibly swell with a pride that overcame his irritation at Lea's presence. 'It was hard,' he jittered: 'hard to do, even when you've worked wi' metal a few year. And Miss Wyre only 'ad a four 'undred year-old picture of the cross to go on.'

'From Camden's 1607 book, *Britannia*,' George added. 'There are two diagrams with minor differences of detail in each, but the inscriptions on both are identical to the engraving reproduced here.'

'Really, really... Mmh, mmh,' Alan croaked in what he considered to be a tone of scholarly contemplation. Despite a good general education and a reasonably broad mind, Alan Forrest's historical and cultural expertise really only extended to the rock music of the late 1960s and 70s, and the Brit-pop era of the mid-Nineties. So as George attempted to justify the accuracy of the forgeries before them, Alan perched his sunglasses on the end of his nose and nodded earnestly. 'And what we find, yes, actually, is that the more dusty old facts you give us about academic texts and archaeological theories, the less we actually listen, and the less chance there is of you getting to the point.'

'This is what the Lady of the Manor gets for trying to treat yokels from the village as equals,' George whispered to Lea, shaking her head with an expression of tested forbearance. 'The point,' she concluded succinctly, having to raise her voice above Lea's laughter, 'is that we should bury these fakes somewhere exposed and hope that someone else finds them. Then Roedan will think that the cross she's after has been found, and there'll be no need to turn Meeting Hill over looking for it.'

'What if,' Lea began, running a hand over her head to enjoy the novelty of stubble against her palm: 'what if Jill Baynes was granted permission to excavate a limited area of Meeting Hill under Earthwork supervision?'

'Then what?' Baz asked bluntly.

Lea picked up one of the crosses and showed surprise at its weight. 'She finds one of these, keeps it quiet, takes it home, festival passes without incident, Earthwork boys wet themselves with happiness, and grateful committee buys Lea Granger huge present. How about that?'

Contented nods from Alan, Ian and Ben. They huddled shoulder to shoulder and applauded Lea with patronising sincerity until the middle finger of her right hand warned them to stop.

'Good thinking,' George replied. She raised an eyebrow and suppressed a smile, indicating that she was about to attempt the kind of teasing that the younger men secretly enjoyed, but which made them cringe when she set about it in polite company. 'And to think, Ben,' she scolded him, 'that you told us Lea was just a doped-up pikey who sits around sponging benefits when she isn't kissing Roedan's arse.'

Lea glared at Ben.

Ben swallowed heavily. 'No I didn't.'

'We should get these crosses looking ancient and weathered and into the ground as soon as possible,' Baz suggested. 'What about tonight, after dark? We could bury at least two on Meeting Hill.'

'Ben and I will do it,' Lea volunteered, though everyone present seemed ready to speak up for the job. 'Doped-up pikeys enjoy hanging around stone circles when they're not sponging benefits, don't we, Ben?'

Hill View

Ben returned to his house with Ian and Lea after the meeting. As Ian's car pulled into the drive a magpie landed on the roof of the house and attacked the peaceful afternoon with its machine gun call of irritated clatter. The bird's plumage matched the Tudor facing of the cottage.

Ben frowned a sudden burden of superstitious anxiety. He saluted discreetly. The bird bobbed its head once, twice, and then dropped smoothly from the roof to plane away across the garden.

Ian unlocked the front door and Lea followed him inside, but Ben remained in the drive a little longer, critically inspecting the home of his youth: a property he had inherited so suddenly, unexpectedly and, it seemed, unfairly, from parents he had abandoned many years before. He winced at the small white windows, the rose bushes climbing the walls around the porch and the horseshoe above the door. It was a trite picture-postcard, and Ben found it offensive to his sense of adult identity, representing everything cosy and secure that he had spent so many years trying to avoid. Now barely even able to claim the dignity of working for a living, Ben felt that his sudden leap onto the property ladder was a betrayal of his politics and previous lifestyle. He shook his head and stepped into the house.

Ben and Ian invited Lea, Ian's parents, George Wyre, Alan and his most recent date to dinner that evening for a house-warming, and the afternoon they spent preparing the meal before their guests' arrival was a welcome distraction from committee business. The tone of Ian and Lea's earlier exchange was replaced by less caustic humour. Ben even felt comfortable enough to leave them alone with the cooking while he cast a critical eye over the sitting room's furniture and décor.

Hill View had not changed in the ten years of Ben's absence, except for certain signs of mild neglect. The familiar interior was haunted by stifling memories, and Ben suddenly wanted to destroy the cream leather settee and hurl its rubble out through an unopened window. He wanted to tear the dusty, sun-faded pictures from the walls and jump on them and paint the beige-and-white wallpaper blood red, or maybe black. Ben could not understand how or why his parents had resisted change to their environment for so many years.

He gripped the back of the settee and squeezed as frustration crowded his mind, still able to remember the last conversation he had held with his parents in this room: an argument, he recalled, concerning his treatment of Eleanor Wyre. He remembered swearing at his parents, and he could clearly picture his father's livid rage and Mum's dejected, powerless sadness. Ben simultaneously wanted to scream and to repent – to hurl punches at Dad's familiar anger and yet sit beside Mum and apologise for everything he had said, and everything that he would go on to do—

'Drinkez vous?'

Ben realised that he was grinding his teeth. He allowed the muscles of his face to relax before turning to Lea, who offered him a large glass of red wine.

'Ca va?' she asked on sight of his reddened cheeks. Pidgin French had become the running joke of the afternoon. Ben couldn't remember what started it, though it had probably been a self-conscious reaction to his first ever purchase of wine. It had made him feel pretentious and hypocritical.

'This house isn't mine,' Ben replied.

'Mais le vin banishé les ghosties, n'est pas?' Lea responded happily, pressing the glass against his arm.

Ben smiled weakly and held up a finger. 'Give me a minute.' He hurried out of the lounge to his old bedroom. Lea heard a squeaky wardrobe door opened and boxes removed, and then Ben reappeared with a rolled up poster and three drawing pins. Lea watched him knock a picture frame from the wall – a desiccated watercolour landscape he had painted for his Mum when he was nine – and pin the poster in its place.

'Kula Shaker?' she observed, deadpan. 'You think the *K* album is going to set the right tone for our *soirée?'*

'Why not? *Temple of Everlasting Light* is one of my favourite songs.'

'No. A true favourite is a song you'd want played at your funeral.'

Ben liked the idea. 'Maybe. But I'd let you decide what's played at my funeral.'

Lea was aghast. 'Fucking presumptuous of you to assume I'd still be around then.'

'Be flattered. Who else would let you control a crowded service devoted to their memory?'

'I'd do a terrible job and make you grateful that you're dead.'

Ben grinned at the reference and returned to the bedroom. Following further moments of rummaging sounds, the opening drums of *Hey Dude* filled the house. Ben accepted the wine from Lea and shuffled around the kitchen, but ceased abruptly when Ian told him that he danced like a cat in a washing machine. He retreated sulkily to the back door.

It was the prospect from this side of the house that earned Hill View its name. The wooded dome of Meeting Hill dominated the estate's rural scenery. The sun was beginning its smooth descent into evening and would reach the horizon just a little short of the hill's northern slope that night. Ben relaxed against the door frame, appreciating the sun's gentle heat, the glow of the wine and the laughter of his friends.

It was the last sunset Ben Marchen ever saw.

Alan's new friend, Carrie, betrayed no discomfort at being the only stranger at the evening's meal, and Alan's buoyant mood was lifted further by her presence. Ian's parents, Philip and Janet Longe, seemed relaxed and adaptable to the humour of the younger company, and enjoyed regaling George, Lea and Carrie with stories of the men's childhood antics. George Wyre seemed the most relaxed of those present, drinking more wine than anyone had ever seen her consume before, and growing wittier with every glassful.

Ben alone seemed unhappy, remaining silent unless singled out. He appreciated the company of his friends and neighbours, but he did not feel at home in Hill View. In consequence, Lea glimpsed visible relief when she caught his eye and tapped her wrist – nine-thirty, and it was dark outside.

The couple drew little attention to their departure. Most members of the party were unaware of their plan, but Ben and Lea did not intend to be away long enough to provoke questions from the lightly inebriated Carrie or the Longes.

Ben carried four items in a backpack as he left the house: a small torch, a trowel and two of the forged relics supplied by the Wyre estate staff. 'But perhaps we should be dressed in black and wearing balaclavas for this sort of caper?' Ben suggested, pulling the front door shut behind him.

Lea also carried a bag, though Ben did not think to ask why. Slung over her shoulder, it bumped rhythmically against Ben as she walked closer to take his hand. The gesture surprised him – Lea had never wanted to hold his hand before. Ben could not disguise his surprise, but he happily returned Lea's grip as they headed south through Carreg's End. 'You're an enigma, Lea Granger.'

'Thank you.'

'Never thought of you as the cosy, walking hand-in-hand type.'

'Cosy? Nah. It's just that you know the road better than I do in the dark, Romeo. I need you to lead me.'

'That's all right. I'd be very disappointed if you were conforming to the slushy behaviour of an *average* couple.'

'You soft sap.'

The road out of Little Arlingham at its southern border rises steadily as the houses and streetlights at either side gave way to darkened fields and woods. Drifting low in the south-eastern sky, the Harvest Moon burnished the world with a smouldering glow the colour of straw.

Ben and Lea felt unquestionably secure in the countryside at night, but as the couple neared the narrow turning to Chiron Dell, Lea stiffened suddenly. She gripped Ben's hand tightly and pulled him to a startled halt. Ben turned to study Lea's fixed expression in the moonlight and found her staring past him, up into the trees lining the road at the very foot of Meeting Hill. A trace of fear lined her unblinking gaze, but more apparent was the curiosity that deepened the intensity of her focus.

Ben stepped back and followed her line of sight, but saw nothing unusual until Lea raised a hand to point. Then, as he gazed into the shadows indicated by her hesitant finger, Ben began to discern a human outline amongst the sylvan silhouettes above them.

Mud caked his skin, but the old man's eyes cast a miasmic reflection of the moonlight.

Ben and Lea held their breath and stared as though frozen by the custodian's glare. Madog maintained his dendroidal stance, his arms outstretched, his elbows bent and wrists angled to blend with the branches he sought to imitate.

A few moments passed in tense silence before Ben tightened his grip on Lea's hand, pulling her away when it became clear that Madog intended to ignore their detection of his presence. The couple resumed their steady pace south, and Madog's head turned slowly to watch them disappear into the night, the amber Moon sailing in his eyes.

After glimpsing *Y Deuddegfed Maen* standing sentinel at the boundaries of his domain, Ben began to suspect that the old man had been awaiting the couple's arrival. 'I can't help thinking that we're following some purpose other than the one we think we've come here for,' Ben whispered, afraid of being overheard by the seemingly omnipresent Twelfth Stone. 'Mad Dog seems to have a way of arranging things so that I end up on Meeting Hill when he has something to say.'

Ben required his torch to negotiate the zigzag path through the trees. Frequent sounds from the depths of the woods revealed the life of the night around them: snaps and rustlings amongst dry undergrowth; the resonant hoot of an owl and the distant bark of a fox; the regular *thock* of acorns as they hit the ground, and the movement of branches that creaked like the tired bones of the ageing year.

Where the path reached the summit at the entrance to the clearing, Ben and Lea stepped back into the rusty glow of the Moon, and Ben swung the light of his torch across the space in which the eleven stones of The Meeting crowned the hill. 'Where shall we bury the first cross?' he asked when he was sure the summit was deserted.

Lea strode forward between the nearest megaliths, pulling Ben behind her. 'In the most obvious spot you'd bury anything in a circular space,' she replied, pacing steadily on through the dew-damp grass until they stood in the centre of the clearing. 'Here,' she decided, and began emptying the contents of her shoulder bag into the grass.

'What's this?' Ben asked, crouching beside her to pull the trowel and one of the replica crosses from his own backpack.

'Respect,' Lea replied, arranging and lighting eleven of the tea-light candles that had so offended Earthwork the night before. She set them in a circle around their position. She lit a roll-up with the eleventh candle and sat down, pulling her sleeves over her hands against the descending chill. 'We're digging into sacred ground,' she explained. 'The stones need a sign that we're doing it for them.'

'Hippy.'

'Twat. Come on, get it over with.'
Lea held the torch as Ben sliced a rough circle of turf with the edge the trowel. He tried to prise it free of the ground in as complete a layer as possible – a turf mat to cover the disturbance once finished – but he struggled against the deep, thickly entwined roots of the grass, and managed to extract only several crumbling clumps. These he set aside and began digging into the exposed soil, piling the dark earth he removed onto a plastic bag beside him. But Ben neglected to maintain the breadth of the hole as he dug deeper, and the cavity was only the width of the trowel by the time he reached a depth of eighteen inches.
'Needs widening,' Lea commentated, 'and it needs to be deep. No one will believe that a relic like this could go unnoticed only a foot from the surface.'
Ben sat back on his heels and silently handed Lea the trowel, but she immediately handed it back. 'Temper, temper. I just want to feel like I'm contributing.'
Ben returned to his task, widening the hole to a circumference greater than the length of the forged cross and digging to a depth of just over two feet. He would have dug deeper still if his trowel had not met resistance. He scraped at a gritty layer with frustrated vigour, noticing that the loamy scent of the earth was being replaced by fouler air. He turned away from the hole to wince at Lea. 'Uur. Do dogs bury their mess this deep?'
Lea cringed in return, her expression gargoyled by deep shadows. 'Smells worse than that. Dead mole? Badger?'
Ben poked at whatever opposed his trowel. He sensed some give in the obstruction, so stabbed the tool vertically into the earth. The metal penetrated a few inches further with a hollow crack, but Ben and Lea left it embedded up to its hilt in the ground when a suffocating stench rose from the hole like a ghoul, forcing them to retreat coughing from the dig.
The couple spent minutes gulping at fresher air until their nausea abated. Ben seemed to recover a little faster than Lea, and he stared thoughtfully across the clearing at their candle-lined excavation. Then he rotated slowly on the spot to search the surrounding trees for any sign that this unexpected turn of events was being observed. 'What are you up to, Mad Dog?' he muttered at the darkness. 'Why are you out tonight? What am I supposed to have found?'
As though in response to some silent reply, Ben turned on his heel and strode back towards the hole in the ground. He drew a deep breath and held it as he neared the circle of candles.
'Perhaps we should leave it,' Lea called after him, surprised by his sudden determination. 'Anything in the ground that stinks like that needs to be left alone, or maybe looked at by the police.'
Ben knelt down beside the hole, paused for a heartbeat and pulled the trowel from the ground. He resumed digging.

'Ben,' Lea called him, approaching the candlelight warily. 'Come away – this could be a fucking crime scene! Do you want your sweat DNA all over the ground if we've uncovered a shallow grave?'
Again, Ben offered no sign that he was listening. The pace of his digging accelerated. Then Lea's own words seemed to echo back at her, and it was at this moment that she began to appreciate the potential, if unintentional, tactlessness of her statement. She spent several repentant moments considering what Ben might be thinking about the discovery, and his work became increasingly frenetic as she watched.
Lea recalled Madog's camouflaged surveillance on the slopes below, and she remembered some of the things the old man had said at Lughnasa. Her conclusions regarding Ben's intense interest in his find began to take shape, and she winced at the possibilities.
Ben's fraught digging and breathing finally reached a distressing pitch of mania, and Lea's fear that Ben suspected some personal connection to the decomposing find was confirmed. 'Ben, I'm sure it can't be what you think,' she said softly, edging closer. 'Just come away. Let's call the police.'
Ben tossed the trowel aside and began to flail at the earth with both hands, scattering soil around him in an indiscriminate shower.
'Ben?' Lea persisted, though her voice cracked, and her continuing attempt at reassurance came in a coarse whisper. 'I know what Madog said about your Dad. I know what you must be thinking about— whatever's here, but you don't know. Just think about it. Could Madog really stand by and watch a man hurt himself, and then just bury him up here?'
Ben was sobbing now, but flinched angrily when Lea touched his shoulder. She stepped away, but could not force herself to withdraw from a clear view of whatever Ben was rapidly revealing in the light of the dropped torch. Lea also felt tears brimming in her eyes: seeing Ben like this was like watching him stumble blindly towards the edge of a cliff.
'Ben?'
Lea was seized by shivering and violent cramps to her stomach. She felt very alone. Ben's passionate focus made him oblivious to all but the frenzied task of exposing the remains before him. One by one, the surrounding candles were disturbed and extinguished by the flying earth. Ben simply tore at the ground with his fingers while his sobs degenerated into a breathless, childish whine.
'Ben?' Lea attempted once more, forcing a little more authority into her voice in an attempt to break his panic. 'Ben!'
The man on his knees before her stopped abruptly and reached for the torch in the grass.
'Don't,' Lea warned him. 'We don't need to see.'
Ben directed the torchlight into the ragged hole and revealed the outline of a human arm. The exposed grey ulna and adjacent radius lay against a dirty

layer of once-white material patterned with helices of green and blue lines, and it was this deteriorating fabric that provoked Ben's broken-minded howl. He released a cry that married a roar of unleashed fury with a doleful plea for mercy. He turned on his knees, pressed his face into Lea's waist and gripped her legs as though survival depended on their stability. In amongst his sobs she thought she heard the word *Mum*.

Lea's own tears came quickly in response, but she did not want Ben to hear her cry, sensing that someone in such distress could only be tormented further by sobs from the person they had turned to for support. She bit her lip, held Ben's shuddering head in her hands and rained tears into his hair with painfully suppressed convulsions.

At some abyssal level of his consciousness, the man kneeling before her registered Lea's overflowing sympathy with an instinctive flicker of gratitude, though too weakly to distract him from the trauma that flooded his reason.

Beneath the tangible shower of Lea's pity, Ben's mind began to dissolve.

Corpán Sídhe

Falling.

Empty.

Arms.
Tears.

Words. Ben?

'Who?'

The boy.

Recognition.
Recognition.

Beckoning.

Resistance.

Why?
Something happened.
When?

Before.

Before this.

What before?

Freedom.

Re*union.*

Better.

Downhill. Steep!

Water. Deep!

Which way up?
Why?

Light, *crimson light.*

Ignore.

Exhale.
Bubbles.

Inhale.

Inhale.

Better.

Fugue

Madog searched the peat-dark flow of the rhyne with a flickering brand that dripped embers like pearls of molten sunset into the reeds at his feet. He saw bubbles cloud and break the placid surface of the water around five feet from the bank, but they moved on with the current and were not replaced. Madog began to worry that this receding breath was Ben's last.

Madog's torch began to die. Its amber flame ebbed to a smouldering carmine. Deepening shadows made the Twelfth Stone's search of the water's unbroken surface seem increasingly hopeless. Then a strengthening breeze revitalised the waning flame, and its renewed brilliance revealed the surfacing of a limp body only a little further downstream. Trailing a length of weed from his waist, the man drifted with the current to rest near the bank and began to rotate slowly in an eddy beneath the roots of a willow.

Madog stooped and demonstrated surprising strength by pulling the man partially free of the water. He laid him face down on the bank and slapped him forcefully in the back.

'Ophelia you're not,' he muttered when the blows provoked no reaction. He fiercely pinched the man's earlobes, watching for any flicker of the eyelids, and then beat at his back until dirty water began to dribble from his pale lips and nostrils. Madog thumped him twice more, but it was a frustrated final slap across the back of the man's head that provoked signs of life. The man tried to sneeze and cough at the same time – a painful combination that induced a contorted expression – then began to leak freely from his mouth and nose. He inhaled deeply and rolled onto his back, his legs still immersed in the rhyne's stealthy flow. Madog nodded and stepped away.

The man opened his eyes. Willow leaves shimmered and flickered above him, moved by a gentle but insistent draught that chilled and dried his skin.

The amber glow by which he viewed these swaying branches also seemed slave to the breeze. Shadows danced.

The man was content with his effortless and hypnotic circumstance. Then Madog cleared his throat. Startled, it was with wide eyes that the man raised his head and met the Twelfth Stone's gaze for the first time. He pulled his legs free of the water and scrabbled backwards until he reached the trunk of the willow. He examined Madog's stern features for any sign of threat, and seemed particularly wary of the way in which the old man brandished a branch tipped by fire, as though it might be used to strike him at any moment.

'Does this cathartic outing mean that you're ready for me now?' Madog asked him evenly. He studied the younger man's fearful expression for some time, but gave up on an answer. 'Stand up.'

Shivering violently but too worried about what the old man might do with the burning club if he did not comply, the man pressed his hands against the roots of the willow and forced himself to his feet. Madog saw the resulting head-rush drain the focus from the younger man's eyes and the strength from his limbs, and the Twelfth Stone dropped his torch just in time to step forward and prevent him from fainting back into the rhyne.

*

Meeting Hill throbbed with the ice-blue light of emergency vehicles.
A cordon of police tape had been strung between traffic cones around Ben's untidy hole in the clearing. Wrapped in a blanket from a paramedic, Lea viewed the scene from beyond the ring of stones hoping to escape attention and questions. She was not allowed to leave.
Ian Longe had been talking to two police officers for the past ten minutes. He had little to tell them. Lea saw the three of them glance her way. Ian nodded about something and then strode towards her.
Lea turned away and gazed into the darkness between the strobe-lit trees. She looked as haunted as when Ian had found her an hour before, and even paler in the turquoise pulse of the lights.
Ian called gently from a wary distance behind her. 'The police really want you to talk to them. They understand you're upset, but they need to know *something*.'
Lea lowered herself to the grass and pulled the blanket tighter around her shoulders. 'It won't help Ben. And it won't help *her*.'
Ian sat beside Lea. 'Then tell me. I can tell them.'
Lea glared at him. 'We dug a hole. We found a body.' She looked away. 'Ben spent twenty minutes gibbering in my arms. Then he went quiet and wandered off. But I couldn't just leave her alone like that, OK? Can we go now?'
Ian fell silent for a moment, but only to relieve pressure before his next question. 'How do you know it's Ben's mum down there?'
'I don't. But Ben recognised the pattern on the mouldy blouse.'
'Was he sure?'
'No,' sarcasm twisted her expression into a snarl, 'he went mute with shock because that could be *anyone's* missing Mum down there wearing her blouse,'
Ian nodded and rose.
'Ian.'
He stopped.
'Don't tell them what we were doing here.'
Ian stared. 'How can I lie?'
'Because I did what Ben and I came here to do. One of the fake crosses is buried inside that cordon.'
Ian dropped back into a crouch beside Lea. 'You interfered with a *crime scene?*'
Lea returned his stare. 'Not really. I didn't disturb her. I planted the cross about

three feet from the hole then threw the trowel downhill.' Her explanation was defiant, and it made Ian fearful that she would be overheard. 'I'll never regret it. That body's fucked things up for Ben, but I don't see why it should fuck up a decent chance to protect The Meeting.'
'But if they find it—'
'Then it'll be an even higher profile discovery than we'd hoped for, and I'll have squeezed one good thing out of the worst night of our lives.'
Propriety prevented Ian from agreeing with Lea at that moment, but he suspected that he would come to discover sense in her reasoning. 'What do I tell them?'
Lea was calmed by complicity. 'Don't mention Ben. They'll want to question him. He's not fit for that.' She paused for a moment. Her ideas raised an expression of satisfaction. 'Tell them I was with you but got sick of your smug *Country Life* soirée, so I came here by myself for a walk and found the hole already there. Let the pigs work out who she is for themselves.'
Ian considered the risk he faced in ferrying lies but already knew that he would do as she asked. 'Stay here. I'll talk to them, then we can head back to Hill View. Perhaps Ben will be home by the time we get there.'

*

Madog returned to the hedge-screened sanctuary of Chiron Dell supporting the rhyne-soaked man, who experienced the stumble across seemingly endless fields as an oneiric assault on his awakening senses. These random, incoherent flashes would become his first hazy memories.
Consciousness had graduated to a more continuous, though still unquestioning, state of awareness for the man by the time his gruff guide lowered him ungently onto a broken bench at a reclining angle and left him blinking into the darkness. He looked up and saw a bottomless ocean of stars.
From a short distance beyond his feet came busy sounds: the brush of long strides through tall grass, a dry clatter of sticks piled and arranged, and then the striking of a match.
The trembling man lowered his gaze to the sound, and a pinpoint of flickering light became the centre of his world. The stars began to fade as the hungry spark ascended from its kindling to devour the conical pyre of wood. The breeze was robbed of its chill as the blaze became a bonfire. Flames filled Chiron Dell with leaping light, ferocious heat and flying sparks, and the man saw his guardian in silhouette wearing only a crude head-dress made of deer antlers and magpie feathers.
Madog assumed an acclamatory role. He gripped a six-foot hazel staff with his left hand and a chipped white cup in the other. The reclining man blinked against the light. When he opened his eyes again, the cup was held before his face and then pressed against his lips.

The man refused to drink: he already possessed a traumatic first memory of liquid that made him hold his breath and struggle. In response, Madog gripped his chin and pushed the beaker forward. The scent of warm spirit seared his nostrils. A shot of something instantly intoxicating filled his mouth. The hand pushed his head back sharply and he swallowed. Madog dropped the cup and stepped away.

The man tried to rescue his faulty balance and clouding clarity by focusing on his busy rescuer. He watched as Madog pissed an apotropaic boundary in a circle around them both. *Y Deuddegfed Maen* bellowed as he walked, challenging the shadows and haranguing the night, daring the world to deny the acclamation, and naming nearby trees as witnesses to it.

Madog's new companion strove to examine his surroundings and the circumstance to which he had surrendered, but he began to perceive these events as a series of blurred, non-consecutive snapshots, and Madog's voice as a distorted booming that induced pain behind his eyes. He felt weaker still, though he strained against paralysis to gaze beyond the man burnished so vividly down one side by the light of the fire. There – a glimpse of impaled animal skulls; a little further away, banners streaming gently from an oak bough; at his feet, a dead magpie, and above all this, the buoyant orb of the golden Harvest Moon.

Madog lowered his voice to a softer, though still didactic, tone. He reached towards the younger man's face with glistening fingers to leave sticky red trails along the ridges of both cheekbones to the corners of his mouth, along the length of his nose, across his chin and above each eye. The hand withdrew, but soon returned to grip the man's head.

'Motherless boy, fatherless son, child of Sulis – your fostering falls to the forces that awakened your will. Gaia, the body of the Earth, you will call Mother. You will kneel to the sun, Lugh, who you will call Father. Meeting Hill you will call Sister, and every stone of The Meeting you will recognise as a Brother.'

The old man paused and gazed doubtfully into the glazed eyes of his initiate, but was reassured when the younger man noticed the sudden silence and glanced up expectantly.

Madog placed a hand on his shoulder and smiled. 'In honour of the waters of the Baltonsborough to Derleigh Rhyne from which you rose, you will be recognised in turn as Balder, *Y Deuddegfed Maen,* the Twelfth Stone of Meeting Hill.

'Lugh awakens to you to light. Cernunnos charges you with the cause that is your Self.'

Madog's hand covered Balder's face. 'Argus aids the watch over your brother stones. Hecate and Ceridwen hone moonlight to illuminate your world.' A hand moved against his chest. 'Gofannon offers the tools you need to survive and fight. Andraste guides the flight of your arrow, the aim of your blade, and sharpens your will to use them.'

Madog stepped away to view the bewildered man by the dancing light of the fire. The spark of pride in the old man's eye began to fade and was replaced by what might have been doubt, or sympathy, or both. He further reduced his voice to a companionable tone. 'Balder, your future begins with whatever I can teach you, and I accept that responsibility. My name is Madog. I have lived this life for more than sixty years, but I will not try to persuade you that this existence is anything other than difficult.

'You will live in poverty, surviving on the charity of a few open-minded villagers and whatever I can teach you about edible plants and wildlife. You will be cold all winter and often on summer nights. Your life is duty: you live only to preserve The Meeting, as *Y Deuddegfed Maen* has done for centuries, and you will be lonely. Get yourself drunk and the *aos sídhe* will flock to your campfire to keep you company, but you will not find the villagers so affable. Tourists will stare and taunt you.

'Your only blessing, as it has been for me, is the chance to recapture a world and a way of life to which the primæval anima within us all wishes to return. I cannot teach you to recognise this world – you know it already. You will remember it as a sense of home in wild places; as an intense nostalgia inspired by the scent of wood smoke; as a love that anyone else would think irrational as you gaze across meadows and woods to the horizon; and finally as the lust provoked by extreme weather, changes of season, the phases of the moon, or the sound of waves against a shingle beach. The difference, Balder, is that unlike the very few and fortunate people who might relate to your longing, you need not experience these emotions in conflict with the life that society demands. All that matters to you is The Meeting. Look around you now and see the world to which The Meeting belongs: step into it, Balder, and know that you are home.'

His sobriety flooded by whatever had laced the whisky, Balder remained aware of Madog's words, though not the sense of them. The old man's statements became lucid echoes whose meanings simply made themselves comfortable in his mind; and all the while he watched, listened and learned. The view he held from his reclining position was transformed by the initiation, and by the way in which Madog's words of enchanted conditioning defined a lasting world view. To Balder's gaze of childlike wonder, the simultaneous distinction and symbiosis of the natural elements became clearly visible to his glittering eyes.

The bonfire before him popped and crackled with a savage, though somehow benevolent, voracity as it consumed the wood, its conscience eased by the grace of sublimation it offered in return. Heat and Light, consort Forces to the matters of Form, gloried in their intense new existence as inspiration to the

Life they motivated. Balder watched the flames flicker their dance of lusty consumption around the glowing timber, and he came to see this movement as the ceaseless scuttling of refulgent orange and charcoal-black salamanders about the pyre.

Sparks rose high above the flames and into the air, which Balder saw blurred and excited by the heat. He saw the thermal drafts and eddies as sylphs that surf their element on etheric wings, diving and darting playfully like swifts in twilight, but drifting peacefully in luxurious tides across the meadow when free of the rising heat. A brackish pond in a corner of Chiron Dell became unsettled by the sylphs' diving passes, and ripples expanded across its surface in the wake of web-fingered undines, quick to shiver at the ticklish contact.

Presiding over this system of ceaseless interaction between elements, the Harvest Moon highlighted Meeting Hill as an elevated focus to the landscape and a wooded vestige for the legendary men and mythological beasts of a disappearing world. Listed by name among Madog's multicultural pantheon, the gods and heroes of ancient epochs and distant nations passed before Balder's enchanted gaze.

This majestically augmented view of the landscape sparked in Balder a realisation and acceptance of his own role within it. For the first time, he became aware of himself as he embraced artless humility, thereby allowing a crystal appreciation of all things guileless and natural to flow through him unobstructed like a warm sunbeam. He smiled and closed his eyes to enjoy the sensation of flowing heat.

When he returned his gaze to the night, the source of the warmth was once again the bonfire before him. The moon was setting, and Madog, seated and recloaked, was eating an apple beside the shrunken fire.

'Everything is alive.' Balder uttered his first words in a hoarse tone of wonderment. 'I've seen…' He tailed off, able only to blink in awe as he gazed around the flickering space of Chiron Dell.

'Yes, it is,' Madog agreed, 'and someone like you, born of Sulis at Harvest Tide, will enjoy the ability to see the forces that accompany and surround us. Of course, an infusion of fly agaric in whisky helps you see them too. Now relax, Balder. I need to talk you through the demands of your role, and there's a lot to tell you.'

Scramble

The Independent, 24th September

The body of a woman was exhumed yesterday from a prehistoric site north of Yeovil, Somerset, after its discovery by caretaker staff. The woman's identity has yet to be released, but the police have confirmed that the circumstances surrounding her death are suspicious.

Police have also confirmed that an object of significant historical interest was unearthed during the exhumation, but have refused to comment on speculation that the artefact is a Twelfth-Century lead cross, said to have marked the grave of King Arthur in the grounds of Glastonbury Abbey. Chief Inspector Wyeth of the Avon and Somerset Constabulary said that the object has been submitted to archaeology experts for examination at the University of Bristol.

The site of these discoveries near Little Arlingham has attracted increasing media attention in recent months. In August, Geoff Marchen, a lifetime resident of the village, made what was described by his neighbours as an 'uncharacteristic' disappearance on the same night that another man was seriously wounded in an unconnected incident nearby. The discovery of human remains has led residents of the area to talk of a curse over the ancient site.

The monument, known locally as The Meeting, has also been the focus of conflicting interests by two opposing agencies: a local action group named Earthwork, which campaigns for the preservation of ancient monuments within their rural environment, and the Glastonbury-based Geophagia, which campaigns for free access to sites of Pagan worship as a human right.

Controversy already surrounds the Earthwork group for perpetrating what observers have described as 'public-funded vigilantism'. Earthwork representatives were last night unavailable for comment.

Roedan pushed the newspaper across the kitchen table towards Sarah Conrad. 'It looks like Little Arlingham is becoming a dangerous place in which to live. Perhaps the superstitious denizens of Arlingham are right: there's a curse on Meeting Hill, and the stones want blood.'

Sarah accepted the paper and read the page-seven article. The text was accompanied by a photograph of The Meeting from the footpath at the edge of the clearing. The eleven stones had been used as boundary markers for a cordon of police tape. For Roedan's benefit, Sarah assumed an expression of indifference. She realised that Roedan intended to expand on her opinions about the story, but a knock at the front door interrupted their breakfast. Wearing only a dressing gown after the couple's late rising, Sarah slid away from the table. 'I'm going to get dressed.' She hurried upstairs and then paused on the landing to listen.

Silence below: Roedan wanted a glimpse of the unexpected visitor through the dining room window before answering. Sarah entered an upstairs bedroom overlooking the front porch and saw a Jaguar parked in the driveway.

The car's owner was a man Roedan had met only once before, at Earthwork's very public meeting in Little Arlingham at the end of August, and she was extremely surprised when she opened the door of Tan Y Bryn to find Brampton Wyre standing there. 'Hello.'

'Miss Baynes,' Wyre nodded formally. 'Or do you prefer your stage name?'

'Jill is fine,' she decided, and then stepped aside as an invitation. 'Mr Wyre, isn't it?'

'Brampton, please.'

'What brings you to Snowdonia?'

Wyre stepped inside and apologised earnestly for the unannounced visit, 'but I would like to discuss something I've only just become aware of.'

The pair shook hands. 'You're very welcome here.' Roedan spoke slowly, and Sarah recognized the smooth and deliberate enunciation her lover reserved for flirting. 'I remember how kind you were at the meeting of your committee in August.'

'You won't be surprised to learn that I'm here regarding that meeting.'

Roedan ushered him along the wide hall and into a spacious lounge. 'You've driven a long way this morning.'

Sarah remained upstairs to dress. She slipped into a pair of loose hiking trousers, a T-shirt and a multi-coloured top whose label said was hand-woven by an isolated tribe in a remote Brazilian village. She did not know why she found this claim reassuring. While dressing, Sarah decided to walk uphill from Pont Cyfyng to Moel Siabod, the mountain she could see from the bedroom window. She put on another warm layer and her walking boots and paced lightly downstairs until she could hear the voice of the visitor in the lounge.

'So the reputation and effectiveness of the group has been left badly dented, which I'm sure you won't be too upset about given their insult to you and your organization.'

'Bearing a grudge would make me an ugly person,' Sarah heard Roedan reply. 'I read a report of these events in one of the nationals only this morning. It must be traumatic for such a close community.'

'That's true,' Wyre went on, 'but the son of the dead woman, Ben Marchen, has suffered the most. He was a member of Earthwork, but now he's rumoured to have lost his mind and memory and gone to shelter – if you can call it that – with the village eccentric.'

'Eccentric?' Roedan asked carefully.

'He spoke against you at the meeting in August – a reclusive old man known as Mad Dog,' Brampton said dismissively. 'He's lived in an overgrown field at the foot of Meeting Hill since anyone can remember. He claims to be some kind of guardian of the standing stones. Perhaps he and Ben deserve each other.'

Roedan paused before making an observation. 'You seem surprisingly cheerful if all this has been such a blow to your committee.'

'I came here with the intention of being completely honest with you. I've heard the accusations levelled at you and I wonder about Geophagia's intentions regarding a festival on Meeting Hill.'

Another pause, a little longer this time. 'I'm very sensitive to the accusations you refer to, but I respect people's concerns. In fact, I've decided to review the location of the October meeting—'

'Because the cross you're accused of searching for has now been found?'

Even from her unseen position in the hall, Sarah sensed the solidifying of Roedan's expression and the bass throb of her unblinking stare. 'Does this mean you share your committee's suspicion of me?'

Wyre adopted a submissive and tactful tone. 'As I said, I'm here to be honest with you. As regards your plans, I'm hoping that my sister and Earthwork are right about you.'

Roedan fell silent.

'Let me make position clear,' Wyre requested, 'and I hope I've not misjudged you – I'm in trouble if I have. The Meeting stands on land that I own, and which I manage with my sister, though we differ in our styles of estate management. George sees the village and estate as a quaint relic to be preserved like a dusty museum piece. The only advantage of this stagnation is the satisfaction of a minority group's unending nostalgia.'

'But you're an entrepreneur,' Roedan said, her tone difficult to judge.

'Not a ruthless one, if at all,' Wyre replied quickly. 'I do not practise unreasonable profiteering, I'm just trying to do what the managing director of any company would do. The Wyre Estate isn't just a nice big garden, it's a business that supports the livelihood of my family and nearly fifty villagers. But businesses, as I'm sure you know, decline and die if they do not review and reinvent themselves in today's competitive and changeable markets. The estate is returning a smaller and smaller profit each year and will soon be worthless if I don't drag it into the 21st Century.'

Roedan nodded. 'Is it true that you once tried to expand your business by advertising land, including Meeting Hill, for sale and development?'

'That's correct.'

'And you founded the preservation committee after the resulting protests – something I assume you now regret?'

'Earthwork has been useful,' Brampton replied. 'Setting up and funding the project during its first year reassured the village. But I do not share the villagers' nostalgic or sentimental view of the land or The Meeting, and I see no value in the site as it stands – except, perhaps, its historical and archaeological significance. But such research is never conclusive or particularly enlightening. The Meeting is not even such a popular tourist draw that I can charge entry to it. '

'Put bluntly, then,' Roedan concluded for him, 'you want the monument removed?'

Wyre tried to disguise the starkness of the statement. 'It boils down to an easy choice: I can sacrifice a small parcel of non-arable estate land, including Meeting Hill, for property development, thereby raising a greater profit than my annual agricultural returns – or I can let the estate slide into debt, in which case all the land might end up being sold off to a city buyer with no local ties, no rural sensibilities, and absolutely no ear for village opinion.'

'And what does this have to do with me?' Roedan asked at last.

'The object discovered on Meeting Hill near the body of Sian Marchen is a fake – a replica of some cross associated with Arthurian legend, planted to give you no reason to lead Geophagia onto the site.'

'Oh?'

'If the genuine article ever existed and was buried on Meeting Hill, then I suppose it might still be there. And if Georgina is right about you wanting to use your organization to unearth it, then any damage caused to the monument in the process might turn out to be beyond repair.'

Roedan exhaled at length. 'Even supposing that these were my intentions, you're asking me to be take responsibility for the destruction of a four-thousand-year-old heritage site.'

'Not at all,' Wyre protested. 'In your hypothetical defence, how are you to predict that your previously well-behaved following will turn into a horde of vandals? Provocation for an unexpected riot might never be discovered – and in his sympathy for you, the owner of the land would never dream of pressing charges.'

Roedan began to lower her guard. 'In light of your confession, I'll admit that these things have already occurred to me. And even if they hadn't, your quiet suggestion and approval of such an outcome would be a sore temptation to an organization like mine. We hold a deep interest in the topic you've raised.'

Brampton Wyre accepted Roedan's reply. He settled back into his chair and relaxed.

From the hall beyond the lounge, Sarah crept quickly and quietly away. She was keen to avoid being seen by Wyre and wanted time to consider the news unearthed by his visit. That Geophagia's leader was actively searching for the funeral cross of King Arthur was not news to Sarah; but the confession that Roedan might be prepared to sacrifice a prehistoric monument to find it was a revelation.

Roedan's longing for the cross became apparent to Sarah soon after their relationship was confirmed as one of lovers. It was one of the many things she unearthed in Roedan during their first eight weeks of intimate discovery. But now she experienced the sense that this honeymoon period had ended with Brampton Wyre's visit, and Sarah suddenly felt sobered, excluded and very alone.

It was in this state of mind that she strode from the grounds of Tan Y Bryn, through the gates of the drive and downhill to the road. To her left was the high stone bridge that carries the lane through Pont Cyfyng – a quiet thoroughfare from which Sarah often watched dippers flitting below Cyfyng Falls. But that day she turned right and headed past Rhôs, the farm bordering Tan Y Bryn, and skirted an old quarry where the road turns into a rough track, climbing steeply through deciduous forest past the ruins of old homesteads. At the crest of this track the dense woodland ends abruptly, preferring root in the moist and sheltered Afon Llugwy valley. Beyond this point only a few wind-twisted thorns brave a living on the exposed mountainside.

The cloud above two thousand feet moved in a steady stream over the mountain that day. The summit of Moel Siabod was occasionally exposed with a crown of blue sky, but obscured again moments later by the shifting grey ceiling.

Sarah contemplated her life in sudden new light as she climbed the last dry-stone wall of the northern slope. She began walking boggier ground, heading uphill in a steep gully that channelled rainwater from the peak, soaking Sarah's legs up to the knees. She tried to consider her options for the future without reference to the past, though news of this threat to The Meeting posed by Roedan and Wyre was a reminder of previous interests in Little Arlingham. She remembered Ian Longe and his attempt to rescue her from Meeting Hill's Midsummer fire. She recalled the originality of his wit and the acuity of his observations. She also remembered him as the best looking man in Little Arlingham (though Ian would not have considered this particularly high praise).

These remained good memories for Sarah, but she had not left Somerset so long ago that she could forget her reasons for leaving. She cringed when she remembered Ian's deadpan humour and the sense of irony he applied to the wry prediction and manipulation of others' behaviour. She recalled Ian's increasing boredom with his own insight and the brutal honesty it spawned – a frankness often used in a way that could be more hurtful than lies.

Particularly disagreeable to Sarah was the way in which Ian's conscience seemed immune to any act performed in the name of Earthwork duty.

From all of this, Roedan offered relief. Twice Sarah had required rescue on Meeting Hill: once from the Midsummer fire, and then from her own distress on the day of Roedan's visit. Ian had tried, of course, and Sarah would never forget it – but Roedan had succeeded where her boyfriend had failed. She accepted that Roedan's intentions towards her were probably as selfish as those of any new lover, and – considering Earthwork's actions at her Midsummer festival – possibly also vengeful. Yet Roedan still treated Sarah with consideration, affection, generosity, and a single-minded attention that no one else had ever shown her.

The hillside grew drier, harder and steeper beneath her feet, and a ridge of rock like an exposed spine began to emerge from the grassy slopes around three-quarters of the way up the mountain, transforming Sarah's ascent from a dogged trudge into a more interesting scramble. She reached the barren plateau of Siabod's summit just after one that afternoon. The southerly wind scouring the mountaintop fragmented the cloud that rode it, and Sarah's reward for such a determined ascent – and the simultaneous scramble through her own unsettled circumstance – was clarity. Despite sudden proof of scheming, Sarah remained content in her relationship with the Priestess of Geophagia, because life and lust in the mountains with someone as exciting as Roedan was indescribably cool, and she intended to enjoy it while it lasted.

The threat to Meeting Hill was a potential injustice she knew she could not ignore; though if alerting the Earthwork at this point meant risking contact with Ian, or compromising her intimacy with Roedan, then Sarah knew she would be able to stifle her conscience until she was sure that she could avoid both.

October 28th

Carreg slept for an hour. He slumbered so deeply that he was not disturbed when heavy rain began to rake the hilltop and seep through the hood of his habit. Water coursed over the contours of the standing stone against which he rested, soaking through the cloth at his back. But Brother Carreg slept on, his breathing deep, slow and contented.

Almost invisible in the darkness, and unheard above the sound of the rain, a mounted man appeared at the southern edge of the clearing on the brow of Meeting Hill. Over a linen top and leggings, Walter Giffard came armoured with a thigh-length shirt of mail, girdled at the waist. He gripped the horse's reins with ironbound gauntlets, and thick leather greaves covered the leggings above his boots. There were spurs at his heels, a sword at his belt, and he drew the blade when he spied the hooded monk against the pale standing stone. He immediately spurred his horse into a gallop. Its hooves bit into the wet turf of the summit, sending sods flying in their wake.

The stallion's eyes grew wide and reeled, expressing its fear of such a pace in darkness. The knight leaned low in his saddle and raised the sword as he bore down on his target.

The sound of the rain and the thundering hooves combined to form a droning bass rhythm, yet Carreg slept on.

A third, unseen, presence on the hilltop was introduced by a higher pitched sound: the searing whip of an arrow, whose flight across the clearing remained invisible until it terminated in the neck of the charging rider.

Walter Giffard fell from the galloping horse. His body hit the ground and tumbled over and over with a series of rolling snaps, until it came to rest against Brother Carreg's legs.

The monk awoke with a yelp, reintroduced to his outlaw status disoriented and terrified. He could not remember where he was, or why, and as he flailed in panic at the broken corpse before him, another figure stepped into sight through the rain. Carreg scrambled to his feet – his knees buckled as he tried to rise. He fell back against the megalith for support, his palms pressed against the cold wet stone for purchase.

Also confused, the dead knight's horse trotted the circumference of the clearing as Carreg fearfully eyed the bow carried by the new arrival.

'Carreg?' the figure asked.

The monk's own breathing at first deafened him to the question. After a long day of running, constant fear, heart-freezing incidents of panic – and now this sudden awakening to darkness, rain and inexplicable death – Carreg's laboured breathing was reduced to a pitiful wheeze.

'You're here to meet me, but we need to be quick,' said the archer, who possessed a dirty, undernourished, unmistakably feminine face.

The monk exhaled panic in a long and shaky breath, squinting into the dark. 'Is your name Marchen?'
'You arrived early. You should have hidden. Others are coming.'
Carreg forced a grip on his composure and pushed himself upright for the last time. After a moment's further thought and a nervous glance around the clearing, he reached inside his rain-heavy habit. 'Each night in the Abbey I dreamed of a chance to run free,' he panted as he pulled a dirty cloth parcel into view. 'But now all I dream of is returning to my cell. Here,' he offered Marchen the bundle, 'it's grown too heavy for me.'
Marchen turned and looked over her shoulder as though startled, but then back at Carreg. 'You saw the exhumation?'
The monk nodded.
'Did you see... Him?'
Carreg nodded again.
'So, Arthur has a grave.'
'If it was him,' Carreg replied. 'But if you destroy this, his death needn't be more than a quiet rumour.'
The monk saw Marchen turn to look across the clearing through the stones. Reacting quickly to whatever she saw, she pulled an arrow from the quiver at her side and notched it against the fletch. She drew the sinew past her ear, paused for a heartbeat and let fly. Carreg felt Arthur's burial marker snatched from his grasp. And then Marchen was gone.
From behind either side of The Meeting's tallest megalith, Baldwin and William of Glaestingaburh appeared and strode through the grass towards Carreg, whom they had hunted since dawn. They drew and raised their swords.
Carreg felt his innards turn cold and liquid. He gazed into the purposeful expressions of both men, made several weak, inaudible pleas for a chance to explain, but soon fell silent beneath the weight of resignation.
Baldwin, the elder of the noblemen, decapitated Carreg without further pause. The monk's body remained standing for a moment – a surprising sight that distracted the knights long enough for William of Glaestingaburh to be dispatched by another arrow from the darkness. His twitching body fell smoothly into the mud even before Carreg's torso had crumpled.
Roaring a challenge at the trees, Carreg's executioner span on his heel to face what he judged to be the source of the arrow's flight. Another missile whistled by and was deflected by the standing stone.
Her quiver now spent, Y Deuddegfed Maen moved stealthily among her sibling stones to accept the knight's challenge from his vulnerable side. Marchen produced a sword of her own and shrugged the cloak from her shoulders, revealing an underfed, though lithe, body clothed in a knee-length tunic, overlaid with a leather jerkin and a belt at her waist.

The swords of Marchen and Baldwin of Glaestingaburh met with a grating clash. The opponents flashed at each other with a series of thrusts and parries that were heard more clearly than seen in the rain-smudged gloom.
'Another Welshman?' the knight laughed as he retreated a little for surer footing.
Marchen mocked a gallant bow, and Baldwin swung heavily at her head. Instead of taking the blow of his larger sword flat against her own, Marchen followed the strike through and let the blade slide away.
'If you're prepared to fight like this for a relic of your sentimental past, why haven't you joined your restless countrymen on the hilly side of the Severn?'
Marchen considered this to be the kind of talk used to provoke violence. With blood already spilt, though, it was just a waste of breath. She advanced and slashed at the air before her, forcing Baldwin into another defensive back-step and giving her time to produce an ornate dagger from her belt. She held the tip of its blade between thumb and forefinger, thrust with her sword to drive Baldwin into a parry, and then sent the dagger spinning towards him.
Baldwin continued the swing of his double-handed parry to deflect the knife with a ringing blow of impressive timing, sending the dagger spinning into the trees.
Yet this seemed to have been Marchen's intention. The sword's momentum swung Baldwin's guard well away to the extreme edge of his fighting arc, exposing the whole left side of his body to Marchen's waiting blade. She stepped forward and punctured the knight's torso between his ribs. Baldwin of Glaestingaburh screamed with a harrowing sadness that destroyed any perception of his cruelty and power, rendering his death at the hands of even a desperate underdog seem like cold-blooded injustice.
But the tears that Marchen shed as she stood over the bodies of the men were not born of sympathy for the English aggressors. Marchen cried for the loss of Brother Carreg, finding a little consolation only in the knowledge that her countryman had died with his mission achieved, and with his lifeblood received by sacred British soil.

'Marchen took Carreg's habit before building him a balefire. I'm sure she took it for practical reasons – even a monk's habit would have been a rich garment for a peasant like Marchen.' Madog unconsciously stroked at his own robe. 'But every Twelfth Stone since 1191 has worn one like it in honour of Carreg's sacrifice.'
With the narrative at an end, Balder's vision of 12th Century intrigue faded from before his eyes. The headless monk was replaced by the sight of his own bare feet in the grass, and the vividly imagined rain evaporated into the softest breeze. Balder glanced at Madog, who crouched against the standing stone that Carreg once used as a pillow. The old man watched him closely.

'Marchen could have saved Carreg,' Balder said.
Madog nodded as though on cue. 'This is what I was afraid of,' he replied, though viewed the innocence of his pupil with some pride. Balder's emerging personality had so far displayed the credulity of a child and the malleability of clay.
'Afraid of what?'
'That you're not thinking with the single-mindedness demanded by this role.'
'But did Marchen need to leave a persecuted man to die?'
'She had to keep the cross away from the Abbot's men,' Madog said. 'Marchen had no choice.'
Balder let his thoughtful gaze wander the circle of surrounding stones. Ben Marchen's clothes were adequate against the cool October air by day – the same denim jacket, Earthwork shirt and grey combat trousers he had been wearing when Madog pulled him from the rhyne nearly five weeks before – but he now required a cloak of his own to feel comfortable beyond early evening.
Balder liked listening to Madog. He naturally and happily accepted the reality with which he was presented, and in which Madog had tutored him patiently for over a month. And yet, after recent dreams and recollections that disturbed and confused him, Balder had learned to ask questions.
'I think she did have a choice,' he said carefully. 'If all these things happened in the way you said, Marchen could have defeated those swordsmen before they got to Carreg.'
Balder displayed a simple, often sentimental, outlook, and Madog had foreseen that the retelling of Carreg's story would provoke discussion along these lines. But it was a conversation he had prepared for: its conclusion was a lesson that Madog had already illustrated from many different perspectives repeated often since his pupil's awakening.
'I disagree. Marchen needed to be able to fight knowing that the cross was already hidden if she lost.'
'Was the cause worth that man's death?' Balder appeared wary of the answer.
'I think his death was a small price to pay for trying to maintain the independence of the western Celts. They were Carreg's people, and Marchen's people, from whom our tradition is derived.'
Balder shrugged. 'I suppose so, if it just comes down to numbers.'
Madog shifted irritably against the stone. His eyes narrowed a little as he regarded Balder's hunched and sulky demeanour. 'The Meeting and countless other megalithic sites across Britain were inherited by the tribes of the Iron Age – the last indigenous people to do so before the Romans came. From the Roman invasion until only two centuries ago, the political and religious powers of this country cared nothing for the scared sites and landscapes of the old religion. That labour of love was taken up by the Welsh some time during

the Dark Ages, though the records and journals handed down to me date only from the eleven hundreds, so listen,' Madog ordered him, and paused until Balder re-established eye contact. 'In 1191, the western Celts were struggling for independence from the English crown, and they would have received the news of their hero's death in the same way that a Christian would react to the discovery of Jesus' body. Carreg died attempting to preserve a legend: the promise of Arthur's return at the moment of his countrymen's greatest need. We shouldn't cheapen his sacrifice.'

The younger man nodded dutifully. 'At least the Twelfth Stone was here to hide the cross. Does every sacred site have people like us watching over it?'

'Good question. I travelled for a while once. I heard rumours, but nothing more. There were guardians at many sites until around the time of the Civil War. Perhaps a few places in England still enjoy a protective influence near the Celtic fringes. Compare the condition of major temples like Boskawen-Un, The Hurlers, The Meeting, Stanton Drew, the Rollrights, Arbor Low and Castlerigg with the few that remain in eastern parts of the country. But even The Meeting had some narrow escapes. The journals of our line record confrontations with some very angry Puritans.'

Madog watched Balder lean back on his arms and gaze uncertainly along the swaying treetops. The trauma and strains of Balder's previous self had been shed with his former name, and now, with the sensitivity of a newborn, Balder was vulnerable to the horror of the fate suffered by Carreg. The younger man would ruminate on such violence if not distracted.

Madog experienced continuing astonishment at Ben Marchen's transformation. The old man soon realised that the emotional crisis suffered by Ben had been a breakdown so devastating, and an exorcism so thorough, that his emergence from the rhyne into which he had stumbled had been a far more literal rebirth than the metaphorical nativity he had first thought it to be. Balder shared only anatomy and a few hazy memories with Ben Marchen, and he regarded life with the awe, muted worship and trepidation of an infant mind.

'You have new eyes for the world,' Madog said gently, tapping Balder's temple, 'but stored away in there somewhere are the instincts of an older man. Successors to the role of Twelfth Stone are not usually old enough to have developed your ethical sensibilities, or learned how to ask the kind of questions that can interfere with difficult decisions. Your single lifelong task will be compromised if you allow yourself to be distracted by other interests, places, or people. There will always be a steady stream of visitors to The Meeting, but you won't need to lurk up here watching all of them. It's those connected with The Meeting, with influence over it, or with ambitions concerning it that you'll lose sleep worrying about. The majority of the gawping public is harmless.'

Balder blinked and turned to his elder. 'Then why do you take such an interest

in the young people who visit the hill alone?'
Unaware of the dark inference loading his question, Balder was surprised by Madog's unsettled expression. The old man caught something in his throat, hacked on it and spat heavily into the grass. 'Blood and sand, boy,' he grumbled sulkily, 'you make me sound like a sweating pervert. If you'd rephrased your question you could have made me sound like a watchful guardian of the innocent and vulnerable – but I'm not the bad man in the woods or a Samaritan. *Y Deuddegfed Maen* does not stand for Justice, Light, Truth, Righteousness, Charity, World Peace, Cutesy Bunnies or any other sentimental clichés. The Twelfth Stone stands for The Meeting.'
Balder shrugged. 'Then why?'
'Children have never needed any particular protection up here in my lifetime – but The Meeting needs protection from them. Of all the casual visitors to this site, the young are most likely to be an impulsive threat to the stones. Earthwork learned that very quickly. But, to answer your question, I have on occasion observed the youngest of Little Arlingham in search of a successor to this role. I'm old, Balder, and I've been old since Ben Marchen was very young.'
Balder's eyes narrowed and darkened, as though his vision was shaded by the cloudy introspection taking place behind them. 'I remember things…'
'I watched Ben as a boy. He was one of the few people who visited The Meeting under my protection, though he never knew it. He was my first choice to succeed me as the Twelfth Stone of Meeting Hill.'
There was a comfortable pause of some minutes as Balder considered Madog's words, the silence relieved by a breeze through the dry, yellowing leaves above.
'I think Ben always realised he was different in some way, even if he didn't know what was planned for him. He was always restless, always provoking, like he was daring the world to put him where he was meant to be. He had a frustrating love of landscape, especially Meeting Hill, but no way of expressing it without feeling emasculated, or sounding irrational and obsessed.' Balder turned to Madog, his face beaming innocent pride. 'Being chosen to succeed *Y Deuddegfed Maen* is like being recognised by The Meeting as worthy of a connection to the site that visiting hippies can only dream about.'
Madog's expression developed a stern edge. 'You're not The Chosen One, you're just the next in a very long line of monomaniacs, and your meagre influence is strictly local.' Madog lightened his tone in response to Balder's wounded glance. 'Of course you should take pride in your role, but you'll soon realise that your life is now one of ceaseless vigilance and isolation, and of trying to see this unending duty as its own reward. Believe me, Balder, you won't feel like Nature's Pagan Messiah when she's doing her best to kill you

in the middle of winter. That was an aspect of this life Sian Marchen struggled with when she considered replacing me.'

Balder's expression changed again, and Madog hoped he had not raised the subject too soon. 'You haven't mentioned this before.'

'I'm mentioning it now.'

Balder nodded. 'Did you ask her directly, or was she— you know, *manipulated* into the role?'

Madog did not react to the accusatory tone of Balder's question. He did not think the younger man capable of spite. 'Actually, Sian Marchen came to me. She climbed Meeting Hill everyday after her son disappeared ten years ago. It was the last place Ben had been seen, and it seemed to be the only place that she felt connected to him. I felt sorry for her. I told her what I knew of Ben's departure, and what I knew was only what I'd seen. We talked. We got to know each other. After three years of visits, of having learned the tradition of the Twelfth Stone – and of my previous intention to offer her son the title – she asked to replace Ben as successor.'

Balder laughed in a way that surprised the old man. 'You accepted a middle-aged married woman as the next Twelfth Stone?'

'A middle-aged married woman with the married surname of Marchen – a family that has offered no fewer than four of its own to the cause of *Y Deuddegfed Maen*. Marchens have watched over The Meeting in the twelfth, thirteenth, sixteenth and seventeenth centuries.'

Balder sat up and pushed his fringe back from his eyes. 'Do you think that might have been a good enough motive for Geoff Marchen to kill her?'

Madog nodded sadly. 'Along with the stress imposed on their marriage by a wayward son, and by Geoff's jealousy of her friendship with me, and by his own attraction to a local nurse. These were things that eased my conscience when I accepted Sian's offer. I knew she was right for this role. She found it easy to express emotions that had only confused and unsettled Ben for years.

'But the situation changed again, and I decided that I owed it to the memory of Sian to see that I made her son my choice after all, even though I knew that convincing him would require sadistic pressure. I admitted my intention to him, but it still took the traumatic unearthing of horrible secrets to make Ben's life unbearable. I hoped that accepting a new one would be his only way of finding relief.'

Scuffed footsteps from the southern path silenced their discussion. Madog and Balder retreated into the woods as Ian Longe strode into view on the other side of the clearing. The two men positioned themselves behind the widest trees at the clearing's edge and peered out through the autumn leaves. Ian paced idly around the circle of stones. Occasionally he glanced at his watch. He stopped at the Monk's Pillow and pressed a palm against the stone, contentedly closing his eyes and raising his face to the sun.

As though he sensed unseen eyes upon him, Ian suddenly opened his own and stared at the nearby trees. Madog and Balder held their breath. He reached for the radio at his belt and began retreating a wary distance.
Balder glanced in every direction because suddenly he could not see Madog. At first he felt startled by the isolation, but then reassured that Ian was unlikely to spot him from the other side of the clearing.
The sound of an engine rose from the brow of the hill; louder, closer, angrier and more unwelcome – and then materialised on the summit in the form of a Land Rover, occupied by Alan Forrest and an unexpected passenger. Alan swerved left and parked at the edge of the monument. He hopped out of the vehicle and asked, 'How was that?'
Ian glanced at his watch. 'Is this the time you want me to record? Nearly five minutes? It's our worst time ever.'
'Don't sweat it,' Alan grinned. 'I slowed down for Halfpenny's sheep at the bottom of the hill. Call it good PR. You OK?'
Ian glanced through the stones. 'Not much birdsong up here this afternoon. I thought there might be someone in the trees. I was getting tingly.'
'A disturbance in The Force? Must be that curry from last night. Mind you,' he went on, lowering his voice, 'there might be *two* spooky voyeurs stalking the shadows up here now. According to the grapevine, Ben didn't lose his mind, he just handed it over to Mad Dog to play with.'
Ian looked at the fresh turf covering the grave. 'I don't want to think about that. As long as Ben's all right we should leave him alone to get his head straight. He'll come to us when he's ready. I'll keep his place together till he does.'
Alan indicated his passenger in the Land Rover. Lea Granger stepped out into the sunlight and lit a roll-up. 'She thinks the same as you. I met her on the path.'
Ian waved at Lea, who winked and blew a jet of smoke in response. 'How is she?'
'Seems fine. She was just talking about giving Ben time to follow some necessary path, realign his chakras and unscramble his tantric bits: the usual harmonics.'
'Has she seen him?'
'Not since— you know. She tried his house half an hour ago. With no one home she came here hoping to bump into us.'
'Us? Did she say anything about Geophagia's reaction?'
'Haven't discussed that yet. She might know something – she wants to see George.'
Ian turned and headed for the car. 'All right, we'll go and see the boss.'
Expressionless, Balder watched all three visitors return to the Land Rover. He saw Ian greet Lea with a brief hug before they climbed into the vehicle. Alan

started the engine, swung the car about and headed downhill.

Balder stepped back into the light and was surprised when Madog emerged from the trees much farther away. The two men wandered into the centre of the circle and Balder contemplated its fresh green turf, avoiding Madog's gaze. 'Those people,' he had difficulty saying: 'that girl: I have a memory—'

'Which doesn't matter,' Madog declared, his face cold and drawn. 'I'm afraid the unusual way in which you came to succeed me, and the pressure we're under to avert a long-standing threat to The Meeting, haven't allowed me to give you a structured introduction to this life. I'm having to improvise lessons as we go along, and you're having to run to catch up – but this is the single most important rule that I can impress on you, Balder. It's the law that will govern your life from this day forward, and you will accept it without question.'

'You won't need to tell me twice,' Balder replied dutifully, as receptive to the old man's words as a flower to sunlight.

'Your one and only concern, from now until the day that someone else inherits your title, is the preservation of Meeting Hill and the circle of stones around us. Any friendships, intimate relationships, material possessions or other activities are only valuable to you if they serve to maintain this site as it has stood for more than four thousand years.'

Balder's haunted expression made Madog realise that his pupil was beginning to understand the enormity of this statement. But Balder still had questions.

News

Alan steered left into the Wyre Estate between the eagle-crowned pillars of the west gate, followed a few moments later by Brampton Wyre's Jaguar, which trailed the Earthwork Land Rover along the poplar-lined avenue towards Arlingham House.
'Poor old Brampton,' Alan grinned when he spied Wyre's car in the wing-mirror, his hands drumming the steering wheel in time to Steely Dan on the radio. 'Loveable Uncle Wyre wants to join our club so much that he's following us around.'
Lea Granger looked over her shoulder at the car. 'Not friends with your landlord?'
'Oh yes,' Alan feigned sincerity, 'to his face. But at the committee meeting in August he gave us a public kicking and practically jumped into bed with your old boss.'
'There's a queue,' Lea muttered, but winced with regret.
Ian snorted a humourless acknowledgement.
'*Ouch,* baby!' Alan exploded, slapping Ian's leg in the throes of his laughter. Ian saw Lea suppress a smile. He pouted a conspicuous sulk.
The courtyard was full of cars. Alan parked as best he could between off-road vehicles and found their drivers seated in the Earthwork barn. They were gathered around the table and almost too engrossed in noisy conversation to notice the field team's arrival. Lea followed them but hesitated at the barn door. 'What's going on? Another meeting?'
'I don't know. Nothing George warned us about.'
'Who are these people?' she asked quietly.
Ian scanned the faces of the crowd filling the dim, timber-scented interior. 'Employees of the Wyre estate,' he said. 'Two of them you already know: Baz, the gamekeeper, and the fidgety old boy next to him is Abel. A few others live and work on the estate, and it looks like they've brought their families. There's a lot of kids in here.'
George Wyre was also present and beckoned to the new arrivals from the other end of the table. Ian, Alan and Lea joined her before the animated crowd.
'Hey, Boss, you should have warned us there was something formal afoot,' Alan scolded George. 'We could have shelved the call-out rehearsal.'
'This wasn't planned.' She winked at Lea. 'Hello. Good to see you without a love-sick Ben trailing after you.'
Lea had expected only expressions of sympathy from those who knew Ben, but she found such convention tiresome and was gratefully surprised by George's playful gesture. Her instinctive suspicion of this particular member of the landed class was transformed into easy respect. She accepted George's gentle humour as a show of faith in her ability to cope. Lea wished that she

cared nothing for Ben, his grief, or for any of the things she had seen. But coping was the next best thing.

George motioned for silence and nodded at Gary Basildon. 'I'm sorry to have kept you waiting. The rest of my team is here now.'

Appointed spokesman for those gathered, Baz rose from his seat. It was like watching a house with a wax jacket relocate itself. Twenty seven heads tilted slowly in unison to follow his face. 'I'm sorry for the way we've turned up all at once like this, but after the things your group has being saying— Word's gone round, and we'd like an update on where we stand.'

'What things?' Ian asked.

The gamekeeper turned a frosty stare on Ian. 'About how the estate will be overrun with travellers in a few days' time.' He gestured at his colleagues and their families. 'Are we going to wake up on November 1st to find our gardens filled with condoms and syringes and shit?'

George was unbalanced by her employees' blunt expression of their fears, but rallied well. 'Chinese whispers. We've never mentioned any travellers—'

'No, you haven't,' Lea said, reflecting Baz's megawatt stare back at him. 'I remember Georgina explaining her concerns very clearly.'

George and Alan exchanged a wary glance. George was afraid of the keeper's response, and Alan was afraid of George's response for being called Georgina in public.

Ian deflected imminent confrontation by shuffling behind Lea, peering over her shoulder and grinning pleadingly at Baz.

'And I think that turning up here at the last minute after months of George's warnings is hypocritical,' Lea told the crowd. 'From what I've heard, no estate employee has offered Earthwork support. Ben Marchen told me that some of you even share Mr Wyre's dislike for this committee, and I think it's no secret that Brampton cares little for The Meeting.'

Several people stood to shout in reply, and many younger members of the gathering enjoyed the excuse to follow their parents' example without necessarily understanding the debate. George stood before Lea and held her lightly by the shoulders. She smelt alcohol on Lea's breath. 'You might want to wait outside. I don't want to see you insulted.'

'I have thick skin.'

George smiled. 'Skin is thinner after a skin-full.'

'I'm not drunk,' she said convincingly above the heckling of the estate staff. 'I only wanted to say what you were thinking.'

'Maybe so, but nobody wants to hear their employer insulted, especially when his sister is present. They'll stick up for me and for themselves. What you said won't help and I really need these people on my side.'

'I get it.' Lea paused. Then, 'I'll say something they'll like.' She pulled a chair from beneath the table and stepped up onto it. 'Everyone, quiet for a minute –

especially you in the baseball cap, you don't know what you're talking about. Listen, there's more for you to know. My name is Lea Granger. I used to belong to the Geophagia Foundation, which is the group that Earthwork has been worried about. I wasn't just a member: my band was one of the headlining acts at Geophagia's festivals, and I can confirm that Roedan did plan to bring her following to Meeting Hill in three days' time.' Unsettled murmurs from the gathering. 'But things have changed. I left Geophagia to protest against their coming here, but they don't seem to have given up on me.' She smiled. 'I still receive their event schedules in the post.' The people around the table fell silent. 'None of you will appreciate how hard it is for me to admit this, but I believe that Earthwork is right to be suspicious. Since a certain artefact was discovered at the monument last month, Geophagia has cancelled its Samhain festival on Meeting Hill.'

George, Alan and Ian exchanged looks of surprise. The small crowd filling the barn became noisy again, but its tone was transformed by relief.

Lea stepped down from the chair. 'Was that better?'

'It's – a surprise,' George replied, sitting down on the chair Lea had vacated. The estate employees chatted in a steady murmur around them.

'It's also a spectacular anti-climax,' Ian decided, staring thoughtfully at his feet.

'But good news,' Alan prompted him. 'We won.'

Brampton Wyre observed this discussion from the barn door. Ian noticed him there when he saw Baz nodding in Brampton's direction. When Wyre returned his stare, Ian waved modestly and looked away.

A man whose name the Earthwork team could not recall rose from his chair. A three-year-old girl clung to his leg with the limpet strength of the youthfully shy. 'Do we know if the cross discovered on the hill is real? I can't be the only one here who finds the timing of it suspicious. Geophagia will think so too.'

Lea shrugged happily. 'Apparently not.'

'The cross was found at a crime scene,' George added, casting empty glances at Abel and Baz. 'The police took it with them but promised to release it to someone qualified at Bristol University.'

This, it seemed, was all that the gathered staff had needed to hear. Baz thanked George on behalf of his colleagues, who all rose from their seats and made for the door.

Brampton Wyre gave his sister a brief and unreadable smile.

The sound of car doors and engines filled the barn for several minutes as the employees and their families vacated the courtyard, dispersing for their homes across the estate. Lea took a seat on the bonnet of one of the Shoguns and watched Earthwork rearranging the chairs around the table. They seemed to be avoiding eye contact with each other, and Lea realised that Ian's description of her news as an anti-climax was a feeling shared by the whole team. For

Earthwork, the cause had lost its urgency, and there was suddenly so much less to think about.

Lea had expected a celebratory reaction to the success of Earthwork's ruse. As the sound of engines faded outside and the Earthwork members contemplated their unexpected victory in awkward silence, she produced cider from her bag and took a seat between George and Ian. 'The last few months' trouble hasn't been your fault. You feel bad because of the knocks your group has taken, but you've put Roedan off coming here, and after your hard work I don't think that Ben or the other lad – Craig? – would begrudge a celebration. You've protected The Meeting, which is exactly what you set out to do.'

Alan cupped his hands and caught the can of cider that Lea threw to him. 'I'm not going to argue with that. You boring bastards,' he said to George and Ian. 'Drink some of this.'

Estate II

Balder found the narrow Sparkford Road into Little Arlingham empty of traffic at ten o'clock the next morning. Tall hedges of moulting thorn and coppiced willow bordered the view northbound along the lane, which was crowned a little less than half a mile ahead by the dome of Meeting Hill. The sky overhead was a clear sapphire blue, but bulbous towers of stainless cloud mushroomed on the rolling horizon, and the autumn colours of Meeting Hill's wooded slopes appeared incendiary against them. The air was fresh, and its smooth northerly breeze carried a hint of loam.
Two days remained until the eve of Samhain: a prehistoric British festival of the dead, now vulgarly remembered as Hallowe'en.
The upright and watchful form of Balder appeared on the tarmac at the junction of Sparkford Road and the lane to Chiron Dell. He glanced in both directions along the narrow lane and then began to walk north.
He wore the only clothes that he owned, except his hooded sackcloth robe, which Madog had presented to him with a reverence that Balder had yet to learn for it. The old man usually insisted that he wear the musty habit as a tribute to Brother Carreg's now legendary sacrifice, but the robe was also a practical item of clothing. A hooded cloak was particularly useful to someone who wished to spend their life in shadow, and this latter reasoning had certainly struck a chord with Balder. He felt a strong urge to hide from the public whenever he was wearing it. But as Balder intended that day's solitary venture to be a mission of friendly introduction rather than stealth, Madog had allowed Balder to leave Chiron Dell without the robe.
When he reached the Wyre Estate's western gateway, Balder pushed his unruly fringe back from his eyes and gazed up at the archway. He was unable to make out the Latin inscription along the upper ledge, upon which two granite eagles had no choice but to remain vigilant. He offered the Wyre coat of arms a nonchalant nod, and then stepped onto the estate.
Madog once told him that this expanse of land had been held by the Wyre family for nearly eight hundred years, and the old man had forbade Balder to set foot on it until he considered him ready to face the challenging individuals he might encounter there. Madog had spoken of people who might question Balder's exclusive commitment to The Meeting, or express concern about his life, and even doubt his name. In fact, the Twelfth Stone still considered Balder ill-prepared for such a challenge, but there was little time left.
'Can I help you?'
Balder halted in mid-step, but he did not immediately turn about. He carried a remarkable self-possession which, while suppressing certain instinctive reactions, offered him unique alternatives. He felt an irrational immunity from threats potentially posed by other people (though he still lived in awe of

Madog). He did not care what other people thought of him, his appeal as a man, his limited attention to personal hygiene or his opinion. And for the rest of his life, Balder would feel self-righteous in nearly all situations when Madog was not present, even times – such as this one – when he was the trespasser

Balder supposed that his unwavering self-confidence was born of the simplicity and all-consuming nature of his purpose – though he also sensed the presence of some greater influence in his life, despite Madog's warning against such grandiose conviction. Balder had not been able to articulate his belief in so many words, but he felt sure that the Earth herself, of which The Meeting was a temple, had buoyed him from her waters to replace Madog as *Y Deuddegfed Maen,* and therefore only the Earth had the authority and power to remove him.

He turned slowly and faced a very tall man carrying an open shotgun. 'What?'

'Oh,' Baz grunted. 'I didn't recognise you. Thought you were in off the road poking about.'

Balder decided that what this man thought about anything had nothing to do with him, so he turned away and strode along the avenue.

A five-minute walk brought him to Arlingham House. Madog had warned him that he would never be greeted warmly if he presented himself at the front door, so Balder rounded the property on its southern side, discovering at its rear a cobbled courtyard bordered by redbrick stables and workshops and a large barn with a Celtic cross painted across its double doors. This was the symbol Madog had told him to look for.

He found the courtyard deserted, but even if he had been confronted by unwelcoming strangers, Balder's sense of immunity would have given him the confidence to stride purposefully towards the barn, which he did. He pulled at one of the doors, splitting the stylised cross exactly in half, and stepped inside, looking for any sign of occupation as his eyes adjusted to the gloom.

Filling the barn to Balder's left were three off-road vehicles, each displaying on its bonnet and doors the same cruciform design painted on the barn. Balder reached into his trouser pocket and retrieved the pewter badge he had always possessed but never understood. He laid it face up on his palm and compared it with the symbol on the nearest Shogun's door. They matched. He blinked at the coincidence and stepped aside to study a display on the wall. Maps of varying scales and a collection of framed photographs hung there, and a portrait dated July of that year received Balder's particular attention. Against a background of familiar standing stones and lush summer trees, four smiling men and two cheerful women in matching uniforms posed for the camera. Their smiles were effortless, their poses relaxed, and the group was huddled companionably, with most members of the party standing with arms around the shoulders of their neighbours.

The portrait made something swell behind Balder's eyes and something else catch in his throat. He looked down to cough, and then up and around the barn to clear his suddenly misty vision.

The barn's walls and cobwebbed rafters enclosed a serene, cosy gloom. The interior's low light was rendered somehow tangible by the scent of the weathered timbers and offered a moist green hue by the moss-filtered sunbeam from the skylight.

Balder appreciated the moment in a profound way, experiencing a deep and inexplicable nostalgia. He immersed himself in this feeling, allowing the indulgent wave to flow over and through him, though he realised that these vague and meaningless memories did not belong to him.

Time seemed to slow while the moment lasted. Balder felt that his consciousness was expanding in every direction, like it was trying to envelope and preserve these peaceful surroundings in a bubble of sensory experience.

'Hello.'

Wrenched from his control, time blurred in its haste to catch up with the lost seconds. He staggered sideways and put one hand against the table for support.

'Are you all right?'

Balder looked up and focused on the new arrival, who studied him with genuine concern. He spent several moments guessing the identity of the mature woman. 'Yes, thank you, Miss Wyre. Just a head-rush. I think sometimes I don't eat enough. Madog is no chef. Nor am I.' Balder looked a little more closely at George's weary expression and winced. Madog had described her as late-middle-aged, but that morning she looked much older.

'Are you all right?'

'I drank too much last night. Some friends of yours stayed overnight. They introduced me to music I've never heard before. I don't know if this team keeps me young or ages me.'

Balder listened politely but felt the conversation distracting him from his purpose. He had ventured there only to introduce himself, aware that he might have to work closely with these people in future. Struggling to assert some control over the encounter, Balder attempted what he thought was a judgemental frown at George's confession, but then realised that he might be feeling a touch of envy.

'I've not seen you for a while. We've all been worried, but we wanted to give you space. Are you staying for a while?' George frowned at Balder's vacant expression.

He nodded silently.

'OK.' George retreated across the courtyard.

She returned only a few minutes later with three younger people: two dishevelled men and a woman with a military lack of hair. The skinhead looked threatening as she drew on a roll-up.

Balder stepped into the sunlight. 'Hello,' he introduced himself before any of them could mistake him for someone else. 'My name is Balder – but I give it no time at all before one of you thinks up a nickname for me.'
The smile Ian managed was a rictus of astonishment.
'What the fu—' Alan breathed abortively.
So it was left to Lea to step forward and offer this familiar, but profoundly changed and soot-etched, face a civil reception. 'Hello,' she said, although she faltered at his name. She ran a hand down one of Balder's arms. 'It's good you're here. We didn't look for you because... well, it's not that I wasn't worried, I just—' Tears came and Lea's voice cracked. 'I heard a rumour that you were being looked after by someone local, maybe—'
Balder stepped closer to Lea. She reached forward to receive his embrace, but lowered her arms again when it became clear that he wished only to speak discreetly. 'I know something about you,' he whispered. 'Before I came here today I learned that you wear your spirituality like a trendy T-shirt. I'm sure your beliefs and reverence are sincere, but I've heard that you use them as an excuse to intoxicate yourself in the name of mind-expansion; you express your environmental concerns as misanthropy, and Ben Marchen worshipped you because self-confidence can look like Enlightenment when you're wearing a crystal round your neck.'
Lea hid her expression behind a cloud of exhaled smoke.
'I've also been told that the time you spend hiding in the countryside has as much to do with your limited social skills and wavering self-respect than any profound need for contact with the Earth. Whatever your reasons, I do believe that you love Meeting Hill, and I'm challenging you like this to squeeze your conscience. The Meeting needs you, and through me it can use you for something more useful than burning incense. Can Meeting Hill rely on you?'
Lea held Balder's gaze in disbelief. She searched his earnest eyes for any trace of humour, but then glanced down at her feet. When she looked up again, her eyes had dried. 'Everyone has to cope with losing their parents some time,' she said. 'But if turning cold and ignorant is the way you want to deal with losing yours, you're going to be very lonely. I think you're a coward, and I'm sorry I started to confuse sympathy for you with something deeper.'
Lea lifted the butt of her roll-up and flicked it at him. He flinched as it bounced off his forehead. Lea walked away without saying goodbye to the others.
Ian did not hear what the man who looked like Ben had said, but he was unable to believe that Lea would react unreasonably given her previous concern for him.
Balder appeared unmoved by the exchange, and for a moment Ian hated him.
Balder stepped forward attempting a smile, but his awkward show of teeth looked more like the result of a lesson from a book called How to Grin. 'I'm

sorry, this introduction hasn't turned out as I wanted. I suppose I should have guessed it would be difficult.'

'I'm sorry too,' Alan muttered.

Balder received the comment like a bullet. He looked at his feet in pain. 'I'm still learning all sorts of things, mostly about what Madog expects of me, and I find it hard to chat about anything else. I think that a relationship with anyone is going to be difficult when I have only one thing in my head.'

'What's that?' George asked.

'The Meeting,' he replied, and said it with such naked innocence that Ian not only believed him, he forgave him for it.

'Looking back,' Ian suggested, 'perhaps that was always your problem,'

'It still isn't safe.'

Alan brightened quickly. 'We can reassure you about that. Lea was with us because we've been celebrating. Geophagia has called off its plans for a festival here.'

Balder shook his head. 'What Lea said might have been true, but probably only for a while – assuming it wasn't just a way of keeping you quiet.'

'Lea was a well-placed Geophagia member,' George defended her. 'She wouldn't tell us something like that lightly.'

George felt patronised when Balder smiled at her. 'I'm not calling Lea a liar. If she's a friend of yours I'm sure she can be trusted – but Madog knows Roedan better than anyone. He says that she will come to Meeting Hill on October 31st, and she'll bring a host of hundreds – maybe more – to help her search.'

The Earthwork members looked at each other. George seemed to age and shrink.

'I think Madog knows even more than he's telling me. He seems so sure about it. He says there's only one way of seeing her off for good: a plan involving me, and probably one of you – but I can't be sure of anything yet.'

Balder was encouraged by the attention Earthwork paid his words. His confidence returned. 'That's all I came to say for now. It's good to have met you. I'll see you again when I have more to tell.'

Madog had suggested that Balder spend the rest of that day exploring the land around Meeting Hill, most of which was arable estate property. *Y Deuddegfed Maen* could only know Meeting Hill as intimately as he should by being acquainted with its form from every perspective.

Balder agreed and obeyed, deciding to navigate this unfamiliar terrain by keeping Meeting Hill to his left, thereby completing his exploration in a wide, meandering circle, and ending up back where he had started.

Despite being a stranger to these tracts of land, Balder became immersed in *déjà vu*. He felt as though he was passing through several dreams at once, and every slope, valley, stream, wood and field seemed stalked by frustratingly familiar, yet nameless, ghosts. He began to feel watched, exposed and vulnerable. When his fear became overwhelming, with cold sweat coating his skin and knots tightening his stomach, Balder discovered that he had only to stop and gaze at the familiar outline of Meeting Hill to feel grounded, secure, and confident enough to move on.

It was not until Balder had reached a position almost north-west of The Meeting, just over half way around his circular route, that he began to fully relax in his own company. He even began to enjoy the isolation.

Balder walked a low ridge bordering the northern extremity of the Wyre estate: the last vantage with any view north before the landscape dropped away into the Somerset Levels, with Glastonbury as the next significant high ground before the Mendips.

He stopped and looked up like an answer to a beckoning, and then moved his head slowly until he faced the source of the wind. He inhaled deeply and rotated on the spot to view the surrounding panorama.

Clouds crept beneath the late-morning sun. Balder watched their shadows travel south across the estate, darkening the green and brown chequer of fields like a gloomy tide, and Meeting Hill's dome of autumn colours was alternately dimmed and ignited by sweeping sunbeams. For the first time Balder saw how Meeting Hill related to the landscape, and his appreciation of this wider view felt like a confirmation of his identity. Away from Madog and his incessant instruction, Balder was better able to think of himself as The Meeting's Twelfth Stone, and not as still aspiring to the title.

His euphoria at that moment cleared his mind of the previous hour's fear, allowing the bright input of his senses to suffuse his consciousness where cloudy rumination had darkened it during much of the walk. Focused, Balder was able to enjoy the freedom of *Y Deuddegfed Maen's* unique perspective. He saw Britain as Madog said it had once been: a boundless vista of wild, uncultivated landscape, unspoilt and unfenced by the dissection of possessive human territories.

The new Twelfth Stone of Meeting Hill, with his privileged vision and singular passion, had enjoyed self-expression (and a name in which to claim it) for little more than a month, though its potential had been incubated as a hopeful dream in the mind of a restless host for over two decades. Ben Marchen was unsettled by its presence since he was eleven years old. As an adult he had been distracted by its gnawing ambition, rendered notoriously nihilistic by its incompatibility with expectations of him, and finally sacrificed to allow Balder's guiltless emergence.

Of all this Balder was aware, and he found himself so breathlessly grateful for it that he knelt and prayed for several minutes without pause or pretence. He prayed to the Earth, to the Sun, to the wilful Air and the Oceans beyond sight, and to the bountiful Life offered form and expression by these elements, thanking each in turn for the pure and simple joy of existence.

Balder felt a selfless and resolute faith that the objects of his reverence were listening, and he prayed with intense emotion and humility for only one favour: that he might be assisted to be worthy of the world he loved; worthy of this unique and dutiful life, and equal to The Meeting's expectation of him.

Such heartfelt supplication exhausted Balder. He remained kneeling for a few minutes more as the sun crossed its meridian, and then rose to walk sedately downhill feeling indescribably older, yet gratefully somehow recognised.

Avalon

While Balder walked the estate around Meeting Hill, Sarah Conrad went shopping. She took Roedan's Audi to Caernarfon rather than the much closer Betws-Y-Coed, just for the change, and made more of the trip by visiting the castle. She drank coffee in a bar opposite.

Sarah realised how quickly she was becoming bored. She knew that when she returned to Tan Y Bryn she had cleaning to do.

The drive back took her through Llanrug, Llanberis, over Pen-Y-Pas, alongside the Llynnau Mymbyr to Capel Curig and then along the Llugwy valley into Pont Cyfyng. Sarah had planned the meal she would prepare for Roedan and herself that evening, so when she struggled through the front door of Roedan's house with groceries at two o'clock, she was disappointed to see a suitcase and several smaller bags in the hall. She guessed their destination but still feigned surprise when she entered the kitchen, found Roedan preparing a packed lunch and already wearing a coat.

'Wherever you're going,' Sarah said, lifting the carrier-bags onto the table, 'I don't think you want me to go with you.'

'I didn't think you'd want to come.'

'Somerset?' Sarah guessed.

Roedan did not know that Sarah was aware of Brampton Wyre's visit. Sarah did not ask Roedan about her visitors, and she did not want to confess to eavesdropping. The older woman nodded.

'Why are you going there? Didn't you cancel your plans for the October festival?'

Roedan looked up with an impatient glance. 'That was my decision until two days ago, but there are more members of Geophagia than there are villagers protesting in Little Arlingham, so who do you think I'm more worried about offending?'

Sarah nodded and began unpacking the shopping. Roedan lightened her tone and sat on the edge of the table. 'I didn't mean to leave you out, but I have noticed how distracted you've been. I thought an invitation to a dance festival on Meeting Hill would be tactless. But of course – you're invited.'

'No, you were right. Why would I want to go back there?' she replied, restocking a cupboard as her mind became flooded with memories: her first encounter with Ian and Alan in Tantric Trading; the Earthwork team faking undercover surveillance on Meeting Hill by standing rigidly in the clearing like standing stones; Ben's and Craig's constant baiting of Abel Mild and Baz on the estate; Alan deafening his team-mates in the Land Rover with Thin Lizzy songs; Ian's complaints about the lack of decent coffee at early morning meetings; Ian imitating Tai Chi in a crop circle; Ian laughing... Ian...

Sarah dropped two tins and gripped the door of the cupboard. Roedan watched her cry for nearly a minute. The house and kitchen were silent but for the sounds of Sarah's sadness and the metallic trundle of a tin crossing the tiles.

Roedan stepped forward to stroke Sarah's hair. 'It's all right to miss them, just don't forget why you left. You described so many good reasons to move up here with me.'

Sarah kissed Roedan's cheek. 'I don't regret anything, but I think we need to talk before you go.'

Roedan stepped back holding her lover's hands. 'Look, I won't go today. The construction team are on the move, but festival set-up doesn't begin until the morning of the 31st. They can manage without me for twenty-four hours. I'll make some phone-calls. Today can be for us.'

Roedan used the phone while Sarah packed the lunch already prepared. They put on walking boots and fleece jackets and headed uphill from the house, though they did not walk far. The couple followed the road south from Tan Y Bryn for a few minutes and turned onto a footpath from Capel Tan-Y-Garth. It climbed steadily through woods to a grassland plateau hosting hut circles and ancient quarries above the valley. They stopped at the edge of the trees and settled themselves beneath a young, wind-bent oak where they relaxed, ate and talked.

The view west, south and east was so impressive that it allowed Sarah to feel justified in avoiding eye contact with Roedan. 'I've missed Somerset and the friends I made in Arlingham. That's strange because I wasn't there that long – not long enough to think of the village as home.'

'You were so upset just now.'

'Arlingham is easy to get attached to. The Meeting's a funny place. It's like an island above everything. You feel like there's no one else in the world while you're up there. You could be in the future or the distant past. But it's not just a pretty landmark. The villagers point at Meeting Hill as a reason to avoid changing anything. It's like a barrier against outside influences and it stops the town expanding. While Carreg's End has something as old as The Meeting on its doorstep, how can Arlingham ever be anything but a quiet rural village? And the monument gets to you. You fall in love with it, so you get pissed off when you visit the site and find a beer can in the grass. No wonder all the villagers are so uptight.'

Sarah turned to meet Roedan's penetrating gaze. 'That's why I got so upset earlier. I don't want you to hold a festival there. You're looking for some Arthurian treasure that might not even exist and I'm afraid for the hill.' She looked away. 'There, I've said it.'

Roedan reddened, though her exertion seemed spent inward. Sarah wondered what might have been said or done had she been anyone else. 'You've been very honest with me. I'm not used to it, but I'm going to share things with you that I've never told anyone.'

Sarah doubted that.

'I love Meeting Hill, too. I lived beneath it with the Meeting's Twelfth Stone for quite a long time. I love all the megalithic sites of the British Isles, as much for what they might have represented when they were first built as the little we know now. Places like The Meeting, Avebury and Wayland's Smithy are imaginative gateways to a lost world. They take us out of our time – and let me tell you, Sarah,' Roedan's voice lowered and sharpened, 'I *hate* our time. Millions of years of human evolution have achieved nothing more than an addiction to pop culture and brand labels. People seem happy to have their values and ambitions defined by television and films and adverts. But I'll tell you what I want: I want to be away from everyone, and feel alone like you can on Meeting Hill. I want to find and hold something that survived from an age when The Meeting was a temple that still channelled the power it was built to focus – when wilderness didn't mean just a little bit of countryside without fields in it. It was Avalon – all of Britain: a free state in which to roam without landowners' fences to cross, or hair-splitting laws to follow or a rat-race to run. When the 5th-Century leader of the British tribes died fighting Saxons – invaders who cared nothing for the identity of this island – that wilderness died too. But a cross was buried with Arthur's body at Glastonbury. To hold that object in your hand would be to possess the epitaph of that age.'

'*If* the cross existed,' Sarah added reasonably.

'It's real,' Roedan insisted.

'So little is known about the time you're talking about. You know that better than I do – you have a degree in archaeology. The picture you're painting is a fairytale.'

'Maybe that's what makes it so attractive. The world's no fairytale today. What meaningful mythology do we have to live by in the 21st Century? Everyone wants to be a celebrity. The cult of cool and the self-centred individual is the most common doctrine now. What cause is there in today's Britain that could bring every citizen together to stand side-by-side in mutual support? People can't even shop in the sales without fighting. Do you think this country is now capable of producing the kind of selfless hero, like Arthur, that everyone would respect?' Roedan's conviction seemed intense, though Sarah thought her argument seemed well-rehearsed. 'Don't you think this country must be missing something if one of our most popular icons is a man who lived fifteen-hundred years ago?'

Sarah did not answer immediately. It gave Roedan a moment to calm herself. When Sarah did reply she remained wary. 'It's a great subject for your stage. Talk of fantasy landscapes and warriors and magic temples must be inspiring at a Geophagia festival – but how can it be a motive for raping what little is left of the landscape you're so nostalgic about?'

Roedan gazed up at the peak of Moel Siabod. 'That's just the difference between you and me, Sarah. If we believed in all the same things you wouldn't be criticising me – you'd be taking notes. I believe that the age of Britain as a wild landscape peopled by environmentally pious tribes is long dead, and even the last surviving patches of it – like this,' she indicated the view around her, 'are too small, fragmented and far from each other to resuscitate it. Avalon exists now only as a lucid dream. It is the Otherworld to which the souls of people who share that dream travel, and I believe that it can only be glimpsed in this life by contact with a relic of its last great leader and protector. An English king was going to use Arthur's burial cross in the Twelfth Century to dishearten the Celts with proof of their hero's death – but I believe that unearthing such a relic today would provide the British with a symbol under which to unite. It would prove to everyone that Arthur once existed, and that the Britain he knew is possible.'

Sarah shook her head and wanted to express reservations about such fierce nationalism, but her conviction faltered as she realised that the debate was now so far removed from reason, and so steeped in Roedan's personal faith, that rational conversation was useless.

It occurred to Sarah that the only way in which she might help those who sought to protect The Meeting was to delay Roedan's departure for Somerset. So she shrugged and smiled as though the conversation meant little to her, and it simply amused her to play devil's advocate. She leaned closer to Roedan and nuzzled her cheek. 'Either way, you can forget about all that for a while. Didn't you say you'd reserve the next few days for us?'

Roedan knew she had made no such promise, but she bought Sarah's compliant silence with a suppression of instinctive denial.

Retirement

Madog and Balder walked to Glastonbury during the early hours of October 30th. They wore their dark hooded robes, and both carried a small shoulder bag. They travelled directly north-west cross-country, following footpaths where possible, roads if necessary, and trespassing frequently. Crossing the channels and rhynes of the Levels, they passed through or near South Barrow, Wheathill, Lydford on Fosse, South Pennard, Baltonsborough, Kennard Moor and Edgarley. They travelled over farms, fields of sheep and cattle, through gardens and, as they drew closer to Glastonbury, through acres of orchards.

The night was overcast and damp and it spawned a grey dawn. Dense fog carpeted the Avalon Vale, clinging to the men's skin, each inhaled breath and the fruit of the trees like apple-infused perspiration. The introduction of weak morning light offered the walkers a short view ahead. Against the glowing ether, the trees of the orchards resembled the bowers from which Arthur Rackham's *Fairies and Elves Pick Apples*.

Balder and Madog stepped clear of the deepest fog on the A361 at Edgarley, almost at the foot of Glastonbury Tor. The sun rose out of the haze and bathed the West Country in stark silver light. The mists clinging to Glastonbury's hills assumed a metallic sheen, giving the Tor and its summit tower a halo of reflected light against a sky of vaporised mercury. The terraced slopes seemed absorb the sunrise and then exude it as a diffuse, but intense outlining aura.

The dazzling scene lasted only minutes. The sun rose quickly into a ceiling of grey cloud and was not seen again that day.

The two men walked into town along Chilkwell Street. They stopped briefly in Well House Lane beside the water spout from the Chalice Well and shrugged off their cloaks, revealing less conspicuous attire beneath. They pushed the robes into their bags, drank mouthfuls of rusty Red Spring water and then decided to walk the Tor, ascending by the longer western footpath. Madog impressed Balder by not needing to pause for breath during the climb, though he coughed with an obstructive rattle and spat thick phlegm at regular intervals. Balder was also as impressed by Madog's appreciation of the view as he was by the view itself. It interested Balder to see a man of confident authority display humility. Madog span slowly as he walked, absorbing the panorama in ascending circles.

Alone on the Tor beside the ruined tower of St Michael, the men were buffeted by a wind felt only at the altitude of the exposed hilltop, allowing the mists of the vale below to recede gently. Three crows drifted and dived about the hilltop.

Madog pointed south-east along the route they had walked. Balder followed his outstretched finger and discerned the dark dome of Meeting Hill against the much larger hillfort at South Cadbury beyond.

'Roedan will arrive in Somerset today or tomorrow, if she's not here already,' Madog predicted. 'She'll visit the Tor at some point and stand where we are now to look along the *ley line* she's always talking about. She'll light a candle and tell Meeting Hill she's coming, or something like that. She likes those kind of gestures.'

Balder listened but displayed no interest. He recognised Roedan as the person who posed the greatest and most immediate threat to The Meeting; but, unless Madog was describing the nature of that threat, Balder received descriptions of her indifferently. He left Madog at the south-east quarter of the Tor and wandered away, rounding the hollow tower until the old man was out of sight and he could feel alone on the windy platform above the Levels.

Just as he had done while exploring land around Meeting Hill the day before, Balder encountered ghosts on Glastonbury Tor. He caught glimpses of the hilltop at different times of day and in very different company, always at the periphery of sight, like stolen memories viewed through an opaque window. This time, though, Balder controlled his reaction to these flashes: he swallowed his fear and gazed resolutely at Chalice Hill until the unnerving flow of déjà vu receded, and the unwelcome recollections drained back into whatever dark neural recess they had seeped from.

Just as before, the relief that came with exercising his will over these unwanted images relaxed his thoughts, thereby unlocking an eidetic faculty that blossomed from his quieted mind. His perception of the view broadened and crystallised; the landscape became changed in every direction. Balder felt his fear renewed as the transformation unfolded because of a smothering sense that these changes were wrought by something placed before his eyes. Again, though, he relaxed, restricting expression of his disorientation to a brief unbalanced stagger.

Growing accustomed to the illusion, he waved experimentally at the air in front of his face, as though he might wipe through the view like condensation on a window. Yet there was no filter to be cleared. The only addition to Balder's view from the Tor was an interpretation of it by his own unique perspective.

With concentration, he noticed the greatest change to the scenery was that certain features of it had been removed: Glastonbury had gone – or, more accurately from Balder's temporal vantage, was not yet conceived of – and the vast network of drainage rhynes, dykes and channels criss-crossing the present-day Levels had yet to be dug.

Balder gazed across tidal fenland and lakes. Water, reeds and rushes surrounded the wooded slopes of the Tor and its adjoining hills, and Balder realised that the prehistoric high ground of future Glastonbury truly once was an island. This inland sea stretched away from the Tor in every direction. It was hedged to the north by the lightly wooded Mendip Hills; it mirrored the pale dawn light in the east where it lapped against the slopes of hills near present-day Pennard and Ditcheat, and was bordered in the south by the Polden Hills and the high ground of Butleigh Wood. To the west, the marshes stretched away to the sea, with only a few distant islands surfacing from the flooded plain.

Balder rotated slowly where he stood and fully appreciated his impression of a long lost isolation. He noticed how a complete absence of urban development expanded the panorama in both scale and majesty, and he attempted to focus on details in the landscape.

But such concentration was also a distraction, and the effort of it blurred, fractured and then shattered the vision. Somerset, present-day – well drained, rurally chequered and littered with towns – was restored to Balder's sight, and he suddenly became wistful for a savage wilderness he had never known.

Madog stepped up beside him and seemed about to say something, but suddenly the world was no longer theirs to wander in dreamy seclusion. A Labrador bounded onto the hilltop plateau from the eastern steps and leapt playfully around the two men in greeting. With the dog's owner following not far behind, Madog guided Balder back downhill along the footpath.

Ten minutes' walk from the Tor, the men passed the northern boundary of the Abbey grounds and stepped onto the High Street. They found an early café, The Blue Note, open and serving. Balder discovered hot chocolate inside and could not disguise his childlike enjoyment of it. He finished it so quickly that it amused Madog to buy him a second cup and sit soberly with his mug of tea watching Balder drink it. The younger man grinned happily.

Glastonbury's preserved antiquity and market-town charm was overwhelmed along the High Street by the proportion of shops catering to the town's trade in New Age merchandise. These establishments were once labelled as an alternative to modern commerce; but, in 1999, Glastonbury boasted so many purveyors of crystals, essential oils, incense, candles, ceremonial swords and meditation music; and so many bookshops selling volumes of shamanistic and Wiccan enlightenment, alien abduction, Reiki healing and folklore, that the only real alternative for local shoppers was the town's modest Woolworth's.

A beggar had appeared outside The Blue Note by the time the men were ready to leave. He was young, but his stubble, dreadlocks, facial tattoo and missing front teeth made him look much older. The man sat on a coat at the edge of the pavement chanting a litany of requests and follow-up abuse at passing pedestrians. 'Spare some change? Just a quid? Fucker.'

It was ten o'clock when Madog and Balder turned left out of the café and headed downhill, following the road east where it swerved to avoid the ancient market cross, until they reached the entrance to the ruins of Glastonbury Abbey. Madog surprised Balder by leading him inside.

Seeing Madog pay for their entry to a Christian site on the Glastonbury tourist trail was one of the unlikeliest events in Balder's short life up to that point, but he resisted the urge to question his guardian, sure that the visit must hold a purpose other than sight-seeing.

Until the Dissolution, Glastonbury Abbey had been one of the wealthiest estates in England. Following its closure in 1540, the building was sold into private ownership and plundered for the next two centuries for road and building materials. But enchanting ruins remain: transepts, archways, a tiny chapel and the Abbot's Kitchen stand today in immaculate green grounds. Madog led Balder around several towering aspects of the weathered ruins to a stone outline in the grass which, according to a nearby sign, was once a building called the Lady Chapel.

As the first and only visitors to the grounds at this early hour, Madog did not restrain himself from a series of theatrical grunts and groans as he lowered himself onto a section of the exposed masonry. He fidgeted until he was comfortable, and then looked up at Balder as though expecting him to do the same.

Balder sat down beside him, watching the old man rummaging through his shoulder bag. Madog pulled from the sack two rectangles of hardboard, pressed tightly together and fastened at each corner by wing-nuts and bolts. This was followed by an unlabelled bottle of golden spirit.

'Why are we here?' Balder asked.

'Think of this as my retirement party,' Madog said, also producing the tin cups from which the men drank at Chiron Dell. He tapped the mugs together, fixed Balder with a devilish grin and half-filled both cups with the unknown – though undoubtedly cheap – brand of whisky.

'No,' Balder replied – the first display of impertinence Madog had ever seen in him. 'You can't retire.'

Madog laughed. 'Isn't it every apprentice's dream to ditch the *Trainee* label and be his own boss?'

'But—' Balder began, and then tactfully tempered his response: 'I mean no. I like being with you, and I'm worried I'm not ready to do this by myself.'

'I'm glad you appreciate the importance of your role, but as the Twelfth Stone, you're fulfilling a self-appointed, voluntary duty under an assumed title, not studying to perform surgery. There's no exam: The Meeting's continued preservation is your certificate of competence.'

'But this job seems so tied up with complicated traditions and worshipping Gods I've never heard of – there must be more I need to know before you disappear. I want to feel like I'm taking the job as seriously as all the others before me.'

'I respect that, Balder,' Madog nodded. 'But you also need to relax. Firstly, *Y Deuddegfed Maen* worships nothing – we show respect for the Will of Nature and whatever form, face or name it chooses to wear, but it is the common respect due any professional relationship. Our modest ritual is offered in return for help with protecting The Meeting. Secondly, you were chosen for this role because I decided that you already had the qualities required, not because you needed teaching them. Look,' he handed Balder a cup: 'you don't have to learn to be *me*. When I leave Meeting Hill and Chiron Dell in your care, you're welcome to forget everything I've taught you – except your one overriding priority.'

'The preservation of Meeting Hill and the stones,' Balder said automatically.

Madog smiled. 'But how you go about it is up to you. Tradition should last only while it's useful. Your methods and style are your own.'

'As of when?'

'Less than forty-eight hours, I hope,' Madog replied, 'after you've completed part of a plan to keep two thousand people off the hill that I can't fulfil myself.'

'Of course. What do you need?'

Madog loosened the bolts fastening the hardboard frame and tilted it gently. Balder gaped as a lead cross, around a foot long and untidily inscribed, slid from between the hardboard sheets and landed with a flat thud in the grass.

'A pension,' the old man announced, cheerfully tapping his tin cup against Balder's. 'Here's to retirement,' he toasted himself.

*

Madog had been right about Roedan. She arrived in Somerset that morning, and as the elderly Twelfth Stone casually revealed the existence of an artefact long thought lost, Roedan parked at the bottom of Well House Lane and strode to the summit of Glastonbury Tor, where she received the wind like an elemental ovation.

She gazed south-east along a straight line of prehistoric monuments, some of which had played host to Geophagia's festivals over the previous nine months. She was not given to prayer, but her reverential stance and breathless expression might have been mistaken for it, especially when she lit a joss stick and planted it in the grass at her feet, hoping that the wind would blow its smoke in the direction of her gaze. Roedan seemed to be whispering something to the distant horizon and was only distracted when a man who shared her ambition approached from the eastern footpath.

'Hi,' said Tom Sutherland. 'I thought I'd find you up here today.'

Roedan turned to glare at the owner of the American accent. She recognised him as her former employee and turned away. 'Fuck off.'

'Oh,' Tom clutched at his chest as though wounded, staggering melodramatically, 'and yeah, I deserve that – but please don't mean it.'

'I mean it.'

'Let me talk, Jill.'

Roedan flinched at such familiar address. 'You insulted me and my work and my beliefs, and then you left me. Nothing has changed.'

'Sure, but I can convince you that I was wrong to go,' he replied, moving to stand within Roedan's field of view. Roedan blinked evasively. 'I never lost my faith in the things you teach, Jill, I just got spooked because I began to realise that the powers you said exist— well, they turned out to be more real than I realised.'

Roedan laughed. 'So what were you doing with me *before* you realised that I'm not full of shit?'

'You employed me as your Press and Promotions Manager – I didn't need to believe anything to work for you,' Tom responded truthfully. 'I was impressed by you and your power over people, and now that I've had time to accept and not fear the things I saw in August, I'd be crazy not to see this thing through. I want to work for you again.'

Roedan sneered cynically. 'Stuck for a job, are you?'

'No,' Tom said quickly. 'Money and work are not a problem right now. I'm just making a professional choice here. I know what you're trying to achieve, and I want to be a part of it. Look, I'm begging for a chance to follow you again, Roedan.'

She closed her eyes and raised her face to the wind. The grey sky was growing darker, and there was a hint of moisture in the air. Roedan casually considered how long it might be before the wind brought rain, leaving Tom to wait an uncomfortable length of time. Then she finally exhaled with a smile, opened her eyes, and with an exaggerated American accent, declared, 'Hell boy, you kiss ass *good*.'

Tom remained silent, wary of pushing his luck.

'Well, I hope you've dealt thoroughly with whatever scared you, Tom, because I want you to remember it all and tell me everything.' Roedan buried her hands in her pockets and hugged herself against the wind. She turned on her heel and paced through the hollow tower of St Michael to the path downhill. 'And I hope you've not lost your persuasive people-skills,' she added, Tom striding triumphantly beside her. 'I have a couple of awkward situations I need you to ease me out of, here and at home.'

*

Already reaching for a refill, Madog made Balder drain his cup as quickly as he had. No one passed them to disturb their conversation or challenge their drinking, and Madog's voice had become slightly raised as the alcohol soaked up his inhibition. 'What do you mean, why do I want *money?*' he asked, making Balder feel ridiculous. 'How am I going to survive away from Chiron Dell? I'll have nowhere to live, and I won't have the food left each week by the few old villagers who respect me.'

Balder was suddenly struck *by* a childlike fear of expressing his thoughts to someone who could make his opinions seem so incredibly naïve. 'But you… against materialism…I thought—'

'No, no, *no!'* Madog winced. 'Please! No more preconceptions about me. I do have some selfish interest – and I'll have even more when Meeting Hill is yours to worry about.'

'So you're going to sell this?' Balder asked, studying the cross before him.

Madog had refilled their cups and was taking a sip from his own, but he almost choked on it in response to the younger man's question. 'No! It's not mine to sell – and how would selling it help Meeting Hill?'

Balder reached out to touch the cross reverently. He hesitated as though expecting an electric shock, but then laid his palm against the metal. It was cold to his touch. Feeling the inscription of the archaic text against his fingers was like stroking a cheese grater. Balder wondered if this was the first time since its discovery that the cross had known contact with the soil of its first ancient burial. 'Is it real?'

Madog burrowed into his shoulder bag again and produced a packet of slim cigars, which he handled with more respect than he had the cross. 'Was this object buried here with the bodies of King Arthur and Guenevere in the Fifth Century? I don't know.'

Balder could not disguise his disappointment.

'But,' Madog went on, fumbling through the bag for matches, 'if you're asking me whether or not this cross was pulled out of the ground we're sitting on in 1191, I can confirm that it is.'

Balder smiled, carefully turning the plate over to study the text on the other side. 'So there was a grave here?'

'Oh yes,' Madog laughed, 'but then this area of the Abbey grounds was a cemetery! There were plenty of political and financial motives for the monks to have faked the discovery of Arthur's body here in the 12th Century – but that doesn't mean the cross isn't immensely valuable in its own right.'

Balder shook his head in wonder, and his innocent pleasure was infectious. Even Madog caught it for a moment. 'Yes,' he smiled, 'it is rather wonderful, isn't it?'

Balder picked up the cruciform plate and immediately became aware that, despite its weight, the lead was malleable. 'Think of all the history this cross has seen, and the blood spilt for possession of it,' he breathed, tracing the flow of its lettering with a finger. 'And to think that these words could have been so wounding to the Welsh.'

Madog nodded thoughtfully. 'Who knows? The theory is sound, but with or without proof of the grave, the Welsh would have believed whatever they'd wanted to about Arthur. Faith satisfies a need, so people believe whatever makes them feel comfortable, whatever century it is. The spirit of a people is bigger than one man – and who's to say that Welsh nationalism might not have been *strengthened* by talk of Arthur's body in English hands? But none of that matters anymore. People will see nothing but financial value in the cross now – except Roedan, who thinks that she only has to touch it to be whisked back through time to a Celtic golden age, when all men were questing warriors in search of The Golden Pants of So-and-So, and all women were High Priestesses of Almighty Cervix.'

Balder frowned, confused. 'But if you're not going to sell it…?'

'I'll leave it with you,' Madog replied, 'and you can do what you want with it.'

'What do you mean?'

'*Y Deuddegfed Maen* has always kept the cross hidden and secure, but you might think that disposing of it in some other way will serve the stones better, especially if people keep wanting to dig Meeting Hill up in search of it.'

Balder shook his head. 'The Twelfth Stone has looked after Arthur's cross for nearly eight hundred years, but you'd let me destroy it?'

'I didn't say you had to destroy it – although if that turns out to be best for The Meeting, then so be it,' Madog shrugged, gazing across the outlines of the abbey's foundations to a lily-covered pond where ducks were nestled in a downy huddle. 'However, destruction need not seem so final,' he suggested thoughtfully. 'My life has been ruled by the natural cycles around me, and I learned from what I saw. For every loss or change I witnessed, something else emerged in its place. I always thought of it as an exchange: sacrifice in return for transformation. That's a concept that you embody, Balder.'

The younger man voiced his interpretation of Madog's meaning. 'An exchange? So perhaps I should give the cross to Roedan if she promises to stay off Meeting Hill?'

The old man studied Balder's expression. 'You could,' he agreed, 'if you and Earthwork fail in all other ways – but wouldn't it be a shame to see Roedan get what she wanted all along?'

'If you knew she was attracted to the site by this cross, why didn't you give it to her before? We could have avoided months of trouble. You always say that The Meeting is all that matters.'

'I'll assume you're joking,' Madog replied indignantly. 'The cross was the ace up our sleeve. Why would I drop such a priceless artefact – and our only bargaining currency – into the private collection of someone so unscrupulous before trying everything else? What do you think Earthwork is for?' He shook his head and grimaced as though chewing something foul. 'And more than that, I've grown to hate Roedan as much as I love The Meeting. She was once in your position, and I had every faith in her – but she robbed me and then abandoned the respect and reverence that defines us to become the treasure hunter she is now. If this cross has to be used in a trade for The Meeting's safety, I accept that – but I won't be the one to hand it to her. I shall retire

when I give it to you, and then you can see this crisis through.'
But Balder was hardly listening now. He stared in vague disbelief at the cross laid in the grass. 'So it's mine?' he wondered aloud.
'No,' Madog snapped, picking up the inscribed plate and sliding it back into its frame. 'It will never be *yours,* just as it was never *mine* – but I'll leave it with you, for the benefit of The Meeting, in exchange for something Roedan stole from me. I need something I can sell for enough money to keep me in cheap whisky and cod-liver oil until I die.'
'And what's that?'
'A dagger: the one lost by Marchen during her fight with Richard of Glastonbury in 1191,' Madog explained. He saw recollection of the story in Balder's wide eyes. 'I found it in 1982. A small tree on the western slope of Meeting Hill was uprooted by my weight as I climbed it, starting a small landslide, and there it was.'
'What does it look like? Balder watched Madog light his cigar with a match in cupped hands.
'Old, but with a very distinctive curving blade. I'll sketch it for you.'
Balder rose and wandered the outline of the foundation around them. 'I suppose this dagger is in Roedan's house?' he guessed, feeling suddenly distanced from his elder, who now seemed so keen to be rid of the responsibility Balder was about to take on.
'Yes,' Madog nodded, 'and I have her address. She wrote to me once, years ago, when we still agreed on a few things. But she took the dagger when she left Chiron Dell.'
'To Wales?'
'If she still has it – but I'm sure she wouldn't sell something like that.'
Balder gaped at the increasingly intoxicated Madog. 'So I have just over twenty four hours to find an object you're not even sure exists?'
Madog shrugged. 'Keep your voice down, boy. I just want my property back. I get the dagger – you get the cross: then you save Meeting Hill in whatever way the situation demands.'
'You want me to be a burglar.'
'Is burglary any worse than what Roedan might do to The Meeting?'
Balder deflated. He looked away and saw the Tor rising above the trees to the north-east. 'I don't know. You still haven't told me what she might do to The Meeting.'
Madog refilled his cup with whisky once more. 'Burglary is a term defined by the society we have chosen to live outside of, but society knows nothing about us, or our cause. This is what's expected of you.'
Madog could not count the number of times he had repeated *Y Deuddegfed Maen's* maxim of social and legal isolation since Balder's Pagan naming. He had continuously hoped that his student would not only hear the words, but

also feel the potentially liberating truth of their acceptance. This time, however, it seemed that Balder had accepted it because he did not respond with his usual obedient nod.

In fact, Balder did not believe that he, or anyone else, could be truly free of society or its laws in Britain. The law recognises no exemptions, of course – but Balder was suddenly struck by the power of even imagining such freedom. Perhaps, as with many aspects of personality, merely behaving as though it were true could make it so – especially in a village like Little Arlingham, which had functioned happily for generations with someone doing exactly that living on the fringe of its community. Madog had spent a lifetime getting away with it.

'All right,' Balder declared confidently, focusing so sharply on his goal that he did not want to waste a moment. 'Then I want to go now. The festival is tomorrow night.'

'You're going to leave right now? Straight from here?'

'Why did you bring me to Glastonbury to announce the plan? I'm helpless here.'

'Because there are lots of pubs nearby where we can celebrate my retirement, and I thought you'd be happier leaving tomorrow.'

Balder gaped. '*Tomorrow?* You wanted me to go North Wales with a hangover, search an obscure address, get back to Arlingham and arrange a deal with Roedan in less than a day? No, I need to get to a telephone. Do you have any change?'

A public telephone stood opposite the Abbey grounds' entrance. Balder dialled the only two numbers he could dredge from second-hand memory. The first – the Marchen house in Carreg's End, where Ian Longe had lived alone since September – rang unanswered. The 1571 message service kicked in and Balder lost 20p.

The second number, an extension to the Earthwork barn on the Wyre estate, was answered by Abel Mild. 'Hello. Is Miss Wyre there? Or Alan? Or Ian?'

Madog listened to Balder's conversation from outside the phone box.

'No, it doesn't matter. Any of them. George is there? Good.'

A long pause, and then Madog laughed when he heard Balder say, 'Can you get her for me, then?'

Balder gave Madog a look of disbelief until he heard a new voice. 'Hello, Miss Wyre? Yes, it is. I need a favour. It's important for us, and for The Meeting. I need a lift to North Wales.'

Madog tapped on the glass and caught Balder's attention. He pointed at himself and then gestured enthusiastically at the nearby George and Pilgrim bar.

When Balder joined Madog ten minutes later the old man was half way through a second pint, and he looked more contented than Balder had ever seen him.

'Georgina had to call me back, I ran out of change.'

Madog lit another cigar. 'Any luck?'

'Ian's coming,' Balder said. 'It's lucky he's self-employed. He's going to get an Earthwork car and come straight here.'

Madog croaked a throaty laugh. 'Did you tell them the plan?'

'No. Ian won't care, but I don't think Georgina Wyre would have passed on the message if she'd known.'

'How long before you leave me here at the mercy of this evil stuff?' Madog asked, taking a mouthful of the ale.

'Ian will be here by one.'

Madog glanced at a clock over the bar. 'Then you have nearly two hours to relax,' he declared, handing him a cigar. 'What do you want to drink?'

Journeys

Lea Granger did not keep a permanent address. She believed that most people are distracted from their ambition and creativity by the nest-building instinct, and she did not like to feel included in a conformist majority.

When in need of a postal address, Lea gave the number of a Georgian townhouse on Hanbury Road in Clifton, Bristol. The house had been converted into spacious flats, one of which was owned by a friend named Simon, who was the lead-guitarist with Kundalini, and whose day job was more profitable than the band's sporadic bookings. Simon let two of the three bedrooms to Bristol professionals, and he let Lea sleep on the sofa in the lounge whenever she wanted to. But he never asked for rent because her presence was barely noticed, though she often stayed for up to two weeks of each month. Lea would arrive very late at night and leave early in the morning, and her only impact on the household bills was the occasional hot shower.

Lea worked behind the bar at The Dungeon in Bristol four nights a week. Employment in a popular nightclub offered her a regular and varied sex life, which naturally led to the provision of a bed somewhere locally, allowing Lea to claim the nomadic lifestyle she expounded so passionately. On other nights, when she was not working or singing with the band, Lea often headed for one of her favourite rural places, in Somerset or north Devon, and camped out. Yet Lea had spent a majority of her nights during the previous four months with Ben Marchen, and so had not seen Simon and the rest of the band as often as she would have liked.

Kundalini often set up and rehearsed their act in the expansive lounge of Simon's flat. Lea was there with them on the afternoon of October 30th when, without warning, the psychological legacy of September's drama finally caught up with her like Dobermans on a complacent intruder. In response to singing the particularly affecting lyrics of Kundalini's favourite ballad, Lea was emotionally savaged in front of her friends.

At news of Lea's withdrawal from Geophagia's future bookings, Kundalini had recruited a new singer, a girl named Jess, to replace Lea at the microphone. Lea felt no rivalry with Jess – Lea would continue to perform with Kundalini at their usual gigs – and it was while teaching Jess some of the band's songs that her usually iron-clad composure crumbled. Lea fled from the room and locked herself in the bathroom, the music of the band faltering behind her.

Lea vomited and clung to the edge of the toilet bowl. Then she washed her face, ate some toothpaste and stared blankly into the mirror, waiting for the spinning zoetrope of dark images to settle in her mind. The unexpected visions were memories of her recent past and had troubled her dreams for weeks: flaming arrows fell from a stormy night sky; hanged magpies dripped blood onto a bone-pale standing stone, and a decomposing limb reached for her from a shallow grave.

Jess's voice and a knock at the bathroom door dispelled the nightmarish replays.

Lea reached for the small bag of toiletries and make-up she kept hanging on the bathroom door and felt able to rationalise her distress. She realised that she missed involvement with the Geophagia Foundation, which had always afforded an acceptable public expression of her Pagan beliefs. She felt confused and frustrated by the betrayal of Roedan. Lea missed the level of contact she usually enjoyed with the Kundalini musicians, who represented a substantial majority of her social life. And she missed Ben.

Until their traumatic separation several weeks before, Lea had been so focused on nurturing Ben's adoration that she had paid little attention to her own need for him. She had neglected to express any affection beyond the physical because she was scared of it. Being young and afraid of commitment is a cliché; and yet, while Lea preferred to avoid clichés, she had been even keener to avoid commitment.

Lea would have been the first to admit that her emotional state could never be described as stable. She had always experienced wild highs, crushing lows, and occasionally a rage of seismic intensity for which the only satisfactory exorcism seemed to have been a cautiously superficial self-harm. But Ben Marchen had shown her the kind of admiring attention and consistent affection she had never dreamed possible. Then, just as she had found herself beginning to trust it, and even take it for granted, Ben's mounting stress, culminating in a mind-melting discovery, had snatched that contentment away.

Lea found powerlessness in the face of irrecoverable change the most frustrating of limitations. Such a situation allows no effective expression of the rage it provokes – but revenge, she suddenly realised, could be a satisfying distraction, surely able to absorb the anger invested in it.

'I'm okay,' she called to Jess. 'Maybe something I ate.'

Galvanised by the birth of a vengeful scheme, Lea returned to the mirror and set about preparing herself for a trip to Little Arlingham. Her hair, still less than an inch long, she could do nothing with; but to her eyes she applied a thick rim of black eye-liner and dark eye-shadow, making the whites of her eyes appear to swim in hollow sockets; and to her lips she applied crimson lipstick which, beneath her gaunt eyes and cold stare, strengthened the projection of her anger.

Feeling invulnerable behind this defiant mask, Lea rejoined her friends in the lounge. They were used to Lea's frequent changes of image, but even they were startled by this rapid and haunting makeover. Simon watched her pack her few belongings, which she hurled into a rucksack like she blamed each item for whatever had gone wrong.

'You don't look ill,' Simon observed from a safe distance. 'You look really pissed off.'
Lea grinned the pitiless rictus of a death's head. 'I won't be when I've taken it out on someone who deserves it. And I already know who.'
'Do you think you should be going out in this mood?'
'Oh yes,' Lea laughed, slipping on her cycling leather and reaching for her helmet. 'I really do.'

*

Ian collected Balder from outside The George and Pilgrim in Glastonbury at just after one o'clock that afternoon, driving one of the Earthwork Shoguns. 'I brought you some of your warmer clothes.'
'Mine?' Balder asked in surprise.
'*Ben's,* then,' Ian said with clear irritation.
It had started to rain, and the sky to the north – the direction in which the men would be driving – looked darker still.
Madog waved a smug farewell from the pub window. Ian returned a suspicious smile as he pulled away. He made a tight U-turn on the High Street and headed for the A39, taking the pair to the A37 at Midsomer Norton and then north through Bristol.
The first few minutes alone in the car together were silent. Balder did not sense any awkwardness, but he was the first to initiate business-like conversation. 'I really appreciate your help. If I can find what I'm looking for in Wales, I can end Roedan's threat to The Meeting like *that.*' He snapped his fingers.
'Good.'
'But what I'm going to do is illegal. You don't need to be involved, I just think you should know that. '
'Of course I'm involved,' Ian said. 'I'm your getaway driver.' Heavy rain flooded the windscreen.
'I'm going to break into a house.'
Ian glanced at Balder's impassive expression. 'Roedan's?'
'Yes. I want to return a knife to Madog that Roedan stole from him. For that he'll give me the cross from Arthur's grave, and I'll give it to Roedan if she promises to go away.'
Ian could not hide surprise. 'Madog has it? Right now? Then why didn't he—'
'I know,' Balder interrupted. 'I went through all that. It was his last resort, and the last resort is what we've come to.'
'Selfish, tricky old bastard… If we've just committed ourselves to becoming outlaws, wouldn't it be easier to mug the old man for it?'
Balder appeared disgusted by the thought. 'That's not the best way to thank him for a lifetime's commitment to the same stones we're trying to protect.

Anyway, he's probably thought of that.'
Ian opened the vents in the dashboard and turned on the fan. 'You smell like a brewery. How long were in the pub?'
Balder ignored the question. 'Did you bring the gear I asked George for?'
Ian stabbed a thumb over his shoulder at the back seat. 'Tent and sleeping bags from the cupboard in yo– *Ben's* old bedroom. They look old.'
Ian turned on the radio after a few moments silence. The men did not speak again until they reached the M32.
Ian looked sideways at Balder and seemed to reach a decision. 'I have to be honest with you, I'm having trouble with this talk of your reincarnation. How is anyone supposed to call you *Balder* with a straight face? Am I really supposed to think of you as a new acquaintance when I know I grew up with you?'
Balder stared through the windscreen. Eventually he said, 'Yes.'
Ian laughed. 'Can you remember anything before the night you found the grave on Meeting Hill?'
'Yes,' Balder said again.
'And you accept that it was the stressful experiences of Ben Marchen that forced this change?'
'That's what Madog thinks too,' Balder agreed.
Ian was surprised by the openness of these answers. 'So wouldn't it be reasonable to conclude that you *are* Ben Marchen, just with a symbolic new name to help put your old life behind you? Does Mad Dog actually believe that Ben died and *you've* taken over his brain?'
Balder hoped to be accepted by people, but he felt no need to justify himself beyond filling the silence of a long drive. 'It doesn't seem so simple to me. My first clear memory is only five weeks old. When I opened my eyes on the edge of the rhyne I knew language, but I'm still learning everything else.'
'Ben Marchen would have laughed his arse off if I jumped into a ditch and came out claiming to be someone else.'
'Then I really can't be him, can I?'

*

As Balder and Ian headed north through Somerset, Lea passed them on the A37, journeying south. Anger inspired her purpose and impatience drove her acceleration. She cruised and cornered the bike at speeds extreme for the conditions, triggering speed cameras in Midsomer Norton and Shepton Mallet. Lea turned west off the A359 just south of Galhampton, rode recklessly through North and South Barrow, and powered along the Sparkford road into Little Arlingham, finally braking with a skid on the wet gravel outside the church of St. Michael.
Lea turned off the bike's engine and removed her helmet with no reaction to

the rain as it instantly soaked her face. Her mascara began to run. She paused to look at the house opposite, whose extension Ben Marchen had rented for much of that year, and then swung herself off the bike and strode towards the church. Beside the sheltered gateway to the churchyard was a weatherproof noticeboard. In the bottom left corner of the display was a section labelled "Altar-gether now – Community News". This section displayed advertisements for church-led events in Arlingham, a few paintings of the building by local school children, and the photograph of Reverend Norton's impromptu waltz with Lea beside the gateway in June. Norton had thought it representative of the Church's relationship with the wider community, but Lea had very different feelings about the picture. It made her nostalgic for the afternoon she had enjoyed with Ben following that dance, and it renewed her anger when she realised that Norton had been scheming against Ben even while dancing with her. The photograph was a portrait of sunny innocence concealing a lie.

Lea studied the chapel for signs of occupation as she muttered rehearsal of the more creative insults she had in mind for the minister. She spied a flickering light through one of stained-glass windows and so strode along the path through the tombstones and pushed open the church door.

The interior was aglow with candlelight and its respectful silence immediately threatened to dull the edge of Lea's temper. She saw Reverend Norton standing beside the pulpit, arranging candlesticks on a decorative throw over the altar.

Nearby, a middle-aged woman and her daughter, who regularly volunteered for the Church, arranged flowers on stands at either side of the aisle in preparation for a wedding the next day.

The chapel's air of reverence and the quiet creativity of those within began to rob Lea of the momentum she needed to execute her plan. She could not release a barrage of abuse in cold blood.

Instead, she returned to an idea she had initially dismissed because it required the presence of at least one witness. Here she found two. With a deep breath and a glare that bore into Norton's neck from across the church, Lea recomposed her advance, adopting an expression completely at odds with her mood. She bounded out from the shadow of the porch and skipped along the aisle. 'Matthew! Matthew!' she cried, dancing past the startled women as Norton turned in surprise. 'It's going to be a boy!'

As well as affecting a very convincing joy, Lea was able to contrive possession of an intellect considerably duller than her own. She hoped that this pretence would help the onlooking women understand why Lea expected witnesses to share her happiness, rather than be scandalised by it. 'I know you said I shouldn't ask what it is, but I couldn't help it! And a son's good? You said a boy would be good 'cause there's so many boys' names in the Bible!'

Lea bounced up the steps to the altar and threw her arms around Norton's neck. His response was predictably rigid – a demeanour Lea used to her advantage as the women behind her stared, expressionless. 'What's up?' she shrank away from him, her face a mask of rejection and pain. 'I told you the scan was today. You didn't want to be there, did you?'
Norton disentangled himself and stepped towards his parishioners. 'Carol? Jenny? Could you give me five minutes, please?' he asked, pessimistically noting their silent response. 'I know this young lady and I know she's angry with me, which explains this indecent act, but I need a little time to discuss it with her.'
'Why, Matthew?' Lea asked, making her voice break satisfyingly at the mention of his name and effortlessly summoning tears. 'I know you wanted to keep it a secret, but it's gone too far for that now. Aren't you proud of me and our baby?' She placed a hand protectively below the belt of her wet jeans.
Norton shook his head. 'Please,' he asked the women again, his tone tightening. 'Let me talk to this confused woman alone. She has issues I can help her with, but I think an audience is making her theatrical.'
By this time, everything Norton said seemed only to deepen his crisis, and Lea's victory was confirmed when the eldest parishioner offered her a reassuring glance. The women left the chapel in silence.
Lea wiped her eyes, smearing dark make-up, and she smiled with humourless satisfaction. 'Methinks the Reverend doth protest too much...'
Norton rubbed at his neck as though in pain. 'What are you doing?'
'You're Madog's brother,' Lea said. 'You helped him in a hate-campaign against Ben Marchen. You turned a decent and vulnerable man into a simple-minded fuck-wit who now believes he's Dungeon Master. I want you to know what you've done, and I want to see you pay for it.'
Norton straightened and responded passionately. Mention of Ben's name was all that he had been waiting for. 'Let me tell you about Ben Marchen: he was an undisciplined rebel who provoked destructive behaviour from other young—'
'Let me tell *you* about Ben Marchen!' Lea ordered him, her voice so loud in the church that Ben's name became lost in its own echo. 'He treated me with more affection and respect than anyone else in the world ever has, and that's all the reason I need to see your reputation buried for what you did to him, you smug, self-righteous—'
The crack in Lea's voice was not a part of the act this time. She cleared her throat and lowered her tone. 'I know you think you had reasons to be angry with Ben, but what happened to turning the other cheek? You antagonised him, criticised him, judged him, harassed him, played on his nerves and insecurities, and wore him down until your brother could brainwash him, you hypocritical bastard.'

Norton glanced away and considered this, suggesting that the presence of revenge within his own actions had only now become apparent. But, 'No, that wasn't it. I don't care about Ben either way – and I don't care about Pagan temples, twelfth stones, Earthwork or any of that business. I'm a Christian minister. To be brutally honest, I really only care about Christians, which I consider to be everyone I meet until they inform me otherwise. Madog also believes in God, albeit in some other form. But he is my brother and I complied with his request. I admit that I went out of my way to highlight Ben's sins, faults and antisocial behaviours – but I do that to my God-fearing parishioners during sermons every Sunday, so why should I treat a troublemaker like Ben differently?' Norton studied Lea's thunderous expression and realised that she was probably too angry to follow his reasoning. 'What did you really come to see me about?' he asked, moderating his tone. 'The demons that drive people like you cannot be exorcised here.'

Lea struggled to resist a growing urge to lash out – to punch, kick, bite, tear and scream. '*The demons that drive people like blah blah blah,*' she imitated him. 'You helped make Ben feel lost. You forced him into your brother's territory where he was open to manipulation for no reason that you care about. You're a cold-blooded shit.'

Norton sighed in frustration, but it sounded to Lea like boredom. She considered bloodying the minister's nose before leaving but knew that this would leave her open to her own severe criticism when she looked back on the exchange later. Instead, satisfied that she had expressed her grievance and given the village some gossip, she settled for spitting at Norton's clerical collar as she turned to leave. Norton did not respond, and nor did he watch Lea stride away along the aisle to the door.

Standing beneath the sheltered gateway at the entrance to the churchyard, Carol and Jenny studied the photograph of Norton and Lea dancing on the notice board. The women glanced back and forth between Lea and the picture as she approached them, and they seemed satisfied by the time she reached the gate. 'I thought I recognised you, even with your haircut,' Carol said, reaching for Lea's leather-clad arm. 'Are you all right?'

Lea slipped smoothly back into character and nodded mournfully. 'Matthew said he liked my hair short,' she sniffed, and then indicated the photograph beneath the rain-soaked panel. 'I met him that day. He said that letting him love me was like letting God love me, and I really thought I could feel it. And then I really got to like him – but now I think I must have been stupid because he's being really horrible to me.'

Lea's tears came easily again in the aftermath of confrontation. She accepted Carol's dignified embrace and sobbed against her shoulder for the loss of Ben Marchen, and for the passionate summer that had died with him.

Cymru

While Matthew Norton contemplated the unexpected visitation of Ben Marchen's vengeance, Ian Longe and Balder passed Dolgellau. They had grown weary of the drive but found the monotony of hours on the A470 compensated by views of increasingly dramatic scenery.
The rain had dried up about an hour before, but then a grey dusk descended quickly.
Ian enjoyed negotiating the tight turns, steep climbs and rolling descents of Cymru in the failing light, and as he drove he maintained conversation with Balder, who seemed as indifferently content to answer Ian's questions as he was to sit in silence, seeming lost in the view.
'This new life of yours,' Ian asked, by then having lost all fear of raising the subject. 'What have you gained from it? I can't help thinking that your new identity is defined by the things you've lost.'
'Like what?'
'Like twenty nine years, for a start, and a comfortable home, a girlfriend, and your—'
'Parents?' Balder added.
'Sense of humour, I was going to say,' Ian finished. 'But what have you gained except a shit name? Did you inherit super-powers with the Twelfth Stone title? Arcane knowledge? Slow-motion martial-arts skills?'
Balder opened the bottle of water and bar of chocolate Ian had bought at the last service station. 'Oh yes,' he said earnestly. 'I can name the meaning of my life.'
Ian slung him a disappointed glance.
'But how many people can do that?' Balder pleaded. 'I have the advantage of a single life-long purpose. I feel no ego and no longing for fashion or material wealth, except for the basics I need to keep me warm, dry and fed. And my view of the world is changed beyond my ability to describe it.'
'Try.'
Balder took a little of the chocolate and gave the rest to Ian. 'I feel amazed all the time, and Madog thinks that's because I've lost Ben's arrogance.'
Ian waited. 'So…?'
'Well, when I consider life, I mean *all* life, I see a miracle. If you could point at an object and make it walk around, you'd call it magic – but that's what life is, isn't it? Animated matter – and not only animated: it's conscious! But people don't notice this incredible fact anymore because life is abundant, common, *normal*.'
Ian agreed but looked disappointed. 'So you can't fly, then? Or turn yourself into stone at will? Maybe your power is thinking that you're special and different to everyone else, even though when I picked you up earlier you were

pissed in a pub.'

Balder fixed Ian's profile with a weary stare and dismissed the conversation with a short laugh.

'Forget it,' Ian said. 'I'm just talking bollocks to get a rise out of you.'

'Then here's an observation in return: I think you're worried that we're going to find Sarah Conrad when we get to Roedan's house. It's not getting caught by her that worries you, it's the confirmation that she and Roedan are still together. But you don't want to talk about that so you're killing time by cross-examining me.'

'Ooh,' Ian nodded. '*Touché.* You think she'll be there, then?'

'I don't know. I suppose she could be if she and Roedan are still together. Sarah might not have wanted to go to Arlingham for the festival.'

'What do we do if she's there?'

Balder shrugged. 'I don't think we can plan for it. Let's just get there, find the campsite nearest Roedan's place and set up for the night.'

With that, Balder settled back in his seat and made Ian feel that further conversation would be an imposition.

Night had fallen. Ian rolled down his window to revitalise the musty air in the car and dared step a little harder on the accelerator.

It was past seven when Ian turned off the A470 at Betws Y Coed and headed west on the A5 for Capel Curig. The 1:25000 scale map of Snowdonia Balder inherited from Ben was old, but it clearly marked Roedan's property, Tan Y Bryn, as the southern-most house of Pont Cyfyng, and Balder found a campsite situated little more than a mile to the east.

Ian spotted it just before they reached Pont Cyfyng: a field in which only three other tents were pitched. A rain-swollen river Llugwy bordered the eastern edge of the site. Ian pulled in over a cattle grid and paused at the gateway. 'Should we find the owner and pay for a night's pitch? Or do we avoid witnesses to our being here?'

'I say we avoid suspicion by acting normally.'

A sign on the gate directed Balder across the road to a farmhouse, Dôl-gam, where he paid the incredulous landowner the asking price of £6. Despite the income generated from a large number of walkers and climbers who used the campsite, the farmer still could not comprehend the appetite for hardship displayed by mountaineers at all times of year. 'Thank you,' the man smiled, 'but you're mad. It's been wet for two days and more's due.'

Ian had unrolled Balder's tent by the time he returned, but setting it up on the boggy ground was a two-man job and the work of fifteen minutes in the beam of the Shogun's headlights. The view of the sky to the north and west was clear, and a pebbledashing of stars allowed the nearby Moel Siabod to rise in conical silhouette against the glittering night, though the stars became more obscured the further east or south the eye travelled. Rain loomed beyond Gwydyr Forest.

Ian and Balder crawled into the tent with sleeping bags, a torch, a flask of tea and the map. 'Plan?' Ian asked, opening Balder's map to familiarise himself with their position. He identified a wide loop in the meandering river where he thought the campsite to be and began to unpack his sleeping bag.

'Kip,' Balder replied. 'You must be knackered after the drive. We need to be fit for tomorrow, it's going to be a long day.'

'All right,' Ian nodded, already yawning. 'But I think we should get up early – really early – to do what we have to do and head south before anyone even knows we were here.'

Balder agreed. 'We'll need time in Arlingham tomorrow to see Roedan off. I don't dare believe that the end of this business will be a simple exchange of artefacts and a merry wave goodbye.'

'Tempting fate there, Baldy?'

'I believe it was fate that dropped me into this circumstance,' Balder replied, unscrewing the cap of the flask. 'If I tempt fate again, do you think she'll turn out just to mess up all her previous hard work? And don't call me that.'

Ian crawled into the sleeping bag fully dressed but for his boots and lay contentedly on his front.

Balder, who did not seem tired at all, sat outside the tent door using an Earthwork waterproof jacket as a mat, setting the torch, map and a bottle of water before him. The evening air was mild and damp and midges busied themselves in the lamplight. The slightest breeze, channelled east along the valley like the Afon Llugwy itself, was thickened and sweetened by the viridescent life of the river's overgrown banks and lichen-slippery rocks.

Ian tasted his tea, winced and rested his chin wearily across his forearms. 'Tea always tastes shit out of a flask. You have it. Listen, give me a kick if you wake up first – and make sure it's early.'

'I'll remember.' Balder watched Ian's eyelids fall as though they were weighted.

He waited ten minutes before breaking his promise. He watched Ian's posture relax into the dead weight of sleep and listened to the deepening of each new breath. Then he looked up warily, studying the sky for any sign that the rain had caught them up. Balder's Maglite was the only illumination that prevented the stars from casting a patina of light over the landscape, so he switched it off and rose from the grass as his eyes readjusted to the night. He gazed east and spied heavy cloud encroaching from beyond Betws Y Coed, so slipped on the waterproof jacket he'd used as a mat. He pocketed the torch and map, quietly zipped up the tent flap and crept away.

Balder crossed the field to the gate and stepped out onto the A5. He turned left, heading west, recalling from the map that another turning half a mile ahead would lead him to the hillside houses of Pont Cyfyng. Balder suspected that the pinpoints of curtain-filtered light to his left marked the area he sought and he became sure that it could be reached more directly cross-country.

A footpath sign pointing into the wide valley basin confirmed that such a route was possible less than two minutes into his walk, and he realised that this alternative would keep him obscured from the local villagers. Balder did not want to be remembered. He stepped through the narrow gap in the dry-stone wall, produced his torch and directed its beam down into the river. Large stepping stones crossed the Llugwy. Chuckling at the thought of city-dwelling tourists shrieking with the insecurity of untested balance as they attempted these slippery islands, Balder stepped down into the thigh-deep water. He leaned against the current and waded over the rocks of the riverbed using the stepping stones as handholds.

A wide stretch of grassland lay beyond the trees on the opposite riverbank and offered Balder easy progress for some distance. Wildlife rustled and fidgeted unseen at his passing. His single glimpse of a local inhabitant was an impressive one: just as his route rejoined the bank of the surging Llugwy, a startled heron emerged from its roost above the water. It beat heavily at the air with expansive wings and drifted silently away to the east, a pale glider against dark riverside trees.

The rain returned, lightly at first, and invisible in the night. Balder sensed the rain as a whisper in the grass and ferns around him before he felt it, but it intensified quickly, drenching in its volume.

A new border of trees to the south offered Balder a winding footpath that he judged would lead him to the tarmac remainder of his route. Once there, he would look for a discreet vantage from which to view Tan Y Bryn.

The path rose steadily from the river basin to skirt the lowest foothills of Moel Siabod, but the trees overhanging the footpath offered no reprieve from the deluge. Reaching the stile that put Balder back onto the Pont Cyfyng road meant being exposed to the saturating sky once more.

He saw a house set back from the lane not far ahead. Balder saw light in a downstairs window, but it did prevent him from crossing the garden to shelter beneath the front porch. Already soaked, Balder sought to keep the map dry as he consulted it for the final time.

Another footpath ran uphill alongside this property into patchy woods. Roedan's house was situated on the other side of them. Balder estimated another ten minutes' walk.

It took him fifteen. He made a wrong turn at a fork in the track, but the mistake was provident, leading Balder to the stone shell of an old building, perhaps an ancient chapel or cottage, just inside the trees. It stood on the border with the grounds of Tan Y Bryn, providing Balder with an excellent

view of Roedan's house, and also of the Eighteenth Century folly, *Pen Annwn*, which was situated on a rise in the lawn to his left,
The ruined building from which Balder chose to survey the area had no roof, and the only cover from the rain was offered by a low doorway in the north-facing wall. From here, Balder's assessment of his task was disheartening.
Roedan's house was large (Balder estimated at least five bedrooms), and the thought of searching it for one small object made him wilt against the damp stones. Worse still, he saw light in two of the downstairs windows. He had accepted the possibility of finding someone home, but until now had not contemplated a way of overcoming such an obstacle.
The best scenario, he decided, would be if those inside went out. The worst, of course, was that they would not, and that he would have to wait until they went to bed. The latter option terrified Balder – but not as much as his intrusion would terrify the occupier if he was heard.
Either way, Balder accepted the possibility of a very long wait at the end of Roedan's garden, exposed, wet, muddy and increasingly cold at the edge of mountain wilderness.
Ben Marchen had spent much of his life feeling as though he occupied this exact position: outside, looking in.Balder also knew that this literal and figurative stance would be one of the defining characteristics of his own existence. The difference between Ben and Balder, of course, was that Ben had resented his perceived exclusion, though he courted it doggedly as an identity, while Balder truly enjoyed it.
Poised, alert, vital and ready to encroach on this domestic scene as a stealthy agent of the Wild, Balder felt confident and justified in his purpose. He even viewed exposure to such challenging weather as a test of his conviction, and one that he considered himself to have passed. Many people claim to enjoy being out in the rain, but Balder decided that this is an easy statement to make with the certainty of a warm house, hot shower and dry clothes to retreat to. Considering this, Balder raised his face to the sky and received the rain in the same way that he would have greeted sunshine, even knowing that all he might expect for hours to come was more cold rain.
Balder heard an electronic noise nearby: a charged click; and then came a wash of light away to his left. *Pen Annwn* suddenly illuminated the surrounding lawn with a ring of rain-triggered intruder lights.
The presence of such a system forced Balder to reappraise the situation. At first glance the tower looked like an ornate, well-preserved, though redundant, antiquity; but Balder realised that the folly's security measures might hint at a valuable purpose or contents.
So he waited several minutes for a response to the light from the house. None came, but still Balder made no move, remaining stationary until the lights went out. As he waited, he reasoned that a security system sensitive enough to be set

off by the weather was probably triggered with trivial regularity. Reassured by this logic, Balder left the ruined walls among the trees and crossed the short distance between the woodland border and *Y Tŵr's* grassy eyrie.

Considerately, the lights came on as he neared the foot of the folly, illuminating its antique red brickwork and a low wooden door. Equally obliging, the door opened when Balder turned the handle, but he would not find out why it was unlocked for another ten minutes.

He closed the door quietly behind him, expecting only darkness, but instead found a dim amber glow emanating from above. Balder was presented with the stone steps of a narrow spiral stairway, but his discovery of interior light made him wary. He listened intently for a minute, dripping rainwater onto the floor, where a pool slowly expanded across the concrete around his boots.

Finally satisfied, Balder crept up the spiralling steps, ascending steeply. Low wattage bulbs set in the wall every ten feet or so illuminated his climb. Twenty steps up, Balder found a door set in what he judged to be the western wall. He opened it to a reveal a dark room containing only a single bed, set beneath a window framed by Mediterranean shutters. Balder shone his torch around the walls and under the bed, and then continued upstairs.

At the top, the spiral stairway pushed its climber up through the polished floorboards of the highest and largest room. The only light entering this attic space came through the trapdoor from the stairwell below, and finding that the eight windows around him were also shuttered, Balder risked the light of his torch. A crystal hanging before the western window caught the beam and refracted a hundred restless pinpoints of light around the room.

An examination of the floorboards made Balder realise that he had discovered a place devoted to ritual, so his decision to search the building was vindicated, though his sense of achievement was tempered by an acknowledgement to fortune. Balder moved the torchlight around the circular outline of a labyrinthine pattern beneath his feet, but quickly stepped aside when he realised that he was leaving damp footprints in the chalk. The rainwater he trailed bled a milky chaos across the maze.

The simple labyrinth, and all the symbols chalked evenly around it, were the leavings of an activity familiar to Balder. Madog had talked at length about the use of such sigils in ritual – in this case, the winding path to a candlelit centre, which replaced the sacred circle of popular magical practise – and if this was indeed the form of divination Madog had described, then Balder also anticipated the presence of four ceremonial objects, each representing one of the classical natural Elements. The expectation of such a find made his pulse quicken – the object usually associated with the element of Fire, he remembered, was a knife or sword.

Balder waved the beam of his torch around the octagonal room and revealed a wooden chest in the darkness. Presciently, Balder knew then that he had discovered exactly what he was looking for, and a feeling that his search had somehow been guided to this safe, successful conclusion laid an emotional foundation for euphoria.

Double-edged sword

Lifting the serpentine blade of Ben Marchen's ancestor from its velvet-lined compartment in the chest, Balder felt himself flooded with a wash of extreme thoughts and emotions.

First to course through him was the immediate satisfaction and relief at having committed this crime without any damage to property, nor confrontation with Tan Y Bryn's inhabitants.

Directly following this release of tension he felt a sudden and unexpected empathy with Roedan's ambition. The Geophagia leader was suspected of planning to break the law in order to acquire an historic artefact – an act that Balder himself was now guilty of, though he assured himself that having this crime in common with her did not amount to an affinity with the priestess. He comfortably justified his actions as a pre-emptive invasion of Roedan's space in order to prevent her from ransacking his.

And then, as Balder rose from his genuflection before the chest to study the dagger closely by torchlight, his feelings became focused as a sense of intimacy with the blade. He realised that his appropriation of the object was not a clear-cut case of theft: it was actually the reclamation of a Marchen heirloom. Balder's childishly open mind and vital spirit were wholly his – but his blood, he had to concede, was Marchen.

This was the short-sword forged and carried by Marchen, *Y Deuddegfed Maen* in 1191, when Carreg carried Arthur's leaden epitaph to Meeting Hill. The blade, almost eighteen inches long, dull and bitten with age, felt at home in Balder's reverent grip.

These heady thoughts and emotions blended warmly to induce in him a dizzying euphoria, and the kind of transcendent gratitude for which there seems to be only one satisfactory expression: Balder needed to pray, and he could think of no better place in which to do it.

He shone his torch across the nearest shutters in the wall, his caution usurped by thoughts of opening a window to gain a view of the landscape. It was then that he noticed a short ladder hooked flat against the ceiling, attached by a hinge at the edge of a trapdoor overhead. Balder's excitement surged.

It was the work of less than a minute to unfasten the ladder, open the trapdoor and climb out into the stormy night sky. Then, stood upon the octagonal rooftop, it took Balder only a few seconds more to undress fervently and completely. He wished to feel immanent in this wind and rain amongst the mountains and share their honesty of being, as though such a state enhanced the intensity of his expression, and laid bare the naked sincerity of his devotion. Balder lifted his head to the wind and turned slightly to receive its force face-on, holding Marchen's dagger flat against his chest with an open palm and speaking his gratitude to the chill October rain.

A bat flickered up from behind him and raced on overhead, as though Balder's prayer had taken form to wing its way into the night.

The security lights were triggered beneath him but Balder was too lost in his communion to notice, expressing his piety to the wilderness with an exhausting pressure of speech until, finally, he began to feel drained.

Balder glanced down and weakly around him, only then becoming aware of the light from below, and he realised with a start that his good fortune might have been about to ebb. He kicked his saturated clothes and boots back through the trapdoor and followed them down on the ladder.

Even as he descended immodestly into the room, Balder realised he was no longer alone. A bulb in the centre of the ceiling came to life and someone was standing by the trapdoor at the head of the stairwell. He did not think to cover himself as he turned to face the new arrival, his expression unreadable, offering neither threat nor surrender.

Surprisingly, the first thing that Sarah Conrad noticed when the man turned and looked at her was that he had lost weight since the last time she saw him. Sharing Madog's frugal living had darkened the shadows between each of Balder's ribs, and the definition of his muscles competed with the hard lines of the bones beneath.

Just as surprisingly, the second thing Sarah realised was that she felt alive with tearful delight at the sight of this unexpected, but wonderfully familiar, face. She strode forward to embrace the man who embodied a link with her longed-for past.

After nearly four months of living in thrall to the subtle, but darkly persuasive, will of a manipulative older woman, Sarah experienced a wave of relief as she hugged the soaked, shivering figure.

Despite his evasive conversation with Ian earlier, Balder had in fact thought about Sarah Conrad and all that he had learned of her. At that moment, finding his face draped by her auburn hair, Balder's conclusions were recalled and confirmed. He and Sarah had much in common: both were casualties of events in Little Arlingham; both had met the climax of their trauma on Meeting Hill, and both of them had been led by their unusual experiences to this tower in the mountains.

Balder maintained his stance impassively for some time as Sarah clung to him. Certain physical sensations, along with a sense of attachment he had never experienced before (but which he knew were an indulgent distraction from his commitment to The Meeting) were reacting to Sarah's embrace in a way that he could not conceal. So he turned his head to look at the blade in his hand as a way of focusing on his purpose.

Sarah withdrew slightly and held Balder's face by the jaw as she stared into his uncertain gaze. 'I've missed you all so much,' she addressed the face that contained Ian Longe, Meeting Hill, Carreg's End, Tantric Trading and nearly six of the most contented months of her life.

'I don't know if anyone's missed you after the way you left,' Balder said blankly, 'but now is be a great opportunity to make it up to them.'

*

Following Balder's assertion of the day before – that Geophagia would soon descend upon Carreg's End, despite Lea's reassurance – George managed to evade the scepticism that infected the rest of her team, instead reacting with a sulky reluctance to accept the continued threat.

Confirmation of Roedan's intentions came that morning when several villagers contacted Wyre with the same urgent report: that a Geophagia site planner had telephoned many local landowners wishing to rent field space as a festival venue on October 31st. Farmers Goddard, Longe, West and Pearce had immediately denied Roedan's group any access and then called Georgina with the news.

Milton Halfpenny had come closer to accommodating Geophagia's needs, but denied Roedan use of his acres when she refused to meet his price.

The local landowners' loyalty had been encouraging, but George did not believe that this would be the end of the matter. She waited patiently for further news, and by the time it arrived she had already predicted the nature of it.

At seven o'clock that evening, a furious Baz, and an especially jumpy Abel Mild, entered the Earthwork barn, where George was lamenting her recent inactivity. She had been so convinced of The Meeting's safety after Lea's announcement that she had neglected to initiate any other defensive measures. When Baz and Abel arrived, George was at least reassured by the fact that these two long-serving employees had turned to her for advice, rather than Brampton, despite their reputation for operating under his close supervision.

'Miss Wyre,' Gary began, clearly uncomfortable with whatever he had to say. 'With respect, your brother has given me orders that I don't want to follow. I've brought the grievance to you because I know what you'd think of me if I didn't. Of course, if you can't argue with Mr Wyre's instructions then I'll understand, but I'll have to give you notice and resign.'

Abel Mild was unable to articulate such a speech, but he had accompanied Baz with the same intention. The engineer was able to stammer a heartfelt, 'Me too!'

'I appreciate that.' George nodded gratefully at the men. 'What's the matter?'

Baz cleared his throat. 'Mr Wyre has asked me to round up the groundsmen and take up the fences between three unploughed fields north and west of Meeting Hill, including the paddock. He wants to create a space large enough for a group called Geophagia to build a dance festival. He's given them permission to arrive and set up early tomorrow morning.'

George shook her sadly. She looked at Abel. 'And you?'
The mechanic fumbled nervously with an oily rag. 'Mr Wyre asked me to help them.'
George began to rub at the tension in her temples, visibly deflating. 'Then I think you'd better do as my brother asks,' she murmured.
Abel and Baz looked at each other in surprise. 'You're giving up?'
'No,' George said, straightening and rising from her chair. 'I think you should give Brampton every reason to believe that you're following his instructions. He wants you to call on every employee for help, and that's what I want too. Talk to everyone on the estate that you think will support us. If it comes to a confrontation, we'll need as many people as possible on our side.'
Baz nodded once, the gesture both a sign of obedience and a statement of firm approval, and turned and strode from the barn. Abel wavered uncertainly as George picked up a telephone from the table and dialled the number of a mobile.
'Alan!' she exclaimed in imitation of the Team Leader's playful answer. 'Are you busy?'

*

'Ian's here.'
Sarah stepped back and watched Balder stare protectively at a small blade he held in one hand. 'Here? Right now?'
'Not far,' Balder replied, stepping into his wet trousers with a shudder. 'There's a campsite down the road. He was expecting to come here with me early tomorrow morning, but I couldn't wait and I left him sleeping. He was prepared to share the risks, but I didn't want to see him in trouble if we were caught burgling the house.'
Sarah pointed at the dagger. 'For that?'
Balder nodded as he wrung out his socks. The water he squeezed from them obliterated at least a third of the chalk labyrinth beneath his feet. 'And you caught me. I'm lucky you didn't just call the police when you realised someone was up here.'
'I didn't realise until I saw your arse descending from the ceiling. I was up here earlier today but I didn't lock the tower when I went to the house for dinner. I knew I'd be coming back up for the sword.'
'You know what it is?'
Sarah nodded. 'Roedan said it belonged to someone called Marchen.'
'And why were you coming back for it?'
Sarah laughed. 'You won't believe this: I was going to drive to Little Arlingham in the morning and give it to you.' She caught Balder's questioning glare and laughed again. 'I wasn't particularly doing it for you, Ben. I just wanted to hurt Roedan in some small way for what she plans to do on Meeting

Hill.'

Balder nodded and chose to ignore the name by which she addressed him. Sarah thought that he was someone else, someone she knew and with whom she was comfortable, and Balder thought it expedient to let her.

Sarah cringed on Balder's behalf as he put on his wet clothes. 'Come back to the house and dry out.'

Balder's eyes flickered indecisively between Sarah and the dagger, and finally his own saturated shirt. 'All right,' he agreed. 'There is more I'd like to talk about.'

Entering Tan Y Bryn via a patio door from the lawn, Balder's response to the wealth of Roedan's possessions and décor was a confusion of admiration and cynicism. He was impressed by the house, its furnishings, artwork and Roedan's collection of archaeological artefacts, but Tan Y Bryn did not feel like someone's home. The leather sofa in the lounge was undented, the kitchen unused, the carpets unworn and the tiles of the central hall highly polished, and such pristine presentation of material wealth seemed at odds with Roedan's claim to a spiritual mission. He smiled when he saw the muddy trail he had left in his wake.

Sarah led Balder through the immaculate kitchen to an equally tidy utility room. She found him a towelling dressing gown to preserve his recovered modesty while he removed his trousers, which he bundled with the rest of his clothes into a tumble dryer.

In the lounge Sarah gestured at the sofa, but Balder's attention was instantly absorbed by three interior-lit cabinets displaying numerous ancient coins, fragile Bronze and Iron Age jewellery, and dozens of flint arrowheads. 'You knew about Marchen's dagger even before I did,' he said.

'It sounds like that pisses you off, but it's not very surprising, is it? I think Roedan told me everything that Mad Dog told her. I even know about the cross she's looking for.'

Balder's eyes narrowed. 'What about it?'

Sarah's eyes sparkled with excitement. 'Roedan is sure that Madog knows where it is.'

'*Y Deuddegfed Maen* has always known,' Balder proudly explained, sinking into a chair opposite her. 'But if Roedan was so sure that Arthur's cross wasn't lost, why has she been using Geophagia as cover to look for it elsewhere?'

Sarah seemed to enjoy the intrigue. 'She hasn't. The other festivals were peaceful and built Geophagia a good reputation. Holding a festival on Meeting Hill lets her use Geophagia as a ransom demand to Madog: Tell me where I can find the cross or The Meeting gets it!'

Balder wilted sadly.

'What?' she asked.

'As of tomorrow an ultimatum like that will be my concern. I have the cross –

or I will when I return this,' he said, lifting the dagger he had rested across his knees. 'But the Twelfth Stone never told me what Roedan suspected.'
'Why would he?'
'Because I'm the Twelfth Stone of Meeting Hill,' he replied, shaking his head when he noticed the way Sarah looked at him. 'It would take too long to explain. Come back to Little Arlingham with us now. However things turn out for me, Earthwork will need all the help they can get.'
'No,' Sarah said. 'I'm not going back now.'
'But you said you've missed it, and I bet you've missed Ian. He's really missed you. He's been terrible company.'
'No!' Sarah said louder. 'I mean yes: I've missed the village, and Ian. But I think we all have to recognise the point of no return. I was going to stop in Arlingham tomorrow to give you the blade and take a last look at the place, but I need something new now.'
'That makes me feel sad,' Balder said, but was not sure if he meant it.
'I don't think letting go needs to be traumatic. Maybe it's more like an exchange: a little sacrifice in return for transformation.'
Balder suddenly sensed the wilful arrival of something as striking, meaningful and as intensely personal as déjà vu, yet of greater influence and wider significance, heralded by Sarah's familiar words. He felt the length of his spine ignited like a trail of magnesium wire. He searched Sarah's expression carefully, wondering if she knew that she had just repeated the words spoken by Madog only nine hours before. After spending weeks in the company of a man who loosed arrows at solitary magpies to ward off ill luck, Balder saw no reason to question the idea that such a perfect coincidence was a message to be interpreted.
'All right,' Balder replied, watching Sarah closely for a few seconds more in case she had anything else synchronistic to say.
'I can give you a lift back to the campsite if you like,' Sarah offered, wondering at his suspicious glare.
'Are you wanting rid of me?'
'No. It's been good to see you. You've made me nostalgic.'
Balder wondered how old memories have to be before their owner can become nostalgic about them, and whether or not any of his qualified.

Sarah steered her Metro off the A5 and into the waterlogged campsite of Dôl-gam at midnight, hoping that her headlights would not wake anyone inside the few tents pitched there. She stopped inside the gate and gazed through the rain-blurred windscreen at one particular tent: a small green dome erected beside a Mitsubishi with familiar Celtic markings. 'I don't want to see Ian and I don't want him to see me. Please don't tell anyone we met, all right?'
Balder nodded and waved the antique blade in reply. 'Likewise,' he said, and

he stepped quickly out of the car. He splashed thoughtfully through the partially submerged grass of the campsite without looking back, failing even to acknowledge Sarah's departure when she reversed out of the gate onto the road.

Preserving his short-sword against the damp by carrying it beneath his freshly dried shirt, Balder crawled into the darkness of the rain-weighted tent and listened to Sarah accelerating along the A5, heading west.

Part Five

Samhain, and The Turning Tide

'Oh Memory, where is now my love,
That rayed me as a god above?

I saw him by an ageing shape
Where beauty used to be;
That his fond phantom lingers there
Is only known to me.'

Thomas Hardy
I Have Lived With Shades

Samhain

The Moon rose a little earlier than the sun on the morning of October 31st. It was two days from full but filled the pre-dawn sky with an ice-white light, smudging the Levels and their island hills with a glassy shimmer. The cloud and rain moved east, exposing Somerset to the freezing void beyond, and the drop in temperature threatened the first frost since March.
The dolmens of Meeting Hill reflected the Moon as a spectral sheen. Traces of quartz scintillated across their weathered surfaces. Rabbits fed and frolicked about the summit, occasionally braving the exposure of the clearing until the hoot of an owl or the bark of a fox sent them dashing for cover.
The stones stretched eleven sliding shadows across the moonlit clearing, and in the silence before sunrise they witnessed an elemental serenity that Meeting Hill would never again experience in its ancient form.
The Meeting's first visitors of the day were already closing in.

Geophagia rose before the sun. Approaching Little Arlingham from almost every direction, the many contractors involved in building and running a large festival – including lighting specialists, scaffolders, stage and sound technicians, fast-food vendors, merchandise sellers, performing artists, as well as D. Romain and Sons' funfair – were already negotiating the narrow lanes off the A303, A37 and the A372 for Arlingham.
And awaiting them at either side of the Wyre Estate's northern gateway were two uneasy parties. With one stood Brampton Wyre, accompanied by many estate employees who cared nothing for the dispute over Geophagia's use of estate land, only for the security of their jobs, and who therefore felt unable to ignore the orders of their senior employer.
Facing them across the track, which led straight onto several acres of unploughed pasture, Georgina Wyre, Alan Forrest, Baz and seven other estate employees of various trades watched the road sternly, fidgeting against the cold. Those who had rallied around George planned to block any attempt by Geophagia's vehicles to enter the estate, though they were realistic about what such a limited number of people might achieve.
'Can't you stop your brother letting people in without your permission?' Alan asked. 'The estate is half yours.'
George glanced across the gateway at Brampton who was, for once, dressed informally. 'You answered your own question there,' she replied sadly. 'If it's half mine, it's half his. He'd have to be doing something illegal before I could think about phoning a lawyer.'
The men around them murmured in disgruntled resignation and turned as one to face the elder Wyre as he approached. Brampton adopted a passive, even amiable expression – but then, George considered, he was in no position to be

defensive. As an intelligent man, Brampton realised that most people suspected his intentions, and that everyone was now aware of the way in which he had negotiated Geophagia's use of estate land without his sister's knowledge. In the public's view, this alone was enough to label him guilty of whatever they cared to accuse him.
George did not wish to make conversation easy. She remained silent until Brampton spoke.
'Good morning,' he nodded at his assembled opposition. 'I know we're all here for the same reason, so let's not pretend otherwise. I'm sorry that I let this land without discussion or notice.'
'Then why did you?' asked one of the men behind George.
'Because I knew that people would protest,' Brampton replied, taking significant note of the man who asked the question. 'I've been the target of public protest before and I don't like it.'
'But people protest for a reason, not for the fun of it. I've helped manage this land for twenty two years. Meeting Hill doesn't interest me much, to be honest – but this job gives me a small leasehold on the estate, and your plan allows hundreds of people to come and dance on my doorstep. What you've done is—'
The man was silenced by a sharp look from George, who did not want any single employee to become a target for reprisals. 'There are reasons for this protest,' George went on. 'You're aware of the reasons for keeping Geophagia away from the monument, as well the effect of the festival on the homes of our staff.'
Brampton shrugged. 'We don't agree on those reasons,' he replied. 'And I don't think that our petty jealousies should restrict the spiritual freedom of so many others. You and I might own Meeting Hill, Georgie, but no one can own The Meeting or dictate what it might mean to a large number of people.'
To this hypocrisy George could reply only silently, fixing her brother with a difficult expression that combined wide-eyed disbelief with a threatening glower, until headlights and traffic noise from the east distracted the small crowd.
George and her supporters offered one another grim glances while Brampton returned to the other side of the track. George and her eight companions stepped forward to block the gate.
The first vehicle to arrive was a Subaru carrying four passengers and towing a trailer of tarpaulin-covered equipment. It turned into the gate and stopped before the groups assembled there. Two more large cars with similar trailers pulled up behind it, one of them playing something loud by Credence Clearwater Revival. The driver of the lead car lowered her window. Brampton Wyre was the first to approach in greeting. 'Good morning.'
A woman using sunglasses as a hair-band leaned out and returned his smile. 'Oh, hello,' she said in surprise. 'I was expecting to see Georgina Wyre.'

Brampton's face straightened and then frowned. He raised an uncertain finger and pointed in his sister's direction.

'There you are!' The driver leaned further out through her window to wave. 'Good to see you again.'

George stepped up to the passenger side and peered through the open window, where a well-built man sporting a goatee beard and a ponytail smiled sleepily.

'Hello, Bere. Hello Carla,' she smiled warmly. 'Thanks for coming. It was short notice, but I knew you were keen to follow up on your work from August.'

Alan's stance of surly defiance relaxed into unexpected relief as he recognised the arrivals. He raised a welcoming hand and Carla saluted in return.

'Who are they?' Baz asked Alan. 'Should I be shaking their hands or slashing their tyres?'

'It's okay, they're the Rainmakers. I wish George had told us they were coming, I wouldn't have got up feeling so bleak this morning. I might even have shaved – see how Carla looked at me?'

The gamekeeper squinted through the windscreen over the glare of the headlights. 'Looks like she's already got enough goatee-bearded rock monsters in her life. What are Rainmakers?'

'Pseudo-scientists,' Alan said a little dismissively. 'Mature students trying to make lights and rain and crop circles with machines that look like Howitzers. Load of bollocks, but someone takes it seriously enough to fund them, and George seems impressed with it all.'

Far from impressed, however, Brampton had begun conferring with his supporters when it became clear that he was not the only Wyre to have made plans for the use of these empty acres.

'Thanks for the invite, Ms Wyre,' Bere said as George stooped beside his car door. 'Do you mind if we set up in the same places as before?'

'I was hoping you would,' George said, glancing through the opposite window to wink triumphantly at Brampton. The elder Wyre recognised his sister's successful manoeuvre with gentlemanly humour. He nodded appreciatively.

Carla, meanwhile, had been searching the ranks of the men around her for one particular face, and now whispered cautiously, 'Is that other guy here? The one who took the piss out of us all day?'

'Craig?' George suggested. 'No, he's not around anymore.'

Gary Basildon had been digesting Alan's information. 'So how do these people's beliefs help us today?' he asked.

Alan replied from George's perspective. 'It's not what they believe, it's what their beliefs lead them to do – in this case, harmlessly occupying land that Geophagia want to build a festival on.'

Baz nodded and a smile softened his granite features. 'All right. I wish George had told us they were coming. I nearly lobbed a brick through their windscreen when they came round that corner. Now I'll have to lead them through this field – some of us laid barbed wire in the grass last night.'

George let her gamekeeper guide the three vehicles into the meadow, watching Baz pace ahead of the cars with his torch directed into the grass.

'Quick thinking,' Alan congratulated her as she rejoined the group.

'Grasping at straws.' George shook her head sadly. 'That's three vehicles versus who-knows-how-many to occupy several acres, and we don't have much else.'

'At least we're making it harder for Roedan when she turns up,' Alan replied, and was about to mention Baz's hint at further booby traps when a man standing beside him asked, 'Miss Wyre? Have you put people on the hill, too?'

All eyes turned south, where the summit of Meeting Hill glowed brightly, emitting the same bleached radiance as the rising moon, though this light was shifting and alive. Headlights shone almost vertically into the pre-dawn sky as vehicles wound their way up the hill's steep track, and other cars on the summit made arborescent silhouettes of the crowning trees.

George looked at Brampton, who returned a smug wink of his own.

Alan saw the look on George's face. 'Tell me this is something else you've arranged,' he begged her.

'I can't,' she replied with tears in her eyes. 'It looks like Brampton has sent Geophagia straight to the hill.'

Angry mutters rose from the men around George and a change came over Alan. The team leader's usual contribution to difficult situations, even Earthwork's most challenging confrontations, was a levity that made people question his ability to take anything seriously. Yet on this occasion his expression framed a fury that distracted even George from the lights on the hill. She watched Alan turn toward Brampton with a stare that scared her. 'You look like you're threatening my brother,' she scolded him. 'Take the look off your face.'

'Can't I wipe the smile off his first?'

George used an uncharacteristic tone on an uncharacteristic Alan. 'How does that solve anything? *Focus.* You are the leader of the preservation committee's field team: I expect you to be objective and professional, not act as Craig Pearce did. Alan, there are unwanted visitors on Meeting Hill. In your professional experience, how should Earthwork react?'

Alan closed his eyes until the red mist began to ebb. 'You're right. The field team would meet at the barn and drive up to the monument to assess and respond.'

'Good,' George nodded. 'Your team's a little under-manned until Ian returns, but I'm sure there are equally professional people here willing to be deputised. Anyone?'

A female voice offered its owner's help from behind the gathered men.

George's staff stepped aside. 'I'd like to help,' Lea Granger said, wincing in the combined light of four torches immediately directed her way. 'I'm already too involved for you to refuse.'
'Hello, Lea,' said Alan. 'Ever driven a Land Rover?'
'Good,' George said again, 'this is better. Half the estate staff is helping Geophagia build a festival on our hill, but this half is going to supervise it. Watch them.'

The hastily assembled Earthwork team reached the courtyard of Arlingham House as dawn breathed a lavender hue into the moonlight, and stars retreated ignominiously before the glowing herald of sunrise. Lea arrived ahead of Alan's car on her motorbike and pulled up in front of the committee barn. Alan parked alongside her but looked quizzically at Baz in the seat beside him when he noticed the heavy padlock fastening the barn's doors. The men stepped out of the car and stared impotently at the lock.
'What?' Lea asked through her helmet visor.
'George didn't lock this, did she?' Alan asked the gamekeeper.
'No. It wasn't locked when I left here this morning.'
Lea removed her helmet and sat it on the saddle of the bike. 'No key?'
'I didn't know there was a lock,' Alan said helplessly.
Baz hummed thoughtfully. He scanned the courtyard around him and stabbed a finger in the direction of the stables. There was a muffled and cowardly squeal from within. A hunched figure emerged at a run with its hands over its head, scampering towards the paddock. Gary blocked Abel's escape and lifted the old man off his feet by the front of his jacket. 'Give me the key.'
'Put me down, you – you – *bas*—'
'I wish Ian was here,' Alan whispered to Lea. ' He'd love this sort of farce.'
'I wish Ben was here,' Lea replied. Then, after a few more seconds of watching the men struggle, she said, 'Shouldn't you restrain Baz? He'll kill the little fellow.'
'No,' Alan said. 'Gary's bigger than me. Anyway, those two are like a double act – Elmer Fudd and Bugs Bunny, only with less Acme dynamite.'
Baz unloaded a double-barrelled glare into Abel's eyes at point-blank range, which made the old man empty his pockets and his bladder. Baz lowered him to the cobblestones and walked away with the padlock key. Snivelling wretchedly, Abel sank to his knees. In a fit of conscience, Lea crossed the courtyard to where Abel was alternately consoling and berating himself in a whining soliloquy. Lea produced her tobacco pouch and offered him a smoke. 'Hard luck,' she said as Abel accepted the roll-up with trembling fingers. 'Wasn't a fair fight, was it?'
Abel laughed maniacally. 'Wh – who would you set against Baz to call it fair?'
The gamekeeper opened the barn doors, but the situation did not improve. The

tyres of the Land Rover and the second Shogun had been slashed. 'What can I do to Abel to make us feel better about this?'

Alan laid a hand on the Shogun as though consoling a hamstrung animal.

'Abel's a pitiful man,' Lea decided as she joined them beside the cars.

'You're too nice,' Baz muttered.

'He doesn't know what he's doing. I'm sure he wants to help us, but he's too scared of Brampton not to do as he's told.'

Baz turned his glare on Lea. 'The old twat's crippled the Earthwork team and you're kissing his arse?'

'What's the matter, Buckshot? Not blown away enough defenceless mammals lately? Well don't take it out on me – or Abel, he's an old man.'

'We need these vehicles,' Alan said. 'They'll set us apart on the hill. We'll make no impression if we stroll up there.'

Baz shrugged. 'Even if Abel grew the spine to help us, he won't be able to produce eight spare wheels.'

'And what about Earthwork uniforms?' Lea added. 'We'll need to look official when we see Roedan and tell her to go fuck herself. I can wear Sarah's old gear, but what about you, Shooter?' she wondered, eyeing Baz. 'Would Craig's old uniform fit? Was he as porky as you? Listen, we're team-mates now so you can tell us: is it all muscle, or mostly fat?'

Meetings

Dawn brightened the West Country, but the lengthening shadow of a towering responsibility darkened Balder's mood.

Ian was similarly distracted as he drove, gnawed by the resentment of having woken at three that morning to find Balder awake beside him and their task already complete. Nevertheless, Ian was able to disguise his mood by drumming the steering wheel in time to songs on the radio.

'You're quiet,' Ian observed as the Shogun approached the Severn Bridge.

'*You're* quiet,' Balder replied. 'Still moody because I committed burglary without you? Like I said, it was easy. Empty house: in and out. I didn't even have to break a window.'

'But if you'd told me before we left that all you needed was a driver,' Ian reasoned, 'I could have asked my mum to give you a lift.'

Balder glanced wistfully through the rear window as the Wye Valley receded into the north. 'I thought I was doing you a favour. You have more to lose than I do from being caught – and it was really wet, Ian. It was a long walk and I nearly froze.'

Ian felt his mood lift at their return to conversation. 'Then you're some kind of hero to suffer for the cause. No pain, no gain, wild man.'

Balder's eyes widened at this statement, reflecting the amethystine glow of dawn before them. He spent two minutes considering Ian's words. 'No pain, no gain: what do you mean by that?'

Ian glanced blankly at his passenger. 'So Ben Marchen bequeathed you his language skills but no memory for clichés?'

Something pleading in Balder's gaze made Ian reconsider his response. 'It's just something people say, isn't it? That the more you sweat and suffer to achieve something, the better the result.'

Balder glanced out of his window at the Severn Estuary beneath them and realised that he was sweating. 'Could that be another way of saying that sacrifice brings about transformation, do you think?'

Ian shrugged. 'If you want. What's the matter?'

Balder wiped his damp palms down the legs of his trousers. 'I've heard the concept of sacrifice and transformation mentioned three times by three different people in less than twenty-four hours,' he said nervously. 'It's stretching the probability of coincidence. It's spooky. I feel like I'm being stalked by an idea.'

'Spooky?' Ian grinned. 'Isn't that part of the territory when you're the Arch Druid of Wicca?'

'It must be important,' Balder breathed, though his words were lost as Ian turned up the radio; 'but I don't want it to be, otherwise I'll be forced to consider something that no Twelfth Stone can have faced before.'

Ian turned off the A37 for Little Arlingham at nine-fifteen that morning. Unusually heavy traffic stretched ahead of them along the narrow lanes, and they would soon discover that many of the vehicles struggling to pass them in the opposite direction had been turned back by police less than a mile from Carreg's End.
'Better put the blade away,' Ian cautioned Balder after nearly twenty minutes in the queue. He glimpsed a constable's fluorescent jacket blocking the lane seven cars ahead. Five of those vehicles were turned back, forced to make messy five or six-point-turns in the narrow lane, and it took Ian another ten minutes to reach the roadblock.
Balder became noticeably animated during this time as the wooded dome of Meeting Hill crept into view through the windscreen. 'I hope the police aren't here to search us,' he quipped, sliding the dagger into his rucksack.
Unfamiliar with Balder's rare and arid attempts at humour, Ian glanced at him nervously and then at the officer before them as he rolled the Shogun forward. 'A checkpoint on this road today can't be good news,' he replied, winding down his window. 'Geophagia must be here.'
A police officer in her early twenties approached the car and studied Ian and Balder with a professional smile. 'No unnecessary vehicle access to Little Arlingham, gents. Road's closed.'
'But we live here,' Ian said indignantly.
'You're not working?'
'No, we live at Hill View in Carreg's End.'
'Who do you work for?'
'We're not working.'
'This looks like a company vehicle,' the officer persisted, indicating the Celtic insignia on the doors and bonnet. 'Are you a Geophagia contractor?'
'Oh, I see,' Ian nodded. 'No, this vehicle is on loan from the Wyre estate. We're volunteers for the Meeting Hill Preservation Committee.'
'Ah,' the officer nodded, turning to a second constable leaning against a marked car ahead of them. 'Here they are!'
Balder picked up his rucksack and opened the car door with a sideways smile at Ian. 'She said no unnecessary *vehicles*,' he reasoned, stepping into the road. 'I'll just go on as a necessary pedestrian.'
'I really need to get to the village,' Ian begged the officer as Balder strode away without a backward glance. 'I think the group I work for is going to be busy today.'
'Yes, I'm aware of your group's activities. I'll let you through because you live here, but we need to talk first. There's trouble in Carreg's End and I want you to explain your intentions.'

Balder discovered a large angry crowd confronting a police line in the road at the foot of Meeting Hill, and he recognised most of the vocal protesters as residents of Little Arlingham. Their calls rang with the time-honoured chants of lively demonstration.

'What do we want? *Roedan gone!* When do we want it? *Now!*'

And from a large minority of younger protesters, who sought to demonise the police for their containment of the demonstration, 'Who let the pigs out? *Who? Who, who?*'

Balder was saddened by the way in which so many articulate individuals were reduced by the whim of the mob to hollering inanities. Whenever people gather to express themselves with one voice, the lowest common denominator will rule – and worse than this, Balder decided, was that the demonstration was self-defeating, attracting hungry local media, thereby earning The Meeting the kind of attention that the protesters had intended to deflect.

But Balder's immediate problem was the obstruction formed by the baying crowd. Two hundred demonstrators restrained by a line of professionally impassive police officers blocked the way ahead. So when a laughing Ian nudged Balder's back with the front grill of the Shogun, Balder's surprise at finding a car behind him was disguised by his relief at the arrival of a possible way through. He climbed back into the car and found Ian's mood revitalised by the challenge before them.

'I didn't hear your engine over the crowd,' Balder said.

'Angry aren't they?' Ian grinned, invigorated by the promise of drama. 'I never would have heard your screams as I drove over you. Do you think Earthwork is lost in there somewhere?'

'I don't care about that,' Balder stated plainly, pointing up at the summit treetops of Meeting Hill. 'We need to be up there. They're letting Geophagia vehicles through – do you think they'll let us?'

Ian affected the arrogant booming laughter of theatrical superiority that always used to amuse Ben Marchen. 'Let us through? Ha! We're *Earthwork,* the renowned saviours of huge lumps of rock! Of course they'll—' He drowned the last words of his cartoon rhetoric in an extended blast of the car's horn.

The nearest ranks of protesters turned instantly and angrily upon the impertinent new arrival, perhaps mistaking it for police reinforcement, or the carrier of an important Geophagia member. Two tomatoes exploded against the Shogun's windscreen before the crowd's fury was checked, and then transformed into a hero's welcome on sight of the Earthwork insignia. Ian and Balder glanced at each other, and this time Ian's humour was infectious.

Ian yelled 'Who brings fruit and veg' to a demonstration anymore?' through Balder's window at the cheering crowd, enjoying the power of popularity. He turned on the windscreen wipers, reached out to dip a finger in the tomato pulp and tasted it. 'I knew it,' he nodded: 'it's fresh! Middle-class rioters…'

Ian edged the car forward at a snail's pace in front of two vans carrying Geophagia's stage equipment, both of which received a hail of eggs. Balder wound up his window and looked embarrassed as the encouraging smiles of villagers beamed between the line of police helmets. 'Go get 'em, lads!' people shouted.

'Idiots,' Balder muttered. 'Do you think they really care? Or is it just hysteria?'

'I can see what you think.'

'People get caught up in things,' Balder decided, 'and they want to be seen to be involved – but how many of these people ever turned up at the monthly committee meetings?'

'Now, now,' Ian responded professionally. 'You might have a point, but as Earthwork representatives we do not mock the mere mortals who fund us. Coming through!' he yelled out of his window. 'How can we scare Geophagia off if we're stuck here?'

One hundred and sixty feet above them, where the ascending footpath of Meeting Hill meets the summit clearing, Georgina and Brampton Wyre stood side by side with Roedan in stiff poses of mutual ignorance. Facing the circle of stones and wearing tense expressions, they presented a convincing illusion of being lined up before a firing squad. Facing them was a TV crew filming for the regional BBC news. A clean-shaven man in his late thirties, wearing a shirt (but no tie) and a designer-label waterproof jacket, was talking into the camera with one eyebrow slightly raised, betraying a metropolitan leer at this quaint provincial matter.

'...Whose expanding society, Geophagia, will conclude its celebration of British Pagan festivals here this evening,' he explained in a singsong tone of forced interest. 'The event will include live music, some unique stage performances by various artists and dancing into the night. So, Roedan, it's going to be quite a party?'

Ted Alexander of South-west Tonight turned as he spoke, making an oily transition from commentator to interviewer.

'Yes it is,' Roedan smiled confidently at Ted, and then at the camera. 'For me, for the members of my group and for the growing number of British pagans, Samhain Eve is an important observance. It's the last day of our calendar, and it marks the ebbing of the sun's power, making this a time to reflect on the darker side of Nature's cycle: the mystery of Death, renewal, transformation and re-emergence.'

'How wonderful,' Ted oozed, completely failing to absorb Roedan's words as they slid off the veneer of his on-screen persona. 'And you've chosen The Meeting in Little Arlingham to host your finale?'

'It's a wonderful site,' Roedan gushed. 'Meeting Hill lies on a ley line that extends from Glastonbury, and it's a sacred place where the Earth's life force rises to the surface and flows across the body of the Goddess. Our interaction with the monument will help raise that energy, expanding the minds of everyone present.'

'Remarkable,' the interviewer nodded like an ecstatic convert as he glanced into the camera. His practised smile said *Sign me up!* while his wide, unblinking gaze cried *Fruitcake!* 'But how do the people of Little Arlingham feel about this take-over of their countryside? Brampton Wyre owns the land hosting Geophagia's festival,' Ted continued, turning to Brampton. 'Mr Wyre, no doubt you'll be looking forward to a treat of a night with no tricks?'

The elder Wyre did not appear comfortable before a camera. His stony smile did not project the forced dazzle of someone embracing his Warholian fifteen minutes; but neither was he nervous. 'My friend Roedan certainly promises an exciting evening,' he agreed, maintaining a reserve appropriate to his rank. 'Given the understandable fears of the villagers concerning preservation of our monument during a gathering of this scale, Roedan has outlined her plans for minimal impact on the site. All the licences required for such an event have been granted by the relevant authorities, and we have reached an agreement with the Somerset and Avon Constabulary to help fund their policing of increased local traffic. With all this in place, it will be a pleasure to see Geophagia practise its religious freedom here.'

'Thank you both for speaking to us,' the interviewer replied, returning his gaze to the camera. 'This is Ted Alexander for South West Tonight, enjoying preparations for the biggest Hallowe'en apple-bobbing Somerset has ever seen.' The word 'seen' allowed Ted to finish with an effortless smile, which he held until the camera was lowered. 'Thanks all,' he nodded at Roedan and Brampton, 'we won't need any more than that. Is there a Starbucks in town?'

'Excuse me,' George approached Ted as Roedan slipped silently away into a crowd of her employees, 'I was expecting a chance to express the community's concern about this festival.'

'Sorry,' Alexander lied, his former sparkle fading. His two colleagues took Ted's microphone and carried all their equipment to a nearby van. 'Wyre and — uh, the other woman used your time. But thanks again, we'll be out of your hair now.'

The Wyres watched the TV crew drive to the edge of the summit, aiming for the footpath downhill. But the van was forced to pause at the edge of the trees as the hastily appointed Earthwork team entered the clearing. Alan, Lea and Baz crested the rise on horseback at a proud trot, followed moments later by Ian and Balder in the only available committee vehicle.

The scene that greeted them as they reached the brow of the hill was one of nightmarish change and confusion for anyone who knew the site well. A swirling tide of heavy vehicles and an army of workers had reduced the green clearing to a slippery mire, criss-crossed by deep vehicle tracks. Scaffolding, stage and lighting rigs in various stages of construction had appeared in and around the circle of megaliths. The hilltop was a hive of activity and noise, and Roedan drifted sedately through it all as though alone with the stones.

Dismounting their horses or stepping out of the Earthwork car, the new arrivals stood together in mutual shock amid the industry. 'We're too late,' Lea said.

'And what are they doing?' Ian asked weakly, pointing at several estate employees with chainsaws on the northern rim of the clearing.

'Well *apparently*,' George enunciated her reply at Brampton before he retreated, 'it's a long overdue brushwood clearance.'

'Shit,' Lea removed her riding hat to scratch her head with a gloved hand. 'Are we really this helpless?'

'No, and we're not giving up,' George responded in what she hoped was an inspiring tone. 'Listen, all of you – this mess is nothing. What do you see here that we can't restore? Churned-up grass? We can get new turf laid in a day, although it'll grow back by spring anyway. Men and machines? They'll be gone by tomorrow. Most of the festival is being built in the field directly below,' George pointed downhill to the north: 'fairground rides, burger vans, merchandise tents, all that. We've got the Rainmakers setting up and obstructing where possible, and they're trying to zap up some rain clouds to drown Roedan this evening. Some of the friendlier estate staff dug trenches and laid barbed-wire in the field last night, but we've managed only limited measures, and I think Geophagia are on schedule – but it's The Meeting we're all worried about, and this is where each of you can make a difference. There's nothing to stop us maintaining a presence up here all day and all night.'

'Two lots of police officers spoke to me about that on the drive in,' Ian said, pleased to be making a contribution. 'They don't like us. They think we're vigilante cowboys looking to provoke a riot.'

George dismissed this opinion. 'I spoke to an inspector here earlier. He seemed decent and I assured him that a riot is the last thing we want. Our role is clear: we report criminal acts to the police. Their concern is the public roads until we do. While the festival is on private land, it's ours to supervise.'

The Earthwork members nodded, their responsibilities a little clearer, but Balder was distracted by the activity of the construction teams around them.

'And now that Geophagia is here,' George suggested without much conviction, 'we could even try to get along with these people and play on their collective conscience. That'll be easier for you, Lea.'

'What about you, George?' Alan asked. 'How are you doing?'

'I'll be up here with you as much as I can,' she replied wearily, 'but I still need to meet up with the committee chairmen and some of the villagers who aren't pelting traffic with groceries. I'm afraid I missed our best chance to plead our case to a wider audience – Roedan used up my TV interview time by talking about the mystery of death and transformation.'

Balder flinched and stared at Georgina like he had been kicked. Ian noticed the coincidence and wondered at Balder's interpretation of it.

'No,' Alan said, a little softer this time, '*how* are you? None of this can be easy on you.'

The others murmured agreement, and their concern brought a grateful lift to George's features. 'Thank you. I'll get through this, and I'll kick and scream tomorrow when it's over. Hello Balder,' she added, turning to greet the silent presence at the edge of the group. 'Was the trip to Wales useful? When we spoke on the phone it sounded as though you might have discovered a lifeline for The Meeting.'

Balder seemed to be struggling beneath the weight of some Atlantean burden. He did not look well, though his eyes were bright and sharply focused, revealing that whatever lay so heavily upon his mind was goading his spirit, not crushing it. But he ignored George's question and asked one instead. 'You have your car back. Thank you for the loan. Can I borrow a horse now?'

There was a moment's pause as the group awaited George's reaction. Then Baz offered Balder the reins of Bucephalus. 'Here – and wear your Earthwork badge if you have it. The police won't let you onto the hill or the estate if they think you're a protester.'

Now consumed entirely by his own plans, Balder silently accepted the reins and swung himself up into the saddle. Sitting astride Bucephalus, he used the advantage of his height to scan the busy hilltop as he turned the horse about and urged him away downhill.

Everyone turned to Ian. Lea asked, 'What was so urgent in Wales?'

'Can't discuss it here,' Ian replied.

'Sounds promising,' George decided.

'Maybe,' Ian said, watching Balder's bobbing head disappear over the brow of the hill. 'But it felt like something might have changed when we were halfway home.'

'Who exactly is he now?' Alan asked bluntly.

Ian laughed, relieved at not being the only person to have asked that question. 'Well you've all seen how he acts: no manners, constantly distracted, disappears without explanation... He's Ben Marchen, only more so.'

The chants of the protesting villagers rose through the trees to meet Balder as he cantered down the steep zigzagging path. The roar angered him, and he was overwhelmed by an urge to escape the noise, the crowd, the unwelcome industry and his own unsettled thoughts.

Balder was forced to step aside and pause as a flat-bed lorry laden with speakers – each nearly as large as one of the standing stones themselves –

laboured up the track, and he spent those moments imagining the route ahead. Allowing for the crowds and the stern police line, he planned the shortest possible path to somewhere green and isolated. He kicked Bucephalus into a gallop as soon as the vehicle had passed.

Balder sensed trepidation in the stallion's pace at each of the blind turns in the track, but on that particular day, when it seemed that everything worth protecting had been made only to be broken, and with some omnipresent will forcing him in a most unexpected direction, Balder found himself daring the path ahead to confront him with unavoidable catastrophe.

The muddy footpath widened, the slope levelled off and the road presented itself. Balder spurred on his wide-eyed mount, and as the view before them became a little clearer he felt the horse's confidence return.

Meeting Hill's only footpath ended between two overhanging oaks. To the right of them were the police-cordoned villagers, and to the left was a Geophagia vehicle awaiting clearance by one of the officers. Bucephalus and Balder galloped into this narrow space, for a moment silencing the chanting crowd. The horse's hooves skidded slightly on the muddy tarmac as they hit the road, but Balder urged him on, accelerating for the unlikeliest of jumps. The police officers turned in response to the surprised expressions of the villagers in time to see a horse and rider leap the roadside border of blackthorn and crab apple.

They landed in wide acres of green freedom. Bucephalus thundered across the open field and Balder welcomed the soil and water kicked up at him by racing hooves. He raised his face to the clear blue sky and let the passing air take the thoughts that pained his conscience. The resumed chants of the protesters faded behind him, and with the slightest tension on the reins, Balder eased Bucephalus into a wide arc of exultant speed past the eastern border of Chiron Dell, across Milford Halfpenny's sheep-grazing acres and along the tree-lined flow of a rhyne he knew well.

The horse tired long before Balder was ready to stop, but the rider dismounted and led the panting animal north along the channel, finally leading him to the water when his surroundings felt familiar. He watched Bucephalus drink his fill, tied the reins to a low willow branch and then retrieved Marchen's dagger from his backpack. He seated himself at the edge of the channel and stared into the dark whirling eddies.

This was how Madog found him fifteen minutes later. The old man appeared beneath the umbrella of cascading willow branches wearing his habit (the time of year when such a garment performed a practical as well as ceremonial role having arrived), and his expression revealed a warmth of feeling for the thoughtful man at the water's edge. 'Hello. I saw you pass the Dell like Herne and his hounds were hunting you. You looked good.'

'Hi,' Balder replied, looking up into the old man's shadow and rising from his seat. 'I wasn't sure I'd be able to find this place again. It's been only a few weeks since you pulled me out of there,' he said, nodding at the leaf-littered flow, 'but it already seems so long ago, and it looks so different in sunlight.'

'This is certainly the spot,' Madog said. He gestured at the ancient blade in Balder's grip. 'I see your journey was fruitful.'

'Yes and no,' Balder said distantly. 'I found my dagger, but something else has happened to make me think that I no longer need to give it to you.'

Madog paused, the humour fading from his face. '*Your* dagger?'

'The sword of Marchen belongs with her descendent,' Balder declared, meeting Madog's piercing gaze with a defiant stare.

Again, Madog paused, tactically denying Balder's confrontational mood any momentum. 'But you are not a Marchen. You are Balder, *Y Deuddegfed Maen*. Your direct ascendant in this role is me, and your blood is the water of the springs of—'

'All right. I have accepted this. And yet neither of us can deny that I inherited the body and blood of a Marchen, and a Marchen hand should hold this dagger. I think it's mine.'

'Is this your reason for not returning the knife? Is one dull antique worth more to you than The Meeting?'

Balder looked away. 'Of course not,' he replied in response to both questions, but Madog gave him no chance to explain.

'And yet you're risking your best chance to preserve the stones by ignoring everything I've taught you!' Madog stepped forward as if to impress his point upon the younger man. 'You are The Meeting's Twelfth Stone and a part of the circle. You share its fate!'

Stood at the edge of the rhyne with the water behind him, Balder did not feel comfortable in Madog's angry proximity. He placed a hand against the old man's chest to request a little distance. But Madog had never before been touched in the course of confrontation. He reacted defensively, and poorly. He tried to knock Balder's hand away and push the younger man backwards.

Being so aware of his precarious stance at the water's edge, Balder anticipated Madog's move and used it against him. He gripped the front of Madog's cloak and leaned into the riverbank as he fell, a manoeuvre that sent the older man swinging about in an opposite arc of startled motion. Balder let go and landed against the trunk of the overhanging willow. Madog plunged into the dyke, his limbs flailing.

The old man's hooded robe buoyed around his spluttering head in domes of trapped air. Balder smiled as his anger subsided. Madog caught his breath and composed himself. He noticed the younger man's humour but pretended not to as his pulled a leisurely breaststroke to the bank.

Balder offered him a hand. Madog accepted it. Out of the water, he stepped away from Balder, shrugged off the heavy robe and paced shivering around the glade. 'So. The student becomes the master, is it?'

Balder disagreed. 'Not exactly Robin Hood and Little John, was it?'

Madog eyed him disapprovingly and stripped himself to the waist. He wrung his clothes until his knuckles turned white. 'It's not too late to replace you,' he muttered. 'You go off on one little treasure hunt and The Meeting gets forgotten for a bauble…'

Balder let Madog pace and mutter himself to a brooding standstill, giving Balder time to phrase his justification. 'I've been more deliberate about this than it sounds. I've come to a difficult decision. It was agony to reach, and keeping the dagger will be my only consolation.'

'A decision to abandon The Meeting?'

Balder suppressed a reflexive denial, and Madog glared at him in shocked silence. 'That can't be it?' Madog asked quietly. 'You can't have decided not to bother?'

Balder was relieved to be able to refute this statement. 'Whatever I will or won't do, I promise you that apathy will play no part in my judgement,' he declared, meeting the old man's glare with confident sincerity. 'I know what's expected of me now. You probably didn't mean to, but you introduced me to the idea, and now a greater Will than ours has ordered it. I can't see what end it will bring about, but I can promise one advantage that you'll be pleased with: Roedan will never possess Arthur's cross. She knows we have it, so she's no longer looking for it. She's coming here to blackmail us for it.'

Madog looked away and stared blankly across the sunny meadow through the fading willow leaves. 'What have you been ordered to do, Balder?' Madog asked carefully. 'And exactly how did you receive these instructions?'

Balder watched him silently for a few moments and laughed as he came to understand the old man's concern. 'I'm not hearing voices, Madog,' he said, self-consciously slipping the dagger into his rucksack. 'I'm not seeing things, and I don't have any grandiose ideas about myself. I don't know which of the gods or powers you told me about arranged the coincidences I've seen, but they were impressive. Just as we both believe that the Earth beneath our feet is the ever-watchful mother of us all, I can believe only that this course has been revealed to me for a good reason.'

Madog turned and studied Balder's pleading expression. He vigorously rubbed the water from his white hair. 'Be very wary of signs, portents and synchronicity, Balder. They're identified by the most fallible system in the world: human interpretation. Remain focused. As for Roedan, whether she's looking for Arthur's cross or coercing us into handing it over, The Meeting as we know it may be spoilt, or even destroyed, if she doesn't get it.'

Balder gazed into the water of his namesake and frowned as he recalled Madog's own familiar, haunting words. 'Perhaps we can't be so black and white about that,' he suggested. 'Nature doesn't recognise destruction in such simple terms. What if we were to think of it as more of an exchange?'

Madog seemed to nod as he sat down on the carpet of fallen willow leaves, or perhaps his head simply dropped in weary defeat.

'A sacrifice, as it were, in return for transformation,' Balder continued. The old man reached out to scratch Bucephalus behind the ears. 'This concept stalked me to Wales and back, and now it's taken on a relevance I can't ignore, even if I don't fully understand it.' As he spoke he reached into his rucksack and produced the robe he had stored there in Glastonbury the day before. He handed it to the shivering Madog and watched the old man put it on.

Some time passed in easy silence before Madog was able to respond to the situation as he saw it. 'I don't know what your plan is,' he said, recapturing a note of his former authority, 'but you now seem more deeply involved in these events than I am.

'I'm going to retire today, just as I always intended to. You've broken the deal we made for Arthur's cross, but I'll give it to you anyway. The Meeting has never been altered during my time as *Y Deuddegfed Maen,* and if I'm going to leave its preservation to you with a clear conscience I need to know that I've left behind everything that might help you continue that success.' Madog rose stiffly and snatched up his wet clothes, but he paused at the curtain of trailing willow branches. 'I'll leave your robe in the hut at Chiron Dell, and I'll hide Arthur's cross beneath the log pile before I go. Don't leave it unattended too long.

'You are now the Twelfth Stone of Meeting Hill, Balder. Please do your best for the other eleven.'

Cutting

A ravenous insectile buzzing filled the air above Meeting Hill. Chainsaws chewed an ever-deepening passage into the northern tree-line, and Lea felt violated on the hill's behalf by the rapacious clearing of undergrowth. The wild tangle in this quarter had provided her with nest-like shelter during many sunset meditations.

Lea discovered that volunteering for Earthwork duty was not as proactive a way of preventing alteration to the site as she had hoped. What she, and many others, considered to be a desecration of this sacred space was simply thought of by a greater number of people as routine land-management. Even Georgina Wyre did not seem particularly bothered by it.

Worse, this did not look like scrub-clearance to Lea. The removal of undergrowth at the edge of the woods might have left a surprising amount of space, but the passage she saw opening above the northern slope could only have been cleared by felling trees.

Lea spent time with Alan watching the progress of the estate's woodcutters, but by mid-afternoon the groundsmen had moved too far into the trees to observe, and the varying pitch of their chainsaws' ceaseless buzzing began to fade, blending with the noise of vehicles, generators, and the calls of construction crews around the hilltop.

But it was not until Lea realised how close to Meeting Brook the estate staff would cut if they continued down the northern slope that she expressed her fear to Alan. 'They're not clearing dead fern and brushwood, are they? They're cutting a footpath.'

'You reckon?' Alan frowned.

'Geophagia's festival arena is in the field below. A path down that slope will give them a perfect short-cut between the fairground and the summit.'

Alan agreed that such a motive was plausible. 'Where are you going?' he asked as Lea strode away.

'I'm going to find out for certain.'

'Do you want me to—'

'I'll be fine,' Lea said. 'But tell George anyway, she won't like it any more than I do.'

Sawdust and wood chips carpeted the grass beyond the northern standing stones, but some larger debris – logs, branches and uprooted undergrowth – had been cleared into the back of an estate van nearby. Looking north, Lea was saddened by the space created before her. Hundreds – perhaps even thousands – of years' worth of wildwood growth had been felled along a route around twelve feet across through the trees, leaving a trail of stumps, dismembered trunks and hewn boughs. Dismayed, she stepped onto the freshly cut path and walked forty feet to the brow of the hill.

Four men were working twenty feet below on the hillside. Even as she watched, a tall silver birch slid sideways into its neighbouring trees. The chainsaws roared victoriously.

Lea flinched at the sight. She turned left from where she stood and fought through piles of uprooted undergrowth at the edge of the track. She walked west around the slope under the cover of the unmolested trees until the sounds of the working men faded. At that point, she headed downhill.

Lea descended until she thought she had reached a point level with the woodcutters. The hillside was at its steepest and most treacherous here, and the root-embroidered slope was slick with wet leaves, but Lea knew this terrain well. It was a route she had scrambled many times before. The hillside grotto hosting Meeting Hill's fragile spring in a concealing ring of sycamores lay only a little further below.

Lea moved carefully, gripping tree trunks and low branches to avoid slipping, and used the soporific bubbling of the spring to guide her. She also discerned a deeper murmuring amid the sound of water. Someone else was visiting the grove. Lea positioned herself behind a holly thicket above the spring and peered down through its prickly nest of branches.

Lea saw Balder kneeling in the shin-deep flow of the stream. He muttered fervently in earnest supplication and bled from a gash across his left hand. As she watched, Balder squeezed his fingers into a tight fist and his face tensed with pain. Then he opened his palm, tilted his hand and poured blood into the water.

Lea was more surprised than alarmed by what she saw, but remained hidden. She remembered feeling irritated when Ben Marchen had invaded her privacy in similar circumstances, and she did not particularly want to meet this relative stranger in such an isolated spot. Yet neither did she withdraw. The scene represented a dramatic role-reversal with the tormented man below.

Several times since their coupling in June, Lea had felt a sense of rivalry with Ben focused on the neuroses by which they were both driven and defined. Lea's undisclosed issues expressed themselves through sullen misanthropy, a sporadic habit of mild self-harm, and a passionate concern for anything over which humankind exercises dominion. Ben Marchen, meanwhile, had presented a more nebulous angst. Lea did not share his bitter nihilism, though she had been able to relate to the frustrating extremes of emotion it provoked in him.

Mutual recognition of these common themes had drawn Lea's attention to the competition developing between them. Both had quietly resented any behaviour in the other that hinted at psychological need, perhaps concerned that their own unique dramas would be upstaged. It seemed at times that a deep-rooted hang-up could be a friend and point of pride – perhaps even worth flaunting as a badge of sufferance, as though evidence of these challenging

urges might render the victim's personality deeper and more interesting.
But whatever rivalry had existed was never given voice, and since the night Ben had been visited by horror that changed him, Lea had known that it never would be. Almost six weeks later, and in full denial of his past and more familiar self, Balder had become a more pious worshipper of the Earth and its pantheon of living faces than Lea had ever been. She recognised and accepted this fact, and so felt cheated of one of her defining characteristics.
Balder muttered with a forcible pressure of speech, though very few of his words reached Lea's straining ears. She could not discern the subject of his speech, but – considering his effusion of tears and whispered distress – Lea quickly recognised the difference between a troubled soliloquy and prayer.
Balder was indeed praying, though such a pained entreaty lacked the dignity in which he believed communion should be made. His muttered litany contained none of the concise, heartfelt praise that the Earth might have come to expect from such a fervent acolyte. Balder was begging forgiveness and, in fear of the plan he believed inspired by the very powers he addressed, was also pleading to be offered some other course of action. He wanted to know why the objects of his adoration wished him to oversee such an unthinkable sacrifice. 'Earth, Lady Mother; sun, Lord Father, why is this necessary? Is there no other way?'
Lea was offered no further insight. Balder's personal Gethsemane was a garden from which he was soon evicted. The sound of chainsaws, this time from below, made Balder twitch in fright. He winced at the sound of living wood chewed by merciless metal.
Balder rinsed his hand in the water of the spring and reached for an object wrapped in what might have been an old T-shirt on the bank of the stream. Wary of making any noise, but not wanting to miss any of Balder's actions, Lea pushed a little further through the branches between them. She watched as he immersed the object in the water, pressed it against the bed of the stream and began working it into the pebbles and clay at his knees.
Finally, apparently satisfied that the bundle was buried, Balder rose dripping from the spring. From the bank beside him he retrieved a tapering length of curved metal, freshly bound at its widest end with a bootlace to create a handle. He shook his head as though he already regretted the prayer, or perhaps suspected that it had been in vain, and stepped out of the water to pull a hooded cloak from a low-hanging branch. (The habit was not a garment that Balder intended to wear as habitually as his predecessor, but on his first day alone as Meeting Hill's Twelfth Stone – and on Samhain Eve at that – this certainly felt like a day to honour the traditional attire of his office). Balder pulled on the robe, fastened it at the front, raised the hood to shade his wan, weary features, and set off carefully downhill through the trees.
Lea watched Balder recede until the dense autumnal foliage between them obscured him from view. When the sounds of his descent had faded, and only

the buzz of chainsaws remained to spoil the peace of the hillside, Lea rose and stared into the spring.

15:43

Meeting Brook cascaded and bubbled down the forested northern slope in a series of waterfalls and plunge pools, and Balder followed it until the hillside levelled off. There, at the foot of Meeting Hill, the trees gave way to the field in which Geophagia was constructing its festival, and Balder saw that it was almost complete.

A few of the larger fairground rides, which Earthwork had spied at previous meetings of Roedan's fellowship, were conspicuous in their absence. Against Brampton Wyre's orders, Baz and his colleagues had not removed the field's border fences in time to make space for them, and several HGVs with equipment had been turned away.

But Balder paid little attention. He was searching for Roedan. He stepped out of the woods at the foot of the hill and wandered in no particular hurry through the industry of busy construction staff, and past the rehearsals of a variety of physical performers.

Passing through a large crowd wearing a monk's habit drew less attention than Balder might have expected, but he did not really care either way.

At the southern edge of the meadow, Balder paused for a moment to consider the activity and equipment of the Rainmakers, who in turn regarded him blankly. They assumed that he was another scowling Geophagia member, angry at their obstruction. Balder surveyed the cannon-like machine they aimed into the sky above Meeting Hill. Only a short distance away, men completed the impressively rapid installation of a fairground Waltzer, a fast-food trailer, a marquee selling Geophagia literature, and two noisy diesel generators.

Moving on across the meadow, Balder passed Georgina Wyre, who was in conversation with Tom Sutherland. George was trying to convince Tom that no one from the New World – even an American who had lived for twenty years in the UK – could possibly feel as strongly about the preservation of prehistoric monuments as someone from a country that actually had some. But they had chosen to hold their heated debate in front of a platform supporting a DJ, his decks and a bank of giant speakers, which broadcast music as a seismological rumble for the staff to work by. George and Tom were forced to holler at each other in competition with Chicane's *No Ordinary Morning*.

Balder eventually spied Roedan in an adjacent field to the north. She was talking to Brampton Wyre, who had crossed the recently ploughed field to reach her in his own Range Rover. Balder followed the fence to a gate and watched their conversation from a distance.

Brampton spoke with Roedan from his seat behind the wheel, and Balder caught a shrill note of Roedan's laughter on the breeze. The pair talked animatedly for several minutes, and Balder saw Roedan touch Brampton's arm

through the car window. Wyre turned the Range Rover about and drove west with bouncing acceleration over the furrowed soil.
The Twelfth Stone waited until Wyre was out of sight, and then he strode confidently into the field towards Roedan. In the time it took him to cross the distance between them, Geophagia's leader seated herself cross-legged on the damp soil, muddying her gown of thin white cotton, and closed her eyes in a pose of indifferent contemplation. Balder did not think that Roedan had noticed his approach, but he still decided that her lotus position had been assumed for the benefit of observers, even though he found it hard to imagine anyone being impressed by a spiritual leader of her reputation doing anything as trite as meditating in a field.
'I hope you have a clean gown for your party tonight,' Balder remarked, effortlessly deadpan. 'Your bouncers might impose a dress code.'
Roedan looked up at Balder wearing a smile that only parodied amusement. Her eyes blinked a glimmer of recognition, though she regarded his hooded cloak uncertainly. 'Earthwork?'
Balder shrugged slightly, but offered a more confident response as he announced, 'I have succeeded Madog as *Y Deuddegfed Maen.*'
Roedan's face replaced its smile with a leer. 'You? Don't bother me,' she muttered in a way that let Balder know he had surprised her. 'You don't know what you're doing.'
She turned away. When Balder lingered silently beside her she was forced to turn back, and then stand up when her position began to make her feel vulnerable. She opened her mouth to speak, but Balder did not let her.
'I don't want to argue, I have nothing to prove to you,' he said, producing a sealed envelope from one of his shirt pockets. He offered it to Roedan, who hesitated, concerned that acceptance of the letter would indicate a loss of control on her part. However, she also considered that snatching it from his hand and tossing it over her shoulder would act as a confident dismissal of him and his opinion of her, so she did exactly that. As the letter landed on the damp soil behind her, Roedan fixed Balder with a glare that demanded, *Now what?*
Balder laughed like he had expected this response. Then he turned and walked away, declaring, 'You'll read it.'
Roedan's instinctive reply was rash, defensive and obscene, so she rejected it before her lips could move to shape the words.
Balder did not see Roedan struggling to restrain her anger as he walked away, but he did experience a glow of satisfaction when, having put what Roedan must have thought a was an inaudible distance between them, he heard the sound of a finger tearing the seal of an envelope behind him.

Jill Baynes,

I will not address you by your assumed name of Roedan. I have discovered what it means and I will not call you 'Guide' in any language.
Besides whatever other intentions you might have while you're here, you are openly threatening the stones by inviting so many people to an entertainment on Meeting Hill.
You are not welcome here.
The Arthurian artefact, which many people now know you're looking for, is in my possession and well hidden. Before he retired, Madog told me that you once attempted (and failed) an apprenticeship to succeed him as *Y Deuddegfed Maen*. You might therefore be interested to know that this title, along with Chiron Dell and the lead cross found with Arthur's tomb, are now mine. Since responsibility for The Meeting has passed to me, I have decided that I will never make any deal that involves giving you what you want, whatever threat Geophagia poses to Meeting Hill.

The cross will never be yours.

If this decision means that you damage the monument in revenge, I will console myself by remembering that every conceivable thing experiences a life cycle, and that nothing dies whose remains are not transformed and renewed. Whatever you choose to do tonight, I believe that a bright new era for Meeting Hill will dawn tomorrow.
If you want your followers to believe that you love Nature's temples as much as you say you do, please leave Meeting Hill alone.

Balder, *Y Deuddegfed Maen.*

*

Following the drama of later that evening, many individuals with influence over Samhain Eve's concatenation of events would eventually search their memories for a point of no return.
At what moment, if any, did that night's tragedy become unavoidable?
In fact, there was such a point at seventeen minutes to four that afternoon.

During the first few seconds of that minute, Roedan finished reading Balder's letter. As she tossed the hand-written message aside, she experienced a new depth of resolve to complete her plan, feeling that she had found further justification for it.

A few seconds later, having spent some time alone watching fallen leaves racing downhill on the water of Meeting Brook, Lea retrieved the Arthurian relic from the pool at the source of the stream. She pulled the lead cross free of its T-shirt wrapping and immediately assumed that it was one of Georgina Wyre's forgeries – perhaps even the same one whose discovery had led to the exhumation of Sian Marchen.

It was at this pivotal moment that Lea finally came to appreciate the cognitive distance separating Balder and Ben Marchen. She was amazed that Balder could not remember having attempted this same ruse only weeks before, and even more surprised that he was trying it again now, with the festival's opening only hours away.

Balder truly had killed Ben Marchen, Lea decided, and such a disheartening insight made the deep dark well of a familiar fury rise and overflow, sending hot tears to her eyes and a terrible energy to her hands. Lea threw the cross up and away into the dense woods of the north-western slope, where its flight was arrested by the trunk of a sycamore just beyond the edge of the grove. It landed with a dry thud on a carpet of browning leaves.

Lea dropped weakly to her knees and wept, scratching at the scars of previous outbursts until she drew blood: a practice that often helped her make other concerns seem comparatively distant.

Simultaneously, the two teams shaving a steep path into the woods of Meeting Hill from above and below met at a point just short of halfway between the field and the summit. As the last slim birch fell sideways from between them, the united workers joked about having been lost in the forest for days, and presumed each other to be Dr Livingstone.

The teams then retraced their steps and unearthed the larger tree trunks obstructing the route. They filled the holes left by them and scattered ferns over the muddier stretches of the path. The rain of the previous days had soaked the hillside, but while it was assumed that frequenters of rural music festivals would not be bothered by mud, the slope was slippery, and now especially treacherous without its ancient network of roots, which had knitted the integrity of the topsoil.

Ironically, the minute in which these events coincided to determine the fate of Meeting Hill was also the point at which Earthwork noticed the temporary truce between Geophagia and the villagers. There had been no formal decision made by the local community to ease pressure on the invaders; but, with construction of the festival almost complete, it began to seem sensible to avoid confrontation with the many hundreds of Geophagia members about to arrive. The revellers might not turn out to be as restrained in the face of protest as the professional contractors had been all afternoon – nor as sober – and the villagers did not want to incite the very riot they had been campaigning to prevent.

Cold, tired, and unconvincingly excusing themselves with this cautious logic, many of the villagers went home.

Those who remained at the foot of Meeting Hill to maintain a vigil over the proceedings were disheartened further by the seventeen young locals among them who, they realised, were followers of Roedan, and who had gathered near the hill only to await the opening of the festival arena.

It was Celtic New Year, the Geophagians explained, and they trusted Roedan to lead them dancing by the light of celebration fires into the smoke-scented mysteries of The Meeting and all that it represents. The summer dies on October 31st, but – as consolation for the loss of the sun's strength – Roedan had promised Geophagia the vitality of the Earth's living aura: an energy to be summoned to the sacred site by the yearning of their prayers and the urging of their dancing feet.

Exposure

The festival's construction crews withdrew from the summit of Meeting Hill by half past four, leaving behind only the completed performance stage, six lighting and sound engineers and a few waiting marshals from Geophagia's security team.
The rear lights of flatbed HGVs and vans could be seen retreating from the village through the trees around the hilltop. Beyond them, snaking in from every direction, were trails of white light formed by queuing inbound traffic. Nearly two thousand members of the Geophagia Foundation waited impatiently at Little Arlingham's borders, in cars and on foot, for the police to open the roadblocks. In response, the number of officers had been increased and redistributed to funnel the many queues of traffic into one large field at the edge of the Wyre estate.
Having returned the horses to the courtyard stables and completed their own separate tours of the sprawling festival site, George, Alan, Ian, Lea and Baz were reunited at the western edge of the clearing on Meeting Hill at five-thirty. The air was cooling rapidly, the breeze stiffening, and the daylight deepening into sunset hues of lament for the summer's passing. Decorative banners suspended from frames lining the edge of the clearing drifted lazily on the air, and as the sun neared the horizon the festival ground was lit in defiance of imminent dusk. A galaxy of restless multi-coloured fairground lights, flickering arena torches and marquee illuminations filled the foreground of the view.
Roedan, accompanied by Brampton Wyre, also chose sunset to reappear on Meeting Hill. A large brazier, gas-fuelled from a canister in the base beneath its telescopic stand, was prepared for their return, and Earthwork watched the pair make a solemn show of its ignition. The festival's DJ played Delirium's *Eternal Odyssey* as a musical accompaniment to their rite, and the torch was elevated above the stage to a height clearing the surrounding trees as the sun began to edge behind the distant Exmoor hills. The flame was visible for miles, offering the Pagan faithful a beacon for which to aim. The gas pressure was increased and the brazier flared as if touched by the final rays of the setting sun, carrying a brand of the summer's fading heat and light into the Samhain night, and with it kindling the dawn of a new year.
The beacon fire also served as a signal to Roedan's staff, declaring the festival's readiness to open. Stewards saw the flame above Meeting Hill. The roadblocks around the village were lifted.
As Roedan and her attendants chanted incomprehensibly to the sky, the five Earthwork members became bored with the self-indulgent ceremony and turned away to appreciate the hilltop's last few minutes of relative peace. They surveyed the panorama of the fiery western skyline, and for a moment seemed

lulled into reverie.

Ian was a little more attentive to the view. He paused, wanting to be sure that he had correctly identified the mounted figure he saw roaming meadows beyond the festival. Then he nudged Lea, pointing into the middle distance.

Balder rode Bucephalus calmly through the crimson dusk along Orchard Ridge. A pale mist formed sedately over the Levels as the sun disappeared from view.

The villagers' interest in Geophagia's event was rekindled when the roadblocks were opened and Little Arlingham became flooded with Roedan's followers. The festival-going motor traffic was well managed, directed by the police straight onto the estate, but those arriving on foot were less easily guided to the festival arena, with many people making diversions in search of village pubs.

As several residents observed that night, Little Arlingham had never been exposed to so many people. The population of the village nearly quadrupled in less than three quarters of an hour, but suspicion of the newcomers was forgotten for a while. Many locals were secretly excited by this admittedly impressive event, especially when the music started. The festival field and the clearing on Meeting Hill echoed with Geophagia's signature tune: an ethereal dance track commissioned by Roedan, and written by the now famous DJ Van Planer. Its bass rhythm rattled windows in Carreg's End, and pint glasses hung above the bar in The Bolt Hole chinked in time to the mid-tempo beat.

Awe inspired by the presence of such a vast celebration briefly defeated the residents' anger at its impact upon them, but the novelty soon wore off. Around an hour after the festival's gates were opened, and with the event well under way, the music and the crowds were no longer regarded as a benign spectacle, but as ravagers of the rural peace. After all, this was a party to which Little Arlingham had not been invited.

So as the last Geophagians to arrive were herded onto the estate, the village was once more animated by the spreading murmur of discontent. Children emerged from their houses to place candlelit pumpkins carved with expressions of grinning menace at their gateways, and then run off in small groups of ghoulishly costumed excitement to play Trick or Treat. Many of their parents, meanwhile, joined a growing number of angry villagers in the village hall to plan their protest anew.

The first Geophagia members to reach the festival appeared among the stones of The Meeting after dark. The attractions of the arena below offered them hours of browsing, but the majority of Roedan's followers believed passionately in the Foundation's stated interests, and they were there to celebrate Samhain on sacred ground, not to shop for bracelets and windchimes, however Authentically Hand-Made In Goa the merchandise might have been.

Earthwork watched the arrivals conspicuously. 'Where's Balder?' Alan asked his friends, using Balder's name without hesitation for the first time, but having to raise his voice against the music. 'As the new Wild Man of the Hill, shouldn't he be up here taking on these people and kicking their arses in turn?'

Ian seemed to enjoy Alan's caricature of Balder's identity and expectation of his abilities. 'Perhaps he's hiding somewhere in the trees, brewing a spell to blow Geophagia away with The Meeting's bucolic energies.'

'Telluric,' Lea corrected him.

'Or at least racking his brains for some last-minute plan to save the hill from pillage by Roedan the tomb-raider and her minions.'

George did not know what they were talking about. 'Listen,' she said, 'there are a few things we need to know before we can plan anything ourselves. Ian and Lea: can you head downhill to the field and see if there's a program drawn up for the event? I'd like to know what time Roedan is due to speak. Alan?'

'Boss?'

'Can you go and find the Rainmakers? There might be time to pull one of their toys up here – perhaps even block the opening to the new path with it,' she suggested. 'Baz, stay with me. I'd like your opinion of an idea.'

Alan hurried downhill along the southern footpath in pursuit of his errand, and he did not have far to search. He found Bere, Carla and Paul operating one of their machines in a field near Chiron Dell, working by the beam of their car's headlights. A small rumbling generator provided power for the mysterious contraption which, Alan observed, did not seem to be doing anything that required electricity. Carla was sitting in it, aiming the antenna-like array into the sky above Meeting Hill.

Bere warmly greeted Alan. 'It's going well!' he declared with childish excitement, addressing the night sky. 'It's building!'

If Alan was baffled by this statement, he did well not to show it. 'Good, good,' he nodded, squinting into the sky with a frown. 'Bere, George would like to ask a favour.'

'Shoot,' Bere replied with a flick of his ponytail, offering Alan his full attention.

'She wants to know if you'll stick one of these—' Alan pointed at the machine, choosing its noun carefully, 'instruments on the hill. It would obstruct Roedan's plan nicely.'

'No – no way,' Bere replied bluntly. 'All three sym-bio accelerators are in mid-cycle now. They're in a perfect equilateral triangle around the monument, and each of them is sending a fierce bio-energy stream into the atmosphere above the stones. In fact,' Bere stepped a little nearer the stoical Alan, lowering his voice to a guilty whisper, 'we're driving these babies well in excess of safety parameters.'

Pausing for a moment to let Bere laugh with playful conscience at his confession, Alan closed his eyes tightly to suppress a rude response. In his opinion, the only thing here operating outside of safety parameters was Bere's sanity.

'With respect,' Alan ventured, 'I thought you came here to help us out.'

Bere seemed startled by the statement. 'What does it look like we're doing?' he asked in a wounded tone, gesturing at the machine and its operator, whose set jaw and expression of narrow-eyed concentration suggested that controlling the accelerator was a mental and physical challenge.

'I have no idea,' Alan said. 'That thing looks like a gun made out of scaffolding.'

'Yeah,' Bere nodded admiringly. 'Isn't it cool?'

With a nod of respect for such revealing honesty, Alan realised that this response probably highlighted a consideration central to the Rainmakers' motivation. 'And I bet that's that important.'

'What's important, Alan, is this: we're confident that this device, and the other two like it, will help you see Geophagia's festival rained off. If we're lucky there might even be some bio-form activity – that'll scare the shit out of the weekend Pagans up there!'

'You're going to make it rain in the next hour?'

Again, Bere was stunned by Alan's doubt. 'Didn't we prove what these accelerators are capable of back in August? What a storm! Isn't that why Miss Wyre asked us back?'

'I think so,' Alan nodded, 'but George has a better grasp on all this than I can manage.'

Bere seemed to understand. 'That's OK,' he shrugged. 'It's hard to get into. Sym-bio research is not an exact science, and not even recognised as science, really, so I'll forgive your scepticism if it doesn't work out tonight. In fact, if we can't make it rain, we'll join you on the hill and stand guard in front of each stone with a big stick. But if we can brew up some damp to make Geophagia uncomfortable tonight, perhaps you'll write us a witness statement for the book we're writing?'

A call from Carla made both men look up into night sky. Above the misty haze of the car's headlights, beyond the distant glow over the festival arena, the starlight was starting to seem a little hazy. Even as they watched, familiar stars were slowly dimmed and lost from view behind encroaching cloud. Bere nudged Alan and winked.

The style of decoration and entertainment for Roedan's Samhain celebration differed vastly from the mode Earthwork had seen at the festival in June. The gathering at South Pennard had been embroidered with bright flags, dazzling lights, fireworks, and energetic dance acts to compliment Midsummer. The event at Carreg's End presented a darker, edgier theme. Both The Meeting and the festival field were lined with ragged black banners, each daubed crudely with the foundation's adopted symbols – the maze, the outline of Arthur's cross, and an eight-pointed sun – in dull shades of red and white. The floodlighting was filtered red, and ultra-violet lamps and flaming braziers were plentiful, as were elevated podiums bearing various kinds of street-theatre style performance. Fire-eaters juggled blazing batons and spat endless jets of flame above the heads of the shifting crowd. Statuesque men and women wore painted period costume and make-up to resemble granite sculptures and occasionally compromised their rigid poses to wink at unnerved passers-by. And everywhere could be seen tireless male and female dancers, most of whom were nude but for a skin-tight covering at the groin, the occasional leather strap or wrist-band, some blue and indigo body paint and a dusting of glitter.

These dancers moved to continuous sounds provided by DJ Van Planer, who had relocated control of his musical set to a pair of decks on Meeting Hill after an unexpected number of Geophagia's members headed straight for the summit. Van Planer liked to see his audience, better able to judge their mood and the best tracks to suit it. Intending to save his more energetic trance and garage for the dancing that would follow Roedan's speech, he initially played a mix of that year's down- to mid-tempo tracks. Van Planer's play-list typically featured music by new and obscure dance acts (he had kick-started the careers of many now popular artists, and was even thought of by some as the John Peel of the club scene), but also included crowd-pleasing favourites from the likes of LHB, Zero 7, Weekend Players, Fragile State and Planet Funk.

Searching for a schedule of the evening's events, Ian and Lea drifted through the crowded arena in guilty awe of the spectacle. Wearing Earthwork uniform, and having no intention of trying to blend in with Roedan's followers, Lea and Ian attracted puzzled glances wherever they walked, and even a few scowls from those who remembered their intrusion at the Midsummer festival.

The Earthwork volunteers passed a base-lit pillar acting as a stage for one female dancer moving slowly and suggestively with a live python. She wore only a headdress of autumn leaves, acorns and sycamore seeds, and a layer of body paint.

'I think we should spend time looking for a timetable right here,' Ian decided, pausing to watch the performance. 'She must be freezing. Doesn't health and safety law apply to open-air dancers?'

'They have outdoor gas heaters everywhere,' said Lea, eyeing the literature of another self-help bookstall. 'I bet she's toasty.'

'No, I think she's really cold. Look.'

Lea pulled at the collar of his jacket. Ian followed reluctantly, though he found the motivation to quicken his pace when he glimpsed similar performers ahead. 'This is a daring new look for Geophagia,' Ian decided, pointing out several podiums that supported dancers of both sexes, many of whom were simulating intimate acts.

Lea stopped and stared at him peevishly. 'Each of Geophagia's meetings has a different theme to suit the season. These dancers perform a new chapter in the story of the natural cycle at each festival, and tonight is all about the end of summer, when the life force withdraws into the Earth. A common symbol for the energy of the sun is the snake, which is why that nice lady painted up to look like Mother Nature back there was cuddling a python. In myth, the sun dies at Samhain and sinks to enter the Underworld until Imbolc.'

Ian digested all this as he watched the writhing of a couple atop a nearby platform. 'I suppose a man might also play the role of the dying sun in a dance like that?'

Lea nodded, turning to follow his gaze. 'Now you're getting it.'

'So's she. It's not hard to interpret. And I can see how that man is keen to enter the underworld. Look, he's going down now.'

Lea stared as her explanation unravelled before her eyes.

'So what does this dance represent?' Ian asked. 'And how many gods in the Celtic pantheon have red demon's horns and wear PVC hot pants?'

Lea conceded defeat and grinned. The pair moved on around the arena, following the tide of moving bodies along an avenue of fairground rides, raising their voices to be heard above the engines and screams. 'Do you miss all this?'

'No,' Lea said. 'I'm here.'

'I mean, do you miss being part of it? You've gone from defending Roedan to wearing an Earthwork uniform in less than eight weeks. If you hadn't met Ben, that might have been you dancing with the snake back there.'

'No way. I wouldn't have bothered with the G-string or the body paint.' Lea enjoyed the look on Ian's face. 'Yeah, I miss it. I was supposed to be here singing with Kundalini tonight, but I can't feel committed to an organisation run by a woman who might want to damage what the rest of us worship.'

Ian raised a smug grin. 'I suppose you know what they say about yesterday's revolutionaries?'

'What about them?'

'Tomorrow's policemen.'

'Fuck off. Ah!' she exclaimed, quickly changing the subject. 'Let's look in here.'

Ian and Lea found exactly what they were looking for in a marquee dedicated to the renewal of Geophagia membership and the sale of booklets filled with Roedan's philosophy. Under the icy glare of the marquee's staff, the Earthwork volunteers pored over a leaflet containing a timetable of the night's events. Then Lea looked up and returned their unblinking stares until Ian had copied much of it onto the back of his hand.

'Roedan goes on stage in less than three hours,' he reported after a glance at his watch. 'Let's tell George.'

Earthwork

Leaving the scene of the Rainmakers' efforts, Alan saw Balder leading Bucephalus along Arlingham Road to Chiron Dell. The horse appeared tired, but Alan was shocked to see that Balder looked haggard. His back and shoulders seemed bent by a weight of years that even Ben Marchen had not known.
'Balder!' Alan called along the lane, and then again when his hail went unanswered. 'Hey!'
With what seemed like incredible effort, Balder raised his head to offer Alan silent, sleepy eyed recognition, followed by a hand in greeting. The exchange lasted seven seconds. Balder looked away and turned right into Chiron Dell with the weary horse in tow.
Despite the questions that he and his Earthwork colleagues still wanted to ask him, Alan did not pursue conversation with Madog's successor, having decided that there must have been a good reason for Balder's apparent withdrawal. What action, he reasoned charitably, could one man take against Geophagia that Earthwork wasn't taking already?
This thought made Alan keen to return to his colleagues and discuss their next move. He crossed the lane and jogged uphill to the clearing.

Balder felt motivated only to sleep, knowing that he lacked the strength and courage to face the consequences of his chosen course. Geophagia's festival might have been called off already, he concluded with a moan of pain and remorse, if only he had paid Roedan with the cross from Arthur's grave.
The shame and regret accompanying this realisation seemed to hang from his heart like a corpse from a gibbet. He clutched at his chest with one hand, and with the other pushed open the gate into the meadow he had lately called home. The creak of the gate's hinge echoed Balder's groan of self-loathing. He considered heading straight for the hut beneath the oak in the south-west corner, as much to hide as to sleep, but sympathy for the faithful Bucephalus prevented him.
Caring for the horse required light, so he led Bucephalus to the embers of the fire Madog had set earlier that day, confident that they would be glowing faintly in their rock-lined pit. A pile of firewood lay nearby; some of it was a little damp, but Madog had taught him that if you maintain a deep bed of hot ash, you can burn just about anything.
Balder crowned the embers with twigs and dry leaves and blew on the ash until its heat rose to the kindling. By the time he was confident enough to add larger sticks to the emerging flames, Balder's gaze had already taken on the flickering mesmerism that fire induces so easily.
But he dutifully resisted the temptation to sit and be lulled by the glow. He

stripped Bucephalus of his reins and saddle and spent some time rubbing down the damp horse's neck, back and flanks with sackcloth. Bucephalus seemed invigorated by the attention; a proud bearing had returned to his stance by the time Balder threw the sack aside and lifted the lid from the barrel of filtered rainwater beside the hut, allowing the horse to drink.
Balder pulled the hood of his robe over his head against the stiffening breeze and assumed a cross-legged squat on the ground before the fire. Bucephalus drank his fill and then wandered a few steps to graze, pulling at the roots of the meadow's grass with a monotonous munching that added a hypnotic rhythm to the flicker of the fire.
Balder sat motionless in this mood until he was startled by an unexpected fluttering. Bucephalus reared and whinnied in fright. A magpie landed on the handle of an axe embedded in the woodpile only a few feet away. It bobbed its head three times as it surveyed the field, its eyes and white plumage reflecting the fire as a tangerine sheen. The bird scolded the seated man with a call like angry castanets, and Balder drew back the hood of his habit to meet the bird's piercing glare. The movement startled the magpie. It leapt off the axe, spread its wings, sailed low over the field and disappeared into the night beyond Chiron Dell's thorn-lined borders.
'One for sorrow' Madog had always said with deep loathing whenever he saw a solitary magpie. Balder found it easy to marry the old man's acceptance of this quaint superstition with an ardent Pagan faith, but simultaneously impossible to reconcile Madog's fear of a magpie's appearance with his derision of other forms of portent.
Balder, however, had no qualms about inferring meaning from coincidence, or believing in folk auguries – especially superstitions remembered in the ancient country rhymes that even Madog respected. During the previous thirty six hours, Balder had experienced a dizzying mix of astonishment and fear at the conspicuous reprisal of a certain subject three times within his hearing, and he was unsettled by that same sense of foreboding now. The nocturnal sighting of a carrion bird was unusual, Balder knew, so he immediately began to suspect that the brief visitation was a message sent by the Will he sought so assiduously to obey. In turn, he found it just as easy to assume that the message would relate to the predicament faced by The Meeting that evening, though Balder would have been much more appreciative of this divine update if he had also been offered more time in which to interpret its meaning.
It seemed far too late for the gods to simply change their minds.
Bucephalus noted his human companion's silent gaze. The horse surveyed the meadow for movement, but dismissed his own momentary panic with a nonchalant harrumph as he bent his head to the grass.

The crowd of Roedan's followers on Meeting Hill had swollen considerably by seven o'clock, but was still too small for Earthwork to meet unnoticed when the team regrouped beneath one of the flickering braziers. Ian and Lea were the last to return, and they felt guilty for having reached the infernally lit hilltop by climbing the route through the trees from the arena.

Four estate employees loyal to George Wyre were also present, between them carrying enough shovels and pick-axes to put ten people to work. Alan, Lea and Ian wondered at the purpose of the tools, as did the Geophagia members who passed them. But questions were delayed until the three Earthwork activists had reported on their errands.

Firstly, Ian produced the pamphlet Lea had found and read it aloud by the light of the flame overhead. 'From six until eight-thirty it's "DJ Van Planer's smooth grooves and classic chill",' he quoted from the timetable, 'and there's "Visionary Conjecture pathworking in the Journey Marquee with Tom Sutherland". At eight-thirty there's "The Summons of the Stones", followed by "Roedan's Samhain address" at nine, and then "Van Planer returns to raise the energy with non-stop garage, trance and old school as our ancestors pass through the veil to walk abroad".'

'Abroad? So we won't see them then?' Alan quipped, frustrated by the team's almost hopeless mood. 'Will they be dancing too? Do spirits have to go abroad to dance?'

George was unable to laugh, though she winked at Alan to approve of his attempt at morale-raising. 'And what about the Sym-bio Research Forum, Alan?' she asked him. 'Are we going to see them up here?'

Alan felt that he had failed in his only useful role of the evening when he said, 'They're staying put below. They're trying to make it rain,' he added a little scornfully, and gaped in surprise when George nodded in satisfaction.

'So far so good, then,' Wyre reassured them, but with little conviction. 'I suppose it's just a waiting game now. Meanwhile, I have a controversial suggestion. I don't like it, and I don't expect any of you to like it either, but we're running short of other ideas. Baz has asked Tony, Paul, Graham and Seb here to help us divert the route of Meeting Brook.'

'What?' Lea erupted. 'Why?'

George looked at her sadly. She had guessed that Lea would offer the strongest protest against the idea. 'I don't want to touch the spring or the grove, of course,' she said quickly. 'I'm just talking about channelling the stream diagonally sideways to flood Brampton's new path. We could start well below the spring, cut a ditch around to the north, and put the path from the arena out of use. If Roedan wants to bring her entire following onto the hill, she'll be forced to send them around the estate along the road, through the village, and up the southern slope – a diversion of half an hour from the festival field. We can restore the stream in the morning.'

After only a few moments' silent consideration, Ian and Alan looked at each other and smiled sadistically, but Lea remained defiant. 'Digging up the hillside will make us as bad as Roedan.'

'I don't quite agree with that,' George said mildly. 'We'd just be making a temporary alteration to the side of the hill where no one will see it, and it'll be well away from the monument. I think that even if the plan works, it will only be a small victory against Geophagia. But that's all we have left to score, isn't it?'

'And everyone else is happy with that?' Lea asked her colleagues.

'Not if you have better ideas,' Baz replied.

Lea fell silent, glaring intensely and pleadingly at each of her companions in turn.

'I think this is the desperate corner we've been backed into,' George said, a little more bluntly. 'Standing here and doing nothing is an option, I suppose, but I think we'll all kick ourselves later if we don't do something now to make it as hard as possible for Roedan to carry out whatever she plans to do tonight.'

Apparently paying more attention to his own thoughts than to George's, Alan nudged her impatiently. 'Even better than just soaking the new path, couldn't we build a small dam and then release the water all at once as the crowd walks uphill?'

Ian cackled appreciatively beside him.

Lea turned away and looked up into the night sky, seeking the diamond brilliance of starlight overhead. She wanted to focus on something distant and safe, and be reminded that there was still beauty that could not be spoilt by such unhappy circumstance. But the sky had clouded over, and there were no stars to lure her wandering thoughts.

Lea knew she could never be persuaded to feel as enthusiastic about Georgina's plan as the others, but Wyre's last-resort reasoning gradually edged Lea into uneasy acquiescence. The need to do something, as the Earthwork leader had said, was the only thing that stopped Lea walking away. Instead, she lifted her hand and accepted a shovel from Paul, the nearest of the estate staff. 'If we have to do it, we have to plan the dig well and stick to it,' she said. 'We need to be surgical.'

Earthwork and its contingent of labourers descended the northern slope via the offending new path. They walked in single file, each of the nine colleagues carrying a pick-axe or shovel, and with Alan in the lead whistling 'Hi Ho, Hi Ho'. A trickle of Geophagia members moved uphill against them, but Earthwork did not have to wait long for the view to clear in both directions when they needed to leave the path unseen.

They proceeded west through the woods with the aid of battery torches, guided by the audible flow of water ahead of them, and they found the stream barely thirty feet in from the footpath.

'Are we below the spring here?' George asked in a hoarse whisper. The voices and torchlight of ascending strangers passed them on the route nearby. Her colleagues murmured their opinion that the spring was a good twenty feet above them. But before she could feel comfortable with their position, George wanted to hear from one member of the group in particular. 'And are you sure, Lea? I don't want to spoil the grove by digging too near it.'

'I'm sure too,' Lea replied quietly. 'Thank you.'

'Then we'll start here. What do you think, Baz?'

'Digging a ditch through woods will be back-breaking wherever we start,' the gamekeeper grumbled, and then raised his voice to address the workers. 'There are tree roots to get past, but we need to dig deep or the channel with overflow too soon. Alan, walk back to the path and drop downhill a little way. We'll spread out in a line towards you and dig a few feet of trench each. Not you, Miss Wyre. Why don't you take a torch and co-ordinate the digging – and try to think of an excuse in case someone wants to know what the hell we're doing? Everyone else, be aware of who's near you when you swing a pick-axe – if it's not Alan, try to miss.'

'Your superior stature is the only thing stopping me from kicking your arse,' Alan declared as he retreated through the trees.

Earthwork and the groundsmen went to work by torchlight. They toiled silently, but for the occasional curse and some light-hearted rivalry between the men, but soon found themselves sweating, panting and having to straighten their backs slowly and painfully at regular intervals. The pick-axes were initially used to break up the thirty-foot stretch of topsoil, and then shovels were employed to remove the earth and leaf-mould and pile it up as a low bank on the lower edge of the deepening trench. They achieved a depth and width of channel almost matching that of the natural stream: around four feet wide, and a little less than two feet at its deepest. Tree roots were exposed, making the work difficult, but where the team could not cut through the ancient network, they scraped earth away from beneath and added it to the growing bank.

By eight-twenty, the back-sore workers had created a channel that the groundsmen considered capable of diverting Meeting Brook, and the team was becoming concerned about the increasing number of people heading uphill.

'If we leave it much longer it won't be worth flooding the path,' Seb observed.

'Everyone will already be up there,'

'You're right,' George agreed. 'Time's up.'

'Thank Christ,' Ian groaned, dropping his shovel to rub at the small of his back. 'Doing this gives a literal new meaning to the title *Earthwork,* doesn't it?'

A foot-wide wall of earth still separated Meeting Brook's natural route from the new trench. Those members of the team not already standing on the higher edge of the ditch moved uphill, and Baz raised his pick-axe to remove the remaining soil.

'Wait!' Lea called.

Everyone turned and directed the beams of their torches towards her, expecting her to point out a fundamental flaw in the plan, or perhaps give voice to logic that would prevent Baz from making this final cut in the hillside But Lea stood and gazed uphill through the trees, appreciating the breeze across her tear-dampened cheeks and the gentle sound of the stream, whose flow had never before faltered or been interfered with.

'Lea?' Ian asked. 'What is it?'

She sniffed and cleared her throat, staring defiantly into the lights of her companions. 'I just wanted to put the last bit off for a minute. Today, the hill has been altered by Brampton Wyre, Geophagia, and now us. When the stream changes course, Meeting Hill will never be the same again. I hate being a part of it, and I hate Roedan even more for forcing us into it.'

There were murmurs of agreement from behind the torches that dazzled her. Lea accepted this validation as some small reassurance, but she still felt as though she were crossing the Rubicon when she stepped over the channel onto the upper bank.

Baz permitted no further delay to the conclusion of their task. He lifted the pick-axe high and swung it hard into the earth. He heaved the axe several more times into the ground, and then Tony and Paul stepped down to shovel loosened soil into the course of the natural stream below the widening junction. Water bulged at the edge of the shallow barrier, brimming against the earth that the labourers stabbed with their spades, and then flowed easily into the new trench, crumbling the last of the obstructing wall as it came.

The men worked intensely for a few minutes more, piling earth into the original waterway below the diversion. By torchlight, the others watched the water of Meeting Brook fill the ditch and surge north to the edge of the woods. Ian and Alan followed the murky flow to the end of the trench and saw the surface of the path begin to reflect their torches as the ground became gorged with water. Puddles expanded across the steep walkway, lively rivulets leaked from them to race downhill – and then the full flow of the spring escaped the ditch in a tumbling cascade of mud. Brampton's freshly cut route to the summit became the new course of Meeting Brook.

'It worked,' Alan called to his colleagues through the trees.

'Right,' George said, 'leave the tools here and let's go.'

'Oh?' Alan contrived a juvenile whine as the others filed passed him. 'Can't we stay to hear the screams?'

But the nine companions did not need to loiter for a reaction to the success of their plan. Earthwork and the labourers heard squeals of surprise a short distance beneath them. They turned and were just able to discern the flailing silhouettes of several people against the floodlights of the festival below. They

heard a succession of wet impacts as the figures dropped from view, followed by a litany of receding cries and curses.
By this time, however, only Alan's boyish sense of humour was able to overcome despondency at their alteration to the hill's northern slope, and he laughed heartily at the fading shrieks.

Geophagia's 'Summons of the Stones' – a gothic dirge created for the occasion by Van Planer – comprised several distinct sounds: a short sample of Gregorian chant, the deep toll of a gong, the hoot of an owl, and a sonar ping, all slightly distorted and layered to create a single mournful tone, dolefully repeated. It was introduced through the speakers on Meeting Hill at eight-thirty as a faint background presence, and its volume gradually increased at the same rate as the music of the arena faded. This process took almost ten minutes, by which time the summons had become the dominant sound across the estate, and people realised that its replacement of the music had been almost imperceptible.
The streets of Little Arlingham became filled with its resonance, and villagers growing accustomed to the dance music stepped outside to wonder at the haunting knell. Meanwhile, Roedan's followers headed for Meeting Hill's new path to answer the call.
Back on the summit, Earthwork found the clearing well populated, around half-filled with Geophagians and flooded with red and ultra-violet light, making focus on detail almost impossible. Cannabis smoke occasionally reached them on the breeze. Accompanied by the loud tedious summons, the combination of sensory experiences was disorientating.
The first members of Geophagia to reach The Meeting sought to stand near one of the standing stones. Every megalith was soon covered by at least twenty people, with each individual sitting on or standing around their chosen stone in a position that offered the most contact with its surface. Their faces expressed a variety of states and behaviours, from blank indifference to breathless wonder, and from animated conversation to deep contemplation. Beneath the UV lights, their teeth and light-coloured clothing (and especially the make-up some people wore for this purpose) glowed a phosphorescent mauve.
Roedan was also present on the summit, standing to one side of the elevated stage awaiting her introduction.
Not knowing what to expect next from the people around them, Earthwork silently surveyed the clearing, the whites of their eyes radiating purple effulgence.
At eight-forty-five, Ian saw a mounted man emerge from the trees that frame the southern footpath. 'About time,' he alerted his companions to Balder's arrival. 'Grizzly Adams has woken up.'
But Lea was the only member of the team to step forward in greeting. She

glanced at her colleagues, who did not know how to react to Balder's presence, and then pushed her way through the excitable crowd towards the horse and its rider. She was surprised by the sudden intensity of her emotions.
Lea still wished to believe that Ben Marchen remained hidden somewhere deep inside Balder, so she felt euphoric at this apparent return to the team. She felt that an offer of co-operation under the shared flag of Earthwork's familiar Celtic cross would be an excellent way of coaxing Ben back into psychological daylight.
Reaching Bucephalus near the southern-most stone of the circle, Lea raised a hand and rubbed the horse's nose. She looked up and exchanged an unreadable gaze with Balder. 'Talk to me?' she asked him, unfazed by the impassive expression he wore beneath the hood of his habit.
Balder considered her appeal for some time, glancing coldly at people around them as they took an interest in the horse. He began to feel uncomfortable as dozens of hands reached out to pat the animal, forming a forest of swaying arms. Rendered conspicuous by the attention, he slid down from Bucephalus' bare back and came face to face with Lea, who seized the chance to speak.
She met Balder's heavily lidded gaze and searched his eyes carefully, but she saw no hint of affection, nor even recognition. 'I just wanted to say that I'm glad you've come back. We thought you'd stopped caring about us, and all this, but—well, you're here.' She stepped forward and kissed Balder lightly on his dry, cracked lips. 'I can see how everything has come between us, Ben, and even between you and yourself, but I think we can leave all the things that haunt us in the past if we're together. There are good reasons to move on. There's something you need to know—'
Against expectation, Balder's expression began to soften. His eyes filled with water. A tear ran the length of his nose. Balder's hands found their way hesitantly to Lea's waist. He opened his mouth to speak, though nothing came.
Lea replaced his awkwardness with a kiss, and this time she felt it passionately returned. For the moments that their lips met and their tongues touched, Balder and Lea experienced the intimacy Ben Marchen had known with Lea.
Balder pulled away far sooner than Lea would have liked. He took a step back and wiped his eyes with a sleeve. 'What you're saying is wonderful,' he admitted. 'But my feelings for you are like a memory I stole from someone else. I just don't think it's possible for me. I'm not the person you knew, and as for all this,' he indicated the festival around them, 'of course I care what's happening. That's actually the whole point, Lea. I can't care about anything else. I'm the Twelfth Stone of The Meeting, and I haven't come here to join your team. There's nothing Earthwork can do now. All that's left is what I can do.'
Balder patted the horse's neck. He could find nothing else to say. He stepped away then and he moved through the fair.

Lea did not turn or follow him. She fixed the space before her eyes with an unfocused gaze, clenched her jaw and winced in the throes of what an observer might have thought was mortal pain. She did not know how long she stood this way. People moved around her in close proximity, either oblivious to her distress or else assuming that she, like many others on the hilltop, had entered a state of personal reflection, worship or intoxication.

Eventually, one pale figure slid into her field of blurred vision and remained there. It took Lea some time to compose her thoughts and senses. When she did, it was Roedan's patient gaze of condescending sympathy that met her eyes. But Lea was now drained of fight, and she did not possess the strength to resist when Roedan slipped a sheet of paper into her passive grip and laid a hand gently on her shoulder. After Balder's brutal rejection, Roedan's presence and touch were almost comforting.

'Hello. We've not had a chance to speak since you left the fellowship,' she crooned. 'I've missed your contribution to Geophagia's interests, and I don't think the girl who replaced you in the band sings your songs half as well.'

Lea's eyebrows flickered but she could not raise a smile.

'Now,' Roedan continued in a more business-like tone, 'it's clear that this local vigilante group have managed to convince you that I'm some sort of ogre. I'm disappointed, of course, but you've a right to act on your conscience. Also, you and I have known each other a long time, so I feel that I should offer you a little advice.'

Lea was lost. She looked at the letter in her hand, and then at Roedan's ingratiating smile. 'What?'

'I saw you with that man, the one who changed his name and stopped washing,' Roedan explained, pointing in the direction of the now vanished Balder. 'It's clear that you're still close, but I think he might be misleading you.'

When the elder woman fell silent, Lea unfolded the piece of paper and read the defiant words Balder wrote that afternoon. Roedan watched her absorb the full meaning of the letter, becoming so engrossed in signs of Lea's deteriorating mood that she was oblivious to Tom Sutherland's arrival at her side.

'Jill?'

Roedan lifted a hand to silence her employee. Tom took a step back.

Lea dropped the letter into the mud. 'I already know that Balder has a funny way of showing his concern for The Meeting,' she said, denying Roedan the satisfaction of surprise. 'And we're not close – I was kissing him goodbye.'

'Well,' Roedan replied, 'then I hope this letter will help you get over him a little quicker. Perhaps he always cared more about Arthur's cross than he did about you,' she went on. 'Perhaps he's even guilty of what I'm being accused of. What if *Y Deuddegfed Maen* cares more for Arthur's cross than he does for The Meeting?'

The anger provoked by Balder's apparent treachery competed with the comfort of Roedan's words for dominance of her mood, making thought confused and difficult, and introducing a frustration that left neither contender a clear winner. 'That cross has ruined everything for so many people,' she cried. 'I tried so hard to love Balder, but even he's corrupted by it.'

Roedan nodded, like she shared Lea's sense of betrayal. 'He rejected you, and now you're in pain.'

Lea flinched, spurred by Roedan's words. She found herself nodding, not only in agreement but in awe of Roedan's insight. 'How did you know? How are you always right? Balder's rejected me, and he's rejected his chance of keeping people off Meeting Hill so he can keep the cross. But you know what?' Lea wiped her eyes, briefly regaining the steely glare that once unsettled even Baz. 'I've heard rumours about you. Everyone says that the founder of Geophagia is a cold-blooded whore who'll fuck anyone to keep them loyal. I also believe that the woman we've followed for so long came here to turn this site over in search of Arthur's cross – but I'm going to save you the trouble and tell you where the cross is anyway.'

Roedan's eyes widened. Tom Sutherland stepped a little closer.

'I found it earlier. Until now I didn't know Balder had the real thing. I thought he'd planted a fake to lure you away, so I threw into the trees. It's at the edge of the grove near the spring on the north slope. Take it away so it can't hurt The Meeting anymore. Let Balder know you have it, and that I helped you find it – but don't ever come here again.'

Lea shouldered Roedan aside and strode away, pushing fiercely past anyone who did not give way fast enough.

Tom Sutherland let Lea disappear before congratulating his companion. 'You were right,' he smiled. 'She knew, and you knew how to get it out of her.'

'She could be lying,' Roedan replied. 'She might seem keen to hurt her boyfriend, but Lea is a true believer. She loves The Meeting and every monument like it, and she'd say anything to make us leave sooner.'

Tom gaped. 'You mean you don't want to look?'

Roedan responded with the measured confidence she knew Tom would appreciate. 'My priority is to my followers, of course,' she said. 'Even the ones I haven't fucked for their loyalty. But after I've given my presentation, perhaps I'll have a stroll downhill while the crowd is distracted.'

'And perhaps not,' Tom said, remembering his errand. 'That's why I came to find you – the new path is impassable. Your speech might have to wait.'

Earth-eaters

Balder moved through the crowd feeling sorrier than the manner of his parting would have suggested, though thoughts of his errand reasserted themselves as he neared the northern trees. Bucephalus drew affectionate attention from the crowd every step of the way, but both Balder and the horse seemed oblivious to their surroundings, until they encountered Earthwork near the new footpath. Like Lea before him, Alan attempted an optimistic greeting. 'Balder.' He grinned widely. 'Good to see you back. We've been busy, and there's a fair bit to tell you. Where have you been?'
Balder inspected the faces of the eight people standing at the edge of the clearing. He recognised four of them and they wore welcoming expressions, but with them were four men he did not know. They looked critical and judgemental. 'I wasn't going to get involved in this,' he confessed, displacing a sudden self-consciousness by reaching out to scratch behind Bucephalus' ears. 'I believed that I was meant to let Roedan and her lackeys come up here and do whatever they wanted.'
'*Meant?*' Ian frowned.
Balder regarded him suspiciously. 'You know: destined,' he said. 'Does that disturb you?'
Ian was used to posing challenging questions, not receiving them. He shrugged.
'Omens scare me,' Balder continued, 'and they scare me even more when I see a sign telling me that I misread the previous one. Fucking magpie. So I have to ignore that now and follow the only purpose I've ever known. I'm going to help preserve The Meeting, but I'm not here to rejoin you.'
'So…?' George asked.
'I'm going to make Roedan the offer she's blackmailing me for and get these people off our hill within half an hour,' he confidently declared. 'Anyone got a torch?'

Roedan spoke to the arena manger on a mobile phone. 'There's another path up here from the road on the other side of the hill. Direct everyone round to it through the village, they won't miss too much.' She handed the phone to Tom without ending the call.
'Do you think Wyre's men disturbed the brook when they were cutting the new path?' Sutherland asked, pocketing the handset.
Roedan laughed. 'No! Do you?'
'Less than half your people are here. Aren't you going to wait for the other half?'
Roedan surveyed the crowd from beside the podium and shook her head. 'There's enough,' she replied. 'The others should have been keener, shouldn't

they? Let's get started.'

Two white spotlights flared to life and were aimed at the platform. Tom Sutherland appeared above the crowd, prepared a microphone at the front of the stage, and then he raised his arms for silence.

The response of those gathered was to cheer the herald of their priestess. Tom was forced to let the roar falter naturally before pressing his mouth to the microphone. 'It's Samhain Eve,' he breathed, provoking further cries and whistles. 'The energies are rising. The veil between this world and the next is weakening, so raise your voices in invitation to our ancestors! Let them walk among us and listen as Roedan talks us into the Feast of Souls!'

Earthwork positioned themselves on the opposite side of the clearing, as far from the speakers as they could manage without descending the hill. They watched avidly, though they felt duty-bound to react critically to everything they heard. 'It's outrageous to suggest that my grandparents would want to drift back onto this mortal plane just to listen to Roedan,' Ian said.

Alan agreed with him. 'Mine wouldn't have liked Roedan while they were alive, and I don't think that being dead will have improved their humour much. What do you think Balder is doing?'

Ian didn't want to commit himself to an answer, or even speculation. The situation seemed more complicated than the plan Balder had described the day before. 'I don't know. I think it has something to do with our trip to Wales.'

'Whatever it is, he sounded confident about it,' George added. 'I just wish he'd decided to do it earlier.'

'Perhaps he was waiting for the best time to hurt Lea again,' Alan suggested. 'I think she's gone.'

'Perhaps Balder will turn all these people into frogs in the next few minutes,' Baz suggested, 'and then we can go for a pint.'

Geophagia raised a cheer of jubilant welcome as their leader appeared on the platform.

Tall narrow podiums had been positioned either side of the stage. Both were draped with banners displaying Geophagia's distinctive motifs, and at the top of each pillar was a dancer – a woman on the left, a man on the right – whose bodies were tanned, toned and oiled well beyond the aspiration or envy of most observers. Van Planer introduced a sixty-second burst of bass-heavy music, to which the dancers energetically performed synchronised moves of Dionysian frenzy. This introduction gave Roedan – who to everyone's surprise had exchanged her usual white gown for a red silk robe – a full minute to bathe in the deafening adulation of her followers.

When the music stopped, engineers dimmed the electric lights around the clearing, leaving only the flames of the gas-fuelled braziers to cast a flickering glow over the event. Flecks of quartz in the standing stones shimmered like fireflies.

Roedan stepped a little nearer the microphone and opened her mouth. The velvet surety of her voice began to flow from the surrounding speakers in smooth waves of mesmerising persuasion, and the Geophagians stood in awe, as in love with Roedan's voice as they were with her philosophy.
From the southern edge of the clearing, a mile-long queue of fellow worshippers began to file into view, and just as the summit was filled to around three-quarters its capacity, the chill night breeze brought rain. A fine spray drifted across the clearing in soaking curtains that made the elevated torches of naked flame splutter, though neither Roedan nor her followers betrayed signs of disappointment. In fact, many of those present welcomed the downpour as a blessing from the benevolent heavens. Those who did not felt compelled to pretend that they did.
'Samhain Eve and all that it represents for us is a challenge to those of our faith,' she began, and the expanding crowd fell silent. 'As we have learned over the course of our meetings, the Solar and Celtic festivals offer us deep insight into the often opposing aspects of our world. We have divined universal truth, defining and reflecting all facets of Life; and we have discovered more personal meaning, which we celebrate as milestones in our individual lives. We have been able to relate to the various themes and associations of the eight-fold year on many levels – but our consistent theme throughout has been veneration of the diverse experiences that fill our lives, if we are open to them. Because of this, Samhain threatens to compromise our reverence. Everything, Nature tells us through this dark festival, whether animate or otherwise, enjoys and suffers a finite period of existence, and then it loses its being in that form. In short: everything dies.'
Very few people in the audience had ever spoken to Roedan personally, but those who had would have noted her consistency of presentation. People often assumed that Roedan was Jill Baynes' stage persona, and that out of the public eye she was probably something of a *prima donna.* Jill Baynes was quick to anger, it was true; yet despite her ambitions, it cannot be said that she was grandiose. What surprised people who met her informally was that she always spoke with the same ceremonial gravity she used on stage, even when discussing mundane subjects. One or two light-hearted Geophagians had attempted impersonations of their leader doing something domestic, and had made even the reading of a shopping list sound like a sermon.
'Death,' Roedan continued, 'is the centre of a maze whose path we all walk, and is the destination of all life. But here, even as we seem to face destruction and the loss of everything we have achieved, the Earth once again offers hope in the form of its annual cycle. Rumours of the immortality of our life force are whispered by the new leaves of trees, which return to vitality after months of standing as corpses. Winter is not just the end of the year – it's the start of the next. Life is not lost, Nature seems to be hinting, it is returned to its Source

and Mother to be transformed— and it is here, my friends, that I lose any further right to speak knowledgeably on the matter.'

As Roedan fell watchfully silent, her followers exchanged bewildered glances, and then spread a murmur of dissent. Of course, no Geophagia member could justify Roedan's right to lecture anyone about anything – except, of course, to point out that over two thousand people had paid to listen to her (and, for the most part, unquestionably accept everything they heard), so this confession of ignorance seemed needlessly modest.

Strategically, Roedan awaited the first hesitant calls of encouragement from the crowd before explaining: 'The experience of consciousness after death is a subject that no living thing is qualified to discuss. It is a subject personal to each individual's reasoning, or faith. Anything I have to say about it can be based only on my own opinion, not on observation of the natural world, upon which all my previous discussions have been founded.'

Again, an expanding chorus of calls from the crowd prevented Roedan from leaving the stage. 'I do not seek credit or blame for my views, even supposing that these opinions could be proved either way – and this, my friends, is the only point that allows me to further discuss our reverence for this dark festival. The potential for experience after death, and before rebirth, remains the deepest mystery. Samhain is a celebration of all our inevitable endings, and of the unknown that follows.

'Personally, I find this mystery liberating,' she smiled, instantly lifting the mood of the gathering. 'Samhain Eve is a long dark night at the end of summer – something that perfectly symbolises the end we all eventually face. But I prefer to see this void as an empty canvas for the imagination. I have always considered true darkness to be the sanctuary of rarer, finer beings, in which everyone here believes, and this is why:

'Utter darkness lies at the beginning and end of all things. It is all that exists before our earliest memories, and it is what we will face following our final breath. Nothing, of course, is deeper than darkness. Darkness with a visible boundary is only shade. True darkness, therefore, is a boundless realm of endless potential: an Otherworld of the infinite Unmanifest, and the great Unmade.

'Light is the Veil that hangs between this world and the Other. Samhain Eve is not the night of the longest darkness – but it is the night of the *deepest* darkness, as the Earth goes into mourning after Her divorce from the summer sun, and so that shimmering Veil is removed. Throughout the night that follows, that which has yet to exist may glimpse Being; those who have lived and passed on into darkness may stand among us, and creative deities are offered the true darkness of Samhain Eve, which for them is an etheric medium that allows them to assume form and walk the wilderness they inspire!'

For everyone present that night, Roedan's reasoning was a licence to fantasise and believe in the visions they conjured.

'Tonight,' she continued in the confident tone of one preaching to the converted, 'I see sprites flicker with the joy of existence within their Element. I see Cernunnos in all his antlered glory throned in a grove of oak. Ceridwen, bent with age and wisdom, stoops over the waters of prophecy and glimpses the light and abundance of the coming year; and as the music of our festival fills the air, I see the stones of The Meeting moved to dance, animated by the energy raised by your love, your gratitude and vision!'

The summit of Meeting Hill was now full. Every member of Roedan's fellowship was present, and the Earthwork volunteers were forced to stand beyond the edge of the circle with their backs against the trees of the northern slope.

George, Ian, Alan and Baz looked at each other nervously. They felt unsettled by Roedan's talk of The Meeting's stones being 'moved' by any force, whether loving, grateful or otherwise, and George became concerned that this was a prearranged command for Geophagian staff hidden in the trees with camouflaged bulldozers to set about toppling megaliths in search of the notorious treasure. She watched the crowd carefully, though there was no discernible increase in activity, nor change in mood.

'We're not much of a deterrent while we're being pushed into the woods,' Alan complained.

George shrugged. 'There's only four of us,' she pointed out, disappointed – but not surprised – that their company of labourers had left when Roedan's speech began. 'What can we do? At least we're dry here,' she added, glancing through the branches at the rain. 'The Sym-bio researchers proved useful.'

Alan rolled his eyes.

'I'm not worried about rain,' said Ian. 'Where's Balder? I never believed he'd be able to kick Geophagia off the hill so quickly, but the half-hour he promised is long gone, and I expected— I don't know. Something. What's happening?'

Exposed to the worsening weather in the clearing, Roedan evoked a fantastical vision for her audience. 'I see the dreams of each and every one of you given form by Samhain's potential to rise as winged sylphs and ride the winds of actualisation!' she claimed wildly, inducing another roar from the crowd. In his sheltered station to the rear of the platform, DJ Planer introduced *Salva Mea* by Faithless as a backing track to zealous oration.

The crowd's euphoria and Roedan's passion were mutually encouraging. With the help of the music, Roedan talked her followers into a state of frenzy, inspiring them to cheers and exultant dancing. In turn, Roedan was inspired further by their reaction, excited by the sight of more than two thousand people dancing in waves of ecstatic rhythm, a sea of hands and faces.

In a demonstration of emergent behaviour, the press of moving bodies began to huddle into itself against the rain and cold. The tight, jumping crowd raised heat, and many members of the foundation stripped themselves to the waist, others even further, to revel in the benevolent hysteria and deteriorating weather. Wet torsos spooned together and synchronised their responses to the music, swaying and jumping as a single body of glistening skin that was burnished by the flickering flames of the torches. The bass thud of music reverberated in the air above the stones and through the earth of Meeting Hill. People heard and felt it several miles away.

'In the shadows of the trees I see Merlin step through the veil between worlds, returning to gaze across the Levels at the terraced slopes of Avalon! And Arthur Pendragon steps into the light beside him, reinforcing the solidarity of our West Country hearts with the eternal majesty of his presence! As the legendary last leader of the Britons and the *King y-crowned in Fairye*, Geophagia honours Arthur as the principle figure in its pantheon of idols. On Samhain Eve, everything he symbolises becomes particularly important, for it was in death that Arthur immortalised the blood of his people and passed the ultimate test of his spirit.'

A brief hiatus in the tempo of the music did nothing to calm the pace of Roedan's speech, nor the fever of her audience.

'In sympathy for Her offspring, the Earth receives the mortal remains of all that lives and dies. In the womb-like incubation of Her soil, death is redefined as transformation, and the traumatic experience of loss is negated by the revelation of rebirth. The body of the past is the fertiliser of the future! Arthur himself was interred in Avalon, the Celtic Otherworld, whose enduring spirit is manifested as the strange, mist-cloaked mires and hills of Glastonbury. His bones are long-since lost, but we are the faithful bearers of his memory, of his principles and his banner, and we are chosen to receive the progeny of his burial. The earth beneath our feet holds the symbol that testifies to the loss of Arthur – but also to the promise of his return, when he will lead the disillusioned British into an age of restored pride and identity!'

Ian Longe, who had been unconsciously nodding and tapping in time to the music, felt his stomach tighten as he glimpsed a possible direction of Roedan's speech. 'Uh-oh.'

His colleagues had not yet inferred the same threat from her fevered preaching. Interpreting Roedan's words only as crowd-pleasing rhetoric, George, Alan and Baz talked contentedly amongst themselves, though they found it difficult. The music grew a little louder every few minutes.

Ian was about to alert them to his suspicion when he noticed new arrivals at the edge of the clearing. Carl Harper, along with the estate employees Tony, Seb, Paul, Graham and Abel Mild, and a number of the Rainmakers, had ascended the eastern footpath at the head of one hundred and fifty villagers, most of them male, and all of them grimly determined.

Concentrating only on the crowd's reaction to her words, Roedan did not notice the angry new arrivals. 'In honour of the ancient festivals, we've danced together since last Midwinter across this myth-soaked landscape, raising its energies, and also our own hopes of a future bathed in the golden light of a halcyon past. Tonight's meeting concludes our tour, and we can retire knowing that the Earth has absorbed the achievement of our efforts, just as She does all things at their end. The passion of our devotion and the sweat of our dancing are accepted by the Earth as a libation, and this elixir renders fertile soil malleable in deserving hands. She will offer up a sign of Her blessing – a token that we may carry at the head of our procession to usher in the Pagan Enlightenment, thereby proving to the world that Geophagia is the herald of its dawn! You, my friends, are Arthur's new Grail-seekers and the arbiters of change. All we need do is reach out…'

Ian obeyed and reached out for Alan's attention, but he was unable to tear his gaze away from Roedan's stage-front frenzy. Instead of grabbing his friend's arm, he succeeded only in cuffing Alan about the head.

'What?' Alan flinched.

'This is it,' Ian said. 'It's going to happen. They know it too.' He pointed at the host of Little Arlingham's residents, which had started edging into the clearing.

The sweat of Roedan's passionate performance soaked her hair and robe more thoroughly from within than the rain did from above. The roaring crowd, much of which was drunk or stoned as well as roused by the speech of their priestess, was slave to Roedan's commands. But such euphoria did not encourage the attention required to untangle their leader's will from her figurative language and metaphors.

'Reach out!' Roedan urged her following. 'Reach out and into the nurturing Earth for Her reward!'

Unused to such direct instruction from someone who could spin a twenty-minute speech out of one or two aphorisms, many members of the fellowship raised their hands into the air as they danced, clearly frustrating their now impatient leader.

'Would a grateful Gaia place our prize overhead, so far out of reach?' she improvised effortlessly. 'The soil is Her womb, where Life and the gifts to Her faithful are nurtured. Arthur himself must have stood amongst these stones, and each of his footsteps was a seed planted in sacred ground – the ground upon which we now stand! Reach down, friends, to reap the harvest of Arthur's passing and the gratitude of the Earth!'

The crowd released a celebratory cheer with every mention of Arthur's name, encouraging Roedan's passion, though foiling her design. 'No!' she finally cried in exasperation. 'Dig!'

Roedan did not have to repeat the order.

There was, of course, a number of people present who realised immediately that Roedan's order was incompatible with her environmental concerns, as well as illegal, and these few Geophagians did their best to distance themselves from the ensuing chaos, pushing their way free of the hysterical mob.

Everyone else dropped to their knees and clawed at the ground with their hands. Many people eyed the stones of The Meeting as potential markers of whatever prize Roedan had referred to, and so began burrowing into the earth beneath them with wide-eyed zeal. People competed violently for the earth at the bottom of countless holes sunk across the muddy clearing like a carpet-bombing of the summit.

The detritus of centuries began to surface from the ravaged earth: discarded drink cans were fought over and revered; animal bones were examined with fervent awe, and the votive offerings of a thousand penitent visitors to the site were held aloft in the rain for Roedan's inspection.

But their leader was not interested in rusty pendants or crystal charms. Seeing her followers committed to the execution of her will at last, Roedan discarded her microphone and dropped lightly from the back of the stage. Tom Sutherland, who had known exactly what to expect from Roedan's performance, seemed shocked nevertheless, but still appeared dutifully at her side.

'Do you think Lea was lying?' Roedan asked her lieutenant, refusing the pointless offer of a towel.

'No,' Tom replied. 'I think she really was bitter enough to tell you the truth. What do you think?'

'I don't know,' Roedan admitted, 'but I'd be stupid to ignore what she said. I'm going to look.' She nodded at the feverish crowd. 'Keep an eye on what they turn up, just in case – and arrange me a lift from the arena in fifteen minutes.'

Equipped with a small torch from one of the stewards, Roedan glanced around quickly in search of conspicuous witnesses, seemed reassured, and then passed unnoticed from the anarchic hilltop into the darkness of the wooded slopes.

DJ Planer was disappointed with the turn of events. He felt no responsibility for the actions of the crowd, but he did see the effect that the music he played had on the revellers. Too late, he realised why Roedan had requested energetic tracks to back her speech, rather than the ambient sounds of previous festivals. Planer had not been aware of Roedan's plan, and he did not approve of it, so he protested against the vandalism in the only way that he could. He silenced the music abruptly and began to pack away his equipment.

But the crowd did not seem to notice the loss of soundtrack, nor the end of Roedan's speech. The roar of her followers continued unabated as they burrowed into the mud, focused only on the task their priestess had set them.

Alan, Ian and Baz dashed forward from their position beneath the trees and

protested impotently. The burly gamekeeper quickly realised that shouting at the hysterical crowd was a waste of breath, so he lifted the nearest digging man bodily from the ground and stared intensely at him until the fanatical glaze in the Geophagian's eyes was replaced by fear.
Alan was happy to follow The Bastard's example, but his anger, once released, was not as restrained as Baz's intimidation. No longer feeling professionally bound to suppress his rage, Alan swung a boot into the ribs of a semi-naked young man in front of him. He hauled a young woman out of the pit she was deepening with several others, punched the man who rose to defend her and hollered a challenge to all the angry, mud-streaked faces that looked up in response.
Ian hurried to Alan's side, fully able to appreciate the futility and danger of provoking a fight with two thousand people, but unable to let Alan stand against them alone. He gaped in shock and horrified awe at a panorama of ruthless, scavenging people, whose restless hands flung the soil of Meeting Hill in every direction. He saw that The Meeting was defiled, and he was suddenly afraid that, from this moment on, it would always remain so for the people who knew it best.
An unexpected sound defused the moment. Baz, Alan and Ian glanced at each other in surprise when they heard laughter, and they turned to see George Wyre wiping tears of hilarity from her eyes. From somewhere to the north came the sound of an approaching helicopter, but it was George's laughter that drew the attention of most people within earshot.
'This is it!' she cried in a breathless combination of amusement and relief. 'This is the worst they can do!'
Alan chuckled lightly in disbelief at Wyre's reaction, and then he laughed with her when he realised that she was right. Alan had an infectious laugh, and being able hear it at that grievous moment struck Ian and Baz as so farcical that they also found it funny.
'They're scratching holes in the mud, and we've been worrying about this festival for months,' George cried. 'We can have the clearing re-turfed in a day!'
The Geophagians ravaged the summit of Meeting Hill with their bare hands and fingernails for a relic they would not find, and through the rain and showers of hand-propelled earth came the sound of Earthwork's defiant laughter.
But the villagers at the eastern edge of the clearing had not yet seen the funny side. Their fury boiled over when they saw the multitude drop to its knees and begin scouring the hilltop. As Georgina Wyre had already realised, there was nothing more that Roedan's followers could do to damage the monument without mechanical aid, but the residents of Little Arlingham could not see beyond the principle of the insult inflicted, which was all they needed to

justify their response.

Abel Mild spurred the one hundred and fifty villagers into action with a hoarse but vehement challenge, followed by a wild berserker charge into the midst of the vandals. Whether his anger was fuelled by his characteristic hatred of outsiders, or by having so much to prove after his former skulking allegiance to Brampton Wyre, Abel was thereafter considered to have redeemed his reputation.

For years following that night, people of the area referred to the skirmish as The Battle of Meeting Hill, and described it as an epic struggle between heroes and barbarians.

In truth, the clash lasted less than ninety seconds. The first Geophagians attacked barely had time to rise and defend themselves before everyone on the hilltop was shocked into cowering silence by a sound of cataclysmic splintering, closely followed by a rising rumble.

The Meeting shuddered.

The rumble grew to a tumultuous quaking of the ground and the air. The woods either side of the new footpath on the northern slope quivered as if in panic, and then the stretch of hillside on which they stood disappeared, taking trees, tall speakers, lighting equipment, two standing stones and twenty three people with it.

The space left behind was momentarily filled with the sparks trailed by a tumbling brazier, a cloud of dust, a shower of autumn leaves, and then only the drifting rain.

People ran for the eastern footpath in a screaming stampede.

Meeting Hill continued to vibrate for ten long seconds, but the panic of the fleeing crowd did not abate with end of the landslide. Villagers ran shoulder to shoulder with Geophagians across the clearing, until almost everyone remaining on the summit was squeezed into a bottle-neck around the footpath in the south-eastern quarter.

But for those who had stood their ground, whether rooted by fear, fascination, or else the selfless wish to be helpful in the aftermath, the calm that descended when the ground stopped shaking was a tangible air of shock and imminent questions. People stood near the summit's new sheer, crumbling border stepped gingerly towards it and peered over the edge.

Georgina Wyre, whom Baz had pushed to the floor and covered with his own body as the trees around them disappeared, patted the gamekeeper's arm gratefully for release and sat up. She saw that a third standing stone had fallen from its stance of millennia and was lying precariously over the jagged edge of the summit.

Alan and Ian crept nearer the verge and looked down. They saw a helicopter landing in the arena below, but it was the carnage of the landslide, heaped in silhouette against the fairground lights, and the distant screams of pain and distress, that drew their horrified attention.

'How did Geophagia cause this?' Alan asked in a shaky whisper, testing the fractured ground before him. 'What did they do to cause subsidence like that?' Ian, who seemed ignorant of all risk as he stepped even nearer the crumbling brink, stared mournfully downhill and seemed to glimpse some hateful insight. 'They didn't,' he said quietly, pulling a mobile phone from his jacket pocket and dialling three nines. 'I think we did.'

Prize

'I'm going to make Roedan the offer she's blackmailing me for and get these people off our hill within half an hour,' Balder declared confidently. 'Anyone got a torch?'

Seb, one of the labourers, provided him with his own. In return, Balder handed him the reins of Bucephalus. 'I can't take him into the woods with me,' the Twelfth Stone explained, smoothing the horse's neck affectionately, and then he walked away, leaving Earthwork on the summit of Meeting Hill in as cold a manner as he had left Lea Granger.

Aiming for the northern-most edge of the clearing, Balder pushed his way through throngs of the excited Geophagians, who competed possessively for contact with the standing stones. Roedan was due on stage in the next few minutes, and her followers were growing impatient. When he reached the border of trees, Balder was heartbroken by the sight of a rough path hewn downhill through the ancient woodland. Starkened by the pallid white light of his torch, the exposed flesh of jagged tree stumps and cropped branches seemed a brutal carnage, and Balder felt that walking the disturbed earth of this ragged corridor was like trampling the soil of a freshly filled grave.

Looking for the spring at the head of Meeting Brook, though disoriented by the path's alteration of the hillside, Balder wandered a little too far down the slope and was further dismayed to find that Meeting Brook had been diverted. The stream emerged from the trees to his left, cutting a scar across the hillside and flooding the slope below. He could see the water's flow eroding the lower lip of its own hastily dug channel, allowing water to escape the trench long before it reached the new path.

Balder's sense of direction had been confused, but the diversion of Meeting Brook was, at least, a guide to its source. He followed the brimming trench uphill and west through the trees to the spring, and he was heartened to find that the grove itself remained unspoilt.

As Balder took off his backpack and set it down beside the pool, he guessed that Earthwork was responsible for the stream's redirection. Perhaps the alteration had been needed to block Geophagia's route uphill, he reflected, or perhaps it was vengefully done to soak the arena below. Whatever its purpose, Balder was surprised to find that he was not particularly angry with the committee. He decided that the stream could probably be restored the next day. In fact, The Meeting's Twelfth Stone was beginning to feel lightly optimistic about the way the evening was unfolding – until he discovered that Arthur's cross had been removed from its hiding place in the bed of the stream.

With the torch clamped tightly between his teeth, Balder moved his hands through the icy water, pushing his fingers deeply into every corner of the plunge pool, and then looked downstream for any sign of the lead cross or its

T-shirt wrapping.

The relic was too heavy for Balder to entertain any thought of it having been unearthed by the gentle flow of the stream – there were coins in the plunge pool that had lain there for months – and he was sure that no one could have known of its burial. Yet it was gone, along with Balder's chances of negotiation with Roedan.

The Twelfth Stone's yell went unheard above the sounds of the festival. Balder screamed his distress into the ink-dark woods. Then he rose from his knees and began a painstaking search of every inch of the stream within the grove, from the gushing fissure in the exposed bedrock to the brook's widening route at the edge of the glade.

The festival became busier and noisier above him as he worked, but it was not until Balder heard Roedan begin her speech that he finally accepted the futility of his search.

Bewildered by the cross's disappearance, and by then feeling weary and defeated by the forces opposing his cause, he trudged back uphill and sank into a despondent crouch beside the spring. From his backpack he removed a tea-light candle, which he set on a flat stone at the water's edge, and then the ancient short-sword of Marchen, which he plunged into the earth at his feet. He also found an open pack of cigarettes and some matches, thereby discovering that Ben Marchen, from whom Balder inherited the bag, had been a smoker.

Balder did not smoke, and he had no second-hand memory of what it was like to do so, but his lungs did not protest when he lit a Marlboro and drew on it experimentally. If ever there was an appropriate time to smoke, he reflected idly, lighting the candle with the same match, then perhaps this was it. His fingers quickly remembered how to hold a cigarette.

The gentle trickle of the spring was a companionable presence and comfort to Balder, even though it was almost drowned by the amplified voice of Roedan, by the increasing volume of the dance music, and the cheers of the crowd from above. The flickering of the candle, which struggled against fine rain in the darkness, turned the hillside grove into a bubble of warm orange light, and Balder blew clouds of smoke and resignation up into the sycamore branches. He listened to Roedan expounding on her seasonal topics, and he dispassionately noted the way in which she toyed with her followers' attention and pandered to their dreams.

Then Balder felt the crawling tingle of déjà vu when the theme of death-as-transformation was raised once more within his hearing. He listened to Roedan say, 'In sympathy for Her offspring, the Earth receives the mortal remains of all that lives and dies. In the womb-like incubation of Her soil, death is redefined as transformation, and the traumatic experience of loss is negated by the revelation of rebirth. The body of the past is fertiliser of the future.'

But such a coincidence no longer carried any suggestion of control over Balder's choice of actions. He knew that no further choice could be made. This further coincidence, if any meaning was to be discerned from it at all, seemed only to confirm the course of events that had been destined all along. At that moment, the message for Balder seemed clear: The Meeting was to suffer in some way, but – as hard as it was to imagine – some compensatory change would come of it.

The first part of this prophecy was soon confirmed. Balder flinched as he heard Roedan command her faithful to dig. He closed his eyes tightly as the roar of the crowd swept through the forest like a shockwave – but opened them again, releasing tears, when the northern slope was assaulted by another noise from above.

A helicopter flew low over the trees. The grove was momentarily flooded with its brilliant white landing light, and the down-draught of its rotor-blades blew out Balder's candle.

Unable to think of anything else that he might do at this late stage, Balder lit another cigarette, tried to ignore Geophagia's ravenous cries, and watched the helicopter circling the festival arena. What was the worst that Roedan's following could do to the monument? he asked himself optimistically, though without enough conviction to stop tears of hopelessness coursing freely down his cheeks.

Meeting Hill was being raped, and there was nothing he could do to prevent it. I tried, he thought defensively against unspoken blame. I did try.

A twig snapped nearby, somewhere to the west. Balder's breath caught in his throat. He searched the darkness through the trees, his gaze guided by a sound of footsteps across the forest floor's carpet of damp leaves.

A cautious scuffing approached, and then someone switched on a torch barely twenty feet away. Its beam stroked the ground in unhurried sweeps of scrutiny, but did not reveal the identity of the silent figure in the dark. Balder groped for the short-sword beside him and rose to a watchful crouch.

The helicopter made another pass. Its landing light dropped a travelling pillar of ghostly brilliance into the sloping woodland. Everything it touched was illuminated for less than a second, including Roedan and her billowing red robe. The Geophagia leader made a florid epiphany against the monochrome trees, but she ignored the helicopter and continued what was clearly a search of the ground by torchlight. Balder could only watch and wonder as she drew nearer.

The Twelfth Stone did not believe that Roedan would indulge his curiosity if he simply asked her what she was doing, but he became impatient, and eventually he decided that announcing his presence and spoiling her search would be a satisfying, if petty, revenge.

Balder switched on his own flashlight and gripped the handle of Marchen's dagger.

Reaching the edge of the grove, Roedan noticed him. She raised her light to identify Balder, but Meeting Hill silenced their questions. A sound like the cracking of a giant nut made both Roedan and Balder duck reflexively and then sway where they stood as the ground beneath their feet slid six inches downhill with a jolt. Roedan redirected her light to the forest floor in surprise. She gasped and lunged for something she saw lying among the leaves.

Balder did not see what she had picked up, but he felt sure he could guess what it was. He leapt forward over the spring and into the trees.

Hugging Arthur's cross tightly to her chest, Roedan aimed the beam of her torch into Balder's eyes and backed steadily away until she felt her spine pressed against a tree.

Balder followed closely, his sword held out before him. 'Give me the cross.'

Roedan recognised the weapon he brandished. 'That's mine! Give it back. You can't threaten me with my own property.'

The trees around them creaked and began moving, as though they were attempting to flee the torrential rumble that emanated from somewhere below. Its intensity was felt as well as heard, and it quickly grew louder, as if the disturbance was racing uphill towards them.

'Give me the cross!' Balder yelled, and he was satisfied to see Roedan flinch. 'I'm not going to let you vandalise The Meeting and then take what you came here for!'

For the first and last time in her life, Roedan found herself lacking a confident response.

'I'll hurt you with this if you don't give me the cross!' Balder hollered, an edge of hysteria now lining his voice. 'You've taken everything I lived to protect and I have nothing left to lose.'

Roedan saw Balder losing control over the quiver in his hands, over the tremor in his voice and even his own saliva, which flew profusely as he bellowed, and this rapid loss of restraint made Balder's threat all the more convincing.

But, 'Didn't you have a friend who got himself into trouble playing with knives?' Roedan asked, surprised at being able to recall and remind him of this fact so calmly. 'Remember what happened to Craig Pearce before you come near me with that.'

Balder seemed suddenly bloated and choked by the rage he experienced at being lectured by the desecrater of his temple. Roedan watched him wrestling with her reasoning and his own fury – a battle between mind and body that made him twitch and wheeze as he struggled to control the hand that held the sword.

The rumble from downhill became a violent vibration, a series of crashes and then a quake, sending Roedan and Balder floundering for support. Roedan fell backwards as the tree behind her toppled sideways, but she sat up and kicked herself away from the collapsing grove.

Balder slid a few feet downhill when the ground cracked, heaved and churned beneath him. He lost both his torch and dagger as a grip on some rooted anchor became more important. But he enjoyed only a few seconds purchase on the bough of a falling sycamore before the lip of the deafening cascade rose to meet him.

In the passing light of the helicopter, *Y Deuddegfed Maen* gaped at Roedan in terror from the very edge of the landslide before he was swallowed by the tide of plummeting earth.

Roedan opened her mouth with an instinctive urge to scream, but no sound emerged as she gripped the trunk of a slim birch and watched the northern face of Meeting Hill fall away. She lay only a few feet from the vertical edge of the landslide. The natural course of Meeting Brook itself seemed to mark the boundary of whatever weakness caused the hill to subside.

Trees standing in silhouette against the damp night sky remained vertical as the earth cradling their roots first began to slide, giving Roedan the illusion that she was being carried uphill. Then, like a sedate wave breaking against the slope in defiance of gravity, the horizontal edge of the landslide passed her on its way up to the clearing, and so the forest floor disappeared. Soil and stones avalanched; trees tumbled like matchsticks, and a number of screaming people skidded by, tumbling and broken in the rubble, until there was nothing left to fall.

The noise and vibration took another thirty seconds to fade, but Roedan did not move for a further minute. She needed time to watch and listen in the shocked silence that followed before she felt safe enough to relax her grip on the tree.

The picturesque grove at the source of Meeting Brook had gone. The tranquil sanctuary was replaced by a jagged, crumbling edge, which ran uphill through the woods only a few feet from where Roedan had cowered. Beyond that was a dark and empty expanse.

The throbbing of her own accelerated heartbeat filled Roedan's ears for a full minute. Then, when her pulse gradually began to ebb, she was able to focus on several other sensations. Firstly the sound of water. The age-old channel of Meeting Brook was lost, but water still emerged from some fractured recess in the section carved from the slope. It had some distance to fall from its new fount, and Roedan heard the echo of its spattering impact against rocks some way below.

Secondly, she discerned the idling engine of the helicopter, which had set down in an open corner of the arena. Roedan's scattered thoughts were shepherded by the sound of whipping blades. She was reminded of her purpose, and of her prearranged flight from the festival.

Finally, Roedan became aware of some discomfort against her sternum, though the feeling turned out to be a reassuring one. She withdrew her embrace of the silver birch. The prize Roedan had held between her chest and the tree throughout the ordeal slid gently into her lap.

Even above the whine of the helicopter's engines, the cries of someone in what might have been mortal agony reached Roedan's ears from below. But when she pressed her palm against the cold metal and engraving of Arthur's burial cross, Geophagia's priestess could not suppress a smile and an ecstatic shiver in the darkness.

The Turning Tide

Many commentators from a wide variety of disciplines had something to say about the events that occurred in Little Arlingham on October 31st, even before the conclusions of the public inquest were published on December 21st. In fact, the issue soon became one of the most closely examined and hotly debated news items of 1999.

In an editorial written during the first week of November, Chris Bay of the Somerset Mail declared, 'Meeting Hill, as the landmark that many generations knew and loved, is gone. Of course, a visit to the monument reveals a remarkable attempt at restoration, and The Meeting remains recognisable, but it can no longer be considered a bold symbol of the kind of Englishness we knew before the advent of political correctness. It is a sad indictment of our liberal culture, which will never have the courage to criticise or blame a religious minority for fear of restricting even destructive freedoms, that those who worked tirelessly for preservation of the stones, and for the solid Conservative principles they embodied, are already being held responsible for their collapse.'

Reading this publication on the day of its release, Sandy Carter, outspoken Labour MP for the Pennard ward, issued a vehement riposte, offended by the media's assumptions concerning Earthwork's political bias. 'Georgina Wyre herself would not deny that she has enjoyed a life of considerable privilege, but this does not justify an instant condemnation of her – or her team of hard-working volunteers – as jealous nobles seeking to curb the weekend fun and freedom of the working class on Wyre land. It serves only to reinforce an archaic cliché, and doing so in this case is particularly offensive. Earthwork is no more Tory than was Robin Hood (though it has to be observed that the man in Lincoln green was a little more successful at preserving his green home and seeing off the bad guys).'

Choosing to ignore the forest of accusing fingers, and instead focus on the damage to Meeting Hill, Shaun Hepburn of the Mercian Archaeological Society wrote, 'The fact that the partial subsidence of Meeting Hill may have revealed one of the most exciting archaeological discoveries of the new millennium should not distract us from the tragedy of having lost a portion of one of the best preserved Neolithic British temples (as well as a number of lives). Due to its excellent condition, The Meeting has always been considered inviolable. The soil of Meeting Hill has lain undisturbed since the stones were erected, and – as keen as many of us have been to explore it – no self-respecting member of the academic community has relished the thought of being the first to dig through the wild flowers of Meeting Hill's pristine summit. Now we finally have our chance, though at heavy cost.'

The ecologist and author Richard Hardy wrote to the BBC's Nature magazine, observing that, 'The confrontation played out on Meeting Hill demonstrates the way in which the modern approach to conservation, of both environment and heritage, has fallen into two irreconcilable camps: one that wishes to plunder our last natural preserves for the material benefit of a few selfish individuals, and a second that seeks to only to sanctify them, putting those areas beyond reach as effectively as the plunderers would. Can there be no middle ground?'

Carla McNeil of the Sym-Bio Research Forum produced a lengthy essay for November's Cerealogy Magazine, in which she lamented, 'Meeting Hill had only just begun to reveal itself as a powerful source of symbiotic biological energy when it was desecrated by reckless profiteers, and the fact that The Meeting was spoilt by those whose stated aim was to venerate the site makes the landslide a particularly tragic end, not least for those who lost their lives.'

And Alan Forrest, formerly the Field Team Leader for the Carreg's End Monument Preservation Committee, was quoted by one of the daily tabloids concisely and explicitly when he described the efforts of his team as, 'A monumental fuck-up. We couldn't preserve jam in a jar.'

The lower temperatures of late October had reassured weather-watchers of Little Arlingham that the traditional properties of the seasons had reasserted themselves that year, and that summer had ended in a way that conformed to the autumns of childhood memory, thereby restoring natural order.

Things seem well when they seem to be the way they were when we were young.

So when November in Somerset turned out to be the mildest of any year since records began, the villagers' growing fear that the world was being turned upside down was all but confirmed for those who continually bemoaned the longevity of summer. Spring flowers were fooled into dazzling blooms five months early. Temperatures did not drop below fourteen degrees centigrade during the hours of daylight until December 8th, and universal condemnation of such a mild start to the winter was silenced only by the fact that these unseasonable temperatures actually stalled the premature appearance of Christmas decorations.

However, after its brief visitation at Hallowe'en, winter finally returned in mid-December, bringing with it a layer of frost that whitened the Levels and thickened a little every night thereafter until the morning of the Winter Solstice.

At twenty minutes to two on the afternoon on December 21st, a lengthy but orderly queue of people at the door of the village hall studied the shimmering white dome of Meeting Hill above the frosted rooftops of Carreg's End. The sensational damage that some of them strained to see lay out of sight on the far northern slope, visible only from the arable plain of the Wyre estate.

Enjoying the illusion of flawlessness that it projected from this perspective, Georgina Wyre also gazed on the pale profile of Meeting Hill through the window of a Shogun driven by Alan Forrest as they negotiated the unusually heavy traffic around the village green. Sitting in the back seat behind George, Ian Longe noticed her wistful stare uphill, but his own attention was soon drawn by the heavy presence of news media around the village hall. Cars filled the centre of Little Arlingham and were parked inconsiderately along the narrow residential roads, leaving no space for the latecomers.

'It's a circus,' George said dismally. 'We're putting ourselves in a goldfish bowl by going in there.'

A few people gathered in front of the village hall turned to study the new arrivals, but Abel Mild had removed the Earthwork insignia from the Shogun nearly six weeks before, allowing its passengers a few moments anonymity.

'You don't have to,' Alan suggested for the fifth time that day, scratching at the full beard he had grown for the winter. 'We'll soon find out what conclusions were drawn.'

'No, no,' George replied, smoothing down her dark skirt in preparation to leave the vehicle. 'I have the lives of fourteen people on my conscience and I'm taking hardly any blame. The least I can do is attend the public inquiry. But you don't need to be there. Or you, Ian. In fact, I really don't think you should be.'

Ian leaned forward in his seat, straightening his tie. 'We're dressed for it now, and I think someone should be in there with you.'

'Rubbish,' George said. 'I've come here to make a dignified show of accepting the conclusions of the inquest, not to wail and beat my breast in the aisles. Please, leave me here. I've managed to keep you clear of blame so far, I don't want to see you pilloried now. I have my mobile, I'll call you after.'

George opened the door and stepped down from her seat, giving her companions no chance to disagree, which Alan was about to do when an extended blast on a car horn made him aware of the angry queue of traffic forming behind. Unable to park or even pause, Alan drove on.

George turned away, bringing herself face to face with the smile of someone she did not recognise.

'Hello, George.'

'Hello,' George nodded formally as she stepped away, but turned back when her memory of familiar features broke the surface of the young woman's outward transformation.

Lea had gained some weight and she looked much healthier for it. She wore no make up that day, but the freezing air had brought a glow to her cheeks. Lea wore a black woollen hat over her inch-long hair, and she was dressed against the cold of Midwinter in a knee-length, fawn-coloured coat, and a multi-coloured scarf that covered her neck to the chin and trailed to her waist.

'Oh! Hello!' George repeated, and she hugged Lea tightly.
The two women studied each other for a moment, and both observed changes in the other that were difficult to voice. Lea could not tactfully express her opinion that George now looked her age, and even appeared quite ill; and George's tone was hesitant when she said, 'Something's different.' The elder woman made another blatant survey of Lea's warmly wrapped form, and then she met her eye. 'Lea, are you—'
'You know me,' Lea interrupted her quickly, stuffing her hands into her pockets. 'I get bored with the way I look every other month. I thought it time for another change of image. I call this one Girl Next Door. I've never tried it before.'
George considered her reply and accepted it tactfully. 'Well, it suits you,' she beamed, and then she pointed at the village hall. 'Are you here for the performance?'
Lea nodded. 'I thought I'd never set foot in Arlingham again, but I heard that a presentation on the archaeological survey was set for today, and when I realised that the inquest's results would be announced as well, I had to come back and find out whether the landslide was our fau—'
George silenced Lea with a cough, glancing nervously at the nearest members of the queue. When she noticed Ted Alexander and a camera crew from the South-west Tonight programme walking purposely towards them, she met Lea's questioning stare with a reassuring smile. 'I'd rather you hadn't come, Lea, as nice as it is to see you,' she said, looping arms with the younger woman and guiding her towards the steward at the door of the hall. 'But as you're here, I'll be much happier if you sit with me.'

The doors of Little Arlingham's village hall were opened to the press and public at five minutes to two. The event attracted a large but sober crowd, and its orderly occupation of the hall allowed representatives of the County Council, the police, and of the scientific disciplines consulted to announce the results of the inquiry into the deaths of fourteen people on Meeting Hill on the evening of October 31st.
The doors of the hall were shut at precisely two o'clock, and Little Arlingham fell silent.
Ian Longe and Alan Forrest played pool in the Bolthole for the duration of the conference. The landlord, Alan's father, was their only company. A poorly defined sense of propriety prevented either of the younger men from enjoying anything stronger to drink than cola, and even from playing their favourite jukebox tunes for some time. But after losing to Alan's unerring cue for the third time in as many games, Ian began to question the morose silence in which the friends had chosen to spend their afternoon. 'Why are we acting like this? They're holding a press conference, not a remembrance service,' he

declared, removing his tie and striding towards the bar. 'Carrying on with my life in the way I want to isn't going to make me feel any guiltier about what happened than I already do.'

'Or any less,' Alan reflected, but still accepted the pint of cider Ian handed him a minute later.

Shadows lengthened and pale surfaces quickly reddened as the Midwinter sun dipped back into view through the Bolthole's low bay windows, and the smoke of Brian Forrest's cigars gradually thickened the air. Ian and Alan drank and played pool in the way they often did on idle afternoons, but the empty tables around them were a reminder of Little Arlingham's sombre distraction that day, and an air of foreboding dulled their humour. Alan frequently checked his mobile phone for messages.

The first person to leave the village hall did so fifteen minutes before the end of the meeting. She had heard enough to feel as informed as anyone with an interest in the festival tragedy might ever hope to be, and more than enough to make her aware of the way in which the Earthwork committee, along with its estate-employed accomplices, would be judged by the public from that day on. Lea Granger crossed the green and entered the Bolthole.

Ian and Alan were conspicuous as the only people present on the drinking side of the bar, but she did not acknowledge them until she had ordered a neat vodka from Brian. 'Oh – no, forget it,' she said, shaking her head irritably. 'I'll have an orange juice.'

Ian and Alan studied the new arrival sternly from beside the pool table, but did not recognize her until she approached them with her drink. 'George said you'd be here,' Lea smiled awkwardly. 'She told me to warn you that the news hounds will be out hunting when the meeting's over. You might want to hide.'

'Lea!' Alan grinned, his surprise and delight provoked easily after four pints of cider, though his impulse to hug her was quelled by Lea's polite reserve and unfamiliar composure. 'You came for the meeting?'

Lea nodded. 'George is going to answer a few questions for the press and then she's going to phone you. She was talking about having us all round for dinner at the house tonight. What have you been up to?'

'We don't have to answer that,' Ian replied. 'We've been through too much together for ice-breaking chit chat.'

Lea glanced at the collection of empty pint glances on the nearby table. She was about to blame them for loosening Ian's tongue, but she remembered that Ian's tongue did not need alcohol if there was anything blunt or socially awkward to be expressed.

'You feel uncomfortable around us because you know we have a guilty conscience. You want to be nice about it, but you're worried about seeming patronising. Meanwhile,' he went on, Alan beside him shaking his head between sips of cider, 'we feel we have to tread carefully now you're here because we know we should have listened to you on Hallowe'en and not dug that trench. And we're not sure if we should mention Ben because we don't know how sensitive you are about it. So what's with the orange juice? I have a picture of the real Lea Granger in my mind: she's got a spliff in one hand and a can of Special Brew in the other.'

'Ah,' Lea stood her drink on the table and sat down in the chair beside it. 'Detox.'

Alan took another mouthful of his cider and admired the glass with a wide toothy grin. '*Re*tox,' he winked, and he sat down beside Lea.

'Aren't you worried about being cornered by the press in here?' Lea asked, glancing through the window at the village hall. She saw people emerging through its doors in a steady stream.

'If George is prepared to put up with it, why shouldn't we?' Ian said.

'Because that's why George didn't want you there,' Lea replied. 'From the way she was talking, it sounds like protecting you is all she thinks about.'

Alan and Ian seemed sobered by the statement. 'We know,' Alan nodded. 'And she's been good at it. I bet the inquest fell short of blaming Earthwork for the landslide.'

Lea blinked in surprise. She nodded.

'But I bet you came expecting to see us blamed for everything,' Ian predicted.

Lea nodded again.

'If we're not in any trouble it's because George swore us all to secrecy,' Ian revealed. 'Believe me, we were more than happy to own up. So was George. But then she realized that Earthwork, you, and all her estate staff would end up in trouble for carrying out a plan she talked us into.'

Lea paused for a moment before pointing out, 'It might have been George's idea, but we didn't have to do it.'

'You *didn't* agree to it,' Ian reminded her, his tone laced with what Lea thought was probably envy, 'which hasn't made it any easier for us to swallow our conscience. But we never mentioned diverting the stream because we didn't want to see George stand trial for criminal negligence or manslaughter.'

Alan nodded. 'Those jokers at the August meeting were right: we turned into the Self-Preservation Society.'

The Bolthole's front door opened in a flurry of cold air, and a steady trickle of villagers entered the bar. The first of them to be served carried his pint to the jukebox and requested a string of seasonal songs, starting with Greg Lake's 'I believe in Father Christmas'. Behind the bar Brian Forrest, who had heard this song at least twice a day every day since the Christmas compilation album was installed on the jukebox, closed his eyes and shook his head.

'To help you leave this business behind, I think you should know what was said at the meeting today.' Lea pulled a folded A4 press release from her pocket, smoothed it open on the tabletop and then paraphrased from its printed pages. 'The inquest concluded that the subsidence of Meeting Hill was caused by a combination of factors. Firstly, the deforestation of the north face, which undermined the integrity of the slope's surface, and which the investigators said may – or may not – have altered the course of Meeting Brook. A number of shovels and pickaxes were found in the rubble at the bottom of the hill, and that aroused some interest. But the estate staff who cleared the trees for the new path couldn't remember how many tools they'd taken onto the hill, and couldn't swear that they hadn't left some behind. Brampton Wyre was identified as having ordered the felling of those trees.

'Secondly, the gathering of nearly two thousand people on the summit around The Meeting, which was not assessed for the suitability of supporting such a large number of dancing people. Brampton Wyre and Jill Baynes were held jointly responsible for failing to seek consultation. And finally, Meeting Hill was saturated by October's above-average rainfall, which made the previous two factors especially risky – but the inquest stopped short of blaming the Rainmakers for that.'

This raised a smile from Alan. But the inquiry's conclusions were not enough to dispel the men's frowns entirely, and Lea did not know what to say next – until she realised how surprised and disappointed she was to find that the Earthwork members had not shown the strength of mind to reach the kind of comfortable justification which had, eventually, allowed Lea herself to sleep soundly at night. 'Look: we didn't divert that stream to kill people in a landslide.' Ian winced and turned away. 'And we certainly didn't intend to collapse a fifth of the hill we were trying to preserve, so I think you should accept the official conclusions, just like everyone else has, and move on. Earthwork still has a monument to protect.'

Ian and Alan brought disbelieving glances to bear on Lea. Ian laughed. 'There's no Earthwork now. The committee succeeded in achieving the *exact* opposite of what it set out to do!'

'But that wasn't your intention,' Lea pleaded in surprise. 'You all tried so hard – you even converted me!'

'Then if anyone can be bothered to try and pick a lesson out of what happened here, perhaps it should be that everyone and everything fails eventually, despite hard work and best intentions, or maybe even because of them. Perhaps everyone should just leave things alone.'

The door to the Bolthole opened again. The bar filled steadily. 'Getting busy,' Lea noted to deflect Ian's sour conclusion.

'This is nothing,' Alan replied after draining his pint glass. 'You should have seen it in November when the forensic people were still examining the hill. It was packed in here every lunchtime. Then a crowd of archaeologists got involved when The Meeting was declared safe, and they came in here everyday spreading rumours about amazing discoveries in the hill. It was like listening to Howard Carter talking about his finds in Egypt.'

'There was a summary of the archaeologists' survey after the inquiry's press conference,' Lea told him, 'but I don't know how the summary compares to the rumours they spread with a beer inside them. What did they say they'd found?'

Alan's eyes glittered for a moment as he quoted, 'Wonderful things…'

Lea nodded happily. 'The experts in the hall couldn't give much away because they're still exploring, but I could see they were excited about what the subsidence had turned up. They had to say it was a tragedy, of course, but I don't think they'll ever regret that it happened.'

Ian turned and stared into the light of the afternoon sun through the bay window. It seemed to have enlightened him with the solution to an ongoing puzzle. 'Sacrifice,' he whispered appreciatively, 'in return for transformation.'

'What about Ben?' she asked unexpectedly, addressing Ian as if unable to trust Alan's sincerity in such a matter. 'Where did they bury him?'

The question – and its answer – made Ian uncomfortable. He examined Lea's expression for some time as if gauging her ability to cope with his reply. 'They didn't find him.'

Lea had not known this, though she did not seem surprised.

'They pulled thirteen bodies out of the rubble, all identified, and the nine injured were Geophagia members. That accounts for everyone, except... But if we're honest with ourselves, we should admit that Ben was lost long before Hallowe'en, on the night he found his Mum.'

Lea cringed at the memory and stared at her shoes.

'What you said about us has to be true for you, too,' Ian added. 'You need to accept and move on.'

Lea parked her small new Peugeot at the foot of Meeting Hill near the opening to the ascending footpath. Beside the car she saw a sign that ordered 'Strictly no vehicles beyond this point'. Lea complied happily, wondering how Earthwork had ever got away with driving large off-road vehicles, whose notorious carbon footprint was not as instantly ruinous as their tyre tracks, onto the summit. She retrieved a bulky holdall from the boot of her car and climbed the zigzagging footpath up the south-eastern slope. Her ascent kept her beneath sight of the setting sun, and yet she did not walk in shade. A ruby glow suffused the woods around her as the sunlight was reflected downhill by the scintillating surfaces of a million frosty branches, and Meeting Hill glittered like Ballard's Crystal World.

Lea found the summit similarly bejewelled, but here the light was harder, and everything, from the eight standing megaliths to each and every frozen blade of grass, cast a long slim shadow. The sunset gave the prickly tangles of ice encasing the surrounding trees a sanguine flush, but the warmth of the light remained a benign illusion. Lea's exhaled breath drifted as steam in the freezing air long after it had passed her awe-parted lips.

And yet the clearing's direct exposure to the deepened light of evening would not have been considered a good thing by anyone who knew Meeting Hill before October 31st. A substantial section of the northern and western tree-lines had disappeared with the slopes in which they had been rooted, leaving a jagged edge and a crumbling escarpment, as well as a conspicuous gap in the Neolithic circle of stones.

But the summit had been re-turfed, and its new north-eastern edge was minimally guarded by a low wooden rail that ran either side of the fallen Monk's Pillow, which Lea approached with her head bowed respectfully, as though nearing an altar. She stopped beside the horizontal stone and peered with a grimace over the edge of Meeting Hill's new cliff-face. Lea could hear a gentle flow of water, and though she could not see where it emerged from the exposed heart of the hill, she was able to view the new crater it had worn in the untidy, tape-lined section of displaced earth below. She could also see that Meeting Brook had eroded itself a new connecting course from the muddy plunge-pool to its original channel through the fields of the Wyre estate, and the two standing stones fallen from the summit had been erected at either side of the stream as a pillared boundary to Meeting Hill's subsided slope.

Lea turned away with tears in her eyes. The vertical section of the hillside and its free-falling stream seemed too much like a gaping wound whose bleeding could not be staunched for Lea to examine it at length. But she blinked the water from her eyes, pulled the holdall from her shoulder, and was about to set the bag on the toppled megalith beside her when she noticed an envelope, clearly addressed to her, laid on the frosty surface of the stone. She smiled and shook her head in surprise, glancing just once around the deserted clearing before lowering her bag and picking up the letter. She sat down on the edge of the Monk's Pillow, opened the envelope and placed a gloved hand over the middle of her coat as she read the handwritten page within.

> Long ago, when the world was fresh and young, and the furthest horizons were untainted by the imposition of his experience upon them, an eleven-year-old boy discovered The Meeting, and his love for the place never allowed him to leave. Ben Marchen grew up, but the shade of his innocence lingered there as something more tangible than a memory, roaming the hill on which the young Ben had experienced his most ardent sense of belonging.
>
> Ben Marchen saw that boy for the first time, I think, on the night his Dad went missing. Ben was on Meeting Hill with you and Madog feeling traumatised by events, and the spirit of his own childhood appeared to him as a reminder of a simpler, happier time. The boy beckoned, which

scared Ben, so he returned to you. But he couldn't resist the chance to lose himself in such innocence again when the boy appeared a second time. You were there on that occasion too, and you were the last person to see Ben Marchen as he pursued his own yearning downhill to the water.

Madog arrived there eventually, but not before Ben had surrendered himself to possession by the simple spirit of his own youth, leaving behind the trials of adulthood to commit himself exclusively to a world symbolised by the awe-struck eleven-year-old.

Renamed Balder, I have been allowed to correct the mistake Ben Marchen made when he gazed beyond the borders of home in search of the source of the passion that Meeting Hill awoke within him.

However, I have one concession to make to those who would doubt that a man might regress and redefine himself so entirely. I am a personality struggling to express itself through a second-hand, well-travelled brain, so this same grey matter is likely to lead me to similar interests and conclusions as its former tenant. Lea, my duty compels me to decline your flattering interest in me, but I have no doubt that familiarity with you would in time have led me to the same intensity of feeling.

I can hear Geophagia gathering on Meeting Hill above me as I write, and I have very little time left to decide how I might best protect The Meeting. But despite my devotion to the site, I'm distracted by regret at the way I've treated you. I really shouldn't expect you to understand, so please don't hate me for it. I hope my behaviour won't leave you unable to accept this note when I try to hand it to you at a later, less stressful date.

Ben Marchen came to love you, Lea, which means that I am bound to love you too.

Balder

Barely half of the sun's smouldering orb was visible above the horizon when Lea lowered Ben's letter and began to cry freely into her gloves. The crystal-dusted hilltop and its crown of wood and stone reflected the sunset's deepening light, and through the shifting filter of Lea's tears the world dissolved into a dense luminous mist.

In the grip of her sadness, Lea did not see the pale branches of a bough halfway up an oak at the edge of the woods begin to fold and retreat, as if withdrawn from the cold by the tree itself. These dendroidal lengths relaxed into a squatting human outline, which lowered itself from the bough and dropped lightly onto the grass. Like the hilltop itself, Madog wore a pale covering of rough texture: the skin of his head, neck and hands was whitened by a coarse, cracked layer of flour; his thick overcoat and trousers had been preserved from a forgotten fashion era when white was in demand; and, to complete the camouflage, his head was bristled by a woven circlet of white-painted twigs.

The Twelfth Stone straightened himself from his landing crouch and paced into the clearing, but he was wary of frightening The Meeting's grieving visitor. 'Hello, Lea,' he greeted her from some distance away.

Lea quickly dried her eyes and stared suspiciously at the bleached old man as he approached.

'I see you got Balder's letter.' He indicated the paper in Lea's hand. 'I came back when I heard what had happened. I found the letter in my hut.'

'Listen to me, Jack Frost,' Lea said. 'Whenever I have a bad day and I start missing Ben all over again, I make myself feel better by imagining all the ways I could hurt you and your brother, so don't expect—'

'I'm sorry,' Madog declared unexpectedly, his gaze meeting hers with unblinking, undeniable sincerity. 'I really am sorry for everything. Just tell me what I can do to prove it. I'll do it.'

'Don't try to get round me by being nice,' she replied, though her softened tone suggested that Madog was succeeding. 'You took advantage of a grieving man and there's nothing you can do to bring him back.' Lea turned away and watched the last sliver of the sun sink into the Levels of Sedgemoor. 'But I suppose you could at least tell me where Ben is now.'

Madog removed his crown of twigs and laid it on the fallen stone. He began to pick and rub at his face, crumbling the mask. 'I'm sure I can't tell you anything that you haven't already heard today,' the old man said gently, his words manifested as a lengthening trail of steam. 'Balder sacrificed himself for Meeting Hill, and now he has become a part of it. The soil beneath The Meeting has received the blood of at least four generations of Marchens over the centuries, and I truly believe that neither Ben nor Balder could have hoped for a more fitting end.'

Lea wiped her face with her gloves, and when she looked up into Madog's sympathetic gaze her expression betrayed a cautious respect.

'Ben Marchen was a chaotic and often reckless young man. His behaviour hurt a lot of people, but he redeemed himself by finally embracing the preoccupation he lived in denial of as an adult.' Madog sat down on the edge of the stone beside Lea. 'I think that becoming Balder, and then dying as him, was simultaneously Ben's prize and punishment for the life he led.'

Lea voiced no agreement, but neither did she object to Madog's opinion. She appreciated the sense of fulfilled narrative and significance that his words offered Ben's life. 'I was in Little Arlingham for the press conference today,' she said, noting Madog's attentive glance. 'Want to hear about it?'

'Certainly,' the Twelfth Stone replied.

'Roedan and Brampton Wyre were blamed for the landslide and deaths at Hallowe'en. Ian took a dim view of the committee's efforts when I spoke to him earlier, suggesting that the only lesson to be learned from what we tried to do is that we shouldn't have tried at all. Brampton Wyre managed to turn himself into a hero at the inquest by expressing his deepest regret, and then he announced that Meeting Hill is to be *returned to the people,* as he put it, by entrusting the site to English Heritage. Of course, it's just as much Georgina's donation as her brother's, and it was probably her idea, but Brampton used it as a PR stunt to deflect the—'

'No, no,' Madog cringed impatiently, 'I don't care about politics and blame. I've been watching academic types dipping in and out of the new hole in this side of the hill for weeks, and they've been very excited. Tell me what they think they've found.'

Lea smiled and nodded – this was a topic she felt happier discussing. 'The landslide uncovered a prehistoric opening and tunnel into the hill. It's so old that it was probably even starting to silt over when the Romans came to Britain.'

Madog spat onto the grass in disgust at her mention of the ancient invaders.

'The entrance is a trilithon, just like the ones at Stonehenge, but set into the side of the hill as an opening to a stone-lined passage,' Lea continued. 'The roof has collapsed about forty feet in, so there'll be even more to explore when they've cleared it, but they've already seen three accessible chambers off one side of the tunnel, and each contains one or more prehistoric bodies surrounded by weapons and ceremonial objects. They're starting to think that Meeting Hill must have been a tomb for very rich and important people in the Neolithic, which is ironic when you think about the interest shown in it by the likes of us since the Sixties.'

Madog was dismissive of this observation. 'So there's a suggestion that the hill itself is man-made?'

'They've not said yet, but they did say that if Meeting Hill does turns out to be, then it'll be the largest prehistoric structure in Europe, almost three times the mass of Silbury Hill. They also said they're applying to have Meeting Hill designated a World Heritage Site, like Avebury, or the Pyramids. I suppose that'll attract thousands more visitors each year, but at least no one will have to lose sleep worrying about the hill's preservation anymore.'

Y Deuddegfed Maen nodded cautiously. 'There's more of Meeting Hill to preserve than its soil and stones. Still, this is all very satisfying,' he admitted, 'and Earthwork and Balder played their parts to bring it about. But I worry that The Meeting will lose a defining element once the Twelfth Stone has gone.'

Lea frowned. 'You're here,' she said. 'You came back.'

'With no one to replace me, I had to. But despite what the children in the village are told about me, I'm not immortal. Lea,' Madog addressed her grandly, rising from the stone and turning to face her, his old white coat and trousers reflecting the diffuse glow of twilight, 'I don't think you'll be surprised to learn that there's a reason I made an effort to meet you here today. I would like you to consider accepting the title of *Y Deuddegfed Maen* as soon as you feel ready, and I can give you three good reasons for doing so. Firstly,' he announced in defiance of Lea's shocked expression, 'you have always appreciated the defence of Meeting Hill in the name of both heritage and spirituality. Heritage, of course, is the conventional, if lightweight, motive for preservation of such a site – but spirituality is the harder motive to admit to, even though it is the deeper of the two, provided it remains true to the prehistoric builders' worship of the natural world. Unlike Ben Marchen, this is a motive that you freely profess, and you don't need the likes of me to help you remember it.

'Secondly,' he continued, watching Lea frown in exaggerated concentration, 'I consider it only natural that you should succeed Balder, seeing how you tried so hard to maintain intimacy with him when he struggled to fulfil this role. And finally,' he concluded, noticing the way in which Lea's expression was settling into relaxed attention, as if she was only now accepting Madog's conviction and the sincerity of his offer; 'I imagine that the child you're carrying was conceived with Ben, so you should accept that no one born with Marchen blood in their veins is able to spend too long away from these stones without going a bit mad.'

Lea touched her belly and offered the old man a faint smile of surprise.

Madog grinned broadly in return. 'A Mum-to-be as proud as you can't hide it. You're radiant. Congratulations, by the way,' he added, and then gazed at her expectantly.

'What?' she asked, also rising from the edge of the stone. 'You've just asked me to live in a cold damp hut and disguise myself as a tree for the rest of my life to spy on tourists, and you expect an answer now?'

Madog shrugged.

'Well you're not going to get one, no matter how insightful you are about my thoughts, or anything else. Thank you, though,' she decided. 'I'll return in a week when I've had a chance to think about such an insane commitment. I'd like to ask you a favour in return now.'

Remembering his earlier promise, Madog agreed.

'I'd like you to leave me alone up here with what's left of the daylight – and I mean alone, Madog, not just out of sight camouflaged as a rabbit or a puddle.'

Madog nodded.

'And then, when I leave in a little while, I'd like you to leave The Meeting to itself for a few minutes, just until the gesture I leave behind has played out.'

'All right,' he said. 'Of course. Take care of yourself and your little one up here in the dark.'

Lea patted the waist of her coat. 'We'll be heading for Arlingham House to see George, Alan and Ian before the light's gone,' she assured him, turning to the large holdall on the recumbent megalith. 'I'll see you later.'

Lea Granger did not hear the Twelfth Stone of Meeting Hill depart, but neither did she need to check to be sure that he had gone. She waited for one silent minute in the scarlet dusk, and then she pulled from the bag a small portable stereo, already loaded with batteries and a compact disc, and placed it with ceremonial reverence in the centre of the fallen stone. She slung the bag over her shoulder and gazed appreciatively around the frosty clearing, smiling in delighted response to the alighting of a magpie, which paused to study her from the tip of the nearest standing stone. Lea considered it a perfect cue to speak.

'You once decided that you would want me to choose the song played at your funeral.' She rotated slowly to address the surrounding stones and trees, the hill beneath her feet, and then Glastonbury Tor on the fiery western horizon. 'It wasn't difficult to choose.

'I checked the local papers for weeks, waiting for a chance to grant your request, but you didn't want to be found. I don't think I blame you. So let this be as close as I can get to a funeral for you, and let this be the place where your child and I can always come to be near you.'

Lea felt better for voicing an optimistic reference to the future. Although she did not consider her short address to be much of an epitaph, her words were expressed as an acceptance of finality and loss, and so it was with cheeks dampened by tears that Lea pressed the 'Play' button on the stereo. Then she looked up and stared for a few more moments into the fading light of the shortest day.

As ascending guitar notes introduced Kula Shaker's *Temple of Everlasting Light* to the freezing air of the clearing, Lea felt pleased to have managed a modest act of personalised commemoration. It was a novel conclusion, and Lea prayed fervently that its fulfilment would offer her lover the serenity that his defining angst had denied him in life.

'Goodbye, Ben,' she whispered at last, and then she returned to the footpath by threading a route between the hopeful stones of The Meeting.

Author's Note

Little Arlingham is a fictitious village, but my description of it and the surrounding area is consistent with the character of its setting at the south-eastern limits of the Somerset Levels, somewhere a little north of Sparkford.

Meeting Hill and its crowning stones do not exist either, but anyone who has visited Avebury in Wiltshire, The Hurlers on Bodmin Moor, or any of the other large prehistoric stone circles scattered across Britain and Ireland will have a clear picture of the monument I imagined for this story.

The novel's snapshots of Carreg's Twelfth-Century flight are my fictitious expansion of events chronicled by Gerald of Wales in his book of 1193, *Liber de Principis Instructione*, and again in *Speculum Ecclesiae* around 1213, in which he described the exhumation of King Arthur's and Guinevere's bones by the monks of Glastonbury Abbey in 1191, two years after a reported tip-off from King Henry II. An excavation of the Abbey grounds by Ralegh Radford in 1962 seemed to confirm the existence – and the Twelfth-Century exhumation – of a grave, but the discovery is generally considered to have been a hoax, and the lead burial cross a forgery. Various motives are offered by scholars for such a hoax, and the one I chose is not one of the strongest, but the theory concerning the grave's use as propaganda against the Welsh proved to be a useful device. James P. Carley's book, *Glastonbury Abbey*, is essential reading for anyone interested in this topic.

After finding many different spellings from a variety of sources during my research, I settled on the Domesday Book's spelling of Glastingberie in the narration of Carreg's story, and I also lifted the names of Carreg's hunters from the Domesday Book's Somerset listings. However, I am responsible for any mistakes or anachronisms.

Printed in Great
Britain
by Amazon